"Laugh-out-loud funny."
—ENTERTAINMENT WEEKLY

W9-CNM-966

"That rarest of long books—
utterly worth it." —ESQUIRE

"There is wit on
every page."
—CHICAGO SUN-TIMES

"A nutty tour de force."
—PUBLISHERS WEEKLY
(starred review)

A Fraction of the Whole
a novel
Steve Toltz

"Rampaging and
irresistible."
—BOOKLIST (starred review)

"Soars like a rocket."
—LOS ANGELES TIMES

"A *Fraction of the Whole* is that rarest of long books—**utterly worth it** . . . The story starts in a prison riot and ends on a plane, and there is **not one forgettable episode** in between . . . It reads like Mark Twain with access to an intercontinental Airbus . . . **This book moves; it bucks and rocks** in a world that feels more than a hemisphere away . . . So comically dark and inviting that you have no choice but to step into its icy wake."

—*Esquire*

"Rollicking . . . laugh-out-loud funny."   —*Entertainment Weekly*

"A rich father-and-son story **packed with incident, humor, and characters reminiscent of the styles of Charles Dickens and John Irving** . . . Occasionally, a big, sprawling first novel fights its way into print with a flourish, at which point its ambition and the eccentricities of its 'first-ness' can become its best marketing tools. Such is the case with *A Fraction of the Whole*, a book that is willfully misanthropic and very funny . . . like Irving, Toltz makes **minor characters leap off the page** . . . He's a superb, disturbing phrasemaker . . . This long novel, which lives or dies in the brilliance of its writing, has a subtle, compelling structure . . . *A Fraction of the Whole* **soars like a rocket**."

—*Los Angeles Times*

"Toltz has made his book rollick. . . . You'll be hard pressed to find as entertainingly tumultuous a 600-page novel."   —*The Globe and Mail*

"**One of the best books I've ever read.** *A Fraction of the Whole* is better than *The Corrections*, and Toltz did it in one book while it took Franzen two to get *The Corrections* out into the world. Granted, you have your whole life to write your first novel, but my God, *A Fraction of the Whole* does things that most writers can't do in a lifetime . . . A **wildly addictive** exploration into a man's soul, a **profoundly moving** experience almost religious in its execution, and possibly one of the sharpest and irresistibly humorous postmodern adventures I've had the pleasure to read . . . Steve Toltz has written **a masterpiece, a smashing debut that will long be remembered as a colossal example of just**

how good fiction can be. He keeps you wired to the page from the jump and he defies gravity all the way to the end." —*Ain't It Cool News*

"First novels these days too seldom dare to raise their voices above an elegant whisper or an ironic murmur. Not so *A Fraction of the Whole*, **a riotously funny first novel that is harder to ignore than a crate of puppies.** This is not a book to be read so much as an experience to be wallowed in. Mr. Toltz's merry chaos—a mix of metaphysical inquiry, ribald jokes, freakish occurrences, and verbal dynamite booming across the page—**deserves a place next to *A Confederacy of Dunces*** in a category that might be called the undergraduate ecstatic. *A Fraction of the Whole* is a sort of Voltaire-meets-Vonnegut tale." —*Wall Street Journal*

"Madcap, exhausting, and true in the way the best lies always are." —*New York Observer*

"Wild . . . an odyssey that's **inspired, sorta stoned, tender, and very funny.** Sometimes all at the same time. Toltz's invention is as breathtaking as the speed of his narrative in a book that seems to have had all the boring parts snipped . . . There is wit on every page . . . Jorge Luis Borges is obviously an influence on Toltz. There is also a bit of John Irving and Tom Robbins here in the wacky characters and narrative drive. *A Fraction of the Whole* even has a touch of the weary philosophizing of Vonnegut, too. In its structure—and especially in its ending—there is even a pinch of Tristram Shandy. Very good company, all." —*Chicago Sun-Times*

"**Hold on tight because you are about to ride a juggernaut of words,** where things will go by very quickly and you better pay attention . . . The real pleasure in reading this book is the pace and the language. What Toltz has done masterfully is have his way with every aspect of modern life. He racks 'em up and knocks 'em down with a laser wit, a fine turn of phrase, and a **devastatingly funny** outlook on everything human." —*Seattle Times*

"An **exuberantly funny debut novel that you should just go away and read** . . . There is plenty to laugh at in A *Fraction of the Whole*—and also, goodness knows, there is plenty of plot and the narrative pace of a puppy with attention deficit disorder. But it also has a heart . . . **A grand achievement** and the debut of a great comic talent."

—*Sunday Times* (UK)

"Sparkling comic writing . . . It gives off the unmistakable whiff of **a book that might just contain the secret of life.**" —*Independent* (UK)

"This **absurdly incident-laden, feverish, farcical** life story bears the watermark of long gestation. What's more, it **stands above the vast majority of debut novels** because it seems so marvelously sure of itself and what it should be . . . Toltz's **fizzing, acid, funny** prose is capable of a kind of broken, lyrical beauty . . . Amid the dizzying whirl of events, Toltz never loses sight of a deep current that runs throughout his story . . . It's a spiritual search that allows a conclusion that finds an affecting depth of feeling. Yes, A *Fraction of the Whole* is **a wildly looping rollercoaster.** But there's much more to it than meaningless exhilaration."

—*Independent on Sunday* (UK)

"With tinges of magical realism and buckets of misanthropic humor it's **a clever and funny debut.**" —*Observer* (UK)

"Very light on its feet, skipping from anecdote, to rant, to reflection, like a stone skimming across a pond . . . There's a section about a labyrinth that you could imagine Borges writing, another about a lottery gone wrong that made me think of Vonnegut, and a strange, lovely account of childhood illness that had echoes of Garcia Marquez. In some ways it **plays like a modern Arabian Nights** . . . The inevitability of disaster is heartbreaking . . . **Brilliant.**" —*Guardian* (UK)

"Toltz goes really big . . . a successor to literary whiz kids like Dave Eggers and Jonathan Franzen. . . . Funny and boisterous. Imagine John Irving only more indulgent." —*The Gazette* (Montreal)

"Toltz is a hugely gifted novelist. A *Fraction of the Whole* is nothing less than a comic masterpiece." —*Ottawa Citizen*

ANCHOR
CANADA

A
FRACTION
of the
WHOLE

STEVE TOLTZ

ANCHOR CANADA

Library and Archives Canada Cataloguing in Publication
has been applied for.

ISBN: 978-0-385-66555-1

Permission for H. L. Mencken quote on page 469 granted by
the Enoch Pratt Free Library and the Estate of H. L. Mencken
in accordance with the terms of Mr. Mencken's bequest.
Book design by Diane Hobbing of Snap-Haus Graphics

Printed and bound in the USA

Published in Canada by
Anchor Canada, a division of
Random House of Canada Limited

Visit Random House of Canada Limited's website:
www.randomhouse.ca

10 9 8 7 6 5 4 3 2

To Marie

A

FRACTION

of the

WHOLE

ONE

You never hear about a sportsman losing his sense of smell in a tragic accident, and for good reason; in order for the universe to teach excruciating lessons that we are unable to apply in later life, the sportsman must lose his legs, the philosopher his mind, the painter his eyes, the musician his ears, the chef his tongue. My lesson? I have lost my freedom, and found myself in this strange prison, where the trickiest adjustment, other than getting used to not having anything in my pockets and being treated like a dog that pissed in a sacred temple, is the boredom. I can handle the enthusiastic brutality of the guards, the wasted erections, even the suffocating heat. (Apparently air-conditioning offends society's notion of punishment—as if just by being a little cool we are getting away with murder.) But what can I do here to kill time? Fall in love? There's a female guard whose stare of indifference is alluring, but I've never been good at chasing women—I always take no for an answer. Sleep all day? When my eyes are closed I see the menacing face that's haunted me my whole life. Meditate? After everything that's happened, I know the mind isn't worth the membrane it's printed on. There are no distractions here—not enough, anyway—to avoid catastrophic introspection. Neither can I beat back the memories with a stick.

All that remains is to go insane; easy in a theater where the apocalypse is performed every other week. Last night was a particularly stellar show: I had almost fallen asleep when the building started shaking and a hundred angry voices shouted as one. I stiffened. A riot, yet another ill-conceived revolution. It hadn't been going two minutes when my door was kicked open and a tall figure entered, wearing a smile that seemed merely ornamental.

"Your mattress. I need," he said.

"What for?" I asked.

"We set fire to all mattress," he boasted, thumbs up, as if this gesture were the jewel in the crown of human achievement.

"So what am I supposed to sleep on? The floor?"

He shrugged and started speaking in a language I didn't understand. There were odd-shaped bulges in his neck; clearly something terrible was taking place underneath his skin. The people here are all in a bad way and their clinging misfortunes have physically misshaped them. Mine have too; my face looks like a withered grape, my body the vine.

I waved the prisoner away and continued listening to the routine chaos of the mob. That's when I had the idea that I *could* pass the time by writing my story. Of course, I'd have to scribble it secretly crouched behind the door, and only at night, and then hide it in the damp space between the toilet and the wall and hope my jailers aren't the type to get down on their hands and knees. I'd settled on this plan when the riot finally took the lights out. I sat on my bed and became mesmerized by the glow from burning mattresses illuminating the corridor, only to be interrupted by two grim, unshaven inmates who strode into my cell and stared at me as if I were a mountain view.

"Are you the one who won't give up his mattress?" the taller of the two growled, looking like he'd woken up with the same hangover three years running.

I said that I was.

"Step aside."

"It's just that I was about to have a lie-down," I protested. Both prisoners let out deep, unsettling laughs that sounded like the tearing of denim. The taller one pushed me aside and yanked the mattress from my bed while the other stood as if frozen and waiting to thaw. There are certain things I'll risk my neck for, but a lumpy mattress isn't one of them. Holding it between them, the prisoners paused at the door.

"Coming?" the shorter prisoner asked me.

"What for?"

"It's your mattress," he said plainly. "It is your right to be one who sets it on fire."

I groaned. Man and his codes! Even in a lawless inferno, man has to give himself some honor, he's so desperate to separate himself from the beasts.

"I'll pass."

"As you like," he said, a little disappointed. He muttered something in a foreign tongue to his cohort, who laughed as they left.

It's always something here—if there isn't a riot, then someone's usually trying to escape. The wasted effort helps me see the positives of imprisonment. Unlike those pulling their hair out in good society, here we don't have to feel ashamed of our day-to-day unhappiness. Here we have someone visible to blame—someone wearing shiny boots. That's why, on consideration, freedom leaves me cold. Because out there in the real world, freedom means you have to admit authorship, even when your story turns out to be a stinker.

•

Where to begin my story? Negotiating with memories isn't easy: how to choose between those panting to be told, those still ripening, those already shriveling, and those destined to be mangled by language and come out pulverized? One thing's for sure: not writing about my father would take a mental effort that's beyond me. All my non-Dad thoughts feel like transparent strategies to avoid thinking about him. And why should I avoid it anyway? My father punished me for existing, and now it's my turn to punish him for existing. It's only fair.

But the real difficulty is, I feel dwarfed by our lives. They loom disproportionately large. We painted on a broader canvas than we deserved, across three continents, from obscurity to celebrity, from cities to jungles, from rags to designer rags, betrayed by our lovers and our bodies, and humiliated on a national then cosmic scale, with hardly a cuddle to keep us going. We were lazy people on an adventure, flirting with life but too shy to go all the way. So how to begin to recount our hideous odyssey? Keep it simple, Jasper. Remember, people are satisfied—no, thrilled—by the simplification of complex events. And besides, mine's a damn good story *and* it's true. I don't know why, but that seems to be important to people. Personally, if someone said to me, "I've got this great story to tell you, and every word is an absolute lie!" I'd be on the edge of my seat.

I guess I should just admit it: this will be as much about my father as it is about me. I hate how no one can tell the story of his life without making a star of his enemy, but that's just the way it is. The fact is, the whole of Australia despises my father perhaps more than any other man, just as they adore his brother, my uncle, perhaps more than any other man. I might as well set the story straight about both of them, though I don't intend to undermine your love for my uncle or reverse your hatred for my father, especially if it's an expansive hatred. I don't want to spoil things if you use your hate to quicken your awareness of who you love.

I should also say this just to get it out of the way:

My father's body will never be found.

•

Most of my life I never worked out whether to pity, ignore, adore, judge, or murder my father. His mystifying behavior left me wavering right up until the end. He had conflicting ideas about anything and everything, especially my schooling: eight months into kindergarten he decided he didn't want me there anymore because the education system was "stultifying, soul-destroying, archaic, and mundane." I don't know how anyone could call finger painting archaic and mundane. Messy, yes. Soul-destroying, no. He took me out of school with the intention of educating me himself, and instead of letting me finger-paint he read me the letters Vincent van Gogh wrote to his brother Theo right before he cut off his ear, and also passages from the book *Human, All Too Human* so that together we could "rescue Nietzsche from the Nazis." Then Dad got distracted with the time-chewing business of staring into space, and I sat around the house twiddling my thumbs, wishing there was paint on them. After six weeks he plopped me back in kindergarten, and just as it started looking like I might have a normal life after all, suddenly, in the second week of first grade, he walked right into the classroom and yanked me out once again, because he'd been overcome with the fear that he was leaving my impressionable brain "in the folds of Satan's underpants."

This time he meant it, and from our wobbly kitchen table, while flicking cigarette ash into a pile of unwashed dishes, he taught me literature, philosophy, geography, history, and some nameless subject that involved going through the daily newspapers, barking at me about how the media do something he called "whipping up moral panics" and demanding that I tell him why people allowed themselves to be whipped into panicking, morally. Other times he gave classes from his bedroom, among hundreds of secondhand books, pictures of grave-looking dead poets, empty long necks of beer, newspaper clippings, old maps, black stiff banana peels, boxes of unsmoked cigars, and ashtrays full of smoked ones.

This was a typical lesson:

"OK, Jasper. Here it is: The world's not falling apart imperceptibly anymore, these days it makes a loud shredding noise! In every city of the world, the smell of hamburgers marches brazenly down the street looking for old friends! In traditional fairy tales, the wicked witch was ugly; in modern ones, she has high cheekbones and silicone implants! People are not mysterious because they never shut up! Belief illuminates the way a blindfold does! Are you listening, Jasper? Sometimes you'll be walking in the city late at night, and a woman walking in front of you will spin her head around and then cross the street simply because some members of your gender rape women and molest children!"

Each class was equally bewildering, covering a diverse range of topics. He tried to encourage me to engage him in Socratic dialogues, but he wound up doing both parts himself. When there was a blackout during an electrical storm, Dad would light a candle and hold it under his chin to show me how the human face becomes a mask of evil with the right kind of lighting. He taught me that if I had to meet someone for an appointment, I must refuse to follow the "stupid human habit" of arbitrarily choosing a time based on fifteen-minute intervals. "Never meet people at 7:45 or 6:30, Jasper, but pick times like 7:12 and 8:03!" If the phone rang, he'd pick it up and not say anything—then, when the other person said hello, he would put on a wobbly, high-pitched voice and say, "Dad not home." Even as a child I knew that a grown man impersonating his six-year-old son to hide from the world was grotesque, but many years later I found myself doing the same thing, only I'd pretend to be him. "My son isn't home. What is this regarding?" I'd boom. Dad would nod in approval. More than anything, he approved of hiding.

These lessons continued into the outside world too, where Dad tried to teach me the art of bartering, even though we weren't living in that type of society. I remember him taking me by the hand to buy the newspaper, screaming at the baffled vendor, "No wars! No market crashes! No killers on the loose! What are you charging so much for? Nothing's happened!"

I also remember him sitting me on a plastic yellow chair and cutting my hair; to him, it was one of those things in life that was so unlike brain surgery he refused to believe that if a man had a pair of hands and a pair of scissors he couldn't cut hair. "I'm not wasting money on a barber, Jasper. What's to know? Obviously, you stop at the scalp." My father the philosopher—he couldn't even give a simple haircut without reflecting on the meaning of it. "Hair, the symbol of virility and vitality, although some very flaccid people have long hair and many vibrant baldies walk the earth. Why do we cut it anyway? What have we got against it?" he'd say, and let fly at the hair with wild, spontaneous swipes. Dad cut his own hair too, often without use of a mirror. "It doesn't have to win any prizes," he'd say, "it just has to be shorter." We were father and son with such demented, uneven hair—embodiments of one of Dad's favorite ideas that I only truly understood much later: there's freedom in looking crazy.

At nightfall, the day's lessons were capped with a bedtime story of his own invention. Yuck! They were always dark and creepy tales, and each had a protagonist that was clearly a surrogate me. Here's a typical one: *Once upon a time there was a little boy named Kasper. Kasper's friends all had the same ideas about a fat kid who lived down the street. They hated him. Kasper wanted to remain friends with the group, so he started hating the fat kid too. Then one morning Kasper woke up to find his brain had begun to putrefy until eventually it ran out his bottom in painful anal secretions. Poor Kasper!* He really had a tough time of it. In that series of bedtime stories, he was shot, stabbed, bludgeoned, dipped in boiling seas, dragged over fields of shattered glass, had his fingernails ripped out, his organs devoured by cannibals; he vanished, exploded, imploded, and often succumbed to violent spasms and hearing loss. The moral was always the same: if you follow public opinion without thinking for yourself, you will die a sudden and horrific death. For ages I was terrified of agreeing with anyone about anything, even the time.

Kasper never triumphed in any significant way. Sure, he won little battles now and then and was rewarded (two gold coins, a kiss, the approval of his father), but never, not once, did he win the war. Now I realize it was because Dad's philosophy had won *him* few personal victories in life: not love, not peace, not success, not happiness. Dad's mind couldn't imagine a lasting peace or a meaningful victory; it wasn't in his experience. That's why Kasper was doomed from the outset. He didn't stand a chance, poor bastard.

•

One of the most memorable classes began when Dad entered my bedroom with an olive-green shoebox under his arm, and said "Today's lesson is about you."

He took me to the park opposite our apartment building, one of those sad, neglected city parks that looked as if it had been the location of a war between children and junkies and the children got their arses kicked. Dead grass, broken slides, a couple of rubber swings drifting in the wind on tangled, rusty chains.

"Look, Jasper," Dad said as we settled on a bench. "It's about time you found out how your grandparents fucked up, so you can work out what you did with the failures of your antecedents: did you run with them or ricochet against their errors, instead making your own huge gaffes in an opposing orbit? We all crawl feebly away from our grandparents' graves with their sad act of dying ringing in our ears, and in our mouths we have the aftertaste of their grossest violation against themselves: the shame of their unlived lives. It's only the steady accumulation of regrets and failures and *our* shame or *our* unlived lives that opens the door to understanding them. If by some quirk of fate we led charmed lives, bounding energetically from one masterful success to another, we'd *never* understand them! Never!"

He opened the shoebox. "I want you to look at something," Dad said, scooping out a pile of loose photographs. "This is your grandfather," he continued, holding up a black-and-white picture of a young man with a beard leaning against a streetlamp. The man wasn't smiling; it looked like he was leaning on that streetlamp for fear of falling.

Dad switched to a photograph of a young woman with a plain, oval face and a weak smile. "This is your grandmother," he said before he flipped through the photographs as if he were being timed. What glimpses of the monochromatic past I caught were puzzling. Their expressions were unchanging; my grandfather wore a permanently angst-ridden grimace, while my grandmother's smile looked more depressing than the saddest frown.

Dad pulled out another photograph. "This is father number two. My real father. People always think biological is more 'real' than a man who actually raised you, but you're not raised by a potent drop of semen, are you?"

He held the photograph under my eyes. I don't know if faces can be the polar opposite of each other, but in contrast to the solemn face of the first grandfather, this one grinned as if he'd been photographed on the happiest day of not just his life but all life everywhere. He wore overalls splattered with white paint, had wild blond hair, and was streaming sweat.

"Actually, the truth is I don't look at these photos much, because all I see when I look at photographs of dead people is that they're dead," Dad said. "Doesn't matter if it's Napoleon or my own mother, they are simply the Dead."

•

That day I learned that my grandmother had been born in Poland right at the unlucky time Hitler annihilated his delusions of grandeur by making them come true—he emerged as a powerful leader with a knack for marketing. As the Germans advanced, my grandmother's parents fled Warsaw, dragged her across Eastern Europe, and, after a few harrowing months, arrived in China. That's where my grandmother grew up—in the Shanghai Ghetto during the war. She was raised speaking Polish, Yiddish, and Mandarin, suffering the soggy diseases of monsoon seasons, severe rationing, and American air raids, but surviving.

After the U.S. troops entered Shanghai with the bad news of the Holocaust, many in the Jewish community left China for all corners of the globe, but my great-grandparents decided to stay, having established themselves as owners of a successful multilingual cabaret and kosher butcher shop. This perfectly suited my young grandmother, who was already in love with my grandfather, an actor in their theater. Then, in 1956, when she was just seventeen, my grandmother got pregnant, forc-

ing her and my grandfather's families to rush through the wedding prepa-
rations as you had to do in the Old World when you didn't want people
to do the math. The week following her wedding, the family decided to
return to Poland, to raise the coming child, the cluster of cells that would
become my father, in their homeland.

They weren't welcomed back with open arms, to say the least. Who
knows whether it was guilt or fear of retribution or simply the unwelcome
surprise of a family ringing the doorbell and saying, "You're in my house,"
but they had been home less than ten minutes when, in front of my
grandmother, her parents were beaten to death with an iron pipe. My
grandmother ran but her husband remained, and he was shot for praying
in Hebrew over their bodies, though he had yet to say "Amen," so the
message wasn't transmitted. ("Amen" is like the Send button on an
e-mail.)

Suddenly a widow and an orphan, she fled Poland for the second time
in her young life, this time on a boat bound for Australia, and after two
months of staring at the daunting circumference of the horizon, she went
into labor just as someone shouted, "There it is!" Everyone ran to the
side of the boat and leaned over the rail. Steep cliffs crowned with clusters of green trees lined the coast. Australia! The younger passengers let
out cries of joy. The older passengers knew that the key to happiness lay
in keeping your expectations low. They booed.

•

"Are you with me so far?" Dad asked, interrupting himself. "These are
the building blocks of your identity. Polish. Jewish. Persecuted. Refugee.
These are just some of the vegetables with which we make a Jasper broth.
You got it?"

I nodded. I got it. Dad continued.

•

Though she could still hardly speak a word of English, my grandmother
hooked up with my grandfather number two after only six months. It's
debatable whether this should be a source of pride or a source of shame,
but he was a man who could trace his family back to the last boatload of
English-born convicts dumped on Australian soil. While it's true that

some criminals were sent down for petty crimes such as stealing a loaf of bread, my father's ancestor had not been one of them—or that is, he might have been, but he also raped three women, and if after raping those women he swiped a loaf of bread on his way home, it is not known.

Their courtship was fast. Apparently unperturbed by acquiring a child not of his own making, within a month, armed with a Polish dictionary and a book on English grammar, he asked my grandmother to marry him. "I'm just a battler, which means it'll be us against the world, and the world will probably win hands down every time, but we'll never give up fighting, no matter what, how does that sound?" She didn't answer. "Come on. Just say, 'I do,'" he pleaded. "It comes from the verb 'to do.' That's all you need for now. Then we'll move you on to 'I did.'"

My grandmother considered her situation. She didn't have anybody to help look after her baby if she went out to work, and she didn't want her child to grow up fatherless and poor. She thought, "Do I have the necessary ruthlessness to marry a man I don't really love for my son's welfare? Yes, I do." Then, looking at his hapless face, she thought, "I could do worse," one of the most ostensibly benign though chilling phrases in any language.

He was unemployed when they married, and when she moved into his apartment, my grandmother was dismayed to discover it was filled with a terrifying potpourri of macho toys: rifles, replica pistols, model war planes, weights and dumbbells. When immersed in bodybuilding, kung fu training, or cleaning his gun, he whistled amiably. In the quiet moments when the frustration of unemployment settled in and he was absorbed with anger and depression, he whistled darkly.

Then he found a job with the New South Wales Prison Services near a small town being settled four hours away. He wasn't going to work in the jail—he was going to help build it.

Because a prison was soon to loom on the town's outskirts, an unkind publication in Sydney dubbed the settlement (in which my father was to grow up) the least desirable place to live in New South Wales.

The road entered town on a descent, and as my grandparents drove in, they saw the foundations of the penitentiary on top of a hill. Set amid huge, mute trees, that half-built prison looked to my grandmother to be half demolished, and the thought struck her as an unpleasant omen. It strikes me as one too, considering that my grandfather moved to this town to build a prison and I am now writing from one. The past is truly an inoperable tumor that spreads to the present.

They moved into a boxy, weatherboard house, and the following day, while my grandmother explored the town, inadvertently frightening the residents with her aura of the survivor, my grandfather began his new job. I'm not exactly sure what role he had, but apparently for the next several months he spoke incessantly of locked doors, cold halls, cell measurements, and grilled windows. As the building neared completion, he became obsessed with everything to do with prisons, even checking out books from the newly established local library on their construction and history. At the same time, my grandmother put as much energy into learning English, and this was the beginning of a new catastrophe. As her understanding of the English language grew, she began to understand her husband.

His jokes turned out to be stupid and racist. Moreover, some of them weren't even jokes but long pointless stories that ended with my grandfather saying things like "And then I said, 'Oh yeah?'" She realized he bitched endlessly about his lot in life, and when he wasn't being nasty, he was merely banal; when not paranoid, he was boring. Soon his conversation made his handsome face grow ugly; his expression took on a cruel quality; his mouth, half open, became an expression of his stupidity. From then on every day was worsened by the new language barrier that had grown up between them—the barrier of speaking the same language.

•

Dad put the photographs back in the box with a dark expression, as if he had wanted a trip down memory lane but when he got there he remembered it was his least favorite street.

"OK, that's your grandparents. All you have to know about grandparents is that they were young once too. You have to know they didn't mean to be the embodiment of decay or even want especially to hold on to their ideas until their final day. You have to know they didn't want to run out of days. You have to know they are dead and that the dead have bad dreams. They dream of us."

He stared at me for a while, waiting for me to say something. Now, of course, I know that everything he told me was merely an introduction. I didn't understand back then that after a good, cleansing monologue, Dad wanted nothing more than for me to prod him into another one. I just pointed to the swings and asked him to push me.

"You know what?" he said. "Maybe I'll throw you back into the ring for another round."

He was returning me to school. Maybe he knew it was there I would learn the second part to that story, that I would inevitably discover another, crucial ingredient to my own distinctive identity soup.

•

A month into my new school I was still trying to adjust to being among other children again, and I decided I'd never comprehend why Dad went from ordering me to despise these people to ordering me to blend in with them.

I had made only one friend, but I was trying to accumulate more, because to survive you needed no fewer than two, in case one was away sick. One day at lunchtime I was standing behind the canteen watching two boys fight over a black water pistol.

One of the boys said, "You can be the cop. I wanna be Terry Dean."

The other boy said, "No, *you're* the cop. *I'm* Terry Dean."

I wanted to play too. I said, "Maybe I should be Terry Dean. It's my name anyway." They looked at me in that snide, superior way eight-year-olds look at you. "I'm Jasper Dean," I added.

"Are you related?"

"I don't think so."

"Then piss off."

That hurt.

I said, "Well, I'll be the cop then."

That grabbed their attention. Everyone knows that in games of cops and robbers, the robber is always the default hero while the cops are fodder. You can never have too much fodder.

We played all lunchtime and at the sound of the bell I betrayed my ignorance by asking, "Who's Terry Dean?"—a question that made my playmates sick.

"Shit! You don't even know who he is!"

"He's the baddest man in the whole world."

"He was a bank robber."

"And a killer!" the other one said, before they ran off without saying goodbye, in the same way as when you go to a nightclub with friends and they get lucky.

That afternoon I went home to find Dad hitting the edge of a cabinet with a banana so it made a hard knocking sound.

"I froze a banana," he said listlessly. "Take a bite . . . if you dare."

"Am I related to the famous bank robber Terry Dean?" I asked. The banana dropped like a chunk of cement. Dad sucked his lips into his mouth, and from somewhere inside, a small, hollow voice I strained to hear said, "He was your uncle."

"My what? My uncle? I have an uncle?" I asked, incredulous. "And he's a famous bank robber?"

"Was. He's dead," Dad said, before adding, "He was my brother."

That was the first time I heard of him. Terry Dean, cop killer, bank robber, hero to the nation, pride of the battler—he was my uncle, my father's brother, and he was to cast an oblong shadow over both our lives, a shadow that for a long time prevented either of us from getting a decent tan.

If you're Australian, you will at least have heard of Terry Dean. If you aren't, you won't have, because while Australia is an eventful place, what goes on there is about as topical in world newspapers as "Bee Dies in New Guinea After Stinging Tree by Mistake." It's not our fault. We're too far away. That's what a famous Australian historian once called the "tyranny of distance." What he meant was, Australia is like a lonely old woman dead in her apartment; if every living soul in the land suddenly had a massive coronary at the exact same time and if the Simpson Desert died of thirst and the rainforests drowned and the barrier reef bled to death, days might pass and only the smell drifting across the ocean to our Pacific neighbors would compel someone to call the police. Otherwise we'd have to wait until the Northern Hemisphere commented on the uncollected mail.

Dad wouldn't talk to me about his brother. Every time I asked him for details he'd sigh long and deep, as though this were another setback he didn't need, so I embarked on my own research.

First I asked my classmates, but I received answers that differed from each other so wildly, I just had to discount them all. Then I examined the measly collection of family photographs that I had seen only fleetingly before, the ones that lay in the green shoebox stuffed into the hall closet. This time I noticed that three of the photographs had been butchered to remove someone's head. The operation could hardly be described as seamless. I could still see the neck and shoulders in two photos, and a third was just two pieces clumsily stuck together with uneven strips of brown packing tape. I concluded that my father had tried to erase any image of his brother so he might forget him. The futility of the attempt was obvious; when you put in that much effort to forget someone, the effort itself becomes a memory. Then you have to forget the forgetting, and that too is memorable. Fortunately, Dad couldn't erase the newspaper articles I found in the state library that described Terry's escapades, his killing spree, his manhunt, his capture, and his death. I made photocopies and pasted them to the walls of my bedroom, and at night I fantasized that I was my uncle, the fiercest criminal ever to hide a body in the soil and wait for it to grow.

In a bid to boost my popularity, I told everyone at school about my connection to Terry Dean, doing everything to broadcast it short of hiring a publicist. It was big news for a while, and one of the worst mistakes I've ever made. At first, in the faces of my peers, I inspired awe. But then kids of all ages came out of the woodwork wanting to fight me. Some wanted to make reputations for beating the nephew of Terry Dean. Others were eager to wipe the proud smile off my face; pride must have magnified my features unappealingly. I talked my way out of a number of scuffles, but one day before school my assailants tricked me by flouting the regulation time code for beatings: it always happens *after* school, never in the morning, before an eight-year-old has had his coffee. Anyway, there were four of them, four bruisers grim-faced and fist-ready. I didn't stand a chance. I was cornered. This was it: my first fight.

A crowd had gathered around to watch. They chanted in their best *Lord of the Flies* manner. I searched the faces for allies. No luck. They all wanted to see me go down screaming. I didn't take it personally. It was just my turn, that's all. I tell you, it's indescribable the joy children get from watching a fight. It's a blinding Christmas orgasm for a child. And this is human nature undiluted by age and experience! This is mankind fresh out of the box! Whoever says it's life that makes monsters out of people should check out the raw nature of children, a lot of pups who haven't yet had their dose of failure, regret, disappointment, and betrayal but still behave like savage dogs. I have nothing against children, I just wouldn't trust one not to giggle if I accidentally stepped on a land mine.

My enemies closed in. The fight was seconds away from starting, and probably as many seconds away from finishing. I had nowhere to go. They came closer. I made a colossal decision: *I would not put up a fight. I would not take it like a man. I would not take it like a battler.* Look, I know people like reading about those outclassed in strength who make up for it in spirit, like my uncle Terry. Respected are those who go down fighting, right? But those noble creatures still get a hell of a clobbering, and I didn't want a clobbering of any kind. Also, I remembered something Dad had taught me in one of our kitchen-table classes. He said, "Listen, Jasper. Pride is the first thing you need to do away with in life. It's there to make you feel good about yourself. It's like putting a suit on a shriveled carrot and taking it out to the theater and pretending it's someone important. The first step in self-liberation is to be free of self-respect. I understand why it's useful for some. When people have nothing, they can still have their pride. That's why the poor were given the myth of nobility, because the cupboards were bare. Are you listening to me? This is important, Jasper. I don't want you to have anything to do with nobility, pride, or self-respect. They're tools to help you bronze your own head."

I sat on the ground with my legs crossed. I didn't even straighten my back. I slouched. They had to bend down to punch me in the jaw. One of them got on his knees to do it. They took turns. They tried to get me to my feet; I let my body go limp. One of them had to hold me up, but I had become slippery and slid greasily through their fingers back onto the ground. I was still taking a beating, and my head was stunned by strong fists pounding at it, but the pummeling was sloppy, confused. Eventually my plan worked: they gave up. They asked what was wrong with me. They asked me why I wouldn't fight back. Maybe the truth was I was too busy fighting back tears to be fighting back people, but I didn't say anything. They spat at me and then left me to contemplate the color of my own blood. Against the white of my shirt, it was a luminous red.

When I got home, I found Dad standing by my bed, staring witheringly at the newspaper clippings on the walls.

"Jesus. What happened to you?"

"I don't want to talk about it."

"Let's get you cleaned up."

"No, I want to see what happens to blood when you leave it overnight."

"Sometimes it turns black."

"I want to see that."

I was just about to rip down the pictures of Uncle Terry when Dad said, "I wish you'd take these down," so of course I kept them right where they were. Then Dad said, "This isn't who he was. They've turned him into a hero."

Suddenly I found myself loving my degenerate uncle again, so I said, "He *is* a hero."

"A boy's father is his hero, Jasper."

"Are you sure about that?"

Dad turned and snorted at the headlines.

"You can't know what a hero is, Jasper. You've grown up in a time when that word has been debased, stripped of all meaning. We're fast becoming the first nation whose populace consists solely of heroes who do nothing but celebrate each other. Of course we've always made heroes of excellent sportsmen and -women—if you perform well for your country as a long-distance runner, you're heroic as well as fast—but now all you need to do is be in the wrong place at the wrong time, like that poor bastard covered by an avalanche. The dictionary would label him a survivor, but Australia is keen to call him a hero, because what does the dictionary know? And now *everyone* returning from an armed conflict is called a hero too. In the old days you had to commit specific acts of valor *during* war; now you just need to turn up. These days when a war is on, heroism seems to mean 'attendance.' "

"What's this got to do with Uncle Terry?"

"Well, he falls into the final category of heroism. He was a murderer, but his victims were well chosen."

"I don't get it."

Dad turned toward the window, and I could tell by the way his ears wiggled up and down that he was talking to himself in that weird way where he did the mouth movements but kept all the sound in. Finally he spoke like a person.

"People don't understand me, Jasper. And that's OK, but it's sometimes irritating, because they think they do. But all they see is the façade I use in company, and in truth, I have made very few adjustments to the Martin Dean persona over the years. Oh sure, a touch-up here, a touch-up there, you know, to move with the times, but it has essentially remained intact from day one. People are always saying that a person's character is unchangeable, but mostly it's the *persona* that doesn't change, not the person, and underneath that changeless mask exists a creature who's evolving like crazy, mutating out of control. I tell you, the most consistent person you know is more than likely a complete stranger to you, blossoming and sprouting all sorts of wings and branches and third eyes. You could sit beside that person in an office cubicle for ten years and not see the growth spurts going on right under your nose. Honestly, anyone who says a friend of theirs hasn't changed in years just can't tell a mask from an actual face."

"What the hell are you talking about?"

Dad walked to my bed and, after doubling over the pillow, lay down and made himself comfortable.

"I'm saying it's always been a little dream of mine for someone to hear firsthand about my childhood. For instance, did you know that my physical imperfections almost did me in? You've heard the expression 'When they made him, they threw away the mold'? Well, it was as if someone picked up a mold that had already been thrown away, and even though it was cracked and warped by the sun and ants had crawled inside it and an old drunk had urinated on it, they reused it to make me. You probably didn't know either that people were always abusing me for being clever. They'd say, 'You're too clever, Martin, too clever by half, too clever for your own good.' I smiled and thought they must be mistaken. How can a person be too clever? Isn't that like being too good-looking? Or too rich? Or too happy? What I didn't understand was that people don't think; they repeat. They don't process; they regurgitate. They don't digest; they copy. I had only a splinter of awareness back then that no matter what anybody says, choosing between the available options is not the same as thinking for yourself. The only true way of thinking for yourself is to create options of your own, options that don't exist. That's what my childhood taught me and that's what it should teach you, Jasper, if you hear me out. Then afterward, when people are talking about me, I'm not going to be the only one to know they are wrong, wrong, wrong. Get it? When people talk about me in front of us, you and I will be able to give each other sly, secret looks across the room, it will be a real giggle, and maybe one day, after I'm dead, you'll tell them the truth, you'll reveal everything about me, everything I've told you, and maybe they'll feel like fools, or maybe they'll shrug and go, 'Oh really, interesting,' then turn back to the game show they were watching. But in any case, that's up to you, Jasper. I certainly don't want to pressure you into spilling the secrets of my heart and soul unless you feel it will make you richer, either spiritually or financially."

"Dad, are you going to tell me about Uncle Terry or not?"

"Am I—what do you think I've just been saying?"

"I have absolutely no idea."

"Well, sit down and shut up and I'll tell you a story."

This was it. Time for Dad to open up and spill his version of the Dean family chronicles, his version that was contrary to the mythologizing gossip of the nation. So he started to talk. He talked and talked nonstop until eight in the morning, and if he was breathing underneath all those words, I couldn't see it or hear it but I sure could smell it. When he'd finished, I felt as though I'd traveled through my father's head and come out somehow diminished, just slightly less sure of my identity than when I went in. I think, to do justice to his unstoppable monologue, it'd be better if you heard it in his own words—the words he bequeathed me which have become my own, the words I've never forgotten. That way you get to know two people for the price of one. That way you can hear it as I did, only partially as a chronicle of Terry Dean, but predominantly as a story of my father's unusual childhood of illness, near-death experiences, mystical visions, ostracism, and misanthropy, followed closely by an adolescence of dereliction, fame, violence, pain, and death.

Anyway, you know how it is. Every family has a story like this one.

Deadlock

I've been asked the same question again and again. Everyone wants to know the same thing: What was Terry Dean like as a child? They expect tales of kiddy violence and corruption in the heart of an infant. They imagine a miniature criminal crawling around the playpen perpetrating acts of immorality between feedings. Ridiculous! Was Hitler goose-stepping all the way to his mother's breast? OK, it's true, there were signs if you chose to read into them. At seven years old, when Terry was the cop in cops and robbers, he'd let you go if you greased his palm with a lolly. In games of hide-and-seek, he hid like a fugitive. But so what? It doesn't mean a predisposition to violence is printed on a man's DNA. Yes, people are always disappointed when I tell them that as far as I'm aware, Terry was a normal infant; he slept and cried and ate and shat and pissed and gradually discerned that he was a different entity from, say, the wall (that's your first lesson in life: you are not the wall). As a child he ran around screaming that high-pitched noise that children scream. He loved reaching for poisonous substances to put in his mouth (an infant's instinct for suicide is razor-sharp), and he had an uncanny ability to cry just as our parents were falling asleep. By all accounts, he was just another baby. I was the remarkable one, if only for my inabilities.

Before Terry arrived, our lives were dominated by illness. It amazes me now how little I knew about my own condition, and how little I wanted to know. The only thing that interested me were the symptoms (violent stomach pains, muscle aches, nausea, dizziness); the underlying causes seemed totally irrelevant. They had nothing to do with me. Encephalitis? Leukemia? Immune deficiency? To this day I don't really know. By the time it occurred to me to get a straight answer, everyone who might have had one was long dead. I know the doctors *had* theories, but I also remember they couldn't make up their minds. I can only recall certain phrases, such as "muscle abnormality," "disorder of the nervous system," and "euthanasia," that made little impact on me at the time. I remember being jabbed with needles and force-fed pills the size and shape of swollen thumbs. I remember that when they took X-rays, the doctors ducked out of the way very quickly, as if they'd just set off a firework.

This all happened before Terry was born.

Then one day I took a turn for the worse. My breathing was short and labored. Swallowing took a century; my throat was a wasteland, and I would have sold my soul for some saliva. My bladder and my bowels had minds of their own. A pasty-faced doctor visited me twice a day, speaking to my anxious mother at the foot of my bed, always as if I were in the other room. "We could take him to hospital," he'd say. "But really, what's the point? He's better off here."

It was then I began to wonder if I would die and if they would bury me in the new town's new cemetery. They were still clearing the trees when I was at death's door. I wondered: Would it be finished in time? If I carked it before it was ready, they'd have to ship my body off to a cemetery in some distant town I had never lived in, whose populace would walk past my grave without thinking, "I remember him." Unbearable! So I thought maybe if I held off death for a couple of weeks, maybe if I got the timing right, I could be the first body to transform the empty field into a functional cemetery, the inaugural corpse. Then I wouldn't be for-gotten. Yes, I was making plans while lying in wait for death. I thought about all the worms and maggots in that field and how they were in for a treat. Don't snack, you maggots! Human flesh is coming! Don't ruin your dinner!

Lying in bed as the sun slid through the crack in the curtains, I thought about nothing else. I reached up and threw open the curtains. I called out to people walking past. What's going on with that cemetery? How's the progress? I was keeping tabs. And it was good news. The trees were gone. Iron gates fastened onto blocks of stone were erected as the entrance to the cemetery. Granite tablets had been shipped from Sydney; all they needed was a name! The shovels were standing by. It was all go!

Then I heard some terrible news. My parents were talking in the kitchen. According to my father, the old woman who ran the local pub had had a massive stroke in the middle of the night. Not a little one, but *massive!* I dragged myself upright. What's this? Yes, my father said, she was barely hanging on. She wasn't just *at* death's door, she was pounding on it! Oh no! A catastrophe! It was going to be a race to the finish line! Who would be first? The old biddy was nearly eighty, so she'd been prac-ticing dying for a lot longer than me. She had nature on her side. I had nothing but luck to hold out for. I was too young to die of old age but too old for infant mortality. I was stuck in the middle, that terrible stretch of time where people can't help but breathe.

The next day, when my father stopped into my room to check on me, I asked how the old woman was traveling. "Not good," he said. "She isn't expected to last the weekend." I knew I had at least another week, maybe ten days in me. I hit the bed. I tore the sheets. He had to hold me down. "What the hell's got into you?" he shouted. I let him in on it, ex-plained that if I were to die, I wanted to be the first in the cemetery. He laughed right in my face, the bastard. He called my mother in. "Guess what your son's been saying to me?" Then he told her. She gazed at me with infinite pity and sat on the edge of the bed and hugged me as if she were trying to stop me from falling. "You won't die, honey. You won't."

"He's pretty sick," my father said.

"Shut up!"

"It's best to prepare for the worst."

The next day my smug father told the men at his worksite what I'd said. They laughed too, the bastards. At night the men told their wives.

They also laughed, the bitches. They thought it was adorable. Don't children say the cutest things? Soon the whole town was laughing. Then they stopped laughing and started wondering. It was a good question, they decided: who *would* be the first? Shouldn't there be a ceremony to commemorate the inaugural corpse? Not just a regular funeral. A real show! A big turnout! Maybe a band? The first burial is a big moment for a town. A town that buries its own is a living town. Only dead towns export their dead.

Queries on the state of my health poured in from all directions. People came in droves to see the exhibit. "How's he doing?" I heard them ask my mother. "He's fine!" she said tensely. They pushed past her into my bedroom. They had to see for themselves. Dozens of faces passed through my bedroom, peering at me expectantly. They came to see me lying prostrate, motionless, dying. Regardless, they were all very chatty. When people think your days are numbered, they're really very nice to you. It's only when you're trying to get on in the world that they bring their claws out.

That was only the adults, of course; the kids of the town couldn't stand to be in the same room as me. That taught me something worth noting: the healthy and the sick are not peers, whatever else they might have in common.

Apparently everyone hassled the old woman too. I heard they crowded around her bed looking at their watches. I couldn't understand why they'd taken such an interest. Later I learned bets had been laid. The old woman was the favorite. I was the long shot. I ran at over 100 to 1. Hardly anyone bet on me. I guess no one, not even in a morbid game of Guess Who'll Die First, liked contemplating the death of a child. It just didn't sit well with anyone.

"He's dead! He's dead!" a voice shouted one afternoon. I checked my pulse. Still ticking. I pulled myself up and called through the window at old George Buckley, our nearest neighbor.

"Who? Who's dead?"

"Frank Williams! He fell off the roof!"

Frank Williams. He lived four houses down on the same street. From my window I could see the whole town running to his house to look. I wanted to look too. I dragged myself out of bed and moved like a greasy slug along the floor of my bedroom, into the hallway, out the front door into dazzling sunlight. Keeping my pajama pants on was an issue, but then it always is. Wiggling across the patchy grass lawn, I thought about Frank Williams, the late entry and surprise winner of our little contest. Father of four. Or was it five? All boys. He was always trying to teach his sons to ride a bike. When it wasn't one son wobbling past my window with a hysterically tense grimace, it was another. I always hated the Williams boys for being slow learners. Now I felt sorry for them. No one should lose a parent through clumsiness. Their whole lives, those boys are going to have to say, "Yeah. My father fell off a roof. Lost his balance. What? What does it matter what he was doing up there?" Poor kids. Clearing gutters is no reason for a man to die. There's just no honor in it.

The curious horde crouching around the dead man took no notice of the sick little worm crawling toward them. I made it through the legs of Bruce Davies, the town butcher. He peered down just as I peered up. Our eyes locked. I thought someone should tell him to get far away from the lifeless carcass of our neighbor. I didn't like the glint in that butcher's eye.

I looked closer. Frank's neck was broken. His head had rolled back in a pool of dark blood and hung limp across the shoulders. When a neck breaks, it really breaks. I looked closer still. His eyes were wide open but there was nothing behind them, just a stupefying cavern. I thought: That will be me soon. Nothingness will envelop me just as it has enveloped him. Because of the contest and my own part in it, I saw this death not just as a preview of my own, but as an echo. Frank and I were in this together, chained to one another in some macabre marriage for all eternity—deadlock, I now call it, the affinity the living have with the dead. It's not for everyone. You either feel it or you don't. I did then and I do now. I feel it profoundly: this sacred, insidious bond. I feel they are waiting for me to join them in holy deadlock.

I rested my head on Frank's lap and closed my eyes and let the voices of the townspeople soothe me to sleep.

"Poor Frank," someone said.

"He'd had a good innings."

"What was he doing up on that roof?"

"He was forty-two."

"Is that my ladder?"

"Forty-two is young. He didn't have a good innings. He had a shit innings."

"I'm forty-four next week."

"What are you doing?"

"Let go of that!"

"This is my ladder. I lent it to him last year, but when I asked about it he swore he'd returned it."

"What about the boys?"

"Oh geez . . . the boys."

"What's going to happen to them?"

"They'll be OK. They still have their mother."

"But they won't have this ladder. It's mine."

Then I fell asleep.

I awoke back in bed, sicker than ever. The doctor said that by crawling half a kilometer to see my first dead body, I had set my health back, as if it were a clock I had adjusted for daylight saving. After he left, my mother sat on the edge of my bed, her unstrung face an inch from mine, and she told me in an almost guilty voice that she was pregnant. I was too weak to say congratulations, and I just lay there as she stroked my forehead, which I really liked and still do, although there's nothing soothing in stroking your own forehead.

•

Over the following months, as my condition gradually worsened, my pregnant mother sat down beside me and let me touch her belly, which was swelling horribly. Occasionally I felt the kick or perhaps head butt of the fetus inside. Once, when she thought I was asleep, I heard her whisper, "It's a shame you won't get to meet him."

Then, just when I was at my weakest and death was licking her lips, something unexpected happened.

I didn't die.

But I didn't live either.

Quite by accident, I took the third option: I slipped into a coma. Bye-bye world, bye-bye consciousness, bye-bye light, too bad death, hello ether. It was a hell of a thing. I was hiding right in between death's open arms and life's folded ones. I was nowhere, absolutely nowhere at all. Honestly, you can't even get to limbo from a coma.

Coma

My coma was nothing like those I've read about since: I've heard of people who fell into a coma in the middle of telling a joke and forty-two years later woke up and told the punch line. For them, those decades of oblivion were an instant of nothingness, as if they had passed through one of Sagan's wormholes, time had curled around on itself, and they had flown through it in a sixteenth of a second.

Describing the thoughts, visions, and sensations I had inside that coma is near impossible. It wasn't the nothingness, because there was quite a bit of somethingness (when you're in a coma, even anyness is good), but I was too young to make sense of the experience. I can say, though, that I had as many dreams and visions as if I'd consumed a canyonful of peyote.

No, I won't try to describe the indescribable, only so much as to say there were sounds I heard that I could not have heard and things I saw that I could not have seen. What I'm about to say is going to sound insane—or, worse, mystical, and you know I'm not that way inclined—but here it is: if you look at the unconscious mind as a big barrel, in the normal run of things the lid is open and sights, sounds, experiences, bad vibes, and sensations pour in during the waking hours, but when there aren't any waking hours, none at all, for months or even years, and the lid is sealed, it's possible that the restless mind, desperate for activity, might reach deep into the barrel, right down to the bottom of the unconscious, dredging up stores of things that were left there by previous generations. This is a Jungian explanation and I don't even know if I like Jung, but there's very little else out there on the shelves that could go any way to explain the things I saw that I could not have seen, to justify the things I heard that I could not have heard.

Let me try to put it another way. There is a short story by Borges called "The Aleph." In the story, the Aleph, hidden under the nineteenth step of a cellar staircase, is an ancient mysterious portal to every point in the universe—I'm not kidding, every single point—and if you look into it, you see, well, absolutely everything. I'm hypothesizing that somewhere in the ancient parts of ourselves there could exist a similar porthole, resting quietly in a crack or a crevice or within the folds of the memory of your own birth, only the thing is, normally we never get to reach it or see it because the usual business of living piles mountains of crap on top of it. I'm not saying I believe this, I'm only giving you the best explanation I've come up with so far for the root of the extraordinarily dizzying hodgepodge of sights and sounds that flashed and whirled before my mind's eye and ear. If the mind can have eyes, why not ears? You probably think there's no such thing as the mind's nose, either. Well, there is. And like Borges in his story, I can't accurately describe it because my visions were simultaneous, and language, being successive, means I have to record it that way. So use your imagination, Jasper, when I tell you one gazillionth of what I saw:

I saw all the dawns come up too early and all the middays reminding you you'd better get a hurry on and all the dusks whisper "I don't think you're going to make it" and all the shrugging midnights say "Better luck tomorrow." I saw all the hands that ever waved to a stranger thinking it was a friend. I saw all the eyes that ever winked to let someone know their insult was only a joke. I saw all the men wipe down toilet seats before urinating but never after. I saw all the lonely men stare at department store mannequins and think "I'm attracted to a mannequin. This is getting sad." I saw all the love triangles and a few love rectangles and one crazy love hexagon in the back room of a sweaty Parisian café. I saw all the condoms put on the wrong way. I saw all the ambulance drivers on their off hours caught in traffic wishing there was a dying man in the backseat. I saw all the charity-givers wink at heaven. I saw all the Buddhists bitten by spiders they wouldn't kill. I saw all the flies bang uselessly into the screen doors and all the fleas laughing as they rode in on pets. I saw all the broken dishes in all the Greek restaurants and all the Greeks thinking "Culture's one thing, but this is getting expensive." I saw all the lonely people scared by their own cats. I saw all the prams, and anyone who says all babies are cute didn't see the babies I saw. I saw all the funerals and all the acquaintances of the dead enjoying their afternoon off work. I saw all the astrology columns predicting that one twelfth of the population of earth will be visited by a relative who wants to borrow money. I saw all the forgeries of great paintings but no forgeries of great books. I saw all the signs forbidding entrance and exit but none forbidding arson or murder. I saw all the carpets with cigarette burns and all the kneecaps with carpet burns. I saw all the worms dissected by curious children and eminent scientists. I saw all the polar bears and the grizzly bears and the koala bears used to describe fat people you just want to cuddle. I saw all the ugly men hitting on all the happy women who made the mistake of smiling at them. I saw inside all the mouths and it's really disgusting in there. I saw all the bird's-eye views of all the birds who think humanity looks pretty active for a bunch of toilet heads . . .

What was I supposed to make of all this? I know that most people would have taken it as a divine vision. They might even have found God in there, jumping out at them like a holy jack-in-the-box. Not me. All I saw was man and all his insignificant sound and fury. What I saw shaped my perspective of the world, sure, but I don't think it was a supernatural gift. A girl once told me that in thinking this I was turning a blind eye to a message from God and I should be walking around filled with a spiritual welling in my soul. That sounds nice, but what can I do about it? I don't have it in me. If it was his intent to tell me something in all that visual noise, God picked the wrong guy. My inability to make a leap of faith is carved into my DNA. Sorry, Lord. I guess one man's burning bush is another man's spot fire.

Six months must have passed in that state. In the outside world I was bathed and fed through tubes; my bowels and bladder were emptied, my appendages massaged, and my body manipulated into whatever shape amused my caretakers.

Then a change occurred: the Aleph, if that's what it was, was unexpectedly and unceremoniously sucked back down into its hiding place and all the visions departed in an instant. Who knows what mechanism was behind the lifting of the lid to the barrel, but it opened a crack wide enough for a stream of sound to come flooding in; my hearing returned and I was wide awake but still blind and mute and paralyzed. But I could hear. And what I heard was the voice of a man I didn't recognize coming through loud and clear, and his words were powerful and old and terrifying:

> Let the stars of the twilight thereof be dark; let it look for light,
> but have none; neither let it see the dawning of the day: Because
> it shut not up the doors of my mother's womb, nor hid sorrow from
> mine eyes. Why died I not from the womb?

I might have been paralyzed, but I could feel my internal organs tremble. The voice continued:

Wherefore is light given to him that is in misery, and life unto the bitter in soul. Which long for death but it cometh not: and dig for it more than for hid treasures; Which rejoice exceedingly, and are glad, when they can find the grave? Why is light given to a man whose way is hid, and whom God has hedged in?

(I later discovered that the voice belonged to Patrick Ackerman, one of our town's councillors, and he was reading me the Bible, from beginning to end. As you well know, Jasper, I don't believe in fate or destiny, but I do find it interesting that the very moment my ears cleared and were primed for listening, these words were the first that greeted them.)

With the return of consciousness and hearing, instinctively I knew that soon would come vision, followed by the ability to touch myself. In short, life. I was on my way back.

But before I returned, there was still a long road to go, and that road was paved with voices. A real cavalcade—old seductive voices, young expressive voices, scratchy throat-cancerish voices—and the voices were full of words and the words were telling stories. Only much later did I learn that the town had taken me on as a sort of community project. Some doctor had pronounced it necessary that I be spoken to, and with our new bush town dying of unemployment, all those semi-altruistic souls who didn't have anything to do with their days turned up in droves. The funny thing was, I asked some of them afterward and not one of them thought I was really listening. But I *was* listening. More than listening, I was absorbing. And more than absorbing, I was remembering. Because the peculiar detail of all this is, perhaps because of the sightless, paralyzed state I was imprisoned in, the books read to me when I was in that coma burned into my memory. This was my supernatural education: the words of those books read to me in my coma I can quote to you word for word.

As it became clear that I wasn't going to die any day soon and might be in this petrified state forever, the voices became fewer and fewer, until only one voice remained: my mother's. The rest of the town gave me up for a block of wood, but my mother kept on reading. My mother, a woman who had only several years earlier left her native land having never read an English book in her life, was now churning through them by the hundreds. And the unexpected consequence was, as she stocked up my mind with words, thoughts, ideas, and sensations, she did as much to her own. It was as though great big trucks filled with words drove up to our heads and dumped their contents directly into our brains. All that unbound imagination brightened and stretched our minds with incredible tales of heroic deeds, painful loves, romantic descriptions of remote lands, philosophies, myths, the histories of nations rising, falling, chafing, and tumbling into the sea, adventures of warriors and priests and farmers and monsters and conquerors and barmaids and Russians so neurotic you wanted to pull out your own teeth. It was a prodigious jumble of legends my mother and I discovered simultaneously, and those writers and philosophers and storytellers and prophets became idols to us both.

Only much later, when my mother's sanity came under scrutiny, did it occur to me what might have happened to her lonely and frustrated head, reading aloud all those astonishing books to her motionless son. What did those words mean to her in the painful quiet of my bedroom with the product of her loins lying there like a leg of lamb? I imagine her mind aching with the pains of growth like a tortured body stretched on a rack. I imagine her dwelling on what she read. I imagine her smashing through the confines of her cemented ideas with all those brutal, beautiful truths. It must have been a slow and confounding torment. When I think of what she transformed into much later, what demented tragedy she had become by the end of her young life, I can envisage in my mother the agonizing delight of the reader who hears for the first time all the ramblings of the soul, and recognizes them as her own.

The Game

Shortly after my eighth birthday, I woke up. Just like that. Four years and four months after I slipped into a coma, I slipped out again. Not only could my eyes see, but I used the lids to blink. I opened my mouth and asked for cordial—I wanted to taste something sweet. Only people regaining consciousness in movies ask for water. In real life you think of cocktails with pineapple chunks and little umbrellas.

There were a lot of joyous faces in my bedroom the week I returned to the land of the living. People seemed genuinely pleased to see me, and they all said "Welcome back," as if I'd been away on a long voyage and any moment I was going to pull out the presents. My mother hugged me and covered my hands in wet kisses that I could now wipe on my pajamas. Even my father was jubilant, no longer the unfortunate man with the freak-show stepson, the Amazing Sleeping Kid. But little four-year-old Terry: he was in hiding. My sudden rebirth was too much of a shock. My mother breathlessly called for him to come and meet his brother, but Terry was a no-show. I was still too tired and weak to be offended. Later, when everything went into the toilet, I was forced to consider what it must have been like for Terry's developing mind to grow up next to a corpse and then to be told "That creepy mummy over there is your brother." It must have been spooky, especially at night when the moonlight hit my frozen face and my unmoving eyeballs fixed on the poor kid, as if they had solidified that way on purpose, just to stare.

On the third day after my resurrection, my father thundered in and said, "Let's get you up and about." He and my mother grabbed my arms and helped me out of bed. My legs were sad, dead things, so they dragged me around the room as if I were a drunk friend they were escorting out of a bar. Then my father got an idea. "Hey! You've probably forgotten what you look like!" It was true. I had. A vague image of a little boy's face drifted somewhere in my mind, but I couldn't be sure if it was me or someone who had once hated me. With my bare feet trailing behind, my father dragged me into the bathroom to look at myself in a mirror. It was a crushing spectacle. Even ugly people know beauty when they don't see it.

•

Terry couldn't avoid me forever. It was about time we were properly introduced. Soon after everyone had lost interest in congratulating me on waking up, he came into the room and sat on his bed, bouncing rhythmically, hands pressed down on his knees as if to keep them from flying away.

I lay back in bed gazing at the ceiling and pulled the covers over me. I could hear my brother breathing. I could hear myself breathing too—so could anyone; the air whistled noisily through my throat. I felt awkward and ridiculous. I thought: He'll speak when he's ready. My eyelids weighed a ton, but I wouldn't allow them the satisfaction of closing. I was afraid the coma was waiting.

It took an hour for Terry to bridge the distance between us.

"You had a good sleep," he said.

I nodded but couldn't think of anything to say. The sight of my brother was overpowering. I felt impossibly tender and wanted a hug, but decided it was better to remain aloof. More than anything, I just couldn't get over how unrelated we looked. I know we had different fathers, but it was as if our mother hadn't a single dominant gene in her whole body. While I had an oily yellow complexion, a pointed chin, brown hair, slightly protruding teeth, and ears pressed flat against my head like they were waiting for someone to pass, Terry had thick blond hair and blue eyes and a smile like a dental postcard and fair skin dotted with adorable orange freckles; his features had a perfect symmetry to them, like a child mannequin's.

"Do you want to see my hole?" he said suddenly. "I dug a hole in the backyard."

"Later on, mate. I'm a bit tired."

"Go on," my father said, scowling. He was standing at the door glaring at me. "You need fresh air."

"I can't now," I said. "I feel too weak."

Disappointed, Terry slapped my atrophied leg and ran outside to play. I watched him from the window, a little ball of energy trampling on flower beds, a little streak of fire jumping in and out of the hole he'd dug. While I watched him, my father remained hovering at the bedroom door, with burning eyes and fatherly sneers.

•

Here's the thing: I had peered over the abyss, stared into the yellow eyes of death, and now that I was back in the land of the living, did I want sunshine? Did I want to kiss flowers? Did I want to run and play and shout, "To be alive! To be alive!" Actually, no. I wanted to stay in bed. It's difficult to explain why. All I know is a powerful laziness seeped into me during my coma, a laziness that ran through my blood and solidified into my core.

It was only six weeks after my groggy reawakening when—even though the pain it caused me to walk was reshaping my body to resemble a eucalypt twisted by fire—my parents and doctors decided it was time for me to return to school. The boy who had slept through a sizable chunk of his childhood was expected to slip unnoticed into society. At first the children greeted me with curiosity: "Did you dream?" "Could you hear people talking to you?" "Show us your bedsores! Show us your bedsores!" But the one thing a coma doesn't teach you is how to blend into your surroundings (unless everyone around you is sleeping). I had only a few days to work it out. Obviously, I failed miserably, because it wasn't two weeks later when the attacks started. The pushing, the beating, the intimidation, the insults, the jeers, the wedgies, the tongue poking, and, worst of all, the agonizing silence: there were almost two hundred students at our school, and they gave me four hundred cold shoulders. It was the kind of cold that burned like fire.

I longed for school to be over so I could go to bed. I wanted to spend all my time there. I loved lying down, the reading lamp shining, just a sheet over me, the blankets bunched up at the bottom of the bed like fat rolls. My father was unemployed then (the prison was completed and had its grand opening while I was in the coma), and he burst into my room at all hours and screamed, "GET OUT OF BED! CHRIST! IT'S A BEAUTIFUL DAY OUTSIDE!" His fury multiplied tenfold when directed at Terry, who would lie in bed too. You see, it might be difficult for anyone to believe now, but somehow, juvenile invalid though I was, I still managed to be a hero to Terry. He adored me. He idolized me. When I lay all day in bed, Terry lay all day in bed. When I threw up, Terry plunged his fingers down his own throat. I'd be under the sheets curled up into a ball, shivering uncontrollably with fever, and Terry would be curled and shivering too. It was sweet.

My father was scared stiff for him, for his actual son, and he concentrated all his mental forces into predicting terrible futures, all because of me.

One day he had an idea, and for a parent, it wasn't a bad one. If your child has an unhealthy obsession, the only way to wean him off it is to replace it with a healthy one. The obsession my father chose to lure Terry away from wanting to be an invalid was as Australian as a funnel-web spider bite on the kneecap.

Sport.

•

It was Christmas. Terry was given a football. My father said to him, "Well, let's you and me go throw the ball around, eh?" Terry didn't want to go because he knew I would stay inside. My father put his foot down and dragged him kicking and screaming out into the sunshine. I watched them through the window. Terry put on a fake limp. Whenever my father threw the ball, Terry hobbled miserably across the field to catch it.

"Now stop that limping!"

"I can't help it!"

"There's nothing wrong with your leg!"

"Yes there is!"

My father spat with revulsion and grumbled his way back into the house, plotting and scheming the way fathers do, out of love. He decided that for a spell he needed to keep his unhealthy stepson away from his healthy actual son; he saw disease as a combination of laziness and weakness, as an inclination, and in our house you couldn't so much as cough without him seeing it as a reflection of your disgusting interior. He wasn't normally an unsympathetic man, and he had his fair share of struggle, but he was one of those people who had never been sick a day in his life (only in his unpaid-bill-induced nausea) and had never even known anybody who had been sick. Even his own parents died without protracted illness (bus crash). I know I've said it before: if my childhood taught me one thing, it's that the differences between the rich and the poor are nothing. It's the chasm between the healthy and the sick that you just can't breach.

The next morning, with my father dragging two suitcases and Terry dragging his leg, they climbed into the family car and disappeared in wild swirls of dust. Two months later, when they returned, Terry told me that they had followed the local football team around the state, going to all the games. After a couple of weeks the team began to notice them, and, touched by the devotion of an apparently lame child, they elected my little limping brother their unofficial mascot. At the first opportunity, my father unburdened his troubles to the players, told them all about me and the insidious influence I had on Terry, and begged them to help him restore the hearty Australian spirit that had left his younger son's left leg. The whole team rose to the occasion and answered the call proudly. They carried Terry onto the unblemished green of the field and in the hot breath of sunshine coached him in the finer elements of the game, inspiring him to limp less and less in his desire to impress them. After two months on the road, he was limpless and a true little sportsman. My father was no dummy. Terry had caught the bug.

On his return, Terry joined the local football club. They played rough in those days—the parents watched the battered heads of their children crash together in chilly autumn dusks, and they writhed in ecstasy. Their kids were proving themselves, and even when they came off the field wearing wigs of dried blood, nobody could have been more pleased. In Australia, as anywhere, rites of passage are no small thing.

It was immediately apparent that Terry was a naturally outstanding player, a star on the field. To watch him tackle, pass, dummy, duck and weave through the skinny legions of little athletes would give your eyes spots. He ran like one possessed, his concentration absolute. In fact, on the field Terry underwent a transformation of character and disposition. Though he played the clown in just about every situation conceivable, he had no sense of humor about the game whatsoever; once the whistle blew, he was as serious about that tough oval ball as a cardiovascular surgeon is about squishy oval hearts. Like me and probably most Australians, Terry had an innate opposition to authority. Discipline was abhorrent to his nature. If someone told him to sit down just as he was reaching for a chair, he'd probably have tossed it out the nearest window. But in the realm of *self*-discipline he was a Zen master. You couldn't stop him. Terry would do laps of the garden even while the magnified moon rose up like a soap bubble. In storms he'd power on with sit-ups and push-ups, and as the sun sank behind the prison, his boots chomped through clumps of thick wet grass and lakes of mud.

In summer Terry joined the local cricket team. Again he shone from the first day. As a bowler he was fast and accurate; as a batter he was deadly and powerful; as a fielder his eye was exacting and his reflexes sharp. It was unnatural how natural he was. Everyone talked about him. And when they opened the new swimming pool, guess who was the first in the water? The guy who built it! And guess who was second? Terry! I ask you: Can a person's body be genius? Can muscles? Can sinew? Can bones? You should've seen him in the pool. And calm! At the start of a race, while the other boys trembled on the swimmer's block, Terry stood there as if he were waiting for a bus. But suddenly the gun fired! He was so quick you wouldn't remember seeing him dive; he glossed through the water as though towed by a jet ski. So that Terry could have his hero cheer him on, I went, always half concealing myself in the back of the stands, roaring louder than anyone. God, those swimming carnivals! It's like I'm there now: the echo of the splashing bodies and the wet feet trotting along the cold sopping tiles of the indoor swimming pool, the pungent stench of chlorine that would make an embalmer nostalgic, the sound of a swimming cap sucked from a head, the dribbling of water emptied from a pair of goggles. And those boys loved it. It was as if someone had said to them, "Human beings need water to live, so get in!" And they got in. And they were happy.

Terry was the happiest of them all. Why wouldn't he be? Football star, cricket star, swimming star. The town had its first local celebrity, made all the more remarkable because he was a seven-year-old boy. Seven! Only seven! He was the Mozart of sport, a prodigy unlike anybody ever seen. The town adored him, all its lovesick eyes caressing him, encouraging him. There's no point denying it was out-and-out worship. The local paper made a big hullabaloo of the amazing Terry Dean too. When one of the city papers did a story on young athletes most likely to make sporting history and Terry was listed among them, my father almost died from delight.

In case you're wondering, there was no sibling rivalry between us, not a speck of jealousy on my part, and even though I felt forgotten like those burned-out cars in derelict suburbs, I was proud of my brother, the sporting hero. But I was concerned too; I was the only one to notice there was more to Terry and sport than mere skill and athleticism.

It wasn't the way he played that keyed me into it, but the way he watched when he was a spectator. First of all, you couldn't get two words out of him before a game. It was the only time in my life I can say I saw him display anything that resembled anxiety. And I've seen him stand in court about to be given a life sentence, so I know what I'm talking about.

We'd arrive to watch a football game and a deep excitement would come over him—for Terry an empty oval was a shadowy, mystical place. The match would begin, and he would sit upright and expectant, his mouth half open and his eyes glued to every action. He was genuinely moved. It was as if he were hearing a language only he understood. He sat with a quiet intensity, like he was seeing something holy—as if scoring a goal in the last thirty seconds was an immortal act. After a game, win or lose, his whole soul seemed filled with satisfaction. He was in a religious fervor! When his team scored a goal, he would actually shudder. I saw him do it with my own eyes, and I don't care what anyone says, a young boy shuddering with religious fervor is just plain creepy. He couldn't stand a draw. You couldn't talk to him after a draw. Bad calls from the umpire set him off into a violent temper too. I'd say, "Can we go home now?" and he'd turn slowly to face me, his eyes full of pain, his breath shallow; he seemed to be suffering. At home, after unsatisfactory games, we all had to walk on tiptoes (which isn't easy when you're on crutches).

As I've said, Terry and I were different in our bodies. His gestures were loose, effortless, honest, and agile while mine were laborious, painful, hesitant, and inept. But our differences were most keenly felt in our obsessions, and contrary obsessions can be a real divider. For example, if you have one friend in a monomania about not having found love and another is an actor who can only talk about whether God gave him the right nose, a little wall comes between them and conversations disintegrate into competing monologues. In a way, this is what was beginning to happen to Terry and me. Terry talked only of sporting heroes. I took some interest, but a significant part of having a hero is imagining his heroic deeds as your own. The fact was, I got only nominal pleasure from imagining myself scoring a goal or running the four-minute mile. Daydreams in which effusive crowds cried, "Isn't he fast?" just weren't that satisfying for me. It was clear I was in need of another kind of hero altogether.

Terry's obsession eventually took over his life; everything from meals to going to the toilet was an unwanted interval between the times he could play, practice, or think about sport. Card games bored him, books bored him, sleep bored him, God bored him, food bored him, affection bored him, our parents bored him, and eventually I bored him too. We started arguing about silly things, mostly about my behavior: now that he was out enjoying life in the company of children who weren't lying in bed moaning, my pervasive negativity and my incapacity for joy became wearisome to him. He started criticizing me for every little thing: he didn't like the way I gently tapped people on the shoulder with my crutch when I wanted to get by them, he didn't like how I quickly discovered the thing a person was most proud of and immediately ridiculed it as a way of undermining them, he was tired of my deep suspicion of everyone and everything, from church doors to smiles.

Sadly, in the space of a few months, Terry finally saw me for what I was: an eleven-year-old grump, a sour, depressive, aggressive, proud, ugly, mean, myopic, misanthropic kid—you know the type. The days of following me around, imitating my cough, and pretending to share in my stabbing abdominal pains were but a sweet, distant memory. Of course, looking back, it's easy to see that Terry's anger and reproaches were born of frustration and love; he didn't understand why I couldn't be as easy and happy in the world as he was. But at the time all I could see was the betrayal. It seemed that all the world's injustices were rushing at me like a strong wind.

•

Now that I was losing my only ally, all I wanted to do was hide, but the fucked thing is that in a small town, there is no such thing as anonymity. Obscurity, yes. Anonymity, no. It's really rotten the way you can't walk down the street without someone saying hello and smiling at you. The best thing you can do is find places everyone hates and go there. And yes, even in a small town there are areas that people avoid en masse— make a mental list, and there you can live your life undisturbed without having to wall yourself into your bedroom. There was a place in our town that Lionel Potts had opened. Nobody ever set foot inside because Lionel was the most despised man in the district. Everyone had it in for him, but I didn't understand why. They said it was because he was a "rich bastard." They thought, "Who does he think he is, not struggling over the rent? What cheek!"

I thought there must be something secret and sinister about Lionel Potts. I couldn't believe people hated him for being rich, because I'd noticed most people were aching to be rich too; otherwise they wouldn't buy lottery tickets and plan get-rich-quick schemes and play the horses. It made no sense to me that people would hate the very thing they aspired to become.

His café was dimly lit, and its dark wooden tables and long wooden benches made it look like a Spanish tavern or a stable for people. There were indoor ferns, paintings of overdressed men on horseback, and a series of black-and-white photographs of a cluster of ancient, majestic trees where the pharmacy now stood. The place was empty from morning to night; I was the only customer. Lionel would complain to his daughter that it wouldn't be long before he'd have to close up and go out of business, while peering at me curiously, obviously wondering why I was the only one in town not adhering to the boycott. Sometimes his daughter stared at me too.

Caroline was eleven years old and tall and thin, and she always stood leaning against the counter with her mouth half open as if in surprise. She had green eyes and hair the color of a golden delicious apple. She was flat-chested and her arms and shoulders were muscular; I remember thinking she could probably beat me in a fight and that would be very embarrassing if it ever came to pass. At eleven, she had that thing that was eventually perfected on Parisian catwalks—a pout. I didn't know it then, but pouts operate like this: they suggest a temporary dissatisfaction that entices you to satisfy it. You think: If only I could satisfy that pout, I would be happy. It's only a recent blip in evolution, the pout. Paleolithic man never heard of it.

I sat in the darkest corner of the café and watched her carry crates of bottles up from the cellar. Neither she nor her father fussed over me or treated me that nicely, considering I was their only client, but I drank milk shakes and Coca-Cola and read books and thought my thoughts, and with an empty notebook in front of me struggled to make sense in words of the visions that had come to me in the coma. Every day she brought me drinks, but I was too shy to talk to her. When she said "Hello," I said "OK."

One day she sat down opposite me with a face that seemed about to burst into cruel laughter. "Everyone thinks your brother is hot shit," she said.

I almost fell over, I was so unused to being talked to. I regained my composure and said wisely, "Well, you know how people are."

"I think he's a show-off."

"Well, you know how people are."

"And up himself."

"Well," I said.

That was it. The one person in town who didn't fall all over my brother was the girl I chose to love. Why not? Even the Kennedys must have had *some* sibling rivalry. Caroline went to the games like everyone else, but I could see she really did hate him, because whenever the crowd jumped and clapped for Terry, she sat as still as a library shelf and only moved to put her hand over her mouth as if stunned by bad news. And the time Terry rushed into the café to take me home for dinner, you should've seen her! She wouldn't talk to him or even look at him, and I'm ashamed to say I found that scene delicious, because for five minutes Terry was getting a little taste of the slimy frog I was forced to swallow day after miserable day.

This is why Caroline Potts goes down in history as my first friend. We talked in that dark café every day, and I was finally able to unleash many of my banked-up thoughts, so I felt a tangible improvement in my mental state. I met her with sweaty palms and prepubescent lechery, and even when I walked slowly toward her, the sight of her smiling, slightly androgynous face was as visceral a shock as if she'd sneaked up on me. Of course I knew she had befriended me because she was friendless too, but I think she really appreciated my snide observations, and we were in total agreement when we compulsively discussed the boundless stupidity of our town's sappy devotion to my brother. I volunteered her the one secret I knew about him: his spooky, religious reverence for sport. It felt good that I wasn't the only one who knew there was something not quite right with Terry Dean, but soon after Caroline and I met, something terrible happened, and then everyone knew.

It was at a birthday party. The host was turning five, a big occasion. I'd missed my own because of the coma, but I wasn't looking forward to it because I anticipated a somber affair, you know, when a child's innocence shows signs of strain and the five-year-old begins, with sadness and alarm, to question why he's suddenly torn between ambition and the desire to sleep longer. Depressing! But I was now off the crutches and could no longer use my illness as an excuse for avoiding life. Terry, on the other hand, was so excited, at dawn he was already standing by the front door in his party clothes. By now you should know the answer to that irritating question, what was Terry Dean like as a child? Was he an outcast? An antiauthoritarian stubborn prick? No, that was me.

When we arrived at the party, the sound of laughter led us through the cool, bright house to the back, where all the children were seated in the large fenceless garden, in front of a magician in an ostentatious black-and-gold cape. He was doing all sorts of cheap tricks. When he exhausted his doves, he went around the crowd and read palms. Trust me, if you haven't experienced it, there's nothing more stupid than a fortune-teller at a children's party. "You will grow up big and strong," I heard him say at one point, "but only if you eat all your vegetables." It was obvious the fraud was taking cues from the parents and scamming the kids with phony futures. It's disheartening to see lies and corruption at a kid's birthday, but it's nothing surprising.

Then we played pass the parcel, in which everyone sits in a circle and passes around some shoddy gift wrapped in newspaper like a dead fish, and each time the music stops, whoever is holding the parcel removes a layer. It's a game of greed and impatience. I caused a stir when I stopped the game to read the newspaper. There was a headline about an earthquake in Somalia: seven hundred dead. The children were screaming at me to pass it on, their bitter recriminations ringing in my ears. I tell you, children's games are no joke. You can't fool around. I passed the parcel to the next boy, but every time another layer was shed, I picked it up hoping to find out more about the earthquake. The other children didn't care about the lives of seven hundred fellow human beings; they just wanted the gift. Finally it was revealed: a fluorescent green water pistol. The winner cheered. The losers cheered through clenched teeth.

The November sun was making us all sweat, so some children leapt into the clear blue swimming pool for a game of Marco Polo, wherein one child with eyes closed swims around trying to catch the children with eyes open. He shouts "Marco!" and they shout "Polo!" and if he says "Fish out of water!" and opens his eyes to see a child out of the pool that child becomes the poor sap who has to swim around with his eyes shut. I don't know how it relates to the life and times of Marco Polo, but there seems to be a criticism in there somewhere.

While Terry joined the others in the pool, I subjected myself to a dreadful thing called musical chairs, another cruel game. There's one chair short, and when the music stops you have to run for a seat. The life lessons never stop at a children's party. The music blares. You never know when it's going to stop. You're on edge the whole game; the tension is unbearable. Everyone dances in a circle around the ring of chairs, but it's no happy dance. Everyone has his eyes on the mother over by the radio, her hand poised on the volume control. Now and then a child wrongly anticipates her and dives for a chair. He's shouted at. He jumps off the seat again. He's a wreck. The music plays on. The children's faces are contorted in terror. No one wants to be excluded. The mother taunts the children by pretending to reach for the volume. The children wish she were dead. The game is an analogy for life: there are not enough chairs or good times to go around, not enough food, not enough joy, nor beds nor jobs nor laughs nor friends nor smiles nor money nor clean air to breathe . . . and yet the music goes on.

I was one of the first to lose, and I was thinking how in life you should always carry your own chair with you so you don't have to share dwindling common resources, when I heard a commotion by the swimming pool. I walked over. Terry's arms were plunged deep into the water and two little hands were reaching up from the crystal depths trying to scratch his eyes out. The scene wasn't open to interpretation: Terry was trying to drown someone.

The other children were now standing on the lawn, all fish out of water. A dismayed parent dived in, pulled Terry off the boy, and dragged both of them out of the pool, where the horrified mother of the half-drowned boy whacked Terry across the face. Later that afternoon, in a huddle of outraged parents, Terry, in his own defense, explained that he had seen his victim cheating.

"I was not!" he cried.

"I saw you! Your left eye was open!" Terry shouted.

"Even so, mate," my father said, "it's just a game."

What my father didn't know was that the phrase "just a game" was never to hold any meaning whatsoever for Terry Dean. To Terry, life was a game and games would always be life, and if I hadn't figured that out, I wouldn't have manipulated the information for my own sad revenge fantasy, which unexpectedly altered the course of my brother's life.

This is one of those memories that I could go blind thinking about—when all the worst of my impulses fused together for one stunningly shameful moment. It was only a month later, when after years of home tutoring between sports practice, Terry finally started at school (an event I had been dreading, as I had been so successful in keeping my spectacular unpopularity a secret from my family). Dave and Bruno Browning, fraternal twins, had tied me to a thick branch of a tree behind the gym. They were not only the official school bullies, they were also thieves, wannabe criminals, and streetfighters, and I always thought they belonged in jail or in graves so shallow that when people walked over them they would actually be stepping on Dave's and Bruno's cold dead faces. As they finished their knots, I said, "How did you know this was my favorite tree? Oh my God, what a view! This is beautiful!" I continued my glib rant as they climbed down. "Honestly, fellas," I shouted, "you don't know what you're missing!" I gave the thumbs-up sign to a small crowd gathered at the base of the trunk.

My frozen smile melted at the sight of Terry's face in the mob, gazing up at me. Because he was an adored sporting hero, the crowd cleared a space to let him through. I fought back tears but kept up the act. "Hey, Terry, this is fantastic. Why don't you come up and see me sometime?"

He climbed the tree, sat on the branch opposite me, and started untying the knots.

"What's going on?"

"What do you mean?"

"Everyone hates you!"

"All right. I'm not popular. So what?"

"So why does everyone hate you?"

"They have to hate someone. Who else are they going to hate, if not me?"

We sat in that tree all afternoon, for five hours, during two of which I had acute vertigo. The bell rang every now and then, and we watched children move from one class to another, obedient yet casual, like soldiers in peacetime. We watched them all day, neither of us talking. In the silence all our differences suddenly seemed unimportant. Terry's balancing on the branch beside me was an enormously significant gesture of solidarity. His presence said to me: You are alone but not utterly alone. We are brothers, and nothing can change that.

The sun moved across the sky. Wispy clouds were transported on fast winds. I looked at my classmates as through a double-glazed bulletproof window and thought: There is no more chance of communication between us than between an ant and a stone.

Even after three, when the school day ended, Terry and I stayed put, silently watching as a cricket game started up below us. Bruno and Dave and five or six other children were arranged in a semicircle, running and jumping and diving in the dirt as if there were nothing fragile about the human body. They let out roars, in crescendo, and occasionally the twins would look up at the tree and call out my name in a singsong voice. I winced at the thought of all the beatings I still had ahead of me, and tears came to my eyes. They were tears of fear. How could I get out of this situation? I watched those two bullies below and wished I had dangerous, mysterious powers that they could feel in their guts. I imagined them singing their taunts with mouthfuls of blood.

Suddenly I had the idea.

"They're cheating," I said to Terry.

"They are?"

"Yeah. I hate cheats, don't you?"

Terry's breathing became slow and irregular. It was a remarkable thing to witness; his face spluttered like hot grease in a pan.

It's not melodramatic to say the entire fate of the Dean family was decided that afternoon in the tree. I'm not proud of myself for inciting my little brother to attack my attackers, and of course if I had had any way of knowing that by manipulating his fanatical reverence for sport, I was effectively ordering dozens of body bags direct from the manufacturers, I probably wouldn't have done it.

I can't tell you much about what happened next. But I can tell you that Terry climbed down, grabbed the cricket bat from an astonished Bruno, and slammed it into the side of his head. I can tell you that the fight had been going for only about fifteen seconds when Dave, the uglier of the nonidentical twins, pulled a butterfly knife and thrust it hard into Terry's leg. I can tell you what the scream sounded like, because it was mine. Terry didn't let out a sound. Even as blood pissed from the wound and I climbed down and ran into the mix and dragged him away, he was silent.

•

The next day, in hospital, an unsympathetic doctor casually told Terry that he'd never play football again.

"What about swimming?"

"Not likely."

"Cricket?"

"Maybe."

"Really?"

"I don't know. Can you play cricket without running?"

"No."

"Then no."

I heard Terry swallow. We all heard it. It was pretty loud. A softness in his eight-year-old face became instantly hard. We witnessed the exact moment he was forcibly disengaged from his dreams. A moment later tears poured out of him and he made unpleasant guttural noises I've had the misfortune to hear once or twice since, inhuman noises that accompany the sudden arrival of despair.

Philosophy

Terry's old wish had been granted: he was a cripple, just like his big brother. Only now that I'd returned to normal health, Terry was on his own. He used my discarded crutches to get from A to B, but sometimes he preferred to stay at A for days on end, and then when he no longer needed the crutches, he switched to a varnished cane of dark wood. He cleared his room of all the sporting paraphernalia: the posters, the photographs, the newspaper clippings, his football, cricket bat, and swimming goggles. Terry wanted to forget. But how could he? You can't run from your own leg, especially a leg that carries the weight of broken dreams.

My mother tried to console her son (and herself) by infantilizing him—making his favorite meal (sausages and baked beans) every day, trying to snuggle him, speaking to him in baby talk, and constantly touching his hair. If he had let her, she would have stroked his forehead until the skin came off. My father was depressed too—sulking, overeating, speed-drinking beer, and cradling Terry's sporting trophies in his arms like dead babies. These were the days my father got fat. In a frenzy, he ate every meal as if it were his last. For the first few months it all pushed out the front and his naturally skinny frame shook with the sudden alteration, but finally it buckled so that his waist and hips fell into line too, expanding to a width exactly one quarter of an inch wider than the average doorway. Blaming me for the calamity cheered him up a little. It wasn't one of those revelations that would need to be drawn out of him in psychotherapy, either. He didn't bury his blame but expressed it outright, over dinner, waving his fork menacingly at me like an exorcist's crucifix.

Fortunately, he was soon distracted by a return to his old obsession: the prison on the hill. He and the warden were drinking buddies and for years they played pool every night, for fun making $100,000 bets on each game. The warden was into my father for an astronomical amount of pretend money. One day my father surprised his friend by demanding he pay up, but instead of insisting his debt be met with money, my father made a strange and dark bargain: he'd forget the $27 million owed to him, and in exchange the warden must bring copies of the inmates' files down from his office. With his son's future blown, the only thing my father was proud of was having helped build that prison, a solid achievement he could see from our front porch. So of course he felt he had a right to know who the guests were. The warden photocopied the files, and night after night my father pored over the case histories of murderers and rapists and thieves and imagined them rattling the bars he himself had welded. If you ask me, this was the beginning of the end for my father, although there was an incredibly long fall yet to come. This was also when he began to rave at my mother in public so much that she could no longer bear being with him outside the house; and so she wasn't, ever again, and on the rare occasion they bumped into each other in the street, an awkwardness fell over them and they were eerily polite. It was only back at home that their normal selves would reappear and they'd yak on insultingly ad nauseam.

Things were strange at school for a while too. As you know, I never fit in; I couldn't even squeeze in. Terry, on the other hand, had been accepted and embraced from day one, but now, after he lost the use of his leg for athletic purposes, he squeezed himself out. I kept an eye on him as he hobbled around the school grounds, squashing the tip of his cane into classmates' toes and putting all his weight on it. Personally, I think it wasn't only his own disappointment that was turning him cold and nasty. It was also a reaction to the endless compassion he had to deal with. You see, people were all very sympathetic to him on account of his loss, plying him with huge dollops of aggravating kindness. It was the worst thing for him. Some people are body-and-soul repulsed at being a figure of pity. Others, such as me, can soak it up greedily, mostly because having pitied themselves for so long, it seems right that everyone else is finally getting on the bandwagon.

Bruno and Dave glared menacingly at Terry whenever they crossed paths. Terry stood his ground and gave them his slipperiest smile. That led into a stare-off, one of those battles of masculinity that looks very silly to a passerby. Later, as I trailed Terry through the school corridors, I realized he followed Bruno and Dave wherever they went. What did he want with them? Revenge? A rematch? I implored him to leave them alone. "Fuck off, Marty!" he spat back at me.

I went back up in the tree. Now I'd put myself there. It had become my secret hiding place. I'd learned a valuable lesson: people almost never look up. Who knows why? Maybe they're looking at the soil for a preview of coming attractions. And so they should. I think anyone who says he looks to the future and doesn't have one eye on the dirt is being short-sighted.

One day I saw a commotion below: the students were running haphazardly around the playground, in and out of the classrooms, calling out. I strained my ears in the weird way humans can strain their ears when they want to. They were shouting my name. I hugged the branch so hard I got a full-body splinter. Every student in school was after me for something. But what now? *What now?* Two students stopped under the tree for a breather and I caught the news: Bruno and Dave had requested my presence behind the school gym. It's about time, I heard the students say. If stabbing my brother was a statement, maybe I was to be the exclamation point. The consensus was that they were going to tear me apart. Everyone wanted to do his bit.

Then one girl caught sight of me, and two minutes later a crowd was carrying me on their shoulders as if I were a hero, but they were really delivering meat to the butcher. They bounced like puppies as they ferried me to Bruno and Dave, who waited behind the gym. "Here he is!" the children cried, dropping me unceremoniously in the dirt. I slowly rose to my feet, just for the hell of it. You could have sold tickets—it was the hottest show in town.

"Martin," Dave shouted, "if anyone . . . *anyone* . . . *ever* . . . touches you . . . or hits you . . . or pushes you . . . or even so much as looks at you funny, you come to me and I will ANNIHILATE them! You understand?"

I didn't understand. Neither did the crowd.

"You are now under our protection, OK?"

I said OK.

The mob was silent. Dave spun around to face them. "Anyone have a problem with that?"

No one had a problem with that. They squirmed like they were all caught on a hook.

"Right." Then Dave turned to me and said, "Smoke?"

I didn't move. He had to put the cigarette in my mouth and light it.

"Now inhale."

I inhaled and coughed violently. Dave patted me on the back in a friendly manner. "You're all right, mate," he said, with a toothy smile. Then he walked away. The crowd was too stunned to move. I struggled to keep my equilibrium. I'd thought I was in for a beating, not a saving.

I was a protected species now. It puffed me up like a blowfish. I turned to the confused horde and offered them a challenge with my eyes. They all looked away, every last eye.

Eight-year-old Terry Dean had made a deal with the devils for his twelve-year-old brother, that's what saved my skin. He'd seen me cowering behind garbage bins one day and suffering the monotonous grind of invisibility the next, so—loyal brother that he was—Terry proposed a deal: if they'd offer me protection, he'd join their demented crew. He suggested that he be their apprentice, a trainee thug. Who knows why they accepted? Maybe they liked his spirit. Maybe they were confused by the audacity of his request. Whatever the reason, when they asked him to write a little memo detailing the arrangement in his own blood, without hesitation Terry cut into himself with a Stanley knife and spelled it out so the pact was all there in red and white.

This was my brother's premature entry into a life of crime. Over the next couple of years he spent all of his after-school time with Bruno and Dave, and since Terry was too young to keep their kind of hours alone, I had to tag along. At first the twins tried to coerce me to run errands for them, but at Terry's insistence I was allowed to sit under a tree and read, even during the street fights. And there were always fights. The gang couldn't sleep well if they hadn't smashed someone's face in at some point during the day. Once they'd fought every likely candidate in our town, Bruno would steal his father's Land Rover and drive them to nearby towns for the face-smashing. There were plenty of kids to fight. Every town has tough guys, a new generation of prison filler waiting to happen.

Each afternoon they taught Terry how to fight. They had constructed a whole philosophical system based on violence and combat, and as Terry's fists formed bony bricks, Bruno and Dave became a double act, one asking a question while the other answered it.

"What are your hands for?"

"Curling into fists."

"What are your legs for?"

"Kicking."

"And the feet?"

"Stomping in a face."

"Fingers?"

"Gouging."

"Teeth?"

"Biting."

"Head?"

"Head-butting."

"Elbow?"

"Jamming into jaws."

Et cetera.

They preached the human body as not only a weapon but an entire arsenal, and as I watched them drum this oily gospel into Terry's head, I thought about my own body in comparison—an arsenal aimed inward, at myself.

When they weren't fighting, they were stealing—anything and everything. With no discerning eye for value, they swiped junked cars, broken car parts, school supplies, sporting goods; they broke into bakeries and stole bread, and if there wasn't any bread they stole dough; they broke into hardware stores and stole hammers and ladders and lightbulbs and showerheads; they broke into butchers' and stole sausages and meat hooks and lamb shanks; they robbed the post office of stamps and uncollected mail; they broke into the Chinese restaurant and took chopsticks and hoisin sauce and fortune cookies; and from the service station they stole ice and frantically tried to sell it before it melted.

If you were unlucky enough to be around after one of their stealing expeditions, you'd have to get ready to go shopping. Their sales technique was impressive. For Bruno and Dave, business was always booming, because they'd found a niche market: terrified children.

Terry got in the thick of it too, crawling through windows and air vents, getting into those hard-to-reach places while I waited outside and pleaded internally for them to hurry. I pleaded so hard I hurt myself. Over the months, while Terry was developing muscles, agility, and hand-to-hand combat skills, I was degenerating again. My parents, fearing a return of my old sickness, called a doctor. He was stumped. "It looks like nerves," he said, "but what does a twelve-year-old have to be nervous about?" The doctor peered curiously at my scalp. "What happened to your hair?" he asked. "Looks like some of it's fallen out." I shrugged and looked around the room as if searching for the hair. "What's this?" my father shouted. "He's losing his hair? Oh my God, what a child!" A Pandora's box of angst opened whenever I witnessed my brother in mid-robbery, but when there was a street fight, I put my whole soul into fretting. Every day when we walked home I pleaded with Terry to break away. I was absolutely convinced I was going to watch my brother die right before my eyes. Because of Terry's age and size, Bruno and Dave armed him with a cricket bat, which he waved in the air as he let out a war cry and fast-limped it to their enemies. Rarely would an opponent stick around to see what he'd do with the bat, although some did stand their ground, and during one fight, Terry got slashed with a knife. Gasping, I ran into the middle of the fight and dragged him away. Bruno and Dave slapped him around to toughen him up, then sent him back in while the blood was still flowing. I screamed in protest until my voice ran out, then I shouted air.

These weren't schoolyard fights, this was gang warfare. I'd look at the snarling faces of the young as they flung themselves into battle, having the time of their lives. Their indifference to violence and pain mystified me. I couldn't comprehend these creatures, rabid with joy, squashing each other into the dust. And the way they adored their injuries—it was baffling. They gazed at their gaping wounds like lovers reunited after a long separation. It was nuts.

Caroline couldn't understand them either. She was livid at me for letting my little brother join these thugs, even though she was happy the gang was protecting me. Her furious words left an afterglow on my cheek: her attention was all I needed. I still admired myself for my friendship with Caroline. Our conversations were the best thing about me and the only thing I loved about my life, especially since every afternoon Bruno and Dave would flick lit cigarettes at me and threaten me with various ingenious tortures, my favorite being that they would bury me alive in a pet cemetery. They never followed up, though, because Terry had made it clear that if I suffered so much as one scratch, he would quit. Clearly the twins could spot talent. They figured he was a criminal prodigy; why else would these two thugs obey him? If you asked them, they might have said it was a mixture of his energy, his sense of humor, his willingness to follow every order, his utter fearlessness. Whatever it was, they felt good having him around, even if it meant putting up with his brooding older brother who'd do nothing but read. Those books of mine really got under their skin. Ironically, they thought *I* was inhuman because of the way I churned through library books.

"How do you know how to pick them? Who tells you?" Dave asked me once.

I explained that there was a line. "If you read Dostoyevsky, he mentions Pushkin, and so you go and read Pushkin and he mentions Dante, and so you go and read Dante and—"

"All right!"

"All books are in some way about other books."

"I get it!"

It was an endless search, and endlessly fruitful; the dead sent me hurtling through time, through the centuries, and while Bruno seethed at my wide-eyed reverence for something as inert and unmanly as a book, Dave was intrigued. Sometimes he'd flop down beside me after a fight, and with blood streaming down his face he'd say, "Tell me what you're reading about." And I'd tell him, keeping an eye on Bruno, who burned with white-hot ignorant hate. More than once he tore my books into shreds. More than once I sat horrified as one of them flew off the edge of a cliff. There goes *Crime and Punishment*! There goes Plato's *Republic*! The pages may have spread like wings as they fell, but they wouldn't fly.

The boys demanded that while reading, I keep one eye out for police and tourists. Terry nudged me in a way that said, "Do this one small thing to keep the peace," so I acquiesced, though as a lookout I was terrible. I was too busy observing the gang and coming to conclusions that I was burning to share. Bruno, Dave, and Terry had smashed their way into supremacy of the district and now were undefeated and bored. They had big plans for themselves; they wanted to climb the underworld ladder—which I suppose is a descent—but they were aimless and drowning in the tedium and didn't know why. *I knew why*, and I couldn't stand it that nobody asked me. After raiding my father's shed, I had even worked out the solution.

One day, despite myself, I spoke up, and pushed my brother in a new terrible direction.

"I know why you're bored," I said.

"He speaks!" Dave shouted.

"Yeah," Bruno said. "Now shut up!"

"Hang on," Dave said, "I want to hear what he has to say. Go on, you sorry sack of shit, tell us why we're bored."

"You've stopped learning," I said. No one responded, so I braved the silence and sliced right through it. "You've peaked. You know how to fight. You know how to steal. You keep doing the same thing day in and day out. You're no longer stimulated. What you need is a mentor. You need someone in the crime scene to tell you how to get to the next level."

Everyone absorbed my advice. I returned to my book, but I was only pretending to read. I was too excited! There was a warm river trickling through my veins. What was this feeling all about? It was brand-new.

Bruno threw a stone so it hit the tree inches above my head.

"Look around, dickhead. This isn't the city. Where the fuck do we find someone like that?"

Without looking up from my book, and concealing my inner fire, I pointed up to my father's proudest achievement—the prison on the hill.

Creation

"So how are we supposed to know who to ask to mentor us?" Dave asked.

"I already know," I said.

My father's shed was furnished with every conceivable detail about the prison and prison life, including, thanks to his whipping the warden at pool, files on the prisoners themselves. After coming up with my idea, I had studied every file on the whole menagerie of scum up there and had stolen the file of the clear winner.

"First I ruled out white-collar criminals, domestic abusers, and anyone who'd committed a single act of passion," I said.

"And?"

"And I also excluded rapists."

"Why?"

"Because there really isn't any money in it."

"Have you bloody picked one or not?" Bruno shouted.

I put down my book and reached into my bag for the file. My heart was beating so wildly I could feel it against my chest. I slid the file across a grassy patch of ground to Bruno and with my mouth dry as a new towel said, "This is your man."

Bruno took a look. The others crowded around. The inmate's name was Harry West; he was doing life. If there was a crime, he'd committed it: shoplifting, assault and battery, breaking and entering, possession of an illegal firearm, malicious wounding, grievous bodily harm, drug possession, drug dealing, drug making, attempting to bribe an officer of the court, successfully bribing an officer of the court, tax evasion, receiving stolen goods, selling stolen goods, arson, larceny, manslaughter, murder—the whole shebang. He'd set fire to brothels. He shot a man on the dance floor of a bar for doing a fox-trot during a waltz. He stabbed a horse at the racetrack. He'd broken arms, legs, feet, toes, broken ligaments, fragments, particles, matter; his charge sheet stretched back fifty years.

"Why him?"

I sprang to my feet. "The criminal underworld runs the industries of gambling and prostitution. Brothels, strip clubs, bars—these are the venues where the action takes place. You need to find someone who has links to all these things. And someone who's a career criminal. You don't want some fly-by-nighter."

You had to hand it to me, I knew what I was talking about. The boys were impressed. They took another look at the life and times of Harry West. It looked like he'd spent more than half his life in a cell. That's a life without a lot of running.

I went on: "It's impossible to know how high up he is in the criminal underworld, but even if he was just answering phones, he's been in it for long enough to know how the whole system operates. I'm telling you, this is the guy!"

I was electrified. No one had ever seen me like that. Their eyes scrutinized me. A little voice in my head tut-tutted me for encouraging them, but I had spent nearly my entire waking life hatching quirky ideas, and no one other than Caroline had ever heard a single one, until now.

"Let's do it," Bruno said, and immediately my stomach tightened. Why? A strange physical reaction was going on inside me. As soon as my idea was embraced, I no longer liked it. It now seemed to be a stupid idea, really awful. I liked it much better when it was in my head all alone. Now that it was going out in the world, I would be responsible for something I no longer had any control over.

This was my first of a lifetime of battles with ideas: the battle of which ones to air and which ones to bury, burn, destroy.

•

It was decided that because Bruno and Dave had juvenile records, it would be safer if Terry went to meet Harry West and report his findings back to the gang. One early morning in the middle of winter, before school, I accompanied Terry up to the prison. I was keen to go, not only because it was my idea, but because I had never been to the Palace (as it was often referred to in our home) that my father built.

You couldn't see it from the town that day. A heavy layer of gray fog swallowed half the hill, including the jail, and snaked down to meet us as we fought our way up toward it. When we reached the halfway mark, we could see the shifting wall of fog in front of us. It curled into knots. We walked right into it, right into the soup. For a good twenty minutes we couldn't get a fix on anything. To make the ascent harder, it had been raining and the winding dirt road that led up to the peak was a river of mud. I was cursing my own head the whole way up. What a big mouth!

When we saw the heavy gates of the prison emerge out of the fog, a long shiver swept over my body. Terry smiled optimistically. Why wasn't he worried? How can the same situation make one person garrote himself with nerves and another person bright and cheery?

On the other side of the gate, a solitary guard was standing erect. He peered curiously at us as we leaned up against the bars.

"We'd like to see Harry West," I said.

"Who shall I say is calling?"

"Martin and Terry Dean."

The guard eyed us suspiciously. "Are you family?"

"No."

"Then what do you want to see him for?"

"School project," Terry said, giving me a surreptitious wink. Behind the gate a gust of wind blew the fog around, and for the first time we saw up close the prison that made a weekend magazine call our town "Least Desirable Place to Live in New South Wales." It didn't look as much like a fortified castle as it did from the town. In fact, it was not one but four large red brick buildings of the same dimensions, as innocuous and ugly as our own school, and without the wire fence in the foreground, it appeared as ordinary as a government office block.

The guard leaned forward, pressing his head against the cold gate. "School project, eh? What subject?"

"Geography," Terry said.

The guard scratched his head listlessly. I supposed the friction on his scalp started his brain like an outboard motor.

"All right, then."

He unlocked the gate and it made a shuddering sound as it opened. I made a shuddering sound too as Terry and I walked into the prison compound.

"Follow the path until you reach the next station," the guard said behind us.

We moved slowly. Two high wire fences ornamented with barbed wire lined the pathway on either side. Behind the fence to the right was a concrete yard where prisoners moved around, swiping at the fog lethargically. Their denim uniforms made them look like blue ghosts floating in a netherworld.

We reached the second guard station. "We're here to see Harry West."

The bearded guard had a sad, weary expression that told us he was underpaid, unappreciated, and hadn't had a hug in over a decade. He plunged his hands into my pockets and rummaged around without so much as a how-do-you-do. His hands went into Terry's pockets too. Terry giggled.

When the guard finished, he said, "All right, Jim, take them in."

A man stepped out of the fog. Jim. We followed him inside the prison. The fog came inside too. It was everywhere, floating through the barred windows and crawling in thin trails along the narrow corridors. We were led through an open doorway into the visiting room.

"Wait in here."

Other than a long table with chairs on either side, the room was bare. We sat down next to each other, expect that Harry West would take a chair on the opposite side, but I started to worry. What if he defied expectation and sat down beside us so we all sat staring at the wall?

"Let's get out of here," I said.

Before Terry could answer, Harry West entered and stood glaring at us from the doorway. His nose looked like it had been squashed, then yanked, then squashed again. This was a face that had a story to tell, a story of fists. As he moved closer, I noted that like Terry (and as I used to), Harry had a terrible limp. He carried his leg like luggage. You know how some animals drag their anuses along the ground to mark it? Well, it seemed to me that Harry was onto the same trick, digging grooves in the dusty floor with that leg. Thankfully, he took a chair opposite, and when I got a front view of him, I realized that his was a terribly misshapen head, like an apple with a bite taken out of it.

"What can I do for you fellas?" he asked cheerily.

Terry took a long time to speak, but when he did he said, "Well, sir, me and my friends, we have this gang in town, and we've been doing a little breaking and entering, and some street fighting, although sometimes it's in the bush, and uh . . ." He drifted off.

I said, "The gang are young. They're inexperienced. They need guidance. They need to hear from someone who's been in the game awhile. In a nutshell, they're looking for a mentor."

Harry sat for a while, thinking. He scratched his tattoo. It wouldn't come off. He stood and walked to the window.

"Damned fog. Can't see a thing. It's a pretty shitty little town you got here, isn't it? Still, I wouldn't mind looking at it."

Before we could say anything, Harry turned and smiled at us, revealing a mouth missing every second tooth.

"Anyone who says the young don't have any initiative has his head up his own arse! You boys restore my faith! I've come across legions of up-and-comers over the decades, and none of them have ever asked me for advice. Not one. I never heard of anyone with the guts to say, 'I want knowledge. Gimme some.' No, those bastards out there, they're loafers. They breeze through life taking orders. They know how to break a leg, sure! But you have to tell them which one. They know how to dig a grave too, but if you're not standing over them, they'd dig it right in the middle of a city park, two blocks from the cop shop. Hell, they'd do it in broad daylight if you weren't standing over them shouting, 'Night, you idiots! Do it at night!' They're the worst kind of drones. And disloyal! Like you wouldn't believe! How many of my former colleagues have visited me since I've been locked up in this miserable place? Not one! Not a letter! Not a word! And you should have seen them before they met me! They were stealing change out of the cups of beggars! I took them in, tried to show them the ropes. But they don't want to know the ropes. They want to drink and gamble and lie all day with whores. An hour or two is enough, isn't it? Hey, have you got guns?"

Terry shook his head. It looked like Harry was warming to his task; he'd had a lot bottled up. The stopper was out.

"Well, that there's your first mission. Get guns! You need guns! You need lots of guns! And here's your first lesson. Once you've got the guns, find hiding places all over town and stash them—in the back of pubs, up trees, down manholes, in mailboxes. Because if you're embarking on a life of crime, you never know when your enemies are going to attack. You're never going to be able to walk through life without glancing over your shoulder. Are you up for that? Your neck gets a lot of exercise, take it from me. Any place you go—the pub, the cinema, the bank, the dentist—as soon as you walk into a room, you better find a wall and stand with your back to it. Get ready. Be aware. Don't let anyone get behind you, you hear me? Even when you're getting a haircut: *always make the barber do it from in front.*"

Harry slammed his hands on the table and bore down on us.

"That's the way of life for us boys. It would shake the foundations of common folk, but we have to be tough and prepared to live against the wall with our eyes blazing and our fingers twitching. After a while it becomes an unconscious act, you know. You develop a sixth sense. It's true. Paranoia makes a man evolve. Bet they don't teach you that in the classroom! Precognition, ESP, telepathy—we criminals have prophetic souls. We know what's coming even before it happens. You have to. It's a survival mechanism. Knives, bullets, fists, they come out of the woodwork. Everyone wants your name on a headstone, so on your toes, boys! It's a cunt of a life! But there *are* rewards. You don't want to be a regular Joe. You just have to look out a window and see. I'll tell you what's out there: a bunch of slaves in love with the freedom they think they have. But they've chained themselves to some job or another, or to a squad of rug rats. They're prisoners too, only they don't know it. And that's what the criminal world is turning into. A routine! A grind! The whole ball of wax lacks spark! Imagination! Chaos! It's sealed from the inside. It's chained to the wheel. Nothing unexpected happens. That's why, if you follow my advice, you'll have an edge. They won't be prepared for it. The smartest thing you can do is surprise them—that's the ticket. Smarts, brawn, courage, bloodlust, greed: all fine, necessary characteristics. But imagination! That's what the criminal world lacks! Just look at the staples: larceny, theft, breaking and entering, gambling, drugs, prostitution. You call that innovation?"

Terry and I looked at each other helplessly. There was nothing stopping this eruption of words.

"God, it's good to see you two boys. You've really pumped me full of piss! And vinegar! And just when things were tasting so stale, you've given me hope! The organization is in ruins. No one wants new ideas. All they want is more of the same. They're their own worst enemies. It's their appetites—insatiable! That leads me to my next tip. Keep your appetites down and you'll live to be a thousand. Accumulate what you need to be comfortable and then go enjoy life awhile. Blaze like a furnace, then hide your light from the world. Have the strength to smother your own flame. You understand? Retreat and attack! Retreat and attack! That's the key! And keep your crew small, that's another tip. Bigger your crew, the more chance one of them will double-cross you and leave you for dead in some shallow ditch. You know why? Because everyone wants to be on top! Everyone! Well, here's your next lesson: don't be on top. Be on the side! That's right. You heard me correctly. Let the others chew through their days charging each other like bulls. You put your heads down and get on with it. There's nothing, you gorgeous unlawful children, nothing I can tell you more important than what I've already said: avoid the treacherous ladder! That's the best advice I can give you. I wish someone had said as much to me when I was your age. I wouldn't be in here. If only I'd known it was the ladder that would get me in the end. That ladder has blades for rungs!"

I struggled to keep up. What was I doing talking to this madman when I should be in school?

"Look. Take it from me, *don't* make a name for yourself, be as anonymous as possible. Everyone will tell you it's all about reputation—that's the trap! Everyone wants to be Capone or Netti or Squizzy Taylor. They want their names to echo through eternity, like Ned Kelly. Well, I'll tell you, the only way to get your name echoing like that is to be massacred in a hail of bullets. Is that what you want? Of course not. Here's a new one: are you ready for it? Don't let the world know who's boss. That will throw them! They'll be eating their hearts out. Be a *leaderless* gang. Give the impression that you belong to a *democratic cooperative of crime!* That'll spin their heads. They won't know who to come gunning for. This is irrefutable advice, boys. Don't be showy! Be a faceless entity! Hell, be a nonentity. You'll show those clowns. Let them speculate, but don't let them know. The paradox of the crime world is that you need a reputation to get things done, but having a reputation gets you killed. But if your reputation is mysterious, if you're in a secret society, like the Templars . . . do you know who the Templars were? Of course you don't. Well—"

"The Templars were an international military order formed in 1118, during the Crusades," I said.

Harry's eyes stuck on mine.

"How old are you?"

"Fourteen."

"A boy with an education! Wonderful! That's what the criminal class lacks! A bit of goddamn smarts."

"I'm just here for moral support. Crime is Terry's thing."

"Ah, a pity, a pity. Well, you make sure your brother gets educated. We don't need any more empty heads running around the industry, that's for sure. Terry, listen to your brother, OK?"

"OK."

"This is just fine. It's a good thing you boys came to me. Anyone else would've told you a bunch of rehashed crap that would get you dead or in here with me."

"Time's up!" a guard shouted from the hallway.

"Well, this looks like the end of class for today. Come back next week and I'll tell you how to obtain and maintain loyalty from the cops."

"I said time's up!" the guard shouted. Now he was standing at the door, blinking irritably.

"OK, boys, you heard the man. Get out of here. Come back, though, I've got lots more stuff. And you never know, maybe we can work together one day. Just because I'm in here for life doesn't mean I won't be out one day. Life doesn't really mean life. It's just a figure of speech. It means an eternity which is actually shorter than life, if you know what I mean."

Harry was still talking when we were escorted out of the room.

•

Bruno and Dave thought Harry's advice was rubbish. An anonymous underworld figure? A democratic cooperative of crime? What was that shit? Of course their names were going to echo through eternity! Infamy was high on their to-do lists. No, the only part of Harry's monologue appealing to Bruno and Dave was his reference to the accumulation and hiding of guns. "We're nothing without guns. We need to move up to the next level," Bruno sang. I shook at the thought of what that level involved, and I didn't know how to reason with them, particularly because I was the one who had suggested they see Harry. I couldn't get my brother out of a life of violence either. It was like trying to persuade a short man to be taller. I knew Terry wasn't cruel, however, only reckless. He wasn't concerned for his own physical well-being, and he extended that indifference to the bodies of others.

He visited Harry once a month, always alone. As much as he wanted me to, and as much as the inmate's rants often seemed to make sense, I refused to return to the prison. I thought Harry was a dangerous maniac and/or an unendurable idiot. I could do without listening to him ever again.

That said, about six months after the original visit I went back up to the prison, this time without Terry. Why? Harry had requested my attendance. I reluctantly agreed because Terry had pleaded with me to go, and when Harry limped into the visiting room, I noticed he had fresh cuts and bruises on his face.

"You should see the other guy. He looks pretty good, actually," Harry said, lowering himself into a chair. He stared at me curiously. I stared back at him impatiently. Our stares were totally different in character.

"Well, Martin, do you know what I see when I look at you? I see a kid who wants to remain hidden. Look. You've covered part of your hand with your sleeve. You're slouching down. Here, I think, is a kid who wishes to be invisible."

"Is this why you wanted to see me?"

"Terry talks about you a lot. He's told me everything about you. You've started to intrigue me."

"That's nice."

"He told me how you don't have any friends."

I didn't know what to say to that.

"Look at the way you're scrunching up your face! It's very slight. Almost nothing. Just in the eyes. You're judging me, aren't you? Well, go ahead, my little misanthrope. Fairly obviously I've been judged before, judged and tried and sentenced! God, I've never met such a disturbed thing in its infancy before. Quite premature, aren't you?"

"What do you want?" I said. "I already told you I'm not interested in crime."

"But I'm interested in you. I want to see how you're managing out there in the big bad world. Certainly not like your brother. He's a chameleon, remarkably adaptable, and a dog, very loyal, happy as a lark. Wonderful disposition your brother's got, even though . . ." Harry leaned forward and said, "There's something unstable about him. You've noticed it, of course."

I had.

"Not much gets past you, I'll bet. No, I won't use that hackneyed phrase that you remind me of myself when I was a boy, because, frankly, you don't. You remind me of myself now, as a man, in jail, and it's pretty frightening for me to be able to make that comparison, Martin, don't you think? Considering, well, you're just a kid."

I could see his point, but I pretended I didn't.

"You and your brother are unique. You are not, either of you, influenced in any significant way by those around you. You don't try to imitate them. You stand apart, even from each other. That kind of fierce individualistic streak is rare. You are both born leaders, you know."

"Terry might be."

"You too, Marty! Problem is, mate, you're in the fucking sticks! The type of followers you might have had just don't grow here. Tell me something—you don't like people very much, do you?"

"They're OK."

"Do you think you're superior to them?"

"No."

"Then why don't you like them?"

I wondered if I should open up to this lunatic. It occurred to me that nobody had ever taken an interest in what I thought or felt before. Nobody had ever taken an interest in *me*.

"Well, for one," I said, "I'm jealous of their happiness. And second, it infuriates me that they seem to have made up their minds without thinking first."

"Go on."

"It seems that they're just keeping themselves busy at any and every task that distracts them from the impulse of thinking about their own existence. Why else would they smash the heads of their neighbors together over different football teams, if it didn't serve the purpose of helping them avoid the thought of their own impending deaths?"

"You know what you're doing?"

"No."

"You're philosophizing."

"No I'm not."

"Yes you are. You're a philosopher."

"No I'm not!" I shouted. I didn't want to be a philosopher. All they do is sit around and think. They grow fat. They don't know how to do anything practical like weed their own gardens.

"Yes, Martin, you are. I'm not saying you're a good one, just that you're a natural one. It's not an insult, Marty. Listen. I've been labeled many times a criminal—an anarchist, a rebel, sometimes human garbage, but never a philosopher, which is a pity because that's what I am. I chose a life apart from the common flow, not only because the common flow makes me sick but because I question the logic of the flow, and not only that—I don't even know if the flow exists! Why should I chain myself to the wheel when the wheel itself might be a construct, an invention, a common dream to enslave us?" Harry leaned forward and I could smell his stale cigarette breath. "You've felt it too, Marty. As you say, you don't know why people act without thinking. You ask why. That's an important question for you. Now I ask you—why the why?"

"I don't know."

"Yes you do. It's all right, Martin. Tell me—why the why?"

"Well, as long as I can remember, in the afternoons, my mother served me up cold glasses of milk. Why not warm? Why milk? Why not coconut juice or mango lassis? I asked her once. She said that this was what children at my age drank. And another time, during dinner, she chastised me for placing my elbows on the table while eating. I asked why. She said, 'It's rude.' I said, 'Rude to who? To you? In what way?' Again she was stumped, and as I went to bed 'because seven p.m. is bedtime for children under seven,' I realized that I was blindly following the orders of a woman who herself was blindly following rumors. I thought: Maybe things don't have to be this way. They could be done another way. Any other way."

"So you feel people have accepted things that may not be true?"

"But they have to accept things, otherwise they can't live their daily lives. They have to feed their family, and put a roof over their heads. They don't have the luxury of sitting around thinking and asking why."

Harry clapped his hands in delight. "And now you take the opposite view in order to hear the counterargument! You're arguing with yourself! That also is the sign of a philosopher!"

"I'm not a fucking philosopher!"

Harry came and sat down beside me, his frighteningly pummeled face close to mine.

"Look, Marty, let me tell you something. Your life isn't going to get any better. In fact, think of your worst moment. Are you thinking of it? Well, let me tell you. It's all downhill from there."

"Maybe."

"You know you haven't a chance in hell of happiness."

That was upsetting news to hear, and I took it badly, maybe because I had the uncomfortable feeling that Harry understood me. Tears came to my eyes, but I fought them. Then I started thinking about tears. What was evolution up to when it rendered the human body incapable of concealing sadness? Is it somehow crucial to the survival of the species that we can't hide our melancholy? Why? What's the evolutionary benefit of crying? To elicit sympathy? Does evolution have a Machiavellian streak? After a big cry, you always feel drained and exhausted and sometimes embarrassed, especially if the tears come after watching a television commercial for tea bags. Is it evolution's design to humble us? To humiliate us?

Fuck.

"You know what I think you should do?" Harry asked.

"What?"

"Kill yourself."

"Time!" the guard called.

"Two more minutes!" Harry shouted back.

We sat glaring at each other.

"Yep, I advise you to commit suicide. It's the best thing for you. There is no doubt a cliff or something you can jump from around here."

My head moved slightly, though it wasn't a nod or a shake. It was a slight reverberation.

"Go alone. When no one is with you. Don't write a note. Many potential suiciders spend so much time composing their final words they wind up dying of old age! Don't let this be your mistake. When it comes to taking your own life, preparation is procrastination. Don't say goodbye. Don't pack a bag. Just walk to the cliff alone one late afternoon— afternoon is best because it sits solidly at the end of a day when nothing in your life has changed for the better, so you aren't suffering the tender illusion of potential and possibility that morning often brings. So then, you're at the edge of the cliff now, and you're alone, and you don't count down from ten or a hundred, and you don't make a big thing of it, you just go, don't jump, this isn't the Olympics, this is a suicide, so just step off the edge of the cliff like you're climbing the steps of a bus. Have you ever been on a bus? Fine. Then you know what I'm talking about."

"I said time's up!" the guard shouted, this time from the door.

Harry gave me a look that set off an intestinal chain reaction. "Well," he said, "I suppose this is goodbye, then."

•

There's no shortage of potential suicide jump points when you live in a valley. Our town was surrounded by cliff walls. I made my way up the steepest I could find, an exhausting, almost vertical climb to a ridge flanked by tall trees. After leaving the prison, I had conceded that Harry was right: I probably was a philosopher, or at least some kind of perennial outsider, and life wasn't going to get any easier for me. I'd separated myself from the flow, ejected my pod from the mother ship. Now I was hurtling through space that loomed endlessly ahead.

The mood of the brightening morning was incongruous to suicide, but maybe that's just what it wanted me to think. I took a last look around. I saw, in the hazy distance, the jagged ridge of the surrounding hills, and above, the sky, which seemed to be a high, unattainable plate-glass window. A light breeze carried the warm fragrance of flowers in waves, and I thought: Flowers really are lovely but not lovely enough to excuse the suffocating volume of paintings and poems inspired by them while there are still next to no paintings and poems of children throwing themselves off cliffs.

I took a step closer to the edge. High in the trees I could hear the sounds of birds. They weren't chirping, they were just moving around making everything rustle. Down near the earth brown beetles were rummaging in the dirt, not thinking of death. It didn't seem to me I'd be missing out on much. Existence is humiliating anyway. If Someone was watching us build, decay, create, degenerate, believe, and wither as we do, he'd never stop laughing. So why not? What do I know about suicide? Only that it is a melodramatic act, as well as an admission that the heat is too hot so I'm getting out of this crazy kitchen. And why shouldn't a fourteen-year-old commit suicide? Sixteen-year-olds do it all the time. Maybe I'm just ahead of my time. Why shouldn't I end it all?

I stepped right out to the edge of the precipice. I thought that when

Caroline saw me afterward she'd cry, "I loved that mashed-up piece of human wreckage." I looked over at the terrifying drop and my stomach lurched and all my joints locked and I had the following horrible thought: You experience life alone, you can be as intimate with another as much as you like, but there has to be always a part of you and your existence that is incommunicable; you die alone, the experience is yours alone, you might have a dozen spectators who love you, but your isolation, from birth to death, is never fully penetrated. What if death is the same aloneness, though, for eternity? An incommunicable, cruel, and infinite loneliness. We don't know what death is. Maybe it's that.

I stepped away from the cliff and ran in the opposite direction, stopping only to trip over a large stone.

·

I went back to see Harry West to give him a piece of my mind. He didn't look surprised to see me.

"So you didn't do it, eh? You think you will wait until you hit rock bottom before taking your own life? Well, let me save you some time. There is no bottom. Despair is bottomless. You'll never get there, and that's why I know you'll never kill yourself. Not you. Only those attached to the trivial things take their own lives, but you never will. You see, a person who reveres life and family and all that stuff, he'll be the first to put his neck in a noose, but those who don't think too highly of their loves and possessions, those who know too well the lack of purpose of it all, they're the ones who can't do it. Do you know what irony is? Well, you just heard one. If you believe in immortality, you can kill yourself, but if you feel that life is a brief flicker between two immense voids to which humanity is unfairly condemned, you wouldn't dare. Look, Marty, you're in an untenable situation. You don't have the resources to live a full life, yet you can't bring yourself to die. So what do you do?"

"I don't know! I'm fourteen!"

"You and me, we're in the same boat. Here in this prison a man cannot live properly. He can't meet girls or cook his own meals or make friends or go out dancing or do any of the skimming-the-surface-of-life things that gather leaves and lovely memories. So I, like you, can't live. And like you, I can't die. I ask you again, what's a man to do?"

"I don't know."

"You create!"

"Oh."

"Can you draw or paint?"

"Not at all."

"Can you make up stories and write them down?"

"No."

"Can you act?"

"No."

"Can you write poetry?"

"Nope."

"Can you play music?"

"Not a note."

"Can you design buildings?"

"Afraid not."

"Well, something will come to you. In fact, I think you already know."

"No I don't."

"Yes you do."

"Really, I don't."

"You know you do. Now hurry up. Get out of here. I'm sure you're in a hurry to get started."

"No, I'm not because I *don't know what you're talking about!*"

I left the prison all dazed and emptied out, on the verge of either a shocking fit or a wonderful discovery. Create, the man said.

Create what?

I needed to think. I needed an idea. Feeling heavy, I trudged into town and walked up and down our five measly streets. When I reached the end of one and almost continued into the bush, I spun around and walked the streets again. Why wouldn't I venture into the bush that surrounded our town on all sides? Well, I wished I could draw my inspiration from Mother Nature's well, but to tell you the truth, the bitch leaves me dry. Always has, always will. I just don't get any great ideas looking at trees or at possums fucking. Sure, the sleeping angel in my breast stirs just like everyone else's when confronted by a breathtaking sunset or a bubbling brook, but it doesn't lead me anywhere. A shivering blade of grass is lovely, but it leaves me with a big mental blank. Socrates must have thought the same when he said, "The trees in the countryside can teach me nothing." Instinctively I knew that I could draw inspiration only from man and manmade things. It's unromantic, but that's just how I'm built.

I stood at the crossroads and watched the people drag themselves about their business. I looked at the cinema. I looked at the general store. I looked at the barbershop. I looked at the Chinese restaurant. That all of this had sprouted from the primordial soup was a profound and impossible mystery. There's nothing perplexing to me about a leafy shrub evolving out of the big bang, but that a post office exists because carbon exploded out of a supernova is a phenomenon so outrageous it makes my head twitch.

Then I had it.

They call it inspiration: sudden ideas that explode into your brain just when you are convinced you're a moron.

I had my idea, and it was a biggie. I ran home thinking Harry was instructing both of us, Terry and me, in different lessons, but to be honest, I don't think Terry got anything out of Harry at all. Oh, a few practical pointers, sure, but none of the philosophy, none of the juice!

First Project

I'm not a handyman by nature. The objects constructed by me that exist in the world are few; scattered in garbage pits across the country lie a misshapen ashtray, an unfinished scarf, a crooked crucifix just big enough for a cat to sacrifice his life for all the future sins of unborn kittens, a deformed vase, and the object I made the night after visiting Harry in his stinking prison: a suggestion box.

I built it optimistically; it was a real cavern, 50 centimeters across, 30 centimeters in depth, enough space inside to fit literally thousands of suggestions. The box looked like an enormous square head, and after I gave it a varnish I took the handsaw and widened the mouth farther, opening up the corners a couple of centimeters on either side so the mouth was smiling. First thing I considered was attaching it to a stick and pounding it into the earth somewhere in the town, but when you're building something for public access, you have to take vandals into account; every place on earth has them, and beyond too.

Consider the layout of our town: one wide, tree-lined main street with four smaller streets running off in the middle. At this crossroads was the epicenter—the town hall. No one could go about his business without passing it. Yes, it had to be the town hall to give the suggestion box an official air. But to achieve permanence, so no one could remove it easily, it had to become part of the structure, part of the town hall itself. It had to be welded, that was obvious, but just try welding wood to concrete! Or to brick!

I scavenged around the backyard for scraps of corrugated iron that hadn't made it onto the roof of my father's shed. With his grinder I cut them into four pieces and with his welding torch I entombed the top, back, and sides of the box. I put a padlock on it, and at three in the morning, when every last person in the town was sleeping and the lights in the houses were off, I welded it to the bottom of the handrail that ran up the steps to the door of the town hall.

I placed the key to the padlock in an envelope and laid it on the front-door step of Patrick Ackerman, our lackluster town councilman. On the outside of the envelope I wrote his name and inside the following words:

> I am entrusting you with the key to unlocking the potential of our town. You are the key master. Do not abuse your privilege. Do not be slow or lazy or neglectful. Your town is counting on you.

I thought it was an elegant little note. As dawn rose over the hills and the prison was backlit by a sinister orange glow, I sat on the steps and composed the inaugural suggestions. They needed to be beauties; they needed to inspire, to excite, and they needed to be within reason. So I refrained from putting in some of my more outlandish and unworkable suggestions, such as that we should move the whole town out of this dismal valley and closer to some water—a good idea, but beyond the jurisdiction of our three-man council, one of whom no one had seen since the last big rain. No, the first suggestions needed to set the tone and encourage the populace to follow suit. They were:

1. Turn to our advantage that desultory tag "Least Desirable Place to Live in New South Wales." We should boast about it. Put up signs. Maybe even exaggerate it in order to turn it into a unique tourist attraction.

2. For Jack Hill, the town barber. While it is admirable that you continue to cut our hair despite the crippling arthritis afflicting you, the result is that this town has more bad, uneven, and downright mysterious haircuts than any town in the world. You are turning us into freaks. Please—retire your vibrating scissors and hire an apprentice.

3. For Tom Russell, proprietor of our general store, Russell and Sons. First off, Tom, you don't have a son. And not only that, you don't have a wife, and now that you're getting on in years, it looks like you will never have a son. True, you have a father and it's possible you yourself are the son your shop refers to, but as I understand it, your father died long ago, decades before you moved to this town, so the title is a misnomer. Secondly, Tom, who is doing your inventory? I was in your shop just yesterday and there exist items that no human being could possibly have any use for. Empty barrels, oversized pewter mugs, thong-shaped fly swatters, and by God your souvenirs are curious: one normally buys a model of the Eiffel Tower in France, at the Eiffel Tower, not in small Australian towns. I know it is a general store, but you have gone beyond that. Your store is more vague than general.

4. For Kate Milton, manager of the Paramount, our beloved local cinema. Once a film has been running for eight months, Kate, you can pretty much take it for granted that we've all seen it. Order some new films, for Chrissakes. Once a month would be nice.

I reread my suggestions and decided I needed one more. A big one.

It's impossible to articulate what I thought was wrong with the people of my town on a level deeper than bad haircuts and vague supermarkets—deeper problems, existence problems. I couldn't think of a suggestion that addressed these directly. It was simply impossible to point to the bedrock of existence, show the crack, and hope that we could all ponder its significance without everyone acting all sensitive about it. Instead I thought of an idea to address it *indirectly*. I guessed that their problems had something to do with priorities that needed shifting, and if so, the underlying cause of that must be linked with vision, with what parts of the world they were taking in and what they were leaving out.

My idea was this: I wanted to adjust their perspective, if I could. That led me to suggestion number five.

5. On Farmer's Hill, build a small observatory.

I offered no explanation, but I threw in the following quotes by Oscar Wilde and Spinoza, respectively: "We are all in the gutter but some of us are looking at the stars" and "Look at the world through the perspective of eternity."

I reread the suggestions and with great satisfaction slid them into the awaiting mouth of my newly constructed addition to the town.

•

The suggestion box became the town's conversation piece. Patrick Ackerman held an impromptu meeting where he read out my suggestions in a solemn voice, as if they had come from above, not below, where I was sitting. No one knew who had put the box there. They guessed, but they couldn't agree. The townspeople whittled their friends and neighbors down to a short list of about eight possibilities, but nobody was a sure thing. They certainly didn't suspect little old me. While I had been out of my coma a good many years, they still saw me as asleep.

Amazingly, Patrick Ackerman was enthusiastic about the whole thing. He was the kind of leader who desperately wanted to be fresh and progressive, but he lacked motivation and ideas and he seemed to adopt my suggestion box as his surrogate brain. He violently shouted down any derision and opposition, and because of his unexpected outburst of enthusiasm, the council, mostly from shock, agreed to every one of my suggestions. It was wild! I really wasn't expecting it. For instance, it was decided that Paul Hamilton, the unemployed one-legged seventeen-year-old son of Monica and Richard Hamilton, would start immediately as Jack Hill's apprentice barber. It was decided that Tom Russell had one year to remove the words "and Sons" from his signs, or marry and reproduce or adopt a child, provided that the son was white and from England or Northern Europe. It was decided that Kate Milton, the manager of the local cinema, should be diligent in procuring at least one new film every two months. It was unbelievable! But the real shock was to come. It was decided that plans should be immediately drawn up for an observatory to be built on Farmer's Hill, and while the budget allocated was a paltry $1000, the spirit was there. I couldn't believe it. They were really going to do it.

Patrick decided that the box would be opened only once a month, by him. He would peruse suggestions to ensure he didn't inadvertently read out anything profane or offensive, and at a public meeting he would announce them to the town, after which there would be discussions and debates and votes on which were to be carried out and which were to be ignored.

It was a tremendous thrill! I can tell you, I've had one or two successes in life thus far, but none has given me the absolute feeling of satisfaction of that first victory.

While the observatory would take some time in planning, my idea of using the dubious title "Least Desirable Place to Live in New South Wales" as a tourist attraction was immediately put into effect. Signs were erected on the road where it fell into town, and on the other side, where it rose out of it.

Then we waited for the tourists to come.

Amazingly, they did.

As their cars pulled into our streets, the townspeople put on dour faces and shuffled their feet.

"Hey, what's it like here? Why is it so bad?" the tourists asked.

"It just is," came the mopey reply.

Day-trippers wandered the streets and saw in every face a look of despair and loneliness. Inside the pub, the locals acted miserable.

"What's the food here like?" the tourists would ask.

"Terrible."

"Can I just have a beer, then?"

"We water it down and charge extra. OK?"

"Hey—this really is the least desirable place to live in New South Wales!"

When the tourists moved on, the smiles returned and the whole town felt like it had played a great prank.

Everyone looked forward to the box's monthly opening, and more often than not, it was brimming. The meetings were open to all, and it was usually standing room only. They routinely began as Councilman Ackerman announced his disappointment at the things found in the box that weren't suggestions—orange peels, dead birds, newspapers, chip packets, and chewing gum—and then he'd read out the suggestions, an astounding array of blueprints for possibilities. It seemed everyone was caught up in the spell of ideas. The potential for the town to reach a higher place, to improve itself, to evolve, had caught on. People started carrying little notepads with them wherever they went; you would see them stop abruptly in the middle of the street, or leaning against the streetlamp, or crouched over the pavement, struck by an idea. Everyone was jotting down his ideas, and in such secrecy! The anonymity of the suggestion box allowed people to articulate their longings and desires, and really, they came up with the strangest things.

First were the practical suggestions pertaining to infrastructure and general municipal matters: dismantling all parking restrictions, lowering taxes and petrol prices, and fixing the cost of beer at one cent. There were suggestions aimed at ending our reliance on the city by having our own hospital, our own courthouse, and our own skyline. There were proposals for entertainment events such as community barbecues, fireworks nights, and Roman orgies, and there were countless suggestions for the construction of things: better roads, a town mint, a football stadium, a horse track, and, despite the fact that we were located inland, a harbor bridge. The list just ran on and on with ultimately useless proposals that our town's council simply wasn't fat enough to satisfy.

Then, when municipal matters bored them, the people began to turn on each other.

It was suggested that Mrs. Dawes shouldn't walk around like "she's better than everyone else," and that Mr. French, the town grocer, stop pretending he was "not good with numbers" when caught out short-changing us, and that Mrs. Anderson immediately cease overexposing her grandson by shoving photographs of him under everyone's noses because while he might be only three years old, "we're all beginning to groan at the sight of him." Things turned so quickly because Patrick Ackerman was struck down with pneumonia and his second-in-command, Jim Brock, took up the task. Jim was old and bitter and mischievous and read out the most profane, personal, idiotic, and provocative suggestions in an innocent voice, but you could hear him smile, even if you couldn't see it. Jim was shit-stirring, and because anonymity guarantees honesty (as Oscar Wilde said, "Give a man a mask and he will tell the truth"), everyone in the town was really letting loose.

One suggestion said: *Linda Miller, you whore. Stop fucking our men or we'll organize a lynch mob to cut your great big knockers off.*

And there was this one: *Maggie Steadman, you old bat. You shouldn't be allowed to park your car anywhere near our town if you can't judge the dimensions of things.*

And this one: *Lionel Potts should stop showing off his money and buying everything in town.*

And another: *Andrew Christianson, you have no neck! I don't have a suggestion for fixing it, I just wanted to point it out.*

And this: *Mrs. Kingston, stop bothering us with jealous concerns about your husband's fidelity. His breath smells like rotten eggs after they've been shat out a runny bottom. You have no worries there.*

And this: *Geraldine Trent, despite your promises of "I won't tell a soul," you are a horrendous gossip and you have betrayed the confidence of just about everyone in town. P.S. Your daughter is a drug addict and a lesbian. But don't worry, I won't tell a soul.*

People came to dread the reading of the suggestions in case they themselves were to be mentioned. They started to feel vulnerable, exposed, and eyed each other suspiciously in the streets until they spent less time socializing and more time hiding in their homes. I was furious. In the space of a few months, my suggestion box had really made our town the least desirable place to live in New South Wales, or for that matter anywhere at all.

•

Meanwhile, the twins had turned sixteen and celebrated the occasion by quitting school. Bruno and Dave were saving up for guns and planning a move to the city, and Terry wanted to join them. As for me, I'd finally managed to extricate myself from the gang. There was no reason for me to pretend I was doing any good watching over Terry, Bruno had finally reached the point of wanting to "vomit his whole stomach up" at the sight of me, and frankly, I'd had a gutful of the whole stinking lot of them. The benefit I derived from my association with the gang was firmly secured; I was left in peace by my schoolmates. I didn't wake with dread every day, so now my mind was free to do other things. It's not until it's gone that you appreciate how time-consuming dread really is.

I spent every spare millisecond with Caroline. I was fascinated not only by her increasingly succulent body but by her idiosyncrasies. She was obsessed with the idea that people were holding out on her. She relentlessly squeezed their stories out of them; she thought that older people, having lived in many places and cities, had experienced all that life has to offer and she wanted to hear about it. She didn't care about the children in the town; they didn't know anything. It was easy to get the adults talking. They seemed ever watchful for a receptacle in which to pour the banked-up untreated sewage of their lives. But after she heard them, she'd incinerate them with an unimpressed look that said very clearly, "Is that all?"

She read too, only she gleaned very different things from books than I did. She obsessed over the lives of the characters, how they ate, dressed, drank, traveled, explored, smoked, fucked, partied, and loved. She longed for exoticism. She wanted to travel the world. She wanted to make love in an igloo. It was comical the way Lionel Potts encouraged his daughter. "One day I'm going to drink champagne hanging upside-down on a trapeze," she'd say. "Good for you! I know you'll get there! It's important to have goals! Think big!" he'd ramble on endlessly. She really set him off.

But Caroline wasn't as totally discontented with her surroundings as I was. She found beauty in things I just couldn't see. Tulips in a flower-pot, old people holding hands, an obvious toupee—the littlest thing would send her squealing in delight. And the women of the town adored her. She was always adjusting their hats and picking flowers for them. But when she was alone with me, she was different. I realized that her sweetness, the way she carried on with the people of the town, was her mask. It was a good one, the best kind of mask there is: a true lie. Her mask was a weave of tattered shreds torn from all the beautiful parts of herself.

One morning I went over to Caroline's and was surprised to see Terry standing outside her house, throwing stones so they landed in the garden bed underneath the front windows.

"What are you doing?" I asked.

"Nothing."

"Terry Dean! Stop throwing stones in our garden!" Caroline shouted from the upstairs window.

"It's a free world, Caroline Potts!"

"Not in China!"

"What's going on?" I asked.

"Nothing. I can throw stones here if I want."

"I guess."

Caroline watched from the window. She waved at me. I waved back. Then Terry waved too, only his was a sarcastic wave, if you can imagine it. Caroline waved ironically, which is totally different in tone. I wondered what Terry had against Caroline.

"Let's go home," I said.

"In a little while. I want to keep throwing stones."

"Leave her alone," I said, annoyed. "She's my friend."

"Big deal." Terry spat, threw down the stones, and walked off. I watched him go. What was that all about? I couldn't figure it out. Of course, back then I didn't know anything about young love. I had no idea, for instance, that it was possible to express love by puerile aggression and spite.

Around this time I went up to see Harry, and I didn't know it then, but it was to be my last visit. He was already in the visitors' room, waiting and gaping at me expectantly, as if he'd put a whoopee cushion under my mattress at home and he wanted to know if it had gone off yet. When I didn't say anything, he said, "You've been really stirring things up down there!"

"What are you talking about?"

"The suggestion box. They've gone crazy, haven't they?"

"How do you know about that?"

"Oh, you can see quite a lot from up here," he said, his voice waltzing in three-four time. It wasn't true. You could see fuck all. "It's all going to end badly, of course, but you can't hate yourself for it. That's why I called you here today. I wanted to tell you not to beat yourself up about it."

"You didn't call me."

"I didn't?"

"No."

"Well, I didn't call the clouds either, but there they are," he said, pointing to the window. "All I'm saying, Marty, is don't let it destroy you. Nothing chews at a man's soul more ravenously than guilt."

"What do I have to be guilty about?"

Harry shrugged, but it was the most loaded shrug I'd ever seen.

It turned out the shrug was right; by creating something as innocuous as an empty box, I had once again nudged my family's destiny in a really unpleasant direction.

•

It started about a month later, when Terry's name first appeared in the suggestion box.

> Mr. Dean should learn to control his son. Terry Dean has fallen under the influence of young men impossible to turn around. But Terry is young. It's not too late. All he needs is some parental guidance, and if his parents can't do it, we'll find some that can.

Everyone in the hall applauded. The townspeople regarded the box as a sort of oracle; because the suggestion didn't come directly out of the mouths of our neighbors but was on paper and pulled ceremoniously from the box and read in the authoritarian tone of Jim Brock, the words were taken more seriously than they deserved, and were often followed with a frightening religious obedience.

"It's not my fault it's a titanic waste of effort raising sons under strict moral guidelines when children are so heavily influenced by their peers," my father said that night over dinner. "One wrong friend and your kid could be knocked off balance for good."

We all sat listening to him with trepidation, watching his thoughts whirl around his head like dust in the wind.

The next day he turned up at the playground at lunchtime. Both Terry and I ran for cover, but he wasn't looking for us. Notebook in his lap, he sat on the swings and watched the children play; he was making a list of young boys he thought suitable to befriend his sons. Of course the children must have thought he was insane (these were the days before they would have simply assumed him a pedophile), but watching his fervent efforts to put me and Terry on the straight-and-narrow made me pity and admire him in equal measure. Every now and then he'd call over a boy and have a chat with him, and I remember being secretly impressed by his commitment to what was a seriously weird idea.

Who knows what they talked about during these informal interviews, but after a week my father's list contained fifteen potentials: fine, upstanding children from good families. He presented us the results of his intensive research. "These are suitable friends," he said. "Go out and befriend them."

I told him I couldn't make a friend out of plasticine.

"Don't tell me that," my father barked. "I know what making friends is about. You just go up and talk to them."

He wouldn't let up. He wanted updates. He wanted results. He wanted to see lifelong friendships parade before his eyes, and that was an order! Finally Terry had his gang "persuade" a couple of unsuspecting kids from the list to come over and hang out in the backyard after school. They came, shaking all afternoon, and for a while my father was placated.

But the suggestion box wasn't. Eyes all over the town could see Terry carrying on with Bruno and Dave as before.

The next suggestion that came was this: *I suggest that while his parents are not religious, Terry could use some spiritual guidance. It isn't too late. Terry can still be reformed.*

Once again my father was furious, though strangely obedient. This was to be the pattern, and as the quantity of the suggestions about Terry's errant behavior increased and our family became a constant object of attention and scrutiny, my father cursed both the box and the "serpent" who put it there, but still he obeyed.

After arriving home from the town hall, my father argued with my mother. She wanted a rabbi to come talk to Terry. He thought a priest would do the job better. In the end my mother won out. A rabbi came over to the house and talked to Terry about violence. Rabbis know a lot about violence because they work for a deity who is famous for his wrath. Problem is, Jews don't believe in hell, so there isn't the same readily accessible chamber of fear the Catholics have up their sleeve to poison the nervous system of their youth. You can't turn to a young Jewish boy and say, "You see that pit of fire? That's where you're going." You have to tell him stories of the vengeance of the Almighty and hope he gets the hint.

Terry didn't, and there were more suggestions to come, but don't think the box was aimed only at my brother. One Monday night in the middle of summer, my own name was mentioned.

Someone should tell young Martin Dean that it's rude to stare, the suggestion began, inspiring the whole room to burst into applause. *He's a*

grumpy boy who unnerves everyone by glaring at them. And he doesn't give
Caroline Potts a moment's peace. I tell you, I'm no stranger to humiliation,
but nothing has ever surpassed that mortifying moment.

A month later another Dean family suggestion was drawn from the
box, this time aimed at, of all people, my mother.

> Mrs. Dean should stop wasting our time with lengthy justifica-
> tions as to why her husband and children are no-hopers. Terry isn't
> just "wild," he's a degenerate. Martin doesn't "march to his own
> drum," he's a sociopath, and their father hasn't got "a healthy
> imagination," he's a bald-faced liar.

There's no doubt about it. Our family was a popular target, and the
townspeople really seemed to have it in for Terry. My mother became
frightened for him, and I became frightened of her fear. Her fear was terrifying. She would sit on Terry's bed and whisper "I love you" as he slept,
from midnight until dawn, as though trying to alter his behavior subconsciously, before it was altered for him. She could see that the townspeople took her son's reformation as one of their top priorities; he had
been their number-one pride and was now their number-one disappointment, and when it was obvious that Terry was continuing to run around
with the gang, stealing and fighting, another suggestion was offered to
tackle the problem: *I suggest the renegade Terry Dean be taken up to the
prison on the hill to talk to one of the inmates and hear the horror of the life
inside. Maybe scare tactics will work.*

For safety, my father forced me along too, in case I took it into my
head to follow my brother into a life of crime. We moved up the hill
toward the prison, our real school, on the dirt road that came down the
hill like an open wound.

It was arranged for us to meet the worst criminal in the prison. His
name was Vincent White. He'd had a bad time inside: stabbed seven
times with a shiv, face sliced open, blinded in one eye and left with a lip
that dangled from his face like a label you just want to tug off. The three
of us sat down in front of him in the visitors' room. Terry had met Vincent once before, with Harry. "Bit surprised you want to see me," Vincent said straightaway. "You and Harry having maritals?" Terry shook his
head imperceptibly, trying to signal him, but Vincent's one functioning

eye was darting around the room, surveying my father. "Who's this you got with you? This your old man?"

My father dragged us out of the prison as if it were on fire, and from that day on the Dean boys were forbidden to visit anyone inside. I tried to return once or twice to see Harry, but I was knocked back. It was a crushing blow. Now more than ever, I desperately needed his advice. I knew things were building to a climax that was obviously not going to go down in our favor. Maybe if I'd had the presence of mind, I'd have encouraged my brother to leave town when, soon after the prison incident, he had an opportunity to escape this awful mess I'd created.

It was a Friday afternoon, and Bruno and Dave drove up in a stolen Jeep loaded with their possessions and also other people's possessions. They honked the horn. Terry and I went out to meet them.

"Come on, mate, we're getting out of this shitty town," Dave called out to Terry.

"I'm not going."

"Why?"

"I'm just not."

"You pussy!"

"You'll never fuck her, you know," Bruno said.

Terry didn't say anything to that.

Bruno and Dave revved the car gratuitously before screeching off. We watched them disappear. I was in awe at how, after all the pain and heartache and drama and anxiety people cause, they so unceremoniously leave your life. Terry looked on the empty road without emotion.

"Who won't you fuck?" I asked him.

"No one," he said.

"Me neither."

The next town hall meeting was on the Monday, and we were all dreading it. We knew the oracle had one more suggestion for Terry Dean. As we entered, we avoided the eyes of all those unfriendly faces, which looked to have experienced a fit of rage in childhood, then harnessed it for their entire lives. They cleared a space for us as we moved through. Four seats were left in the front, and my parents and I took three of them. Terry had stayed at home, sensibly boycotting the proceedings. I sat on the uncomfortable wooden chair with my eyes half closed, peering beneath my eyelids at a photograph on the wall of the Queen on her twenty-first birthday. She looked to be in a state of dread too. The Queen and I waited impatiently as we listened to the other suggestions. They held Terry's off until last. Then it came.

I suggest Terry Dean be taken to Portland Mental Institution and be treated by a team of psychiatrists for his violent, antisocial behavior.

I hurried out of the hall into the unexpected brightness of the evening. The night sky was lit by a huge moon, not full so much as fat, hovering above deserted streets. My footsteps were the only sound in town, other than the barking of a dog that followed me for a while, excited by my panic. I didn't stop running until I reached the house—no, I didn't stop there. I charged through the front door and barreled down the hall into our bedroom. Terry was sitting on the bed reading.

"You have to get out of here!" I shouted. I found a sports bag and threw his clothes into it. "They're coming! They're going to put you in a mental institution!"

Terry looked up at me quietly. He said, "Stupid bastards. Was Caroline there tonight?"

"Yes, she was, but—"

I heard footsteps tearing down the hallway. "Hide!" I whispered. Terry didn't move. The footsteps were almost at the door. "Too late!" I shouted uselessly. The bedroom door swung open and Caroline ran in.

"You have to get out of here!" she shouted.

Terry gazed at her with bright eyes. That threw her off balance. They stared at each other, unmoving, looking like strangely arranged mannequins. I was utterly isolated from the energy in the room. This was a shock to me. Caroline and Terry had a thing for each other? When did this happen? I resisted a strong impulse to pluck out my eye and show it to them.

"I'm helping him pack," I said, breaking the moment. My own voice was unrecognizable. Caroline liked Terry, maybe even loved him. I was furious! I felt drenched by all the world's rain. I coughed impatiently. No one looked at me, or gave any hint that I was among them.

She sat on the edge of his bed and drummed her fingers on the blankets. "You have to leave," she said.

"Where are we going?"

I looked to Caroline to see what her response would be. "I can't go," she said finally. "But I'll visit you."

"Where?"

"I don't know. Sydney. Go to Sydney."

"And hurry up about it!" I shouted so loudly that we didn't hear the second round of footsteps.

Two men came in, eager early members of a lynch mob. They took on the role of a strong-arm taxi service. Terry put up a futile struggle while more people filed into our house, all with hostile, determined faces. They dragged him outside, his face bled white in the moonlight.

Caroline didn't cry but held her hand over her mouth in a twenty-minute gasp while I was in a frenzy, screaming myself hoarse at my parents, who stood helplessly by.

"What are you doing? Don't let them take him!"

My mother and father cowered like frightened dogs. They were afraid of going against the oracle's command and the unstoppable will of the townspeople. Public opinion had them on the back foot.

My father said, "It's for the best. He's unbalanced. They know how to fix him."

He said this as he signed the necessary paperwork and my mother looked on, resigned. Both wore obstinate grimaces you couldn't have removed with a hammer.

"He doesn't need fixing! I think he's already fixed! He's in love!"

No one listened to me. Caroline and I stood together as they dragged Terry away to a mental asylum. I looked at my parents incredulously, at their inexorably tepid souls. All I could do was uselessly shake a clenched fist and think how people are so eager to become slaves it's unbelievable. Christ. Sometimes they throw off their freedom so quickly, you'd think it was burning them.

Transcendence

It's not that insanity is contagious, although human history *is* littered with tales of mass hysteria—like the time everyone in the Western world was wearing white loafers with no socks—but as soon as Terry disappeared into the crazy house, our own house became a place of darkness as well, starting with my father, who came to his senses a week later and did everything in his power to spring Terry from the hospital, only to discover that once you put someone under forced psychiatric care, the administrators take that care as seriously as the money the government pays them to do the caring. My little brother was judged to be a danger to himself and others—the others mostly being the hospital staff he fought to break himself out. My father petitioned the courts and consulted numerous lawyers but soon realized he'd lost his son in a tangle of red tape. He was stuck. As a result, he started drinking more and more, and though my mother and I tried to slow the momentum of his downward spiral, you can't stop someone from taking the role of alcoholic father simply by telling them it's a cliché. Twice in the months following Terry's internment he lost his temper and hit my mother, knocking her to the floor, but you can no more easily wean a man off the part of Wife Beater than you can convince a woman to flee her own home by assuring her she has Battered Wife Syndrome. It just doesn't do any good.

Like my father, my mother oscillated between madness and sadness. A couple of nights after Terry was taken away, I was preparing for bed and said aloud, "Maybe I won't brush my teeth. Why should I? Fuck teeth. I'm sick of teeth. I'm sick of my teeth. I'm sick of other people's teeth. Teeth are a burden, and I'm sick of polishing them every night like they're the royal jewels." When I threw my toothbrush down in disgust, I saw a shapely shadow outside the bathroom. "Hello?" I said to the shadow. My mother came into the room and stood behind me. We looked at each other in the bathroom mirror.

"You talk to yourself," she said, placing her hand on my forehead. "Do you have a temperature?"

"No."

"A little warm," she said.

"I'm a mammal," I mumbled. "That's how we are."

"I'm going to the pharmacy, get you some medicine," she said.

"But I'm not sick."

"You won't be if you catch it early."

"Catch what early?" I asked, examining her sad face. My mother's reaction to having put her son away in a mental asylum was to become a maniac for my welfare. It didn't happen gradually but all at once, when I found I couldn't pass her on the stairs without her crushing me in an embrace. Nor could I leave the house without her buttoning up my jacket to the top, and when that still left a little expanse of neck exposed to the elements, she sewed an extra button on so I would be always covered to the lower lip.

She went to the city almost every day to visit Terry and always came home with good news that somehow sounded bad.

"He's doing a little better," she said in a distraught voice.

I soon discovered these were nothing but lies. I had been forbidden to go to the hospital because it was assumed that my weak psyche wasn't up to a battering. But Terry was my brother, so one morning I went through all the motions of a boy preparing for school, and when the bus thundered by I hid behind a thorny bush I later burned for pricking me. Then I made my way to the asylum by hitching a ride with a refrigerator repairman who laughed snidely the whole way about people who don't defrost.

Seeing my brother was a shock. His smile was a little too wide, his hair unkempt, his eyes vague, his skin pale. They made him wear a hospital gown so he might remember at all times that he was too unstable for a zipper or button-up fly. Only when he joked about the electricity bills for his shock therapy was I convinced that this experience wasn't going to destroy him. We ate lunch together in a surprisingly cozy room filled with potted plants and with a large picture window that had the perfect view of a teenager with a persecution mania.

Terry turned dark in reference to the suggestion box. "What fucking tit put that there, I'd like to know," he growled.

At the end of the visit he told me that he had not had one visit from our mother and that while he wasn't blaming her, he thought mothers were supposed to be better than that.

When I arrived home, she was in the backyard. It had rained all afternoon, and I saw she had her shoes off and was digging her toes in the mud. She urged me to do the same because cold mud oozing through toes is a pleasure greater than anyone could imagine. She was not lying.

"Where are you going every day?" I asked.

"To visit Terry."

"I saw him today. He said he hasn't seen you."

She said nothing and squelched her feet as deep in mud as they would go. I did the same. A bell rang out. We both looked up at the prison and watched it a long time, as though the sound had woven a visible path across the sky. Life up there was regulated by bells that could be heard inside every house in town. This bell signified it was time for prisoners' afternoon exercise. There would be another bell shortly to stop it.

"You can't tell your father."

"Tell him what?"

"That I've been to the hospital."

"Terry said you haven't."

"No, a regular hospital."

"Why?"

"I think I've got something."

"What?"

In the silence that followed, her eyes fell to her hands. They were white wrinkled things with blue veins the width of telephone cords. She let out a little gasp. "I have my mother's hands!" she said suddenly with surprise and disgust, as if her mother's hands hadn't actually been hands but hand-shaped lumps of shit.

"Are you sick?" I asked.

"I have cancer," she said.

When I opened my mouth, the wrong words came out. Practical words, none of the words I really wanted to say.

"Is it something they can take out with a sharp knife?" I asked.

She shook her head.

"How long have you got?"

"I don't know."

It was a dreadful moment that got more dreadful with every passing second. But hadn't we had this conversation before? I felt a strange sort of déjà vu. Not the type where you feel as though you've already experienced an event, but the feeling that you've already experienced the déjà vu about the event.

"It's going to get bad," she said.

I didn't say anything, and I was starting to feel as though something frosty had been injected into my bloodstream. My father shuffled out of the back door in his pajamas and stood there glumly with an empty glass in his hand. "I want a cold drink. Have you seen the ice?"

"Try the freezer," she said, then whispered to me, "Don't leave me alone."

"What?"

"Don't leave me, with him, alone."

That's when I did an incredible thing that to this day I still can't get my head around.

I took my mother's hand in mine and I said, "I swear I'll stay with you until the day you die."

"You swear it?"

"I swear it."

As soon as I'd said it, this seemed like a very bad, even self-castrating idea, but when your dying mother asks you to pledge undying devotion, what are you going to say? No? Especially since I knew that her future was the exact opposite of prosperity. What would it entail? Slow periods of deterioration broken by intermittent periods of false hope and convalescence, then recontinued degeneration, all under the weight of increasing agony and the terror of approaching death, which wasn't sneaking up silently but was coming forward from a great distance trumpets blaring.

So why did I make this pledge? It's not that I felt pity or was overwhelmed by emotion. It's just that I seem to have at base a revulsion to the idea of a person being left alone to suffer and die, because I myself would hate to be left alone to suffer and die, and this revulsion is so deeply embedded within me that there was nothing fine about pledging devotion to my mother, as it constituted not a moral choice but rather a moral reflex. In short, I'm a sweetheart, but I'm cold about it.

"Are you cold?" she suddenly asked me. I said no. She pointed to the goose bumps on my arm. "Let's get you inside," she said, and swung her arm over my shoulder as if we were old drinking buddies going inside to rack up a game of pool. As we walked up toward the house and the prison bell rang out again across the valley, I felt that either a wall had come down between us or one had been taken away, and I couldn't work out which it was.

•

With Terry in hospital, I spent almost every afternoon with Caroline. Not surprisingly, we talked about Terry interminably. Christ, when I think of it, there hasn't been a time in my life when I haven't had to talk about the bastard. It's hard to keep loving someone, even after they're dead, when you have to keep jabbering about them.

Whenever Caroline mentioned Terry's name, heart molecules broke off and dissolved into my bloodstream—I could feel my emotional core getting progressively smaller. Caroline's dilemma was this: should she be the girlfriend of a crazy gangster? Of course the drama and romance of it tickled her pink, but there was a sensible voice in Caroline's head too, one that had the effrontery to seek her happiness, and that was the voice that was getting her down. It made her miserable. I listened without interrupting. Soon enough I was able to read between the lines; Caroline had no problem envisaging Bonnie and Clyde–style escapades, but she obviously didn't hold out much hope for Terry's luck. He was already behind bars and he hadn't even been arrested yet. That didn't sit well with her plans.

"What am I going to do?" she'd cry, pacing this way and that.

I was in a pickle. I wanted her for myself. I wanted my brother's happiness. I wanted him safe. I wanted him free of crime and danger. But most of all I wanted her for myself.

"Why don't you write to him and give him an ultimatum?" I said with trepidation, not really knowing whose cause I was aiding. It was the first concrete suggestion I'd made, and she pounced all over it.

"What do you mean? Tell him to choose between crime and me?"

Love is powerful, I'll admit, but so is addiction. I was wagering that Terry's absurd addiction to crime was stronger than his love for her. It was a bitter, cynical wager I made with myself, a bet I had no probable way of winning.

Because I spent so much time at Caroline's house, Lionel Potts became our family's only ally. In an attempt to get Terry released from the institution, he made phone calls to various legal firms on our behalf, and when that failed, he arranged through an associate for the most renowned psychiatrist in Sydney to go have a chat with Terry. That's the psychiatrists' version of doing a quote: they turn up in casual pants and chat like old friends. This psychiatrist, a middle-aged man with a floppy, worn-out face, even made his way to our house to pass on his findings. We all drank tea in the living room as he told us what he'd found under Terry's hood.

"Terry has made it easy for me, far easier than most of my patients, not necessarily with his own self-awareness, which, to be honest, is nothing special, but with his candor and total willingness to answer without pause or detour any question I put to him. Actually, he may be the most straightforward patient I've ever had in my life. I would like to say at this point, you have done a tremendous job in raising a truly honest and open person."

"So he's not insane?" my father asked.

"Oh, don't get the wrong idea. He's crazy as a coconut. But open!"

"We're not violent people," my father said. "This whole thing is a mystery to us."

"No man's life is a mystery. Believe me, there is order and structure in the most ostensibly chaotic skull. There seem to be two major events in Terry's life that have shaped him more than any others. The first I would not have believed had I not unwavering faith in his honesty." The doctor leaned forward and said, almost in a whisper, "Did he really spend the first four years of his life sharing a bedroom with a comatose boy?"

My parents looked at each other with a start.

"Was that wrong?" my mother asked.

"We didn't have any room," my father said, annoyed. "Where were we supposed to put Martin? In the shed?"

"Terry described the scene so vividly it actually gave me shivers. I know shivers aren't a professional reaction, but there you have it. He talked about eyes rolled back that would spontaneously roll forward and stare. Sudden jerks and spasms, incessant drooling . . ." The psychiatrist turned to me and asked, "You would be the boy who was in the coma?"

"That's me."

He pointed a finger at me and said, "My professional opinion is that this faintly breathing corpse gave young Terry Dean what I can only diagnose as the permanent willies. This more than anything made him retreat into his own private fantasy life, in which he is the protagonist. You see, there are traumas that affect people, traumas that are sudden, but there are also prolonged, lingering traumas, and often they are the most insidious, because their effects grow alongside everything else and are as much a part of the sufferer as his own teeth."

"And the second thing?"

"His injury, his inability to play sport. Deep down, although he was very young, Terry was convinced that excelling at sport was the reason he was here on earth. And when he was robbed of that, he turned from a creator to a destroyer."

Nobody spoke—we all just soaked it up.

"I think at first, when Terry found he could no longer play football or cricket or swim, he embraced violence as a perversion of what he knew—to display skill. He wasn't out to do anything other than show off, pure and simple. You see, his useless limping leg was an insult to his self-image, and he couldn't accept the powerlessness without restoring his ability to act. So he acted, violently, the violence of the man who is denied positive expression," the psychiatrist said with a pride that felt inappropriate for the occasion.

"What the hell are you talking about?" my father said.

"So how does he cease to be crippled?" I asked.

"Well, now you're talking about transcendence."

"Transcendence that could be, for instance, found in the expression of love?"

"Yes, I suppose so."

This conversation was really puzzling for my parents, as they had never seen my brain before. They'd seen the shell, but not the goods inside. The answer to all this was obvious to me: a doctor couldn't turn Terry around, nor a priest nor a rabbi nor any god nor my parents nor a fright nor a suggestion box nor even me. No, the only hope for Terry's reform was Caroline. His hope was love.

Eternity

I hadn't noticed it going up. You couldn't see it from the town, owing to the high wall of thick leafy trees at the summit of Farmer's Hill, but on Saturday night everyone wound up the track toward it for its opening. You should've seen us, all filing out of town as if in a fire drill no one believed in. No one was carrying on with the usual banter; there was something different in the air. We all felt it—anticipation. Some didn't even know what an observatory was, and those who did were rightly excited. The most exotic thing in bush towns is the dim sum in those ubiquitous Chinese restaurants. This was something else.

Then we saw it, a large dome.

All trees had been removed from directly in front of it, because where telescopes are concerned, even a single leaf of an overhanging branch can obscure the galaxy. The observatory was painted white; the building walls were framed with two-by-fours and covered with roofing metal. The telescope itself I knew little of, other than it was thick, long, and white, had a simple spherically curved mirror, stood on an isolated pier for a stable platform to prevent the transmission of vibrations, was designed to include expansion capabilities, weighed in excess of 250 pounds, was 10 degrees from the southern horizon, could *not* be pointed down into the girls' bathroom in the school gymnasium, was encased in a fiberglass dome, and had a glass roof that lifted on a hinge. To move the telescope, if you wanted to peek at another corner of the galaxy or follow the transit of celestial objects across the sky, the idea for rotation motors was dropped in favor of "putting your back into it."

We all stepped up, one by one, to the big eye.

You had to climb up to it on a little stepladder. Each person pressed against the eyepiece, and when their time was up, they stepped down in a sort of trance, as though lobotomized by the vastness of the universe. It was one of the strangest nights I ever had in that town.

I had my turn at the telescope. It exceeded my expectations. I saw huge numbers of stars: faint and old and yellow. I saw brilliant hot stars, clusters of young blue stars. I saw streaks of globules and dust, sinuous dark lanes winding through luminous gas and scattered starlight, reminding me of all the visions I had seen in the coma. I thought: The stars are dots. Then I thought of every human being as a dot too, but realized sadly that most of us could barely light up a room. We're too small to be dots.

Still, I returned to the telescope night after night, familiarizing myself with the southern sky, and after a while I understood that watching the universe expand is like watching grass grow, so I watched the townspeople instead. After they stepped up silently, poked around in the farthest reaches of our galaxy, let out a whistle, and stepped down, they came outside and smoked cigarettes and talked. Probably their ignorance of astronomy helped move the conversations onto other things; this is one of those areas where lack of trivial, useless knowledge—the names of the stars in this instance—is a huge benefit. The important thing is not what the stars are called but what they imply.

People began with some marvelous understatements of the universe, such as "Pretty big, isn't it?" But I think they were purposefully laconic. They were filled with awe and wonder, and like a dreamer who has woken but lies unmoving in bed trying to return to the dream, they didn't want inadvertently to shake themselves awake. But then, slowly, they began to talk, and it wasn't about the stars or their place in the universe. I listened with astonishment as they said things like

"I should spend more time with my son."

"When I was young, I used to look up at the stars too."

"I don't feel loved. I feel liked."

"I wonder why I don't go to church anymore."

"My children turned out differently than I expected. Taller, maybe."

"I'd like to take a holiday with Carol, like we did when we were first married."

"I don't want to be alone anymore. My clothes smell."

"I want to accomplish something."

"I've gotten so lazy. I haven't learned anything since I was at school."

"I'm going to plant a lemon tree, not for me but for my children's children. Lemons are the future."

It was thrilling to hear. The incessant universe had made them look at themselves, if not from the perspective of eternity, then at least with a bit more clarity. For a few minutes they were stirred to the depths, and I suddenly felt rewarded and compensated for all the damage my suggestion box had done.

It made me think too.

One night after I had come down from the observatory, I found myself frozen in the garden at midnight fretting on the future of my family, trying to come up with ideas of how to save them all. Unfortunately, the idea bank was empty. I had made too many withdrawals. Besides, how do you save a dying mother, an alcoholic father, and a criminally insane little brother? Anxiety threatened to damage my stomach lining and also my urethra.

I carried a bucket of water from the house and poured it in a shallow ditch at the end of the garden. I thought: I might not be able to make a better life for my loved ones, but I can still make mud. The dirt met the water and thickened appropriately. I plunged my feet in it. It was cold and gooey. The back of my neck tingled. I thanked my mother aloud for instructing me in the glories of mud. It's so rare that people give you real, practical advice. Normally they say things like "Don't worry," and "Everything will be OK," which is not only impractical, it's exasperating, and you have to wait until they're diagnosed with a terminal disease before you can say it back to them with any pleasure.

I sank deeper into the mud, using all my force, all the way to the tops of my ankles. I wanted to go farther into the cold sludge. A lot farther. I thought about getting more water. A lot more. Just then I heard footsteps running through the bush and I saw branches shuddering as if repulsed. A face popped out and said, "Marty?"

Harry stepped into the moonlight. He was wearing his prison denims and was badly cut and bleeding.

"I escaped! What are you doing? Cooling your feet in mud? Hang on." Harry came over and sank his bare feet in the ditch next to mine. "That's better. Well, there I was. Lying in my cell, contemplating how the best years of my life were behind me and how they weren't that good. Then I contemplated how all I had to look forward to was decaying and dying in jail. You've seen the prison—it's no sort of place at all. I thought: If I don't at least try to make a break for it, I'll never forgive myself. Fine. But how? In movies, prisoners always escape by smuggling themselves inside a laundry truck. Could it work? No. You know why? Because maybe in the old days prisons sent out their laundry, but we did ours in-house! So that was out. Second option, digging a tunnel. Now, I've dug enough graves in my time to know it's tedious, backbreaking work, and besides, all my experience is in the first six feet, enough to hide a body. Who really knows what lies deeper? Molten lava? An unbreakable shelf of iron ore?"

Harry looked down at his feet. "I think the mud's setting. Help me out of here," he said, holding out his arm as if it were for sale. I helped him out and he collapsed on a small mound of grass.

"Get me something to wear, and a beer if you've got it. Hurry up," he said.

I went inside and sneaked into my father's closet; he was sleeping facedown on the bed, a deep drunken sleep with such a shattering snore I almost stopped to check his nose for an amplifier and lead. I picked out an old suit, then went to the fridge for beers. When I returned, Harry was ankle deep in mud again.

"First thing I did was fake an illness: stabbing abdominal pains. What else was I going to use? Back pain? Middle-ear infection? Was I going to complain that I saw a drop of blood in my urine? No, they needed to think it was a matter of life and death. So I did it and found myself sent to the infirmary, at three in the morning, when only one man was on duty. So I'm in the infirmary, doubled up in pretend pain. At about five the guard on duty goes out for a piss. At once I leap out of bed and break the lock of the medicine cabinet and steal all the liquid tranquilizers I can. I jab the guard when he comes back and then go around looking for another guard to help me get out of there. I knew I'd never get out without a guard's help, but these bastards were unbribable, for the most part. Not that they weren't corrupt, they just didn't like me. But a couple of weeks before, I called in all my old favors and got one of my cronies to supply me with information about a certain guard's family. I chose one of the newer guys—Kevin Hastings is his name, he's been with us only two months, so he was less likely to know his arse from his elbow. It's hilarious how these bastards think they're anonymous in prison. You can really freak them out when you tell them you know precisely what positions they use with their wives, duration, et cetera. Anyway, Hastings turned out to be perfect. The man has a daughter. I wouldn't have done anything, but I had to scare the life out of the bugger. And even if he didn't bite, what did I have to lose? Would they really bother giving me *another* life sentence? I already have six!" Harry paused here a moment, reflecting, and said quietly, "I'll tell you something, Marty, there's freedom in forever."

I nodded. It sounded true.

"So anyway, I go right up to Hastings and whisper in his ear, 'Get me out of here now or else your lovely little daughter Rachael will enjoy the pleasure of a very diseased man I know.' His face went white and he slipped me the keys, let me bang him on the noggin so he wouldn't be under suspicion, and that's all there was to it. I don't feel proud of myself, but it was just a threat. When I'm safely hidden away, I'll call him and ease his mind that his daughter is safe."

I said, "Good one."

"So what's next for you, Marty? I don't suppose you want to come with me? Be an accessory. What do you say?"

I told Harry about the bond I'd made with my mother that prevented me from leaving town at present.

"Wait, what kind of bond?"

"Well, it was more like an oath."

"You made an oath with your mother?"

"Well, what's so strange about that?" I asked, annoyed. What was the big deal? It's not like I had confessed to *sleeping* with my mother, I merely pledged allegiance not to leave her side.

Harry didn't say anything. His mouth was half open and I could feel his eyes tunneling deep into my cranium. He slapped his hand on my shoulder. "Well, can't talk you out of an oath, can I?"

I agreed that he couldn't.

"Well, good luck, old boy," he said before turning and disappearing into the dark bush. "See you next time," his disembodied voice called out. He left without even asking after Terry.

•

A week later my mother came into my room with big news. "Your brother's coming home today. Your father's gone to collect him," she said, as if he were a long-awaited parcel. Terry had become a sort of fictitious character to us in the year he'd been gone, and the psychiatrist, by reducing him to a catalogue of psychological symptoms, had robbed my brother of his individuality. True, the complexity of his psychosis impressed us—he was collateral damage in a war waged between his deeper instincts—but it posed a question that plagued us: which Terry would be coming home? My brother, my mother's son, or the impotent destroyer desperate for transcendence of the self?

We were all on pins and needles.

I wasn't prepared for the sight of him walking through the back door—he looked so happy you'd have thought he'd been in Fiji sipping margaritas out of a coconut. He sat at the kitchen table and said, "So what kind of welcome-home feast you got planned for the prodigal son? Some fattened calf?" My mother was in such a state she cried, "Fattened calf? Where am I going to get that?" and Terry jumped from the table and hugged her and spun her around the room and she almost screamed in terror, she was so frightened of her own son.

After lunch Terry and I walked the narrow dirt road that led into town. The sun beat violently down. All the flies in the district came out to greet him. He brushed them away and said, "Can't do that strapped to a bed." I related the story of Harry's shifty escape and his appearance that night in the mud.

"And have you seen Caroline?" he asked.

"Now and then."

"How is she?"

"Let's go see."

"Wait. How do I look?"

I gave him the once-over and nodded. As usual, he looked good. No, better than good. Terry was already looking like a man, whereas I, more a man in age than he was, looked more like a boy with an aging disease. We moved silently toward town. What do you say to someone who's just got back from hell? "Was it hot enough for you?" I think in the end I blurted out something like "How are you?" with an emphasis on the *are*, and he muttered that the "mongrels couldn't break me." I knew he'd suffered through an experience he'd never be able to communicate.

We reached town and Terry gave every person on the street a challenging stare. There were bitterness and anger in that stare. Clearly the hospital "treatment" had done nothing to quiet his anger. He had it in for everyone. Terry had chosen not to blame our parents for his sentence but had fixed his fury on everyone who followed the word of the suggestion box.

Except one. Lionel Potts came bounding up, waving his arms wildly. "Terry! Terry!" He was the only person in town happy to see my brother. It was a welcome relief to feel the force of Lionel's childlike enthusiasm. He was the sort of man you talk to about the weather and you still walk away smiling. "The Dean boys, together again! How are you, Terry? Thank God you got out of that hellhole. Cunt of a place, wasn't it? Did you give that blond nurse my phone number?"

"Sorry, mate," Terry said. "You'll have to get committed yourself if you want that action."

So Lionel had been up to see Terry.

"Maybe I will, Terry. She looked worth it. Hey, Caroline's in the café, smoking. She pretends to hide it from me and I pretend to be fooled. Have you seen her?"

"We're on our way now," Terry said.

"Excellent! Wait here!" Lionel pulled out a packet of cigarettes. "These are lights. See if you can wean her off the Marlboro full-strengths, would you? If it doesn't bother you, a little collusion."

"Not at all. How's your back?"

"Crap! My shoulders feel like clamps. A town masseuse, that's the kind of suggestion that would do some good," Lionel said as he massaged his own shoulders with both hands.

Terry and I arrived outside the café. It was closed. It was always closed now; the boycott had won in the end. Caroline was lurking inside; the café was her private hideout until her father managed to sell it. We saw her through the window: she was lying on the bar smoking, trying to blow perfect smoke rings. It was adorable. The rings came out as whirling semicircles. I tapped on the glass and reached out to put my hand on Terry's shoulder in brotherly support, but my hand met with nothing but air. I turned to see Terry's back moving away from me fast, and by the time Caroline had unlocked the door and stepped out on the street, Terry was gone.

"What's up?" she asked.

"Nothing."

"Do you want to come in? I'm smoking."

"Maybe later."

As I walked away I noticed a bad smell in the air, like dead birds rotting in the sun.

I found Terry sitting beneath a tree, holding a pile of letters in his hands. I sat beside him and didn't say anything. He stared down at the letters.

"They're from her," he said.

So, Caroline's letters! Love letters, no doubt.

I stretched out on the grass and closed my eyes. There was no wind, and next to no sound. I had the impression of being inside a bank vault.

"Can I take a look?" I asked.

A masochistic streak in me was dying to get my hands on those stinking letters. I was frantic to see how she expressed her love, even if it wasn't for me.

"They're private."

I could feel something crawling on my neck, maybe an ant, but I didn't move—I didn't want to give it the moral victory.

"Well, can you summarize?" I asked.

"She says she only wants to be with me if I can give up crime."

"And are you going to?"

"Yeah, I think so."

I felt myself shrink a little. Of course I was pleased that Terry would be saved by the woman he loved, but I couldn't rejoice. One brother's success is another brother's failure. Dammit. I didn't think he had it in him.

"Only, the thing is . . ." he said.

I sat up and looked at him. His eyes were heavy. Maybe the hospital had changed him after all. I wasn't sure how, exactly; maybe inside him something fluid had hardened, or something solid had melted. Terry gazed out in the direction of the town center. "There's one thing I need to do first," he said. "Just one little illegal thing."

One thing. They all say that. Just one and he'll be on to the next, and before you know it he'll be like a snowball rolling downhill gathering yellow snow.

"Well, you'll do whatever you want," I said, not strictly encouraging him, though not discouraging him either.

"Maybe I shouldn't do it," Terry said.

"Maybe."

"But I really want to."

"Well," I said, choosing my words very carefully, "sometimes people need to do things, you know, to get the things that they need to do out of their system."

What was I saying? Absolutely nothing. It was simply impossible to recommend to Terry a course of action; this was my defense for the unconscionable act of bad brothering I was doing.

"Yeah," he said, lost in thought, and I stood there like a stop sign, even though I was saying, Go!

Terry picked himself up and brushed the grass off his jeans. "I'll see you a bit later on," he said, and walked off slowly in the opposite direction from Caroline's café. He was really dawdling, I think because he wanted me to stop him. I didn't.

Betrayal wears a lot of different hats. You don't have to make a show of it like Brutus did, you don't have to leave anything visible jutting from the base of your best friend's spine, and afterward you can stand there straining your ears for hours, but you won't hear a cock crow either. No, the most insidious betrayals are done merely by leaving the life jacket hanging in your closet while you lie to yourself that it's probably not the drowning man's size. That's how we slide, and while we slide we blame the world's problems on colonialism, imperialism, capitalism, corporatism, stupid white men, and America, but there's no need to make a brand name of blame. Individual self-interest: that's the source of our descent, and it doesn't start in the boardrooms or the war rooms either. It starts in the home.

Hours later, I heard the explosion. Out my window I saw thick billows of smoke spiraling into the moon-drenched night. My stomach tightened as I ran into town. I wasn't the only one. The entire populace had congregated in the main street outside the town hall. They all looked horri-fied, the preferred expression of a crowd of spectators who gather specifi-cally for tragedies. My poisonous suggestion box was gone. There were bits of it all over the street.

An ambulance had arrived, though not for the broken box. A man was stretched out on the pavement, his face covered with a white cloth soaked in blood. At first I thought he was dead, but he removed the cloth to reveal a face of blood and powder burns. No, he wasn't dead. He was blind. He'd been reaching into the box to place a suggestion when the whole thing exploded in his face.

"I can't see! I can't fucking see!" he was shouting, panicked.

It was Lionel Potts.

There were more than fifty men and women on the scene, and in their eyes was a sort of thrill, as if they had come to dance in the streets on an enchanted evening. Through the crowd I saw Terry sitting in the gutter with his head between his legs. The horror of his badly timed act of vandalism was too much for him. Lionel had been the one bright light in a world full of dim ones, and Terry had torn his eyes out. It felt strange to see shards of my suggestion box strewn all over the road, and the way my brother was slumped in the gutter, and Lionel sprawled on the pave-ment, and Caroline hunched over him; it seemed to me that my loved ones had all exploded too. Smoke still hung in the air, curling in the bluish light, and it smelled very much like firecracker night.

Only five days later our family was dressed in its Sunday best.

Juvenile courtrooms are just like regular courtrooms. The state tried a number of charges on Terry like a rich woman trying suits on her fa-vorite gigolo: attempted murder, attempted manslaughter, malicious wounding—the prosecutors couldn't decide. They should have arrested me too. I don't know if egging on a crime for love is an offense punish-able by law, but it should be.

In the end, Terry was sentenced to three years in a juvenile detention center. When they took him away, he gave me a little wink. Then he was gone, just like that. The rest of us stood hugging each other in the court-room, totally bewildered. I tell you, the wheels of justice may turn slowly, but when the state wants you off the streets, the wheels that carry you away spin like comets.

Democracy

After Lionel's blinding, I found myself haunted by questions, and after Terry's incarceration, I felt those questions pressing down on me from all sides. I had to do something. But what? I had to be someone. But who? I didn't want to imitate the stupidity of the people around me. But whose stupidity should I imitate? And why did I feel sick at night? Was I afraid? Was fear making me anxious? How could I think clearly if I was anxious? And how could I understand anything if I couldn't think clearly? And how was I going to function in this world if I couldn't understand anything?

It was in this besieged state that I arrived at school, but I couldn't make my way through the gates. For a good hour I stood staring at the ugly brick buildings, the dim-witted students, the trees in the playground, the brown polyester pants of the teachers making a swishing sound on their fleshy thighs as they marched between classes, and I thought: If I study hard, I'll pass my exams, but so what? What do I do between *that* moment and the moment of my death?

When I got home, neither my mother nor my father seemed to care very much that I had quit school. My father was reading the local paper. My mother was writing a letter to Terry, a long letter, forty pages or more. I had sneaked a peek but couldn't get past the uncomfortable first paragraph, in which she wrote: "I love you I love you my darling son my life my love what have you done my love my lovely son?"

"Didn't you hear me? I said I've quit school," I repeated in a hurt whisper.

They didn't react. What was conspicuously lacking in the silence was the question, What are you going to do now? "I'm going to join the army!" I shouted ludicrously, for effect.

It worked, though in the manner of a firework that sizzles and sparks on the ground, then abruptly dies out. My father actually said "Ha!" while my mother half turned her head to me and said in a quiet, stern voice, "Don't." And that was it.

In retrospect, I see how desperately I needed attention after a lifetime of being small print to my brother's headlines. I can think of no other reason for my stubborn, impetuous, self-destructive decision to follow up on my threat. Two days later, in the Australian Army Registration Office,

I found myself answering stupid questions with stupider answers. "Tell me, sonny, what do you think makes good army material?" the recruiting officer asked. "Light cotton?" I offered, and after not laughing for ten straight seconds, he grudgingly sent me down to the doctor. Unfortunately, that was the end of my adventure. I failed the mandatory physical examination with flying colors. The doctor probed me with an astonished look on his face and concluded that he had never seen a body in as bad a shape as mine outside of wartime.

Against all reason, I took the rejection badly and plunged into a deep depression. What followed was a period of lost time: three years, during which I felt myself circling the questions that had been circling me, though I never found the answers I needed. While searching, I went for walks. I read. I taught myself the art of reading while walking. I lay under trees and watched the clouds creep across the sky through a veil of leaves. I passed whole months thinking. I discovered more about the properties of loneliness, how it is like the slow squeeze of testicles by a hand that has just been in a refrigerator. If I could not find a way to be authentically in the world, then I would find a superior way of hiding, and to that end I tried on different masks: shy, graceful, pensive, buoyant, jovial, frail—they were the simple masks that had one defining characteristic. Other times I tried on more complicated masks, somber and buoyant, vulnerable yet cheerful, proud yet brooding. These I ultimately abandoned as they required too much upkeep on an energy level. Take it from me: complex masks eat you alive in maintenance.

The months groaned by, turning into years. I wandered and wandered, going mad with the uselessness of my life. Having no income, I lived cheaply. I gathered unfinished cigarette butts from pub ashtrays. I let my fingers turn a rusty yellow. I gazed stupidly at the people of the town. I slept outside. I slept in the rain. I slept in my bedroom. I learned valuable lessons about life, such as that a person who is sitting is eight times more likely to give you a cigarette than a person who is walking and twenty-eight times more likely to give you a cigarette than a person inside a car stuck in traffic. No parties, no invitations, no socializing. I learned that detaching is easy. Retreat? Easy. Hiding? Dissolving? Extraction? Simple. When you withdraw from the world, the world withdraws too, in equal measure. It's a two-step, you and the world. I didn't look for trouble, and it wore me down that none found me. Doing nothing is as tumultuous for me as working on the floor of the New York

Stock Exchange on the morning of a market crash. It's how I'm made. Nothing happened to me in three years and it was very, very stressful.

The townspeople began to look on me with something resembling horror. I'll admit, I cut a strange figure in those days: pale, unshaven, scraggly. One winter's night I learned that I had been unofficially proclaimed the town's first homeless lunatic, despite the fact that I still had a home.

And still the questions remained, and each month my demand for answers became louder and more insistent. I went on an uninterrupted bout of inward stargazing, where the stars were my own thoughts, impulses, and actions. I wandered in the dirt and the dust, cramming my head with literature and philosophy. The first true hint of relief had come from Harry, who first introduced me to Nietzsche back when I saw him in prison. "Friedrich Nietzsche, Martin Dean," he said, making the introductions while throwing a book. "People are always angry at anyone who chooses very individual standards for his life; because of the extraordinary treatment which that man grants to himself, they feel degraded, like ordinary beings," he said, quoting his idol.

I had since devoured many philosophy books from the library, and it seemed that most philosophy was petty argument about things you just couldn't know. I thought: Why waste time on insoluble problems? What does it matter whether the soul is made up of smooth, round soul atoms or of Lego, it's unknowable, so let's just drop it. I also found that, geniuses or not, most of the philosophers undermined their own philosophies, from Plato onward, because almost no one seemed willing to start with a blank slate or endure uncertainty. You could read the prejudices, the self-interest, and desires of every single one. And God! God! God! The most brilliant minds coming up with all these complicated theories and then they say, "But let's just assume there's a God and let's assume he's good." Why assume anything? To me, it was obvious man created God in his own image. Man hasn't the imagination to come up with a God totally unlike him, which is why in Renaissance paintings God looks like a skinny version of Santa Claus. Hume says that man only cuts and pastes, he doesn't invent. Angels, for instance, are men with wings. In the same way, Bigfoot is man with big foot. This is why I could see in most of the "objective" philosophical systems man's fears, drives, prejudices, and aspirations written all over them.

The only thing of value I did was read books to Lionel, whose eyes were irrevocably damaged, and one rainy afternoon I almost lost my virginity to Caroline, an event that precipitated her leaving town in the middle of the night. Here's how it happened:

We were trying to read a book together to her father, but he kept interrupting to convince himself that his life had changed for the better. Lionel was doing his best to take blindness in his stride. "Judgmental faces! Condescending eyes I've felt on me since the day I moved into this rotten town! I'll never have to see them again! Thank God—I was sick of the sight of them!" Lionel was finally letting loose on the people's automatic antipathy to him as though his personality were an extension of his bank balance. They didn't want to know him or his story. They didn't care that two years before moving to our town, Caroline's mother was discovered to be hoarding a basketful of inoperable tumors growing like plums in her insides. They didn't care that she had been something of a cold, neurotic woman, and the process of dying had not turned her into a sweetie. They didn't believe that a man with so much money could have human qualities worth sympathizing with. He was up against the smelliest prejudice in existence: wealth-haters. At least a racist, a man who hates black people, for instance—at least he isn't harboring a secret desire to *be* black. His prejudice, while ugly and stupid, is at least thorough and honest. Hatred of the well-off, from those who would jump at the chance to swap places, is a textbook case of sour grapes.

"Hey—I'll never have to see another disappointed face either! Now when I let someone down, if they don't say, 'Awwwww,' I'll never be burdened with it! Fuck disapproving eyes! I've escaped!"

Eventually he talked himself to sleep. While Lionel snored as if he were all nose, we crept silently into Caroline's bedroom. She had decided to forget all about Terry, but she talked about forgetting him so much, it was the only thing on her mind. She rambled on, and as much as I loved the sound of her spongy voice, I just had to switch off. I lit a half-smoked cigarette I'd found in a puddle and dried in the sun. As I sucked on it I felt her eyes on me, and when I looked up, I saw her lower lip curl a little, like a leaf when hit with a single drop of rain.

Suddenly she lowered her voice. "What's going to happen to you, Martin?"

"To me? I don't know. Nothing bad, I hope."

"Your future!" she gasped. "I can't stand to think of it!"

"Well, don't."

She ran over and hugged me. Then she pulled away and we looked into each other's eyes and breathed into each other's nostrils. Then she kissed me with her eyes closed—I know because mine were wide open. Then she opened her eyes too, so I shut mine quickly. The whole thing was unbelievable! My hands went for her breasts, something I'd wanted to do even before she had them. Her hands, meanwhile, went straight for my belt, and she fumbled to undo it. For a split second I thought she wanted to hit me with it. Then I got into the swing of things, and reached up her skirt and pulled off her underpants. We crashed on the bed like fallen soldiers. There we struggled together, laboring to rid ourselves of unwanted garments, until she suddenly pushed herself from me and screamed, "What are we doing!" Before I could answer, she ran out of the room crying.

I lay bewildered on her bed for half an hour, smelling her pillow with my eyes closed, engrossed in the spectacle of a lifelong dream slipping away. When she didn't return, I got dressed and went to sit under my favorite tree to think suicidal thoughts and tear up weeds.

I avoided Caroline for the next week. Since she was the one who went hysterical, it was up to her to find me. Then on Saturday, Lionel phoned me in a panic. He couldn't find his toothbrush, and while he might be blind, that didn't mean he wasn't afraid of gingivitis. I went over and found it floating in the toilet bowl, specked with feces. I told him I was very sorry, he'd have to kiss that toothbrush goodbye, but not literally.

"She's gone," he said. "I woke up yesterday morning and there was a strange person breathing in my bedroom. I can recognize a person by their breathing patterns, you know. It gave me the fright of my life. I shouted, 'Who the fuck are you?' Shelly was her name, a nurse Caroline had organized to look after me. I shouted at Shelly to get out, and she left, the bitch. I don't know what I'm going to do. I'm afraid, Martin. Darkness is boring and surprisingly brown."

"Where did Caroline go?"

"Damned if I know! Still, I'll bet she's having fun. That's what you get when you give your child a liberal upbringing, I suppose. Liberation."

"I'm sure she'll be back soon," I lied. I didn't think she was ever coming back. I always knew Caroline would vanish one day, and finally that day had come.

Over the following months we received postcards from her from all over. The first was of a river in Bucharest, the word "Bucharest" stamped across it, and on the back Caroline had scrawled, "I'm in Bucharest!" The same kind came every second week from Italy, Vienna, Warsaw, and Paris.

Meanwhile, I visited Terry often. It was a long journey, from our town by bus, through the city by train, then another bus to a poor outer suburb. The detention center looked like a low-rise residential block. Each time I signed in, the administrator greeted me like the patriarch of a distinguished family and took me personally to the visiting room, through a long series of corridors, where I felt physically threatened at all moments by young criminals who never stopped looking furious, as if they'd been arrested after crossing the Himalayas on foot. Terry would be waiting for me in the visitors' room. Sometimes he had fresh purple bruises around his eyes. One day I sat down with him to see the imprint of a fist on his cheek, which was only slowly beginning to fade. He looked at me with great intensity. "Caroline visited me before she left, and she said that even though I blinded her father, she'll always love me." When I didn't respond, he talked about his crime of blinding Lionel as a one-way ticket into a criminal life. "You don't burn your bridges with normal society," he said. "You blow your bridges up." He spoke quickly, as if dictating in an emergency. He was eager to justify, to confide, to seek approval from me for his new plan. You see, he was picking up the pieces of that suggestion box and with it building the story of his life. He'd fit the pieces together into a pattern he could live with.

"Can't you just keep your head down and apply yourself to studying?" I pleaded.

"I'm studying, all right. A few of us, we got big plans when we get out of here," he said, winking. "I've met a couple of blokes who are teaching me a thing or two."

I left wringing my hands, thinking about detention centers, boys' homes, prisons; it's through these punishments that up-and-coming criminals get to do most of their schmoozing. The state is always going about the business of introducing dangerous criminals to each other; they plug them right into the network.

•

If my father had an idea of how to accelerate his own deterioration, taking a job at a pest extermination business was it. For the past few years he had become the town handyman, mowing lawns, fixing fences, doing a little brickwork, but now, finally, he'd found the perfect job for himself: exterminating vermin. He breathed toxic fumes all day, handling poisonous substances such as bug powder and lethal little blue pellets, and I got the impression he was delighted by his own toxicity. He'd come home, his hands out, and say, "Don't touch me! Don't come near me! I have poison on my hands! Quick! Someone run the taps!" Sometimes if he was feeling especially mischievous, he would run at us with his poisonous hands outstretched and threaten to touch our tongues. "I'm going for your tongue! You're done for!"

"Why don't you wear gloves?!" my mother screamed.

"Gloves are for proctologists!" he'd say back as he chased us around the house. I deduced that this was his bizarre way of dealing with my mother's cancer, pretending she was a sick child and he was the clown called in to cheer her up. She'd finally told my father the bad news, and while he had become compassionate enough to stop hitting her when he was drunk, her cancer, treatment, remission, and relapse cycle had made him increasingly unstable. Now, as my father threatened us with his poisonous hands, my mother would stare at me long and hard, making me feel like a mirror that reflects death back on the dying.

That's how it was in our house; with my mother fading, my father becoming a carrier of lethal toxins, and Terry going from mental hospital to prison, what had previously been a poisonous environment only metaphorically became one literally too.

•

When at last Terry was released from the detention center, for no good reason I had renewed hope he'd be rehabilitated, and might even want to come home and help with our dying mother. I went to an address he'd given me over the phone. To get there I had to travel the four hours to Sydney, then change buses to ride another hour to a suburb in the south. It was a quiet and leafy neighborhood; families were out walking dogs and washing cars, and a newspaper boy pulled a yellow cart up the street, casually tossing newspapers so they landed with admirable accuracy on the doormat of every home with the front-page headline facing up. The house where Terry was residing had a beige Volvo station wagon parked in the driveway. A sprinkler languidly watered an immaculately manicured lawn. A boy's silver bicycle rested against the steps leading up to the front porch. Could this be right? Could Terry have been adopted by a lower-middle-class family by mistake?

A woman with rollers in her brown hair and a pink nightgown answered the door. "I'm Martin Dean," I stammered with uncertainty, as though perhaps I wasn't. Her kind smile disappeared so quickly, I wondered if I hadn't imagined it. "They're out the back," she said. As the woman led me down a dark hallway, she threw off the rollers with the hair too—it was a wig. Her real hair, tied up in a tight bun and fastened with bobby pins, was flaming red. She dropped the pink nightgown too and revealed black lingerie hugging a curvy body that I wanted to take home as a pillow. When I followed her into the kitchen, I saw there were bullet holes in the walls, the cupboards, the curtains; sunlight streamed through the tiny perfect circles and stretched diagonally across the room in golden rods. A plump half-naked woman sat at the table with her head in her hands. I stepped past her and went out into the backyard. Terry was turning sausages on a barbecue. A shotgun was leaning against the wooden fence next to him. Two men with shaved heads lay on banana chairs drinking beers.

"Marty!" Terry screamed. He strode over and gave me a bear hug. With an arm over my shoulder, he made enthusiastic introductions. "Boys, this is my brother, Marty. He got all the brains. I got whatever was left. Marty, this is Jack, and this timid-looking bloke over here is Meat-ax."

I smiled nervously at the powerfully built men, thinking an ax was rarely necessary when cutting meat. Looking at my vigorous, muscular brother, I automatically straightened my back. Sometime over the last few years I had become conscious that I'd developed a slight hunch, so I looked, from a distance, approximately seventy-three years old.

Terry said, "And now for the grand finale . . ."

He removed his shirt and I reeled in shock. Terry had gone tattoo mad! Head to toe, my brother was a maze of crazy artwork. From visiting days, I had already seen the tattoos crawling down his arms below the shirtsleeves, but I'd never before seen what he'd done to his body. Now I could make out, from his Adam's apple to his belly button, a grinning Tasmanian tiger, a snarling platypus, an emu growling menacingly, a family of koalas brandishing knives in their clenched paws, a kangaroo dripping blood from its gums, with a machete in its pouch. All those

Australian animals! I never realized that my brother was so horribly patriotic. Terry flexed his muscles, and it appeared as though the rabid animals were breathing; he'd learned to contort his body in particular ways to make the animals come alive. It had a frightening, magical effect. The swirling colors made me dizzy.

"It's getting a bit crowded here in the old zoo, isn't it?" Terry said, anticipating my disapproval. "Oh, guess who else is here!"

Before I could answer, a familiar voice cried out from somewhere above me. Harry was leaning out an upstairs window, smiling so widely, his mouth seemed to swallow his nose. A minute later he joined us in the yard. Harry had aged badly since I saw him last. Every hair had turned a gloomy gray, and the features on his tired, wrinkled face looked to have been pushed deeper into his skull. I noticed that his limp had gotten worse too: he dragged his leg behind him like a sack of bricks.

"We're doing it, Marty!" Harry cried.

"Doing what?"

"The democratic cooperative of crime! It's a historic moment! I'm glad you're here. I know we can't coerce you to join up, but you can be a witness, can't you? God, it's wonderful to have your brother out. I'd been having a shit of a time. Being a fugitive is lonely." Harry explained how he eluded the police by phoning in anonymous sightings of himself. There were patrols conducting street-by-street searches in Brisbane and Tasmania. Harry exploded with laughter at the thought of it. "The police are so easy to throw off the scent. Anyway, I was just biding my time until Terry's term was up. And now here we are! It's like the Greek senate! We meet every afternoon at four by the swimming pool."

I looked over at the pool. It was an aboveground number, the water a snaky green. A beer can floated in it. Democracy obviously had nothing to do with hygiene. The place was a sewer. The lawn was overgrown, there were empty pizza boxes strewn about and bullet holes in everything, and in the kitchen I could see the whore sitting at the table listlessly scratching herself.

Terry smiled at her through the window. I put my hand on his shoulder. "Can I have a word with you?"

We walked around to the other side of the swimming pool. On the brick barbecue the sausages had been incinerated and were withering in the sun.

"Terry," I said, "what are you doing? Why don't you give up crime, go get a normal job somewhere? The cooperative is never going to work, you must know that. Besides, Harry's mad," I added, though I knew I wasn't convinced. The truth was, as I gazed at Terry's wild eyes I began to suspect that my brother was the real madman and Harry just an old goat with strange ideas.

"What about you?" Terry asked.

"What about me?"

"What are you doing with *your* life? I'm not the one trapped in a cage—you are. I'm not the one living in a town I hate. I'm not the one ignoring his potential. What's *your* destiny, mate? What's *your* mission in life? You don't belong in that town. You can't hang around there forever. You can't protect Mum from Dad, or from death. You've got to cut them loose. You've got to get out of there and live your life. My life is mapped out, more or less. But you—you're the one sitting around doing nothing."

That struck me cold. The little bugger was right. I *was* the one trapped. I had no clue where to go or what to do. I didn't want to get locked into some grind, but I wasn't a criminal either. Plus I had made that unbreakable bond with our mother, and I was beginning to strain against it.

"Marty, have you thought about university?"

"I'm not going to university. I didn't even finish school."

"Well fuck, mate, you have to do something! Why don't you start by leaving that shit hole of a town?"

"I can't leave town."

"Why the hell not?"

Against my better judgment, I told Terry about the promise I had made. I explained that I was stuck in no uncertain way. Viciously and immovably stuck. What could I do? Leave my mother alone to die with my unfeeling father? The woman who read to me while I lay in a coma all those years? The woman who had risked everything for my sake?

"How is she?" Terry asked me.

"She's OK, considering," I said, but that was a lie. Impending death was having a strange effect on her. Occasionally she crept into my room at night and read to me. I couldn't stand it. The sound of a voice reading a book reminded me of that other prison, that rotten living death: the coma. Sometimes in the middle of the night when I was sound asleep I was woken by a violent shaking. It was my mother, wanting to make sure I hadn't fallen into another coma. It really was impossible to sleep.

"What are you going to do?" Terry asked. "Stay there until she's dead?"

It was an awful thought, both that she would one day die and that I'd made this vow that was now strangling me. How could I go on in this way without succumbing to the ugliest thought: "Hey, Mum. Hurry up and die!"

Terry discouraged me from visiting his house again. At his insistence, we met at either cricket or rugby games, depending on the season. During these games Terry filled me in on the democratic cooperative's antics: how they changed their modus operandi all the time, never doing the same job twice, or if they did, not doing it in the same way. For instance, once they did two bank jobs in a row. The first was at the end of the day, and they all ran in wearing balaclavas and forced customers and staff facedown on the floor. The next job they pulled at lunchtime, and they wore gorilla masks, spoke only in Russian to each other, and made customers and staff hold hands and stand in a circle. They were fast. They were successful. And above all they were anonymous. It was Harry's idea for the gang to learn a couple of languages—not the whole thing, but just the kind of vocabulary you'd need in a robbery situation: "Get the money," "Tell them to put their hands up," "Let's go," that kind of thing. Harry really was a genius at throwing people off the scent. It was a mystery how he'd spent so long in jail. He also found a couple of police informers and fed them misinformation. And the one or two enemies they had to deal with from Harry's old days, they attacked when they were most vulnerable: when they had more than two items on the stove.

The only problem was that the establishment of the democratic cooperative, the fulfillment of Harry's dream, seemed to inflame his world-class paranoia. You couldn't get behind him! He'd slide against the wall, and if he was ever in an open space, he'd spin like a top. He panicked in crowds, and when he was caught up in the throng, he'd really go into violent spasms. The funniest thing was when he had to take a piss outdoors. He wouldn't go behind a tree, because his back was exposed; Harry leaned against the tree facing out, one hand on his dick, the other holding a .45. And at home he rigged up bells and ropes so you couldn't enter his bedroom without setting off an alarm. He checked the newspapers every day to see if he got a mention. He flicked through them frantically, eyes bulging.

"Don't underestimate the value of the daily news," Harry said to me

once. "It's saved many a wanted man's skin. The police are always trying
to prove they're making progress: 'Oh, we have a sighting here, we've
picked up this clue or that one.' Put that together with the public's indefatigable hunger for news that has nothing to do with them, and
you've got the best thing for a fugitive out on a crime spree. You think
I'm paranoid? Check out the general public. They demand up-to-date
news on investigations because they think the authorities are holding
out on them, hiding information about criminals who are in their backyards with their guns and cocks out, ready to party."

He accused the others in the cooperative of harboring mercenary
thoughts. He said he could smell greed on all of them; he said it clung to
them like beads of sweat. "A thousand dollars in your hand isn't good
enough?" he'd scream. Harry predicted that their little Greek senate
would go down in flames. Democracy in crime was turning out no different from democracies everywhere: a sublime idea in theory, soiled by the
reality that deep down nobody really believes that all men are created
equal. The cooperative was getting into constant disputes over the share
of profits and the distribution of dirty jobs like filing the serial numbers
off a thousand stolen cameras. Its members were learning that, like their
manifestations in whole countries, profit-driven democracies create im-
balances, encourage greed and impatience, and because no one's going
to vote to be the one who cleans the public toilets, lead to faction-
splitting and ganging up on the weakest and most unpopular members.
Moreover, Harry smelled that anonymity was frustrating them. That's
how Harry discovered everything, through his nostrils. "You're the
worst!" he'd say, pointing at Terry.

"Mate, I didn't say a word," Terry said.

"You didn't have to! I can smell it!"

And maybe he *could* smell it. What did Harry once say about long-
term paranoia earning a man telepathic powers? Maybe he was really
onto something there. Maybe Harry *was* seeing the future. Or maybe he
was just stating the bloody obvious: that my brother had ideas, and those
ideas were going to destroy him and everyone along with him. To be honest, though, it wasn't obvious to me then. I just didn't see it coming. Well,
maybe Bob Dylan was wrong. Maybe you do have to be a weatherman to
know which way the wind blows.

Second Project

Normally, there is your life, and you turn on the television and there is news, and no matter how grave it is, or how deep in the toilet the world has fallen, or how relevant the information might be to your own existence, your life remains a separate entity from that news. You still have to wash your underpants during a war, don't you? And don't you still have to fight with your loved ones and then apologize when you don't mean it even when there's a hole in the sky burning everything to a crisp? Of course you do. As a rule, there's no hole big enough to interrupt this interminable business of living, but there *are* exceptions, grim instances in the lives of a few select unlucky bastards when the news in the papers and the news in their bedrooms intersect. I tell you, it's a daunting and appalling moment when you have to read the newspapers to find out about your own struggle.

It started far from home. One morning headlines shouted that key players in the Australian cricket team had been caught taking bribes from bookmakers to underperform in international matches. It was big news, perhaps bigger than it deserved, mostly because if sport is Australia's national religion, as it has been said, then it was like all the Christian fundamentalists finding out that God made the trees and mountains without first washing his hands. It rocked a lot of cores. There was public outcry and mass disappointment and saber-rattling and everywhere people said it was disgusting and rotten and corrupt and an unremovable stain on sport. The voices on the radio bayed for blood. They wanted to hear the snapping of necks: the necks of the bookies and the necks of the real traitors, the players themselves. The politicians cried for justice and vowed to get to the bottom of things, and even the prime minister promised "a thorough and exhaustive inquiry into corruption in sport."

For me, this sporting scandal was mere background noise. I was too preoccupied with my own problems: my mother was dying and shutting herself up like a mad queen, my father was disappearing into a bottle, and my brother was tearing through the world with a gun in one hand and an ax in the other.

The next Saturday that Terry and I met at a game, it was Australia vs. Pakistan. There had been a question as to whether it would still be on, considering the scandal, but the innocent-until-proven-guilty technicality meant it was going ahead as scheduled. The sky was bright and the air full of spring—the kind of day that lulls you into a false sense of security, but I still felt the apprehension I always feel in groups of thirty-five thousand people apt to pool their collective fury at a moment's notice.

When the players walked onto the field, the crowd started to boo like mad, because these were the men implicated in the scandal. Some of the players ignored the crowd, while others gave the fuck-you sign, the one where you use both arms. It was a hoot. I love booing. Who doesn't? Some of the boos were chock-full of fury, while others were more light-hearted boos mingled with laughter. Beside me Terry didn't make a sound.

When the captain came out to bowl, there wasn't just booing but hissing, and people started throwing things, like beer cans and shoes—their own shoes! One of the spectators jumped the fence, ran onto the field, and tried to tackle the captain. Then a crowd spilled out too. Someone blew a whistle, and the game was clearly over when Terry turned to me and said, "Let's go." I thought he meant "Let's go home," so I agreed, but before I knew what was happening, Terry was bolting down the grandstand toward the cricket oval. I tried to follow, but for a long time I couldn't see him in the madness of the crowd that had come from all sides and blocked the teams' exit. It was all very tribal and nerve-jangling. You know how rioting mobs are.

Then I heard some yelling that was different in character from the stock murmuring of the furious mob. I saw what they were looking at, an image that has never left the inside of my eyelids: Terry had pulled out a gun and was pointing it at the Australian captain. Terry's eyes were wide and clear, his face refreshed, as if he'd just bathed in crystal waters. He wore an uncharacteristic look of self-admiration. The mob watched on, frozen. They wanted to run, but curiosity wanted them to stay. Curiosity won. Police were fighting their way down the grandstand steps when my brother shot the captain of the Australian cricket team in the stomach.

•

I don't know how we got out of there. I remember Terry seeing me in the crowd and waving. I remember running. I remember Terry laughing and suggesting we split up and just before disappearing into the crowd saying, "Let's see if he can underperform his own death!"

There was no bigger story in Australia, before or since. Not even the Federation got as much press. And the worst thing was, they had pictures. Someone took a beauty of Terry standing there, eyes shining, arm outstretched, the gun held out in front of him and a friendly smile on his face, as if he were about to give the captain an amiable piece of advice. Every newspaper and television station ran that picture. From then on, he was a wanted man. This was the real beginning of Terry's infamy.

Our little town was inundated with police and reporters. The reporters were a nuisance. They wouldn't take "Fuck off" for an answer. The police were irritating too. They asked me all sorts of questions, and for a while I was under suspicion. I admitted having gone to the game with my brother but said I'd lost him as soon as he ran into the crowd. No, I said, I didn't see the shooting. No, I said, I hadn't heard from him since. No, I said, I didn't know where he lived. No, we weren't close. No, I didn't know who his friends or associates were. No, I didn't know where he got the gun. No, I didn't even know he had a gun. No, I didn't expect to be hearing from him again. No, if I did hear from him I wouldn't call the police, because after all, he was still my brother. Yes, I had heard of obstruction of justice. Yes, I knew what being an accessory was all about. Yes, I would be willing to go to jail, but I'd really rather not.

The police gave my mother a good grilling too, but she wouldn't answer their simplest questions—when the chief detective asked, she wouldn't even tell him the time.

Terry could never come home again. That was the thing that killed my mother. She cried inconsolably, and from then on slept most nights in Terry's old bed. She made one of his favorite dishes every mealtime, and, perhaps to punish herself, she stuck the newspaper article with Terry's picture to the fridge under a pineapple magnet. She obsessed over that picture, even going so far as to measure it with a ruler. One morning I came down and saw my mother studying it. I said, "Let me throw that away." She didn't say anything, but when I reached over to take it she elbowed me in the stomach. My own mother! Later, around four in the morning, I woke to see her sitting at the edge of my bed.

"What's wrong?"

"Do you remember *William Wilson* by Poe? And *The Double* by Dostoyevsky?"

These were books she'd read to me while I was in the coma. I remembered them perfectly, almost word for word.

"I think Terry has a double," she said.

I shook my head and said, "I don't think so."

"Listen to me. Everyone has a double somewhere in the world. That's what's happened here. Terry didn't shoot anyone. It was him, the double!"

"Mum, I was there. It was Terry."

"I admit it looks like him. That's what doubles are. Look-alikes. Identical look-alikes. Not look-a-little-alikes."

"Mum . . ."

Before I could say any more, she was gone.

So where was Terry? At Harry's? The next morning at breakfast I decided to go see for myself. When I stepped outside I saw that the reporters had gone home, but on the bus to the city it occurred to me I was probably being followed. I peered at the cars on the road. Sure enough, I saw it: a blue Commodore following. I got off at the next stop and went into the movies. It was a comedy about a husband who dies but comes back as a ghost and haunts his wife whenever she looks at another man. Everyone was laughing but me; I found it grotesque, and it made me really hate the dead, the selfish pricks. Two hours later, when I stepped into the sunshine, the car was still there. I knew I had to lose them, to "shake my tail," so I ducked into a shop. It was a tailor's. I tried on a black dinner jacket and I looked good but the sleeves were just a little too short. Out the window, through mannequin legs, I could see my blue hound dog. I asked if they had a back entrance, even though I wanted to use it as an exit. They had one. In the alleyway there was another Commodore, only this one was white with leather seats that I could almost smell. I fast-walked it down the street and looked for another shop to duck into.

The whole day passed in this way. It was very, very irritating. I just couldn't shake them. They seemed always to guess my every move. Dejected, I caught the bus back home and decided I'd try it again when the Terry Dean story had died down a little, when it wasn't so fresh. It had to peter out eventually, I reasoned. The public has attention deficit disorder. It's famous for it. But what I hadn't figured was that the Terry Dean story wouldn't stop there because Terry Dean wouldn't stop there.

The next day there was more news, and more police and more reporters. The two bookies named in the affair had been found shot dead in their apartments. Witnesses had seen a young man of Terry's description leaving the scene. In the newspapers and on the radio, language

used to describe Terry Dean indicated a subtle shift in public opinion—
he was no longer a "lone madman." He was now a "vigilante."

Meanwhile, the eyes of the nation were fixed sharply on the inquiry
into corruption in sport, which was being conducted with uncustomary
speed. It had escaped nobody's attention that any bookie or cricketer
named in the report would become a potential target for Terry Dean,
Vigilante at Large.

The report of inquiry into corruption in sport was released and made
a matter of public record. It named names. Three more cricketers were
mentioned: some for throwing games, some for passing on match information. More bookies were named too. Everyone was on guard. They
were put on twenty-four-hour police surveillance. The police thought
they were ready to catch Terry, because if they had deduced one thing, it
was that he had started something he felt he had to finish. But Terry was
one step ahead of them.

The thing was, no one really paid close attention to the inquiry into
corruption in sport. They read about the cricketers and waited eagerly
for Terry to make his move. But the prime minister had promised an exhaustive inquiry, and they delivered an exhaustive report that also contained sections and subsections detailing corruption in horse racing,
rugby league, rugby union, Australian rules, soccer, the Commonwealth
Games, lawn bowls, snooker, cycling, rowing, boxing, wrestling, yacht
racing, hockey, basketball . . . If it involved an Australian running or
sweating or handling balls not his own, it was in there.

The first time Terry showed the breadth of his passion was with the
murder of a jockey named Dan Wonderland; he was found beaten and
force-fed enough horse tranquilizer to kill a stampede. I gazed searchingly at the photograph of this man whose life my brother had taken, in
the hope of seeing something evil, something that rose up out of the picture signaling unequivocally that the fucker deserved to die. It was taken
after winning a race, and in it Dan Wonderland was beaming and holding up his arms in triumph. Even if I hadn't known my brother had killed
him, I'd have seen something infinitely sad in the face of this jockey, the
look of a man who has just achieved a lifelong dream only to realize that
his dream was really nothing special.

The next day there was another killing: middleweight champion
Charlie Pulgar, who'd taken a very obvious dive in the ring, falling when,
at the sound of the bell, his opponent smacked his gloves together. With

Terry's help, Charlie Pulgar took his last dive—off the roof of his seventeen-story apartment building into a steady flow of traffic.

Just as investigators started anticipating Terry's next moves, he changed tactics once again. The inquiry into corruption in sport had also uncovered a phenomenon seeping into the world of professional sport: performance-enhancing drugs. With a little detective work, Terry ascertained who was purchasing and administering them: the coaches. Men who had always worked tirelessly behind the scenes shifted from the background to the foreground; their square jaws and haggard faces appeared more and more in the papers, as one by one they turned up dead.

But the most dangerous aspect of Terry's crusade was that, understandably, the bookies did not go quietly. Their links to the underworld guaranteed them guns and protection, and reports of gun battles in the backs of restaurants and bars filtered through the news. Terry had broken the last of Harry's laws—not only was he as far from anonymity as a person could be, but he had won the ire of the criminal world. He was not just on the ladder, he was shaking it. Along with the state and federal police, the criminal superstructure wanted him dead.

My parents dealt with the situation in their own way. Rather than face up to the awful truth, they extended their delusions about their son. While my mother doggedly pursued her double theory, my father put a positive spin on the whole dirty mess, turning rationalizing into a high art. If Terry shot a policeman in the leg, my father praised his mercy for not going for the heart; if Terry shot a policeman in the heart, my father praised his aim. To hear him talk, his son's eluding the police was evidence of his brains, his craftiness, his blanket superiority.

Lionel Potts was calling me five times a day, begging me to come to his house and give him updates. As I read him every newspaper report, he would remove his dark sunglasses. His dead eyes seemed to see for miles, and he'd lean back and vigorously shake his head. "I know a great lawyer—he'd defend Terry. I'm only sorry I didn't recommend him last time. I was a little pissed off. He did blind me, after all. Still, this lawyer would be perfect for him." I sat listening to Lionel go on and on, gritting my teeth. I couldn't stand it. As crazy as it sounds, I was overcome with jealousy. Terry was doing something with his life. He had found his calling; insane and bloodthirsty as it may have been, it was still a calling, and he was pursuing it vigilantly.

Every morning I ran to the corner shop for the newspaper to read about his atrocities. Not all his victims were dead. The snooker player who allegedly sank the white after the black accidentally on purpose only had his right hand broken, and strangely, he, along with some of Terry's other victims, came out in support of Terry's crusade. Through a public emotional hazing, they confessed their sins and said that Terry Dean was cleaning up an institution that had once been pure but had become soiled by the lure of big money. They weren't the only ones.

Sportsmen, commentators, intellectuals, talk-show hosts, writers, academics, politicians, and radio shock jocks—everyone was talking about sporting ethics, ideals, heroes, and the Australian spirit. Terry had jump-started a dialogue in the nation, and all the sportsmen and -women were on their best behavior.

•

One day during this chaos, Caroline came back into town, dragging a suitcase. I was sitting on the town hall steps counting the lines on my index finger when I spotted her coming down the street. She saw me, dragged that suitcase in a run, and threw her arms around me, plastering my cheeks with platonic kisses. I knew then and there that we would never discuss that night in her bedroom. I took a good look at her. She had really blossomed into a woman, but there were strange changes too: her hair was a lighter color, almost blond, and though her face was fuller and her lower lip more mature, there seemed to be something that had left her, a light or a glow. I thought maybe on her travels she had seen something that had scared it away.

"You heard about Terry?" I asked.

"It's incredible."

"Is that why you came home?"

"No, I only heard when I saw a newspaper at the airport, and the bus driver filled me in on the rest. You don't hear about Australia in Europe, Marty. It's strange. No one knows anything about us."

That's when I first discovered that living in Australia is like having a faraway bedroom in a very big house. All the better for us, I thought.

"I only came to pick up Dad. I'm taking him back overseas."

"Where?"

"Paris."

I drew my name on the ground with a stick. Martin Dean. Little clumps of earth lay in brown piles around it.

"Have you heard from him?" she asked.

"No."

"He's going to get himself killed."

"That seems likely."

Next to my name I wrote her name in the dirt. Our names were lying side by side.

"He's doing something important," she said.

"He's a murderer."

"But he believes."

"So?"

"So nothing. He believes in something, that's all."

"Rapists and pedophiles believe in something too. Hitler believed in something. Every time Henry the Eighth cut off another wife's head, he believed in something. It's not hard to believe in something. Everyone believes in something."

"You don't."

"No, I don't."

The words had left my mouth before I realized what I'd said. On reflection, I could see that this was absolutely true. I couldn't name a single thing I believed in. For me, 1 percent of doubt has the same effect as 100 percent. So then, how could I believe in anything when what might not be true might as well not be true?

I drew a heart around our names in the dirt.

"If you'd heard from Terry, you'd tell me, wouldn't you?"

I quickly covered our names with dirt. I was being foolish. She didn't love me. She loved him. I suddenly flushed with embarrassment.

"You've heard from him."

She grabbed my wrist, but I jerked it away from her.

"I haven't."

"Yes, you have!"

"I haven't, I tell you!"

She pulled me toward her and grabbed my face with both hands and gave me a long, long kiss on the lips. She pulled away, leaving me stunned and speechless. I couldn't open my eyes.

"If you see Terry, give him that for me."

That opened my eyes. I smiled to stop myself foaming at the mouth. I hated her. I wanted to throw her in the dirt. I said something like "I hate you and will hate you for all remembered time" and walked away, toward home, even though home was the last place I wanted to go. It had transformed into a place of minor historical importance, like the restaurant toilet Hitler used before the Reichstag fire, and thus the reporters were back with their bad manners and zero empathy, shouting their inane questions through the front windows.

When I got home, it became clear that my father had had enough. He was standing at the door, swaying on his feet, drunk. His face was stiff, as if he had lockjaw.

"You want to come in, you cunts? *Well, come in!*" he shouted.

The reporters looked at each other before stepping tentatively into the house. They thought it was a trap. It wasn't. It was merely a man teetering off the precipice of his sanity.

"Here. Take a shot of this," my father said, opening the kitchen cupboards. He ripped up the floorboards. He led them into our bedroom. He shoved a pair of Terry's underpants under their noses. "Sniff it! Sniff it!" He turned everything inside out. "You need to see where he originated from." My father unbuttoned his fly, pulled out his penis, and waved it around. "Here, you maggots! He was a delinquent sperm! Beat the other sperms to the egg! He came out of here! Film it! Film it, you grubby parasites!" The reporters laughed while my mother chased them around the house. But they didn't want to leave. They were having a high old time doubled over in laughter. This man's drunken maudlin despair was the best thing they'd seen in ages. Couldn't they see my mother crying? Oh yes, they could see it all right; they could see it through the zoom lens.

Once we got them back out onto the front lawn, I tried talking reasonably with them.

"*Please* go home," I pleaded.

"Where's your brother?" they asked.

"There he is!" I shouted, pointing behind them. They spun their heads around like fools. When they turned back to me I said, "Made you look."

A petty victory.

•

I hadn't lied to Caroline. All this time I'd had no word from Terry or Harry and I still hadn't managed to get myself over to the suburban hideout. I felt cut off, and my natural curiosity was burning steadily inside me. I was sick of relying on unreliable newspaper reports and talk-back gossip. I wanted the inside scoop. I suppose there was also a part of me that wanted to join in somehow, if not in the actual killing, then at least as a witness. Everything that happened in Terry's life up to this point had included me in one way or another. I wanted back in. I knew that the moment I stepped into his world, my life would be altered forever.

And I was right.

It was time to try again. I couldn't assume the police had tired of watching me. I spent the afternoon threading a labyrinthine trail through the bush, then I made my way on foot across a wide, empty clearing, spinning around to check behind me every few minutes. Nothing. Nobody there. Just to be safe, I walked the five miles to the next town and caught the bus from there.

I was surprised to see that the front lawn of the suburban hideout was no longer immaculately groomed. The station wagon in the driveway was gone. The blinds were drawn. It looked as if the nice normal family they'd been emulating had fallen on hard times.

The door opened as soon as I turned up the driveway. Harry must have been watching from the window.

"Quick! In! In!"

I hurried inside, and Harry dead-bolted the door behind me.

"Is he here?" I asked.

"No, he's fucking not, and he'd better not set foot within my periphery if he doesn't want a bullet in the head!"

I followed Harry into the living room, where he flopped down on the sofa. I flopped too. "Marty, your brother is an attention-grabber. I can't stop him. The cooperative is in ruins! It's a shambles! My dream! The whole thing's a downright failure. Terry's fucked it. He wants to be famous, doesn't he? He's turned his back on all my advice. I thought he was like a son to me. But no son of mine would piss in my face like that. I mean, I don't have children, but when you have kids you don't expect a golden shower! The first couple of years, sure, but after that you let down your guard. And look at what he's blown it all for! He's attacking sportsmen, football players, bookies! He's not even robbing them, he's just ripping them apart for no reason! Where the hell's the money in that? And you know what else? Have you seen the papers? The world thinks it's his gang! Not mine, his. Well, it's not his. It's mine! Mine, dammit! OK, sure I wanted us to be anonymous, but we all have to be anonymous, and if we can't, then I want the credit I deserve! Now it's too late. He's casting a shadow over me. And crims I've known for fifty years think I'm working for him! How's that for a slap in the face? It's humiliating! But I've got a plan. I need your help. Come in here, I want to show you something."

Harry got to his feet and limped off in the direction of his bedroom. I followed him in. This was the first time I'd been in Harry's bedroom. Other than his bed, there was nothing in it. Nothing at all. He was anonymous even in his own room.

He reached under his mattress and pulled out a thick wad of paper.

"I thought just maybe the anonymous democratic cooperative of crime might be a unique gift to give to the world. But now I see it was doomed from the start. It was never going to work. You can't help human nature. People think they need limelight to grow. No one can stand anonymity. So here's Plan B, a backup I've been working on for ten years. It's something that's never been done. No one's ever thought of it. This is going to be my legacy. This is it, Marty. But I need help. I can't do it on my own. That's where you come in."

He hit me in the chest with the stack of pages.

"What is this?"

"This, my boy, is my opus. A handbook for criminals! Everything I've learned I've written down here. It's going to be a book! A textbook! I've written the textbook on crime! The definitive work!"

I took the collection of handwritten pages and picked a page at random.

Kidnapping

If the media catches whiff of the story, you're in deep trouble if you haven't picked your victim wisely. Never take someone young and attractive, the last thing a kidnapper needs is a public outcry . . .

. . . find a suitable location to stash your victims . . . avoid the temptation to use motel or hotel rooms in case the victim breaks free long enough to order room service or fresh towels.

"As you can see, Marty, I need these thoughts to be expanded and put into chapters . . ."

I picked up another page.

Burn, Baby, Burn: Arson and You

Everyone likes to watch a fire, even you. Avoid the temptation! After you've set a building alight, don't peek from around the corner so you can admire the conflagration . . . It's a common trap . . . most arsonists have been caught within meters of the scene of the crime and police are always on the lookout for shady characters standing around saying to bystanders, "Some fire, huh?"

His masterpiece was written on scraps of paper, on the backs of receipts, on napkins, paper towels, newspapers, toilet paper, and hundreds of loose-leaf pages, reams of the stuff. There were instructions, diagrams, flowcharts, thoughts, reflections, maxims, and aphorisms on every possible aspect of the criminal life. Each thought had an underlined title, which was the only hint at how one might make some order of the chaos.

Home Break-in

Don't enter a home unless you're sure the resident hasn't just gone out to pick up a carton of milk . . . be quick . . . don't stop to browse in the bookshelves . . .

"Of course there've been countless books on the subject of crime, but they're either sociological studies or written to help criminologists and police. Crime-fighting, basically. No one's written a book by and for the criminals themselves." He stuffed the papers into a brown satchel and cradled it like a baby. "I'm entrusting this to you."

I took the satchel. It was heavy, the weight of the meaning of Harry's life.

"I'm not doing this for the money, so I'll split the profit with you fifty-fifty, straight down the line."

"Harry, I don't know if I want to do this."

"Who cares what you want? I've got a lot of knowledge to impart! I have to get it out there in the world before I die! Otherwise my life will have been for nothing! If it's money you're thinking about, then forget the fifty percent. Take it all! I don't care! I really don't. Here."

Harry ran to the bed and grabbed a pillow and shook it until money fell out of the pillowcase, spilling onto the floor. On his one good leg, he squatted and bounced around the room, scooping up the money. "You want cash? You want the shirt off my back? You want the heart from my chest? Name it. It's yours. Only for God's sake, help me! Help me! *Help me!*" He thrust the money in my face. How could I refuse him? I took the money and his opus but thought: There's always time to change my mind later.

That night, in my father's shed, I pored over Harry's scrawls in amazement. Some of his notes were short and appeared to be written with morons in mind.

Car Theft
If you can only drive an automatic, don't steal manuals.

Others were more in-depth and not only concentrated on how to perform the crime but included psychological insights into the intended victim.

Mugging
Be prepared! Despite what common sense tells us, people *will* risk their lives to chase after the two dollars in their wallets or handbags . . . and if the mugging takes place in broad daylight, they are especially incensed . . . the audacity of a criminal to steal while the sun is high in the sky is so irritating to them, they will run at you like an action hero, even if you are holding a knife or a gun . . . also, it seems the hassle of canceling a credit card and the thought of applying for a new driver's license are so unbearable to the majority of the general public, they are more than willing to die to avoid it . . . in their minds, a slow agonizing death by knife wound is infinitely preferable to dealing with the bureaucracy of the motor registry . . . that's why you need to be as fit as a long-distance runner.

This was either rubbish or it was brilliant, and I couldn't decide which. I stood up from the table, intending to have a break, but I found myself standing hunched over Harry's notes reading through them fever-ishly. Something about this insanity got under my skin. There seemed to be a pattern forming: my father built a prison; Terry became a criminal influenced by a prisoner he met in the prison my father built. And me? Maybe this was my role. Maybe this book was finally something I could stake my life on, something to take with me into the cold, abandoned furnace of death. I couldn't drag myself away. The pages were beckoning me like the glint of light from a coin at the bottom of a swimming pool. I knew I had to dive in to see if the coin was valuable or if it was just some aluminum foil blown in by the wind.

I lit a cigarette and stood at the door of the shed and looked up at the sky. It was a dark night with only three stars visible, and not the famous ones. I put a hand in my pocket and felt the scrunched-up wads of cash. After all the lectures I'd given Terry about crime, how could I do this? Wouldn't that make me a hypocrite? And so what if it did? Is be-ing a hypocrite such a terrible thing? Doesn't hypocrisy actually demon-strate flexibility in a person? If you stand by your principles, doesn't that mean you're rigid and close-minded? Yes, I have principles, but so what? Does that mean I have to live my life unbendingly by them? I chose the principles unconsciously to guide my behavior, but can't a person assert his conscious mind to override the unconscious? Who's the boss here, anyway? And am I to trust my young self to dictate the standards of my behavior throughout my whole life? And might I not be wrong about everything? Why should I bind myself to the musings of my own brain? Am I not now, at this moment, rationalizing because I want the money? And why shouldn't I rationalize? Isn't the benefit of evolution that we possess a rational mind? Wouldn't the chicken be happier if he had one too? Then he could say to mankind, "Would you please stop chopping off my head to see if I will run around without it? How long is that going to amuse you?"

I rubbed my head. I felt an existential migraine coming on, a real blinder.

I went out and walked along the dark road into the town. With his newfound celebrity, Terry had given the criminal world a face. With this book, Harry and I would be giving it a brain. It felt good to be a part of something bigger than myself. The lights from the town were flicking off, one by one. I could see the silhouette of the prison on the hill. It loomed large and grotesque, like an enormous stone head of some long-dead god eroding on a cliff. I spoke out loud: "Why shouldn't I do what I want? What's stopping me?"

I felt a lump in my throat the size of a fist. It was the first time I'd ever questioned myself so rigorously, and it seemed as if the questions were being articulated by someone older than myself.

I continued to speak out loud: "People trust too much in themselves. What they take for truth, they let rule their lives, and if I set out to find a way to live so I will be in control of my life, then I actually lose control, because the thing I have decided on, my truth, becomes the ruler and I become its servant. And how can I be free to evolve if I'm submitting myself to a ruler, any ruler, even if that ruler is me?"

I was scared by my own words, because their implications were beginning to sink in. "Lawlessness, aimlessness, chaos, confusion, contusion," I said to no one, to the night. I was talking myself in circles. My head throbbed. I was thinking the kind of thoughts that caused throbbing.

All of a sudden, with blinding clarity, I knew that Harry was a genius. A prophet, maybe even a martyr—that would be decided later, depending on the nature of his death. He was innovating. That's why Harry chose me to bring his asinine tablets down from the mountain. He was showing me the way. By example, he was showing me that it doesn't take a god to innovate, create, invert, destroy, crush, and inspire; a man can do the job just as well, and in his own good time. Not in six days, like You-Know-Who. It needn't be a rush job. And even if, at the end of my toils, I wound up inspiring only hatred or indifference, I knew then and there it was my duty to try, because this was my awakening, and that's what an awakening is all about: getting up. There's no use having an awakening and then hitting the snooze button and going back to sleep.

These were big thoughts, really obese. I found a half-smoked cigarette on the ground. I picked it up. It felt strong in my hand, like an Olympic torch. I lit it and walked around town. It was cold. I stamped my feet and held my hands under my armpits to keep warm. This book of Harry's was the first small step in a nameless revolution that was taking place, and I had been chosen because of the excellence of my mind. I wanted to praise myself without guilt. I wanted to kiss my own brain. I felt thousands of years old. I felt older than soil. I was overcome with the strength and power of words and ideas. I thought about my first father, father number one, back in Poland, and I thought about his insanity: dying for a god. What a stupid reason to die: for a god, a lousy god! I shouted loudly to a tree, "I want to die because I am a creature with a sell-by date! I want to die because I am a man and that's what men do; they crumble, decay, disappear!" I walked on, cursing my father's blind stupidity. I screamed, "To die for an idea! To take a bullet for a deity! What an idiot!"

Our town had streetlamps only on the main street—the roads leading into and out of it were left to the mercy of the moon and the stars, and when there were neither it was black through and through. The trees rattled in the wind that blew from the west. I walked to a house and sat on the veranda and waited. For what? Not what: who. I was at Caroline's house. I realized suddenly that romantics are dickheads. There's nothing wonderful or interesting about unrequited love. I think it's shitty, just plain shitty. To love someone who doesn't return your affections might be exciting in books, but in life it's unbearably boring. I'll tell you what's exciting: sweaty, passionate nights. But sitting on the veranda outside the home of a sleeping woman who isn't dreaming about you is slow moving and just plain sad.

I waited for Caroline to awaken and come out onto the veranda and wrap her arms around me. I thought the power of my mind was so strong I could will her from her slumber and draw her to the window. I would tell her my ideas and she would finally know who I was. I thought I was as good as my mind and she would be bowled over by both; I forgot entirely about my body and my face, which were not so hot. I stepped up to the front window and saw my reflection and changed my mind. I stepped away and walked back home. This was my awakening, Jasper! Harry, poor Harry, he was enormously important for me: an unfettered mind. Up until I met him, all the minds I knew were fettered, shockingly fettered. The freedom of Harry's mind was exhilarating. It was a mind absolutely true to itself, that ran on its own steam. I'd never before encountered a timeless mind, impervious to the influence of its surroundings.

I went home and sifted through Harry's notes some more. They were impossibly silly! This book, his handbook for criminals, it was an aberration. It shouldn't exist. It couldn't exist. That's why I had to help him bring it to life. I had to! I divided the book into two major sections: Crime and Punishment. Then within these sections I made chapters, an index, and added footnotes, just like in a real textbook. I was completely faithful to Harry's notes. Every now and then as I typed I'd come across a passage and I'd laugh out loud, a huge belly laugh. It was wonderful! His words were stupendous! They bored right into my brain.

On Home Break-ins

Once inside, be fast and methodical. Wear gloves and keep them on. Never take them off under any circumstances. You'd be surprised at how many burglars remove their gloves in order to pick their nose. I cannot stress this strongly enough: Don't leave fingerprints anywhere! Not even in your nose!

I typed it all up, word for word. I didn't leave anything out. I did the whole thing without sleep. There was electricity running through me. I couldn't turn it off. Here's another one I remember:

On Bribery

When bribing officers of the law, a common technique is to drop the money on the floor in front of the officer in question and say in a casual voice, "Did you drop that?" This is risky because of the possibility of the officer saying, "Yes I did. Cheers," and arresting you after he's pocketed the money. While no bribery ploy is guaranteed, I recommend just coming out and saying, "So. You take bribes or what?" This way, if he doesn't, and charges you with attempting to bribe an officer, you can defend yourself by explaining that you never actually offered a bribe, which you didn't; you were inquiring about the honesty of the person arresting you and were simply on the lookout for hypocrisy.

His logic was infallible. Even the chapter headings made me whirl with joy:

Motiveless Crimes: Why?
Armed Robbery: Laughing All the Way from the Bank
Crime and Fashion: Balaclavas Are Always In
The Police and You: How to Spot a Crooked Cop by His Shoes

The chapter titled "Pickpocketing: An Intimate Crime" had a line in it that said, *"If you have to unzip it, it's not a pocket. Remove your hand im-*

mediately!" Can you argue with that? No, you can't. I can remember some of the other chapter headings. There was

> Assault: Bruising Your Enemies
> Blame: Framing Your Friends
> Manslaughter: Oops!
> Escaping Custody: Walk, Don't Run
> Love: The Real Informer
> Crimes of Passion: Hot-Headed Murder
> Crimes of Perversion: For Lovers Only

It was an exhaustive tome. He'd left nothing out. No crime was too small, as was covered in Chapter 13: "Misdemeanors and Other Non-profit Crimes: Jaywalking, Loitering, Graffiti, Littering, Joyriding, and Public Nudity." When Harry said this was to be the definitive work, he wasn't kidding!

I left the house at dawn, buzzing with speculation. Would Harry ever get this crazy book published? Who would publish it? How would the public react?

When I stepped outside, I noticed a campfire smoking in the cold morning and, beside it, four sleeping reporters camped out under the trees. When did they get there? A shiver ran through me. Their presence meant one of only three things: either Terry had committed another crime or he'd been arrested or he was dead. I wanted to shake them awake and ask them which it was, but I didn't dare, not when I was on my way over to Harry's—a lesser fugitive, sure, but a fugitive all the same. I let the reporters have their sleep, wished them all nightmares, and walked to the bus stop.

I heard footsteps behind me. I grimaced, expecting police or a gaggle of reporters. It was neither. It was my mother in her beige nightgown and bare feet. She looked as if she hadn't slept in decades. She must have sneaked past the reporters too.

"Where are you going at this hour of the morning? Are you going to see Terry?"

"No, Mum, I don't know where he is."

She gripped me by the arm. I saw something terrible in her eyes. They looked like they'd been crying, draining her body of salt and other essential minerals. Her illness was taking its toll. She was already thinner, already old. She said somberly, "There's been another attack. It was on the radio. This time another cricketer—they found him with his head bashed in and a cricket ball stuffed in his mouth. They're saying your brother did it. Why, why are they saying he did it?"

"Because he probably did it."

She slapped me hard across the face. "Don't say that! It's a lie! Find Terry and tell him to go to the police. If he hides, it just makes him look guilty."

The bus came while she was still babbling hysterically. "And if you can't find Terry, then for God's sake, find that double!"

I stepped onto the bus and found a seat. As it drove off, I looked out the window at my mother. She rested one hand against a tree while picking gravel off the soles of her feet with the other.

I arrived at Harry's to see him glaring at me through the front window. As I entered, I resisted a powerful urge to hug him.

"What are you doing here?" Harry shouted in my face. "I was hoping I wouldn't see you until you finished! You've changed your mind, haven't you? Fucker! Traitor! You've had an attack of conscience! Why don't you get out of here and go join a monastery, you bloody hypocrite!"

Resisting a smile, I pulled the manuscript from the brown satchel and waved it in his face. His eyes widened.

"Is this . . ."

My smile couldn't contain itself any longer. I let it explode.

"So quick?"

"I had great words to work with."

Harry dived for the manuscript and flicked through it excitedly. When he reached the end, he turned back to the front page. I stood there awhile before realizing that he was going to read the thing to the end. I went into the backyard, which was drenched in sunlight. The pool was now an enormous fetid swamp. The lawn was overgrown with weeds. The metal frames of the banana chairs were brown with rust. I stretched out on one and looked up at the sky. Clouds shaped like pregnant bellies were floating through it. My lids closed and I drifted languidly into sleep. Before I got there, in the half dreamworld, I thought I saw Terry hiding out in one of the clouds. I saw him pull the soft fluffy veil over his face whenever a plane sailed by. Then I fell asleep.

I woke sweating. The sun was sitting on me. Blinking through the bright light, I could see the silhouette of Harry's head. It seemed enormous. When he leaned into the shadows, I saw him beaming at me. He sat on the edge of my banana chair and locked me in a tight embrace, covering me in kisses. He even kissed me on the mouth, which was revolting, but I took it in the spirit it was given.

"You've done me a wonderful service, Martin. I'll never forget it as long as I live."

"There was another attack," I said.

"Yeah, heard it on the radio. Stupid bugger."

"Any word from him? Any idea where he might be?"

Harry shook his head sadly. "He's become a true-blue celebrity. He can't avoid the coppers too much longer. Famous faces make lousy fugitives."

"Do you think, if they catch up with him, he'll go quietly?"

"Not bloody likely," he said, picking up his manuscript and stroking it as though it were a thigh. "Come on. Let's go make some noise of our own."

•

Finding a publisher wasn't going to be easy, and not only because of the risky content. Harry was a fugitive. If we went to a publisher with Harry's name plastered all over the manuscript, we might get more than a simple rejection. It was possible one of the publishers might call the police. A double rejection! After much arguing, I managed to persuade Harry that we should keep his identity secret until the last possible minute— right up to the moment of printing we'd withhold the author's name. But Harry still wanted to come along to choose the publishing house most worthy of his tome. It seemed impossible. He was a wanted man—not in Terry's league, but police don't forget to look for escaped criminals just because the press isn't in love with them. On top of that, Harry's leg had gotten so bad he could hardly walk. Unfortunately, nothing I could say would dissuade him from personally guiding his legacy into print. It was all too vital to leave in my inexperienced hands.

We went out the following day. With his limp and scraggly beard, he looked like a castaway. I suggested he shave and make himself more presentable, but he insisted that authors always look unfit for society so it was actually to our benefit that he looked like shit. He threw on an old coat despite the hot sun and hid a sawed-off shotgun in the inside pocket. I didn't say anything. "Let's go then, eh." I offered my services as a human crutch and he put all his weight on me, apologizing profusely. It felt like I was lugging a dead body.

The first publisher's building looked like it would cost you just to enter it, and inside, the lobby was full of mirrors that proved you were a slob. We made our way up to the twentieth floor, sharing the elevator with two suits that had men trapped inside them. The publisher's offices hogged the whole floor. The top of the receptionist's head asked if we had an appointment. What little of her face we could see was smiling cruelly as we fumbled a no. "Well, he's too busy to see you today," she said in a nonnegotiable voice. Harry went into his thing.

"See here. This is one of those opportunities you'll be kicking yourself about. Just like the publisher who rejected that famous book which went on to sell a gazillion copies. What was the name of that book, Martin? You know, the one that got rejected and went on to sell a gazillion copies?"

I didn't know but thought I'd better play along. I joined in by naming the best seller of all time.

"The Bible, King James edition."

"Yes, by God, that was it. The Bible! The receptionist wouldn't let the apostle through, even though he had a gold mine in his hands."

"Oh for God's sake," the receptionist said, sighing. She glanced down at her appointment book. "He has an appointment at the end of the day, and if that runs short, you can see him for five minutes before he goes home."

"Good enough, kind lady," Harry said, winking. I helped him to a chair in the waiting room.

We waited.

Harry was shivering and his hands were hiding deep inside his coat, which made me nervous, knowing what else was in there. His teeth were clenched together as if someone had asked him to smile for a photo twelve hours earlier and hadn't taken it yet.

"Are you OK?" I asked him.

I could tell his paranoia was firing on all circuits. His eyes circled the room while his neck swung his head from doorway to hallway. Around lunchtime I noticed that Harry had his fingers in his ears. When I asked him about it, he muttered something about a noise. I couldn't hear anything. A split second later there was a loud bang. I craned my head and through one of the doorways saw a young man kicking the life out of a photocopier machine. I looked at Harry incredulously, and remembered again that when Terry and I had first gone to the prison to meet him, Harry had mentioned something about telepathy being highly developed in the minds of career criminals. Long-term paranoia earns people a certain level of ESP, he had said, or something to that effect. Was it true? I hadn't taken him seriously then, but now? I didn't know what to think. I scrutinized Harry's face. He nodded at me with an almost imperceptible smugness.

At five minutes to five we were ushered into the publisher's office. Everything about it made you feel small and unimportant. It was spacious and quiet and air-conditioned and newly carpeted, and instead of a window there was a wall of glass you couldn't open and jump out of, even if you wanted to; at best you could press your face against it and dream of falling. The publisher looked as if someone had told him if he smiled he'd lose everything he had ever worked for.

"You've written a book. I publish books. You think that means we're a match made in heaven. It doesn't. I have to be bowled over by whatever you've got, and I don't fall easily," he said.

Harry demanded that the publisher take a quick look while we waited. The publisher laughed without smiling. Harry tossed in the line about missing golden opportunities that went straight to the man's heart, the one in his back pocket. He picked up the manuscript and browsed through it, clicking his tongue as if he were calling his dog. He stood and walked to the glass wall and read it while leaning against it. I worried the glass would crack and send him tumbling into the street. After a minute he threw the manuscript at us as if it were making his hands dirty.

"Is this a joke?"

"I assure you it's not."

"To publish this would be suicide. You're instructing people how to break the law."

"Why is he telling me what my book is about?" Harry asked me.

I shrugged.

"Get out of here before I call the police!" the publisher screamed at us.

In the elevator on the way down, Harry shook with fury. "That cunt," he muttered.

I felt similarly dented, and I didn't know much about the publishing world, but I tried to explain to him that we had to expect some rejections. "This is normal. It would have been too much to expect that the first place fell all over it."

At the second floor the elevator stopped. "What are we stopping for?" Harry yelled at me.

The doors slid open and a man stepped in. *"You can't walk down one fucking floor?"* Harry shouted, and the man leapt out again just before the doors closed.

On the street it was impossible to get a cab. It was really not advisable to be lingering on the street like this with a known fugitive, but neither of us seemed able to make a taxi materialize just by wishing it.

"We've been made!" he whispered.

"What?"

"They're onto me!"

"Who?"

"All of them!"

He was out of control. He was trying to hide behind me, but the crowd was on all sides. He circled my body like a shark. He was drawing too much attention to himself in his panicked attempt to remain inconspicuous.

"There!" he screamed, and pushed me into a stream of traffic, into a taxi. Cars halted and honked their horns as we jumped in.

I really put my foot down after that. Harry was to stay at home. I simply refused to help him anymore if he insisted on coming along. He put up a struggle, but it was a weak one. The last incident had added seventeen years to his face. Even he could see it.

•

The following weeks were a nightmare. I tripped from office to office in a blur. They were all the same. I couldn't get over how quiet they were. Everyone spoke in a whisper, and the way they tiptoed around, you'd think you'd wandered into a sacred temple if it weren't for the telephones. The receptionists all wore the same condescending sneers. Often I sat in waiting rooms with other authors. They were the same too. They all emanated fear and desperation and looked so hungry they would have signed away the rights to their children for a lozenge, poor bastards.

In one of the publishing houses, where I waited all day for two days in a row and still wasn't granted an audience with the king, a writer and I swapped manuscripts to pass the time. His was set in a small country town and was about a doctor and a pregnant schoolteacher who passed each other on the street every day but were too inward to say hello. It was unreadable. It was almost all description. My spirits lifted when, on page 85, he'd deigned to put in a smattering of dialogue between the characters. His novel was a real struggle to wade through, but he was sitting right beside me so I had to persist, out of politeness. Every now and then we glanced at each other to see how we were getting on. Finally, around lunchtime, he turned to me and said, "This is a peculiar book. Is it a satire?"

"Not at all. Yours is interesting too. Are the characters mute?"

"Not at all."

We each handed back the other's manuscript and looked at our watches.

Every morning I endured the four-hour bus ride into Sydney, where I spent the day going from publisher to publisher. Most laughed right in my face. One guy had to come out from behind his desk to do it because my face was too far away. It was discouraging. Also, the publishers didn't like the idea of my hiding the author's name from them right up to the day of printing. It made them suspicious. Many thought it was some kind of plot to drop them in the shit. You never met a greasier bunch of paranoid, unimaginative, dull-witted merchants in your life. The ones who took the manuscript seriously, who didn't think it was a hoax or a prank or a plot, called me the worst possible names. They thought the work was an abomination and I was a dangerous, irresponsible anarchist for trying to peddle it. Before they threw me out on the street, they all said the same thing: this book would never be published, not in their lifetimes. I guess that meant that once they were dead, the world could fall into the toilet for all they cared about it.

Harry took it badly. He flew into fits, accused me of being lazy or sabotaging the meetings with ineptitude. That burned. I was slaving my guts out peddling that book of his, but it was the book they didn't like, not me. Then, and after the tenth rejection, he started cursing the Australian publishing industry instead of me. "Maybe we need to take this to America. Freedom of expression is big over there right now. They have a thing called the right to free press. They have amendments enforcing it. Ideas are encouraged to flourish. Here the industry's as stale as week-old bread crusts. This country's so fucking conservative it makes you want to puke. It's a wonder anyone gets anything published at all." He might have had a point. Maybe the local publishers were just scared. He started talking about buying me a plane ticket to New York, but I shot that idea down the best I could. I didn't want to go to New York. I couldn't leave my sick mother or Terry, wherever he was. I was convinced that someday, soon, Terry was going to need me, maybe to save his life. I had to be on hand.

Caroline felt no such duty. She and Lionel arrived at my front door in the near-darkness of twilight to say goodbye. They had sold the house and were moving off. Lionel gave me a hug while Caroline stood shaking her head. "I'm not going to hang around and see Terry killed," she said. "No one's asking you to," I said back, although I did think about it. It began to rain softly. She gave me a hug too, though it wasn't the squeeze I needed, and as I watched her guiding her blind father out into the night, I felt as though I had renounced my humanity. I called out "Bye!" as she disappeared into the darkness, but it was as though I meant, You go ahead, I'm not a man anyway. There's nothing human about me, so you be off.

A week later I was at Harry's watching television when Terry called. After giving him an earful, Harry threw me the phone.

"How are you holding up?" I asked frantically. "They're saying you got shot."

"In the ankle! Who shoots ankles? Look, don't worry about me, mate. I got a bird who does wonders with iodine. I'm tired, that's about it. Otherwise I'm OK."

"You're famous."

"Isn't it wild?"

"It's going to get you caught."

"I know."

"So what are you going to do?"

"Look. Maybe I started this thing without too much thought, but I realized pretty quick that I'm doing something here, something I feel is important. Everyone's on their best behavior. No one's cheating. No one's playing dirty. No one's ripping anyone off. No one's screwing anyone. Sport's going through a reformation. Everyone's taking the ethics seriously."

"How can you talk about ethics! You're a cold-blooded murderer! I think you should give yourself up."

"Are you nuts? This is who I am! This is what I was put here to do!"

"Caroline came home."

There was a sharp intake of breath. I could hear Terry moving around, dragging a chair across the floor. Then I heard him sit.

"Where is she? Does she know? Can you take her a message?"

"She left again."

He took another breath, this time deeper, and I waited a full thirty seconds before I heard him let it out. He cracked open a can of something, then swallowed maybe half by the sound of it. He still didn't say anything. Caroline's absence seemed to weigh more heavily on both of us than murder.

"So are you going to stop or not?" I asked.

"Listen, Marty, one day you'll understand all this. The day you believe in something. Oops. Gotta go. Pizza's here."

"Hey, I believe in—"

Click.

I put down the receiver and kicked the wall. It's normal to think that the laws of physics don't apply when you're angry, that your furious foot will pass through brick. Nursing my injured toe, I felt extremely agitated. The sound of profound gratification in Terry's voice was enough to put me on edge. He didn't give me a chance to tell him I'd found my belief. I was doing something important too. He didn't know I'd been irresistibly drawn to Harry's book and was instrumental in getting it published. Well, how could he? I wasn't getting it published. And why not? Terry was doing everything possible to murder those sportsmen, but was I really doing everything I could for the book? The idea began gnawing at me that I didn't have it in me to go all the way, to go with total devotion down a road on which it was impossible to do a U-turn. Terry was displaying absolute ruthlessness and obstinacy in pursuit of his goal, and I needed to apply the same ruthless obstinacy to follow my path incessantly; otherwise I was just another frightened worthless hypocrite unwilling to put himself on the line for his cause.

I made a groundbreaking decision.

If the next publisher rejected the book, I simply wouldn't accept his rejection. I would reject his rejection. I wouldn't take no for an answer. I wouldn't take never for an answer. I'd *demand* he publish it, and if that meant holding him hostage until it was in the stores, then so be it. It would be easy enough to get my hands on a gun. You only had to open a cupboard at Harry's or plunge your hand deep into the sugar bowl to find a semiautomatic. Of course, I despised guns and all the baggage that went along with them, like bullet wounds and death, but on the other hand, I liked the idea of breaking another one of the Ten Commandments, especially since I didn't honor my father either. They couldn't very well force you to suffer for *two* eternities, could they?

That night before going home, while Harry was out cold on vodka and sleeping pills, I plunged my hand deep into the sugar bowl. The pistol inside came out covered in sticky crystals. I brushed them off into a cup of tea and drank it. I could taste the gun.

The next day I left my house when it was still dark. Terry hadn't made a whisper in the world for at least a week and there were no reporters camping in our yard, although their cigarette butts were wet with dew. I took the bus into the city. The office building of the next publisher on the list was across the road from Central Station. Before going in, I studied the train timetable in case I might need to make a hasty getaway. One train or another was leaving every three minutes, if I wasn't too particular about the destination. I bought a whole bunch of tickets, gateways to everywhere.

The lobby had a blackboard under glass listing the building's residents in white letters. There, on the fourth floor, was the name of my last hope. Strangeways Publicati ns. The "o" was missing. It wasn't too difficult to see why. On the sixth floor was a company called Voodoo Cooperative Clothing, while on the second floor resided another company called Ooooops! Stain Remover Inc.

I took the elevator to the fourth floor. There was a bathroom at the end of the corridor. I went inside and hung my head over the toilet bowl for a good twenty minutes, strategizing, before going back out into the corridor and making my way to the door of Strangeways Publications. Before knocking, I reached into my bag. The gun was still there, but the sugar was gone. There was nothing sweet about it anymore.

I knocked. I heard a voice say, "Come in."

A man was sitting behind a desk reading. Without looking up, he motioned for me to sit down. I was too nervous to sit. My knees wouldn't bend. They hardened. I looked around the office. It was no bigger than a closet, and was a pigsty. Newspapers were stacked up from the floor to the ceiling. A pile of clothes and a brown suitcase sat in one corner. The window was shut and there was no air in the place. The publisher was in his forties. Whatever he was reading made him smile like a senile goat. There was a toothbrush and a white bowl filled with green water on the desk. The toothbrush made me sick. It had a hair in it.

"What can I do for you?" he asked, looking up.

I reached into my bag, felt the gun, and pulled out the manuscript. I plopped it on his desk and went through my routine. The author, I said, who shall remain anonymous for the moment, was seeking the right publisher for his groundbreaking masterpiece, and because of the sensitive nature of the subject matter, I couldn't possibly leave the manuscript with him, but if he had an ounce of curiosity and didn't want to miss out on the most sensational opportunity of a lifetime, he'd really need to look through the manuscript now, while I waited. I had made this speech so many times I said it without thinking. He stared at me the whole time, with half-drunk eyes, smiling that old-goat smile as if he were thinking of bubble baths.

"Well, let's have a look at her then, shall we?"

He turned to the first page. Through the window behind him I could see a train snake into the station. The publisher flicked to the middle of the manuscript, giggled at something, then put it down.

"A satire, eh? I love a good satire. It's well written and it's pretty funny, but to be honest, not really in my line."

My hand, grasping the gun, was all sweat.

"Thanks for coming in anyway."

I didn't move. A minute dragged by. He made gestures with his eyes that directed me out the door. I ignored them.

"Look," he said. "Things are a bit rough for me right now. I couldn't afford to publish my own obituary if I wanted to, so why don't you fuck off."

I didn't move. It was as though the air in the room had turned solid and trapped me where I was standing.

"You know what I was reading when you came in? No? Nothing—that's what! I was pretending to read so I'd look busy. Sad, huh?" When I still didn't so much as visibly breathe, he said, "Take a look at this."

A pile of books towered beside his desk, and he picked the top one and handed it to me. I took a look. It was a biology textbook.

"Back in London I was working for the tabloids. That was a long time ago." He came around and sat on the edge of his desk, his eyes darting around the room. "This is a small publishing company. Nothing too flash. We publish science textbooks. Physics, biology, chemistry, the usual suspects. Me and my wife, we shared this business fifty-fifty. Her money, inherited from her father, and my money, saved through blood and sweat. So ten years we ran our little company, and sure, we had our domestic disputes, and I had my indiscretions, but I was discreet about them, so what was the harm? Look at this. Feast your eyes on the instrument of my destruction!" He motioned to the biology textbook in my hands and said, "Page ninety-five."

I turned to page 95. It was a picture of the human body, with all the parts labeled and their functions explained. It looked like a booklet of stereo instructions. "See anything unusual?" he asked.

I couldn't. It looked like a pretty standard human body. Sure, it was lacking some common elements like love handles, wrinkles, and stretch marks, but otherwise it was relatively comprehensive.

"She did it on purpose. She knew I'd be too pissed to check through it before printing."

"I don't see anything."

"The brain! Look at what she's called the brain!"

I looked. It said "The Testicle." And where the testicles were, it was labeled not just "The Brain" but "Stanley's Brain." In fact, now that he'd pointed it out, almost every organ in the human male was a critique of Stanley's drinking, gambling, and womanizing: the heart, the kidneys, the lungs, the intestines, you name it, she had accompanying notes that described his excessive alcohol consumption, his bad diet, his aggressiveness and poor sexual performance. It went on and on. I could see how this wouldn't be appropriate for certain schoolchildren.

"She sabotaged me. All on account of me sleeping with a barmaid at our local. OK, I shouldn't have done it, but to ruin my livelihood! Ten thousand books I can't sell! And I can't sue anyone because I signed the approval form. I delivered the book to the printers myself. Of course she lost everything too, but she doesn't care. That's how vindictive women are. It was worth it, she says, just to put me in the ground. Have you ever heard such venom? You're not likely to. Now I'm waiting for the creditors to come knocking. I can't even pay the rent on this office. So as much as I'd like to publish your delightful little satire . . ."

"It's not a satire."

"It's not?"

"No."

He looked down at the manuscript and thumbed through it quickly. "This is on the level?"

I nodded.

"Then this would be a textbook for young criminals?"

I nodded again.

"You could get both of us arrested for publishing this."

"I'm willing to risk it if you are."

He leaned back into his chair and said, "How about that." He looked at the manuscript again, and a little while later he said, "Well, well."

He closed his eyes a moment before opening them again. The moment seemed endless, but it was probably only half that.

"What made you come to me?" he asked.

"Everyone else said no."

"Of course they did," he said, chuckling. That seemed to please him no end.

His mouth widened into a smile, and he jumped up as though answering a call to duty, that smile just kept on widening and widening, until my mouth hurt.

•

I ran all the way to Harry's and stumbled up the front steps. I was so excited I almost forgot the secret knock. It was too elaborate. Four knocks, a pause, one knock, a pause, three knocks, then my voice saying, "Hey, Harry. It's me, Martin." If you ask me, we could've done just as well without the knocks, but Harry was inflexible about it. I fumbled the knocks all right: two . . . pause . . . three—no, better start again . . . I heard the ominous sound of a shotgun pumping into readiness. "It's me, Harry!" I said in a fluster. Realizing my mistake, I ducked down, waiting for the spray of bullets. They didn't come. A series of clicks and slides. Harry was going through the tedious routine of unlocking the dead bolts. It took longer than usual. He must've added a couple of new ones. The door crept open. Harry stood there in his underwear, shotgun in one hand and an ax in the other. His eyes were full of fire and fear. I couldn't wait. I told him the news.

"I found a publisher! He loves it! He's from England, so he grew up on a diet of scandal! He's not afraid to put himself on the line. He loves your book! He's putting everything into it! The book's going straight into publication!"

Harry was too stunned to speak. He was frozen solid. Have you ever seen a man congeal from good news? It's hilarious.

"Waaa—what did you say?"

"We did it! Your book is going to be a book!"

Relief and fear and love and terror and elation crowded his face. Even the most self-confident egotists have a secret part of themselves that doubts anything will ever go right. That part of Harry was going into tumult. It was just so unexpected. Harry's ESP had a blind spot because of that pessimistic voice, which shouted louder than the prophetic whispers of his third eye. He laughed and cried and raised his shotgun in the air and fired. The ceiling came down in large plaster chunks. It was terrifying. He hugged me. We danced around the hallway, but it was hard to enjoy it because Harry still held the shotgun and the ax. He tried to kiss me on the mouth again, but this time I was ready for it. I gave him my cheek instead. He kissed my ear. As we kept on spinning, Harry's dead leg swung around and knocked over the side table. This was it! His book! His baby! His legacy! His immortality!

•

The next few weeks passed in a blur. Thrilling times! I went into Stanley's office almost every day. We did everything together: chose the typeface, reorganized the chapters. He asked me to ask the mystery author to pen a preface and Harry went to work on it, day and night, guarding it from my eyes. Stanley had sold everything he owned to get the money to pay the printers. "They won't know what hit them," he kept saying. "They'll be in an uproar when it lands on the shelves. Then it'll be banned. Free publicity! There's nothing like censorship to boost a book's sales. There'll be moral outrage! Banned copies will pass surreptitiously from hand to hand! The book will live in the shadows and grow like mushrooms in the dark and the damp! Then a lone voice, someone will say, 'Ho! This is genius!' Then the other heads who were shaking in disgust will start nodding in assent! Our champion will be someone who may not believe a word of what he's saying. That doesn't matter to us. Luckily, some critics just have to go against the grain, no matter what the grain is. The grain could be 'Love your neighbor' and the critic will say, 'No! Detest him, the worm!'"

Stanley went into this rant every day. It was always the same. He was predicting big things for Harry's book, although he kept pressing me to reveal the author's name. "Nothing doing," I always said. "On the day of printing, all will be revealed." Stanley hit the desk. He did everything he could to wheedle it out of me. "I'm putting myself on the line here, Marty—how do I know the author isn't a pedophile? I mean, scandal is one thing, you know I'm not afraid of it, but no one would touch the book if the author's hands had been all over some kid."

I gave him my word Harry was just an ordinary run-of-the-mill murdering thief.

•

One day Stanley's wife came in to see what he was up to. She was a thin attractive woman with a pointy nose that didn't look sculpted so much as it looked like it had been sharpened on a grinder. She circled the office and tried to take a peek at the manuscript on his desk, but he threw a newspaper on top of it.

"What do you want, hag?"

"You're up to something."

He didn't answer, just gave her a smile that said, "Maybe I am, you rotten wench, but it's none of your fucking business."

She turned to me and started examining. "I know you from somewhere."

"I don't think so."

"Did you ask me for money on a train once?"

I said I had never asked anyone for money on a train, which was not true, because once I had asked someone for money on a train.

"All right, visit over," Stanley said, grabbing her by the shoulders and pushing her out of the office.

"OK, OK! I just came to ask you for a divorce!"

"Whenever you want. Although I'd prefer to be a widower."

"Fuck up and die, you bastard!"

Once he had her in the corridor, he slammed the door in her face and said to me, "Call a locksmith. We have to get the locks changed, then let's get back to work."

Stanley had given Harry a couple of little tasks to do. The first was the title, and Harry had handed me a sheet of paper with his suggestions. I sat down and read over the list. *A Handbook for Criminals, A Handbook for Young Criminals, The Handbook of Crime for Young Criminals and Toddlers, Crime: How to Do It, Breaking the Law by Numbers, Felony for Dummies, Step-by-Step Guide to Crime, Lawlessness Is Easy!* . . . The list went on.

Then came the problem of the preface. Harry had given me his first draft and asked me to pass it on to Stanley untouched. I couldn't touch it even if I wanted to. It was the outpouring of a man on the edge. It went like this:

> There are men put on this earth to make laws designed to break the spirits of men. Then there are those put here to have their spirits broken by those put here to break them. Then there are those who are here to break the laws that break the men who break the spirits of other men. I am one of those men.
>
> —*the author*

Stanley sent it back and told him to try again. Harry's second attempt was no better.

> They have you in their sights. They have you on their list. They want to turn the product of your semen's blood into steam engines that churn out power to light up their lives. Well I'm here to tell you if you read this book and follow its advice you can fill your own pockets with gold for a change and let someone else's children carry the stone tablets for the corpulent Egyptian taskmasters. I say, why not get them first?
>
> —*the author*

Stanley didn't think anything that sounded bitter or insane would be good for sales. I could see his point. I gently asked Harry to take one more crack at it. His third attempt I opened and read as the bus rolled toward the city. It read simply:

Ah-ha! Worship me! You cunts!
                                  —*the author*

I tore it up and composed my own preface and put Harry's name to it.

The world's a fat place, so fat you'd think there's enough to go around. There isn't. So some have to grab what they can without following the rules because the rules state that they get next to nothing. Most stumble along this path unguided, unmapped. By writing this book, I am not trying to cause a revolution, just giving some roadside assistance to the disadvantaged on the road less traveled by lighting it a little, showing the potholes and the pitfalls, putting up entry and exit signs and speed limits.

Drive well, you young thugs, drive well . . .
                                  —*the author*

Finally the day of printing arrived. I had to go to Stanley's office and disclose the author's name. Harry and I sat in the backyard smoking cigarettes for breakfast. He had gone beyond anxiety; his hands were shaking vigorously. We both tried not to notice it, and when I had to light his cigarette for him, we pretended it was because I was his long-serving houseboy. I said, "There you go, sir," and he replied, "Thanks, boy."

Above us the sky was a strange color, the same algae green as his swimming pool.

"This publisher. Can we trust him?" Harry asked.

"Implicitly."

"Is he going to screw us?"

"No."

"When you speak to him next, tell him I've killed seventeen men, two women, and a child."

"You killed a child?"

"Well—a young adult."

Harry handed me a sheet of paper. On it was a list of acknowledgments. I took it and went off to fulfill our destinies, hitting the streets with my arms swinging at both sides. That's how you walk when you're doing destiny's dirty work.

I met Stanley at his office. He was too excited to sit. In the first two minutes after I arrived, he went from the door to the window three times, making strange gestures with his hands as if strangling chickens.

"This is it, mate—the printers are standing by. I'm ready for the name now."

"OK, here it is. The man who wrote The Handbook of Crime is Harry West."

Stanley's mouth opened and stayed that way as he let out a long throaty exhale.

"Who?"

"Harry West!"

"Never heard of him."

I ran through his rap sheet, not leaving anything out. "Harry West," Stanley said as he wrote the name down, sounding a little disappointed. Then, as I fed him information, Stanley composed a biography for the "about the author" section. It ran like this:

> Harry West was born in Sydney in 1922. For the next fifty-five years he broke every law in the Southern Hemisphere. He escaped from custody and is currently a fugitive from justice.

"And Harry's written a list of acknowledgments he wants to go in the front," I said.

"Fine."

Stanley took a look at it. It was just your standard page of thanks that precedes a life's work.

> I would like to acknowledge my father for giving me a taste for violence, my grandfather for giving my father a taste for violence, who in turn gave it to me. I have no children, so I've had to give it to acquaintances and passersby. I would also like to acknowledge the New South Wales criminal justice system for teaching me about injustice, the New South Wales police force for their inde-fatigable corruption and tireless brutality, violence in cinema for desensitizing my victims so they take longer to say ouch, my victims for losing, my victors for showing me there is no dishonor in a bul-let in the thigh, and finally my editor, friend, and brother in isola-tion, Martin Dean.

"Are you sure you want your name on this?" Stanley asked me.

"Why not?" I asked stupidly, knowing why not. I was practically admitting to a crime: harboring a known fugitive and editing his opus. "I think so," I said.

"Think about it a second."

I thought about it. Was I making a mistake? It was obvious there was no real reason my involvement needed to be mentioned in any way. But this was my work too. I had broken my back to get this book this far, and I wanted the world to know it.

"Yeah, leave it in."

"OK then, well, we're all ready to go. I'm going to run this down to the printers. Afterward, can I meet him?"

"I don't know if that's such a hot idea right now."

"Why?"

"He's not well at the moment. He's a little . . . on edge. Maybe when the book's out in the stores. When will that be, by the way?"

"Three weeks."

"I can't believe it's really happening."

"You bet your arse," he said, and just before he left the office, Stanley turned to me with a strange, far-off look on his face and said, "Tell Harry I think he's a genius."

I said that I would.

•

"What did he say when you told him my name? What was the look on his face? Tell me everything. Don't leave anything out," Harry said breathlessly from his front door as I headed up the drive.

"He was impressed," I lied. "He'd heard of you."

"Of course he's heard of me. A man doesn't kill steadily for fifty years without making a name for himself. So when's it in the stores?"

"Three weeks."

"Three weeks! *Fuck!*"

There was nothing left to be done but wait. Everything was sorted. I had that feeling of satisfaction and anticlimax that comes with the completion of a job. Now I knew how all those Egyptian slaves must have felt when the pointy stone was put on top of the pyramid of Giza and they all had to stand around waiting for the cement to dry. Also I felt a sense of disquiet. I had been involved in something meaningful for the second time in my life, after the suggestion box; now what the fuck was I going to do? The ambition rising in my chest had no further outlet. That was annoying.

After a few hours of forecasting our phenomenal success one minute and dismal failure the next, I dragged myself back home to look after my mother. The chemotherapy and regular bombardments of radiation left her fatigued all the time, she had lost weight and some of her hair, and moved around the house by groping the walls. It was clear the body she was inhabiting was fast becoming uninhabitable. The only pleasant surprise was my father, who actually turned out to be not that dissimilar to a human being, and one of the nice ones too. He became kind to my mother, loving, and supportive at a level far deeper and more committed than either she or I had expected of him. So did I really need to linger there all the time? Now that I had been in the world, every fiber of my being revolted at the idea of spending another second in that miserable town. That's why you should never make an unbreakable bond. You never know what the fibers of your being are going to feel like doing later on down the track.

Those weeks of waiting were an intricate and elaborate torture. I'd always known there are 1,440 minutes in a day, but during those three weeks I *felt* them, profoundly. I was as jumpy as naked wires. I could nibble, but I couldn't eat. I could close my eyes, but I couldn't sleep. I could stand under the shower, but I couldn't get wet. The days stood their ground like monuments to timelessness.

Somehow, magically, the day of publication arrived. At three in the morning, I caught a bus into the city. On the way I had the smug feeling that I was a famous person who had sat down in a public place and was only waiting for someone to turn around and scream, "Hey! There's so-and-so!" That was me: I was So-and-So. It felt good.

A city is a strange place for dawn. The sun just can't seem to make any headway in the cold streets, and it took two hours to get sunny. I walked down George Street past a crowd of partygoers falling over each other and kissing and cursing the unwanted arrival of daytime. They sang in my face as they walked by, a drunken song, to which I did a little dance that must have been OK because they all cheered me. I cheered them back. It was cheery.

Dymocks bookshop had promised to put a copy in the window. I was two hours early. I smoked some cigarettes. I smiled, just for something to do. I pushed the crescent moons of my fingernails down into the fingers. A thread from my shirt took me through from eight to eight-thirty. Then, at a few minutes to nine, a woman appeared inside the shop. I don't know how she got in. Maybe there was a back entrance. Maybe she slept there overnight. But what was she doing in there? She was just leaning against the counter, as if she were a customer. And then, why was she messing around with the cash register? Why was that important *now*? When bookstores have a new book to put in a window, that should be the first priority. It's obvious!

She got down on her knees and cut open the lid of a cardboard box with a knife. She took a handful of copies and walked toward the window. This was it! Stepping up on the little podium, she placed the copies on an empty stand. When I saw the books, my heart fell out.

This is what I saw:

> *The Handbook of Crime*, by Terry Dean

What's this? What's this? I had to take a closer look. Terry Dean? Terry Dean! How the hell did this happen? I ran to the doors. They were still locked. I banged on the glass. The woman inside the shop peered at me from the other side.

"What do you want?"

"That book! *The Handbook of Crime*! I have to see it!"

"We don't open for another ten minutes."

"I need it now!" I shouted as I pounded on the door. She muttered a cruel insult under her breath. I think it was "book lover." There was nothing I could do. She wouldn't open the door. I ran back to the window and pressed my eyeballs against the glass. I could see the front cover. It said, in color with a star around it,

> A book by fugitive Terry Dean—written on the lam!

I couldn't work it out. Nowhere on the cover was there any mention of Harry. Shit! Harry! He'd . . . A steel door slammed shut inside my head. My brain wouldn't let me think about Harry. It was too perilous.

On the nose of nine o'clock the store opened and I rushed inside, grabbed a copy of *The Handbook of Crime,* and flicked through it frenetically. The "about the author" section was entirely different. It was Terry's life story, and the dedication said simply, "To Martin, my brother and editor."

Stanley had double-crossed us! But how? I'd never mentioned that I was Terry's brother! I pushed some money at the clerk and ran out of the store without waiting for change. I ran all the way to Stanley's office. When I burst through the front door, he was standing at his desk, talking on the phone, saying, "No, he can't give an interview. He just can't. He's a fugitive, that's why."

He hung up and beamed at me triumphantly. "The phone's been ringing off the hook! There's a shit storm! It's better than I ever anticipated!"

"What have you done?"

"I guarantee every copy will be gone by this afternoon. I've just ordered another fifty thousand to be printed. First day, and it's a hit!"

"BUT TERRY DIDN'T WRITE IT!"

"OK, come on, Martin. The cat's out of the bag. I know you're Terry's brother. You tried to keep that secret from me, you naughty boy. Actually, believe it or not, you know what put me onto the idea? My fucking ex-wife! She recognized you from the papers. It hit her a couple of hours after she left that day and she called me, demanding to know what I was publishing with Terry Dean. Then it hit me. Of course! It was so obvious! Harry West was a pseudonym for Terry Dean! It's not clever like an anagram or anything, but it is bullshit. Problem is, pseudonyms aren't going to sell books, my friend. Not when the author is as famous as your brother is!"

I moved closer to Stanley's desk, wondering if I was strong enough to pick it up and squash him with it.

"Listen to me, you dopey bastard," I growled. "Terry didn't write it! Harry did! Oh my God! Harry! Harry is going to explode!"

"Really. And who is this Harry?"

"He was Terry's mentor."

Stanley looked at me curiously for a long time. "Come on, mate, give it up."

"I'm telling you. You've fucked up! Harry's going to go on a rampage! He'll tear us all to pieces, you idiot!"

Stanley's face looked as if it were tossing up between smiling and frowning and finally settled for an uncomfortable combination of the two. "Are you serious?"

"Deadly serious."

"You're saying, then, that Terry didn't write this book?"

"Terry can't write his name in the snow with his piss!"

"Really?"

"Really!"

"Oh," Stanley said, before burying his face behind a pile of papers. He picked up a pencil and started scrawling something. I went over and ripped it out of his hands. This is what he'd written: "Oops!"

"Oops! Oops? You don't know! You don't know Harry! He'll kill me! Then he'll kill you! Then he'll kill Terry and then he'll kill himself!"

"Why can't he be first?" Stanley cried absurdly. He stood, buttoned up his jacket, unbuttoned it, and sat down. He finally had the sense to panic.

"Didn't you think of at least *checking* my story? Didn't you think to find out about Harry?"

"Now, hang on . . ."

"Call them back!"

"Who?"

"The press! The publishers! Everyone!"

"Now, wait a tic!"

"Do it!"

"I can't!"

"But it's a lie!"

"Sit down. Calm down. We have to think about this. Are we thinking? Let's think. OK. Think. Are you thinking? I'm not. I don't have a thought in my head. Stop looking at me for a second. I can't think when someone's looking at me. Turn around. I mean it, Martin, turn around."

Reluctantly, I half swiveled my body so I was facing the wall. I wanted to smash my head against it. I couldn't believe it! Here was Terry again! Taking center stage again! What about me? When was it going to be my time?

Stanley rattled off thoughts that stank up the room. "OK. OK. OK. So . . . what we had, with *The Handbook of Crime*, was a literary scandal. Spectacular. Controversial. Polemical. That we already have. But now it turns out the author is in fact not the author. That means . . . what we *now* have, on top of the scandal . . . is a literary hoax."

"A what?"

"OK. You can turn around now."

When I swiveled back, Stanley was beaming at me triumphantly. "Two in one!" he shouted joyously.

"Stanley—" I started.

"This is brilliant! It'll serve us well. Tell Harry to be patient—in a year or two, we'll leak out the truth. He'll be famous."

"A year or two!"

"Sure, what's the rush?"

"You still don't get it! Harry will think I was in on this. He'll think I've betrayed him. This is his legacy to the world! You have to tell him! You have to tell him it was your own fault, that you made a mistake! You fool—he's going to kill us!"

"So what? Let him come. I'm not afraid! If I have to die, let it be for a book. Yes, I like it! Let it be for *this* book. Yes! Bring him on!"

Stanley held his fist up in the air as if it were an award he'd just won. Can you beat that? This was the worst crisis imaginable, and I was in the company of a man right at the time he'd found something to die for. He looked disgustingly, inappropriately peaceful. I wanted to tear his lips off.

•

I took a cab to Harry's, thinking I was going to have to tread very, very carefully. Harry loved me, and I loved him, but that didn't mean he was above putting a bullet between my eyes. That's what love is all about, after all. I rolled down the taxi window. Outside, the air was supernaturally still, as in a windowless room. Nothing stirred. It was as if the hatch on the world had been hermetically sealed and we were, all of us, shut in.

I did the secret knock and then the not-so-secret knock, the one anyone can do. I hollered his name. I hollered an apology. It was a waste of hollering—he wasn't home. What should I do? A cab sailed past and I hailed it and went back into the city, where I wandered aimlessly through the streets, deep in my tumult. The level of activity made my head spin, and it irritated me that no one else looked lost. A little sad and lonely, maybe, but they knew where they were going. I bumped into people on purpose, in the irrational hope of eliciting some kind of sympathetic reaction. The faces of a city take on a supremely cruel and indifferent quality when you wander through it in the midst of a personal crisis. It's depressing that nobody stops to hold your hand.

I went into a pub, the Park View, took a seat at the bar, and didn't dwell on the lack of a park or a view. I ordered a beer. A song was on the radio, a nice cheery love song that clashed with my mood. I drained the beer quickly. The pub was empty except for two old drunk men who were bickering about someone named Gazza; one of the old men thought Gazza was pussy-whipped by his new bride, while the other thought Gazza had her on the ropes. Either way, the upshot was that Gazza wasn't coming out to the pub as often as he used to, and it just wasn't the same without him. I nodded in sadness, and stared at my empty glass as if it had wronged me for the last time.

Then the news came over the radio and my ears went into high alert. Fugitive Terry Dean had written a scandalous book instructing would-be criminals on how to break the law. The most recent development in the story: the publisher of *The Handbook of Crime* was under arrest.

So! Stanley was under arrest! Just as well, I decided. At least that would keep him safe from Harry for a while. I supposed they couldn't hold him long. When the police are hunting for someone they can't find, it just gives them relief to arrest someone connected to him.

While I contemplated Stanley behind bars, and the possibility that as the credited editor, I might be the one they came for next, the last story of the news came on: fugitive Harry West had climbed to the top of the Harbor Bridge armed to the teeth and was threatening to jump. The story added a little afterthought which put it all into perspective: if Harry West plummeted to his death, he would be the first person to commit suicide from the Sydney Harbor Bridge on live television. Yes, it made perfect sense. Terry had robbed him of the democratic cooperative, and Stanley had pulled *The Handbook of Crime* from under his feet. Harry was desperate to leave his legacy, any legacy. First person to be broadcasted suiciding off Sydney's bridge and in color too. No wonder Harry had taken his arsenal up there. Anyone tried to jump first, Harry would shoot them before they got a toe near the edge.

I ran out of the pub, leapt into a moving cab, and hightailed it to the bridge. If he was armed I supposed there'd be a chance he'd shoot me, but I had to explain that this was a mistake that could be cleared up in a day or two. I had the nauseating feeling that something terrible was going to happen on that bridge. He was going to toss himself into the drink; that seemed unavoidable. But knowing Harry, he'd want to drag as many souls into the abyss with him as possible. He wanted to turn the harbor red, I just knew it.

The midday sun was in my eyes, and through the glare I saw the bridge in the distance. Police blocked entry on either side and were scratching their heads over what to do with commuters trapped in the middle. Panicky policemen were directing people all over the place, but there was too much chaos. One of the bewildered cops seemed to be pointing in the direction of the water.

As I left my cab in the traffic jam, the driver made it clear he didn't like it that I was ending our relationship so unexpectedly. People in uniforms were pouring in from everywhere. More policemen, firemen, ambulances, and media trucks weaved through parked cars. The emergency services were in a muddle. None of them knew what they were supposed to do. The intended victim was also the alleged perpetrator. It was confusing. On the one hand, he had a gun, but on the other hand, he was only threatening to use it on himself. They wanted to shoot him down, but can you shoot a man threatening suicide? That's just what he wants.

I ran through the narrow passageway between halted cars and quickly found myself at a line of policemen. I ran right through their long yellow ribbon of tape and explained to the cop screaming at me that I was a close friend of Harry West and might be able to talk him down. In their confusion, they let me through.

I could see him, way up top. He was just a little speck up there, like a little plastic groom on a wedding cake. It was a long way up, but I had to go to him.

A tremendous wind was blowing. It was difficult to hold on. As I climbed, my stomach became the dominant organ, and I could feel nothing but its grind. Below I could see the ocean, the green suburbs, a smattering of houses. The wind made the whole bridge creak and did her best to throw me off balance. I thought: What am I doing here? It's not my business! I wondered why I didn't just let him take his big dive. I felt this was my fault, he was my responsibility, as were the people he might kill. But why? How do I fit in? I'm no Christ figure. I don't have a savior complex. The whole human race could get acute angina for all I care.

Ruminations such as these and the realization that the men in my life,

Harry and Terry and Stanley, with their little projects were dragging me with them down into the void, should be kept for after the event, over a mug of hot chocolate, not during the event, at the edge of a terrifying precipice. I had stopped my ascent to contemplate the existential meaning of it all. As usual, I couldn't help myself. On that shaky metal stepladder I thought: One man's dream is another man's anchor. One swims, the other sinks, and in the swimmer's pool too—a double insult. Meanwhile, the wind was threatening to toss me into the harbor. I knew then and there that pondering the significance of an action in the middle of the action is just not right.

I climbed on. I could hear him now. Harry was yelling, the wind carrying his voice to me before I could even see his face. At least I think it was Harry. Either that or the wind had just called me a bastard.

My shoe slipped. I looked down at the water and trembled from top to bottom. It looked like a flat blue slab of concrete.

"Thanks for the backstab, mate!"

Harry was leaning against a steel rail, the one I was white-knuckled clutching for dear life. To drag his leg all the way up that bridge must have been a nightmare. Maybe it was out of exhaustion that he let himself sway, and nearly topple over, with the wind.

His face was all shriveled up. He'd frowned so much he'd actually broken his face. His worry lines had snapped.

"Harry, it was a mistake!" I shouted.

"It doesn't matter anymore."

"But we can fix it! Come down and everyone will know the book is yours!"

"It's too late, Martin! I've seen it!"

"Seen what?"

"The hour of my death!"

"When?"

"What time is it now?"

"Harry, don't jump!"

"I won't! I'll fall! You can't tell a person not to fall! That's gravity's business, not mine!" He was laughing from fear, from hysteria. His eyes were on all those guns pointing up at him from below. His paranoia had finally reached enlightenment. The paranoid fantasies and reality were experiencing absolute fusion.

"I fall . . . I'm gone . . . there's another war . . . an earthquake . . . and the return of the Madonna . . . only now she's a singer . . . but still a virgin . . . and now sexual revolution . . . and marble-wash jeans . . ."

His ESP was reaching into the infinite, blinding him to the present. His small, twitchy eyes, which usually darted around in their sockets, had finally frozen solid; they were traveling, exploring and seeing everything. Everything.

"Computers . . . everyone has one . . . in their homes . . . and they're fat . . . everyone's so fat . . ."

He was out of control, prognosticating like crazy! He could see the whole of human future mapped out. He was flicking through the pages! It was too much for him. "She's dead! She's dead!" Who? He couldn't make sense of what he was seeing. "A third world war! A fourth! A fifth! A tenth! It never ends! They're dead!" Who's dead? "The astronaut! The president! The princess! Another president! Your wife! Now you! Now your son! Everyone! Everyone!" It went on for hundreds of years, perhaps thousands. So humanity was going to persist after all. His eyes were pushing through space and time. He wasn't missing a thing.

Harry's line of communication with the infinite was broken by the wail of sirens starting up again. We looked down and saw the police and the media trucks backing away. Everyone was leaving.

"Where the fuck are you going?" Harry screamed to the world below.

"Hang on," I said. "I'll go see."

Halfway down I ran into a petrified reporter who'd been overcome with vertigo during his climb and couldn't move up or down the rail.

"What's going on?"

"Haven't you heard? They've got Terry Dean trapped! He's taken hostages! There's going to be a showdown!"

The reporter's voice was excited, but he had the kind of deadpan face you usually see behind the wheel of a hearse. I climbed back up to Harry.

"What is it?" he asked.

"Terry," I said, dreading his reaction.

Harry lowered his head, watched wistfully as the last of the reporters sped away.

"Mate," I said, "I have to go and see if I can help Terry."

"Fine. Go."

"I'm sorry, I—"

"Go!"

I climbed down, my eyes focused on the handrail and my feet, and before I reached the bottom I heard the blast of a gun, the sound of a body whistling through the air, and a splash below that was really more of a thud.

That was it.

That was Harry.

Goodbye, Harry.

•

The police had Terry cornered in a bowling alley. I knew the whole of Australia would be rushing there as if they were water and my brother was the drain, so I jumped in a taxi and promised the driver untold riches if he could get as close to the speed of light as a V6 will get you. When you're hurrying off to save your brother's life you don't fret over pennies, so every time his foot touched the brakes, I threw money in his lap. When he reached for the street directory, I tore exactly one third of my remaining hair out. It's a bad sign when the driver cranes his head back to look at a street sign he's just passed.

No directions were necessary, though; a real cavalcade of vehicles and bodies was surging through the streets in one direction: police cars, ambulances, fire engines, army Jeeps, media trucks, ice cream vans, spectators, gardeners, rabbis, anyone in Sydney who owned a radio and wanted to take part in a historical event.

Everyone wants a ringside seat for history in the making. Who'd turn down the opportunity to watch the back of Kennedy's head explode if given a ticket to Dallas in '63, or the falling of the Berlin Wall? People who *were* there speak as if their clothes were stained with JFK's cerebrum, as if the Berlin Wall fell from their own persistent nudging. No one wants to have missed anything, like sneezing during a small earthquake and wondering why everyone is screaming. The capture and possible killing of Terry Dean was Australia's biggest earthquake in fifty years, which is why they got to that bowling alley any way they could.

I leapt from the taxi and slid ungracefully over the bonnets of cars, cracking my hip on the side mirror of a Ford. I could see it: the bowling alley. It looked like the whole New South Wales police force was there. Snipers were taking their positions on the roof and in the trees in the children's park opposite. One sniper was climbing up the jungle gym, two were balancing on a seesaw.

I couldn't get through the mob. I was stuck. I shouted, "I'm Martin Dean! Terry Dean's brother!" They caught on. They cleared a path and let me through, then I got stuck again. A few people around me made getting me inside their life's mission, lifting me up on top of the crowd— I rode on a hundred shoulders like a rock god. I was getting closer, but sometimes the crowd pushed me in different directions. At one point I was going across, not forward. I shouted, "Forward! Forward!" as if I were Captain Ahab and that bowling alley was my great white whale.

Then I heard the crowd shouting something new: "Let her through! Let her through!" I craned my neck around. I couldn't see who they were referring to. "It's his mother! Terry Dean's mother!" they cried. Then I saw her: my mother, coming from the opposite direction, rising and falling on the roll of the human sea. She waved to me. I waved back. We were both being propelled toward our family's destiny. I could hear her now. She was shouting: "It's the double! The double! We've got him cornered!" She was off her head! And the crowd was rushing us so fast now we almost collided. They dropped us on the ground in front of the police, who were trying to keep the crowd and the media back at the same time. Both groups were screaming outrage. We had to squeeze into the circle of police and start answering questions. We showed them ID. I just wanted to get inside, but my mother wasn't helping with her crazy ranting about the doppelgänger. She *was* Terry Dean's mother, she said, but the man inside was not her son. They couldn't work it out. I had to shout over her: "I can get him to come out peacefully! Just give me a chance!" But the cops had different ideas. It dawned on me that they didn't want him to leave that bowling alley alive. I had to snap into action. I said, "So what, you want to make a martyr out of him? You want his name to go down in history as another outlaw massacred by the police? If you kill him, no one will remember his crimes! You'll turn him into a hero! Like Ned Kelly! And you'll be the bad guys. Let him go to trial, where all his brutality will come to light. Then the hero will be the man who captures him alive! Anyone can shoot a man, just as anyone can shoot a wild boar, then run around screaming, I got him! I got him! But capturing a wild boar with your bare hands—that takes guts!"

I had to say this whole speech with my hand over my mother's mouth, and she was biting me viciously. She'd really gone crazy. "Shoot to kill!" she screamed when I took my hand away. "Aren't you his mother?" they asked, confused. They couldn't grasp the meaning of this evil-twin business.

Holding my brother's fate in the balance, the policemen conferred among themselves, whispering malignantly, almost violently.

"OK, you can go in," they said to me, and unfortunately, they let my mother in too.

The bowling alley was on the second floor. There was a policeman on every step of the concrete staircase, eyes glowering. I thought: These men are unspeakably dangerous, like understudies waiting to be called to be the star, their raging egos determined not to be undone by performance anxiety. On the way up, a detective filled us in. As far as he knew, Terry had gone into the alley while Kevin Hardy, the three-time world champion, was rolling a few. There were unsubstantiated rumors that during competition Hardy had paid someone behind the pins to take out those he missed with the end of a broomstick. Because the accusations were shaky, Terry hadn't gone in there to kill him, only to snap his bowling fingers, including the pinkie, just in case he was one of those rare bowlers who used the pinkie for extra spin. Afterward, Terry was tempted by a pair of pretty girls working behind the counter. The groupie phenomenon, the undeniable perk of celebrity, had always been too much for Terry to resist. Unfortunately, once he'd made his choice between the two girls, the jilted one called the police almost immediately, so by the time Terry had broken Kevin's hand, had sex with the groupie, and was ready to leave, he was already trapped.

Now Terry was kneeling down in the middle of the last lane, gun in his hand, using four hostages as a human shield. Police were positioned at every point of the bowling alley; you could even see the black nozzle of a sniper's rifle poking out between the pins. They had him covered, and I knew instantly that if they could take the shot, they would, but he was well hidden behind a row of faces contorted in terror.

"You!" my mother shouted. The police held her back. They didn't trust Terry not to shoot his own mother, especially given her crazy story that he was not her real son but some insidious clone.

"Terry," I shouted, "it's me, Marty." I didn't get the chance to say anything else before my mother started up.

"Who are you?" she cried.

"Mum? Shit, Marty, get her out of here, will you?"

He was right, of course. When a man is staging his final bloody showdown, he doesn't want his mother loitering around.

I tried persuading her to leave, but she wouldn't hear of it.

"Stop cowering behind those poor people, you impostor!" she screamed.

"Mum, get out of here!" Terry shouted.

"Don't call me Mum! I don't know who you are or how you got my son's face, but you can't fool me!"

"Terry, give yourself up!" I shouted.

"Why?"

"They'll kill you!"

"And? Look, mate, the only thing that's bugging me is that this whole scene is getting a bit boring. Hang on a sec."

There was frantic whispering over at the human shield. Suddenly they started to move. They edged to the bowling ball racks, then back to the lane. Then it went! A ball flew down the center of the lane. Terry was bowling! The policemen's eyes watched the ball fly toward the pins. There was a profound silence that verged on the religious. A strike! Terry had done it! He took out all ten pins! The crowd seemed to shout with one voice, reminding me how man is often stupid alone, but in packs he is absolutely cretinous. They might have been police at the dénouement of a long manhunt, but they were also sport-loving Australians—and nothing starts the heart beating faster than a victory, no matter how bloodthirsty the victor.

At the moment the ball hit the pins, a bullet hit Terry. That ball was Terry's ploy to make a run for it, but not all police are that gullible or even like bowling.

He lay on the lane, smeared in his own blood, shouting, "My ankle! Again in the ankle! The exact same spot, you mongrels! That's never gonna heal!" and he lay there while overcome by forty policemen all competing to be the one to walk him outside in the bright flashing glare of the paparazzi, to get their little dose of immortality.

Farewell

I'm no expert on linguistics or the etymology of words, so I have no idea if the word "banana" really was the best-sounding collection of syllables around to describe a long yellow arc-shaped fruit, but I can say that whoever coined the phrase "media circus" really knew what he was talking about. There's simply no better description of a bunch of journalists clamoring for quotes and photographs, although "media primates," "media rioting mob," or "explosion of a media supernova" might do just as well. Outside the courthouse where Terry's trial was to take place, there were hundreds of them—sweaty-faced leering men and women of the press, pushing and elbowing and jeering and by their appalling behavior generally degrading the human race in the name of public interest.

Inside, the courtroom was standing room only. As Terry denied none of the charges, it was more a process than a trial, and his court-appointed barrister was there to navigate Terry through the bureaucracy of the system rather than aid him in an actual defense. Terry had no defense. He admitted everything; he had to—his infamy was tied up in it. To deny what he had been trying to do would have been like the crusaders explaining their journey into the Islamic world by saying they were just out for a long walk.

Terry sat defiantly next to his lawyer, and when the judge began his deliberations, he rubbed his hands together as though he were about to be sentenced to two scoops of vanilla ice cream. Speaking slowly and solemnly, like a seasoned actor getting his one and only chance to deliver Hamlet's soliloquy, the judge projected his voice to the back of the courtroom with the words, "I sentence you to *life imprisonment*." It was a bravura performance. Everyone let out the typical murmur that follows sentencing, though it was just for show. No one was surprised. There was no other way it could have gone down. What did come as a surprise, however—though you'd think by now I would've been accustomed to the taste of ironies squeezed from the cosmic juicer—is that the prison Terry was sentenced to was the one in our hometown.

That's right.

Our prison. In our town.

Automatically, I looked to my father. Terry was sentenced to spend the remainder of his life in the prison his father had built, the prison that lay 1½ miles from our front door.

●

With their prodigal son home but not home, detained in a building that we could see from both the front veranda and the kitchen window, the sweaty grip that my mother and father had on their sanity began to loosen at an alarming rate. While there was some comfort having him safe from eager police snipers, to have him so tantalizingly out of reach was a torment that made it impossible to tell which of my parents had drifted further from light and life; they were dissolving so fast, each in his or her own sad way, you'd have thought it was a competition. It was like living with two ghosts who had recently accepted their death, who had given up trying to blend with the living. They had finally recognized their transparency for what it was.

With a curious, crazed look of joy on her face, my mother took up a new project: she framed every photograph of Terry and me as children and nailed them to every available wall space in the house. There was not a photo in the house of us over the age of thirteen, as if by growing up we had betrayed her. And I can see my father now too, sitting on the far right corner of the veranda, which allowed a view of the prison unobscured by treetops, binoculars pressed up against his eyeballs, trying to catch a glimpse of his son. He spent so many hours a day peering through those binoculars that when he finally put them down to rest, his eyes strained to see us. Sometimes he'd shout, "There he is!" I'd come running out to see, but he always refused me permission to use his precious binoculars. "You've done enough damage," he'd say inexplicably, as if my gaze were like that of an ugly Greek witch. After a while I stopped asking, and when I heard my father shout, "There he is again! He's in the yard! He's telling a joke to a group of inmates! They're laughing! He looks like he's having a ball!" I didn't move a muscle. Of course, I could've gotten my own binoculars, but I didn't dare. In truth, I didn't think he could see anything at all.

Our town became a place of pilgrimage for journalists, historians, students, and scores of curvy women with teased hair and excessive makeup who turned up at the prison gates to visit Terry. Most were turned away and wound up wandering around town, many clutching first and only editions of *The Handbook of Crime*. The book had been ripped from the shelves on the day of publication and quickly banned for all time. It was already a collector's item. The obsessive fans were searching the town for guess who? *Me!* They wanted me, as credited editor, to sign it! At first it gave me a thrill to finally be the focus of attention, but I rapidly couldn't stand it. Every autograph fiend hounded me with endless questions about Terry.

Again, Terry.

It was in this throng of star-hungry morons that I ran into Dave! He was wearing a suit but no tie, and his hair was neatly combed back. He'd really cleaned himself up. He was going for a new life. Apparently he'd found God, which made him less violent but no less unendurable. I couldn't get away from him; he was hell-bent on saving me. "You like books, Martin. You always did. But have you read this one? It's good. In fact, it's the Good Book." He held a Bible so close to my face I didn't know if he wanted me to read it or eat it.

"I saw your brother this morning," he said. "That's why I've come back. I led him into temptation and now I've got to lead him out." This Biblical talk was making me irritable, so I switched subjects and inquired after Bruno. "Bad news there, I'm afraid," Dave said sadly. "He was shot dead during a knife fight. Martin, how's your family? In all honesty, seeing Terry was only half my mission. I've also come to see your parents and beg their forgiveness."

I strenuously advised him against it, but he was unswayable. It was God's will, he said, and I couldn't think of a persuasive argument against that, apart from saying I'd heard otherwise. Religious nuts! It isn't enough that they believe in God, they have to go all the way, seeing into his vast mind. They think faith gives them access to his glorious to-do lists.

Dave didn't come up to the house in the end; by chance he ran into my father outside the post office, and before he'd so much as pulled his Bible from his back pocket, my father's hands were already wrapped around the poor bastard's throat. Dave didn't fight back. He thought it was God's will he be strangled on the post office steps, and when my father pushed him to the ground and kicked him in the face, he thought that was God's afterthought.

You see, my father really did have a list, and Dave was on it. The list fell out of his pocket during the fight. I picked it up. There were six names.

People who destroyed my son
(in no particular order)
1. ~~Harry West~~
2. Bruno
3. Dave
4. The inventor of the suggestion box
5. Judge Phillip Krueger
6. Martin Dean

Given that he hadn't been shy in blaming me with every look and gesture for most of my life, I wasn't surprised to see my own name on the list, and it was only fortunate for me that my father didn't realize I actually appeared on it twice.

After the fight, my father stumbled off into the dark, muttering threats. "I'll get every last one of you!" he shouted to nobody, to the night. The police wandered up as they always do, like garbagemen after a street party, and as soon as Dave's breath returned, he shouted, "I don't want to press charges! Let him come back! You're impeding God's will!"

I grimaced, hoping for Dave's sake that God wasn't listening to his presumptuous rant. I don't imagine God likes a sycophant any more than anyone else.

To tell you the truth, that episode saved me from death by boredom. With *The Handbook of Crime* finished and promptly buried, with Caroline gone, Terry locked away, and Harry dead, the town had little to recommend itself to me. My loves were all out of reach and I had nothing to keep me occupied. In short, I had no projects left.

Yet I couldn't leave. True, I couldn't stand cohabitating with the living dead too much longer, but what to do about my regrettable oath not to leave my mother under any circumstances? Certainly while she was decaying so unpleasantly, it seemed impossible.

There was nothing I could do to help her condition or ease her physical suffering in any way, but I was very aware that my presence in the house gave my mother considerable peace of mind. Jasper, do you know the burden of being able to make someone happy by your mere presence? No, probably not. Well, my mother was always visibly affected by her sons—the light in her eyes was unmistakable, every time either Terry or I entered a room. What a heavy load for us! We felt we had to enter said room or else be held responsible for her sadness. What a drag! Of course, when someone needs you to the point that your very existence acts as a sort of life support, it's actually not bad for your self-esteem. But then, Jasper, do you know what it's like to see that same loved one deteriorate before your very eyes? Have you ever tried to recognize someone across the street in a heavy rain? It became like that. Her body became too thin to support life. And with her approaching death came the approaching death of that need for me. But it wouldn't go quietly. Not by a long shot. The course of her life had produced two things: me and Terry, and Terry had not only slipped through her fingers long ago, he was now languishing indefinitely just out of her reach. That left me. Out of her two boys, whom she once said she wished to "pin to her skin so as never to lose them," I was the only one left, the only thing that gave her any meaning. I wasn't going to abandon her, no matter how revolting the notion that I was only waiting in that dusty house for her to expire.

Besides, I was broke. I couldn't go anywhere.

Then a letter delivered by courier complicated matters. It was from Stanley.

Dear Martin,
    Well! What a shit storm!
    The book is out of print, out of the stores, out of circulation. The state is suing me, the bastards. You're in the clear, though, for about five minutes. If I were you, I'd make myself scarce for a while. Go overseas, Martin. I've been listening very carefully to these clowns. They're not done yet. They will come after you. I told you not to put your damn name on the book! Now they've got you for harboring a known fugitive and correcting his syntax. But you've got a little breathing time left. The cops don't know the first thing about publishing. They're looking for a way to beat the defense that the whole thing was done by mail. Plus, how about this for a kick, they don't want to know about Harry. They slap me in the face every time I mention his name. They refuse to believe that Terry didn't write the book. I guess they figure it gives the case a bigger profile. No wonder the world's a mess. How can you trust anyone to act decent when all they want is to push you out of the way so they can get to the spotlight? Oh well.
    Honestly, Martin, listen to me on this one. GET OUT OF THE COUNTRY. They're coming for you with a briefcase full of bullshit charges.
    I'm giving you everything from the initial sales. Don't think I'm being generous. The truth is, there's no point in me holding on to it, the courts are going to take it all anyway. But I know how much you put into it. I know how much it meant to you. Plus, I want to thank you for the ride of my life. We did something! We made some noise! I felt for the first time that I was involved in something meaningful. For that, I thank you.

Enclosed is a check for $15,000. Take it and go. They're
coming for you, Martin. They're coming soon.
Warm regards,
  Stanley

I shook the manila envelope until something nice fell out. The check.
There it was: $15,000. Not a huge amount of money, but by the stan-
dards of a man who was in the habit of recycling old cigarettes, it was
considerable.

So that was that. I was leaving. The hell with my unbreakable bond—
I was breaking it. I didn't think I'd be doing my mother any good rotting
in jail next to her other rotting son. Besides, jail was Terry's thing. I
wouldn't last one shower.

I hadn't even been up to see him since he'd been in. That may sound
strange, after all the fretting and running around I did after him, but to
tell you the truth, I was sick to death of everything to do with Terry
Dean. The public accolades had got to me in the end. And now there
wasn't anything more I could do for him. I needed a breather. I had, however, received a note, and I remember thinking it was the first time I'd
seen his handwriting.

Dear Marty,
  What's this shit about a book? No one will shut up about it.
If you get a sec, straighten that out, will you? I don't want to be
known as a writer. I want to be known as a vigilante who liber-
ated sport from the dirty hands of corruption. Not for scribbling
some stupid book.
  Prison—blah. Still, I can see our house from up here. The
warden treats me well on account of me being a kind of
celebrity and he lent me his binoculars the other day, and guess
what I saw? Dad looking at me through a pair of binoculars!
Weird!
  Anyway, don't forget to get the hell out of town and do
something with your life. Politics, mate. I reckon that's for you.
You're the only one with brains in this whole silly circus.
Love,
  Terry
P.S. Come up and see me sometime.

I started packing immediately. I dug out an old brown suitcase and threw a few clothes into it, then looked around my bedroom for memorabilia, but stopped when I remembered that the purpose of memorabilia is to trigger memory. Fuck that. I didn't want to be lugging my memories all over the place. They were too heavy.

"What are you doing?" my mother asked. I spun around, shamefaced, as if she'd caught me masturbating.

"I'm going," I said.

"Where?"

"I don't know. Maybe Paris," I said, surprising myself. "I'm going to track down Caroline Potts and ask her to marry me."

She didn't say anything to that, just swayed back and forth on her feet.

"Lunch in half an hour."

"OK," I said, and when she was gone, the gaping mouth of my open suitcase looked up at me accusingly.

After a silent lunch, I made my final journey up the hill to say goodbye to Terry. It was the hottest day of summer, so hot you could fry bacon on a leaf. The wind was hot too, and it felt like I was walking into a hair dryer. Sweat ran into my eyes. As I passed through the gates, the blistered hands of nostalgia gave my heart a good squeeze and I realized you miss shit times as well as good times, because at the end of the day what you're really missing is just time itself.

The guard wouldn't let me in.

"No visitors. Terry's in solitary confinement," he said.

"Why?"

"Fighting."

"Well, how long is he going to be in there for?"

"I dunno. A month?"

"A month! In solitary confinement! Is that legal?"

"I dunno."

Christ! I couldn't wait a month just to say goodbye. I was terrified of putting the brakes on my momentum.

"Well, can you tell him his brother came to say goodbye?"

"But his brother hasn't been here."

"I'm his brother."

"Oh. And what's the message?"

"Tell him I've gone overseas."

"But now you're back, eh. How long have you been away?"

"I don't know. A couple of years maybe. But when you tell him, put it in the future tense, OK?"

"Why?"

"Private joke."

"All right. I'll say his brother is *going* overseas for a couple of years," he said, winking at me.

"Perfect," I said, and turning away from the prison, I made the steep descent down the treeless hill and took in a full, unobscured view of our town. Nice town. Nice little town.

Fuck you, nice little town.

I hope you burn.

I walked through the streets, entertaining various revenge fantasies of returning one day rich and successful, but I quickly got over that idea. In truth, all I ever wanted was for everyone to like me, and coming back to a place rich and successful never won anyone any hearts.

As I was thinking these pointless thoughts, I noticed a queer sensation in my interior, and an odd noise that sounded like a little man was gargling mouthwash in my abdomen. The sensation quickly developed into an awful pain. I doubled over and rested my hand against a streetlamp. What was this? It felt as if all the glands in my body had started secreting battery acid.

Just as suddenly the pain subsided, and feeling light-headed, I groped my way back home.

When I got into my bedroom, the pain returned worse than before. I lay down and shut my eyes with the thought that a twenty-minute nap was all I needed to get over this.

But it was just the beginning.

By the morning I was still unwell. Some crazy sickness had struck me down suddenly, with debilitating stomach cramps, vomiting, then fever. At first I was diagnosed as having the flu, but my mother and I were worried; these were the symptoms I'd had as a child that had led me into the black arms of the terrifying coma. Once again I was confined to bed, and I feared that my brief flicker of light was growing prematurely dim, and every time I shat my pants from the stomach cramps, I shat my pants from fear. There's no two ways about it. Sickness and fear were making me incontinent. It was while lying in bed that I realized that illness is our natural state of being. We're always sick and we just don't know it. What we mean by health is only when our constant physical deterioration is undetectable.

Now I want you to know, I do not agree with the theory that all illness is made in the mind. Whenever someone says that to me, and blames all sickness on "negative thoughts," I think one of the ugliest, most uncharitable, angriest thoughts in my ugly, uncharitable, angry thought repertoire. I think: I hope to see you at your child's funeral so you can explain to me how your six-year-old daughter fabricated her own leukemia. Like I said, not nice, but that's how furious that particular theory makes me. Old age means nothing to those theorists. They think matter decays because it's down in the mouth.

The problem with people is that they are so in love with their beliefs that their epiphanies have to be absolute and comprehensive or nothing. They can't accept the possibility that their truths may have only an *element* of truth in them. It follows, therefore, that it's possible that some illnesses *are* born in the mind, and since desperation makes a man still more desperate, I was even willing to consider a supernatural cause for my deteriorating state.

When you're lying in agony, it gives you some relief to diagnose yourself; you get some of the illusion of power back. But if you know as much about the intricacies of the human body as you do about jet engines, you have to get creative. First, I meditated on plain old simple anxiety. But other than a exhausted concern for my mother and an unease about the possibility of being charged in a police investigation, I really wasn't that anxious. In truth, the slamming of the cell door in Terry's face was an enormous relief to me. That cell door signified the end of my days of fretting. I was relieved he was shut away.

The second tier of investigation brought me to the spiritual world. My thinking was this: I had sought to break the bond I had made with my mother, and if this was the cause of my illness, I had psychological and supernatural roots to choose from. Perhaps unconsciously I had made myself sick about it. Maybe my body revolted at the act of betrayal. Or, supernaturally, possibly the link with my mother was so strong, our bond had doomed me to keeping my word. Perhaps I had been suckered into a Polish mother's curse, and I didn't know it.

Either way, I was really sick. Name a symptom, I had it: vomiting, diarrhea, stomach cramps, fever, dizziness, shortness of breath, blurry vision, aching joints, groaning muscles, sore toes, chattering teeth, white tongue. I had everything short of bleeding from the eyeballs, and I didn't doubt that was next. I was so weak, I couldn't stand up to go to the bathroom. Beside my bed were two white bowls, one for vomit, one for piss and shit. I lay in a stupor, eyeing my half-packed suitcase and watching through a blurry haze a parade of noxious childhood memories pass before my eyes. I was right back where I started! That was the most painful part of being ill again, realizing that I had come full circle, and all I could think about was how I'd squandered my years of good health by just moping around and not climbing Everest.

My mother came into my room with an armful of books and began reading to me again, just like in the old days. Barely alive herself, she sat in the thin light of the lamp and read to me, beginning with an ominous choice, *The Man in the Iron Mask.* Lying in that dazed state, I had little trouble imagining a similar metallic apparatus constricting my own poor head. She read from morning to night, and after a while began sleeping in Terry's old bed next to mine, so there was hardly a time that we weren't together.

Her conversation often drifted to her early life in Shanghai, before she was pregnant with me, when she was still pregnant with possibility. She spoke often of Father Number One and remembered moments of intimacy between them when he stroked her hair while saying her name as if it were a sacred thing. It was the only time she liked the sound of her own name. She told me I had a similar-sounding voice, and one night she asked me to call her by her first name. It made me very uncomfortable, as I was already familiar with the works of Freud, but I did it to make her happy. Then she began unburdening herself by my bedside with lots of awful confessions like this one:

"I feel like I took a wrong turn but went so far down the road I didn't have the energy to turn back. Please, Martin, you must remember this. It's never too late to turn back if you make a wrong turn. Even if it takes you a decade to backtrack, you must do it. Don't get stuck because the road back seems too long or too dark. Don't be afraid to have nothing."

And this one:

"I have stayed faithful to your father all these years, even though I don't love him. Now I see I should've fucked around. Don't let morality get in the way of living your life. Terry killed those men because that's what he wanted to do with his life. If you need to cheat, cheat. If you need to kill, kill."

And this:

"I married your father because of fear. I stayed because of fear. Fear has ruled my life. I am not a brave woman. It's a bad thing to come to the end of your life and discover you are not brave."

I never knew what to say when my mother unloaded herself in this way. I only smiled into her face that was once a well-tended garden, and patted her bony hands not without some embarrassment, because it is embarrassing to watch a life that scrutinizes itself at the end and realizes all it has to take into death is the shame of not having fully lived.

One day I imagined I was at my execution after a long and costly trial. I thought: On a clear day you can see me dying. I was thinking of Caroline too, that I might never see her again, that she would never understand the width and depth of my feelings. I thought about how I was dying a virgin. Damn. I took a deep breath. There was a repulsive, sickening smell in the air. It was me.

Was I dreaming? I didn't hear them come in. Standing over me were two men in brown suits, jackets off, sleeves rolled up, sweat dripping into their eyes. One had a jutting-out jaw so extreme I didn't know whether to shake his hand or his chin. The other one had small eyes set in a small head, and a small nose sitting above a small mouth with lips so thin they looked drawn on by a pencil, a 2B.

"We want to talk to you, Mr. Dean," the chin said, and that sentence was notable for being the first time in my life I was called Mr. Dean. I didn't like it. "Can you hear me? What's wrong with you?"

"Childhood illness," my mother said.

"Isn't he a bit old for that?"

"Listen, Mr. Dean. We'd like a statement from you concerning the exact nature of your editing of the book."

"What book?" I groaned obtusely.

The small one wiped sweat from his face and smeared it on his pants. "Let's not play games, Mr. Dean. You did considerable work editing *The Handbook of Crime* for Terry Dean."

"Harry West," I said.

"What?"

"*The Handbook of Crime* was written by Harry West, not Terry Dean."

"The guy who took a dive off the harbor bridge," the chin said to the thin lips.

"Blaming it on a dead man because he can't corroborate your story is a little too convenient. I don't like it."

"Do you have to like something before it becomes fact?" I asked, and before they could respond, I said, "Excuse me a minute." I could feel my lunch coming up for air. I grabbed a bowl and threw up into it. A long silver thread of saliva connected my lower lip to the edge of the bowl.

"Listen, Dean. Are you going to make a statement or not?"

I motioned to the bowl and said, "I just made it."

"Look. There's no need to be hostile. We're not charging you with anything, we're just making some preliminary inquiries. Could you tell us how exactly you edited the book? Where did you and Terry meet?"

"Your brother isn't the most educated man in the world, Mr. Dean. There must have been a lot of spelling mistakes, grammatical errors, and the like."

I looked over to my mother, who was staring out the window in a sort of trance.

"We've looked into it. Editors work closely with their authors."

"Did your brother have any accomplices? We're investigating some new crimes."

I said nothing, but I too had read the small print in the newspapers. Just like artists, murderers are seduced by the dazzling, unexpected fusion of originality and success, and one or two would-be criminals had taken to plagiaristic copycat killings in the months after Terry's arrest, but they lacked spark and innovation. When the Australian chess champion was found with the bishop and two pawns lodged in his throat, the nation gave it scant attention, not least because the wannabe vigilante hadn't realized that chess is a game, not a sport.

Observing that I was in no state to answer their questions, one of the detectives said, "We'll come back when you're feeling a little better, Mr. Dean."

After they left, my father shuffled down the hallway in his pajamas and paused at the door, looking from me to my mother and back at me, with a look on his face that I couldn't quite read, before shuffling off again. For the record, I did not see the look as something sinister, and for all his bitterness and resentment toward me, I was still his son in a way. I never gave too much weight to his infamous list, nor to the possibility that his madness had taken him to a place where he could actually, willingly do me harm.

The following morning I heard my mother's voice calling me in a half whisper, half gurgle, and when I opened my eyes, I saw that my suitcase was now fully packed and sitting by the door with my brown boots beside it, toes pointing into the corridor. My mother, with her paper-white face, was peering down at me. "Quick. You should go now," she said, staring at me fixedly, but not at my eyes—at some other point on my face, perhaps my nose. "What's happening?" I croaked, but she just pulled the sheets off the bed and tugged at my arm with surprising force. "Time to go, Marty. You go catch the bus now." She kissed my sweaty forehead. "I love you very much, but don't come back here," she said. I tried to get up, but I couldn't. "We came a long way together, Marty. I carried you, remember? But I can't carry you this time. You have to go on your own. Come on, get a move on. You're going to miss the bus." She cupped her hand around the back of my head and gently eased me upright.

"I don't understand," I said.

We heard footsteps in the hallway, the floorboards creaking. My mother threw the sheets over me again and leapt into Terry's bed. My father's face appeared at the door, and he saw me still half propped up in bed.

"Feeling better?" he asked.

I shook my head, and when he left, I swiveled my head to see my mother's eyes closed; she was pretending to be asleep.

Later I had only a vague, fleeting memory of all this, but the residual feeling remained, a feeling like walking into the middle of a Harold Pinter play and being asked immediately by a tribunal to explain it or be executed. My mother, for her part, seemed to remember none of it, and when I brought it up she told me I had been laid up all night in a crazy fever, babbling like a lunatic. I didn't know what to believe.

Then things went from worse to cataclysmic.

It was hot, 104 degrees. A blazing southerly wind blew through the open window. I tried to eat some vegetable soup my father had made. My mother brought it in. I drank only two spoonfuls, but I couldn't hold it down. I reached for the bowl and threw it all up. My head hung over the bowl and I left it there, staring stupidly into the kaleidoscopic face of my own vomit. There, in the spew, I saw perhaps the most horrifying thing I have ever seen in my entire life, and since then I've seen dogs sawn in half.

This is what I saw:

Two. Blue. Pellets.

That's right, rat poison.

That's right, rat poison.

I struggled for a while to figure out how I may have inadvertently swallowed them myself. But having not put one foot out of bed since my illness began, I just had to rule it out. That left only one answer. My stomach tightened like a vise. I'm being poisoned, I thought. He, my father, is poisoning me.

•

Let's not beat around the bush: human feelings can be ridiculous. Thinking back to that moment, to how I felt at the realization that my stepfather was slowly murdering me, I did not feel anger. I did not feel outrage. I felt hurt. That's right. That this man who I'd lived with my whole life, the man who married my mother and was for all practical purposes my father, was maliciously poisoning me to death *hurt my feelings*. Ridiculous!

I dropped the bowl so the vomit spilled onto the carpet and dribbled down the cracks in the floorboards. I looked and looked again, each time confirming that I was not hallucinating, as my mother had assured me the previous night.

My mother! What was her part in all this? She obviously knew—that was why she wanted me to escape, a desire that ended abruptly when she feared that if the murderer knew I was fleeing, he would abandon his languid plan on the spot and just take a knife to my guts or a pillow to my face.

Christ! What a pickle!

Keeping your calm while your stepfather tries to kill you is quite impossible. Watching your murderer scrunch up his face in disgust as he silently cleans up your vomit may have its darkly comic elements, but it's also just so damn chilling, you want to curl into a fetal position and remain there until the next ice age.

I couldn't take my eyes off him. I was consumed by a perverse curiosity to see what he'd do. I should say something, I thought, but what? Confronting your own assassin is a tricky business; you don't want to trigger your own murder just for the sake of getting something off your chest.

"Next time, try to get it into the bowl," he said blandly.

I said nothing, just stared at him as if he'd broken my heart.

When he was gone, my rational mind came home. What the fuck was I going to do? It seemed sensible, as the intended victim, to remove myself from the scene of the crime, so as to avoid the crime. Yes, it was time to test the theory of superhuman strength being bestowed on people in life-threatening situations. Because my body was no use, I was counting on my will to live to get me out of this Shakespearean family drama. I swung my legs over the side of the bed and got to my feet, using the side table for balance. I winced through the pain as my stomach contracted and twisted horribly. I went for my suitcase and noted it was still packed from the episode the night before. My feet struggled into my boots, and with great effort I began to walk: when you haven't worn footwear in a while, even sandals feel as heavy as cement blocks. Trying to sneak out without a sound, I crept down the hallway. I could hear arguing from the living room. They were both screaming, my mother crying. There was the sound of breaking glass. They were fighting, physically. Maybe my mother had confronted him about his plot! At the door, I put down the suitcase and headed for the kitchen. What else could I do? I couldn't leave my mother in my father's psychotic hands. My course was clear. I had to kill my father (by marriage).

I tell you, I've taken more time choosing an item on a menu than I took making the decision to end my father's life. And as someone who has always battled the pernicious vice of indecision—beginning the moment my mother dangled the raw nipples of two milk-filled tits in my face and said, "Choose one"—I found that having suddenly made a quick choice, however dreadful, gave me a supremely satisfying sense of empowerment.

In the kitchen I grabbed the carving knife. It smelled of onions. Through a crack in the door, I could see my parents struggling. They were really going for it. He'd hit my mother before many times, always late at night, in the privacy of their bedroom, but not since she'd told him she had cancer. My mother was clawing at him as best as she could in her half-dead state, and in return he gave her such a backhander, she fell to the floor in a crumpled heap.

My strength flowing, I burst through the door unsteadily but kept a clean, tight grip on the knife handle. They saw me—first my mother, then my father—but paid no attention to the knife in my hands. I might just as well have been holding a feather, they simply were so deep in their own private nightmare.

"Martin! Get out of here!" my mother wailed.

At the sight of me, my father's face did something I've never seen a face do before. It contracted to half its normal size. He looked back at my mother, picked up a chair, and smashed it to pieces on the ground so the fragments shattered around her.

"Get away from her!" I yelled, my voice cracking and wobbling at the same time.

"Martin . . ." he said in a strange voice.

My mother was sobbing hysterically.

"I said get away!" I repeated.

Then he said, in a voice like a grenade, "Your fucking crazy mother has been putting rat poison in your food!"

I stood there like a wall.

"It was *you*," I said.

He just shook his head sadly.

I turned, confused, to my mother, whose face was partially covered by her hand. Her eyes streamed with tears; her body heaved with sobs. Immediately I knew it was true.

"*Why?*" my father yelled, punching the wall next to her. She screamed. He looked at me with tenderness and confusion and sobbed, "Martin, why?"

My mother was shivering. Her free hand clutched a copy of *The Three Musketeers*, by Alexandre Dumas. That was the next book she'd planned on reading to me. "So she could look after me," I said, almost inaudibly.

He looked at me blankly. He didn't get it. He didn't get it at all.

"I'm sorry, son," he said, in the first display of love he'd ever shown me.

It was all too much. I stumbled through the kitchen and down the hall and, grabbing my suitcase, burst through the front door.

If I'd been in any kind of reasonable state at all, I would've immediately noticed something wrong in the world around me. I walked in a daze, feeling the heat of the day on my face. I walked and walked, fast, as if carried by a strong current. My thoughts broke in half, then replicated—anger dividing into horror and rage, then again into pity and disgust, and so on. All the time I kept walking, feeling stronger and stronger with every step. I walked to the top of Farmer's Hill.

Then I saw it.

The sky.

Fat cones of dense smoke spiraled into thin trails. Layers of hazy orange overlapping gray fingers stretching out from the horizon.

Then I felt it. The heat. I winced. The land was on fire!

A bushfire!

A big one!

Standing on top of the hill, I saw another in a quick series of searing images that I knew at once would never leave my mind. I saw the fire split. One half raced toward my parents' house, the other to the prison.

I don't know what possessed me as I watched that fire encircle my town—but I became convinced that it was within my power to rescue at least part of my family. I knew that I probably couldn't help Terry, and that he die violently and unpleasantly in the prison my father helped build just so cleanly rounded off the issue, my choice was clear. I would go and try to save my mother, even though she had just tried to kill me, and my father, even though he had not.

The bushfire season had started early that year. Soaring temperatures and strong winds saw to it that small fires had sprung up along the periphery of northwestern New South Wales throughout the summer. It takes only one sudden gust of searing wind to fan the isolated fires, pushing them rapidly into raging uncontrollable infernos. That's how it always happens. The Fire had some shifty strategies up its flaming sleeve: It threw embers into the air. The embers were then couriered by winds to a destination a few miles ahead, with the intention of starting fresh fires, so by the time the main Fire caught up, its child was already raging and taking lives. The Fire was no dummy. It evolved like crazy.

Smoke crept over the town in an opaque cloud. I ran toward my parents' house, passing fallen trees, poles, and power lines. Flames crept along both sides of the road. Smoke licked my face. Visibility was zero. I didn't slow down.

The fallen trees made the road impassable. I took a path through the bush. I couldn't see the sky; a thick curtain of smoke had been drawn over it. All around me was a sound, a crackle, like someone was jumping on old newspapers. Burning debris blew across the tops of trees. It was impossible to know which way to go. I went on anyway until I heard a voice call out, "Stop!"

I stopped. Where was the voice coming from? It was hard to tell if it was from far away or inside my own head.

"Go left," the voice said. "Left!"

Normally, demanding voices who don't introduce themselves would have had me go the other way, but I felt this voice had my best interests at heart. Terry was dead, I just knew it, and the voice was his, his last words to me on his way to the other world.

I went left, and as I did, I saw the right-hand path consumed by flames.

Around the next bend I came across a group of men shooting water into the trees. They held swollen wild pythons that jutted from the bellies of two firetrucks and wore wet rags over their mouths. I wanted one. Then I thought: There's almost no situation you can get yourself into when you don't want what the other guy has.

"Martin!" a voice called.

"Don't go that way!" another shouted.

"My mum and dad are in there!" I shouted back, and as I ran on, I thought I heard someone call out, "Say hello for me!"

I saw the fire jumping a dry creek bed. I passed the flaming carcass of a sheep. I had to slow down. The smoke had thickened to a gray wall; it was suddenly impossible to tell where the flames were. My lungs seared. I knew if I didn't get a whiff of air soon, this was the end. I gagged and vomited smoke. There were carrots in it.

When I reached my street, a jagged wall of flame blocked the entrance. Through it I could make out a group of people standing on the other side. The wall of fire stood like fortress gates. I squinted against the intense glare as yellow-black smoke billowed over the people.

"Have you seen my parents?" I shouted.

"Who are you?"

"Martin Dean!"

"Marty!" I thought I heard my mother's voice. It was hard to tell. The fire swallowed words. Then the air grew very still.

"The wind!" someone screamed. They froze. They were all waiting to see which direction the fire would run next. A flame whirling up behind them, standing tall, was ready to pounce. I felt like a man about to be guillotined hoping that his head could be stuck back on later. A hot breeze touched my face.

Before I could scream, the flames leapt on top of me. In a split second my head was on fire. And then, just as quickly, the wind changed direction and the flames leapt away toward the group of people. This time it kept going.

Though the fire was gone, my eyes and my lungs were filled with smoke and my hair was in flames. I wailed at the pain of it. I tore the clothes off my body, threw myself on the ground, and rubbed my head in the dirt. It took a few seconds to extinguish myself, and by then the fire had devoured an ear and scorched my lips. Through puffed-up eyelids I could see the flaming hurricane sweep over the group of people, my parents included, and devour them. Naked and burned, I dragged myself to my knees and screamed in a helpless, frenzied rage.

•

Most of the prisoners had made it out, except those in solitary confinement. They were blocked in on the lower level of the prison, and there wasn't time to save them.

As I suspected, Terry was gone.

While small fires still burned away from the town, the media wasted no time in making a big deal of Terry Dean's perishing in the prison. He was nothing but a pile of ashes. After the police photographers had taken photos of the cell, I went in. The bones were there too. But all the good stuff was in the ash. With a broom, a pan, and a small cardboard box, I scooped up my brother. It wasn't easy. Some of Terry's ashes mingled with the ashes of the wooden bunk beds. Poor Terry. You couldn't distinguish him from a bed. That's just sad.

I left the bones. Let the state bury them. I took the rest. Like I said, all the good stuff was in the ash.

Outside the prison, black cinders whirled crazily in the air, climbed into the sky, and when the wind died down settled on the ground and on the cars and on the journalists. Red-hot sparks lay on the hot bitumen. I looked at the smoking black acres of burned grassland and the parched hills. Everywhere was smoldering ashes. Every house was filthy with ash and burned debris. Every smell was acrid. Every color eerie.

Mother dead. Father dead. Brother dead. Harry dead. Caroline gone. Lionel gone. Town gone. Oath gone too; the sacred bond finally broken.

Free.

A man was heard to be barbecuing a steak on the embers of his own home. Reporters were all crowded around him. They thought it was hilarious. I suppose it was.

A brief thunderstorm came. A group of survivors standing in the remains of town were talking about the origin of the fire. What had started it this time? I had just assumed it was arsonists. It's nearly always arsonists. What is it with these fucking arsonists? I supposed they are less likely to be malignant smudges of evil than just dumb and bored: a deadly combination. And whatever happens in their upbringing, they emerge from adolescence with no sense of empathy whatsoever. These dumb, bored, unempathetic people are all around us. We can't trust anyone to behave himself. We always have to be on the lookout. Here's the case-winning example: it doesn't happen every day, but every now and again, *people shit in public swimming pools.* That just says it all to me.

But no, the survivors were saying, this time it wasn't arsonists.

It was the observatory.

My blood turned cold.

I moved closer. This is what I heard:

Over the years, the novelty of the observatory had worn off; the whole thing had gone to seed, left to ruin up there on the hill, abandoned to nature. The roof of the observatory lifted on a hinge. *Someone had left it open.* The lens had concentrated the summer sun's rays into a hot beam of light and ignited the structure, the wind came in to do her bit, and we ended with this current catastrophe.

It was the observatory.

My observatory!

The observatory I had suggested into existence was the direct cause of my mother's, father's, and brother's deaths. It was the final nail in the coffin of that odious suggestion box of mine, that slimy box that had turned the town against my family, put my brother in a mental institution, then into a young offenders' home, and now into the grave (figuratively speaking; literally speaking, into a cardboard box that had once contained seedless grapes). I had thought that with the observatory I could change people's souls for the better, but instead I succeeded only in accelerating their obliteration. When my brother went into the hospital, I should have destroyed the suggestion box that put him there; and when *he* destroyed the suggestion box, blinding our only friend, I should have then and there destroyed everything connected to the box, the box that suddenly reminded me of the box that was now in my hands, the box with my brother in it.

I walked on.

I didn't forget Stanley's warnings, or the detectives and their determination to prosecute me. Time to leave for good. Besides, there was nothing more to learn here. Time to travel to new lands to practice old habits. New longings! New disappointments! New trials and failures! New questions! Would toothpaste taste the same everywhere? Would loneliness feel less bitter in Rome? Would sexual frustration be less of a grind in Turkey? Or Spain?

This I thought as I moved through the silence of the dead town, the dreamless town, the town that was charred and black like burned toast. Don't scrape it! Don't save it! Toss my town into the garbage. It's carcinogenic.

The embers of my childhood were fading to cold, hard lumps. No wind could fan them to life now. It was gone. I had not a person in the world. Australia was still an island, but I was no longer marooned on it. I was finally adrift. And it was endless, the sea beyond. No horizons.

No one knew me where I was going, no one knew my story, my brother's story. My life was reduced to no more than a secret anecdote I could reveal or keep hidden for all time. That was up to me.

I walked the long, windy, dusty road out of town.

I had the feeling of leaving an amusement park without having been on any of the rides. While I'd always hated the town, the people, their lives, I had existed beside them nonetheless, and yet I had not immersed myself in the stream of life, and that was regrettable, because even if it's the worst amusement park in the world, if you're going to take the trouble to spend twenty-two years there, you might as well at least have a go. The problem was, every ride made me sick. What could I do?

Then I remembered that I still held Terry in a cardboard box.

I was definitely not going to have a nervous breakdown deciding what to do with the ashes of my downsized little brother: I would just get rid of them, quickly, secretly, without ceremony. If a child passed me in the street, I would give him the box. If I saw a suitable ledge, I would leave it on the ledge. I continued this line of thought until I became so fascinated by the overall idea of ashes that I got thirsty.

Up ahead I saw a gas station and grocery store. I went inside. The fridge was at the back. I walked down the aisle and grabbed a Coke.

Turning back, I saw beside me a shelf that contained small jars of Indian spices, cayenne pepper, and Italian herbs. Obscured from the shop-keeper's view, I opened up the jars one by one and emptied half their contents onto the floor. Then I poured Terry's ashes into the jars with lit-tle precision, spilling much of him on my feet, so that when I finished, I walked out with my brother on my shoes. And then—I have this image in my head forever—I wiped my brother off my shoes with my hands and finished him off by washing him into a nearby puddle, thereby leaving my brother's last remnants floating in a shallow puddle of rainwater on the side of the road.

It's funny.

People have always asked me, "What was Terry Dean like as a child?" but no one has ever posed the more pertinent question, *What was he like as a puddle?*

The answer: still, copper-brown, and surprisingly unreflective.

The End!

Out the window I could see a pink dawn sky covering the backyard and probably farther, at least to the corner store. The morning birds, unaware of the concept of sleep-ins, were chirping their usual dawn chirps. Dad and I sat in silence. Talking for seventeen hours and covering almost every minute of his first twenty-two years on earth had worn him out. Listening had done the same to me. I don't know which of us was more exhausted. Suddenly Dad brightened and said, "Hey, guess what?"

"What?"

"The blood's congealed!"

Blood? What blood? Oh, that's right—I *was* in a fight, wasn't I? I did get beaten senseless by my peers, didn't I? I reached up and felt my face. There was a hard, crusty substance on my lower lip all right. I ran to the bathroom mirror to look. Woo-hoo! Yes, sometime during Dad's story the blood on my face had turned black and globular. I looked revolting. I smiled for the first time since way before the story began.

"You want me to take a photo before you wash it off?" Dad called from my room.

"Nah, there'll be plenty more blood where that came from."

"Too true."

I got the corner of a towel and held it under hot water and sponged off the crusted blood. As I cleaned up my face and the water turned the black blood red and stained the white towel too, I thought about Dad's story: the story of Terry Dean. It seemed to me I hadn't learned as much about Uncle Terry as you'd think you would in a seventeen-hour monologue, but I had learned an awful lot about my father.

I had the uneasy feeling that maybe every word he said was true. Certainly he believed it all. There's something disturbing about a thirty-two-year-old man putting his thirty-two-year-old soul into the mouth of a child, even if that child is himself as a boy. Was my father an eight-year-old anarchist? A nine-year-old misanthrope? Or was the boy in the story an unconscious reinvention, a man with a man's experience of the world trying to make sense of his childhood, obliterating along the way any of the thoughts or perspectives he would really have experienced during that time? Maybe. After all, memory may be the only thing on earth we can truly manipulate to serve us, so we don't have to look back at ourselves in the receding past and think, What an arsehole!

But Dad was not one to airbrush his memories. He liked to preserve everything in its natural state, from his hair to his past. That's how I knew every word he said was true, and why I still feel sick when I remember the shocking revelation that came after this one, the crazy bombshell about the most important woman who was never in my life: my mother.

TWO

I was taking a forty-five-minute shower. I know I was being unforgivably inconsiderate of the environment, but I'd read in New Scientist that in a couple of billion years the expanding universe will have stretched to breaking point and will start contracting like a rubber band, time will run backward, and (therefore) the water will eventually return to the showerhead.

"Jasper! I completely forgot!" I heard Dad shouting.

"I'm in the shower!"

"I know. Do you know what the date is?"

"No."

"Guess."

"The second of December."

"No. It's the seventeenth of May! I can't believe I forgot all about it! Hurry up!"

The seventeenth of May, my mother's birthday. Inexplicably, Dad always bought her a present. Inexplicably, he'd make me unwrap it. I never knew whether to say thank you. Usually it was a book or chocolates, and after I opened it and said something like "Good one," Dad would suggest we give it to her in person. That meant a trip out to the cemetery. This morning, since the significance of the date had slipped his mind, Dad ran around the house looking for something to wrap. In the end he found a bottle of whisky with two decent sips left. I stood there on edge while he wrapped it, and moments later he stood there eagerly while I unwrapped it and said, "Good one."

My mother was buried in a Jewish cemetery, a possible nod to my grandparents. In case you don't know, the Jewish religion wants you to put an old rock on the grave of your loved ones. I never saw any reason to quibble with oddball ancient traditions as cheap as this one, so I went outside and wondered what kind of filthy rock my dead mother might want as a token of my devotion.

When we finally got to the cemetery, we couldn't find the grave. The maze of gray stones confused us, but in the end we found her lying where she always was, between Martha Blackman, who had breathed in and out for a tedious ninety-eight years, and Joshua Wolf, whose heart had unfairly stopped beating at the age of twelve. We stared at a slab of stone with her name on it.

Astrid.

No last name, no date of birth nor date of death—just her name all alone on the headstone, speaking volumes of silence.

I tried to imagine what life would have been like with a mother around. I couldn't picture it. The mother I mourned was an amalgam of manufactured remembrances, photographs of silent movie actresses, and the warm, loving image of the maternal archetype. She transmogrified constantly, a vision in constant motion.

Beside me, Dad was bouncing on his toes as if waiting for a game result. He stepped forward and brushed the star-shaped autumn leaves off the headstone.

I looked at him. I looked at his feet. "Hey!" I shouted.

He turned to me, startled, and snapped, "Don't make sudden loud noises in a cemetery, you ghoul. You want me to die of fright?"

"Your feet!" I shouted, pointing at them. He lifted up the heels to inspect for dog shit.

"You're standing on her!"

"No, I'm not."

He was. He was standing right on top of my mother. Any fool could see it.

"You're fucking standing on her grave! Get off!"

Dad smiled but didn't do anything to make his feet move. I grabbed his arm and dragged him off to the side. That only made him laugh.

"Whoa. Relax, Jasper. She's not in there."

"What do you mean, she's not in there?"

"She's not buried there."

"What do you mean?"

"I mean there's a coffin. Only it's empty!"

"An empty coffin?"

"And you want to know the worst part? You still have to pay the same price as if there was actually a body inside! I guess I assumed it was done on weight, but apparently not."

I looked at his cheerless face, aghast. He was shaking his head, mourning the loss of his money.

"WHERE THE FUCK'S MY MOTHER?"

•

Dad explained that she had died in Europe. He wouldn't say much more about it. He had purchased the burial plot for my benefit, reasoning that a boy has the right to mourn his mother in the appropriate setting. Where else was he going to do it? At the movies?

Over the years, when the topic came up, Dad had told me nothing about her other than that she was dead and the dead can't make you dinner. What I can't believe now is how fully I'd repressed my curiosity. I suppose because he didn't want to talk about it, Dad had convinced me that it was rude to go poking into finished lives. My mother was a topic he put on the high shelf, out of reach of questions. I had accepted this at face value, that under no circumstances did you ask about the destruction of someone who was supposed to be indestructible.

But now, suddenly, with the revelation that all along I'd been grieving over an empty hole, anger mutated into a burning curiosity. In the car on the way home from the cemetery, I told him that if I was old enough to mourn, at nine years old, I was old enough to know something about her.

"She was just this woman I saw for a little while," Dad said.

"*Just this woman?* Weren't you married?"

"Oh God, no. I've never even gone near an altar."

"Well, did you, you know, love her?"

"I don't know how to answer that question, Jasper. I really don't know how."

"Try."

"No."

Later that night, I heard the sound of hammering and went into the bathroom to see Dad putting up curtains on the bathroom mirror.

"What are you doing?"

"You'll thank me for this one day," he said.

"Dad, just tell me about her. What was she like?"

"Are you still harping on about that?"

"Yes."

"That oughta do it."

Dad finished hammering, put up the rod, and pulled the beige curtains across the mirror with a drawstring.

"Why do people need to look at themselves while they brush their teeth? Don't they know where their teeth are?"

"Dad!"

"What? Christ! What do you want to know, factual information?"

"Was she Australian?"

"No, European."

"From where, exactly?"

"I don't know, exactly."

"How can you not know?"

"Why are you so interested in your mother all of a sudden?"

"I don't know, Dad. I guess I'm just sentimental."

"Well, I'm not," he said, showing me a familiar sight: his back.

•

Over the following months, I pushed and pressed and squeezed and, in dribs and drabs, managed to extract the following scant information: my mother was beautiful from certain angles, she was widely traveled, and she disliked having her photograph taken as much as most people dislike having their money taken. She spoke many languages fluently, was somewhere between twenty-six and thirty-five when she died, and though she had been called Astrid, it was probably not her real name.

"Oh, and she absolutely *hated* Eddie," he said one day.

"She knew Eddie?"

"I met Eddie more or less at the same time."

"In Paris?"

"Just out of Paris."

"What were you doing just out of Paris?"

"You know. The usual. Walking around."

Eddie, Dad's best friend, was a thin Thai man with a sleazy mustache who always seemed to be smack bang in the middle of the prime of life and not a day over. When he stood next to my pale father, they looked less like friends and more like doctor and patient. It was clear now that I was going to have to interrogate Eddie about my mother. Finding him was the trouble. He made frequent and unexplained overseas trips, and I had no idea whether he went for business, pleasure, restlessness, genocide, or on a dare. Eddie had a way of being categorically unspecific—he would never go so far as to tell you, for example, that he was visiting relatives in the Chiang Mai province of Thailand, but if you pressed, he might admit that he had been "in Asia."

I waited six months for Eddie to resurface. During that time I prepared a list of questions, running and rerunning the interview with him in my head, including his answers. I anticipated—wrongly, as it turned out—a lurid love story wherein my saintly mother martyred herself in a Romeo and Juliet–type scenario: I imagined that the doomed lovers had made a tragically romantic double suicide pact but Dad had pulled out at the last minute.

Finally one morning I was in the bathroom brushing my teeth with the curtains drawn when I heard Eddie's syrupy voice calling out. "Marty! You here? Am I talking to an empty apartment?"

I ran into the living room.

"Here he is," Eddie said, and as usual, before I could say "Please don't," he lifted the Nikon dangling from his neck and took my photo.

Eddie was a photography nut and couldn't go five minutes without taking my photograph. He was a great multitasker: with one eye on the lens of his Nikon, he could smoke a cigarette, photograph us, and smooth down his hair at the same time. Although he said I photographed well, I couldn't disprove him—he never showed us the results. I didn't know if he ever developed the photos or not, or even if he had film in his camera. It was just another example of Eddie's pathological mysteriousness. He never talked about himself. Never told you how things were in his day. You didn't even know if he had a day. He was, body and soul, aloof.

"How's your dad? Still around, is he?"

"Eddie, did you know my mother?"

"Astrid? Sure, I knew her. Shame about her, wasn't it?"

"I don't know. Was it?"

"What do you mean?"

"Tell me about her."

"All right."

Eddie plopped himself on the couch and patted the cushion next to him. I leapt on it excitedly, unaware of how intensely unsatisfying our conversation would be: in all my anticipating, I had completely forgotten that Eddie was the world's worst storyteller.

"I met her in Paris, with your father," he began. "I think it was autumn, because the leaves were brown. I think the American name for autumn, 'fall,' is really beautiful. Personally, I like fall, or *the fall*, as they say, and also spring. Summer I can only tolerate for the first three days and after that I'm looking for a meat freezer to hide in."

"Eddie . . ."

"Oh. I'm sorry. I got sidetracked, didn't I? I forgot to tell you how I feel about winter."

"My mother."

"Right. Your mother. She was a beautiful woman. I don't think she was French, but she had the same physique. French women are small and thin with quite small breasts. If you want big breasts, you have to cross the border into Switzerland."

"Dad said you met my mother in Paris."

"That's right. It was in Paris. I miss Paris. Did you know that in France they have a different word when something disgusts you? You can't say 'Yuck!' No one will know what you mean. You have to say 'Berk!' It's weird. The same goes when you hurt yourself. It's 'Aie!' not 'Ow!' "

"What was my dad doing in Paris?"

"He was doing nothing in those days, the same kind of nothing he does now, except then he was doing it in French. Well, actually he didn't do nothing. He was always scribbling in his little green notebook."

"All of Dad's notebooks are black. He always uses the same kind."

"No, this one was definitely green. I can see it in my mind's eye. It's a shame you can't see the pictures I've got showing in my mind's eye right now. They're so damn vivid. I wish we could project all the mind's eyes onto a screen and sell tickets. I think how much you could expect the public to pay would really determine your self-worth."

I eased myself off the couch, telling Eddie to go on without me, walked to my father's bedroom, and stood at the open door, staring stupidly at the vast chaos and disorder that may or may not have been hiding the secret story of my mother in a green notebook. Normally I don't enter my father's bedroom, for the same reason you don't walk in and chat with a man when he's on the toilet, but this was important enough to force me to break my own rule. I stepped into my father's open bowels, his howling sandstorm; that he slept in here was an achievement in itself.

I set about my task. First I had to navigate my way through a yellowing archive of newspapers that would rival those stored in the public library. They were stacked up and pushed into the dark corners of the room, the stacks so numerous they carpeted the floor all the way to the bed. I stepped on the newspapers and over things I could only imagine he'd pulled out of garbage bins and those I imagined he'd dragged out of people's mouths. On the way I found things I had long considered missing: the tomato sauce, the mustard, all the teaspoons, the soup spoons, and the big plates. I opened up one of his wardrobes, and under a heap of clothes I found the first pile of notebooks—there must have been a hundred of them. They were all black. Black, black, black. In the second wardrobe I found another hundred, again, disappointingly, all black. I stepped inside the wardrobe—it was very deep. There I found a pile of magazines but tried not to linger on them. From all the photographs inside, Dad had cut out the eyes. I tried not to dwell on this. A man can read a magazine and might be inclined to remove the eyes if he feels they are staring at him insolently, can't he? I ignored them, and moved deeper inside the wardrobe (it really was a deep wardrobe). Yet another box revealed yet another pile of notebooks, as well as all the cut-out eyes from the magazines. They watched me pitilessly as I rummaged through the notebooks, and seemed to widen with mine at the sight of, wedged under the cardboard flap at the bottom of the box, a green one.

I took it and got the hell out of his suffocating room. I could hear Eddie in the living room, still talking to himself. I went to my own room to examine the green notebook.

The edges of it were worn. I opened it to see that the ink had run in parts, but not so the writing was illegible. The handwriting went from small and neat to large and loopy, and in later passages, when it ran diagonally down the page, it was as though it had been written while on the back of a camel or the bow of a ship tossed around in bad weather. Some of the pages were barely hanging on by a staple, and when the notebook was closed, the corners stuck out like bookmarks.

There was a title page, in French: *Petites misères de la vie humaine.*

This doesn't mean little miseries either, as I first thought, but translates, more or less, to "Minor irritations of human life." It gave me a sick feeling, although it served well to brace me for the story of how I came to be, the story that was located in the following journal, which I reprint here for you to read.

Petites misères de la vie humaine

11 May

Paris—perfect city to be lonely & miserable in. London too grim to be a sad sack with any dignity. O London! You grisly town! You cold gray cloud! You low-lying layer of mist & fog! You dense moan! You drizzling forlorn sigh! You shallow gene pool! You career town! You brittle town! You fallen empire! You page-three town! Lesson from London—hell isn't red-hot but cold & gray.

And Rome? Full of sexual predators who live with their mothers.

Venice? Too many tourists as dumb as believers feed Italian pigeons, whereas in their own cities they snub them.

Athens? Everywhere mounted policemen ride by, pausing only so their horses can shit on cobblestone streets—horse shit lying in such mammoth piles you think there must be no better laxative in the world than bales of hay.

Spain? Streets smell like socks fried in urine—too many Catholics baptized in piss. Tho the real problem with Spain is you're constantly frustrated by fireworks—sexual stink of exploding fiestas salt in wound of loneliness.

But Paris—beautiful poor ugly opulent vast complex gray rainy & French. You see unbelievable women, umbrellas, beggars, tree-lined streets, bicycles, church spires, Africans, gloomy domes, balconies, broken flowerpots, rudeness that will ring through eternity, aimless pedestrians, majestic gardens, black trees, bad teeth, ritzy stores, socialists moving their hands up the thighs of intellectuals, protesting artists, bad drivers, pay toilets, visible cheese smells, witty scarves, shadows of body odors in the metro, fashionable cemeteries, tasteful transvestites, filtered light, slums, grime, desire, artistic lampposts, multicolored phlegm of passive chimney smokers, demented cobblestone faces in terrace cafés, high collars, hot chocolates, flashy gargoyles, velvet berets, emaciated cats, pickpockets running away with glittering entrails of rich German tourists, & great phallic monuments in the squares & the sex shops.

It's no rumor: prancing arrogant Parisians sit cross-legged in cafés & philosophize uninvited—but why is it that when I hear someone make a great philosophical argument I get the same feeling as when I see someone has put clothes on his dog?

With me is Caroline's last postcard. Typical Caroline. "I'm in Paris" & an address, some grimy suburb just out of the city. I'll go there & tell her my brother's dead, the man she loved, and then . . . But NOT YET—clumsy love declarations are a high heart risk. Should I see her? Should I wait? The problem with most people is they've NEVER been torn in half, not really not right down the middle like I have, NEVER ripped themselves to shreds NEVER listened to the warring factions BOTH make their case so convincing AND so right & they don't know what it is to have your brain & your body want TWO things each that's FOUR compelling ideas all at once.

I wonder if I'm reaching out for Caroline in particular or just for someone who knew me before five minutes ago.

4 June

This morning woke to sound of children laughing—that shit me. Even worse—found decision had taken place in my head overnight—Today Martin Dean will go to Caroline Potts & declare undying love & devotion. I lay in bed stuffing stomach w/ butterflies. Thought how all my life-altering decisions are command decisions made from the highest peak of hierarchy of self—when orders boom from commander in chief what can you do? I showered shaved drank stale wine & dressed. In head 2 fragmented Caroline memories 1. her smile, tho not her smiling face, just the smile like a suspended pair of dentures 2. her handstands—plaid skirt hanging down to her armpits—jesus how that innocent childlike act made me want to pounce on her in brutal tho heartfelt manner.

Went into bowels of city then suffocating metro ride out of Paris. Saw four horse-faced people. 14-year-old toughie tried to pick my pocket making me realize I don't know French word for Hey!

Finally sat on low stone wall opposite small many-windowed building, all shutters closed as if forever. Hard to believe this dirty apartment building housed the woman I love. Commander sensing I was about to linger screeched in my ear so I marched to front door & pounded. Bit my lower lip too tho commander hadn't ordered it.

Door handle turned slowly & insensitively to prolong immaculate agony. Finally opened to reveal short, stout woman as wide as she was long—in other words, a perfect square.

—Oui?

—Caroline Potts, she is here? I said in perfect English translation of grammatically correct French. The woman blabbered away in her tongue & shook head. Caroline was no longer there.

—And Monsieur Potts? The blind man?

She looked at me blankly.

—Blind. No eyes. No eyes, I repeated idiotically, thinking Well, can I come in & smell her pillow?

—Hello! a voice called out from the upstairs window. An Asian face was hanging there looking for a body to match. Wait there! the face said & ran down breathlessly.

—You are looking for the girl & the blind man?

—Yes!

—I'm Eddie.

—So?

—So nothing. The girl left a month ago, after the blind man died.

—Died? Are you sure?

—Of course I'm sure. I was at the funeral. What's your name?

—Martin. How did he die?

—I used to watch them from my window. Every day she walked him to the shops so he would know where the holes were in the street, but this one day he went alone. He must have got disoriented because he walked right into the middle of the road and just stood there.

—He was hit by a car?

—No, he had a heart attack. He's buried up at the local cemetery. You want to see his grave? I could take you. Come on, he said buttoning up his coat, but I hesitated. Something in his manner was unsettling: his hands made delicate gestures & in his voice a conciliatory tone as if we'd argued & he wanted to make it up to me.

—Shall we go and see your dead friend? he asked sweetly & I thought I don't like this man not that I had any real reason for disliking him but so what? I've been disliked by people who couldn't even pick me out of a police lineup.

Under gray sky we walked up the same color road in dead silence to the top of the hill. The cemetery was only 100 meters away—convenient place to die. The grave had only his name & lifespan & nothing else no little witticisms nothing. I wondered if Lionel died instantly or w/ final breath made a banal plan like Must buy milk. Then I thought about all the deaths I knew—how Harry chose his & how Terry was probably shocked by his & how my parents' deaths must have come to them as a disagreeable surprise like a bill in the mail they thought they'd already paid.

Eddie invited me in for hot wine. His small sparsely furnished room smelled like a combination of burned orange peel & old woman's cheek you're forced to kiss at a family reunion. Carpet covered in big oily stains, the room spoke eloquently of spills of the clumsy fuckers who'd once lived there.

We had sandwiches & hot wine. Eddie was one of those people adept at summing up their lives in less than a minute. Born in Thailand. Studied medicine—never practiced. Traveled widely. Now trying Paris.

Nothing to say to that.

Conversation flowed like water down flushed toilet. He stared at me so intensely I felt my eyes were pocket-sized mirrors & he was checking his hair.

Night came quickly—it unnerved me he didn't put on lights. Glanced at switch on the wall but was afraid to move if this fool preferred the airless joy of shadows then so would I. Finally he reached behind him & put on a lamp. Small light burned & grew huge in my eyes.

—So, you had a disappointment today, he said.

—Yes, I thought she'd be here.

This made him laugh in violent spasms, a laugh like a congenital defect.

—I meant the death of your friend.

—Oh, yes, that too.

—You love this girl?

—She's an old friend from home.

—Australia, he said blandly making the name of my country sound like an old thing he'd once owned but had since thrown away. I said Uh-huh & he continued w/ questions. What was I doing in Paris? How long would I stay? Where did I live? Did I work? Why not? & so on. He offered to help me in any way I needed. Money or a job or a place to stay. I thanked him & said it was getting late.

—Would it bother you very much if I took your photo?

It would.

—Oh, come on. It's just this little hobby of mine, he said smiling. I looked around the room for proof of this claim—a photograph maybe—but the walls were bare & when he went into the next room to get his "apparatus" as he called his camera that made me shudder because whenever someone says the word apparatus I see enormous gleaming pincers w/ single plump drop of blood at its tip.

—I think I should be going, I said.

—Just one little photo. I'll be quick, he said w/ fixed smile like a window painted shut.

As he set up I felt convinced he was going to ask me to take off my clothes. He was talking all the while saying You really must tell me if there's anything I can do for you, convincing me not only was he going to ask me to take off my clothes, he was going to pull them off himself. He switched on another light—a single bulb blared a trillion watts & he took my photo sitting in the chair & standing up & putting on my coat & walking out the door.

—Come by for dinner tomorrow night, he said.

—OK, I lied & hurried out & on the way home swung by the cemetery for a final farewell to Lionel where I tried to be solemn & feel REMORSE SADNESS LOSS SOMETHING I took a deep breath didn't do any good I couldn't feel ANYTHING other than pure disgust at myself—I procrastinated so long I missed what might have been a turning point in my life when is the next one going to be? I'd pictured our reunion a zillion times Caroline had been the focal point of my being in Europe or to put it plainly of being alive and through fear & indecision I'd missed her.

I kicked the headstone in a fit of impotent rage but then remembered Lionel. Tried to be sad again but had no room in my heart for mourning him. Too busy mourning love.

Unfeeling tribute to my old friend broken by soft footsteps on grass—Eddie at the bottom of cemetery hands in pockets staring. I pretended I didn't see him & rushed off into night thinking of pincers.

Me Again

Can't pretend other people's minor misfortunes aren't of great amusement to me because they are—not death or sickness but when someone's money is swallowed by a public telephone which then refuses to make a call it's fucking funny. I can watch people hitting telephones all day.

I've found an ingenious place to think—inside cool, dark cathedrals of Paris. Of course believers as dumb as patriots make conversations but conversations quiet as they're w/ God. Stupid how we think God only hears our thoughts when we address them to him in particular & not when we think our dirty little thoughts in everyday scenarios such as I hope Fred dies soon so I can have his office, it really is much nicer than mine. The meaning of faith is our understanding w/ Creator that he will not eavesdrop on our mind's whisper to itself unless invited.

Café Gitane

Months since last written. Crazy with solitude crazy with indecision crazy with imaginary eyes. Days filled w/ walking thinking reading eating drinking smoking & generally trying to pick the padlock of life but it's difficult when you're the blunt weapon left out of every war. Hope I won't suffer same problems in the future, can't think of anything worse. (Not that I've anything against problems, I don't—expect to have them all my life—just don't want them to be the same problems. Hope for different horrific affliction to mark each new year.) I think your early twenties must be the age you stumble onto patterns that will ruin your life.

A Thursday

Talk about volatile combinations now LUST & LONELINESS have fused in a haunting unbearable way my body screams my soul screams to touch to be touched around me are countless chiseled & flawless couples look like they're off to start new unendurable race of ex–soap stars there MUST be someone for me somewhere.

2:30—Midweek?

Every day—same café, different book to read. I don't speak to ANYONE & keep my eyes in strange places when I order my coffee but they know my face here. The patrons smoke anything flammable & the bartender asks you what you want to drink as if you might be his old nemesis from high school but he isn't sure & I sit at a small table near the radiator thinking here I am again wanting to be invisible then furious when ignored.

Out the large window I look at life. What a fucking lot of bipeds! Australia—bipeds throwing a ball. Paris—bipeds in turtleneck sweaters. Pessoa called humanity "variable but unimprovable"—hard to find a better description than that. The waiter comes by with the bill. I argue w/ him & lose quickly. No wonder key existentialists were French. It's natural to be horrified at existence when you have to pay 4 dollars for coffee.

Undated Time

I imagine Judgment Day to be God calling you into a tiny white room w/ an uncomfortable wooden chair that you sit in & splinter yourself as you shift anxiously. He comes in smiling like a train conductor who found you without a ticket & he says I don't care what good you did or what evil & I don't care if you believed in me or in my son or in any other member of my extended family & I don't care if you gave generously to the poor or if you gave to them stingily with closed fists but here is a minute-by-minute account of your time on earth. Then he produces a piece of paper 10,000 kilometers long & says, Read this & explain yourself. Mine would read as follows:

June 14th

9:00 am	*woke up*
9:01 am	*lay in bed, staring at ceiling*
9:02 am	*lay in bed, staring at ceiling*
9:03 am	*lay in bed, staring at ceiling*
9:04 am	*lay in bed, staring at ceiling*
9:05 am	*lay in bed, staring at ceiling*
9:06 am	*lay in bed, staring at ceiling*
9:07 am	*lay in bed, staring at ceiling*
9:08 am	*rolled over onto left side*
9:09 am	*lay in bed, staring at wall*
9:10 am	*lay in bed, staring at wall*
9:11 am	*lay in bed, staring at wall*
9:12 am	*lay in bed, staring at wall*
9:13 am	*lay in bed, staring at wall*
9:14 am	*lay in bed, staring at wall*
9:15 am	*doubled over pillow, sat up to see out window*
9:16 am	*sat in bed, staring out window*
9:17 am	*sat in bed, staring out window*
9:18 am	*sat in bed, staring out window*
9:19 am	*sat in bed, staring out window*

Then God would say Life is a gift & you never even bothered to unwrap it. Then he would smite me.

New Year's Eve

All Paris counting down to Christmas now counting down to New Year proving that not only are we more obsessed with time than ever we just can't stop counting everything. Our perception is that time is moving forward but scientists tell us we are wrong wrong wrong in fact they say we are so wrong they feel a little embarrassed for us.

It's New Year's Eve & I've NOTHING to do NOBODY to touch NO ONE to kiss.

January 1

What a night! If anyone feels sudden potent tremors in the world they come from me having finally sideslipped into the aromatic hairy pocket of the other gender. Yes it's official—I am a fornicator!

Sat on bench in Montmartre cemetery opposite Nijinsky's grave & made a list of resolutions. The usual bunk—quit smoking & be happy with what you have & give to beggars but not pleaders & don't grovel even to yourself & piss wine & shit gold blahblahblah. Banal list of promises to myself numbered an even fifty & as I tore them up I thought New Year's resolutions are a confession that all along we know the fault of our unhappiness lies w/ us & not w/ others.

Walked the streets until midnight among the people of Paris gorging on joy & I felt stupid & inadequate in my unhappiness & it seemed very clear to me that loneliness is the worst thing in the world & people should ALWAYS be forgiven for all the compromises they make in love.

At midnight I put my fingers in my ears but it didn't do any good—I could still hear it. The countdown to the New Year was the worst thing I'd ever heard.

I walked on. The window of regular café shone out of the fog in a circle of dotted lights. As I entered fat bartender poured me champagne smiling. I took it & wished him a happy New Year in French. Regular patrons all turned eager to know who I was & plied me w/ questions & let out gasps of shock when I said I was from Australia—my country to them no closer than the moon. Got drunk & returned questions w/ questions & found out who had children who was divorced who had bowel cancer who won a small literary prize for a poem entitled "The Tripe of Life" who had crushing financial difficulties & who belonged to the Freemasons but don't tell anybody.

4 am—noticed a woman standing at the other end of the bar. Hadn't seen her come in. She had a beautiful angular face & wide brown eyes & wore a black furry hat & when she removed it hair fell out all over the place over her face into her champagne. She had a lot of hair. It went down her back. It went into my mind. It covered her shoulders & my thoughts.

I watched her as she drank & thought her face was one that you have to earn—there was a world-weariness in that face as if it had seen all the acts of creation & all the acts of destruction & had gotten stuck in the bottleneck of history & crawled out naked over miles & miles of broken bodies & machine parts & wound up here in this bar for a quick glass of champagne to rinse the taste of holocaust from her mouth.

The alcohol gave me courage & I went over without preparing an opening line.

—Bonsoir, mademoiselle. Parlez-vous anglais? I asked.

She shook her head as if I were a policeman interrogating her after a rape so I backed away & resumed my place at the end of the bar. Humiliated, I downed champagne in one go & when I finished saw her coming over.

—I do speak English, she said settling herself on stool beside me. Hard to place her accent, European but not French. Caught her looking at my scarred ears, not subtle about it, & before I knew what was happening she had her finger on my scar & I liked that there was no pity in her eyes only mild curiosity. Pity is the awful lost dazed brother of empathy. Pity doesn't know what to do with itself so it just goes Awwwwwww.

She surprised me further by not asking about it.

—Do you have any scars? I asked.

—I don't even have any scratches, she answered softly as tho a hand was over her mouth.

Her cardigan was open just enough to reveal a tight black T-shirt concealing small thrilling breasts like hard-boiled eggs.

I dangled my weak smile in front of her & asked what she was doing in Paris.

—Nothing mostly.

Nothing <u>mostly.</u> Those strange words played in my mind for a while rearranged themselves (mostly nothing) & finally died there.

Lust reaching astonishing proportions I felt my secret thoughts broadcast through a megaphone. She asked me where I was from & I told her & watched her eyes fill with the visions of a land she'd never seen. I always wanted to go to Australia she said but already I've traveled too much. We talked about the earth for a while & there was hardly a country I could think of she hadn't been lost in. She told me she speaks English French Italian German Russian. Mastery of languages impresses my lazy Australian brain.

Was this woman accepting my advances? Even reciprocating them? There's a hidden agenda here, I thought. She wants me for some banal purpose like to help her move furniture.

—Do you want to kiss me? she asked suddenly.

—As a start.

—Then why don't you?

—What if you reel backwards and make a scene?

—I won't.

—Promise?

—I promise.

—And hope to die?

—Above all things, I hope to die.

—In general, or if I kiss you?

—What's wrong with you?

—I don't know. Here I come.

I leaned forward & she grabbed my face & her long fingernails against my cheek were sharper than they looked & we kissed for a long time I think I was doing something wrong because our teeth kept colliding. When we finished the kiss she said laughing, I can taste your loneliness—it tastes like vinegar.

That annoyed me. Everyone knows loneliness tastes like cold potato soup.

—What can you taste of me? she asked playfully.

—I can taste your insanity, I said.

—What does it taste of?

—Blue cheese.

She laughed & clapped her hands then threw them around me & clutched my hair so it hurt.

—Let go.

—Not until you kiss me again. I want to taste some more of your loneliness, she said loudly. I was glad no one in the bar could speak English—this was embarrassing crazy talk & I didn't want anyone in the café thinking about the flavor of my lonely soul.

—Let's get another drink, I said.

We drank for another hour & I mutilated many of my most coherent thoughts by putting them into words.

I don't remember how we ended up back in her apartment. I remember her hands resting on my arms as she talked & I remember kissing in the street & afterwards hearing the sound of immature whistling nearby. I remember her telling me to stop whistling.

I remember that the sex was good. To prolong the moment I thought of mass graves & syringes & gum disease. I don't know what she thought of or if she even wanted to prolong the moment.

It was unofficially my first time. Officially too.

Now five in the morning. She fell asleep before me & I'm writing this very drunk & propped up in bed beside her. O Whatever Your Name Is! You sleep deeply like a beautiful cadaver & your ghostly white face sits there strangely on the pillow like a piece of the moon.

Still January 1, Later

Woke up feeling her breath on the back of my neck. The whole night played out in my head in Technicolor. I dragged myself along the sheets & turned & I looked at her dark eyebrows & big lips & long brown hair & thin body & small breasts & her beautiful angular face so still so chalky. I wanted to leave the bed without waking her & looked around the room for an object within reach of same approximate density of own body to replace myself w/ but could see only a coat rack which I discounted out of respect for my self-image. I lifted myself from the bed & quietly dressed. She is the first woman I have ever slept w/. She is a delicate flower I thought as I snuck out the door.

Odor of Paris in my mouth, mint with a chewy center. The sky a vast foreign country. The setting sun in my eyes but too happy to blink. Must have slept heavily all day—the sleep of a human body depleted of semen?

I have returned to my café taller from the previous evening's conquest. Me conquered? Her conqueror? The moon has just risen. I feel lazy & hungover, the warm sensation of pleasant exhaustion slowly contracting. Edges of my old miserable self coming home.

I know I'll never see her again.

January 2 (Night)

Saw her again. She came into the café & sat opposite me. My brain scrambled for excuses why I snuck out of her apartment but she didn't appear to require one—she just began talking in her strange accent as if we'd arranged to meet. Behind her eyes I could tell she was happy to see me. That was surprising. Then I could tell she was unhappy that I was surprised at her happiness. Then she fell into awkward silence & she grinned w/ pain behind it & tried to stare at me but her eyes looked away.

She cleared her throat & in an uncertain voice told me that the way to make French people uncomfortable is to talk about money. When I still said nothing she said I don't want to disturb you. Go on reading & she removed a sketchbook & pencil from her bag & started drawing my face & ordered a coffee & drank it slowly as she stared w/ strange big eyes, drawing me.

Was grateful to her for removing my virginity but it was gone now & I couldn't see any further purpose to her. Like having dinner with doctor after successful operation. What's the point?

—I can't concentrate with you staring at my head like it's a sculpture.

That made her giggle.

—Do you want to go for a walk? she asked.

Head whispered no. Mouth said yes.

On way out she told me her name was Astrid & I told her mine & I wondered if I should've given a fake name but it was too late for that now.

Luxembourg Gardens. Cold & windy & naked trees, frightening against the white sky. She kicked piles of leaves so they flew around us in the wind, an act of childlike joy she made seem violent. She asked me how tall I was. I shrugged this off w/ a sneer—every now & again someone asks me this asinine question & is flabbergasted that I don't know. Why should I know? What for? Knowledge of your own height serves no useful purpose in our society other than to be able to answer that question.

I asked <u>her</u> personal questions, she was evasive & her eyes on me felt like cold rain. Where was she from? Her family was always moving she said—Spain Italy Germany Bucharest the Maldives. But where was she born? She was born on the road, she said, eyes half closed. Her family treated her badly & she doesn't want to return to them, not even in her thoughts. The future is an unbearable topic also. Where will she go? What will she do? She shook her head as if to say these are the wrong questions.

Then in an excited voice she started boring me with lengthy historical discourses HONESTLY what do I care if Louis XVI cut himself shaving the morning before he was guillotined? DO I REALLY WANT TO KNOW that an eyewitness at the stake where Joan of Arc was burned heard her speaking to God through the flames saying You can be pleased! I didn't renounce you! & God saying back Stupid woman! What do I care what these people think? In the end while I like reading about history, something inside me rebels at being told it as if I were a slow-witted schoolboy who can't be trusted to open a book.

As if sensing my boredom she suddenly went silent & her eyes fell to the ground & I thought there's something about her that's way too adhesive. Occurred to me if I didn't get away that very second I'd be prying her off later with a bottle of mentholated spirits & a naked flame but she invited herself back to my place & I accepted.

She came in & stood in the center of the room in a way that made me think of cows & horses who sleep standing up. We made love in the bedroom in the dark, only sometimes the moonlight hit her face & I'd see her eyes were not just closed but squeezed tight.

Afterwards I watched her delight in tearing the plastic off a fresh packet of cigarettes as if picking daisies. She seemed to be relaxed now & as she smoked she talked passionately about everything her eyes fell on: ceilings & windows & curtains & faded wallpaper as if she'd been contemplating these objects for centuries & I was impressed by her knowledge & insights & asked if her intensity was European in character.

—No, it's just me she said smiling.

Then she asked me if I loved her. I have waited a long time to say it honestly to Caroline, so I said no. I wanted to say more, to hurt her so she'd never come back, so I said Maybe you should leave now before your angular face cuts something.

She exploded, tearing me apart, critiquing everything about me. The subtext was clearly You don't love me, tho in my defense should a person even need a defense for not loving someone, I had only known her two days.

She stormed out & I wondered what she wanted with my hollow life. Did she want to fill it & by filling it empty herself?

A Few Nights Later

This is how it works: She turns up uninvited & stands in front of me like those dozing cows & sometimes we make dinner & sometimes we eat it & sometimes we make love & sometimes she cries during it & I really hate that.

Often she takes my arm even as we walk around the apartment and as she speaks I keep losing track. Her English is fluent but often I have no idea what she means as if she's expressing an abridgment of her own thoughts. Sometimes she tells stories laughing & while she does have a genuinely sweet laugh I can never work out for the life of me what's so funny. She laughs at what I say too but at such odd moments, for all I know she might well be laughing at the word "the." Her laugh is so enormous and sustaining I'm afraid I'll be sucked into her mouth & wind up on the wrong side of the universe.

& she believes in God! I never imagined I would be with someone who <u>believes</u>—out of boredom I start a little argument about him, lazily throwing out the old chestnut If there's a God why is there so much misery & evil in the world, & she bores me right back w/ God's facetious smarty-pants answer to Job: Where were you when I created the heavens & the earth? THAT'S AN ANSWER?

I think her love for me has nothing to do with me except proximity—wrong place, wrong time. She loves me as a starving man loves whatever slop you put in front of him—not a compliment to the cooking but a testament to his hunger. I'm the slop in this analogy.

I want to be in love w/ her but not. I mean she's v. beautiful especially when exclaims surprise or shock which is why I'm constantly jumping out at her but I can't bring myself to love her. I don't know why. Maybe because she's the first nonrelated/nonmedical person to see me naked and vulnerable or maybe because she often seems *so* genuinely pleased simply to be with me—something inside me irritated at the idea that I have the capacity to make someone else happy just by existing when my existence has never done anything for me.

Yesterday she told me to call her Pauline.

—I fake a new name depending on what country I'm in, she said.

—So what are you telling me, Astrid isn't your real name?

—It's real if you call me & I answer to it.

—What's your name?

—Pauline.

—No, that's your French name. What's your original name?

—There are no original names. They've all been used before.

I gritted my teeth & thought what am I doing with this nutcase? She talks too much & her crying frustrates then bores me & every day I grow more & more convinced she's spent some time in a mental hospital & if not she should really think about it.

Blahblahblah

Tried closing myself off to her but it doesn't do any good. Astrid or Pauline or whatever her name is has sneakily gone about understanding me by finding passages I've underlined in books. The other day she found this one in Lermontov: "*I was gloomy—other children were merry and talkative. I felt myself superior to them—but was considered inferior: I became envious. I was ready to love the whole world— none understood me: and I learned to hate.*" This one struck her especially as it was underlined circled highlighted & annotated with the words My childhood! Must be more careful in leaving soulglimpses lying around like that.

Going to have to end this thing tho don't know how when it's my indifference that's probably made her fall deeper in love with me— if I wanted to stay she'd probably throw me out on my ear but since she can tell I want to leave she doesn't. She knows pleasure of pushing someone out the door is weakened considerably when w/ slightest nudge they break into a run.

An Ugly Day

Eddie's back. Standing on Rue de Rivoli wondering if I stole just *one* hot roasted chestnut would the vendor bother chasing me for it when I had the weird sensation that I was being talked to in a language not of words but of energy and vibrations. Turned to see his wry Asian face peering at me—we stared at each other, neither moving. After loooonng time he waved meekly & came through crowd to shake hand resting in my pocket. He had to pull it out. We chatted amiably & I was surprised to find how pleased I was to see a familiar face. Familiarity is important in a face. Don't like Eddie's face tho it's clean & sparkling like a bathroom tile in a ritzy hotel. Don't know how we found each other again—when I say goodbye to someone I expect it to stick. We walked in cold air & wintry light & Eddie told me he's working down by the docks & asked me if I have a job & what have I been doing without one? I told him I'd found a woman because that's the only external thing that has happened to me—some internal things have happened but they're not his business & besides they're incommunicable.

—What does she look like? he asked.

I'm not good at describing people & wind up sounding like an eyewitness in a police interview. She's 5'7" brown hair Caucasian . . .

Eddie said he'd like to meet her, trying again to worm his way into my life. I sense he is trouble, he's too nice too genial too helpful too friendly. Trouble. He wants something. Don't know why but I invited him to dinner then thought Now I'll never get rid of him.

—Get rid of who? Eddie asked & as streetlamps came on I realized that somewhere along the way I'd developed habit of thinking out loud.

Possibly a Weekday

Changing my opinion of Eddie. Tho he's constantly chilling me w/ his suspicious pursuit of friendship I like his contradictions—he's a man at the peak of fitness who refuses to walk anywhere & he hates all tourists especially when they obstruct his view of the Eiffel Tower & while his clothes are always immaculately washed or dry-cleaned the man just doesn't brush his teeth. What I like about him most tho is that he seems genuinely interested in everything about me & always seeks my thoughts & opinions & laughs at my jokes & every now & then actually calls me a genius. Who wouldn't like a fellow like that?

A strange threesome—Eddie & Astrid & me. At first when we ate dinner together you could see them freeze when I went to do something & it made me laugh to myself to see two grown people loath to be left in the same room. But soon quasi-friendship developed based on laughing together at my clumsiness & forgetfulness & lax attitude toward hygiene—amusement at my faults is common ground on which they both stand.

Sometimes three of us walk by the Seine. Buy cheap wine & bread & cheese & we talk about everything but I'm always impatient w/ other people's opinions because I'm sure they're just repeating something they heard somewhere or else regurgitating ideas fed to them in childhood. Look, everyone's entitled to their own opinion & I'd never shut anyone down who was expressing one but can you be sure it's really theirs? I'm not.

Catastrophe!

Tonight Astrid Eddie & me went to do laundry & to pass the time we tried to guess the origins of each other's stains. Astrid thought every wine stain was blood & every coffee stain a splattering of tuberculosis. It was cold out & the window of the laundromat was all fogged up & we couldn't see outside & Eddie was bent in front of the dryer lifting his clothes to his nose & sniffing each item with pleasure before folding it in a meticulous fashion as if preparing to send his underpants off to war.

—Hey, what the fuck? Eddie suddenly shouted as he sniffed his clothes his face contorting with each enormous whiff. There must have been something in the machine! These smell of shit!

He waved his garments under Astrid's nose.

—I don't smell anything.

—How can you not smell anything? Maybe you don't smell what I smell but you must smell something.

—I don't smell anything bad.

—Martin. You don't smell shit?

I reluctantly took a sniff.

—It smells fine.

—Shit smells fine?

Eddie put his head in the clothes dryer sniffing. I was laughing & Astrid was laughing & it was a good moment. Then Astrid said I'm pregnant & Eddie hit his head on the inside of the dryer.

A baby! A fucking baby! A defecating pea-brained unformed biped! A horrible toothless homunculus! An incarnation of ego! A demanding serpent of need! A bald whining primate!

My life is over.

Help!

The topic of the moment: abortion. I am a passionate advocate. I hear myself in conversations w/ Astrid extolling virtues of abortion as if it were a new time-saving technology we can't afford to live without. Like everything else her responses alternate between vague & fuzzy & downright mysterious. She says an abortion would be probably pointless—whatever that means.

Sex: the match that sets off human firework. In our loveless palace we've built a child. Suddenly being almost broke filled w/ new & daunting meaning compounded by the terrible discovery that I have not the heart/cunning/spine/amorality necessary to simply slip out of the country without a word and never return. To my horror principles have wormed their way into fabric of my being. I can't recall a single instance of my parents showing strong moral fiber, but still it's there inside me & I know I can't leave Astrid. I'm stuck. Hopelessly stuck!

Much Later

Haven't written for months. Astrid very pregnant. The fetus expands persistently. The invader draws near. My own private population explosion: spinal injury of my independence. Do I care if it dies?

The only good I can imagine from having a child: what I can learn from him, not from nauseatingly cute attempts at walking talking shitting which thrill every parent so they repeat their discoveries to you ad nauseam until you despise not only all children everywhere but even find you're struck by sudden & irrational distaste for kittens & puppies. But it occurs to me I could learn from this child something about the nature of humanity—and if I accept Harry's pronouncement that I am a born philosopher then this baby could be an ambitious philosophical project! What if I reared it in a cupboard without light? Or in room full of mirrors? Or Dali paintings? Apparently babies have to <u>learn</u> to smile so what if I never taught him or showed him laughter? No television of course no movies maybe no society either—what if he never saw another human other than me or not even me? What would happen? Would cruelty develop in that miniature universe? Would sarcasm? Would rage? Yes I could really learn something here tho why stop at one child? Could have a collective of children or "family" & alter variables in environment that will govern life of each one to see what's natural what's inevitable what's environmental & what's conditioning. Above all <u>I will strive to raise a being that understands itself.</u> What if I gave child head start by encouraging self-awareness at an unnaturally young age, maybe 3? Maybe earlier? Would need to create optimum conditions for flowering of self-awareness. This child will know a lot of solitude that's for sure.

Yuck

If a girl Astrid wants to name the child Wilma for some reason—if a boy, Jasper. God knows where she got these names—all the same to me. If raised properly at a certain age he'll/she'll choose his/her own name to reflect who he/she thinks he/she is to feel entirely comfortable in his/her own skin—nothing worse than hearing your name called & feeling a dispassionate shudder or being left cold when you see your own name in print which is why most signatures are barely legible scrawls: the unconscious rebeling against the name, trying to smash it.

Worried about money. Astrid is too. She says she has been broke before in more countries than I can name in such poverty I cannot imagine but she's never done it with a baby & she's worried my inherent laziness will ensure our mutual starvation. Clearly criticism is the new fire that will not die. To have a child is to be impaled daily on the spike of responsibility.

Christ!

Idiocy (or is it insanity?) redefined in what I saw when I came home today: Astrid fixing the fuses in the kitchen while standing in a small puddle of water. I threw her over my shoulder and tossed her on the bed.

—You trying to kill yourself? I screamed.

She looked at me as if I had put my face on inside out & said in small bored voice If I could think of a really clever way to commit suicide, I would.

Suicide?

—How can you even think about suicide when you're pregnant? I said surprising myself w/ pro-life thoughts.

—Don't worry. Suicides often fail, anyway. When I was a girl my uncle jumped off a cliff and then waved from the bottom, his back broken. And my cousin took an overdose of pills and just wound up vomiting for a week. My grandfather put a gun in his mouth, pulled the trigger, and somehow managed to miss his brain.

—This is the first thing you've told me about your family!

—Is it?

—Did every member of your family attempt suicide at one point?

—My father never did.

—Who was your father? What was his name? What did he do? Is he still alive? What country did he come from? What country do you come from? What is your first language? Where did you grow up? Why don't you talk about anything? Why won't you tell me anything? Did something terrible happen to you? What . . .

A cold glaze came over her—she was receding fast. Her soul on an express train, back to nowhere.

Strange Days Indeed

Things w/ Astrid worse than ever. Icy wall dividing us. She does nothing all day, just stares out window or at own puffiness. On rare occasions she says anything her opinions are as bleak & sterile as mine were before I got sick of them. (I haven't grown optimistic merely bored with pessimism so now I think light pretty thoughts for variety—sadly this is starting to get dull too—where next?)

209 A Fraction of the Whole

I say We should get out a bit.

She says To do what?

I say We could go sit in a café & look at people.

She says I can't look at people anymore. I've seen too many.

Life's lost its appeal. Nothing I can suggest to break her from catatonic spell. Museums? She's been to every one. Walks in the park? Already strolled under every color of the leaf. Movies? Books? No new stories only different character names. Sex? She's done every position untold times.

I ask her Are you sad?

—No, unhappy.

—Depressed?

—No, miserable.

—Is it the baby?

—I'm sorry. I can't explain it, but you're being so lovely, Martin. Thank you she says squeezing my hand & staring at me w/ her wide glassy eyes.

One night she cleaned the whole apartment & went out & returned w/ wine & cheese & chocolates & a fedora hat for me which I wore w/ no clothes on & it made her laugh hysterically & I realized just how much I missed her laugh.

But by morning she was miserable again.

Remembering how on the morning after our relationship began she'd drawn my face in pencil I went out & bought paints & a canvas spending all the money I had in vain hope that she might take out burning misery on blank canvas instead of on me.

When I unveiled the gift she cried & smiled in spite of herself then moved the canvas by the window & began painting.

That set off something new.

Each painting a rendition of hell, she has many hells & she paints them all. But hell is just a face, and it is just the face she paints. One face. One terrible face. Painted many times.

—Whose face is it? I asked today.

—It's nobody. I don't know. It's just a face.

—I can see it's a face. I said it was a face. I didn't say Whose hand is that?

—I'm not a good painter, she said.

—I don't know much about painting but I think it's very good.

But that's not what I'm talking about. I want to know who the face belongs to.

—I painted it, she said. It belongs to me.

You can see there was no talking to her like you talk to a normal person. You had to be tricky.

—I've seen that face before, I said. I know him.

—He is not a man. He is not in the world, she said & my suspicions hardened into conclusions: that this woman is insane.

Always small canvases, always the same painting, only the colors differ browns & blacks & muted reds. I can see her frenzy in that face.

Later I study the painted faces hoping that in the hallucinatory state in which she paints slips of her subconscious have dropped clues onto the canvas. The paintings perhaps elegantly symbolic maps that can lead me to epicenter of her morbid condition. My eyes train on them, dissecting them furtively under the weak lamplight. But I can't see anything in that face other than her horror of it that fast has become my own. It really is a horrible face.

Yesterday

Whatever religious sentiments she has banked up in her interior stirred up in all this painting. Sometimes she'll be lost in painting & she'll call out Forgive me Lord! then go about chatting to him in half whispers leaving lengthy pauses presumably where he responds. When today she said Forgive me Lord! I did his part & said OK. You're forgiven. Now shut up.

—He doesn't believe in you, Lord.

—He's right not to believe in me. I'm not very believable. Besides, what have I ever done for him?

—You have led him to me!

—And you think you're such a gift? You aren't even honest with him!

—Yes I am, Lord, I am honest with him.

—You don't tell him anything about your past.

—I tell him about my feelings.

—Oh for fuck's sake. Go and take him a beer. He's thirsty! I shouted & a few seconds later she entered the room carrying the beer smiling sweetly & kissing me all over & I didn't know what to think.

Curiouser & Curiouser

This is how we communicate. How I'm finding out a little more about her. Is there really a possibility she doesn't know it's me doing the part of God?

This morning she painted as I sat beside her and read.

—Oh Lord! How long! she shouted suddenly.

—What?

—How much longer!

—How much longer what? Astrid, what are you talking about?

She wasn't looking at me she was looking up at the ceiling. I thought for a few minutes then went into the next room & half closed the door & peering through the crack tried this experiment and shouted back How much longer for what? Be specific, my child. I'm not a mind reader.

—The years! How much longer will I live?

—A long time! I said and watched the light behind her face galloping away.

I couldn't get any more out of her after that.

& Curiouser

Only when painting her ghastly sickening faces does it happen. I was sitting on the toilet when I heard from the living room Lord! I am afraid! I am afraid for this baby!

I opened the door a little so she could hear me.

—That's ridiculous! What's there to be scared about?

Speaking as God from the toilet lent the whole situation some authenticity, the acoustics made my voice echo just like his would.

—Will he be a good father? she asked.

—He'll do his best!

—He won't stay. I know it. One day he'll go and I'll be alone with this baby this sick baby!

—There's nothing wrong with the baby.

—You know he must be sick like me.

Then she laughed long & horribly & lapsed into silence.

These chat sessions with the Lord i.e. me seem to take on proportions of a fabulous opera. Calling out from across the room, she confides in me as never before.

—Lord?

—Talk to me.

—My life is a waste!

—Don't say that.

—I have wandered everywhere! I have no friends! I have no country!

—Everyone has a country.

—I moved too fast! I saw too much! I forgot nothing! I am incapable of forgetting!

—Is that such a bad thing? So you've got a good memory. Listen, whose face are you painting?

—My father.

—Really!

—My father's father.

—Well, which is it?

—My father's father's father.

—Listen, Astrid. Do you want me to smite you?

She said nothing more. I'd put the fear of Me into her.

Sigh

Eddie & I discussed tonight my pathetic financial situation & he offered to give me money not as loan but as gift. Out of fictitious pride I refused it biting my inner lip. Wandered streets randomly picking cafés & asking in patchy French if I might work there. Answers came in wordless sneers. What am I going to do? Clock's ticking. A nine-month gestation period just isn't enough preparation time. I pray the baby won't be premature—undercooked people are trouble.

Love Is Hard Work

I was in the kitchen & Astrid in the living room painting her soul's leftovers & I heard her shout Dieu!

—What?

—Dieu! Vous êtes ici? Pouvez-vous m'entendre?

—English, my child.

—I saw a child's corpse today, oh Lord.

—Yuck. Where?

—Outside the hospital. A couple were carrying him in their arms to the emergency room, they were running but I saw that the child was already dead.

—That's hard, I said.

—Why did you take him, O Lord?

—Why blame me? I was nowhere near that kid!

She fell silent for ten minutes then said Where are you, Lord?

—In the bathroom.

—WHERE ARE YOU, LORD?

—IN THE BATHROOM!

—What if after the baby's out, nothing's changed?

—Are you nuts? A baby changes everything.

—But inside me? In my blood.

—Astrid, have you been to the doctor's?

—Yes, God, I've been to doctors in Austria & in Italy & in Greece & in Germany & in Turkey & in Poland & they all say the same thing. I have the healthiest blood they've ever seen.

—Well, there you go. Did you really go to a doctor in Turkey? Did he wash his hands?

—I'm doomed.

—You're imagining it. There's nothing wrong with you. Everyone says so. You've been given a clean bill of health. You can't go on imagining there's something wrong with your blood. That's just crazy talk, OK?

—OK.

—Are we together on this?

—Yes, Lord.

—Good. Now what's for dinner?

Three in the Morning

Tonight I worked!

Eddie—without consulting me—convinced someone to give me a job.

—I didn't authorize you to do that.

—You're almost out of money. You've got a child to think about now.

—Well, all right then, what will I be doing?

—You'll be working with me. Loading crates.

—That sounds all right.

—It's hard, backbreaking work.

—I've heard about that kind of thing I said wondering why people always boast about doing something that breaks your back.

Pont Neuf at dusk—no boats. Dark waters of the Seine, not flowing. We waited on the stone banks of the river & watched the brown water just sit there.

—What do we do now? I asked.

—We wait.

Boats & barges ambled languidly by. A soft rain fell & night fell down with it. Colored city lights reflected on the body of the river. Rain fell unabated.

Two hours later Eddie said Here we are then.

The boat came forward relentlessly, a nightmare littered with heavy packing crates. Two men stepped off, faces hardly visible between where beanies stopped & scarves began. We worked wordlessly in the anonymous night clearing crates one by one from the boat & carrying them up the ramp to the street where truck was waiting. Driver of truck had sluggish dozy eyes & as we worked I tried guessing his inner sufferings but couldn't come up with anything other than "hates to work at night." Eddie & I unloaded those heavy crates for hours while others shouted orders to each other in harsh whispers. By end as the empty boat putted out to sea my everything hurt.

Driver of truck gave Eddie envelope & we walked off together sweating in the cold moonlight. Eddie handed envelope to me, in an attempt to get me to keep all the money to feed my sudden & unwanted family but I gave him half—my greedy self chafing against my principled self.

I came home & was distressed to see I was spotless after heavy night of toil. Imagined my face would be covered in black soot but there's just no soot in lifting crates no matter how heavy they are.

—How was it? Astrid asked as if I'd been to see a much-hyped movie. I looked at her belly & it occurred to me there was nothing inside not a baby not even a digestive system just a vacant hollow shell puffed up with air & I walked over & put my hand on her growth which she took as a loving gesture & she kissed my hand which made me feel cold all over & I thought I am incapable of loving this woman the mother of my child, and maybe I won't be able to love the child either. And why am I like that? Is it because I have no self-love? I have self-like but is it enough?

A Week Later an Accident

We work night after night, silent silhouettes sweating in the dark. The hours grind by & I make time pass by imagining I'm an Egyptian slave constructing one of the lesser pyramids. My reverie broken when I mistakenly articulate it to Eddie by saying when we drop a crate for the third time Come on Eddie, for the love of Ra!

Tonight when I came home Astrid was on the floor.

—Are you OK? What happened?

—I fell down the stairs.

First compassionate thought was for the baby—his head will be dented & all squashed in at one side I thought.

I took her to bed & fed her & read to her like my mother read to me tho she was by all appearances unharmed by the fall. She lay in bed staring with only the whites of her eyes. Her pupils lay there like little broken pieces of night. She told me not to fuss. Do you think the baby's all right? I asked. Should we take your stomach to the hospital?

—You don't want this baby, she said not looking at me.

—That's not true! I shouted defensively. I didn't want this baby but now that it's coming I've accepted the inevitable I lied hoping to talk myself into stoic fortitude. It didn't work.

Tonight

Something happened tonight. Laboring away as usual, a useless moon shedding diffused light through a thin veil of clouds, the night like a bite of cold apple—it made my teeth sting. Tied the boat to the pier & thought how if someone bottled smell of wet rope & sold it over the counter I'd buy it.

Sudden shouting. Above us a group of four Arabs descended the steps walking closely together—a tough-guy walk, a mean bounce. Long black coats & longer faces. The Arabs shouted something & our guys shouted back & stopped working & grabbed whatever was handy, pipes crowbars metal hooks. The two groups argued in a spattering of French & Arabic. I didn't know what they were arguing about but tension chewable. The two groups menacingly close to one another & there was a little show of pushing & shoving & they looked so much like rival football supporters full of beer the whole scene made me homesick.

Eddie said to me We should keep out of it. What do you think?

Didn't tell him what I thought because what I thought was this: Everyone here but Eddie & me has a beard.

Couldn't pick up the meaning of all those guttural sounds—only the hostility was clear. After the group broke up & climbed back up the sloping ramp the leader of the Arab group spat on the ground, a gesture that always says to me I'm too scared to spit in your face so I'm just going to put some phlegm about half a meter from your left shoe OK?

Dawn

Am I changing? Is a man's character changeable? Imagine an immortal. Revolting to think he might be making the same old boo-boos over the centuries. To think of the immortal on his 700,552nd birthday still touching the plate even when someone has told him it's hot—surely we have deep capacity for change but our 80 years doesn't give us ample opportunity. You have to be a fast learner. You have to cram infinity into a handful of lousy decades.

This morning passed horribly deformed beggar who was for all practical purposes merely a torso rattling a cup—was it really me who gave him 100 francs & said Take the day off? It wasn't me, not exactly. It was one of my selves, one of the multitudes. Some of them laugh at me. Others bite their nails in suspense. One snorts with derision. That's how they are, the multitudes. Some of the selves are children & some are parents. That's why every man is his own father & his own son. With the years if you learn enough you can learn how to shed your selves like dead skin cells. Sometimes they come out of you & walk around.

Yes I'm changing. Change is when new selves come into foreground while others recede into forgotten landscapes. Maybe definition of having lived full life is when every citizen in the hall of selves gets to take you for a spin—the commander the lover the coward the misanthrope the fighter the priest the moral guardian the immoral guardian the lover of life the hater of life the fool the judge the jury the executioner—when every last soul is satisfied at moment of death. If only one of the selves has been nothing but a spectator or a tourist then the life is incomplete.

My commander, that highest voice in the hierarchy of my head, is back—tyrannical bastard. He orders me to stay w/ Astrid & ride it out. No wonder am in confusion. Am oppressed by totalitarian police state in which I live. There must be a revolution one of these days. A revolt of all my selves—but I'm not sure I have the one needed to lead them: a liberator.

Escape!

Baby escaped! Fluid has become flesh. No turning back now. We've named it Jasper.

A cause for celebration & fear & trembling. Astrid proud mother—me semiproud. Never been much of a collaborator. Baby was joint project & my personal stamp hard to ascertain.

Today baby on a blanket kicking chubby legs in the air. Told Astrid to keep him off the floor—would be embarrassing if he was eaten by rats. Bent over baby & looked but really wanted to peer into his skull to see if any evil or cruelty or intolerance or sadism or immorality in there. A new human being. Am not impressed it's mine.

Can't help thinking that in this baby we've forged an absurd monument to our passionless relationship—we've created a symbol of something not worth symbolizing: a crazy edifice of flesh that will grow in equal proportion to our dwindling love as it dies.

The smell! The smell!

There's more feces here than in the Marquis de Sade's prison cell.

Silence

Baby doesn't cry. I don't know anything about babies except that they cry. Ours isn't crying.

—Why is he so damn quiet? I asked.

—I don't know.

Astrid sat in the living room all pale staring out the window. Can't help but look at this baby & see not a child or a new human being but an old one. A sickening idea has taken hold—*this baby is me prematurely reincarnated.* I loathe this kid—I loathe it because it is me. It is me. It will surpass me. It will overthrow me. It will know what I know, all my mistakes. Other people have children. Not me. I have given birth to something monstrous: to myself.

—I think he's hungry, I said.

—So?

—So get your tit out.

—He's sucking me dry.

—OK, OK. Maybe I'll just give him some normal milk.

—No! That's no good for him!

—Well, fuck, this is not my field of expertise. All I know is the baby needs some kind of nourishment.

—Why don't you read to him? she said laughing. Last night she'd caught me reading him passages from Heidegger.

—He doesn't understand, she'd howled.

—I don't either! I shouted back. Nobody does!

A very bad situation. Of the three of us, it's clear whose welfare must be provided for at all costs, who is the most important here.

Me.

I Almost Died Tonight!!!!!!!

The boat's never on time so we wait & read the newspaper & then it arrives like the four horsemen of the apocalypse on a moonlight cruise. The darkness broken by bobbing lights of the boat heading toward us & as it moors the rigid faces of our employers wedged tightly in the dark.

Tonight Eddie & I were lifting a particularly heavy crate that just wouldn't budge & I'd only got it a quarter of an inch off the ground when I realized in a panic I wasn't bending my knees. Fearing for longevity of my spine I lowered the crate & stepped away from it & tho it was too late I bent my knees.

—What are you doing? Eddie asked.

—Let's have a break, I said & pulled out a book from my back pocket & started to read—a novel I'd bought at one of the stalls next to the Seine: *Journey to the End of the Night* by Céline.

Didn't read more than a line—my eye caught dark mass moving toward us, a group of men you'd think were out for a brisk walk if not for guns in their hands.

A shot fired in the air. Our coworkers fled in all directions running up & down the bank of the Seine. It's funny watching people's stony indifference disappear when their lives are at stake.

Eddie & I walled in behind a tower of crates. Our only escape route would have been the freezing Seine or the sudden appearance of a golden staircase to the clouds. We ducked down behind crates.

—What have you gotten me into? I asked Eddie eager to assign blame.

Eddie ran forward & untied the ropes mooring us to the bank & pushed with his foot & ran back & joined me behind the crates. The boat slowly drifting.

We listened to the footsteps as they came closer to the boat & we listened to the footsteps as they jumped onto the boat now gliding down the Seine.

—Come out of there, a gruff voice said.

Maybe he's not talking to us I thought optimistically & was annoyed at Eddie's automatic compliance. He stood his hands high in the air like he's done this before.

—You too, the voice said to someone, hopefully not me. Come on, I can see your shadow.

I looked across at my shadow & realized it's only the head that gives you away. Otherwise crouched down you could be any old sack of potatoes.

I stood hands in air but felt too clichéd so turned palms inward.

Our would-be assailant had a beard that reminded me of an Alaskan husky & was generations past me & it filled me with outrage. I'd always expected to be done in by a young punk—wild & misguided & angry at the world.

He pointed the gun at me. Then he looked up at my hand & tilted his head slightly.

—Journey, he said. I had forgotten I was still holding the book.

—Céline, I said back in a whisper.

—I love that book.

—I'm only halfway through.

—Have you got to the point where—

—Hey, kill me, but don't tell me the end!

He lowered his gun & said You won't understand it unless you take it as a whole. It doesn't work episodically. Who else do you like?

—The Russians.

—Well yeah, the Russians. What about the Americans?

—Hemingway's OK.

—I like his short stories. Not his novels. You like Henry James?

—Not much. I love his brother though.

—William James! He's a genius!

—Absolutely.

He put down his gun & said Shit let's get this boat back.

Eddie & the Alaskan & I started up the boat & drove it back to the riverbank. Saved by a book!

—What's all this about? I asked him.

—We're competitors. My boss wants your boss to pack up shop.

—Well, shit, that doesn't mean you have to go around shooting does it?

—Yeah, it does.

That figures. Most people are killed by their jobs slowly over decades & I had to land one that's likely to do me in within the week.

Life with Baby

MAJOR problems at home. Astrid sleeps insatiably—her fatigue indefatigable & maybe because of this she treats poor baby as if he's someone else's dentures. Her love for me has gone all flabby too. I'm an irritant to her now.

Sometimes I find baby on floor, sometimes behind couch, once I came home & he was in the empty bath his head resting on drain. Other times she takes up her maternal role & lets the baby suck on her nipples her face a big blank. I ask if it hurts & she shakes her head & says Don't you notice anything, you idiot?

There's no understanding her.

Just five minutes ago she was on the couch her knees bunched up under her arms. I merely cleared my throat & she let out a scream. What if all relationships are like this behind closed doors?

—It was the only thing I hadn't done she said. I thought this baby would change something inside me.

—It is a big change.

—I meant deep inside.

—I think you've changed.

—I mean right deep down at the bottom of the core of me.

I don't know what she means. She's mad. I'm gobsmacked when I think about HER secret minions. What dissent going on in that woman! Total fucking pandemonium! I think she's suicidal—intestinal wall to intestinal wall crammed tight with treacherous extremists clamoring for the end.

I pick up the baby & comfort him.

I don't know what to do.

I say to Astrid I've heard about this. Postpartum depression.

She laughs loudly at the idea tho it isn't <u>that</u> funny.

An Extraordinary Day!

As usual went out & dragged anxieties along the boulevards until found a café to sit when anxieties wanted coffee & a cigarette. Paris all around me. A drunk pissing like he was nothing but a bladder in a hat, his ribbon of urine snaking its way through cobblestones. Two policemen paced the boulevard because to march would give off wrong impression.

Walked to the Seine & sat down beside it.

On bench next to me a woman had her legs stretched out catching a rare dose of sun. Nice legs—long & sinewy. She was looking at me while I was looking at her legs. I did a combination shrug & smile & before my brain recognized her, my mouth did.

—Caroline! I cried.

—Marty!

We leapt up at the same time & gazed at each other with deep surprise and joy.

—I went to find you! I shouted.

—Dad died!

—I know! I saw his grave!

—It was awful!

—Everyone I love is dead too!

—I know!

—Everyone! Mum! Dad! Terry! Harry!

—I heard! I rang home when Dad died and my uncle in Sydney told me the news!

—It was awful!

—I'm married! It's terrible!

—No!

—Yes!

—Well, I'm a father!

—No!

—That's what I said!

—Marty, let's run away together!

—I can't!

—Yes you can!

—I have to fulfill my parental duty!

—Well, I can't leave my husband either!

—Why not?!

—I still love him!

—So we're stuck!

—Hopelessly stuck!

—You look good!

—You look beautiful!

We both took a breather & laughed. I had never been so excited. She cupped my face in her hands & kissed me all over.

—What are you going to do? I asked.

—Let's rent a hotel room & make love.

—Are you sure?

—I'm sorry I ran out on you.

—You were in love with my brother.

—I was young.

—And beautiful.

—Let's get that room.

A small hotel above a restaurant, we made love all afternoon. I won't go into specifics except to say I didn't disgrace myself at all— duration was respectable & thunderstorm raged outside as we left the curtains open & I knew that this would hang hazy in our minds as a half-remembered dream & we would step back afterwards into our lives & when I thought this my heart painfully contracted there in the dark.

—So you're the father of a French child, she said.

Strangely that thought had never occurred to me before & while I love the French & theoretically am indifferent to my own country, one's roots hold a strange grip. Suddenly unpleasant my son wouldn't be Australian. There's no better country in the world to run away from. Fleeing from France is fine when German tanks are rolling in but in peacetime why would you bother?

We held each other giddily she was thin & so smooth I could've skipped her across a lake & she squeezed me in spasms & I kept kissing her as a way to stop her looking at the time as day turned to night. I couldn't waste this opportunity & I couldn't bear to hate myself again so I said that I didn't position myself deliberately in the path of love but it happened and to that end I would leave Astrid and the child so we could be together. She lapsed into a long silence her face barely visible in the dark. Then she spoke softly You cannot leave your son and mother of your child I couldn't handle the guilt besides I love my husband (a Russian named Ivan of all things). These people were insurmountable obstacles she said then added I love you too, but more as an afterthought hers was an I love you couched in conditions. It was not unconditional love. There were clauses and loopholes. Her love was not binding. I smiled, as if my mouth were compelled by tradition to do so.

I felt a violent mood swing coming on.

She and Ivan were going to visit his family in Russia for a while maybe six months or longer but when we said goodbye we arranged to meet again in exactly one year not on top of the Eiffel Tower but on the side & see if anything's changed. She said I love you again & I tried to take her at her word & after we said goodbye I walked aimlessly feeling like my heart had swung open briefly then shut before I had a chance to see what was inside. I walked for a couple of hours wanting desperately to cry on someone's shoulder but when I reached the Seine the sight of Eddie my only friend made me protective of my secret.

—Where have you been? You're late.

—The boat isn't here yet, is it?

—No he said absently gazing out upon the silent Seine.

One day I think history will judge me badly or worse accurately.

Night

It's night now & am watching Astrid sleep & am thinking of van Gogh. When he was fired from an early job he wrote When an apple is ripe a soft breeze will make it fall from a tree.

Love is like that. Love was inside banked up & has poured out at <u>her</u> arbitrarily. I say that because I realize dammit I love her I love her but I don't like her I love the girl I don't like. That's love for you! It goes to show love has little to do with the other person it's what's inside you that counts—that's why men love cars mountains cats their own abdominal muscles that's why we love sonsofbitches & bloodlesscunts. I don't like Astrid one bit I love her.

Maybe Caroline's tacit rejection of me had the same effect on my love for Astrid as the cooling of the universe had in aiding the formation of matter. & who would have guessed the heart is spacious enough to love not one but two people at once? Maybe three? Maybe I can love my son too.

The End!

This is the end!

Everything has changed drastically & permanently. Last big change—life will never be same again.

It started ordinarily enough. Was in Shakespeare & Co. bookshop leafing through secondhand paperbacks when I heard a voice Hey Céline!

A familiar voice, a familiar ugliness. The Alaskan husky striding toward me not slowing down the way people normally do but walking at full speed stopping abruptly an inch from my face.

—I've been looking for you. Don't go to the pier tonight, he said.

—Why not?

—Have you finished Journey yet?

—Not yet, I lied.

—Shit's going down tonight. I can't say any more than that.

—Go on.

—OK. We're going to blow your boat out of the water.

—Why?

—You're our rivals.

—Not me. I don't even know what's in those crates.

—That's why you shouldn't show up.

Ran around all afternoon trying to find Eddie & wrote notes & left them for him everywhere at his house at his favorite restaurant with his barber. Notes all identical:

> Stay away from work tonight. They're going to blow up the
> boat into a trillion pieces.

Even left note at my house on the kitchen table for Astrid telling her to pass on message should she see Eddie. She wasn't home. Why was I so terror-stricken that Eddie might die? Friendships are an unforeseeable burden.

At 4 went to a movie then passed by Eddie's place once more on my way home but he wasn't there & when I came home I opened the door to see him sitting in my kitchen a beer in his hand as though it were just an average day tho I spotted gaps in his tireless optimism. I caught him sighing wearily.

—You just missed Astrid, he said.

—I looked all over for you today. What a business you got me into!

—Back pain again? Anyway, I thought we'd walk together.

—What do you mean? Didn't Astrid tell you about the note?

—No, she said she was going down to the Seine.

I stood thinking for a few seconds before I got it. I looked at my watch. 7:40.

Left baby w/ Eddie & ran out of house & along wet pavement covered in a frosty sweat. Stumbling, I hurled myself toward the mighty Seine. What is she thinking? Ran palpitating, my feet hitting the wet pavement like little heartbeats. What is she going to do? I ran & suddenly I was not alone: along came the shame of a man who all at once discovers he's been ungrateful so we ran the three of us—me & shame & ingratitude running together like three shadows of three men who were running just ahead. I know what she's thinking. Almost out of breath. Are my lungs half empty or half full? Don't know what to do with my appetites. Astrid loved me greedily & I loved her back in reluctant nibbles. I thought I was as small as I could be but was wrong having once more shrunk in my own eyes. I know what she's going to do!

Suddenly I could see her just up ahead. A little thing in a black dress she was ducking & weaving in & out of streetlamps' pools of light a willowy figure slipping into darkness and out again. Of course she's crazy I know this I know she wants to kill herself in original fashion she's been looking for. She's running to do it—that makes sense. No one saunters to her own death. You don't keep Death waiting like that. You don't dawdle.

I lose her & then see her again running along bank of the Seine. Streetlamps cover the river in glitters. Boat's chugging in. Above I see the Alaskan hiding behind a wall. He holds up a grenade w/ one hand and shoos me away w/ the other. Boat docks & our guys tie it up to the pier. Three Arab men come running down pistols blazing & grenades in hands. Astrid jumps on the boat. They yell at her but she ignores them & the killers don't know what to do. They don't want to kill a civilian, no extra money in it.

She's on the boat refusing to move.

One of the men sees me. Takes a shot & I duck down behind the stone wall.

A siren.

The men consult each other in guttural screams. No time to lose. It's now or never. I look up at Astrid & her face is small & colorless & braced for death. Her whole face contracted like expecting boat's explosion to be nothing but loud pop.

—Astrid! Get out of there! I scream.

She looks up & smiles at me eloquently conveying the message that the lacerating misery of her life is taking its final bow. There was an *adios* in that smile, it was no au revoir.

A second later the boat went up in a series of little explosions. Just like Terry's suggestion box. Astrid in the middle of it, a wholly unique suicide. Pieces of her everywhere. On the bank. In the Seine. She couldn't be more scattered if she'd been dust.

People gaping, terribly excited to have witnessed my tragedy.

•

I walked home leaving Astrid in a million little pieces. No one looked at me. I was unlookable. But from every face I asked forgiveness. Every face was a link in a chain of faces, in one face broken up. Regrets came up & asked me if I'd like to own them. Declined them for the most part but took a few just so I wouldn't leave this relationship empty-handed. NEVER would've imagined that the dénouement of our love affair would be Astrid blown up into bits. I mean metaphorically maybe.

Never imagined she would ACTUALLY EXPLODE.

Death is full of surprises.

Under the arch I stop & think The baby! Am now sole caregiver me cursed & unclean w/ soul like forgotten limb on battlefield. Thought for first time maybe I should go back to Australia. Suddenly & for no good reason I missed my sun-beaten countrymen.

Back in the apartment her smell everywhere. I told Eddie to go home then went to the baby in bedroom asleep, unaware that his mother's head & her arms & her face were all in separate locations.

Just me & this grimacing baby.

He woke up screaming from hunger or existential angst. What am I going to do? It's not like there are any breasts in the refrigerator. I opened up a carton of milk & poured him a cup & then took the cup back to Jasper & poured a little milk into his mouth thinking I'm a widow of sorts. We weren't married but a baby is a fleshier contract than a flimsy piece of paper.

Found note taped to the bathroom mirror:

> I know you will worry how to be a father. You only have to love him. Don't try to keep him safe from harm. Love him, that's all you have to do.

Rather simplistic, I thought folding the note. Now I see it was her plan all along even if she herself didn't know it. To have this child & then dispose of herself.

Astrid dead. Never really knew her. Wonder if she knew I loved her.

Went upstairs & threw some clothes into a bag & then went back into the room & looked at the baby. That's what I'm doing now. Looking at this baby. My baby. Poor baby. Jasper. Poor Jasper.

I'm sorry I'm sorry I'm sorry what terrible tomorrows we'll have together what shabby luck your soul fell into the body of my son my son your father is love's lonely cripple. I'll teach you how to decipher all the confused faces by closing your eyes & how to cringe when someone says the words "your generation." I will teach you how not to demonize your enemies & how to make yourself unappetizing when the hordes turn up to eat you. I'll teach you how to yell with your mouth closed & how to steal happiness & how the only real joy is singing yourself hoarse & nude girls & how never to eat in an empty restaurant & how not to leave the windows of your heart open when it looks like rain & how everyone has a stump where something necessary was amputated. I'll teach you how to know what's missing.

We'll go.

We'll go home, to Australia.

& I'll teach you that if ever you're surprised you're still alive to check again. You can never be too sure about a thing like that.

•

That was it. The last entry.

I closed the notebook, sick to my stomach. The story of my birth shattered into rubble in my brain. Each broken piece of debris reflected an image from the journal's story. So, then—out of loneliness, insanity, and suicide, I was laboriously born. Nothing surprising about that.

•

The following year, on the morning of my mother's birthday, Dad came into my bedroom while I was dressing.

"Well, mate, it's the seventeenth of May again."

"So?"

"You be ready to go after lunch?"

"I have other plans."

"It's your mother's birthday."

"I know."

"You're not coming to the grave?"

"It's not a grave. It's a hole. I don't mourn holes."

Dad stood there, and I noticed there was a present in his hand. "I got her something," he said.

"That's nice."

"Don't you want to unwrap it?"

"I'm late," I said, leaving him alone in my bedroom with his sad and pointless gift.

Instead I took myself to the harbor to look at the boats. During the year that had passed, I thought against my will of all that was in my father's journal. No piece of writing before or since has burned so permanently into my memory. Despite the clever tricks in the art of forgetting my mind knows, they have no impact here. I remember every frightening word.

I sat all day, watching the boats. Or else I looked down at the rocks and the slick, shiny coat of oil floating on top of the water. I stayed there a long time. I stayed until the moon rose and a curtain of stars was drawn across the sky and the lights on the harbor bridge shone out of the darkness. All the boats nodded gently in the dark.

My soul is ambitious and mercenary in its desire to know itself. Dad's journal left this aim unsatisfied, and my mother's story was more of a mystery than when I knew nothing at all. I had ascertained that my mother was probably insane and of unknown origins. Other than that, my investigation had led only to more questions. About my father, it didn't surprise me that I had been violently unwanted. The only concrete thing I learned about *her* was that my birth was the final item on her to-do list, and once she'd checked it off, it allowed her to die. I was born to clear the obstacles on her pathway to death.

It got cold. I shivered a little.

The rhythms of the universe were perceptible in the way the boats were nodding at me.

•

A few years later I went back to the cemetery. My mother's grave was gone. There was someone new there, wedged in between old Martha Blackman and little Joshua Wolf. Her name was Frances Pearlman. She'd been forty-seven years old. She left behind two sons, a daughter, and a husband.

Since finding the journal I had read it over several more times.

The most disturbing element in that unpleasant little book was his assertion that I was possibly a premature reincarnation of his still living self, that *I was my father*: what did it all mean? That somewhere inside him, the man feared my autonomy would be the death of him?

I thought this staring at the grave of Frances Pearlman.

There were fresh flowers spread out over her grave. This was no misshapen love or empty coffin. I thought about my father, and how one of us was the host, the other the parasite, and I did not know who was who. It seemed to me we could not both survive. It seemed to me that one day, inevitably, one of us had to go. It seemed to me we were going to fight each other for supremacy of the soul. It seemed to me I'd be willing to kill him to survive.

They were creepy thoughts, but I was in a cemetery, after all.

THREE

In the newspaper and television reports made immediately after my father's death, much was made of the years of the early to mid-1990s, the period covering the worst excesses of his so-called insanity. Not only was this epoch notable for the arrival of Anouk Furlong (as she was known then)—a woman who played no small part in provoking his mental collapse—but this was the eventful slab of years that included strip clubs, mental asylums, plastic surgery, arrests, and what occurred when my father tried to hide our house.

Here's how it all happened:

One day without warning Dad struck a resounding blow to our peaceful squalor: he got a job. He did it for my sake and never stopped reminding me. "I could milk the social welfare system dry if it was just me, but it's insufficient for two. You've driven me into the workforce, Jasper. I'll never forgive you!"

It was Eddie again who found him work. A year after Dad's return from Paris, Eddie turned up at our apartment door, which surprised Dad, who'd never had an enduring friendship in all his life, certainly not one that spanned continents. Eddie had left Paris just after we did and had returned to Thailand before moving to Sydney.

Now, eleven years later, he had found Dad employment for the second time. I had no idea if this new gig was with equally murky characters and just as dangerous. Frankly, I didn't care. I was twelve years old, and for the first time in my life, Dad was out of the apartment. His heavy presence was suddenly lifted from my life, and I felt free to eat my cornflakes without hearing over and over again why man was the worst thing that had ever happened to humanity.

Dad worked all the time, and it wasn't that his long hours away from me were making me lonely (I was lonely already), but there was something to it that didn't feel right. Of course, it's not unusual for fathers to work all the time because they are bringing home the bacon, and it can't be helped that the bacon lurks in offices and coal mines and building sites, but in our home there was a mystery regarding the location of our bacon. I started thinking about it every day. Where the hell's our bacon? I thought this because my friends lived in houses, not apartments, and their fridges were always full of food while ours was full of space. Dad worked all day every day, even on weekends, but we didn't seem to have any more money than when he was unemployed. Not a cent. One day I asked him, "Where's all the money go?"

He said, "What money?"

I said, "The money you make from your job."

He said, "I'm saving."

I said, "For what?"

He said, "It's a surprise."

I said, "I hate surprises."

He said, "You're too young to hate surprises."

I said, "All right, I like surprises, but I also like knowing."

He said, "Well, you can't have both."

I said, "I can if you tell me and then I forget it."

He said, "I'll tell you what. I'll let you choose. You can have the surprise, or I can tell you what I'm saving for. It's up to you."

That was a killer. In the end, I decided to wait.

While I waited, Eddie let it slip that Dad was managing a strip club in Kings Cross called the Fleshpot. A strip joint? My dad? How could this happen? And as a manager? My dad? How could Eddie have convinced his shady connections to hire Dad for such a position? With responsibilities? My dad? I had to see it for myself.

One night I wound through the Cross, up side streets that were nothing more than long public urinals, past the drunken English tourists, a couple of glassy-eyed junkies, and a skinhead who looked weary of his own persona. As I entered the bar, a middle-aged hooker shouted something about sucking, her croaky voice lending the suggestion a nauseating picture of withered lips. A bouncer grabbed me by the shirt and squeezed the collar until I told him I was here to see my father. He let me in.

My first time in a strip club and I was visiting family.

It wasn't what I imagined. The strippers were shaking their bodies, unenthused, bobbing up and down to repetitive dance music under glaring spotlights in front of leering muted men in suits. Sure, I felt elated to see so much smooth, pliable flesh in one place, but I wasn't as aroused as I'd expected. In real life, almost naked women straddling poles just isn't as sexy as you'd think.

I spotted Dad yelling into the phone behind the bar. As I walked over, he sent a frown to intercept me.

"What are you doing here, Jasper?"

"Just looking around."

"Like what you see?"

"I've seen better."

"In your dreams."

"No, on video."

"Well you can't stay in here. You're underage."

"What do you actually do here?" I asked.

He showed me. It wasn't easy. There was the running of the bar, and while there were naked women floating in front of it, it had to be run just like a regular bar. He chose the women too; they came and auditioned for him. As if he knew anything about dancing! Or women! And how could he stand it, all those supple sexual creatures bending and flaunting their haunting slopes and curves day in, day out? The life force is like a hot potato, and while impure thoughts may make you burn in hell for all eternity once you die, here in life what gets you baked and fried is your inability to act on them.

Of course, I don't know everything. Maybe he indulged his lecherous fantasies. Maybe he fucked every dancer there. I can't picture it, but then, what son could?

So working in this lovely den of sin was how he chose to support his family—me—and save. But for what? To help stave off my curiosity, Dad broke into his bank account to buy me a little present: four bloated fish in a grubby little tank. They were like goldfish, only black. They survived in our apartment just three days. Apparently they died from overfeeding. Apparently I overfed them. Apparently fish are terrible gluttons with absolutely no self-control who just don't know when they've had enough and will stuff themselves to death with those innocuous little beige flakes imaginatively labeled "fish food."

Dad didn't join me in mourning their passing. He was too busy with his strippers. For a man who had spent the majority of his working life not working, he was really working himself to the bone. It turned out I had to wait more than a year to find out what he was saving for. Sometimes it drove me crazy wondering, but I can be tremendously patient when I think the reward might be worth the wait.

It wasn't worth the wait. Really, it wasn't.

•

I was thirteen when I came home one day to see my father holding up a large glossy photograph of an ear. This, he explained, was what he'd been saving for. An ear. A new ear to replace the one that had been scarred in the fire that consumed his town and family. He was going to a plastic surgeon to undeform himself. This is what we'd been sacrificing for? What a letdown. There's nothing fun about a skin graft.

Dad spent one night in hospital. The pressure was on to buy flowers even though I knew he wouldn't appreciate them. Flora always seemed to me a non sequitur of a present for someone in pain anyway (how about a flagon of morphine?), but I found a couple of huge sunflowers. He didn't appreciate them. I didn't care. The important thing was that the operation was a success. The doctor was very pleased, he said. That's a tip for you: never bother asking after the patient; it's a waste of time. The important thing is to discover how the doctor is feeling. And Dad's was on top of the world.

I was there when the bandages came off. To tell you the truth, the anticipation had built to such a level I was sort of expecting something on a grander scale: a colossal ear that doubled as a bottle-opener, or a time-traveling ear picking up conversations from the past, or a universal ear hearing for everyone alive, or a Pandora's ear, or an ear with a tiny red light that showed when it was recording. Basically, an ear to end all ears. But it wasn't like that at all. It was just a regular ear.

"Speak into it," Dad said. I moved around to the side of the bed and leaned into the new arrival.

"Hello. Testing. Testing. Two. Two. Two."

"Good. It works," he said.

When he was released from hospital, he ventured out in the world eager to catch a glimpse of himself. The world provided. Dad lost the ability to walk in a straight line. A to B was now always via the side mirrors on passing cars, shop windows, and stainless-steel kettles. When you obsess about your appearance, you notice just how many reflective surfaces exist in the cosmos.

One night he came to the doorway of my room and stood there, breathing loudly.

"Feel like playing around with my camera?"

"Are you making porn?"

"Why would I be making porn?"

"That's between you and your biographer."

"I just want you to get a few snaps of my ear, for the album."

"The ear album?"

"Forget it." Dad made a beeline for the hall.

"Wait."

I felt bad for him. Dad didn't seem able to recognize himself. The outside of him may have been more presentable, but the inside shrank down a size. I felt there was something ominous in all this, as if by adding on a new ear, he'd actually broken off a fundamental part of himself.

•

Even after the plastic surgery, he worked every day. Once again there was no money. Once again our lives were unchanged.

I said, "OK. What are you doing with the money now?"

He said, "I'm saving again."

I said, "Saving for what?"

He said, "It's a surprise."

I said, "The last surprise sucked."

He said, "This one you'll like."

I said, "It better be worth it."

It wasn't. It was a car. A slick red sports car. When I went outside to look at it, he was standing beside it, patting it as if it had just done a trick. Honestly, I couldn't have been more shocked if he had blown the money on political donations. My dad? A sports car? Pure lunacy! It wasn't just frivolous, it was meticulously frivolous. Was it a distraction? Was he announcing his dissolution? Was it a surrender or a conquest? Which part of him was this meant to fix? One thing was clear: he was breaking his own taboos.

It was comical, the sight of him getting into that sports car, a 1979 MGB convertible. Then, strapped into his seat, he looked as apprehensive as the first astronaut.

Now I think it was a brave attempt, an ingenious act in total defiance of himself and the voices within him intent on categorizing him. Dad in that sports car was a man reinventing himself from the outside in. A rebirth doomed to miscarriage.

"Are you coming?"

"Where?"

"Let's take her for a spin."

I get in. I'm young. I'm not a machine. Of course I love the car. I fucking love it. But there's something about it that just isn't right, like if you walk in on your kindergarten teacher getting a lap dance.

"Why did you buy this?" I asked him.

"Why?" he repeated, picking up speed. He's trying to leave himself behind in the dust, I thought, and on some level I could already hear the tendons and joints of his sanity split and tear. His job, his regular hours, his suit, his new ear, and now his car: he was creating unbearable tension between the selves. Something's going to give, I thought, and it won't be pretty.

II

Then it gave. It wasn't pretty.

We were in a crowded Chinese restaurant and Dad was ordering lemon chicken.

"Anything else?" the waiter asked.

"Just some boiled rice and the check."

Dad always liked to pay before he ate so the second he finished swallowing he could leave. There was something about sitting in a restaurant not eating that he just couldn't stand. Impatience seized him like a fit. Unfortunately, some restaurants make you pay at the end no matter what. In those situations Dad stood next to the table to show that he no longer wanted anything to do with the table. Then he called for the bill as if he were pleading for mercy. Sometimes he'd carry his plate to the kitchen. Sometimes he'd wave money under the waiter's nose. Sometimes he'd open the cash register, pay the bill, and give himself change. They hated that.

This night Dad had a table by the window and was staring out, his face set on "boredom incarnate." I was there, but he was eating alone. I was on a hunger strike for some heroic cause I can't remember now, but this was probably in the period we ate out eighty-seven nights in a row. Dad used to cook in the old days, but they were old, those days.

We both looked out onto the street because it required so much less effort than talking. Our car was out there, parked behind a white van, and beside it a couple were fighting as they walked. She was pulling his black ponytail and he was laughing. They came right up to the window and fought in front of us, as if they were putting on a show. It was a bold performance. The guy was bent over with a big grin on his face, trying to get her to let go of his hair. It looked painful, having your hair pulled like that, but he wouldn't stop laughing. Of course, now that I'm older, I know why he had to keep laughing like that; I know he'd have kept on laughing even if she'd pulled his whole head off and dropped it in the gutter and pissed on it and set it on fire. Even with the sting of piss in his dying eyes, he'd have kept on chuckling, and I know why.

The lemon chicken arrived.

"Sure you don't want any?" Dad asked, a taunting lift in his voice.

The smell of hot lemon made my stomach and my head mortal

enemies. Dad threw me a look that was smug and victorious and I gave him one back that was conceited and triumphant. After a grueling five seconds, we both turned our heads quickly to the window, as if for air.

On the street, the fight was in intermission. The girl was sitting on the bonnet of a black Valiant; the guy was standing beside her, smoking a cigarette. I couldn't see her hands because she had them bunched up under her arms, but I imagined they were clutching pieces of his scalp. Then I heard scraping metal. There was a figure in the background, behind the couple, someone in a red parka, hunched over Dad's car. The red parka moved alongside the car slowly. It was hard to tell exactly what he was doing, but it seemed that he was scratching the paint off with a key.

"Hey, look!" I shouted, and pointed out the scene to Dad, but his lanky body was already up, running for the door. I leapt out of my chair and followed his trail. This was to be my first chase scene through the streets of Sydney. There have been others over the years, and I'm not always the one in pursuit, but this was the first, so it remains special in my memory.

We did not run gracefully, of course; rather we staggered at great speed, down the main strip, almost toppling over, bursting through couples who strolled absently toward us, ricocheting off them. I remember humming a tune while I ran, a spy tune. We sped through the city like men on fire. People looked on as if they'd never seen running before. Maybe they hadn't. Outside a cinema, businessmen and -women indistinguishable from each other stood their ground as we approached, as if that square meter of pavement had been handed down to them by their ancestors. We pushed them aside as we ran through. Some of them shouted. Maybe they'd never been touched before either.

The man in the red parka had feet like a gust of wind. He blew across a congested street, dodging the steady stream of traffic. I had taken only one step off the pavement when Dad's hand grabbed my wrist and almost yanked it off.

"Together," he said.

Beware the father and son in pursuit of the mysterious villain in the red parka. Beware the menacing duo who hold hands as they make chase. We turned a corner and came into an empty street. Our presence somehow deepened the emptiness of it. There was no one in sight. It felt as though we had stumbled upon a remote and forgotten part of the city.

We took a moment to catch our breath. My heart pounded on my chest wall like a shoulder trying to break down a wooden door.

"In there," Dad said.

Halfway down the street was a bar. We walked to the front. There was no sign on the window. Evidently the bar didn't have a name. The windows were blacked out and you couldn't see in. It was a place made dangerous by low lighting. You could tell from the outside. It was the kind of place where nefarious characters knife anyone who asks them for the time, where serial killers go to forget their troubles, where whores and drug dealers exchange phone numbers and sociopaths laugh at the times they've been confused with naturopaths.

"Do you want to wait outside?"

"I'm coming in."

"Things might get ugly."

"I don't mind."

"OK, then."

Only a few steps in and we were at the cloakroom—we could see the red parka swinging on a hanger, swinging like a tune.

There was a band on the stage, the singer's voice like the feeling of biting tinfoil. Musical instruments were stuck on the wall above the spirit bottles at the bar—a violin, an accordion, a ukulele. It looked like a pawnbroker's. Two exhausted bartenders paused every now and then to pour themselves tequila shots. Dad ordered a beer for himself, lemonade for me. I wanted a beer too, but I got lemonade. My whole life's been like that.

Dad and I kept one eye apiece on the cloakroom and spent a couple of hours guessing who might be our man, but you can't pick a vandal from a room of faces any more than you can pick an adulterer or a pedophile. People carry their secrets in hidden places, not on their faces. They carry suffering on their faces. Also bitterness, if there's room. We made our guesses anyway, based on what, I don't know. Dad chose a short nuggety guy with a goatee. He's our man, Dad insisted. I begged to differ and picked a guy with long brown hair and an ugly purple mouth. Dad thought he looked like a student, not a vandal. What's he studying, then?

"Architecture," Dad said. "One day he'll build a bridge that will collapse."

"Will people die?" I asked.

"Yes, a thousand."

While I contemplated the thousand dead, Dad ordered another drink and noticed a woman with peroxide blond hair and lipstick-stained teeth leaning on the bar. He gave her the number-three smile, the one usually reserved for getting out of speeding fines. She looked him over without moving her head.

"Hi," Dad said.

As a response she lit a cigarette, and Dad scooted over a stool to get closer.

"What do you think of the band?" he asked. "It's not really my type of music. Can I buy you a drink? What do you think of the band?"

She let out a laugh that was more like gargling in that it never left her throat. After a whole fat minute when nothing happened, Dad got sick of staring at her profile, so he scooted back to his original stool. He drank his beer in one go.

"Do you think you'll ever get married?" I asked.

"I don't know, mate."

"Do you want to?"

"I'm not sure. On the one hand, I don't want to be alone forever."

"You're not alone. I'm here."

"Yeah, that's right," he said, smiling.

"What's on the other hand?" I asked.

"What?"

"You said, 'On the one hand, I don't want to be alone forever.' "

"Oh, um. Shit. I can't remember. It's gone."

"Maybe there's nothing on the other hand."

"Yeah, maybe."

I watched Dad's eyes follow the blonde as she moved from the bar to a table of women. She must have said something about us, because they all looked over, and it seemed pretty obvious they were mentally spitting on Dad. He pretended to drink from his empty glass. The whole scene made me sick, so I turned one eye back to the cloakroom and the other to the mean, purple, murderous mouth of the architecture student, and I imagined him high up in an office, looking down on a thousand dead bodies and the silver arms of his broken bridge.

The red parka was still hanging around, killing time. It was getting late. I was tired. My eyelids wanted closure.

"Can we go?"

"What time does this bar close?" Dad asked the bartender.

"About six."

"Fuck," Dad said to me, and ordered another drink. Clearly he would stay out all night if need be. And why shouldn't he? There was no one at home waiting up for us. No forehead crinkled with worry. No lips waiting to kiss us goodnight. No one to miss us if we never went back at all.

I laid my head on the bar. There was something wet and sticky under my cheek, but I was too tired to move. Dad sat erect on the bar stool, vigilant, watching the cloakroom. I drifted off to sleep. I dreamed of a face floating out of the dark. Nothing more than a face. The face was screaming, except the dream was silent. It was terrifying. I woke with a damp cloth at my nose.

"Move your head, please."

It was the bartender wiping down the counter.

"What's happening?"

"I'm closing up."

I tasted salt. I reached up and wiped my eyes. I'd been crying in my sleep. This confused me. I don't remember the face being sad, only scary. The bartender gave me a look that said I wouldn't be a real man as long as I cried in my sleep. I knew he spoke the truth, but what could I do about it?

"What's the time?"

"Five-thirty."

"Have you seen my—"

"He's over there."

Dad was standing beside the cloakroom, bouncing on his toes. I craned my neck and saw the red parka still hanging around. There was only a handful of people left in the bar: the guy with the purple mouth, a woman with an angry face and a shaved head, a bearded man with a face full of rings, a Chinese girl in a jumpsuit, and a guy with the biggest potbelly I'd ever seen.

"I'm closing up now," the bartender shouted to them. "Go home to your wives and children."

That made everyone laugh. I didn't see what was so funny about it. I went over and waited with Dad.

"How did you sleep?" he asked.

"I feel sick."

"What's the matter?"

"What are you going to do when you find him?"

Dad indicated with his eyebrows that he found my question ignorant. The patrons started leaving one by one. Finally the girl with the shaved head leaned on the cloakroom counter.

"That's mine," she said, pointing. "The red one."

This was our man—or I should say woman. The culprit. The vandal. The clerk handed her the parka. Now what?

"Hello," Dad said.

She turned her face to him. We got a good look at her. She had bright green eyes set in the boniest face I'd ever seen. I thought she should thank God for those eyes; they were the only beautiful things about her. Her lips were thin, almost nonexistent. Her face was gaunt and pale. She'd be nothing more than white skin stretched over a long skull if it weren't for those eyes. They were translucent. Dad said hello again. She ignored him, opened the door with her foot, and went into the street.

Outside, a light rain was falling from a metal-yellow sky. I couldn't see it but I knew the sun was around there somewhere—its yawn had lit the air. I took a deep breath. There's no doubt about it, the dawn smells different from the rest of the day; there's a certain freshness about it, like when you take a bite out of a head of lettuce and put it back in the fridge bite side down so no one will notice.

The girl was standing under the awning, doing up her famous red parka.

"Hello there." Dad's voice had no impact on her. I thought clearing my throat might help. It did. Her bright green eyes shone a spotlight on Dad and me.

"What do you want?"

"You scratched my car," Dad said.

"What car?"

"My car."

"When?"

"Earlier tonight, around a quarter to nine."

"Says who?"

"Says me," Dad said, then moved a step closer to the red parka with the green headlights. "I know it was you."

"Get the fuck away from me before I call the police."

"Ho-ho, you want to call the police, do you?"

"Yeah, maybe I do, moneybags."

"What did you call me?"

"I called you moneybags, moneybags."

"Every time you open your mouth, you're incriminating yourself. Why do you think I'm a moneybags unless you've seen my car?"

Good one, Dad, I thought. She's on the run now.

"Your suit looks like something a fat rich bastard would wear."

Good one, Green Eyes. She got you there, Dad.

"For your information, I'm not a moneybags," Dad said.

"I don't care what you are."

This ludicrous evening seemed to be reaching a dead end. Dad had crossed his arms and was trying to stare down Green Eyes, but she had crossed *her* arms and was glaring right back at him with eyes so wide they were positively lidless. Was that it? Could we go home now?

"How old are you?"

"Fuck off."

"I only want two things from you."

"Well, you aren't getting them."

"I want a confession and an explanation. That's all."

This is exactly the kind of thing a single man can do at five-thirty in the morning, I thought—this is exactly why people have wives and husbands and girlfriends and boyfriends, so they don't allow themselves to get too creepy. But leave a man alone for long enough and there is nothing odd he won't do. A life lived alone weakens the mind's immune system, and your brain becomes susceptible to an attack of strange ideas. "I want a confession and an explanation," Dad repeated, and placed his hand on her shoulder as if he were a security guard surprising a shoplifter. She started screaming, "Help! Police! Rape!"

Then Dad had yet another dubious idea: he started shouting for the police too. He nudged me. He wanted me to join in. I shouted along with the other two, calling out rape, calling for the cops. But I didn't stop there. I called for a SWAT team too. I called for helicopters. I called for Satan. I called for the ground to swallow the sky. That quieted her down. She stepped off the pavement into the rain. Dad and I walked into the street beside her without talking. Every now and then Green Eyes took a peek at me.

"What are you doing with this fuckwit?" she asked me.

"I don't know."

"Is he your father?"

"He says he is."

"That doesn't mean anything."

"Hey, vandal. Don't you talk to him. You have some confessing to do."

"You can't prove anything, moneybags."

"Can't I? Can't I? Well, vandal, you have in your pocket a key of some description, don't you? Wouldn't take more than a couple of seconds for a forensic scientist to match the specks of paint on your key to the missing paint from the side of my car."

Green Eyes pulled a key from her pocket and dropped it in a puddle of water.

"Oops, clumsy me," she said, kneeling down beside the puddle, scrubbing the key, then wiping it on the sleeve of her parka. She put the key back in her pocket. "Sorry, moneybags," she sang.

We crossed Hyde Park as it went through a transformation of light and color. Dawn was melting into the shadows of the trees. As Green Eyes strode briskly, Dad took my hand and urged me to keep up the pace. At the time I couldn't comprehend what was going on. Now, looking back at his determination to follow this strange woman, it seems as if he somehow understood the mess she was going to make of our future, and he was not going to let her wriggle out of it.

When we reached the top of the park, guess who we saw hanging over Taylor's Square? The huge deep orange blazing sun, that's who. Green Eyes lit a cigarette. The three of us watched the sunrise in silence, and I thought: One day the earth is going to get sucked into that lurid sun, and all the Chinese restaurants and all the peroxide blond women and all the seedy bars and all the single men and all the vandals and all the sports cars will be obliterated in a brilliant white flash and that will be that. Suffice it to say, it was a hell of a sunrise. I felt like a naked eyeball standing there, an eyeball the size of a boy, an eyeball with ears and a nose and a tongue and a thousand nerves sticking out like uncut hairs touching everything. I was all the senses at once, and it felt good.

Suddenly I was glad there was no one at home waiting up for us. Normal fathers and sons can't stay out all night to watch the sun rise if there's a wife and mother fretting by an open window, her long bony finger hovering over the button that speed-dials the police. I turned to Dad and said, "It's good that you're alone."

Without looking at me he said, "I'm not alone. You're here."

I felt Green Eyes staring at me, before she fixed her stare on Dad. Then she walked on. We followed her up Oxford Street and into Riley. We followed her to a terrace house in Surry Hills. "Thanks for walking me home, moneybags. Now you know where I live. Now you know where my boyfriend lives too. He'll be home soon and he'll make a meal out of you. So fuck off!" she screamed. Dad sat on the front porch and lit a cigarette.

"Can we *please* go home now?" I begged.

"Not yet."

About twenty minutes later, Green Eyes came back out in tracksuit pants and a yellow undershirt. She was holding a jug of water with something floating in it. On closer look, it was a tampon. A used tampon floating in the jug. A thin trail of blood wove through the water, dissolving into layers of misty red.

"What are you going to do with that?" Dad asked, horrified.

"Calm down, moneybags. I'm just watering my plants."

She stirred the tampon in the jug and then poured the red water over what looked like marijuana plants sitting on the railing.

"That's sick," Dad said.

"From this body I give life," she said back.

"Why did you scratch my car?"

"Piss off," she spat; then, turning to me, "Do you want a drink?"

"Not if it's out of that jug."

"No, from the fridge."

"What have you got?"

"Water or orange juice."

"Orange juice, please."

"Don't give your dad any. I'm hoping he'll die of thirst."

"I know what you mean."

Dad's hand slapped the back of my head. Hey! Why shouldn't I say stupid things? I was tired and embarrassed and bored. Why wasn't Dad tired and embarrassed and bored? It was a weird thing we were doing, hanging out on a stranger's porch waiting for a confession.

The front door opened again. "Remember what we talked about, now," she said, handing me a glass of orange juice.

"I won't give him a drop," I promised.

She smiled warmly. In her other hand was a black sports bag. She knelt down beside Dad and opened the bag. Inside were envelopes and letters. "If you're going to stalk me, might as well make yourself useful. Put these in envelopes."

Dad took the envelopes without a word. He made himself comfortable and started licking envelopes as if it were the most natural thing in the world to lick envelopes on a stranger's porch, his tongue working like it was the tongue's reason for being, the reason we came all the way over here at six in the morning.

"What about you, kid, you want to help us out?"

"My name's Jasper."

"You want to lick some envelopes, Jasper?"

"Not really, but OK."

The three of us sat on the porch stuffing envelopes with deftness and precision. It was impossible to articulate what exactly was happening here; it was as if we were all actors improvising in a student play, and every so often we'd all look at each other with barely concealed amusement.

"How much do you get paid for doing this?" Dad asked.

"Five bucks for every one hundred envelopes."

"That's not so good."

"No, it's not."

As she said this, I noticed how her serious, severe face had become serene and gentle.

I asked, "Why do you hate rich people so much?"

She narrowed her green eyes and said, "Because they get all the breaks. Because poor people are struggling while the rich complain about the temperature of their pools. Because when ordinary people get into trouble, the law fucks them over, and when the rich get into trouble, they get an easy ride."

"Maybe I'm not rich," Dad said. "Maybe I have a red sports car but it's the only thing of value I own."

"Who cares about you?"

"My son does."

"Is that true?" she asked me.

"I suppose."

There was something about this conversation that wasn't working. It was as if language were failing us when we needed it most.

"We need a housekeeper," Dad said suddenly. Green Eyes's tongue froze mid-lick.

"Is that so?"

"Yeah. It's so."

Green Eyes put down the envelopes and her face hardened again. "I don't know if I want to work for some rich bastard."

"Why not?"

"Because I hate you."

"So?"

"So it'll be hypocrisy."

"No, it won't."

"It won't?"

"No, it'll be irony."

Green Eyes thought about that awhile, and her lips started moving soundlessly, to let us know that she was thinking it over. "I have a boyfriend, you know."

"Does that prevent you from cleaning?"

"Plus you're much too old and much too ugly for me. I'm not going to sleep with you."

"Listen. I'm just looking for someone to clean our apartment and cook for Jasper and me occasionally. Jasper's mother is dead. I work all the time. I don't have time to cook. Also, for the record, I'm not interested in you sexually. Your shaved head makes you look sort of mannish. Plus your face is oval. I only like round faces. Oval turns me off. Ask anyone."

"Maybe I will."

"So you want the job?"

"All right."

"Why did you scratch my car?"

"I didn't scratch your car."

"You're a liar."

"You're a weirdo."

"You're hired."

"Fine."

I looked at Dad who had a strange look on his face, as if we had trekked all night to arrive at a secret waterfall and this was it. We kept on with the envelopes as the dawn became morning.

•

The first night Anouk came in to cook and clean, her confusion was hilarious; she was expecting a wealthy man's spacious house, only to step into our small and disgusting apartment, which was rotting like the bottom of an old boat. After she cooked us dinner she asked, "How can you live like this? You're pigs. I'm working for pigs," and Dad said, "Is that why you cooked us this slop?" She was furious, but for reasons that I've never completely understood (there *are* other jobs), she came back week after week, returning to us always with tireless and aggressive disapproval and a face that looked like it had just sucked a basket of lemons. She came in, opening curtains and dumping light into our hole in the wall, and as she stepped over Dad's overdue library books, which carpeted the floor, she looked searchingly at me, as if I were a captive she was considering freeing.

At first Anouk came in for a few hours on Mondays and Fridays, though gradually the routine fell apart and she just started turning up whenever she felt like it, not only to cook and clean but often to eat and make a mess. She ate with us regularly, argued with us constantly, and introduced me to a breed I'd never encountered before: a left-wing, art-loving, self-proclaimed "spiritual person" who chose to convey her gentle ideas about peace and love and nature by screaming at you.

"You know what your problem is, Martin?" she asked Dad one night after dinner. "You're choosing books over life. I don't think books are supposed to be a substitute for life, you know. They're more of a complement."

"What do you know about it?"

"I know when I see someone who doesn't know how to live."

"And you do?"

"I've got some ideas."

In her view, Dad and I were problems waiting to be solved, and she began by trying to turn us into vegetarians, parading pictures of howling mutilated animals in front of us while we were in the middle of tucking into a juicy steak. When that failed, she sneaked meat substitutes onto our plates. And it wasn't just food; Anouk dished out all forms of spirituality like a Hun: art therapy, rebirthing, therapeutic massage, strange-smelling oils. She recommended we go and get our auras massaged. She dragged us to criminally obscure plays, including one where the actors performed with their backs to the audience during the entire production. It was as if a lunatic were holding the key to our brains, stuffing things inside like crystals and wind chimes and pamphlets advertising lectures by one mystical left-wing levitating Gucci guru after another. That's when she started with escalating urgency to critically assess our way of life.

Every week she inspected a new corner of our airless lives and gave us a review. It was never a rave. We never got a thumbs-up. The thumbs were always pointing to the sewer. After she discovered that Dad was managing a strip club, the reviews became savage, starting on the outside and working in. She critiqued our habit of impersonating each other on the phone, and the way, whenever there was a knock on the door, we both froze in terror as if we lived in a totalitarian regime and were running an underground newspaper. She pointed out that living like art students while Dad had an expensive sports car was borderline insane; she shot down Dad's habit of kissing books and not me, as well as the way he'd go weeks without acknowledging my existence, then weeks when he wouldn't give me a moment's peace. She picked apart everything, from the way Dad slouched in his chair, to how he'd spend an hour weighing the advantages and disadvantages of having a shower, to his sociopathic manner of dressing (it was Anouk who first spotted that Dad was wearing his pajamas underneath his suit), to his lazy way of shaving, so he left tufts of hair sprouting in random patches on his face.

Maybe it was her arctic, belittling tone of voice, but he'd just stare sullenly into his coffee as she unveiled her latest damning report from the front lines. Her most unsettling and damaging form of reproach, though, was when she critiqued Dad's criticism; that sent him reeling. You see, he'd spent nearly his whole life honing his contempt for others and had nearly perfected his "guilty" verdict on the world when Anouk came in and leveled it. "You know what your problem is?" she'd say (that's how she always began). "You hate yourself and so you hate others. It's just sour grapes. You're too busy reading and thinking about big things. You don't care about the little things in your own life, and that means you're contemptuous of anyone who does. You've never struggled like they have, because you've never cared like they do. You don't really know what people go through." Often as she dished it out Dad would be strangely quiet, and he rarely rose to his own defense.

"You know what your problem is?" she asked after Dad told her his life story one afternoon. "You're rehashing your old thoughts. Do you realize that? *You're quoting yourself,* your only friend is a sleazy sycophant"— Eddie—"who agrees with everything you say, and you never air your ideas in a forum where they might be challenged, you just say them to yourself and then congratulate yourself when you agree with what you said."

She went on and on like this, and over the following months, as I squeezed uncomfortably into adolescence and my relationship with Dad weakened daily, as if it had osteoporosis, Anouk didn't just pour acid all over *his* ideas, hopes, and self-esteem, she took aim at me too. She was the one who told me I was only good-looking enough to attract about 22 percent of the female population. I thought that was a dismal figure, really abominable. It wasn't until I was able to spot the loneliness in the faces of men that I realized that being attractive to 22 percent of women is a whopping success story. There are legions of ugly, wretchedly lonely, hopelessly inept sociopaths out there who fall in the 0–2 percent category—armies of them—and every one would kill for my 22 percent.

Oh, and she also berated me for neglecting the second batch of fish.

You see, Dad's bank balance was swelling again, and undaunted by the previous episode of fish homicide (suicide?), he bought three more fish, this time simple goldfish, as if he thought that the ownership of fish went through degrees of difficulty depending on the species and the previous disaster had been caused by the fact that he had bought me fish that were simply too hard for my level. To him, goldfish were fish with training wheels: immortal, impossible to kill.

He was wrong. In the end I disposed of those fish quite easily too, though this time from underfeeding. They starved to death. But we argued right up to and including the day Dad died on the issue of whose fault it was. I went away for a week to stay at my friend Charlie's house, and I swear to God, as I was leaving the apartment I said to Dad, "Don't forget to feed the fish." Dad remembers it very differently, and in his version, when leaving the apartment I had actually said, "OK, bye." Whatever the case, sometime during my weeklong absence the fish came down with a bad case of starvation and, unlike humans in the same fix, did not think to resort to cannibalism. They just let themselves waste away.

Anouk took Dad's side on this one, and I noticed that the only time Dad enjoyed the benefits of a ceasefire was when he could team up with Anouk against me. I have to admit, their relationship perplexed me. They were an improbable pairing, as if a rabbi and a man who raised pit bulls were marooned together on a desert island; incompatible strangers thrown together during a time of crisis, only Dad and Anouk's was a nameless crisis without beginning or end.

•

A year into her employment with us, Dad received an unexpected phone call.

"You're kidding," he said. "Jesus Christ, no. Absolutely not. Not if you raped and tortured me. How much is a lot? Well, all right, then. Yes, yes, I said yes, didn't I? When do I start?"

It was good news! An American film production company had heard of the Terry Dean story and wanted to make it into a Hollywood blockbuster. They wanted Dad's help to make sure they got it right, even though they were setting it in America as the story of a dead baseball player who comes back from hell to take revenge on his teammates who battered him to death.

So it seemed Dad could make good money off his memories, but why now? There had already been a couple of wildly inaccurate Australian movies based on the story, and Dad had refused to cooperate with any of them. Why this surrender, this sudden willingness to exploit his private dead? It was another in an alarming series of abrupt about-faces, allowing a writer to come with a nice check in exchange for picking the scabs off Dad's brain to see what was underneath. Anouk, with her uncanny gift for identifying the worm in the apple, said, "You know what your problem is? You're living in your brother's shadow," and when the twenty-three-year-old gum-chewing writer bounded cheerily into the apartment the following week, he only had to say, "So, tell me what Terry Dean was like as a child," for Dad to grab him by the shirtsleeves and throw him exuberantly out the door with his laptop after him. One court appearance later, his new "job" cost him $4,000 and some unwanted press. "You know what your problem is?" Anouk said that night. "You're a fanatic, but you're fanatical about everything. Don't you see? You're spreading your fanaticism too thin."

But you want to know what our real problem was? You can't drift blissfully along in a blind haze when someone's standing beside you shouting: That's lust! That's pride! That's sloth! That's habit! That's pessimism! That's jealousy! That's sour grapes! Anouk was stuffing up our deeply entrenched custom of scraping and wheezing our way unenthusi-astically around our claustrophobic apartment. The only way we knew how to get ahead was to plod toward our paltry desires and pant loudly to get attention. And the endlessly optimistic Anouk wanted to turn creatures like us into superbeings! She desired us to be considerate, help-ful, conscientious, moral, strong, compassionate, loving, selfless, and brave, and she never let up, until gradually we fell into the regrettable habit of watching what we did and what we said.

After months of her boring us and boring into us, we no longer used plastic bags, and rarely ate anything that bled; we signed petitions, joined fruitless protests, inhaled incense, bent ourselves into difficult yoga posi-tions—all worthy ascents up the mountain of self-improvement. But there were crap changes too, deep plummets into the gorge. Because of Anouk, we lived in fear of ourselves. Whoever first equated self-knowledge with change has no respect for human weakness and should be found and bitten to death. I'll tell you why: Anouk highlighted our problems but didn't have the resources or the know-how to help us fix them. We certainly didn't know. So thanks to Anouk, not only were we stuck with the slippery menagerie of problems we already had, we were now imbued with an appalling awareness of them. This, of course, led to new problems.

III

There was something really wrong with my father. He was crying; he was in his bedroom, crying. I could hear him sobbing through the walls. I could hear him pacing back and forth over the same small space. Why was he crying? I'd never heard him cry before; I thought he couldn't. Now it was every night after work and every morning before work. I took it as a bad omen. I felt that he was crying prophetically—not for what had happened but for what was about to take place.

In between sobs he talked to himself. "Fucking apartment. Too small. Can't breathe. It's a tomb. Must wage war. Who am I? How can I define myself? Choices are infinite and therefore limited. Forgiveness is big in the Bible, but nowhere does it say you should forgive yourself. Terry never forgave himself, and everyone loves him. I forgive myself daily, and nobody loves me. All this dread and insomnia. I can't teach my brain how to sleep. How's your confusion these days? It's put on weight."

"Dad?"

I pushed open his door a little, and in the shadows his face was severe and his head looked like a bare lightbulb hanging from the ceiling.

"Jasper. Do me a favor. Pretend you're an orphan."

I closed the door, went into my bedroom, and pretended I was an orphan. It didn't feel too bad.

Then, as abruptly as it started, the crying stopped. Suddenly he started going out at night. That was new. Where did he go? I followed him. He was walking the streets with a bounce in his step and waving to people as he passed. They didn't wave back. He stopped at a small, crowded pub. I peeked through the window and saw him perched at the bar, drinking. And he wasn't sulking alone in a corner either; he was chatting to people, laughing. That was brand spanking new. The color of his face had gone all·rosy, and after he polished off a couple of beers, he stood up on the bar stool and turned off the football game and said something to the crowd while laughing and shaking his fist like a dictator telling a joke at the execution of his favorite dissident. When he finished he bowed (though nobody applauded) and went to another pub, shouting "Hello there!" as he entered, then "I'll see what I can do!" as he left. Then he popped into a dimly lit bar and paced around in circles before leaving without ordering anything. Then a nightclub! Christ! Is this what Anouk had driven him to?

He disappeared up the escalator of the Fishbowl, a concept disco designed as an enormous glass bowl with a platform around its perimeter. I climbed up onto the platform and peered into the bowl. At first I couldn't see him. At first I couldn't see anything but immaculately sculpted beautiful people illuminated in brief moments under strobe lights. Then I spotted him. *He was fucking dancing.* He was soaked with sweat and gasping for breath, moving clumsily and making strange, drowsy arm movements, like a lumberjack chopping trees in space, but he was having *fun.* Or was he? His smile was twice the size of normal smiles and he was gazing lustfully at cleavage of all sizes and religions. But what was this? He wasn't dancing alone! He was dancing with a woman! Or was he? He was dancing behind her, gyrating at her back. She was ignoring him a little too effortlessly for comfort, so he swiveled around so he was in front and tried to sweep her up in that mile-wide smile. I wondered if he was going to invite her back to our sad and filthy apartment. But no, she wasn't taken in. So he moved on to another woman, a shorter, rounder one. He swooped down and escorted her to the bar. He bought her a drink and handed over the cash as if he were paying a ransom. As they talked, he placed his hand on her back and drew her toward him. She resisted and walked away and Dad's smile grew even wider, making him look like a chimpanzee who'd had peanut butter smeared on his gums for a television commercial.

A flat-nosed, no-neck bouncer in a tight black T-shirt arrived. His Goliath's hand wrapped around the back of Dad's neck, and he forcefully escorted him out of the club. On the street, Dad told him to fuck his mother if he hadn't already. That did it for me. I'd seen enough. It was time to go home.

At around five in the morning he banged on the door. He'd lost his key. I opened up to see him sweating and yellow and in the middle of a sentence. I went back to bed without hearing the end of it. That was the only night I followed him, and when I recounted the story to Anouk, she said it was either "quite a good sign" or a "very bad sign." I don't know what he did the rest of those nights out on the town. I can only assume they were variations on the same fruitless theme.

A month later he was home again, crying. But what was worse, he started watching me sleep. The first night he did it he came into the room just as I was drifting off and took a seat by the window.

"What is it?" I asked.

"Nothing. You just go to sleep."

"What, with you sitting there?"

"I'm going to read in here awhile," he said, holding up a book.

He turned on the lamp and started reading. I watched him for a minute, then put my head back down and shut my eyes. I could hear him turning the pages. A few minutes later I sneaked one eyelid open and almost recoiled. He was staring at me. My face was in shadows, so he couldn't see I was watching him watching me. Then he turned the page again. I realized he was *pretending to read*, as an excuse for watching me sleep. This happened night after night, Dad pretending to read in my bedroom while I stayed awake with my eyes closed, feeling his eyes on me and listening to the sound of turning pages in the quiet. I tell you, they were some eerie, sleepless nights.

Then he started shoplifting. It began well enough. Dad came home, his bag stuffed with avocados and apples and fat nobs of cauliflower. Fruit and vegetables, nothing to complain about. Then he stole combs, throat lozenges, and Band-Aids—pharmaceutical goods. Useful. Then he stole nonsense items from gift shops: an old piece of driftwood with the words "My home is my castle" etched onto a plaque, a thong-shaped flyswatter, and a mug that said "You never know how many friends you have until you own a beach house," which might be fun to put in a beach house, if you had one. We didn't.

Then he was in bed crying again.

Then he was watching me sleep again.

Then he was at the window. I don't know when exactly he took up post there, or why, but he was vigilant about his new role. Half his face was looking out the window, the other half buried in the bunched-up curtains. We should have had venetian blinds, the perfect accessory for sudden outbursts of acute paranoia; there's nothing quite as atmospheric as those slits with their thin bars of shadow falling across your face. But what was he looking at out the window anyway? Mostly the backs of people's shitty apartments. Mostly bathrooms and kitchens and bedrooms. Nothing fascinating. Man with pale skinny legs stands in underwear devouring apple, woman puts on makeup arguing with person unseen, old couple brushes teeth of uncooperative German shepherd, that kind of thing. Staring out, Dad had a dark look in his eye. It wasn't jealousy, that much I know. For Dad, the grass was never greener on the other side of the fence. If anything, it was browner.

Everything had taken a darker turn. His mood was dark. His face was dark. His vocabulary, dark and menacing.

"Fucking bitch," he said one day at the window. "Fucking cunt."

"Who?" I asked.

"Bitch across the way looking at us."

"Well, you're looking at her."

"Only to see if she's looking."

"Is she?"

"Not now."

"So what's the problem?" I asked.

Here's the problem. He used to be funny. I mean, I know I'd complained about him my whole life, but I missed the old Dad. What happened to his lighthearted godlessness? That was funny. Reclusion is hysterical. Rebellion, a thousand laughs! But crying is rarely funny, and sociopathic rage never gets a chuckle—not from me, anyway. Now he was keeping the curtains humorlessly closed all day. No light penetrated the apartment. There were no longer middays or mornings or seasonal fluctuations of any kind. The only change was in the darkness. There were things breeding in it. Whatever mushrooms existed in his psyche were thriving in that dark, damp place. Not funny.

One night I spilled coffee on my bed. It was coffee, I swear, that soaked through the sheets and seeped into the mattress, but it looked like urine. I thought: Anouk will think it is urine. I tore the sheets off my bed and hid them. I went to the cupboard for clean sheets. There were none there.

Where did all the sheets go?

I asked Dad.

"Outside," he said.

We didn't have an outside. We lived in an apartment. I puzzled over this mystery awhile before arriving at a frightening conclusion. I went to check. I opened the curtains. *There was no outside world.* What I saw was sheets; he had hung them over the windows from the outside, maybe as a white flapping shield to hide us from prying eyes. But no, they weren't white. They weren't a shield either. They were a sign. There was something written on the other side of the sheets, in red. The words "Fucking Bitch."

This was bad. I knew this was bad.

I took down the sheets and hid them with the others, the ones with urine on them. Shit, I wrote that, didn't I? OK. I admit it. It *was* urine (it is not attention-seeking that makes children wet their beds, but fear of their parents).

Just so you know, you don't have to be religious to pray. Prayer is not so much an article of faith anymore as it is something that is culturally inherited from film and television, like kissing in the rain. I prayed for my father's recovery as a child actor might pray: on my knees, palms locked, head bowed, eyes closed. I went so far as to light a candle for him, not in a church—you can take hypocrisy only so far—but in the kitchen late one night, when his nocturnal rumblings had reached a fever pitch. I hoped the candle would unwrap whatever it was that bound him so tight.

Anouk was in the kitchen with me, cleaning it from top to bottom, muttering that she wanted to be not only paid but praised, and, citing mouse poo and cockroach nests as evidence, she implied that by cleaning the kitchen she was saving our lives.

Dad was stretched out on the couch with his hands covering his face.

She stopped cleaning and stood in the doorway. Dad could feel her staring at him and pressed the palms of his hands harder into his eyes.

"What the fuck is going on with you, Martin?"

"Nothing."

"Do you want me to tell you?"

"God, no."

"You're wallowing in self-pity, that's what I think. You're frustrated, OK. Your aspirations are unfulfilled. You think you're this special person who deserves special treatment, only you're just starting to see that no one in the whole wide world agrees with you. And to make matters worse, your brother is celebrated like the god you think you are, and that's finally dropped you in this kind of bottomless pit of depression where all these dark thoughts are gnawing at you, feeding on each other. Paranoia, persecution complex, probably impotence too, I don't know. But let me tell you. You have to do something about this before you do something you'll regret."

It was as excruciating as watching someone light a firecracker, then peer over it thinking it's a dud. Only Dad wasn't a dud.

"Stop bad-mouthing my soul, you meddlesome bitch!"

"Listen to me, Martin. Anyone else would get the hell out of here. But someone has to talk some sense into you. And besides, you're scaring the kid."

"He's OK."

"He's not OK. He's pissing his bed!"

Dad lifted his head over the top of the couch so all I could see was his receding hairline.

"Jasper, come here."

I went over to the hairline.

"Haven't you ever been depressed?" Dad asked me.

"I don't know."

"You're always so calm. It's a façade, isn't it?"

"Maybe."

"Tell me, what gnaws at you, Jasper?"

"You do!" I shouted, and ran to my room. What I didn't yet under-stand was that Dad's unhinged state had the potential to send me down the same precarious path.

Soon after that evening, Anouk took me to the Royal Easter Show to cheer me up. After the rides and the fairy floss and the show bags, we wandered over to see the judging of livestock. While staring at cattle, I suddenly pretended to be suffering from a bout of chronic disequilibrium, a new pastime of mine that involved bumping into people, stumbling, falling into shop displays, that kind of thing.

"What's wrong?" she shrieked, grabbing me by the shoulders.

"I don't know."

Her hands clasped mine. "You're shaking!"

It's true, I was. The world was reeling, my legs bending like straw. My whole body was vibrating out of control. I'd worked myself into such a lather, the fabricated illness had taken over, and for a minute I forgot there was nothing wrong with me.

"Help me!" I screamed. A crowd of spectators rushed over, including some officials from the show. They hovered over me, gawking (in a real emergency, a thousand eyes pressing against your skull isn't actually that helpful).

"Give him some air!" a voice cried.

"He's having a fit!" exclaimed another.

I felt bewildered and nauseated. Tears rolled down my face. Then all of a sudden I remembered I was only playing around. My body relaxed, and the nausea was replaced by a fear of discovery. The eyes had moved a couple of feet back, but the force of their gaze was undiminished. Anouk was holding me in her arms. I felt ridiculous.

"Get off me!" I screamed, pushing her away. I returned to the cattle. They were being judged by a panel of leathery-looking folk in Akubra hats. I leaned over the fence. I heard Anouk whispering frantically be-hind me, but I refused to look. After a minute she joined me.

"You OK now?" she asked.

My answer wasn't audible. We stood side by side, in silence. A minute later a brown cow with a white stain on his back won first prize for being the juiciest-looking steak in the paddock. We all applauded as if there were nothing absurd about applauding cows.

"You and your father are quite a pair," Anouk said. "I'm ready to go as soon as you are."

I felt terrible. What was I doing? So what if his head was an empty seashell in which you could hear the torment of the sea? What did that have to do with my mental well-being? His gestures had become crazy birds banging into windows. Did that mean mine needed to be too?

A couple of weeks later, Dad and I drove Anouk to the airport. She was going for a few months to be massaged on a beach in Bali. Just before she went through the departure gate, she took me aside and said, "I feel a little guilty leaving you at the moment. Your dad's about to fall off the edge."

I think she wanted me to say, "No, we'll be fine. You go enjoy yourself."

"Please don't go," I said.

Then she went anyway, and a week later he fell off the edge.

•

Dad went through his monthlong cycle of crying, pacing, screaming, watching me sleep, and shoplifting, though suddenly all within a week. Then it was compressed further and he ran through the whole cycle in a day, each stage taking about an hour. Then he went through the cycle in an hour, sighing and groaning and muttering and stealing (from the corner newsstand) in a blaze of tears, running home and tearing off his clothes and pacing naked in the apartment, his body looking like spare parts assembled in a hurry.

Eddie came banging on the door. "Why hasn't your dad been coming into work? Is he sick?"

"You might say that."

"Can I see him?"

Eddie went into the bedroom and closed the door. After half an hour, he came out scratching his neck as though Dad had given him a rash and said, "Jesus. When did this all start?"

I don't know. A month ago? A year?

"How do we fix him?" Eddie asked himself. "We've really got to brain-storm. Let's see. Let me think."

We stood in a swampy silence for a full twenty minutes. Eddie was brainstorming. I was sick at the way he was breathing through his nostrils, which were partially blocked by something I could see. After another ten minutes Eddie said, "I'm going to think some more about this at home." And then he left. I didn't hear from him after that. If he had any brilliant ideas, they just didn't come fast enough.

A week later there was a knock on the door. I went into the kitchen and made some toast and started shaking. I don't know how I knew the universe had vomited up something special for me; I just knew. The banging on the door persisted. I didn't want to overtax my imagination, so against my better judgment I answered it. A woman with a sagging face and big brown teeth was at the door, wearing a look of pity on her face. There was a policeman with her too. I guessed it wasn't the policeman she felt sorry for.

"Are you Kasper Dean?" she asked.

"What is it?"

"Can we come in?"

"No."

"I'm sorry to tell you this. Your father is in the hospital."

"Is he all right? What happened?"

"He's not well. He's going to stay awhile. I want you to come with us."

"What are you talking about? What happened to him?"

"We'll tell you about it in the car."

"I don't know who you are and what you want to do with me, but you can go fuck yourselves."

"Come on, son," the policeman said, clearly not in any mood to follow my suggestion.

"Where?"

"There's a home you can stay in for a couple of days."

"This is my home."

"We can't leave you alone here. Not until you're sixteen."

"Oh, for Christ's sake. I've been taking care of myself forever."

"Come on, Kasper," the policeman barked.

I didn't tell him my name was Jasper. I didn't tell him that Kasper was a fictional character of my dad's invention and that Kasper had been killed off many years ago. I decided to play along until I worked out just what the situation was. I knew this much: I wasn't sixteen, and that meant I had no rights. People are always talking about the rights of the child, but it's never the rights you need when you need them.

I went with them in the police car.

On the way they explained that Dad had driven his car through the window of the Fleshpot. It was an act that might have been taken as an unfortunate accident, only when he got through the window, he locked the steering wheel in a tight circle and spun the car around the dance floor, into tables and chairs, smashing up the place, destroying the bar. The police had to drag him out of the car. Clearly he'd gone mad. And now he was in the madhouse. I wasn't surprised. Denouncing civilization takes its toll when you continue to exist within it. It's OK from a mountaintop, but Dad was smack bang in the middle, and his berserk contradictions had finally butted each other insensible.

"Can I see him?"

"Not today," the woman said. We pulled up to a house in the suburbs. "You'll stay here a couple of days, until we see if any of your relatives can come and get you."

Relatives? I didn't know anyone like that.

The house was a one-story brick number and looked just like a regular family home. From the outside you couldn't tell this was where they warehoused the broken-off pieces of shattered families. The policeman honked the horn when we pulled up. A woman with one enormous bosom came out with a smile that I predicted I would see again and again in a thousand awful nightmares. The smile said, "Your tragedy is my ticket to heaven, so come here and give me a hug."

"You must be Kasper," she said, and she was joined by a bald man who kept nodding as if *he* were Kasper.

I didn't say anything.

"I'm Mrs. French," the single-bosomed woman said, as if boasting, as if to be Mrs. French were a hard-earned achievement in itself.

When I didn't respond, they walked me through the house. They showed me a bunch of kids watching television in the living room. Out of habit, I surveyed the female faces in the room. I do this even among the fragmented. I do this to see if there is any physical beauty I can dream about or lust over; I do this on buses, in hospitals, at the funerals of dear friends; I do this to lighten the load a little; I will do this as I lie dying. As it happened, everyone in the place was ugly, at least on the outside. All the kids peered at me as though I were up for sale. Half of them looked resigned to whatever it was their fate was dishing up to them; the other half snarled defiantly. For once I wasn't interested in their stories. I'm sure they all had perfectly awful tragedies that I could weep over for centuries, but I was too busy aging ten years with every passing minute in this limbo for children.

The couple continued with their tour. They showed me the kitchen. They showed me the backyard. They showed me my room, a glorified closet. The people may have been nice and kind and soft-spoken, but I preferred to save some time and just assume they were perverts awaiting nightfall.

As I dropped my bag on the single bed, Mrs. French said, "You'll be happy here."

"You've got to be kidding," I said back. I don't like people telling me when and where I am to be happy. That's not even for me to decide.

"So what now? Do I get my one phone call?" I asked.

"This isn't prison, Kasper."

"We'll see."

I telephoned Eddie to see if I could stay with him. He admitted that he had overstayed his visa and was illegal and therefore unable to make any application to be my legal guardian. I called Anouk's house to hear her flatmate tell me what I already knew—she was still sunning herself in a Buddhist meditation center in Bali and wasn't due home until her money ran out. I was stuck. I hung up the phone and went back to my little slab of darkness and cried. I'd never thought negatively about my future until that moment. I think that's the real loss of innocence: the first time you glimpse the boundaries that will limit your own potential.

There wasn't a lock on the door, but I managed to wedge the chair under the handle. I sat awake all night, waiting for that ominous rattle. At about three in the morning I fell asleep, so I can only assume they came to sexually abuse me when I was far gone, dreaming of oceans and the horizons I would never reach.

IV

The next day, accompanied by Mrs. French, I went to see Dad. I admit, shamefully, that when we hopped in the car I was excited. I'd never been inside a mental hospital—was it like in the movies, with a symphony of high-pitched inhuman screams? I even went as far as to hope the patients were not too heavily sedated to bang wooden spoons against the back of saucepans.

In the car on the way, I didn't say anything. Mrs. French kept glancing at me impatiently, irritated that I wasn't pouring out my heart to her. Silence dogged us all the way to the hospital. She pulled over at the newsagent's and said, "Why don't you pick up your father some magazines to read?" and she gave me $10. I went inside and thought: What does a man who's fallen off the brink want to read? Pornography? Entertainment news? I picked up an equestrian magazine but put it down again. That wasn't right. In the end I settled for a book of puzzles, mazes, anagrams, and teasers to give his brain a workout.

Inside the hospital we heard the kind of frenzied screams you generally associate with boiling rivers of blood. Stepping out of the elevator, I could see patients walking aimlessly through the corridors, legs twitching, tongues hanging out, mouths open wide as if at the dentist's. I could see something yellow in their eyes. I could smell a smell unlike any smell I've ever smelled. These were people who had been tossed in the darkness, human leftovers starring in their own nightmares, covered in flimsy white gowns, their psyches poking through like ribs. They were the embers of a fire dying out. Where in the world could they go where they made sense?

The doctors walked briskly on the way to strip the patients of their crazy laughter. I studied the faces of the nurses: how could they work here? They must be either sadists or saints. They couldn't be anything else, but could they be both? They and the doctors looked tired: draining heads of wrong ideas is obviously an exhausting business.

I thought: What human thing could emerge out of this edifice of violent nightmares and say, "OK, now back to work!"?

The nurse at reception sat eerily still with a pained expression, as if bracing herself for a punch in the face.

"Jasper Dean to see Martin Dean," I said.

"Are you family?"

When I didn't say anything for a while, she said, "I'll call Dr. Greg."

"I hope that's his last name."

She picked up a phone and paged Dr. Greg. I searched Mrs. French's face for some acknowledgment that I hadn't referred to myself as Kasper. If she had heard me, she wasn't giving anything away.

A couple of minutes later, Dr. Greg arrived, looking sharp, smiling like someone who thinks he is always well liked, especially at first sight.

"I'm glad you're here. Your father won't talk to us," he announced.

"And?"

"And I was wondering if you could come into the room and help us out."

"If he doesn't want to talk to you, it means he doesn't care what you think. My presence won't change that."

"Why doesn't he care what I think?"

"Well, you probably said things to him like 'We're on your side, Mr. Dean,' and 'We're here to help you.' "

"What's wrong with that?"

"Look. You're a psychiatrist, right?"

"And?"

"He's read books written by your predecessors: Freud, Jung, Adler, Rank, Fromm, and Becker. Those guys. You need to convince him that you're cut from the same cloth."

"Well, I'm not Freud."

"And there's your problem right there."

Mrs. French waited in the reception area while I followed the doctor through the gloomy corridors and the opening and closing of countless locked doors. We got to Dad's room and he unlocked it with a key. Inside was a single bed, a desk, a chair, and half-chewed morsels of indefinable food mangled on a plate. Dad stood with his back to us, staring out the window. Watching him was like looking at a naked tree in winter.

"Look, Martin. Your son's here to see you," Dr. Greg said.

When he turned, I let out a little gasp. It looked as if all the bones and muscles in his face had been taken out.

"How are you?" I asked, as if we were meeting for the first time. He stepped forward with the dazed look of a mother after childbirth.

Any vow of silence Dad had taken he abandoned at the sight of me. "Jasper. Listen. You can never really kill your old selves. They lie there in a mass grave, buried alive, one on top of the other, waiting for the opportunity for resurrection, and then, because they've once been dead, they drive you like a zombie, as they themselves are zombies. Do you see what I'm getting at? All your old failures squirming to life!"

I looked over at Dr. Greg and said, "You wanted him talking. Well, he's talking."

Dad sucked in his lip as a sign of defiance. I went over to him and whispered, "Dad, you have to get out of here. They've got me in a state-run home. It's horrible."

He didn't say anything. Dr. Greg didn't say anything either. I looked around the room and thought it was the worst possible environment for a collapsed mind, as it would give him more time to reflect, and if his disease had a cause, it was excessive reflection; too much thinking had broken his brain. I looked back at Dr. Greg: he was leaning against the desk, as if watching a play where none of the actors knew whose turn it was to speak.

"Here. I brought you something," I said, handing Dad the book of puzzles. He gave me a sad glance as he took it and then began studying the book and making little "hmm" sounds.

"A pencil," he said in a scratchy whisper, holding out his hand without looking up.

I stared at Dr. Greg until he reluctantly fished in his shirt pocket and handed me a pencil as delicately as if it were a machete. I gave it to Dad. He opened the book and started going through the first maze. I tried to think of something to say, but I didn't come up with anything other than "You're welcome," even though he hadn't said thank you.

"Done," he said to himself when he finished.

"Martin," Dr. Greg said. Dad flinched, turned the page, and started on the second maze. From where I sat the book was upside down, and I got dizzy watching him.

After a minute he said, "Too easy," turned the page, and began to tackle the third maze. "They get progressively harder as you go through the book," he said to no one.

He was now attacking the puzzles compulsively. Dr. Greg gave me a look as if to say, "What made you give a mentally confused man a compendium of conundrums?" and I had to agree I would've done much better with my first instinct, to buy porn.

"Eddie says you can come back to work when you're ready," I said.

Without looking up, Dad said, "Son of a bitch."

"He's being pretty good to you, I think, considering you smashed up his club."

"The first day I met him in Paris he offered me money, then he offered me a job. Then he found me a job. Then later he followed me here to Australia and gave me money to feed you. Not much, a hundred here, a hundred there, but he keeps helping me out."

"Sounds like you have a very good friend," Dr. Greg said.

"What do you know about it?" Dad snapped.

Enough of this small talk, I thought. I walked close to Dad and tried whispering in his ear again. "Dad, I need you to get out of here. They've put me in a home." He didn't say anything, and turned to the last maze in the book and started working through it. "It's dangerous. Some guy made a pass at me," I lied.

He still didn't say anything, only scrunched up his face in annoyance, not at my distasteful lie but at the puzzle he was failing to solve.

"Martin," Dr. Greg chimed in, "don't you want to look at your son?"

"I know what he looks like," Dad said.

It was clear that Dr. Greg's lacerating mediocrity was suffocating Dad. The doctor was treading the unlit terrain of Dad's mind with muddy boots, trampling over everything, understanding nothing. As I said, Dad wanted to be prodded by a Freud or a Jung, and if there was no further evidence of his unhinged mind, expecting that an undiscovered genius would be languishing here in this state-run hovel was proof enough.

He was still having trouble with the last maze. His pencil worked through it, but he kept hitting dead ends. "What the fuck?" he said. He was grinding his teeth so loudly we could hear it.

"Martin, why don't you put the book away and talk to your son?"

"Shut up!"

Suddenly Dad jumped up and stamped his foot. He grabbed a chair and held it above his head, breathing so deeply his whole body heaved. "Get me out of here now!" he screamed, waving the chair in the air.

"Put it down!" Dr. Greg shouted. "Jasper, don't be afraid."

"I'm not afraid," I said, although I was a little afraid. "Dad," I said, "don't be a dickhead."

Then the reinforcements arrived, like they do in the movies. An orderly ran in and grabbed Dad and pushed him onto the table. Another grabbed me and pushed me out of the room. I could still see Dad through the little window in the door. The orderlies had him pinned to the table and were sticking a needle in his arm. He was kicking and screaming; whatever was in that needle was taking its time. Dad's stubborn hyped-up metabolism was slow to react, his agitation far too electric. Then I couldn't see his face because one of the orderlies was in the way, and I thought how when the apocalypse comes there's bound to be someone with big hair standing in front of me. Finally the orderly moved to the side, and I saw that Dad was all slobbery and drowsy and medicated into ambivalence. When, a couple of spasms later, he was blissfully at peace, Dr. Greg came out to talk to me. His face was red and sweaty, and I detected a subtle look of exhilaration behind his eyes, as if he were saying to himself, "This is what it's all about!"

"You can't keep him here!" I shouted.

"Actually, we can."

He showed me some paperwork. There was plenty of technical mumbo jumbo. I couldn't understand it. It was all pretty dull. Even the font was boring.

"Listen. What will it take to get him out of here?"

"He needs to be better than he is now."

"Well, fuck, can you be more specific?"

"More balanced. We need to be confident he's not going to do any harm to himself, or to you, or to others."

"And how do you intend to do that? Be specific, now."

"By getting him to talk to me. And by medicating him to maintain his stability."

"This all sounds time-consuming."

"It isn't going to happen overnight."

"Well, how long? An estimate."

"I don't know, Jasper. Six months? A year? Two years? Look at him— your father's pretty far gone."

"Well, what the fuck am I supposed to do? Live in a fucking state-run home?"

"Don't you have any relatives who can look after you?"

"No."

"Uncles or aunts?"

"Dead."

"Grandparents?"

"Dead! Dead! Everyone's fucking dead!"

"I'm sorry, Jasper. This is just not something that can be moved along quickly."

"It has to."

"I don't see how."

"That's because you're an idiot," I said, and stormed down the corridors, not stopping to contemplate the loud groaning on either side. At the reception area, Mrs. French was studiously examining her fingernails like someone who doesn't like to be left alone with her thoughts. Those fingernails were a way out. I left her with them and crept silently to the elevator. On the way down, I thought of all the people I'd heard pompously call themselves crazy and I wished them lots and lots and lots of bad luck.

I caught a bus home. The other passengers looked as tired and worn-out as I felt. I thought about my problem: this hospital, rather than being a road to wellness, would only accelerate the decay of his body, mind, and spirit, and if Dad was going to get well, he had to get out of there, but to get out of there, he needed to be well. To get him well, I needed to discover exactly what had made him sick, the means by which he had rendered himself useless.

•

Back in the apartment I searched for Dad's more recent notebooks. I needed an idea, and no textbook could better aid me than one he wrote himself. But I couldn't find them. They weren't in his wardrobe, or under his bed, or wrapped in plastic bags and hidden in the top of the toilet—none of his usual hiding places. After an hour of general ransacking, I had to admit they weren't in the apartment at all. What had he done with them? I turned the bedroom upside-down again, which only transformed it from one state of chaos to another. Exhausted, I lay on his bed. The atmosphere reeked of Dad's collapse, and I did my best to avoid the sticky notion that this was not the beginning of the end but the actual definitive conclusive end, the end of the end.

On Dad's bedside table was a postcard from Anouk. It had "Bali" printed in bold red letters over a picture of rice workers in a field. On the other side she had written "You guys need a holiday," and that was all. We sure did.

I rolled over. Something in his pillowcase dug into my skull. I shook the pillow—out fell a black notebook! There were 140 pages, all numbered. Okay, I was the only one who could free Dad, and this book was going to tell me how. The problem was, entering my father's mental state implied a certain danger, because his was the kind of thinking that closed around you, not slowly or surreptitiously but quick like the snap of a rusty bear trap. My defense, then, was to read ironically, and with this in mind, I braced myself and began.

Not surprisingly, it was a profoundly uncomfortable experience, as all journeys into dissolution and madness must be. I read it through twice. There were general frustrations, as on page 88:

I have too much free time. Free time makes people think; thinking makes people morbidly self-absorbed; and unless you are watertight and flawless, excessive self-absorption leads to depression. That's why depression is the number-two disease in the world, behind Internet porn eyestrain.

and disturbing observations pertaining to me, as on page 21:

Poor Jasper. Watching him sleep while I'm pretending to read, I don't think he realizes yet that every day his pile of minutes lightens. Maybe he should die when I die?

and observations about himself:

My problem is I can't sum myself up in one sentence. All I know is who I'm not. And I've noticed there is a tacit agreement among most people that they'll at least try to adjust to their environment. I've always felt the urge to rebel against it. That's why when I'm in the movies and the screen goes dark I get an irresistible impulse to read a book. Luckily, I carry a pocket torch.

The most recurrent thoughts were Dad's desire to hide, to be alone, to be isolated, not to be bothered by noise and people. The usual Dad rant. But surprisingly, there were also hints at a megalomania I hadn't heard him articulate before, passages in his notebook that alluded to a longing to dominate and change the world—this appeared to be an evolution of his obsessive thoughts—which shed new light on his usual longing to be alone. I understood it now as a desire to have an isolated headquarters where he could plan his attack. There was, for instance, this:

No symbolic journey can take place in an apartment. There's nothing metaphorical about a trip to the kitchen. There's nothing to ascend! Nothing to descend! No space! No verticality! No cosmicity! We need a roomy, airy house. We need nooks and crannies and corners and hollows and garrets and staircases and cellars and attics. We need a second toilet. The essential important idea that will shift me from Thinking Man to Doing Man is impossible to apply here. The walls are too close to my head, and the distractions too many—the noise of the street, the doorbell, the telephone. Jasper and I need to move to the bush so I can lay the plans for my major task which I have lying in egg form. I am also lying in egg form. I am a halfway man, and I need a place of intense concentration if I am to whisper into a golden ear and change the face of this country.

and this:

> Emerson understood! "The moment we meet with anybody, each becomes a fraction," he said. That's my problem. I'm ¼ of who I should be! Maybe even ⅛th. Then he said, "The voices which we hear in solitude grow faint and inaudible as we enter into the world." This is my problem exactly: I can't hear myself! He also said, "It is easy in the world to live after the world's opinion; it is easy in solitude to live after your own; but the great man is he who in the midst of the crowd keeps with perfect sweetness the independence of solitude." I can't do this!

And then, on my second reading, I found a quote that was so frighteningly to the point, I actually shouted "Ah-ha!" which is something I'd never said before and have never said since. It was this, on page 101:

> Pascal notes that during the French Revolution, all the nuthouses were emptied. The inmates suddenly had meaning in their lives.

I closed the notebook and walked to the window and looked down at the twisted roofs and roads and the city skyline, then moved my eyes to the sky, to the clouds dancing on it. I felt as though I had drawn a new and fresh source of strength into my body. For the first time in my life, I knew exactly what I had to do.

•

I caught the bus to Eddie's and trod a narrow path winding between expensive jungles of fern to the front of his sandstone house. I rang the bell.

You couldn't hear its call from the outside. Eddie must have made a lot of money himself from strip clubs—only rich people can afford to mute like that; the silence is due to the thickness of the door, and the more money you have, the chunkier your door is. It's the way of the world. The poor get thinner and the rich get chunkier.

Eddie opened the door, combing his thin hair. Gel dripped off the comb in large dollops I could smell. I cut straight to the point.

"Why are you always so good to my father?"

"What do you mean?"

"You're always offering money and help and kindness. Why? Dad says it started the day you met him in Paris."

"He said that?"

"Yes."

"So I don't understand—what is it you want to know?"

"This generosity of yours. What's behind it?"

Eddie's face was strained. He finished combing his hair while searching for the right words to answer me.

"And while you're answering that one, answer this: why are you always taking photographs of us? What do you want with us?"

"I don't want anything."

"So it's just plain friendship."

"Of course!"

"Then you might be able to give us a million dollars."

"That's too much."

"Well, how much can you get?"

"Maybe, I don't know, a sixth of that."

"How much is that?"

"I don't know."

"Well, Dad's been saving, and I don't know how much he's got, but it won't be enough."

"Enough for what?"

"To help him."

"Jasper, you have my word. Whatever I can do, or give you."

"So you'll give us a sixth of a million dollars?"

"If it would help you and your father."

"You're crazy."

"I'm not the one in hospital, Jasper."

I suddenly felt bad about harassing Eddie. He really was a rare person, and clearly their friendship meant a lot to him. I even got the impression he thought it contained a deep spiritual quality that was in no way lessened by the fact that Dad occasionally hated his guts.

When I went back to the hospital, Dad was strapped to a bed in the same olive-green room. I peered over him. His eyes rolled around in his head like marbles tossed into a teacup. I bent over and whispered in his ear. I wasn't certain he was listening, but I whispered myself hoarse. Afterward, I pulled the chair up next to him and put my head on his rising and falling stomach and fell asleep. When I woke, I realized that someone had put a blanket over me and a croaky voice was talking. I don't know when Dad had started his monologue, but he was already in the middle of a sentence.

". . . and that's why they said that architecture was like reproducing the universe, and all the old churches and monasteries were attempting the divine task of replicating heaven."

"What? What's going on? Are you OK?"

I could see only the odd shape of his head. He was straining to hold it up. I stood, turned on the light, and undid the bed straps. He turned his head from side to side, trying out his neck.

"We are going to construct a world, Jasper, of our own design, where no one can come in unless we ask them."

"We're going to build a world of our own?"

"Well, a house. All we have to do is design it. What do you think of that?"

"I think that's great," I said.

"And you know what else, Jasper? I want this to be your dream too. I want you to help me. I want your input. I want your ideas."

"OK. Yeah. Great," I said.

It had worked. In his sandstorm, Dad had found a new project. He'd decided to build a house.

V

Per his instructions, I brought Dad every book on the theory and history of architecture I could find, including weighty tomes on animal buildings such as birds' nests, beaver dams, honeycombs, and spiders' burrows. He took the books with delight. We were going to build a container for our moldy souls!

Dr. Greg came in and noted the piles of architectural literature. "What's going on here, then?"

Proudly, Dad told him the idea.

"The Great Australian Dream, huh?"

"Sorry?"

"I said, you're going to pursue the Great Australian Dream. I think that's a very good idea."

"What do you mean? There's a collective dream? How come nobody told me? What is it again?"

"Owning your own home."

"Owning your own home? *That's* the Great Australian Dream?"

"You know it is."

"Wait a minute. Haven't we merely appropriated the Great *American* Dream and just substituted the name of our country?"

"I don't think so," Dr. Greg said, looking worried.

"Whatever you say," Dad said, rolling his eyes so we both could see it.

●

A week later I went back. The books were open and pages torn up and scattered all over the room. When I entered, Dad held up his head like a hoisted sail. "Glad you're here. What do you think of manifesting the symbolic paradise of the womb, a house huge and glistening, and we'll bury ourselves inside where we can really rot in privacy?"

"Sounds good," I said, moving a pile of books off the chair so I could sit down.

"Tell me if any of these say anything to you: French chateau, English cottage, Italian villa, German castle, peasant simplicity."

"Not really."

"But geometric simplicity, OK? Fundamentally simple, uncluttered, loud, pretentious, and gaudy, without being dispiritingly tasteless."

"Whatever you like."

"Above all, I don't want anything angular, so maybe it should be round."

"Good idea."

"You think so? Do you feel like living in an orb?"

"Yeah, that sounds fine."

"What we want is to blend into the natural surroundings. An organic synthesis, that's what we're after. And inside I think two bedrooms, two bathrooms, a living room, a kitchen, and a dark room, not to develop photos, just so we can sit in the dark. Now, what else? Let's talk about the threshold."

"The what?"

"The portal into the home."

"You mean the front door?"

"How many times do I have to say it?"

"Just once would be good."

Dad's eyes narrowed into thin slits and the edges of his mouth curled downward. "If you're going to be that way about it, we'll just scrap the whole design. What about living in a cave?"

"A cave?"

"I thought we agreed we'd live in a uterine symbol."

"Dad."

"Well, what if we live in the trunk of an old tree, like Merlin? Or wait. I know. We could construct platforms *in* the trees. What do you say, Jasper—are we tree-dwellers?"

"Not especially."

"Since when don't you want to live in leafy sensuality?"

Dr. Greg had come into the room. He was ogling us like a Supreme Court judge watching a couple of neo-Nazis wash his car at traffic lights.

"Dad, let's just have an ordinary house. Just a nice, normal, ordinary house."

"You're right. We don't need to go over the top. OK. Which do you prefer? A cubical ordinary house or a cylindrical ordinary house?"

I sighed. "Cubical."

"Have you ever seen the Tower of Samara in Iraq?"

"No. Have you?"

"OK. Here's a structural dilemma we have to overcome. I want to hear the echo of my own footsteps, but I don't want to hear yours. What can we do about that?"

"I don't know."

"All right, then. Let's talk ceilings. Do you want high ceilings?"

"Of course. Why would anyone want a low ceiling?"

"To hang yourself. OK? Hang on a sec. Let's see . . ." Dad rummaged through his books. "Tepee?"

"Come on, Dad, what's happened to your brain? You're all over the place."

"You're right. You're right. We need to focus. We need to be sensible. We need to be logical. So let's be logical. What are the objectives inherent in the design of a house? To meet your physical needs. Eating, sleeping, shitting, and fucking. That translates to comfort, utility, efficiency. But our psychological needs? The same, really. In fact, I don't see why we should separate ourselves from primitive man in this. Our goal should be to exist in a consistent climate and to keep out predators."

"Great."

"Just remember that the form of our habitat will inflict undue influence on our behavior. We have to be smart about this. What about an igloo?"

"No."

"A house on wheels! A drawbridge! A moat!"

"No! Dad! You're out of control here!"

"OK! OK! Have it your way. We'll do something simple. The only thing I insist on, though, is that the ideology behind the design of our house should be the old Italian proverb."

"What proverb?"

"That the best armor is to keep out of range."

This idea was clearly backfiring. Dr. Greg looked on quietly through these brainstorming sessions with half-closed, judgmental eyes. Dad had become luminous with ideas, but he'd made the undesirable leap from manic-depressive to obsessive-compulsive.

Meanwhile I decided to play along and be a good provisional orphan, so I returned to the house for lost children. It made sense, because if I played truant they'd be lying in wait for me every time I visited Dad in hospital, and breaking into an insane asylum is just as difficult as breaking out. I also had to return to school. Mrs. French drove me in the mornings, and throughout the school day I scrupulously avoided telling anyone about Dad's meltdown or about how my father and I were now living in separate homes for cracked eggs—talking about it would have meant surrendering myself to reality. I just went on as if it were business as usual. Of course, returning from school every afternoon was a nightmare, though as it happened, absolutely everyone at the house neglected to sexually abuse me in any way, and nothing of interest occurred there except I eventually gave in to my gnawing curiosity and listened to everyone's stories, which were far worse than mine. In this way all the abandoned children robbed me of self-pity. That's when I really bottomed out. Without being able to feel sorry for myself, I had nothing left.

And worse, every now and then the fools at the hospital granted Dad access to a telephone. I'd answer it and suffer through a conversation like this:

My voice: "Hello?"

Dad's voice: "Here's a spatial dilemma: how to arrange the house so that at the same time it is comfortable for us but discourages guests from staying more than forty-five minutes."

Mine: "Not sure."

Dad's: "Jasper! This is to be a hard, practical exercise! No messing about! Something that reflects my personality, no, my dilemma, my lie, which is, of course, my personality. And the color. I want it white! Blindingly white!"

Mine: "Please, can we do something simple?"

Dad's: "I couldn't agree with you more. We want something simple that can be eroded by the elements. We don't want anything more durable than we are."

Mine: "OK."

Dad's: "Open living space. No. That discourages human intimacy. No, hang on, I want that. I want . . ."

Long silence.

Mine: "Dad? You still there?"

Dad's: "Bullfighting ring! Gothic cathedral! Mud hovel!"

Mine: "Are you taking your medicine?"

Dad's: "And no mantelpieces! They always make me think of urns with ashes in them."

Mine: "OK! Jesus!"

Dad's: "Which do you prefer, a porch or a veranda? What's the difference, anyway? Wait. I don't care. We'll have both. And I'll tell you something else. Ornamental detail can go to hell. *We are the ornamental detail!*"

Then I'd hang up and curse myself for sending Dad down what I thought was another ruinous path. These conversations certainly did not prepare me for the abrupt change that was about to follow.

•

One day I visited the hospital and was shocked to see that Dad had arranged the books into a neat pile. All the pages of erratic designs had been thrown away, and when I sat down in that eerily organized room, he presented me with a single piece of paper with a shockingly normal design for a shockingly normal family home. No moats, drawbridges, igloos, or stalagmites. No bullfighting rings, indoor slides, trenches, or underwater grottos. It was just a normal house. The construction was clear and simple: a classic boxy structure with a central living space and several rooms arranged off it. I might even go so far as to say it summed up the national character, right down to the veranda on all sides.

He had finally seen his situation clearly: to build his house he must get out, and to get out he must convince the powers that be that he was once again mentally healthy and fit for society. So he faked it. It must have been a strenuous period for him, putting all his energy into pretending to be normal; he did this single-mindedly, and talked about the Great Australian Dream and interest rates and mortgage repayments and sports teams and his employment prospects; he expressed outrage at the things that outraged his countrymen: taxpayer-funded ministerial blowjobs, corporate greed, fanatical environmentalists, logical arguments, and compassionate judges. He was so convincing in his portrayal of Mr. Average that Dr. Greg swallowed every droplet of bullshit my father sweated out for him, swelling with triumph at the conclusion of each session.

And so, four months after he entered the hospital, he was released. Dad and I went to Eddie's house and secured his loan, which really consisted of Dad saying, "So you got the money?" and Eddie saying, "Yeah."

"I'll pay you back," Dad said, after an uncomfortable silence. "Double. I'll pay you back double."

"Martin, don't worry about it."

"Eddie. You know what Nietzsche said about gratitude."

"No, Marty, I don't."

"He said a man in debt wants his benefactor dead."

"OK. Pay me back."

After we left Eddie's, Dad tore his design for his dream house into pieces.

"What are you doing?"

"That was just a hoax. That was just to make those bastards think I was normal," Dad said, laughing.

"But you're better now, aren't you?"

"Yeah. I feel good. This house idea has really got me back on top."

"So if that was a hoax, where's the real design for our house?"

"There isn't one. Look. Why bother fucking around with building your own house? That sounds like an enormous pilgrim's headache."

"So we're not getting a house?"

"Yeah. We're just going to buy one."

"OK. Yeah. That sounds really good, Dad. We'll buy a house."

"And then we're going to hide it," he said, smiling so proudly I finally understood why pride is one of the seven deadly sins, and such was the repellent force of his grin, I wondered why it shouldn't be all seven.

VI

According to him, it was an idea that arrived in one piece, completely formed: we will buy a house and hide it in a maze. The idea came to him during a psychological game of word association with Dr. Greg.

"Health."

"Sickness."

"Ball."

"Testicle."

"Ideas."

"Complexity."

"Home."

"House. Hidden in a labyrinth of my own design that I will build on a large property in the bush."

"What?"

"Nothing. I have to go back to my room for a while. Can we continue this later?"

And why did he get the idea in the first place? Maybe because labyrinths have always been a facile metaphor for the soul, or the human condition, or the complexity of a process, or the pathway to God. I discounted these as being too profound, and if I know one thing, it's that men don't do things for profound reasons—the things they do are sometimes profound, but their reasons are not. No, I must have inspired this whole ridiculous plan by making a gift of that silly book of mazes. The failure to complete a child's puzzle infuriated him so that it lodged in his brain, and when the idea for designing and constructing a house came in, it either merged with the idea of the maze or wrapped around it, somehow fusing so that the two ideas became one.

"Dad. Can't we just get a house like everyone else and *not hide it?*"

"Nah."

No one could talk him out of it, not me or Eddie and especially not Dr. Greg, who learned the truth when Dad went back for a checkup. He told Dad in no uncertain terms that a labyrinth wasn't the Great Australian Dream, which is quite right, it isn't, but in the end no one objected too strongly, because no one but me really thought he would actually build it.

We went looking at properties out of Sydney in all directions, and each time he dashed out along the property lines, exploring the bushland, nodding his head approvingly at the trees and the space and the potential for solitude. The houses themselves seemed to be unimportant to him, and he took only a cursory look through them. Colonial? Federation? Victorian? Modern? He didn't care. He only required that the house be surrounded on all sides by dense bushland. He wanted trees and bushes and rocks fused together, bushland so dense that even without the labyrinth walls, the natural landscape would be almost impassable.

While searching for the perfect site, he accumulated dozens of mazes from everywhere from puzzle books to old manuscripts of the labyrinths of antiquity, from Egypt to medieval England, using them mainly as inspiration, not wanting merely to copy an existing design. He labored furiously in pencil to invent a complex pattern of his own imagining that he would actually reproduce on the land. This was his first major step in altering the existing universe with his own brain, so he obsessed about the structure of the house: not only did it need to be locked up in the protective custody of the maze, but it had to serve as a palace of thinking, where Dad could wander and plot without interruption—a base for his "operations," whatever they were. He also wanted dead ends and passages where an intruder, or "guest," would be forced into making several critical choices between paths, resulting in disorientation and/or starvation and madness. "The unpassable path!" became his new motto. "Bloody hell!" became mine. Why? Those designs stalked my nightmares. It seemed all our future disasters were prefigured in them, and depending on which he chose, we would suffer a different disaster. At night I pored over the designs myself, trying to read our impending calamities in them.

One afternoon we went to inspect some land half an hour northwest of the city. To reach the property you had to take a private road that was a long wiggling dirt track, over which you had to bounce unevenly through burned-out forests, their charred tree trunks a warning: by living in the bush, you are living in a war zone during an unreliable ceasefire.

The property seemed custom-built for his purpose: it was dense, dense, dense. Hills with steep climbs and sudden descents, twisting gullies, large rocky outcrops, winding creeks you had to wade across, a foliage of thick scrub and waist-high grass that would require special footwear. As we surveyed the property we got lost straightaway, which Dad took as a good sign. Standing on ground that sloped gently downward, he looked at the dirt, the trees, the sky. Yes, he even examined the sun. He looked right into it. He turned to me and gave me the thumbs-up. This was the one!

Unfortunately, the house wasn't subjected to examination at all. Me, I would've failed it mercilessly. It was a drafty, dilapidated old thing—no more than your classic two-story shoebox. The shag carpet was thick and ugly, and crossing the living room floor felt like walking on a hairy chest. The kitchen stank like a toilet. The toilet, covered in moss, looked like a garden. The garden was a cemetery for weeds and dead grass. The staircase creaked like drying bones. The ceiling paint had dried midbubble. Each room I encountered was smaller and darker than the room before. The upstairs hallway narrowed as you moved down it, so much that the very end of it was almost a point.

Worst of all, to get to school I would need to trek a half a kilometer through the maze, then down our long private road to the nearest bus stop so I could travel twenty minutes to the train, then ride a further forty-five minutes to the coast, where my school was located, but the bus came only three times a day, only once in the morning, and if I missed it, I missed it. I rejected Dad's suggestion that I move to a new school in the area, because I couldn't be bothered with the hassle of making a whole new set of enemies. Better the bully you know, I reasoned.

Dad signed the papers that afternoon, and I had to accept that this insane folly was going to happen. I knew I wouldn't last long in exile on this property, and it was only a matter of time before I'd have to move out and leave him alone, an uncomfortable thought that made me feel wretchedly guilty. I wondered if he realized it too.

He wasted no time hiring the builders, and the fact that he was not the kind of man who had any business at a building site (even if it was his own) did not stop Dad from aggravating them. They gritted their teeth as he passed on his gigantic compositions. Dad had adjusted his maze designs to fit into the natural configurations of the landscape and insisted that few trees were to be harmed. He had narrowed down his mazes to four, and instead of reducing the choices to one, he incorporated them all in one section of the property or another, so that four equally confounding conundrums were to be forced onto the land: mazes within mazes, and in the center our rather ordinary house.

I won't go into all the dull details—the zoning ordinances, the building codes, the delineation of boundaries, the delays, the unforeseen problems like hailstorms and the unrelated disappearance of the builder's wife, but I will say the labyrinth walls were constructed from hedges and countless rocks and massive stones and boulders and sandstone slabs and granite and thousands and thousands of bricks. Because Dad mistrusted the workmen intensely, he broke up the design and gave each section to a different team to construct. The men themselves frequently got lost among the thousand alleys and paths that emerged, and Eddie often joined us on our search parties. He would always photograph their irritated faces when we found them.

Gradually, though, the tall stone walls and oversized hedges were erected, and the house was hidden from sight. A synthesis of house and shell. Psychologically complex. Virtually inaccessible. We moved inside, willing victims of Dad's vast and hazardous imagination.

•

When Anouk came back from Bali, she wasn't surprised so much as absolutely furious that she'd missed everything: the collapse, the home for children, the mental hospital, and the building of this outrageous place.

But, incredibly, she came back to work as if none of it had happened. She made Dad install an intercom system so that when she or any wanted visitors arrived, we could go and lead them through the maze to our fortified homestead. I'll never understand that woman, I thought, but if she wants to cook and clean in a place of endless wanderings, that's her choice.

So this is where we lived.

We were cut off and had only the natural sounds of the bush to placate, stimulate, and terrify us. The air here was different, and I surprised myself: I loved the quiet (as opposed to Dad, who developed the habit of leaving the radio on all the time). For the first time I felt the truth that the sky begins a quarter of an inch from the ground. In the mornings the bush smelled like the best underarm deodorant you ever smelled, and I quickly got used to the mysterious movements of the trees, which heaved rhythmically like a man chloroformed. From time to time the night sky seemed uneven, closer in points, then smoothed out, like a tablecloth bunched up, then suddenly pulled taut. I'd wake up to see low-lying clouds balanced precariously on the tops of trees. Sometimes the wind was so gentle it seemed to come from a child's nostril, while other times it was so strong all the trees seemed held tenuously to the earth by roots as weak as doubled-over sticky tape.

I felt the promise of catastrophe weaken, even break, and I dared to think optimistically again about our softly stirring futures.

During a long walk around the grounds the idea hit me like a mud slide: the most striking difference between my father and me was that I preferred simplicity and he preferred complexity. Not to say I often, or ever, succeeded in achieving simplicity, only to say that I preferred it, just as he enjoyed muddying everything when he could, complicating everything until he couldn't see straight.

•

One evening he was standing in the back garden staring out. It was a liquid night and the moon was just a smudge out of focus.

I said, "What are you thinking about?"

He said, "It's a surprise."

I said, "I don't like surprises. Not anymore."

He said, "You're too young to—"

I said, "I'm not kidding. No more surprises."

He said, "I'm not going to get another job."

I said, "How will we live?"

He said, "We'll live fine."

I said, "What about food and shelter?"

He said, "We have shelter. Eddie said he's not in a hurry for me to pay back the loan, and thanks to him, we own this property."

I said, "And what about Anouk? How will you pay her?"

He said, "I'm giving her the back room to use as a studio. She wants somewhere to sculpt."

I said, "And food? What about food?"

He said, "We'll grow food."

I said, "Steaks? We'll grow steaks?"

Then he said, "I'm thinking about cleaning up the pond."

In the back garden, there was a pond in the shape of a figure eight with small white stones around its perimeter. "And I might put some fish in it," he added.

"Shit, Dad, I don't know."

"But this time *I'll* take care of them, OK?"

I agreed.

As promised, he cleaned up the pond and put in three rare Japanese fish. They were not goldfish; they were so big and colorful they must have been the most advanced form of fish before great white sharks, and Dad fed them once a day, sprinkling the flakes in a semicircle across the pond as if in a simple, dignified ceremony.

A month or two later, I was in the kitchen with Anouk and I could see Dad in the back garden with a tub full of a white substance that he was dishing into the pond in large spoonfuls. He was whistling contentedly.

Anouk pressed her face against the window, then turned to me with a stunned look. "That's chlorine," she said.

"Well, that can't be good for the fish," I said.

"MARTIN!" Anouk screamed through the window. Dad turned swiftly, with an air of perplexity. You could see in his face, even from that distance, that the man had tasted the collapse of his own mind, a taste that hadn't yet left his mouth. "WHAT ARE YOU DOING, YOU GREAT BIG IDIOT?" Anouk shouted. Dad continued to stare at her as if she were a puppet he had made out of wood that had startled him by speaking.

We ran outside. It was too late. The three of us stood over the dead fish, which lay on their sides, eyes bulging with disbelief.

"You know what your problem is?" Anouk asked.

"Yes," Dad said in a soft voice. "I think I do."

That night I was numb with cold. The fire was dying out, so I went upstairs to bed fully clothed and piled blankets on top of me. From my bed I could see a soft glow emanating from the back garden. I went to the window and looked out. Below, Dad stood in his pajamas holding a kerosene lamp that bobbed in the dark.

He was mourning those fish. He went so far as to stare at his hands in a dramatic show of guilt, looking like he was in a student production of *Macbeth*. For a while I watched him standing down there in the back garden, the thin sliver of moon casting a pale light on his minikingdom. The wind cut through the trees. The cicadas sang a monotonous song. Dad threw stones in the pond. I felt disgusted, but it was compelling, the sight of him.

I heard a noise behind me.

There was something in my room: a bat, a possum, or a rat. I knew I'd never sleep until it was dead or removed; I knew I'd be lying in bed in the dark awaiting the sensation of sharp, jagged teeth on my toes. That was our new house for you. Our house, where from every little crack and orifice, every hole and slit, a living thing crawled out.

I went downstairs and made myself comfortable on the couch just as Dad came in from the garden.

"I'm going to sleep down here tonight," I said.

He nodded. I watched him browsing along his bookshelves for something to read. I turned over on my side and thought the completion of his project had introduced a new danger—he might once again render himself susceptible to a lethal twiddling of thumbs. What was he going to do now? With all that activity in his head? The house and the labyrinth had sustained him for a time and would continue to sustain him for a while longer, but they would not do so forever. Sooner or later he'd need a new project, and if one considered the progressive scale of the projects he'd already embarked on—the suggestion box, *The Book of Crime*, the construction of the labyrinth—it was clear that the next one would have to be enormous. Something that would, ironically, sustain him to his death and probably be the thing that killed him.

Dad settled into the reclining chair and pretended to read. I knew exactly what he was doing; he was watching me sleep. It used to bother me, that creepy habit of his. Now I found it strangely comforting—the sound of turning pages in the quiet, his wheezy breathing and heavy presence filling the corners of the room.

He turned the pages quickly. Now he was not only pretending to read, he was pretending to skim-read. I felt his eyes like a sandbag on my head, and I stretched out on the couch, let out a little moan, and after a believable period of time, pretended to dream.

FOUR

It must have been that the maze outside infected everything within. Why else would Dad leave scraps of paper around the house with nonsensical messages written on them, such as "Can't love ear and not your open ugly raw room onto old maps!"? These messages were easily decoded by using the most basic system of cryptology, the first letter of each word in the text spelling out the real message.

"Can't love ear and not your open ugly raw room onto old maps!"

becomes

"Clean your room!"

Then he started with transposition, where the letters were jumbled and their normal order rearranged.

"Egon ot het sposh. Kabc ralet."

becomes

"Gone to the shops. Back later."

Then one night, a few weeks after my sixteenth birthday, I found the following message stuck to the bathroom mirror:

rezizsl ta ta ixs em teme

It took me a while to decode it, because he'd rearranged the words as well as the letters. After a few minutes of scrutiny, I cracked it:

"Meet me at Sizzler at six."

Sizzler was where we preferred to eat to celebrate good news—that is to say, we'd been there once before, five years earlier, after Dad won $46 on lotto. I rode my bike through the labyrinth to the main road and took the bus into the city to the Hotel Carlos. This particular Sizzler was located on the top floor, although you didn't need to stay in the hotel to eat there. You could if you wanted to, of course, but truth be told, once you'd finished eating and paid your bill, they didn't really care where you slept.

When I got there, he was already sitting at a table by the window, I suppose so we could gaze out across the cityscape during the inevitable lulls in conversation.

"So how's school?" he asked as I sat down.

"Not bad."

"Learn anything today?"

"The usual stuff."

"Such as?"

"You know," I said, and became nervous when I realized that he wasn't looking at me. Maybe he'd heard someone say you're not supposed to look directly into the sun and took it the wrong way.

"I have something to show you," he said. He laid an envelope on the table and drummed his fingers on it.

I picked up the already torn-open envelope and removed the note inside. The letterhead was from my high school. As I read it, I feigned confusion, but I think it came across as a confession.

> Dear Mr. Dean,
>
> This is to officially inform you that your son, Jasper Dean, has been involved in an assault that took place on a train in the afternoon of the twentieth of April, after school. We have indisputable evidence that your son, while wearing school uniform, assaulted a man without provocation. In addition, we are writing to inform you that your son has chosen of his own volition to leave school.
> Yours sincerely,
> Mr. Michael Silver
> Principal

"Why did they write that you were wearing your school uniform? Why is that important?"

"That's how they are."

Dad clicked his tongue.

"I'm not going back," I said.

"Why not?"

"I've already said my goodbyes."

"And you attacked someone? Is that true?"

"You had to be there."

"Were you defending yourself?"

"It's more complicated than that. Look, everything I need to know I can teach myself. I can read books on my own. Those fools need someone to turn the pages for them. I don't."

"What will you do?"

"I'll think of something," I said. How could I tell him that I now wanted what he had once wanted—to travel on trains and fall in love with girls with dark eyes and extravagant lips? It didn't matter to me if at the end of it I had nothing to show but sore thighs. It wasn't my fault that the life of the wanderer, the wayfarer, had fallen out of favor with the world. So what if it was no longer acceptable to drift with the wind, asking for bread and a roof, sleeping on bales of hay and enjoying dalliances with barefooted farmgirls, then running away before the harvest? This was the life I wanted, blowing around like a leaf with appetites.

But unfortunately Dad didn't like the concept of his only son floating aimlessly through space and time, as he came to describe my life plan. He leaned back in his chair and said, "You have to finish school."

"*You* didn't finish school."

"I know. You don't want to follow in my footsteps, do you?"

"I'm not following in your footsteps. You don't own the rights to quitting school."

"Well, what are you going to do?"

"I'm going to put my soul on the open road. See what happens."

"I'll tell you what happens. Road rage."

"I'll risk it."

"Look, Jasper. All I know is the exact pathway to frozen dinners and unwashed laundry. I left school. I wandered aimlessly over the whole earth. I gave myself no choice but to remain exiled from society. But I put you back in school for a reason: so you could have a foot in both worlds, ours and theirs. There's no reason to leave now as if from the scene of a crime. Stay. Finish. Then do what you want. You want to go to university? You want to get a job and settle down? You want to travel to some of the world's most exciting dictatorships? You want to drown in a foreign river during a monsoon? Whatever. Just give yourself the option. Stay within the system for now, OK?"

"You didn't. How many times have I heard you say, 'Fuck the system'? Well, that's all I'm doing. Fucking it."

Pity us, the children of rebels. Just like you, we have the right to rebel against our father's ways, we too have anarchies and revolutions exploding in our hearts. But how do you rebel against rebellion? Does that mean turning back to conformity? That's no good. If I did that, then one day my own son, in rebellion against me, would turn out to be my father.

Dad leaned forward as though about to confess a murder he was particularly proud of.

"Well, if you're going out to put your soul on the open road, I'd like to give you a warning," he said, his eyebrows arching unattractively. "Call it a road warning. I'm just not sure how to word it."

Dad put his thinking face on. His breathing became shallow. He spun around and shushed the couple at the table behind us. Suddenly he proceeded with his warning.

"People always complain about having no shoes until they see a man with no feet, then they complain about not having an electric wheelchair. Why? What makes them automatically transfer themselves from one dull system to another, and why is free will utilized only on details and not on the broad outlines—not 'Should I work?' but 'Where should I work?' and not 'Should I start a family?' but 'When should I start a family?' Why is it we don't suddenly swap countries so that everyone in France moves to Ethiopia and everyone in Ethiopia moves to Britain and everyone in Britain moves to the Caribbean and so on until we have finally shared the earth like we were supposed to and shed ourselves of our shameful, selfish, bloodthirsty, and fanatical loyalty to dirt? Why is free will wasted on a creature who has infinite choices but pretends there are only one or two?

"Listen. People are like knees that are hit with tiny rubber hammers. Nietzsche was a hammer. Schopenhauer was a hammer. Darwin was a hammer. I don't want to be a hammer, because I know how the knees will react. It's boring to know. I know because I know that people *believe*. People are proud of their beliefs. Their pride gives them away. It's the pride of ownership. I've had mystical visions and found they were all so much noise. I saw visions I heard voices I smelled smells but I ignored them just as I will always ignore them. I ignore these mysteries *because* I saw them. I have seen more than most people, yet they believe and I do not. And why don't I believe? Because there's a process going on and I can see it.

"It happens when people see Death, which is all the time. They see Death but they perceive Light. They feel their own death and they call it God. This happens to me too. When I feel deep in my guts that there's meaning in the world, or God, I know it is really Death, but because I don't *want* to see Death in the daylight, the mind plots and says *Listen up you won't die don't worry you are special you have meaning the world has meaning can't you feel it?* And I still see Death and feel him too. And my mind says *Don't think about death lalalala you will always be beautiful and special and you will never die nevernevernever haven't you heard of the immortal soul well you have a really nice one.* And I say Maybe and my mind says *Look at that fucking sunset look at those fucking mountains look at that goddamn magnificent tree where else could that have come from but the hand of God that will cradle you forever and ever.* And I start to believe in Profound Puddles. Who wouldn't? That's how it begins. But I doubt. And my mind says *Don't worry. You won't die. Not in the long term. The essence of you will not perish, not the stuff worth keeping.* One time I saw all the world from my bed, but I rejected it. Another time I saw a fire and in that fire I heard a voice telling me I would be spared. I rejected that too, because I know that all voices come from within. Nuclear energy is a waste of time. They should go about harnessing the power of the unconscious when it is in the act of denying Death. It is during the fiery Process that belief is produced, and if the fires are really hot they produce Certainty— Belief's ugly son. To feel you know with all your heart Who made the universe, Who manages it, Who pays for it, et cetera, is in effect to disengage from it. The so-called religious, the so-called spiritualists, the groups that are quick to renounce the Western tradition of 'soul-deadening consumerism' and point out that comfort is death think it applies only to material possessions. But if comfort is death, then that should apply most profoundly to the mother of all comforts, *certainty of belief*—far cushier than a soft leather couch or an indoor Jacuzzi, and sure to kill an active spirit faster than an electric garage door opener. But the lure of certainty is difficult to resist, so you need one eye on the Process like me so that when I see the mystical visions of all the world and hear the half-whispered voices, I can reject them out of hand and resist the temptation to feel special and trust in my immortality, as I know it is only the handiwork of Death. So you see? *God is the beautiful propaganda made in the fires of Man.* And it's OK to love God because you appreciate the artistry of his creation, but you don't have to believe in a character because you're impressed by the author. Death and Man, God's coauthors, are the most prolific writers on the planet. Their output is prodigious. Man's Unconscious and Inevitable Death have co-penned Jesus, Muhammad, and Buddha, to name but a few. And that's just the characters. They created heaven, hell, paradise, limbo, and purgatory. And that's just the settings. And what more? Everything, maybe. This successful partnership has created everything in the world but the world itself, everything that exists except for what was originally here when we found it. You get it? Do you understand the Process? Read Becker! Read Rank! Read Fromm! They'll tell you! Humans are unique in this world in that, as opposed to all other animals, they have developed a consciousness so advanced that it has one awful by-product: they are the only creatures aware of their own mortality. This truth is so terrifying that from a very early age humans bury it deep in their unconscious, and this has turned people into red-blooded machines, fleshy factories that manufacture meaning. The meaning they feel becomes channeled into their immortality projects—such as their children, or their gods, or their artistic works, or their businesses, or their nations—that they believe will outlive them. And here's the problem: people feel they need these beliefs in order to live but are unconsciously suicidal because of their beliefs. That's why when a person sacrifices his life for a religious cause, he has chosen to die not for a god but in the service of an unconscious primal fear. So it is this fear that causes him to die of the very thing he is afraid of. You see? The irony of their immortality projects is that while they have been designed by the unconscious to fool the person into a sense of specialness and into a bid for everlasting life, the manner in which they fret about their immortality projects is the very thing that kills them. This is where you have to be careful. This is my warning to you. My road warning. The denial of death rushes people into an early grave, and if you are not careful, they will take you with them."

Dad stiffened, and his tempestuous face sent me torrents of inexhaustible anxiety while waiting for me to say something complimentary and obedient. I stayed mute. Sometimes there's nothing as snide as silence.

"So, what do you think?"

"I have no idea what you just said."

His breathing got loud, as if he'd just run a couple of marathons with me on his back. In truth, his speech made an impression on my mind so deep, a surgeon could probably still make out the grooves. And not just because it planted a seed that would eventually make me distrust any feelings or ideas of my own that might be viewed as spiritual, but because there's nothing more distressing or uncomfortable to look at than a philosopher who's thought himself into a corner. And that was the night I first got a good, clear look at his corner, his terrible corner, his sad dead end, where Dad had inoculated himself against having anything mystical or religious ever happen to him, so that if God came down and boogied right in his face, he'd never allow himself to believe it. That was the night I understood he was not just a skeptic who doesn't believe in a sixth sense, but he was the über-skeptic, who wouldn't trust or believe in the other five either.

Suddenly he threw his napkin in my face and growled, "You know what? I wash my hands of you."

"Don't forget to use soap," I said back.

I guess there's nothing unusual about it—a father and son, two generations of men, growing apart. Still, I thought back to how it used to be when I was a kid, when he carried me on his shoulders to school, sometimes right into the classroom. He'd sit on the teacher's desk with me balancing on his shoulders and ask the shocked kids, "Has anyone seen my son?" If you compare times like that with times like this, it just makes you sad.

The waiter came by. "Can I get you anything else?" he asked. Dad stabbed him with his eyes. The waiter backed away.

"Let's go," Dad snapped.

"Suits me."

We pulled our coats off the chairs. A crowd of haunted eyes followed us to the door. We walked out into the cold night air. The eyes stayed in the restaurant, where it was warm.

I knew why he was upset. In his own paradoxically neglectful way, he'd always made a significant effort to try to mold me. This was the first night he saw clearly that I wanted nothing to do with his mold. He saw me spit inside it, and he took offense. The thing is, education was the first great battle of our relationship, our continuous duel, which is why he always vacillated between threatening the public school system with arson and abandoning me to it. By leaving school of my own volition, I had made a decision that he couldn't. That's why he gave me that speech: after all the confused and contradictory lectures Dad had bombarded me with over the years, on topics ranging from creation to gravy to purgatory to nipple rings, wherein he tried on ideas as if he were in a dressing room trying on shirts, he had finally let me hear the core idea on which his life was based.

What neither of us knew then, of course, was that we were on the verge of another scarcely credible sequence of disasters that could be traced back to single events. They say endings can be read in beginnings. Well, the beginning of this ending was my quitting school.

•

So why did I really quit? Because I always wound up sitting next to the kid with the baffling rash? Or because whenever I walked into class late, the teacher made a face as if he were defecating? Or was it simply the way every authority figure was so scandalized by my behavior all the time? No, on second thought, I quite liked that; one teacher's veins throbbed in his neck: the height of comedy. Another one turned purple with rage: a zinger! Back then nothing was funnier to me than outrage, nothing got me feeling lighter or bouncier.

No, if I'm to be honest, all those irritations only stuck me in a grinding hell of dissatisfaction; no reason to walk away from that, that's just regular unhappiness a person is lucky to have. My true motivation for quitting school began with all those pesky suicides.

Our school was pushed as far up against the eastern seaboard as possible without actually being in the water. We had to keep the classroom windows shut to avoid the distraction of the roaring sea below, but on summer days the stifling heat left us no choice but to open them, and the teacher's voice could hardly compete with the crashing of the waves. The school buildings, a series of connected red brick blocks, were positioned high above the water, on the edge of the Cliffs of Despondency ("Cliffs of Despair" was already taken by a bleak cliff-face a few beaches around the headland). From the end of the school oval, treacherous paths led down to the beach. If you were disinclined to take the paths, if you were impatient or you didn't want to brave the steep descent, or if you despised yourself and your life and saw no hope for a brighter future, you could always jump. Many did. Our school averaged one suicide every nine or ten months. Of course, youth suicide isn't uncommon; young men and women have always been sneezing to their deaths from various influenzas of the soul. But there must have been some mythical hypnotic call drifting through those half-open classroom windows, because we really had more than our share of kids propelling themselves through the celestial gateway. Not that there's anything unusual about teenagers calling it quits, as I said, but it's the funerals that wear you down. Christ, I should know. Even now I still dream about one particular open casket, one that might not have happened if I hadn't had to write an essay on *Hamlet* for my English class.

Hamlet's Paralysis
by Jasper Dean

The story of Hamlet is an unambiguous warning of the dangers of indecision. Hamlet is a Danish prince who can't decide whether he should avenge his father's death, kill himself, not kill himself, etc., etc. You wouldn't believe the way he goes on about it.

Inevitably, this tedious behavior sends Hamlet mad, and by the end of the play everyone is dead, too bad for Shakespeare if he decided later he wanted to write a sequel. The brutal lesson of Hamlet's indecision is one for all humanity, although if your uncle has murdered your father and married your mother, you might feel it is especially relevant.

Hamlet's name is the same as his father who is also called Hamlet and who died unpleasantly when his brother poured poison in his ear. In his ear! Not nice. Clearly, sibling rivalry was what was rotten in the state of Denmark.

Later, when his dad's ghost beckons Hamlet to follow him, Horatio advises against it in case the ghost tries driving Hamlet insane, which he does, and Horatio also notes that everybody looking down from an unprotected large height thinks about jumping to their death which made me think, Good, it's not just me then.

In conclusion, Hamlet is about indecision. The truth is, indecisiveness affects us all, even if we are one of those people who have no trouble making decisions. In other words, impatient shits. We suffer too. Waiting for someone else to make a decision, for example, in a restaurant when the waiter is standing right there is among life's greatest horrors, but we must learn patience. Tearing the menu out of your date's hand and shouting "She'll have the chicken" is no way to combat this affliction, and it certainly won't get you sex.

That was it. I suppose I shouldn't have been surprised when my English teacher, Mr. White, failed me. What more could I have expected from him, or from any other of the sluggish educators who haunted that school? I can see them even now. One teacher looks like all his vital organs not only have been removed but are being held for a ransom he can't afford to pay. Another looks like he entered a party two minutes after everyone left and can still hear their laughter tormenting him from down the street. One sits there defiantly, like a sole ant who refuses to carry a bread crumb. Some are as cheerful as despots, others as giddy as idiots.

Then there was Mr. White: he was the teacher with the small patch of gray hair that sat on his head like the ash of a cigarette, the one who often looked like he'd just glimpsed his future in a single-sex nursing home. But worse, *he was the teacher with the son in our class.* OK, you can't plan for happiness in life, but you *can* take certain precautions against unhappiness, can't you? At the beginning of every class, Mr. White had to do roll call. He had to call out his own son's name. Can you imagine anything more ridiculous? A father *knows* whether his own son is in the room or not, surely.

"White," he'd say.

"Here," Brett would answer. What a farce.

Poor Brett!

Poor Mr. White!

How could either of them stand it, to have to suppress their intimacy to the extent where one pretends daily not even to recognize the face of his own kin? And when Mr. White growled at the students for their stupidity, how did Brett feel to be mauled by his own father like that? Was it a game to them? Was it real? During Mr. White's tirades, Brett's face was too emotionless, too frozen—I'd say he knew as well as we did that his father was a petty tyrant who treated us students as though we had deprived him of his vital years and, as revenge, predicted our future failings, then failed us to prove himself prophetic. Yes, Mr. White, you were unquestionably my favorite teacher. Your awfulness was the most comprehensible to me. You were the one visibly raging in pain, and shamelessly you did it in front of your own child.

He handed me back my *Hamlet* essay with a livid face. He actually gave me a mighty zero. With my essay, I'd made a joke of something that was sacred to him: William Shakespeare. Deep down, I knew that *Hamlet* was an extraordinary work, but when I'm ordered to complete a task, I find myself straining dumbly at the leash. Writing garbage was the form of my petty rebellion.

That night I made the mistake of showing the essay to my father. He read it squinting, grunting, nodding—basically, as if he were lifting heavy timber. I stood beside him, waiting for approval, I suppose. I didn't get it. He handed it back to me and said, "I read something interesting today in Voltaire's *Philosophical Dictionary.* Did you know before the Egyptians embalmed their pharaoh, they took his brain out? Yet they expected him to reemerge later on down the centuries. What do you think they imagined he'd do there, without his brain?"

It had been a long time since my father had tried to educate me him-

self. To make up for abandoning me to a system he had nothing but contempt for, Dad routinely dumped piles of books in my room with little
Post-it notes ("Read this!" or "This man is a motherfucking god!") pasted
onto the covers: Plato, Nietzsche, Cioran, Lawrence, Wittgenstein,
Schopenhauer, Novalis, Epictetus, Berkeley, Kant, Popper, Sartre, Rousseau, and so on. He seemed especially to favor any writer who was a pes-
simist, a nihilist, or a cynic, including Céline, Bernhard, and the ultimate
pessimist-poet, James Thomson, with his darkly frightening "The City of
Dreadful Night."

"Where are the women?" I asked Dad. "Didn't they think anything
worth writing down?"

The next night I found Virginia Woolf, George Sand, Ayn Rand,
Gertrude Stein, Dorothy Parker, Simone de Beauvoir, Simone Weil, Mary
McCarthy, Margaret Mead, Hannah Arendt, and Susan Sontag waiting
on my pillow.

In this way I was not self-educated so much as I was force-fed, and in
truth I liked them all well enough. The Greeks, for example, had fine
ideas about how to run a society that are still valid today, especially if
you think slavery is wonderful. As for the rest of them, all unquestion-
able geniuses, I have to admit that their enthusiasm for and celebration
of one kind of human being (themselves) and their fear and revulsion of
the other kind (everyone else) grated on my nerves. It's not just that they
petitioned for the halting of universal education lest it "ruin thinking,"
or that they did everything they could to make their art unintelligible to
most people, but they always said unfriendly things like "Three cheers for
the inventors of poison gas!" (D. H. Lawrence) and "If we desire a certain type of civilization and culture, we must exterminate the sort of people who do not fit into it" (G. B. Shaw) and "Sooner or later we must
limit the families of the unintelligent classes" (Yeats) and "The great majority of men have no right to existence, but are a misfortune to higher
men" (Nietzsche). Everyone else or, in other words, everyone I knew was
nothing more than a corpse rotting upright mainly because of his preference for watching football over reading Virgil. "Mass entertainment is
the death of civilization," those highbrows spat, but I say, if a man giggles
at something puerile and his body glows from the joy, does it matter that
it was caused not by a profound artwork but by a rerun of *Bewitched*?
Honestly, who cares? That man just had a wonderful inner moment, and
what's more, he got it cheap. Good for him, you ponderous fuck! Basi-

cally they thought it would be lovely if the dehumanized masses, who made them literally sick, would please either pass into history or become slaves and be quick about it. They wanted to create a race of superbeings based on their own snobby, syphilitic selves, men who sit on mountaintops all day licking their inner god into a frenzy. Personally I think it wasn't the "plebeian desire for happiness" of the masses they hated so much, but the secret, sour acknowledgment that the plebes sometimes found it.

That's why, just as my father had abandoned me, I'd abandoned his learned friends, all those wonderful, bitter geniuses, and at school I'd settled in comfortably doing the bare minimum. Often I'd give myself the day off and walk around the throbbing city to watch it throb or to the racetrack to watch the horses eke out their unfortunate existence under the arses of small men. Occasionally the administration would send grave, unintentionally humorous letters to my father about my attendance.

"Got another letter," Dad would say, waving it in the air like a $10 note he'd found in an old pair of pants.

"And?"

"And what do you have to say for yourself?"

"Five days a week is too much. It's draining."

"You don't have to be the first in the state, you know. Just scrape by. That's what you should be aiming for."

"Well, that's what I'm doing. I'm scraping."

"Great. Just make sure you turn up enough to get the little sliver of paper with your name on it."

"What the hell for?"

"I told you a thousand times. You need society to think you're playing along. You do what you like later, but you need to make them think you're one of them."

"Maybe I am one of them."

"Yeah, and I'm going to the office tomorrow morning at seven."

But he wasn't always able to leave it alone. In fact, I had achieved a certain notoriety among the faculty because of the universally dreaded and personally mortifying visits of my father, whose face would appear suddenly pressed against the frosted glass of the classroom door.

The day after I showed my father my *Hamlet* essay, he came into my English class and took a seat in the back, squeezing himself into a wooden chair. Mr. White had been writing the word "intertextualization" on the blackboard when Dad came in, so when he turned back to us and saw a middle-aged man among all of us fresh-faced dopes, he was confused. He glowered at my father disapprovingly, as if getting ready to chastise one of his students for spontaneously aging in the middle of a lesson.

"Bit sluggish in here, isn't it?" Dad said.

"Pardon me?"

"I said, it's a bit difficult to think in here, isn't it?"

"I'm sorry, you are . . ."

"A concerned parent."

"You are a parent of a student in this class?"

"Maybe the word 'concerned' is an understatement. When I think of him under your tutelage, I start bleeding from the eyes."

"Which child is yours?"

"I'm not ashamed to admit it. My son is the creature labeled 'Jasper.' "

Mr. White shot me a stern glance just as I was trying to merge with my chair. "Jasper? Is this your father?"

I nodded. What choice did I have?

"If you would like to speak with me about your son, we could make an appointment," he said to Dad.

"I don't need to talk to you about my son. I know my son. Do you?"

"Of course. Jasper has been in my class all year."

"And the others? So they can read and write: well done. That's a lifetime of shopping lists taken care of. But do you *know* them? Do you know yourself? Because if you don't know yourself, you can't help them know *themselves*, and you're probably pissing away everyone's time here simply training an army of terrified copycats like all you lackluster teachers in this state-run fleapit are prone to do, telling the students what to think instead of how, and trying to fit them into the mold of a perfect taxpayer-to-be instead of bothering to find out who they are."

The other students laughed, out of confusion.

"Keep quiet!" Mr. White yelled, as if it were the Day of Reckoning and he had the crucial role of sorting all the souls. We shut up. It didn't do any good. Silence that has been commanded is still very noisy.

"Why should they respect you? You don't have any respect for them," Dad continued, and to the students he said, "To bow down to an authority figure is to spit in your own face."

"I'm going to have to ask you to leave."

"I'm looking forward to that moment."

"Please leave."

"I notice you have a crucifix around your neck."

"What of it?"

"Do I really need to spell it out for you?"

"Simon." Mr White addressed one of the baffled students. "Would you kindly run down to the principal's office and explain to him that we have a disturbance in the classroom and the police should be called."

"How can you encourage your students to think for themselves with an open mind if you've got an outdated belief system crushing your own head like an iron mask? Don't you see? The flexibility of your mental movement is constricted by stringent dogmatic principles, so you might think you're standing there telling them about *Hamlet,* but what they really hear is a man in fear of stepping outside the tight circle that was drawn around him by long-dead men who sold his ancestors a bunch of lies so they could molest all the little boys they wanted in the privacy of their confessional booths!"

I shot a look at Brett. He sat in his chair silently; his face was slender and delicate-looking, and I thought if it were not for the hair, eyes, nose, and mouth, his face could be a pianist's hand. Brett caught me staring at him, but I don't think he knew I was composing similes about his face, because he smiled at me. I smiled back. If I'd known that two months later Brett would take his own life, I would've cried instead.

•

We actually spoke the morning of his death.

"Hey, Brett, do you have that five dollars you owe me?"

"Can I pay you tomorrow?"

"Sure thing."

People are amazingly adept at faking happiness. It's almost second nature to them, like checking a public phone for coins after making a call. Brett was a champ at it, right up until the end. Hell, I spoke to a girl who chatted with him ten minutes before he jumped, and she said they talked about the weather!

"Hey, Kristin, d-do you think it's a southerly wind?" Brett had a slight stutter that came and went in relation to fluctuating social pressures.

"How the hell would I know?"

"It's p-p-pretty strong, eh?"

"Why are you talking to me, zitface?"

I don't want to make a bigger production out of Brett's death than it was for me. He wasn't my closest friend or even my confidant. We were allies, which in a way made us closer than friends. Here's how it happened:

One lunchtime a small crowd had formed a circle in the quadrangle, standing so close to each other they looked woven together like an ugly quilt. I winced in anticipation. There are no private humiliations in the schoolyard; they are all mercilessly public. I wondered who was being shamed this time. I peered over the flattop haircut of the shortest link to see Brett White on the ground, blood dribbling from his mouth. According to several delighted spectators, Brett had fallen while running from another student, Harrison. Now, peering down at Brett, all the students were laughing because their leader was laughing. It's not that these were particularly cruel children; they'd just abandoned their egos to his, that's all, submitted their will to the will of Harrison, a bad choice. Why groups never follow the sweet, gentle child is obvious, but I wish it would happen just once. Man, as Freud noted, has an extreme passion for authority. I think his secret yearning to be dominated could really work nicely, if he would just once allow himself to be dominated by a real sweetie. Because the truth is, in a group dynamic the leader could scream, "Let's all give the bastard a tender kiss on the cheek!" and they'd run at the poor kid with their lips pursed.

As it was, Brett's front teeth lay on the concrete. They looked like Tic Tacs. He picked up the teeth. You could see him struggling not to cry.

I looked at the other students and despaired that none had enough compassion to go about their business. It was painful to watch all those meager spirits harassing Brett in this way. I bent down beside him and said, "Laugh like you think it's funny."

He followed my advice and started laughing. He whispered in my ear, "Can they put them back in?" and I laughed loudly too, as if he'd made a joke. Once I'd gotten him to his feet, the humiliations persisted. A soccer ball came flying at his face.

"Open your mouth wide, I want to get it through the posts!" someone yelled.

It was true that his teeth looked like goal posts.

"Is that really necessary?" I shouted, pointlessly.

Harrison stepped out of the crowd and, towering over me, said, "You're Jewish, aren't you?"

I groaned. I had told just one person that my grandfather was slaughtered by Nazis, and I'd never heard the end of it. Generally speaking, there wasn't too much anti-Semitism at school, just the usual jokes about money and noses, noses and money, great big noses with money falling out of them, grubby Jewish hands stuffing money into their big Jewish noses. That kind of thing. After a while you don't care about the ugly sentiments behind the jokes, you just wish they were funnier.

"I think you have a stupid face, Jew."

"And I'm short too," I said, remembering that Dad once told me the way to confuse your enemies is to respond to their insults with your own.

"Why are you so stupid?" he asked.

"I don't know. I'll get to that after I work out why I'm so ugly."

Brett caught on fast and said to me, "I'm uglier than you, and I have bad hand-eye coordination."

"I can't run without tripping over," I said back.

"I've never kissed a girl and I probably never will."

"I have bad acne on my back. I think it will leave lifelong scars."

"Really? Me too."

Charlie Mills pushed through the mob and started up too. "That's nothing," he said. "I'm fat, ugly, smelly, stupid, *and* adopted."

Harrison stood there, confused, thinking of something to say. We all looked at him and burst out laughing. It was a good moment. Then Harrison stepped toward me with the confidence of someone who has biology on his side. He pushed me, and I tried shifting my weight onto my front foot, but it made no difference. I wound up facedown on concrete. For the second time I went home with my white shirt splattered with blood.

Eddie, Dad, and Anouk were on the veranda drinking tea, looking exhausted. There was a heavy stillness. Something told me I had just missed a heated argument. The smoke from Eddie's clove cigarettes hung in the air. As I approached, the sight of my blood reanimated them. They all leapt to attention, as if they were three wise sages who had waited ten years for someone to ask them a question.

Anouk shouted first. "Are you being picked on by a bully? Why don't you give him my phone number and ask him to call me? I'm sure meditation would really calm him down."

"Pay him money," Eddie said. "Go back and talk to him with a paper bag filled with cash."

Not to be outparented, Dad shouted from his armchair, "Come here, boy, I want to tell you something!" I walked up the veranda steps. He slapped his knee to indicate the all-clear to sit on it. I preferred to stand. Dad said, "You know who else used to get a rubbishing? Socrates. That's right. Socrates. That's right. This one time he was out philosophizing with some mates, and this bloke who didn't like what he was saying came right up to him and kicked him in the arse so hard he fell to the ground. Socrates looked up at the man and smiled at him benignly. He was taking it with amazing calm. An onlooker said, 'Why don't you do something, or say something?' and Socrates said back, 'If you were kicked by a mule, would you reprimand him?' "

Dad broke into howls of laughter. His body shook so badly I was glad I had opted not to sit on his knee. It was bouncing like a rodeo bull. "Get it? Get it?" Dad asked me through peals of laughter.

I shook my head, although in secret I did get it. But truth be known, I would absolutely reprimand a mule for kicking me. I might even have it put down. It's my mule, I can do what I want. Anyway, the point of the story is I got the point of the story, but it didn't help my situation any more than Eddie's or Anouk's impossible suggestions. I tell you, Dad and Eddie and Anouk, the lights I had to guide me through childhood, did nothing but lead me into brick walls.

•

A few weeks later I went to Brett's house. He'd lured me there with the promise of a chocolate cake. He said he wanted to try out his teeth. As we left the school grounds, he explained how, by wiring them back into his gums, the dentist had managed to prevent the nerve from dying. To finish the job he'd had root canal treatment, during which the dentist gave him lots of gas but not quite enough to make it worthwhile.

When we arrived at his house I was disappointed to find there was no cake, and shocked when he said we'd have to make it ourselves. I thought it best to come clean with him.

"Listen, Brett. You're OK, but I feel a little funny baking a cake with you."

"Don't worry. We're not really baking anything. We're going to make the batter and just eat that. We won't even use the oven."

That sounded OK, but really in the end it was not that dissimilar to making a proper cake, and when he started sifting the flour, I nearly made a run for it. I didn't though. I held out. We finished the mixture and were just digging into it with large wooden spoons when we heard the front door open and a voice say, "I'm home!"

My body froze and stayed that way until the kitchen door opened a crack and Mr. White's head came through the door.

"Is that Jasper Dean?"

"Hello, Mr. White."

"Hi, Dad," Brett said, which struck me as odd. I had stupidly assumed he called his father Mr. White at home.

Mr. White pushed the door open and came into the kitchen. "You two making a cake?" he asked, and, looking at the mixture, added, "Let me know when it's ready and maybe I can have a piece."

"Ready? It's almost finished," Brett said, beaming at his father.

Mr. White laughed. First time I'd ever seen his teeth. They weren't bad. He came over and stuck his finger into the bowl and tasted the thick chocolate.

"So, Jasper, how's your father?"

"You know, he is what he is."

"He certainly gave me a run for my money," he said, chuckling to himself.

"I'm glad," I said.

"The world needs passionate men," Mr. White said, smiling.

"I suppose," I said, and as Mr. White went upstairs, I thought of all Dad's long catatonic periods when passion meant remembering to flush the toilet.

Brett's room was more or less a typical teenager's room, except it was so neat I felt my breath might make a mess. There were a couple of framed photographs on the desk, including one of Brett and Mr. White standing with their arms around each other's shoulders on an oval—they looked like actors from a mushy television movie about a father and son. It didn't look in the least bit real. Above Brett's bed was a great big crucifix hanging on the wall.

"What's that for?" I asked in horror.

"It was my mother's."

"What happened to her?"

"Stomach cancer."

"Ouch."

Brett walked to the window with slow, hesitant steps, as if crossing unfamiliar terrain at night.

"You don't have a mother either, do you? What happened to yours?"

"The Arab mafia."

"OK, don't tell me."

I took a closer look at Jesus strung up there, his long-suffering face looking down at an angle. He appeared to be studying those sentimental photographs of Brett and his father. His unhurried eyes seemed to be contemplating them with a certain sadness. Maybe it made him think of his own father, or of how sometimes you get resurrected when you least expect it.

"So you guys are religious?" I asked.

"We're Catholics. You?"

"Atheists."

"Do you like school?" Brett asked suddenly.

"What do you think?"

"It's not forever. That's what I keep thinking. It's not forever."

"Just be grateful you're not fat. Once you're out in the real world, you'll be fine. No one hates a thin man."

"Yeah, maybe."

Brett sat on the edge of his bed, biting his fingernails. I admit now, there must have been a fog in my perception that day. I missed all the signs. I didn't interpret the nail-biting as a cry for help or as an indication that he would soon be rotting dumbly in the earth. After Brett's death, I dissected that afternoon in my head countless times. I thought: If only I'd known, I could have said something, or done something, *anything*, to change his mind. Now I wonder, why do we wish our loved ones back to life if they were so obviously miserable? Did we really hate them that much?

•

The day of Brett's suicide, a Monday.

It was recess and everyone was fondly reminiscing about a Saturday night party. I was smiling because I felt lonely and unwanted, and it seemed to me that everyone in the phone book from A. Aaron to Z. Zurichman had been invited except me. I imagined what it would be like to be popular for an afternoon, and decided it meant I'd have to high-five everybody as I walked down the hallways. I wouldn't like that, I was thinking, when I heard a voice shouting, "Somebody jumped! Somebody jumped!"

"Another suicide!"

The school bell rang and wouldn't let up. We all crossed the oval and ran toward the cliffs. A teacher ordered us to return, but there were too many of us. You've heard of mass hysteria—mass curiosity is even more powerful. There was no turning us back. We reached the edge of the cliff and peered down. The waves were smashing up against the rocks, as if digesting: there was a body down there, all right, a student. Whoever it was, all the bones must have shattered on impact. It seemed as if all we were looking at was a school uniform tossed about in a washing machine.

"Who is it? Who is it?"

People were crying, grieving for someone. But who? Who were we grieving for? Students were already climbing down the steep path to see.

I didn't have to see. I knew it was Brett. How did I know? Because Charlie was standing beside me on the cliff edge, and the only other friend I had was Brett. I had personalized the tragedy; I knew it was something for *me*—and I was right.

"It's Brett White!" a voice confirmed from below.

Mr. White was standing right there, peering down like the rest of us. He straightened up and swayed on his feet. Before he ran down the path and waded into the sea and took his dead son in his arms and sobbed until the police pried Brett from his cold, wet hands, there was a long moment when everyone gaped at him and he just stood there on the cliff edge crumbling, like a Roman ruin.

II

Brett's suicide note fell into the wrong hands. It was found in his locker by a couple of nosy students, and before it was turned in to the proper authorities it had passed around the whole school. This was it:

Don't be sad for me unless you're prepared to be sad your whole lives. Otherwise forget it. What good's a couple of hard weeks of tears and regret if a month later you're laughing again? No, forget it. Just forget it.

Personally, I thought Brett's suicide note was pretty good. It cut right to the heart of the matter. He had measured the depth of human feeling, found it shallow, and said so. Well done, Brett, wherever you are! He didn't fall into the trap of most suicide notes—people are always assigning blame or asking forgiveness. Rarely does anyone leave any helpful tips on what to do with his pets. I suppose the most honest and lucid suicide note I ever heard of was by the British actor George Sanders, who wrote:

Dear World, I am leaving you because I am bored. I feel I have lived long enough. I am leaving you with your worries in this sweet cesspool. Good luck.

Isn't that gorgeous? He's so right. It *is* a sweet cesspool. And by addressing the note to the world, he doesn't worry about leaving anyone out. He's succinct and clear in his reasons for ending his own life, makes a final poetic insight, then generously and considerately wishes us luck. I'm telling you, this is the kind of suicide note I could really go for. It's a hell of a lot better than the crappy suicide note I once wrote. It said:

So what if life's a gift? Haven't you ever returned a gift? It's done all the time.

That was it. I thought: Why not be a surly smarty-pants right to the end? If I was all of a sudden magnanimous, it just wouldn't ring true. But really, I'm not even the suicidal type. I have this stupid habit of thinking things are going to get better, even when all evidence is pointing to the contrary, even when they get worse and worse and worse and worse.

•

Brett was buried in tan slacks and a blue shirt. Smart casual. Mr. White had bought the clothes two days earlier. They were on sale, but I heard he wanted to pay full price. I heard the clerk had argued with him. "Ten percent off," he'd said, and Mr. White refused the discount and the clerk laughed as Mr. White threw the full amount on the counter and ran out, demented with grief.

Brett laid out in his coffin, hair combed back. Odor? Hair gel. Expression molded on his half-bled white face? Peaceful slumber. I thought: This is your unblinking eclipse. The long frozen plunge. Your soft awkward stutter cured by oblivion. So what's to be sad about?

The morning of the funeral was bright and sunny. A gentle fragrant wind made everything seem frothy and not worth worrying about, almost suggesting that grief was an overreaction. The whole class had the morning off; students in other years could come too, but it wasn't compulsory. The cemetery was conveniently located only a kilometer from the school, so we all walked together, about one hundred students and a few teachers who were there either to mourn or to supervise—both, if they had it in them. Most of the group wouldn't have said hello to Brett while he was alive, but now they were lining up to say goodbye.

We all gathered around the grave waiting for the priest to begin, standing in the kind of silence that's so silent the clearing of a throat can frighten you to death. I thought our school uniforms made us look like postal workers congregated to mail a colleague back to God. I imagined "Return to Sender" stenciled neatly on the casket.

The priest began. His eulogy reached me as though through a coffee filter. I got drips. He described Brett as "weary of this world" (true), "mortal and weak" (also true), and "eager to join his Lord, Our Savior" (unlikely). Finally he said melodramatically that "suicide is a mortal sin."

Now hang on a sec!

OK, Brett took his own life, but he also answered Hamlet's question without tearing himself all up inside, and even if suicide *is* a sin, surely decisiveness is rewarded. I mean, let's give credit where credit is due. Brett answered Hamlet's dilemma as straightforwardly as ticking a box.

I knew this sermon was just an ancient scare tactic that had survived intact through the ages while practices like draining someone's blood with leeches when they have a runny nose had long ago been dismissed as old-fashioned. If there is a God, I doubt he is such a hard-liner. Rather, I imagine him greeting the men and women who take their own lives like a police chief surprised when a wanted criminal turns himself in. "You!" he might say, not angry so much as slightly disappointed that he won't get the credit or the satisfaction for the capture.

The casket was lowered, and the sound of hard clumps of dirt hitting its lid made it sound empty. Brett was thin. I'd told him that no one hates a thin man. No one, I thought now, except hungry worms.

Time passed. The sun like a golden lozenge dissolved as it slid across the sky. I watched Mr. White the whole time. He stood out as luminously as if he'd been highlighted in yellow fluorescence. He was suffering the ultimate public humiliation: through neglect or faulty parenting, he'd lost his son, as surely as if he'd put him on the roof of his car and driven away without remembering to take him off.

After the sermon, the principal, Mr. Silver, walked over and placed his hand on Mr. White's shoulder. He twitched violently and shrugged off the hand. As he walked away, I thought: Well, Brett, there goes your father, there he goes to pack away your hollow shirts and your empty pants.

That's what I really thought.

Back at school, a special assembly was held in the quadrangle. A counselor stood up and talked about youth suicide. He asked us all to reach out to our wobbly peers and be on the lookout for signs. His description of a suicidal teenager sent little shockwaves through the crowd. He had described every person there. That gave them something to think about. The bell rang and everyone wandered off to class except our year. The decision from above was that we were just too sad to learn calculus. I felt understandably unsettled. I could feel Brett's presence. I saw him on the podium, then his face in the crowd. I was certain that pretty soon I'd be seeing his head on my own neck. I knew I'd have to abandon that place, just leave it behind and not look back. I could see the school gate was wide open, tempting me. What if I made a run for it? Or even better: *what if I walked?*

My reverie was interrupted by the sound of some metaphysical finger-pointing. Several students were discussing the possibilities of Brett's current location. Where was he now? Some said he was in heaven; others supposed he was back where he started, in the subarctic darkness, wondering when he'd move up in the reincarnation queue. Then someone with Catholic tendencies said, "His soul will burn forever, you know," and I couldn't let such a nasty thought sit there without spitting on it, so I said, "I think you should find whoever does your thinking for you and ask them to update."

"Well, what do you think happened to Brett's soul, then?"

"Nothing. Because he hasn't got one. Neither have I. Neither have you."

"Yes I do!"

"No you don't!"

"Do too!"

"Do not!"

"You don't believe in the soul?"

"Why should I?" I asked.

You should've seen the looks I got! When you say you don't believe in the soul, it's hilarious! People look at you as if the soul, like Tinker Bell, needs to be believed in in order for it to exist. I mean, if I have a soul, is it really the kind of soul that needs my moral support? Is it as flimsy as all that? People seem to believe so; they think that doubting the soul means you are the Soulless, the one lone creature wandering the wasteland without *the magic stuff of infinity* . . .

III

So did I quit school out of some sort of magnanimous allegiance to my dead friend? A symbolic protest prompted by my heart? I wish.

It didn't happen that way at all.

I suppose I'd better come clean.

The afternoon of the funeral I received a package in the mail. It contained a single red rose and a short letter. It was from Brett, my cold dead friend.

> Dear Jasper,
>   There's a tall, beautiful girl with long red flaming hair in the year above us. I don't know her name. I've never spoken to her. I'm looking at her right now as I write this. I am staring right at her! She's reading. She's always so engrossed in reading, she doesn't look up, even as I sit here mentally undressing her.

Now I have her right down to her underwear! It's infuriating how she just keeps on reading like that, reading in the sun. Stark naked. In the sun.

Please hand her this rose and tell her I loved her, and will love her, always.

Your friend,

Brett

I folded the note and placed it in the bottom of a drawer. Then I went back to Brett's grave and laid down the rose and left it there. Why didn't I give it to the girl he loved? Why didn't I carry out the dead kid's final wish? Well, for one thing, I've never been a big fan of the idea of running all over town dotting i's and crossing t's for the deceased. Secondly, it seemed to me unreasonably cruel to implicate this poor girl in a suicide, this girl who never even knew he was alive. Whoever she was, I was sure she had enough on her plate without having to wear the guilt of the death of someone whom she couldn't have picked out of a crowd of two.

The next day I went up to the plateau above the school—the flat, treeless patch of parched earth where the eldest students loitered arrogantly. That's how they were. They held themselves above the rest of the school, as if making it all the way to the final year was comparable to surviving a third tour of duty in Vietnam. I went out of curiosity. Brett had taken his life while in love with a tall girl with red hair. Was she the cause? Who was she? Did he really die, not from the torment of bullies, but from frustrated desire? Secretly I hoped so, because every time I saw Harrison around school it made me sick to think that Brett had died because of him. I was eager to replace him with a worthier cause of death. That's what I was searching for. A girl worth dying for.

Unfortunately for me, I found her.

•

While I've got a pretty good memory, I'm the first to admit that some of my recollections should be called in for questioning. The fact is, I'm not above deluding myself and getting away with it, which is why, as I visualize the girls from my high school, I can only guess that I'm romanticizing. In my mind's eye they look like sexy-celebrity-hooker-fantasy-music-video schoolgirls. That can't be right. I see them wearing white unbuttoned shirts with exposed black lacy bras and dark green miniskirts and long cream socks and black buckled shoes. I see them floating on pale legs through narrow halls, their hair billowing behind them like flames in a strong wind. That can't be right either.

This I am sure of: the girl Brett loved was tall and pale-skinned, with flaming red hair falling down her back, shoulders as smooth as eggs, and legs as long as an underground pipeline. But her dark brown eyes, often hidden behind an unevenly cropped fringe, were her secret weapon: she had a look that could have toppled a government. She also had a habit of running her tongue around the tip of her pen. It was very erotic. One day I stole her pencil case and kissed every last biro. I know how that sounds, but it was a very intimate afternoon, just me and the pens. When Dad came home he wanted to know why my lips were stained with blue ink. Because she writes in blue, I wanted to tell him. Always blue.

She was half a foot taller than me, and with that flaming red hair she looked like a skyscraper on fire. Thus I called her the Towering Inferno, but not to her face. How could I? That beautiful face and I hadn't been introduced. I couldn't believe I hadn't seen her before—maybe because I took every third day off school. Perhaps she did the same, only on alternate days. I followed her around the school grounds at a distance, trying to see her from every conceivable angle to get the three-dimensional mental image my fantasies deserved. Sometimes, as she moved lightly through the grounds, seeming to weigh only slightly more than her own shadow, she sensed I was there, but I was too quick for her. Whenever she turned I'd pretend to be looking at the sky, counting clouds.

But shit! I could suddenly hear my father's grating voice telling me I was looking to deify the human because I hadn't the stomach for God. Yeah, maybe. Maybe I was in a bid for self-transcendence, projecting onto this tall succulent woman in order to release myself from my solitary carnival of despair. Fine. That was my right. I just wish I could've been oblivious of my unconscious motivations. I wanted just to enjoy my lies like everyone else.

I couldn't think of anything other than her and the components of her. For example, her red hair. But was I so primitive I let myself be bewitched by hair? I mean, really. Hair! It's just hair! Everyone has it! She puts it up, she lets it down. So what? And why did all the other parts of her have me wheezing with delight? I mean, who hasn't got a back, or a belly, or armpits? This whole finicky obsession serves to humiliate me even as I write it, sure, but I suppose it isn't *that* abnormal. That's what a first love is all about. What happens is you meet a love object and immediately a hole inside you starts aching, the hole that is always there but you don't notice until someone comes along, plugs it up, and then runs away with the plug.

For a while the roles in our relationship were easily definable. I was the lover, the stalker, the sun-worshipper. She was loved, stalked, worshipped.

A couple of months passed in that way.

•

After Brett's suicide, Mr. White went right back to teaching. It was a bad decision on his part. He didn't do what everyone should do after a monumental personal tragedy—run away, grow a beard, sleep with a girl exactly half your age (unless you are twenty). Mr. White didn't do anything like that. He just came into class, same as before. He didn't even have the sense to order the removal of Brett's desk—it just sat there, empty, tipping his scales of grief all the way over.

On his better days, he looked like he'd been woken from a deep sleep. Mostly like he'd been exhumed from his own grave. He didn't yell anymore. We suddenly found ourselves straining to hear him, as if trying to pick up the beat of a weak pulse. Even though he was obviously suffering to the point of becoming a caricature of suffering, he got (not surprisingly) little empathy from his pupils. They only noticed that before he had been industrially furious and now he was utterly remote. Once he lost the essays the class had written. He pointed listlessly to me. "They're somewhere in my car, Jasper, go look for them," he said, throwing me the keys. I went to his car. A Volkswagen covered in dust. Inside I found empty food containers, wet clothes, and a prawn, but no essays. When I went back empty-handed, he gave the class an exaggerated shrug. That's how he was. And at the sound of the bell, when the students rapidly stuffed their books into their bags, wasn't Mr. White packing up his things faster than anyone? It was almost like a competition, and now he always won. Yet for some reason he stayed on in his job, day after miserable day.

One day after class he asked me to wait behind. All the other students winked at me to signify they thought I was in trouble and it pleased them to know it. But it was only that Mr. White wanted the recipe of the chocolate cake Brett and I had made that day. I told him I didn't know it. Mr. White nodded for an unnaturally long time.

"Do you believe in the Bible, Jasper?" he asked suddenly.

"In the same way I believe in 'Hound of the Baskervilles.' "

"I think I understand."

"The problem is most of the time when God's supposed to be the hero, he comes across as the villain. I mean, look at what he did to Lot's wife. What kind of divine being turns a man's wife into a pillar of salt? What was her crime? Turning her head? You have to admit this is a God hopelessly locked *in* time, not free of it; otherwise he might have confounded the ancients by turning her into a flat-screen television or at least a pillar of Velcro."

From the look on Mr. White's face, I could tell he wasn't following the lucid argument I was, not proudly, plagiarizing from one of Dad's midnight sermons. Anyway, what was I talking about? Why was I haranguing a man who looked like the rotting stump of an old tree? It seemed I was able to do anything for a suffering man except be nice to his Deity.

What I should've said was this: "Why don't you quit? Get out of here! Change schools! Change jobs! Change lives!"

But I didn't.

I let him go on thrashing about in his cage.

"Well, anyway, I guess you'd better get to your next class," he said, and the way he fiddled with his tie made me want to burst into tears. That's the problem with people who suffer right in your face. They can't so much as scratch their noses without its being poignant.

•

Not long after that, Dad came to pick me up from school. That wasn't as rare as you might think. After exhausting his daily activities—waking up (an hour), breakfast (half hour), reading (four hours), walking (two hours), staring (two hours), blinking (forty-five minutes), he'd come and get me as "something to do."

When I arrived at the school gate, Dad was already waiting for me in his unwashed clothes, his face carelessly shaven.

"Who is that grim man gaping at me?" he said as I arrived.

"Who?"

I turned to see Mr. White peering at us from the classroom window in a trance, as if we were doing something strange and fascinating, and I suddenly felt like a monkey to Dad's organ grinder.

"That's my English teacher. His son died."

"He looks familiar."

"He should. You harassed him for about forty minutes one day."

"Really? What do you mean?"

"You came into the class and abused him for no reason. You don't remember?"

"Honestly—no. But who keeps track of things like that? You say he lost his son, eh?"

"Brett. He was my friend."

Dad looked at me with surprise. "You didn't tell me that."

"He wasn't my best friend or anything," I said. "We were just, you know, hated by the same people."

"How did he die? Drug overdose?"

"Suicide."

"Suicide by drug overdose?"

"He jumped off a cliff."

Dad turned back to Mr. White's sad face peering out the window. "I think I might go and talk to him."

"Don't."

"Why not? The man's grieving."

"Exactly."

"Exactly," Dad agreed, though to a totally different idea from mine, because the next thing I knew he was striding over to the classroom window. The two of them stared at each other through the glass. I could see it all. I could see Dad tap on the window. I could see Mr. White open the window. I could see them talking amiably at first, then seriously, then Mr. White was crying and Dad had his arm through the window, resting it on Mr. White's shoulder, even though the angle was awkward and unnatural. Then Dad came back over to me, his lips pursed as if whistling, though he wasn't. He was just pursing his lips.

After this shadowy conference, Mr. White went crazy in class. Of course, after his outburst, no matter how much they made short gasping sounds and said things like "I don't believe it!," no one on the staff was really surprised, and they couldn't even see what I could see all over Mr. White's sudden eruption: Dad's influence.

It happened like this: One morning Mr. White came to class with the face of a thumb that had soaked too long in the bath. Then he com-menced the lesson by staring wide-eyed and penetratingly, singling out students with his eyes without letting up, then moving on to the next student. No one could match him. You couldn't sustain eye contact with a pair of peepers like his. All you could do was lower your eyes and wait for him to pass over you, like the Angel of Death. He was leaning against his desk, this hollow man with the X-ray eyes. It was morning and I remember the windows were open; a layer of milky mist wafted in, and the air was so thick with the sea you could almost taste the plank-ton. There was an oppressive silence, just the sound of the ocean rising up and falling on the shore. The students watched him in breathless suspense.

"It's funny that you need training to be a doctor or a lawyer but not to be a parent. Any dolt can do it, without so much as a one-day semi-nar. You, Simon, you could be a father tomorrow if you wanted."

Everyone laughed, and rightly so. Simon was not someone you could imagine fucking anyone, ever.

"Why are you here? Not just in this class, but in the world? Do you think your parents wondered why they had you? Listen to what people say when they have new babies: 'It's the best thing I ever did in my life,' 'It's magical, blahblahblah.' They've done it for their own enchantment, to sa-tiate their own emotional needs. Have you ever noticed that? That you're a projection of other people's desires? How does that make you feel?"

No one said anything. It was the right thing to say. Mr. White moved through the desks to the back of the classroom. We didn't know whether to keep our eyes forward or to turn them toward him or to tear them out.

"What do your parents want of you?" he shouted from the back. We swiveled to face him. "They want you to study. Why? They're ambitious for you. Why? They look at you as their personal fucking property, that's why! You and their cars, you and their washing machines, you and their televisions. You belong to them. And not one of you is any more to them than the opportunity to fulfill *their* failed ambitions! Ha-ha-ha! Your par-ents don't love you! Don't let them get away with saying 'I love you'! It's disgusting! It's a lie! It's just a cheap justification for manipulating you! 'I love you' is another way of saying, 'You owe me, you little bastard! You represent the meaning of my life because I couldn't give it to myself, so don't fuck it up for me!' No, your parents don't love you—they *need* you! And a hell of a lot more than you need them, I can tell you that!"

The students had never heard anything like it. Mr. White stood there breathing noisily, as if through a clogged tube.

"Christ, I'm getting out of here," he said suddenly, and left the room.

Unsurprisingly, within hours the whole school had feasted on the scandal, only it came all distorted: some said he had attacked his students; other said he tried to whip a whole bunch of them with his belt. And more than a few whispered that unmentionable word that people hate (read, "love") to mention these days: pedophile!

•

I wish that was the end of it. I wish I could end on that happy note. Happy? In comparison with what happened next, yes. What took place that same afternoon sits solidly in history as my first official regret, remaining to this day number one. Any good I'd done in my life up to that afternoon was about to be demolished, and any good I've done since has been an attempt to make up for what I did.

Here's what I did: I followed the Towering Inferno all day. I watched her reading in the sun, as Brett described, pulling compulsively at her stockings with her cobalt-blue fingernails. I followed her across the school grounds as she clutched the hand of a girl with a face like a spade. At lunch I stood behind her in the canteen while she ordered a meat pie, and when the woman wasn't looking she grabbed a handful of squeezable tomato sauce packets and shoved them in her pocket, then sauntered off, having adorably stolen complimentary items.

In the afternoon I trailed Mr. Smart, the biology teacher, as he chased her through the musty halls. When he caught her, she held her head as if it were an heirloom.

"Why weren't you in class?" he demanded.

"I have my period," she replied defiantly, with a look that said, "Prove I don't." Good one! The broken man cast his eyes to the floor, wishing he were at home with that weird collection of moss he brought in one time.

After school we used to stand around at train stations for hours (try doing that into your twenties—the thrill is gone, believe me). The train guards were always telling us to go home, but there's really no law against standing on the platform not catching trains. That afternoon I shadowed the Towering Inferno to the far end of the station. She was standing with her usual crowd and I was gaping from behind a pylon thinking my usual obsessive thoughts: wishing she would fall into some danger so I might rescue her, spitting on myself for fetishizing a girl I'd never met, longing to take a personal memento from her as a holy relic, indulging in a sexual fantasy in which we intersect at right angles, and generally planning a systematic exploration of her cathedral-like edifice.

She and her friends kept edging farther down the platform, so to keep my eyes on her I had to step out from my hiding place. One of her friends—Tony, a boy with a slight hunch I knew because he had once taken a pack of cigarettes from me in exchange for the observation that my eyes were set too close together—unzipped his fly and gyrated his crotch in the Towering Inferno's general direction. She turned away in disgust and found herself trapped in my stare. It caught us both off guard. Then a strange thing happened: *she stared back.* Her eyes, unblinking and wild, dared me not to look away. The moment stretched its way into infinity, then snapped back to about a nanosecond and rebounded, so all in all it lasted about eight and a half seconds.

I turned away and moved to a public phone. I put some coins in the slot and dialed a number at random.

"Hello?"

"Hello."

"Who's this?"

"It's me. Is that you?"

"Who is this? What do you want?"

"Never mind that," I said. "How are you?"

"Who is this?"

"I told you. It's me."

I could still feel the Towering Inferno's eyes on me. I knew what to do: I shook my head vehemently and laughed a loud, unnatural laugh before pausing to nod sagely, as though the person on the other end of the phone had made a funny yet offensive comment that on further reflection proved wise. I turned casually to face her, but her back was turned. I felt a tiny thorn prick my ego.

It was getting dark. Everyone wordlessly agreed that loitering on the station platform had gone stale—until tomorrow—and when the next train arrived, we all filed in.

At the other end of the packed carriage there was a commotion, and a small crowd formed a circle—bad news for someone. Circles of people always are. Honestly, sometimes I think human beings should be prohibited from forming groups. I'm no fascist, but I wouldn't mind at all if we had to live out our lives in single file.

I heard happy cheers and joyous laughter. That meant someone was suffering. My heart felt sick for the poor sucker. Thankfully Charlie was home sick and Brett was dead, so whoever they were humiliating this time had nothing to do with me. Still, I pushed through the crowd to see who it was.

Mr. White.

The students had torn the hat off his head and were waving it in the air, asserting their power over him. Mr. White was trying to get the hat back. Ordinarily even the most rebellious young crackhead can't physically assault a teacher—emotionally and psychologically, sure; physically, no—but Mr. White was a teacher made evil by gossip, and that made him fair game.

"Hey!" I shouted.

Everyone looked over at me. This was my first stand against the bullies, against the ruthlessness of the human pack animal, and I was determined not to disappoint myself. But then four things happened in quick succession.

The first was that I noticed the person holding the hat was the Towering Inferno.

Second, my shouting "Hey!" was interpreted not as a heroic "Hey" but a "Hey, throw *me* the hat."

She threw it to me.

I caught it with my cheek. It rolled on the floor, toward the door. Mr. White trudged through the carriage after it.

The third thing that happened was that the Towering Inferno yelled out, "Get it, Jasper!"

She knew my name. Oh my God. She knew my name. I ran like a maniac for the hat. I grabbed it. Mr. White stopped midcarriage.

Then the fourth thing, the final painful event, was her delicate high-pitched voice commanding me again: "Throw it out!" I was under a spell. I half pushed open the train door, enough for my hand to hang outside the carriage. The brim of the hat danced a waltz with the wind. Mr. White's face had frozen with a sort of forced nonchalance. I felt sick.

Sick. Sick. Sick. Self-hatred was at an all-time high. Why was I doing this? Don't do it, Jasper. Don't do it. Don't.

I did it.

I let go of the hat. The wind picked it up and threw it out of sight. Mr. White ran toward me. I bolted for the door at the end of the carriage. Rain smacked me in the face. I opened the door of the next carriage, ran in, and closed it behind me. He tried to follow, but I blocked the door with my foot. He stood in the rain on the tiny rattling platform between the two carriages, trying to force it open. I tied the strap from my bag to the door handle, held it down with my other foot, and let physics do the work. In no time he was drenched to the bone. He swore through the glass. Finally he gave up and turned back. The others had blocked the other door. It rained harder. He turned back to me, banged on the glass door again. I knew if I let him in, he'd have me for lunch. He was stuck. It rained even harder, a stiff hard rain. Mr. White stopped screaming and just looked at me with old-dog eyes. I felt something in me sink, but there was nothing I could do. At the next stop we both watched the Towering Inferno step onto the platform. Through the dusty window, she gave me a smile that said, "I'll never forget what you did for me, Jasper Dean, Destroyer of Hats."

•

The following morning I walked through the long, airless hallways and silent stairwells into the quadrangle for a special assembly. The headmaster stepped up to the podium. "Yesterday afternoon, our English teacher, Mr. White, was terrorized by students *from this school!*" A murmur snaked through the crowd. The headmaster continued his diatribe. "I would like the students involved to please step forward." Everyone looked around to see if anyone was owning up. I looked around too. "Right. We'll just have to find you. And we will find you. You are all dismissed. For now."

I walked away thinking that my time at this school was almost up, and it wasn't twenty minutes later in the science lab that the bell rang and rang and rang, and I heard that old delighted cry of "Someone's jumped! Someone's jumped!" I ran out of the classroom while the bell kept on ringing. It was the suicide bell—I think we were the first school in the country to have one; now they're all the rage. Like inquisitive sheep, all the students ran to the cliff edge to see, and I had not just a bad feeling but the worst one, that feeling of dread, because I knew who it was and that I had put him there myself.

I peered over the cliff edge and saw Mr. White's slumped body thrashed by the waves on the rocks.

That afternoon it was as if I were looking at life through a rolled-up newspaper. I had drained the remaining dregs of innocence from my heart. I had put a man in the ground, or at least aided his descent, and I loathed myself into the future and beyond. Well, why shouldn't I? You shouldn't forgive all your trespasses. You can't always go too easy on yourself. In fact, in some circumstances, forgiving yourself is unforgivable.

I was sitting behind the gym with my head in my hands when a school prefect, a sort of benign Hitler youth, came up and told me the principal wanted to see me. Well, that's that, I thought. I walked to the principal's office and found that his pliable face had been shaped into a picture of weariness.

"Mr. Silver," I said.

"I understand you were a friend of Brett's."

"That's right."

"I was wondering if you wouldn't mind reading a psalm at Mr. White's funeral."

Me? The murderer reading a psalm at the funeral of his victim? As the principal went on telling me about my role in the funeral proceedings, I wondered if this weren't some sort of clever punishment, because I felt transparent sitting there, maybe even more see-through than that—I felt like the site of an archaeological dig, my old clay pot thoughts revealing all about the civilization that had ruled there in its ignorant and doomed way.

I said that I would be honored to read a psalm at the funeral.

What else was I going to say?

•

That night I read it over. It had everything you'd expect in a psalm: heavy-handedness, hit-you-over-the-head metaphors, and Old World symbolism. I tore it out of the Bible thinking: I'm not lending my voice to this oppressive nonsense. Instead I chose a passage from one of Dad's favorite books, one he'd horrified me with a couple of years earlier, one that had seared my brain. It was a passage by James Thomson from his book of poetry, *The City of Dreadful Night*.

The morning of the funeral, I was called again to the principal's office.

I went thinking he wanted to go over the running order of the event. I was surprised to see the Towering Inferno waiting outside his office, leaning against the wall. So we'd been fingered for the crime after all. It's just as well, I thought.

"We're fucked," she said.

"We deserve it," I said back.

"I know. Who'd have thought he'd react so badly?"

"No talking," Mr. Silver snapped as he opened the door and beckoned us in. The Towering Inferno flinched as though slapped, and I wondered at what age she had discovered she possessed the power to convince men to throw hats out of trains. If I asked her now, would she remember the day? The moment? The event? What I wouldn't give to exchange the tale of her strength for the saga of my weakness.

In the office there was a skinny middle-aged woman sitting with her hands in her lap, her narrow eyes closing a quarter of an inch with every step I took into the room.

"Well, you two," the principal said, "what do you have to say for yourselves?"

"She didn't have anything to do with it," I said. "It was me."

"Is that true?" he asked the Inferno.

She nodded guiltily.

"That's not true," the woman said, pointing at me. "He did it, but she was ordering him around."

I took offense at that, because it was true. I stood up and placed my hands on the principal's desk. "Sir, just take one second and look at the girl you are accusing. Are you looking at her?" He was looking at her. "She's a victim of her own beauty. Because why? Because beauty is power. And as we learned in history class, power corrupts. Therefore, absolute beauty corrupts absolutely."

The Towering Inferno stared at me. Mr. Silver cleared his throat.

"Well, Jasper, it's unforgivable what you've done."

"I agree. And you don't have to suspend me, because I'm quitting this place." He bit his lip. "You still want me to read at the funeral?"

"I think you should," he said, in a cold, serious voice.

Damn. I knew he was going to say that.

•

The funeral was more or less a repeat of Brett's: everyone standing there as if dignity mattered, the polished smile of the priest making your eyes squint, the sight of the coffin closing in on you. The Towering Inferno was staring at me, though I didn't want to be stared at just then. I wanted to be alone with my guilt. Despite myself, I looked at her, the Angel of Death with great legs. Without even knowing it, she was the central figure in demolishing a family.

I peered over the cold body of Mr. White and silently pleaded: Forgive me for throwing your hat out of the train! I didn't know your head was still inside! Forgive me! Forgive me for throwing you out of a moving train!

The priest nodded at me, the nod of a man tight with Omniscience. I got up to read.

They were all expecting the psalm. Instead, this is what I read:

"Who is the most wretched in this dolorous place?
I think myself; yet I would rather be
My miserable self than He, than He
Who formed such creatures to his own disgrace.

"The vilest thing must be less vile than Thou
From whom it had its being, God and Lord!
Creator of all woe and sin! Abhorred,
Malignant and implacable! I vow

"That not for all Thy power furled and unfurled,
For all the temples to Thy glory built,
Would I assume the ignominious guilt
Of having made such men in such a world."

I finished and looked up. The priest was gnashing his teeth just as it's described in his favorite book.

IV

After returning home from Sizzler, I stood alone in the labyrinth, staring at the moon, which looked to be just an empty wreck of a rock, burned out, as if God had done it for the insurance.

"I'm worried," Dad said, coming up behind me.

"What about?"

"My son's future."

"I'm not."

"What are you going to do now?"

"Go overseas."

"You don't have any money."

"I know I don't have any money. I know what an empty pocket feels like. I'll make some."

"How?"

"I'll get a job."

"What kind of job? You don't have any skills."

"Then I'll get an unskilled job."

"What kind of unskilled job? You don't have any experience."

"I'll get some."

"How? You need experience to get a job."

"I'll find something."

"Who'll employ you? No one likes a quitter."

"That's not true."

"OK, then. Who likes a quitter?"

"Other quitters."

Dad left me with a melodramatic sigh that trailed after him like a smell. I don't know how long I stood in the cold trying to see past the veil covering my future. Should I be a baker or a male stripper? A philanthropist or a roadie? A criminal mastermind or a dermatologist? It was no joke. I was caught in a brainstorm, and ideas were clamoring for prime position. Television presenter! Auctioneer! Private investigator! Car salesman! Train conductor! They arrived without invitation, made their presentation, then made way for the others. Some of the more persistent ideas tried to sneak back in. Train conductor! Television presenter on a train! Car salesman! Train salesman!

I spent the next day staring into empty space. I get a lot of joy out of air, and if sunlight hits the floating specks of dust so you see the whirling dance of atoms, so much the better. During the day Dad breezed in and out of my room and clicked his tongue, which in our family means "You're an idiot." In the afternoon he came back in with a loaded grin. He had a brilliant idea and couldn't wait to tell me about it. It had suddenly occurred to him to throw me out of the house, and what did I think of his brainwave? I told him I was concerned about him eating all his meals alone, because the clinking of cutlery on a plate echoing through an empty house is one of the top five depressing noises of all time.

"Don't worry. I have a plan for throwing you out. We, you and me, are going to build you a hut to live in. Somewhere on the property."

A hut? "How the hell are we going to build a hut? What do we know about building? Or huts?"

"The Internet," he said.

I groaned. The Internet! Ever since the Internet, complete idiots have been building huts and bombs and car engines and performing complicated surgical procedures in their bathtubs.

We settled on a clearing in the maze next to a circle of sinewy gum trees and only a few meters from a freshwater creek, and the following morning, under an orange-copper sky, we started chopping trees as if we were mythic Germanic creatures in an early Leni Riefenstahl film.

I couldn't stifle the thought that my life had taken a disappointing turn—I had only just left school and I was already doing hard manual labor. Every time the blade of the ax hit timber I felt my spine move a couple of millimeters to the left, and that first day for me was all about raising complaining to a high art. The second day was even worse—I dislocated my shoulder. The third day I said I needed to look for work and so I went into the city and saw three movies in a row, all of them bad, and when I returned I was shocked to see that an enormous amount of work had been done on the hut.

Dad was leaning on his ax, wiping sweat from his brow onto his pants. "I worked like a bastard today," he said. I looked steadily into his eyes and knew at once that he had called in outside help.

"How's the job hunt?" he asked.

"I'm closing in."

"Attaboy." Then he said, "Why don't you have a crack at construction tomorrow? I'm going to spend the day in the library."

And so I dug into the savings he kept in a hollowed-out copy of Rousseau's *Confessions* and called a builder of my own.

"Just do as much as you can," I said.

And in this manner the place was built. We'd alternate. One day I'd pretend to build the hut single-handed, then the next day he'd pretend to build the hut single-handed, and I don't know what any of this meant, only that it proved we both had damaged, underhand characters. The upshot was, the shack was taking shape. The ground was cleared. The frame erected. The floor laid. The roof beams raised. The door fastened on with hinges. Windows where windows should be. Glass in them. The days growing longer and warmer.

During this time I went for a job with an advertising agency, even though there was something condescending about the way the ad wanted a "junior." I entered a sterile cement shanty, shuffled along dark, joyless corridors where a large clone army slid by me, smiling with urgency. In the interview, a guy named Smithy told me I'd get four weeks off a year for cosmetic surgery. The job was data entry clerk. I started the next day. The ad didn't lie—I entered data. My coworkers were a man who smoked cigarettes that were mysteriously lipstick-stained in the pack and an alcoholic woman who tried very hard to convince me that waking up in the revolving door of the Hyatt Hotel was something to be proud of. I loathed that job. The good days passed like decades, the so-so days like half centuries, but mostly it felt as if I were frozen in the eye of an everlasting time-storm.

The night the hut was finished, Dad and I, two lying fakers, sat on the front porch and toasted the achievement that was not our own. We saw a star fall and tear a long thin strip of white in the black sky.

"Did you see that?" Dad asked.

"Shooting star."

"I made a wish," he said. "Should I tell you what it was?"

"Better not."

"You're probably right. Did you make a wish?"

"I'll make one later."

"Don't wait too long."

"As long as I don't blink, the power of the star is still good."

My fingers held my eyelids wide open while I contemplated my wishing options. It was an easy choice. I wanted a woman. I wanted love. I wanted sex. Specifically, I wanted the Towering Inferno. I worked all this into one wish.

Dad must have read my mind, or made a similar wish, because he said, "You're probably wondering why I've been single most all my life."

"It's kind of self-explanatory," I said.

"Do you remember I told you one day about a girl I once loved?"

"Caroline Potts."

"I still think about her."

"Where is she now?"

"Europe probably," he said. "She was the love of my life."

"And Terry was the love of hers."

We finished our beers and listened to the gurgling of the creek.

"Make sure you fall in love, Jasper. It's one of the greatest pleasures there is."

"A pleasure? You mean like a hot bath in winter?"

"That's right."

"Anything else?"

"It makes you feel alive, really alive."

"That sounds good. What else?"

"It confuses you so you don't know your arse from your elbow."

I thought about that. "Dad," I said, "so far you've described love as a pleasure, a stimulant, and a distraction. Is there nothing else?"

"What more do you want?"

"I don't know. Something higher or deeper?"

"Higher or deeper?"

"Something more meaningful?"

"Like what?"

"I'm not sure."

We had reached an impasse, and turned our eyes back to the heavens. The night sky just disappoints after a falling star has fallen from sight. Show's over, the sky says. Go home.

•

That night I wrote a nice little blackmail note to the Towering Inferno:

I'm considering changing my story and telling the principal it was you who orchestrated the hat incident on the train. If you would like to talk me out of it, come to my house anytime. Come alone.

You don't think you can blackmail a woman into loving you? Well, maybe you can't, but it was my last card and I had to play it. I perused the note. It was just the way a blackmail letter should read: concise and demanding. But . . . my pen wriggled in my hand. It wanted to add something. OK, I conceded, but I remembered that brevity is the soul of extortion. I wrote: P.S. *If you don't show up, then don't think I'll be waiting like a fool. But if you do come, I'll be there.* And then I wrote on a little; I wrote about the nature of expectation and disappointment, about lust and memories; and about people who treat use-by dates as though they were holy commandments. It was a fine note. The blackmail element was short, only three lines. The P.S. was twenty-eight pages long.

On my way to work I popped it in the mailbox outside the post office and five minutes later almost broke my hand trying to get it out. Honestly, they knew what they were doing designing those mailboxes—you really can't get into them. I tell you, those little red fortresses, they're impenetrable!

Two days later I was in a deep sleep, trapped in an unpleasant dream where I was at a swimming carnival and when it came my turn to swim they drained the pool. I was on the swimmer's block and the crowd booed me because I wasn't wearing anything and they didn't like what they saw. Then all of a sudden I was in a bed. My bed. In my hut. Dad's voice had dragged me into consciousness, away from the disapproving eyes. "Jasper! You have a visitor!"

I pulled the covers over me. I didn't want to see anyone. Dad started up again. "Jasper! You in there, son?" I sat up. His voice sounded funny. I couldn't work out what it was at first, but then I realized. He sounded polite. Something must be up. I put a towel around me and stepped outside.

I squinted in the sun. Was I still dreaming? A vision soaked my eyes with cool delight. She was here: the Towering Inferno, in my home, next to my father. I froze. I couldn't reconcile the two figures standing side by side. It was all so out of context.

"Hi, Jasper," she said, her voice wriggling down my spine.

"Hi," I countered. Dad was still standing there. Why was he still standing there? Why wouldn't he move?

"Well, here he is," he said.

"Come on in," I said, and by her hesitant eyes remembered I was wearing only a towel.

"Are you going to put clothes on?" the Inferno asked.

"I think I can dig up some socks."

"There's a bushfire up in the mountains," Dad said.

"We'll stay away from there. Thanks for the tip," I said dismissively, turning my back on him. As we walked into my hut, I whipped my head around to make sure Dad wasn't going to follow us in. He wasn't, but he winked at me conspiratorially. It annoyed me, that wink. He had given me no choice. You can't not accept a wink. Then I saw Dad look at her legs. He glanced up and saw me see him looking at her legs. It was a weird moment that could've gone either way. Despite myself, I couldn't help but smile. He smiled too. Then the Inferno looked up and caught us smiling at each other. We both glanced at her and caught her looking at us smiling at each other. Another weird moment.

"Come in," I said.

As she stepped into the hut, the swoosh, drag, lift of her footsteps advancing on the wooden floorboards would have driven me to drink had there been a bar in my bedroom, and had it been open. I went into the bathroom and threw on jeans and a T-shirt, and when I came out she was still standing at the doorway. She asked me if I really lived in this place.

"Why not? I built it."

"You did?"

I showed her where I'd cut myself helping my builder put in a window. It felt good showing her my scars. They were man scars.

"Your father seems nice."

"He's not really."

"So what are you doing with yourself?"

"I got a job."

"You're not going back to school?"

"Why should I?"

"A high school certificate is a pretty handy thing."

"If you like paper cuts."

She gave me a half smile. It was the other half I was worried about. She said, "So then, how does it feel to be a working man?"

"I don't know," I said. "You might as well come up to me in a seven-story parking station and ask how it feels to be on the fourth level when before I was on the third."

"I got your note."

"We drove a man to suicide."

"You don't know that."

She was only inches away. I couldn't breathe. I was experiencing one of those horriblebeautifulterrifyingdisgustingwondrousinsaneunprecedentedeuphoricsensationaldisturbingthrillinghideoussublimenauseating-exceptional feelings that's quite hard to describe unless you happen to chance upon the right word.

"Do you want to take a walk in my labyrinth?" I asked.

"I really don't have much time."

"I'll give you the no-frills tour."

Outside, everything shone brightly in the sun and there were no clouds spoiling the blue except one shaped like a goat's head, a solitary cloud as if God had wiped down the sky and missed a spot. We walked to the creek and trailed along it and looked at the faces of half-submerged rocks. I told her they were called stepping-stones because man likes to think that all of nature was set up especially for his feet.

We followed the creek to where it poured tirelessly into the river. The sun was hammering away so you couldn't look at the water without squinting. The Inferno knelt down beside the river and put her hand in it.

"It's warm," she said.

I picked up a flat stone and threw it away from the river. I would've skipped it across the water, but that scene was too cute for me. I was past all that. I was at the age where boys would put a body in the river, not a stone.

We walked on. She asked me how I found my way around the maze. I told her I had got lost for a long time, but now it was like navigating through the digestive system of an old friend. I told her I knew every wrinkle in every living rock. I was bursting to tell her the names of the plants and the flowers and the trees, but I wasn't on a first-name basis with flora. I pointed out my favorites anyway. I said, There's the silvery gray shrub with large clusters of vivid yellow ball flowers like bright furry microphones, and the small bushy bronze tree with white globular fruit I wouldn't eat even for a dare, and this one has leaves glossy like they've been covered in contact paper, and a crouching shrub that's wild and tangled and smells like a bottle of turpentine you drink at two in the morning when all the bottle shops are closed.

She looked at me strangely, standing there like my favorite tree: straight and tall, slim-stemmed and graceful.

"I'd better get going. Just point me in the right direction," she said, putting a cigarette in her mouth.

"So I see you're still smoking like an inmate on death row."

Her eyes fixed on mine as she lit her cigarette. She had just taken the first puff when something black and nasty floated down to her face and landed on her cheek. She wiped it off. We both looked up at the sky. Ash was falling softly, dark ash falling and whirling crazily in the hot bright air.

"Looks like a bad one," she said, looking at the orange glow over the horizon.

"I suppose."

"Do you think it's close?"

"I wouldn't know."

"I think it's close," she said.

All right, so what if we live in a flammable land? There's always a fire, always houses lost, lives misplaced. But nobody packs up and moves to safer pastures. They just wipe their tears and bury their dead and make more children and dig in their heels. Why? We have our reasons. What are they? Don't ask me. Ask the ash that sits on your nose.

"Why are you looking at me like that?"

"You've got some ash on your nose."

She wiped it off. It left a black smear.

"Is it gone?"

I nodded. I wouldn't tell her about the black smear. A raw, hungry silence descended, swallowing whole minutes.

"Well, I really have to go."

"Why don't you take your pants off and stay awhile?" I wanted to say but didn't. There's little doubt that when the defining moments arise in which character is molded, you'd better make the right decision. The mold dries and sets quickly.

We walked through a small clearing where the grass was so short it looked like green sand, and I led her to a cave. I walked in and she followed me. It was dark and cool inside.

"What are we doing in here?" she asked suspiciously.

"I want to show you something. Look. These are cave paintings."

"Really?"

"Sure. I did them myself just last week."

"Oh."

"Why do you sound so disappointed? I don't see why you have to be fifty thousand years old to paint on a cave wall."

That's when she leaned forward and kissed me. And that was that.

V

A few weeks later the Towering Inferno and I were lying in bed and I was feeling as secure as if we were both stored in a large vault. She was on her side, propped up on one elbow that was tireless, like a steel pole. She had her pen poised on a notebook, but she wasn't writing anything.

"What are you thinking about?" I asked.

"I'm thinking about what you're thinking about."

"That's no answer."

"Well, what are you thinking about?"

"What you're thinking about."

She snorted. I didn't press it. She was secretive, like me—not wanting anyone to know her every thought in case he used it against her. I imagined she'd discovered, as I had, that what people want from you is confirmation that you're toeing the line, living by the same rules they are, and that you're not going off on your own or awarding yourself any special privileges.

"I'm trying to write a birthday card," she said. "It's Lola's birthday. You remember Lola, from school?"

"Oh yeah, Lola," I said, not knowing who Lola was.

"Do you want to write something to her?" she asked.

"Sure," I lied.

Just before I put pen to card the Inferno said, "Write something nice." I nodded and wrote: "Dear Lola, I hope you live *forever.*" I handed the card back. The Inferno scrutinized it but didn't say anything. If she knew my message was a curse and not a blessing, she didn't let on.

Then the Inferno said, "Oh, I almost forgot. Brian wants to talk to you."

"Who?"

"His name's Brian."

"That may be so, but I don't know who you're talking about."

"He's sort of my ex-boyfriend."

I sat up and looked at her. "Sort of?"

"We went out briefly."

"And you still speak to him?"

"No, I mean, the other day I ran into him," she said.

"You ran into him," I repeated. I didn't like the sound of this. No matter what anybody says, I know that people don't really just run into each other.

"Well, why does he want to talk to me?"

"He thinks you might be able to help him get his job back."

"His job? Me? How?"

"I don't know, Jasper. Why don't you meet him and find out?"

"No, thanks."

She looked annoyed, rolled over, and turned away from me. I spent the next ten minutes watching her naked back, her red hair spilling over her shoulder blades, which jutted out like surfboard fins.

"I'll think about it," I said.

"Don't put yourself out," she said back.

•

Our honeymoon period mostly consisted of staring at each other's faces for hours on end. Sometimes that's all we did for the whole day. Sometimes her face drifted in and out of focus. Sometimes it looked like an alien face. Sometimes it didn't look like a face at all, but a bizarre compendium of features on a blurry white background. At the time I remember thinking that we'd fastened onto each other in such a sticky fashion it would be impossible to separate without one of us losing a hand or a lip.

Things weren't perfect, of course. She hated it that I'd not yet dropped the habit of mentally noting all the famous actresses I'd like to sleep with when my ship came in.

I hated it that she was *too* open-minded and half believed in a creationist theory that had God go "Ta-da!"

She hated it that I didn't hate fake breasts.

I hated the way when she was mad or upset, she'd kiss me with her lips closed.

She hated the way I'd try everything to open them—lips, tongue, thumb and forefinger.

Whenever I'd heard anyone say "Relationships are work," I'd always scoffed, because I thought relationships should grow wild like untended gardens, but now I knew they *were* work, and unpaid work too—volunteer work.

•

One morning a couple of weeks into the relationship, Dad ran into my hut as if he were taking refuge from a storm.

"Haven't seen you in a while. Love must be pretty time-consuming, eh?"

"It is."

He looked to be bursting with bad news that he couldn't hold in much longer.

"What?" I asked.

"Nothing. You enjoy it while it lasts."

"I will."

He stood there like stagnant water and said, "Jasper, we've never talked about sex."

"And thank God for that."

"I just want to say one thing."

"Get it over with."

"Even though using a condom is as insulting to the senses as putting a windsock on your tongue before eating chocolate, use one anyway."

"A windsock."

"A condom."

"OK."

"To avoid paternity suits."

"OK," I said, although I didn't need a sex talk. Nobody does. A beaver can make a dam, a bird can build a nest, a spider can spin its web at the first attempt without even fumbling. Fucking is like that. We're born to do it.

"Want to read anything on love?" Dad asked.

"No, I just want to do it."

"Suit yourself. Plato's *Symposium* won't be much use to you anyway, unless your girlfriend is a thirteen-year-old Greek boy. I'd avoid Schopenhauer too. He wants you to believe you've been had by the unconscious desire to propagate the species."

"I don't want to propagate anything. Least of all the species."

"Attaboy." Dad put his hands in the tattered pockets of his old tracksuit pants and went right on nodding at me with a half-open mouth.

"Dad," I said, "remember how you said love is a pleasure, a stimulant, and a distraction?"

"Uh-huh."

"Well, there's something else you didn't mention. And that's that if you could save the person from ever having another splinter in her finger, you'd run around the world laminating all the wood with a fine, transparent surface, just to save her from that splinter. That's love."

Dad said, "Huh. I'll make a note of that."

The next night when I got into bed, I found something bulky under the pillow. It was thirteen books, from Shakespeare to Freud, and after staying up all night and skim-reading at least half of them, I learned that, according to the experts, you cannot be "in love" without fear, but love without fear is sincere, mature love.

I realized I'd completely idealized the Towering Inferno, but so what if I had? Sooner or later we have to idealize something—being lukewarm to everything is inhuman. So I idealized her. But did I love her or not? Was it a mature love or an immature love? Well, I had my own method of working it out. I decided: I know that I love and am in love when suddenly I fear her death as sharply as I fear my own. It would be lovely and romantic to say I fear hers more than mine, but that would be a lie, and anyway, if you knew how deep and complete is my desire to perpetuate through the eons with every particle intact, you'd agree it was a romantic enough fear, this terror of the death of the beloved.

•

So I called her sort-of-ex-boyfriend, Brian.

"It's Jasper Dean here," I said when he answered the phone.

"Jasper! Thanks for calling."

"What's this about?"

"I was wondering if we could meet for a drink."

"What for?"

"Just for a chat. Do you know the Royal Batsman, near Central Station? We could meet tomorrow at five?"

"Five twenty-three," I said, to exert some control over the situation.

"Done."

"What's this about me helping you get your job back?" I asked.

"I'd rather tell you face-to-face," he said, and I hung up the phone thinking he must have either a low opinion of his voice or a high opinion of his face.

For the next twenty-four hours my whole body pulsated with curiosity; this idea that I could help him get back his job confounded me. Even if it was somehow possible, why assume I'd want to? The worst thing you can say about someone in a society like ours is that they can't hold down a job. It conjures images of unshaven losers with weak grips watching sadly as the jobs slip free and float away. There's nothing we respect more than work, and there's nothing we denigrate more than the unwillingness to work, and if someone wants to dedicate himself to painting or writing poetry, he'd better be holding down a job at a hamburger restaurant if he knows what's good for him.

I only just got through the doors of the Royal Batsman when I saw a middle-aged man with silver hair waving me over. He was in his late forties and wore a flashy pin-striped suit, almost as flashy as his hair. He smiled at me. That was flashy too.

"Sorry, do I know you?"

"I'm Brian."

"You're the ex-boyfriend?"

"Yeah."

"But you're old!"

That made him smile unpleasantly. "I guess she has a little something for celebrities."

"Celebrities? Who's a celebrity?"

"Don't you know who I am?"

"No."

"Don't you watch television?"

"No."

He looked at me, puzzled, as if I'd actually said no to the question "Don't you eat, shit, and breathe?"

"My name's Brian Sinclair. I was on Channel Nine television for a couple of years. As a current affairs journalist. I'm taking a hiatus now."

"Well so what?"

"Beer?" he asked.

"Thanks."

He went to the bar and fetched me a beer and I was swept up in a sort of panic, dazzled by his silver hair and matching suit. I had to remind myself that he needed my help, and that put me in a position of power which I was free to abuse at any given time.

"Did you see the game last night?" I asked when he returned.

"No. What game?"

I didn't answer. I didn't know what game—I was just making conversation. And he had to ask what game? Who cares what game? Any game. There's always a game.

"So what can I do for you?" I asked.

"Well, Jasper, as I said, I used to be a current affairs journalist for Channel Nine. And I was fired."

"What for?"

"Are you sure you don't know about this? It was big news for a while. I was interviewing a twenty-six-year-old father of two who was not only not meeting his child-support payments but living off the dole so he could maintain his obsession with daytime television. I was just asking him a few simple questions, and right in the middle of the interview—"

"He pulled out a gun and shot himself."

"Hey—I thought you didn't watch television."

"It's the only way it could have gone down," I said, although the truth was, I do sometimes watch television and I suddenly recalled seeing a repeat of that suicide in slow motion. "This is all very interesting," I said, "but what's it got to do with me?"

"Well, if I had a news story that no one else had, that could make me a valuable commodity again."

"And?"

"And your father has never given an extensive interview about his brother."

"Jesus."

"If I could get the inside scoop on the Terry Dean story—"

"What are you doing now? Are you working?"

"In telesales."

Ouch. "That's a job as good as any other, isn't it?"

"I'm a journalist, Jasper."

"Listen, Brian. If there's one thing my father doesn't want to talk about, it's his brother."

"But can't you—"

"No. I can't."

Brian suddenly looked as though life had worn him down, literally, with an enormous nail file. "All right." He sighed. "What about you? You probably know a few things about the story that the rest of us don't."

"Probably."

"Would you agree to an interview?"

"Sorry."

"Give me something. *The Handbook of Crime.*"

"What about it?"

"There's a theory your uncle didn't write it."

"I really wouldn't know," I said, and watched his face tighten into a fist.

•

When I got home, Dad was curled up on the couch, reading and breathing heavily. Instead of saying "Hello, son, how's life?" he held up the book he was reading: it was called *A History of Consciousness.* Instead of saying "Hi, Dad, I love you," I sneered and started searching the bookshelf for something to read myself.

As I browsed, I could detect the sweet, sickly odor of clove cigarettes. Was Eddie here? I heard muffled voices from the kitchen. I opened the door to see Anouk and Eddie huddled together, speaking in low tones. They looked surprised to see me, and while Eddie hit me with one of his dazzling smiles, Anouk beckoned me over with one finger over her lips.

"I just got back from Thailand," Eddie said in a whisper.

"I didn't know you'd gone," I whispered back.

He frowned unexpectedly—the frown surprised his own face.

"Jasper, I've got bad news," Anouk said in a barely audible voice.

"Say it all at once."

"Your dad's depressed again."

I looked through the door at Dad. Even when there were people in the house he still came across as a complete recluse.

"How can you tell?" I asked.

"He's been crying. Staring into space. Talking to himself."

"He always talks to himself."

"Now he's addressing himself formally as Mr. Dean."

"Is that all?"

"You want a repeat of the last time? You want him to go back to the mental hospital?"

"The man's depressed. What can we do?"

"I think it's because his life is empty."

"And?"

"And we need to help him fill it."

"Not me," I said.

"Jasper, you should talk to your father more," Eddie said with surprising sternness.

"Not at this juncture," I said, leaving the room.

My father's depression could wait a couple of days. At present I was suddenly interested in having a look at *The Handbook of Crime*, by Terry Dean (Harry West). I figured that since my relationship with the Towering Inferno had begun with blackmail, maybe the book had some other relationship advice. I found it in a pile on the floor, in the middle of an unsteady igloo of printed word. With the book in hand, I wound through the labyrinth to my hut.

In bed, I flicked through the table of contents. Chapter 17 caught my eye. It was called "Love: The Ultimate Informer." *If there's one thing a lawbreaker needs in his inventory, it's secrets, and if there's one enemy of secrets, it's love,* the chapter began.

The names of your informers, what backstabbing campaigns you're embarking on, where you store your guns, your drugs, your money, the location of your hideout, the interchangeable lists of your friends and enemies, your contacts, the fences, your escape plans—all things you need to keep to yourself, and you will reveal every one if you are in love.

Love is the Ultimate Informer because of the conviction it inspires that your love is eternal and immutable—you can no more imagine the end of your love than you can imagine the end of your own head. And because love is nothing without intimacy, and intimacy is nothing without sharing, and sharing is nothing without honesty, you must inevitably spill the beans, every last bean, because dishonesty in intimacy is unworkable and will slowly poison your precious love.

When it ends—and it will end (even the most risk-embracing gambler wouldn't touch those odds)—he or she, the love object, has your secrets. And can use them. And if the relationship ends acrimoniously, he or she will use them—viciously and maliciously—against you.

Furthermore, it is highly probable that the secrets you reveal when your soul has all its clothes off will be the cause of the end of love. Your intimate revelations will be the flame that lights the fuse that ignites the dynamite that blows your love to kingdom come.

No, you say. She understands my violent ways. She understands that the end justifies the means.

Think about this. Being in love is a process of idealization. Now ask yourself, how long can a woman be expected to idealize a man who held his foot on the head of a drowning man? Not too long, believe me. And cold nights in front of the fire, when you get up and slice off another piece of cheese, you don't think she's dwelling on that moment of unflinching honesty when you revealed sawing off the feet of your enemy? Well, she is.

If a man could be counted on to dispose of his partner the moment the relationship is over, this chapter wouldn't be necessary. But he can't be counted on for that. Hope of reconciliation keeps many an ex alive who should be at the bottom of a deep gorge.

So, lawbreakers, whoever you are, you need to keep your secrets for your survival, to keep your enemies at bay and your body out of the justice system. Sadly—and this is the lonely responsibility we all have to accept—the only way to do this is to stay single. If you need sexual relief, go to a hooker. If you need an intimate embrace, go to your mother. If you need a bed warmer during cold winter months, get a dog that is not a Chihuahua or a Pekingese. But know this: to give up your secrets is to give up your security, your freedom, your life. The truth will kill your love, then it will kill you. It's rotten, I know. But so is the sound of the judge's gavel pounding a mahogany desk.

I closed the book and lay in bed thinking about honesty and lies and decided that my feelings were honest but I was toes to eyeballs with secret stories and secret thoughts, none of which I had revealed to the Towering Inferno. Why had I been instinctively following the book's advice, a book written for criminals? Well, how could I reveal all the unimpressive things I'd done, like the time I was cornered by bullies and pretended to sleep through the beating they gave me? Or the time, just a week into our relationship, I was so jealous at the thought of the Towering Inferno sneaking off and sleeping with someone else that I went off and slept with someone else just so I wouldn't have any right to be jealous? No, I wasn't even going to tell her the good stuff, like how some mornings I came out of the labyrinth to the main road to find the streetlights still humming above me, an early wind tickling the trees, and the familiar scent of jasmine leading to a friendly confusion of the senses so it was as if my nose were full of the soft, heady smell of a light pink eyelid. I felt so fantastic bouncing in the warm morning air, I picked up a garden gnome from someone's lawn and put it on the lawn across the street. Then I undid a garden hose from that family's lawn and placed it on their neighbor's front porch. I thought: We're sharing today, people! What's his is yours! What's yours is his! Only later it did seem like a strange thing to have done, so I kept the story from penetrating my lover's inner eardrum.

And because it was apparent to me just how thoroughly I was infected by Dad's mistrust of everything, including his own thoughts, feelings, opinions, and intuitions—leading me to mistrust my own thoughts, feelings, opinions, and intuitions—neither could I tell her that every now and then I enter some dreamy trance state in which it's as if all the opposing forces of the universe submit to a sudden and inexplicable ceasefire and melt together until I feel like I have a piece of creation stuck between my teeth. Maybe I'm out walking in the street or simply erasing porn site addresses from my Internet browser's history, when suddenly it's as if I am wrapped in a soft golden mist. What is it, exactly? A period of superconsciousness, where the I of Me becomes the Us of We, where We is either Me and a Cloud or Me and a Tree and sometimes Me and a Sunset or Me and the Horizon but rarely Me and Butter or Me and Chipped Enamel. How could I explain it to her? To attempt to communicate uncommunicable ideas is to risk oversimplifying them, and the organic thrill is just going to come off sounding like an organic cheap thrill, and what would she think of these enchanting incomprehensible hallucinations anyway? She might rush to the conclusion that I am actually at one with the universe while others are not. It's like Dad said: moments of cosmic consciousness could simply be a natural reaction to a sudden unconscious awareness of our own mortality. For all we know, the feeling of unity might be the greatest proof of separateness there is. Who knows? Just because they *feel* like genuine apprehensions of Truth doesn't mean they are. I mean, if you mistrust one sense, you must mistrust them all. There's no reason the sixth sense might not be as misleading as smell or sight. That's the lesson I've learned from my father, the headline news from the corner that he thought himself into: direct intuitions are as untrustworthy as they are potent.

So you see? How could I tell her about these things when I wasn't sure whether I'd just put one over on myself? Neither could I tell her that sometimes I was certain I could read my father's thoughts and other times I suspected he could read mine. Sometimes, I tried to tell him something just by thinking it, and I'd feel I could hear him respond in the negative; I sensed a "Fuck you" traveling through the ether. Nor could I tell the Inferno that more than once I'd had visions of a disembodied face. I first dreamed of the face in my childhood, a tanned, mustached, thick-lipped, wide-nosed face floating out of a dark void, his piercing eyes giving off an aura of sexual violence, his mouth contorted into a silent scream. I'm sure this has happened to everyone. Then one day you see the face even when you're awake. You see it in the sun. You see it in the clouds. You see it in the mirror. You see it clearly, even though it's not there. Then you feel it too. And you stand up and say, "Who's there?" And when you receive no answer, you say, "I'm calling the police." And what is this presence anyway if in fact it's not a ghost? The most likely explanation: a fully exteriorized and manifested idea. There were things crawling inside my brain itching to get out, and, worse, they were getting out and I had no control over where and when.

No, why air every ugly, negative, loopy, idiotic thought that floats through the head? That's why when you're standing by the harbor and your lover says, in a tender embrace, "What are you thinking about?" you don't respond, "That I hate people and I wish they'd fall down and never get up." I'm telling you. You just can't say it. I don't know much about women, but I do know that.

•

I fell asleep, and at four in the morning I woke with a shocking realization: I'd never told the Towering Inferno that Terry Dean was my uncle.

I stared at the clock until eight a.m. without looking away once, then called Brian.

"Who is it?"

"How did you know I was Terry Dean's nephew?"

"Jasper?"

"How did you know?"

"Your girlfriend told me."

"Yeah, I know, I was just checking. So, um . . . you and her, then . . ."

"What about us?"

"She said you went out with her for just a little while."

He didn't say anything. In the silence I heard him breathing like someone who knows he has the upper hand, and I wound up breathing like someone stuck with the lower hand, and then he began telling me not just about him and her but things about her she had kept secret— her whole life, it seemed: how she ran away from home at fifteen and stayed two months with a drug dealer in Chippendale named Freddy Luxembourg and how she went back home one abortion later and changed schools and how when she was sixteen she started going out by herself to bars and that's where they met and she ran away from home again and lived with him for one year until she caught him with another woman and totally freaked out and ran back home again and her parents sent her to a psychologist who declared her a human time bomb and how she'd been calling him and leaving strange messages on his answering machine about her new boyfriend who was going to kill him if he ever showed his face in her life again. It surprised me to learn that the killer boyfriend was me.

I took all this with pretend calm, saying things like "Uh-huh" and trying not to show alarm at the unsettling conclusions I was drawing. That she had been calling her old boyfriend and leaving surly messages on his phone meant that she was probably still hung up on him, and that he in return was talking to her about getting his old job back meant that he was probably still hung up on her.

I couldn't get my head around it. She'd lied to me! *She* had lied to *me!* *Me!* I was supposed to be the liar in this relationship!

I hung up and threw my legs over the side of the bed like two anchors. I didn't get up. I sat on that bed for hours, breaking the spell only to call in sick to work. At around five I finally got out of bed and sat on the back veranda emptying tobacco out of my cigarette and into a pipe. I stared at the sunset because I thought I saw a face in it, a face in the sun, that old familiar face I hadn't seen in a long time. All around me cicadas were making a racket. It sounded like they were closing in. I thought about catching one and fixing it into the pipe and smoking it. I was wondering if it would get me high when I saw a red flare shoot into the sky. I put down the pipe and set off in the direction of the trail of vapor that hung in the air. It was her. I had given her a flare gun because she often got lost in the maze.

I found her near a large boulder and took her back to the hut. When we got inside, I told her everything Brian had told me. She looked at me, her eyes death-empty.

"Why didn't you tell me you lived with him for a year?" I yelled.

"Well, you haven't been honest with me either. You didn't tell me that your uncle is Terry Dean!"

"Why would I? I never met him! It was a long time ago. I was minus two years old when he died. What I want to know is, why didn't you tell me that you knew about my uncle?"

"Look. Let's be honest with each other from now on," she said.

"Yes, let's."

"Scrupulously honest."

"We'll tell each other everything."

The door was wide open. Neither of us stepped through it. It was the time to ask questions and answer them, like two informants who'd just discovered that each had made separate immunity deals with the public prosecutor.

"I'm going to have a shower," she said.

I watched her walk across the room, and when she bent over to pick up a towel from the floor, I noticed how the back of her jeans curved away from her body, like an evil grin.

VI

After this incident I got into the bad habit of treating her with courtesy and respect. Courtesy and respect are advisable when addressing a judge right before he sentences you, but in a relationship they signify discomfort. And I was uncomfortable because she still hadn't gotten over Brian. This was not baseless paranoia, either. She had started comparing me to him, unfavorably. For instance, she said I wasn't as romantic as Brian, just because I'd once said in an intimate moment, "I love you with all of my brain." Is it my fault she didn't understand how the heart has stolen credit from the head, that wild passionate feelings actually come from the ancient limbic system in the brain, and that I was just trying to avoid referring to the heart as the actual storehouse of all my feelings when it is, after all, only a soggy, bloody pump and filter system? Is it my fault people can't enjoy a symbol without turning it into a literal fact? Which is why, by the way, you should never waste your time giving the human race an allegorical tale—in less than one generation they'll turn it into historical data, complete with eyewitnesses.

Oh, and then there was the jar.

I was at her place, in her bedroom. We'd just had sex very quietly because her mother was in the next room. I enjoyed doing it quietly because when you can make all the noise you like you sort of go faster. Silent sex makes you slow down.

Afterward, when I was fishing on the floor for all the coins that had fallen from my jeans pockets, I saw the jar underneath her bed, mustard-sized, with a misty liquid floating in it, like cloudy water from a Mexican tap. Removing the lid, I sniffed tentatively, irrationally expecting the odor of sour milk. It smelled of nothing at all. I turned and watched her thin body settle on the bed. "Don't spill it," she said, before giving me another in a long dynasty of perfect smiles.

I dipped my finger in the jar, whipped it out, and licked it.

Salty.

I thought I knew what that meant. But could it really mean what I thought it meant? Was I actually, in reality, holding a jar of tears? Her tears?

"Tears, huh?" I said, as though everybody I knew collected their own tears, as if the whole world did nothing but forge monuments to their own sadness. I could imagine her pressing the little jar against her cheek, when the inaugural tear looked like the first raindrop sliding down a windowpane.

"What's it for?" I asked.

"Nothing."

"What do you mean, nothing?"

"I just collect my tears, that's all."

"Come on. There's something more."

"There's not. Don't you believe me?"

"Absolutely not."

She stared at me a moment. "OK—I'll tell you, but I don't want you to take it the wrong way."

"OK."

"Promise you won't take it the wrong way?"

"That's a hard promise to make. How will I know if I'm taking it the wrong way?"

"I'll tell you."

"OK."

"OK. I'm collecting my tears because . . . I'm going to make Brian drink them," she said.

I gritted my teeth and looked out the window. Outside, the drooping autumn trees looked like golden brown shrugs. "You're still in love with him!" I shouted.

"Jasper!" she screamed. "You're taking it the wrong way!"

About two weeks later she heaped another insult on top of the last one. We were in my hut, making love, making a hell of a racket this time, and as if going out of her way to confirm my worst suspicions, right in the middle of it she called out *his* name. "Brian!" she moaned breathlessly.

"Where?" I asked, startled, and started looking around the room for him.

"What are you doing?"

I stopped when I realized my stupid error. She gave me a look that deftly combined tenderness with revulsion. To this day the memory of that look still visits me like a Jehovah's Witness, uninvited and tireless.

She climbed naked out of bed and made herself a cup of tea, grimacing with guilt.

"I'm sorry," she said, her voice shaking.

"I don't think you should close your eyes during sex anymore."

"Hmm."

"I want you to look at me the whole time. OK?"

"You don't have any milk," she said, squatting in front of the bar fridge.

"Yes, I do."

"It's lumpy."

"But it's still milk."

She hadn't finished sighing when I went out of the hut and walked in the darkness to Dad's house. We were always breaking into each other's houses to steal milk. It has to be said: I was the better thief. He would always come in while I was sleeping, but because he was paranoid about sell-by dates, I would awake to the sound of thunderous sniffing.

The night was the kind of thick, all-encompassing black that renders concepts such as north, south, east, and west unusable. After I'd stumbled over tree stumps and been slapped in the face by thorny branches, the lights of Dad's house welcomed me and depressed me at the same time; they meant he was awake and I'd get stuck talking, that is, listening to him. I groaned. I was aware of our growing estrangement. It had started after I quit school and gradually worsened. I'm not sure why, but he'd unexpectedly resorted to normal parenting, especially in the use of emotional blackmail. He even once said the phrase "After all I've done for you." Then he listed all that he'd done for me. It sounded like a lot, but many were small sacrifices such as "bought butter even though I like margarine."

The truth was, I could no longer stand him: his unrelenting negativity, his negligence of both our lives, his inhuman reverence for books over people, his fanatical love for hating society, his inauthentic love for me, his unhealthy obsession with making my life as unpleasant as his. It occurred to me that he hadn't made my life distressing as an afterthought, either, but had gone about dismantling me laboriously, as if he were being paid overtime to do it. He had a concrete pylon for a head, and I just couldn't take it anymore. It seems to me you should be able to look at the people in your life and say "I owe you my survival" and "You owe me your survival," and if you can't say that, then what the hell are you doing with them? As it stood, I could only look at my father and think, "Well, I survived in spite of your meddling, you son of a bitch."

The light was on in his living room. I peered through the window. Dad was reading the newspaper and crying.

"What's the matter?" I asked, opening the sliding doors.

"What are you doing in here?"

"Stealing milk."

"Well, steal your own milk!" he said.

I walked in and tore the newspaper out of his hands. It was one of the daily tabloids. Dad got up and went into the next room. I looked closer at the newspaper. The story Dad had been reading was about Frankie Hollow, the recently murdered rock star who, coming home from a tour, had been confronted by a crazed fan who shot him twice in the chest, once in the head, and once "for good luck." Every single day since then the story had managed to make the front page, despite there being no additional facts after day one. Some days the papers included interviews with people who didn't know anything and who in the course of the interview revealed nothing. Then they squeezed every last drop of blood out of the story by digging up the dead star's past, and when there was absolutely, positively nothing left to report, they reported some more. I thought: Who prints this toe jam? And then I thought: Why is Dad crying over this celebrity death? I stood there with a thousand belittling phrases swimming in my head, trying to decide if I should lay the boot in. I decided against it; death is death, and mourning is mourning, and even if people choose to shed tears over the loss of a popular stranger, you can't mock a sad heart.

I closed the paper, more clueless than before. From the next room I could hear the television; it sounded like Dad was testing the volume to see how high it could go. I went in. He was watching a late-night soft porn series about a female detective who solves crimes by showing her clean-shaven legs. He wasn't looking at the screen, though; he was staring into the tiny oval mouth of a can of beer. I sat next to him, and we didn't talk for a while. Sometimes not talking is effortless, and other times it's more exhausting than lifting pianos.

"Why don't you go to bed?" I asked.

"Thanks, Dad," Dad said.

I sat there trying to think of something sarcastic to say in retort, but when you put two sarcastic comments side by side, they just sound nasty. I went back into the labyrinth and to the Inferno in my bed.

"Where's the milk?" she asked as I crawled in beside her.

"It had lumps in it," I said, thinking of Dad and the lumps within. Anouk and Eddie were right—he had slipped back into a depressed state. Why this time? Why was he grieving over this rock star he'd never heard of? Was he going to start mourning every death on the planet Earth? Could there be a more time-consuming hobby?

In the morning when I woke up, the Inferno was gone. That was new. We had obviously fallen to a new low—in the old days we would've shaken each other out of a diabetic coma to announce our departure. Now she sneaked out, probably to avoid the question "What are you doing later?" My hut had never felt so empty. I buried my head in my pillow and shouted, "She's falling out of love with me!"

To distract myself from this sour-smelling reality, I picked up the newspaper and browsed through it, cringing. I've always hated our newspapers, mostly for their insulting geography. For example, on page 18 your eyes fall on the story of a terrible earthquake in some place like Peru with an insult hidden between the lines; twenty thousand human beings buried under broken rubble, then buried again, this time under seventeen pages of local blabber. I thought: Who prints this gum disease?

Then I heard a voice. "Knock knock," the voice said.

That put me instantly on edge. I shouted back. "Don't stand at the door and say 'Knock knock'! If I had a doorbell, would you stand there saying, 'Brrrring'?"

"What's wrong with you?" Anouk asked, entering.

"Nothing."

"You can tell me."

Should I confide in her? I knew Anouk was having troubles in her own love life. She was in the middle of a messy breakup. In fact, she was always in the middle of a messy breakup. In fact, she was always breaking up with people I never knew she'd even been seeing. If anyone had an eye for the beginning of the end, it would be Anouk. But I decided against asking for her advice. Some people sense when you're drowning, and when they step forward to get a clear view, they can't help putting their foot on your head.

"I'm fine," I said.

"I want to talk to you about your dad's depression."

"I'm not really in the mood."

"I know how to fill his emptiness. His notebooks!"

"I've snooped enough in his notebooks to last a lifetime! His writings are the stains of dripping juices from all the tangled meat in his head. I won't do it!"

"You don't have to. I already did."

"You did?"

Anouk pulled one of Dad's little black notebooks from her pocket and waved it in the air as if it were a winning lottery ticket. The sight of the notebook produced in me the same effect as the sight of my father's face: an overwhelming weariness.

"OK," Anouk said, "listen to this. Are you sitting down?"

"You're looking right at me, Anouk!"

"OK! OK! Jesus, you're in a bad mood."

She cleared her throat and read: " 'In life, everyone's doing exactly what they're supposed to. I mean, look closely when you meet an accountant—he looks exactly like an accountant! Never did there exist an accountant who looked like he should have been a fireman, a clerk in a clothing store who looked like a judge, or a vet who looked like he belonged behind the counter at McDonald's. One time at a party I met this guy and I said, "So then, what do you do for a crust?" and he said loudly, so everyone could hear, "I'm a tree surgeon," just like that, and I took a step back and gave him the once-over and I'll be damned if he didn't fit the image precisely—he *looked* like a tree surgeon, even though I'd never met one before. This is what I'm saying—absolutely everyone is as they should be, and this is also the problem. You never find a media mogul with the soul of an artist or a multibillionaire with the raving, fiery compassion of a social worker. But what if you could whisper in a billionaire's ear and reach the raving, fiery compassion that's lying dormant and unused, where empathy is stored, and you could whisper in his ear and fuel that empathy until it catches alight, and then you douse that empathy with ideas until it's transformed into action. I mean, excite him. Really excite him. That's what I've been dreaming about. To be the man who excites rich and powerful men with his ideas. That's what I want—to be the man who whispers thrilling ideas into an enormous golden ear.' "

Anouk closed the notebook and looked at me as though expecting a standing ovation. Was this what she was excited about? His megalomania was old news to me. I'd learned the same when I'd helped him out of the asylum. Of course, it was just a lucky break that time—taking the contents of those insane notebooks literally and using them on its owner was a very hazardous business—as we were about to find out.

"So what?" I said.

"So what?"

"I don't get it."

"You don't get it?"

"Stop repeating everything I say."

"It's the answer, Jasper."

"It is? I've forgotten the question."

"How to fill your dad's emptiness. It's simple. We go out and find one."

"Find what?"

"A golden ear," she said, smiling.

VII

That night, on my way over to Anouk's house, I thought about her plan. The golden ear she had decided on belonged to the head of Reynold Hobbs, who, in case you live in a cave that doesn't get cable television, was the richest man in Australia. He owned newspapers, magazines, publishing houses, movie studios, and television stations that recorded sporting events that he broadcast through his cable networks. He owned football clubs, nightclubs, hotel chains, restaurants, a fleet of taxis, and a chain of record companies that produced music that he sold in his music stores. He owned resorts, politicians, apartment buildings, mansions, racehorses, and a yacht the size of the Pacific island of Nauru. Half the time Reynold lived in New York, but he was so secretive, you never knew which half. He was the rare sort of celebrity who didn't have to worry about the paparazzi because he owned them. I tell you, Reynold Hobbs could take a shit off the Harbor Bridge and you'd never see a picture of it in the paper.

I don't know how long Anouk had been planning this unpromising mission, but she showed me an article that said Reynold and his son, Oscar, were going to be in the Sydney casino that night to celebrate their purchase of it. Her plan was for us to go to the casino and try to convince Reynold Hobbs, Australia's richest man, to meet with Dad, Australia's poorest.

At this time Anouk was back living with her parents in a nice house in a nice neighborhood in a nice cul-de-sac with a nice park next door and lots of children playing in the street and neighbors chatting over fences and big front lawns and big backyards and swings and a nice comfortable family car in every driveway and dogs who knew where to shit and where not to shit and in nice symmetrical piles too, like a Boy Scout's campfire. It was the kind of middle-class exterior people love to peel back the layers of, looking for worms—and the worms are there, sure. Where aren't there worms? And yes, Anouk's family had a worm. They had a big worm. A worm that wouldn't go away. It was Anouk. She was the worm.

Her father was working in the garden when I turned up. He was a healthy man in his fifties, so healthy that the sight of him always made me resolve to do fifty push-ups every morning. Muscles bulging, he was bent over the flower bed ripping up weeds, and even his workman's crack was taut and glowing rosily underneath strong, virile tufts of bum hair.

"Hey, Jasper, what are you all dressed up for?"

"Anouk and I are going to the casino."

"What the hell for?"

"To break the bank."

He chuckled. "You can't beat those corrupt bastards. They've got it rigged."

"There aren't many corrupt bastards you can beat."

"Too true."

Anouk's mother, a beautiful woman with streaks of gray through her thick black hair, came out with a glass of water that she might have intended for her husband but that she gave to me.

"Here you go. Hey, am I shrinking or are you still growing?"

"I think I'm still growing."

"Well, don't stop now!"

"I won't."

I liked Anouk's family. They didn't make a great effort to make you feel welcome, they just looked at you as though you'd always been there. They were honest and earnest and enthusiastic and cheerful and hardworking and never had a bad word to say about anyone. They were the kind of people it's impossible not to like, and often I've felt like marching them up and down the street, daring people not to like them.

"Where's Anouk?"

"In her room. Go on in."

I walked through the nice cool house, up the stairs, and into Anouk's bedroom. Anouk always returned here after unsuccessful outings into the world—usually after jobs or relationships went bust. They kept it for her. It was strange to see her here in her family home, and in the bedroom of a fifteen-year-old girl. Let's be clear—Anouk was now thirty-two, and each time she moved out, she swore she'd never return, but things always had a way of going sour for her, and she was never able to resist going back for a while, to take a breather.

I had been to several of Anouk's apartments, and she was always in the middle of throwing out a man who'd disgusted her, or washing the sheets because a man she'd been sleeping with had been with someone else, or waiting by the phone for a man to ring, or not answering the phone because a man was ringing. I remember one who refused to leave; he'd tried to invoke squatter's rights in her bedroom. In the end she got rid of him by throwing his mobile phone out the window, and he followed closely behind it.

When I went in, Anouk was in her walk-in closet getting changed.

"I'll be out in a minute."

I snooped around. There was a photograph beside her bed of a man with a square head and dark sunglasses and the kind of sideburns that killed Elvis.

"Who's this horror show?"

"He's history. Throw him in the bin for me, will you?"

I had considerable satisfaction tossing his photograph in the bin.

"What happened with this one?"

"I'll tell you what happened. I have no luck. My relationships always fall into one of two categories: either I'm in love with him and he's not in love with me, or he's in love with me and he's shorter than my grandmother."

Poor Anouk. She couldn't stand being eternally single and she couldn't stand that she couldn't stand it. Love was tantalizingly absent from her life, and she was trying her best not to conclude that she was three-eighths through an eighty-year losing streak. She was humiliated to have joined the legions of single women obsessed with trying not to obsess about their singular obsession. But she couldn't help obsessing. She was now in her thirties and single. But it wasn't a question of the biological clock. It was a question of the other ticking clock—*the* clock, the Big Clock. And while she was always looking deep into herself for answers, just as the sages advise, what she came up with wasn't one single reason, and it wasn't as if she were stuck in a vicious circle, but rather in a pattern of several conjoined vicious circles. In one, she always singled out the wrong type—either "bourgeois yuppie bastards" or just "bastards," or, more often than not, a "man-child." In fact, for a while she seemed to be meeting only men-children in various guises. She also had a habit of being the other woman and not *the* woman. She was the kind that men like to sleep with but not have a relationship with. She was one of the boys, not one of the girls. And I don't know the psychology behind it, but anecdotal evidence proves it: *she wanted it too much.* But because no one seems sure how it works, you just have to go about trying to beat this mysterious force by pretending not to want what you really want.

Anouk stepped out of her closet looking spectacular. She was wearing a diaphanous green dress with a floral print and a black slip underneath. It looked like she had bought it two sizes too small on purpose; it showed every curve of her body. They were hairpin curves. My God, she was voluptuous, and if you had the right kind of imagination you couldn't think of anything other than sleeping with her, if only to get her off your mind. I admit I'd enjoyed masturbatory fantasies about her from the age of fourteen onward, ever since she had tired of her phase as shaven-headed, Doc Martens–wearing, pierced angry girl. The green eyes were still shining, but over the years she had grown her black hair out so it was long and flowing. She removed her piercings and went from stick-thin to spongy and now sauntered around like a promiscuous cloud in a tight dress. Even though I was there to help combat my father's depression and encroaching suicide, I couldn't help but think: Maybe it's high time Anouk and I slept together. Should I try to seduce her? Can you seduce someone who's seen you go through puberty?

"Maybe you should give relationships a break for a little while," I said.

"I don't want to be celibate, though. I like sex. I've slept with a lot of men and I want to keep sleeping with them. I tell you, whoever talks about the carnality of human beings and excludes women should come by my place one night and see me at it."

"I'm not saying you should be celibate. You could find a lover, like they have in France."

"You know, that's not a bad idea. But where do I find a no-strings-attached lover?"

"Well—and don't say no straightaway—what about me?"

"No."

"Why not?"

"Because you're like a son to me."

"No, I'm not. We're more like distant cousins secretly checking each other out."

"I've never checked you out."

"You should think about it."

"What about your girlfriend?"

"I think she's falling out of love with me. You see, I need a confidence boost, and I think if we became lovers, that would do it."

"Jasper, I don't want to."

"Is that any reason?"

"Yes."

"Haven't you ever slept with someone as a gesture of goodwill?"

"Of course."

"Or out of pity?"

"More often than not."

"Well, I don't mind if it's a charity fuck."

"Can we drop the subject?"

"I never knew you were so selfish and ungiving. Didn't you volunteer one year with the Salvation Army?"

"Collecting money door to door, not screwing the down and out."

We were at an impasse. Well, I was at an impasse.

"Come on, stupid," she said, and with Anouk leading the charge, we made our way to the Sydney casino.

•

Let's not mince words: the interior of the Sydney casino looks as if Vegas had an illegitimate child with Liberace's underpants, and that child fell down a staircase and hit its head on the edge of a spade. At blackjack tables and sitting in front of poker machines were tense and desperate men and women looking like droids, who didn't seem to be gambling for pleasure. As I watched them, I remembered the casino was famous for having its patrons lock their children in their cars while they gambled. I had read a news story about it, and I hoped all these sad, desperate people rolled the windows down a little while they put their rent money in the pockets of the state government, which rakes in huge profits and then puts half a percent of it back into the community for counseling services for gamblers.

"There they are," Anouk said.

She pointed to a crowd of paparazzi, businessmen, and politicians. Obviously Reynold Hobbs, a seventy-year-old man with square wire-framed glasses and a perfectly round, bald, Charlie Brown head, had taken some advice that it might be good for his public image if he tried to pass himself off as an "ordinary guy just like you," which was why he was hunched over the $10-minimum blackjack table. The way his shoulders were slumped, it seemed as if he'd lost his posture in the last hand. Anouk and I walked up a little closer. He might be Australia's richest man, but it didn't look like he had got there by gambling.

His son, Oscar Hobbs, was a few meters away, trying his luck at a poker machine, holding himself upright as only a celebrity can—a man that can be photographed at any moment, that is, a man not picking his nose or shifting his genitals. I quickly gave myself a stern warning: Don't compare your life to his! You haven't a chance! I looked around the room for a comparison I could live with. There. I saw him: old guy, not many teeth, not much hair, boil on his neck, nose like a conch shell; he would be my anchor. Otherwise I'd be in trouble. There was no way I could stand comparison to Oscar Hobbs, because it was a matter of public record that with women he was the luckiest son of a bitch alive. From my furtive readings of tabloid magazines I had seen his string of girlfriends—a long, beautiful, enviable string. If you saw some of the honeys he'd been intimate with, you'd eat your own arm up to the elbow. Fuck. I can't even stand to think about it. He wasn't a social-butterfly kind of heir apparent; you'd never see him at art openings or A-list bars or movie premieres. Oh sure, every now and then you'd see the corner of his chin in the social pages of the Sunday papers, but even from the way the chin was looking out at you, you'd just know he'd been caught unawares, like a thief surprised by a security camera in a bank. But the women! After seeing photos of them, I'd go back into my bedroom and tear at my pillow savagely. More than once I tore it to shreds, literally to shreds, and it is very hard to actually tear a pillow.

"So how do you want to tackle this?" I asked Anouk.

"We should attack on two fronts. One of us takes the father, the other one the son."

"This is never going to work."

"You want to try Reynold or Oscar?"

"Neither, but I suppose I'll try Reynold. I want to ask him something anyway."

"OK. But what should I say to the son? What kind of opening do you think will work?"

"I don't know. Pretend you met before."

"He'll think I'm trying to pick him up."

"Then insult him."

"Insult him?"

"Dissect him the way you always do. Tell him what's wrong with his soul."

"How do I know what's wrong with his soul?"

"Make it up. Tell him his soul's got one of those stains on it that smudges when you try to wipe it clean."

"No, that's no good."

"All right. Then tell him he's so rich he's cut off from reality. That'll get him going. Rich people hate that."

"But he *is* so rich he's cut off from reality."

"Anouk, believe it or not, financial hardship is not actually the one official reality."

"Let's not argue. Let's just get going on this."

"OK. Good luck."

I went over to the table where Reynold Hobbs was hunched, but there were no empty seats. I stood around, breathing on the players' necks. A security guard eyed me suspiciously, and with good cause too. I was acting suspicious, muttering to myself, "What the hell am I going to say to this media giant? How can I convince him to see my father? As an act of charity? Reynold Hobbs is a famous philanthropist, sure, but his is the kind of charity you phone in."

A reporter sitting next to Reynold finished an interview, stood up, and shook his hand. I took the opportunity and squeezed in beside him. Reynold smiled cordially at me, but I immediately sensed his discomfort. Some people are just no good talking to anyone under twenty years old, and the closer you are to zero, the greater their discomfort. He turned away from me and became instantly engrossed in a conversation with his lawyer about the average point size of small print in a legal contract. Reynold wanted to put in some clause in Times New Roman but drag it down to four points. His lawyer was debating the ethics of the proposed move, and argued that any print needs to be no smaller than seven points to be "all aboveboard."

"Excuse me, Mr. Hobbs?" I said.

He turned slowly, as if to say "Everything I breathe on turns to gold, so I'm doing you a big favor just facing in your direction," and when his eyes reached me, they did so with an infinite stillness that told me in no uncertain terms that despite our proximity, he was inaccessible.

"What is it?"

"You own some of our newspapers, don't you?"

"And?"

"Well, I thought power was supposed to corrupt, Mr. Hobbs. But what you do isn't corrupt—selling diarrhea isn't corrupt, it's just a baffling waste of power. With all the influence you exert, with the infinite choices you have up your sleeve, you could print anything, and yet you choose to print armpit sweat. Why?"

Reynold didn't know what to say. I looked over to see how Anouk was doing. She seemed to be faring better than I was. Oscar had an embarrassed look on his face. I wondered what she was saying.

Reynold was still ignoring me. I said, "OK, you want to sell papers. I get it. You sell fresh phlegm because the public has an indefatigable taste for fresh phlegm. But can't you make your papers a little bit liberating? What about sticking in a quarter page of Tibetan wisdom between the rehashed headlines and the daily horrorscopes? Would it kill sales?"

The security officer's hand rested on my shoulder. "Come on," he said. "Let's go."

"It's OK," Reynold said, without taking his eyes off me.

I pushed on. "Take the shamelessly sensationalist rehashing of the Frankie Hollow story. You don't have any more insight than you had on the first day, but you plop it on the front page anyway, turning it round and round, now from the point of view of the turd in the hotel toilet, now that of a bird flying past the window. Honestly, Mr. Hobbs, it's like reading dick cheese. How can you live with yourself? You must hire someone to look in the mirror for you."

"Listen to me, sonny, whoever you are. A newspaper is there to report, not to enlighten men's souls. Tabloids are sensationalist because men's lives are not sensational. That's the long and the short of it. The death of a celebrity is the best paper-seller we have. Do you know why? Because it's as if the headline reads: 'Gods Die Too.' Do you get me?"

"Sure. Can I borrow thirty thousand dollars?"

"What for?"

"To wander aimlessly over the whole earth. Ten thousand would get me started."

"How old are you?"

"Seventeen."

"You shouldn't be looking for handouts. You should be inspired to do it on your own."

"There's nothing inspiring about minimum wage."

"Yeah, well, I started on minimum wage. I never got a handout. I worked for what I have."

"That's a good speech. It's a shame you can't give your own eulogy."

"OK. My patience has run out now."

He nodded to the security guard, who helped me to my feet by squeezing my neck.

"One more thing!" I shouted.

Reynold sighed, but I could tell he was wondering what I was going to say. "Make it quick," he said.

"My father wants to meet with you."

"Who's your father?"

"Martin Dean."

"I never heard of him."

"I didn't say he was famous. I just said he wants to meet you."

"What about?"

"Why don't you let him tell you in person?"

"Because I don't have time. My plate's full right now."

"You're rich enough. Buy a bigger plate."

Reynold nodded again, and the security officer dragged me from the table. Someone took my picture as I was "escorted" outside. I waited for Anouk on the casino steps for an hour, and to pass the time I swung by the car park to check for suffocating children. There weren't any.

I came back up just as Anouk was coming out. I had never been flabbergasted before, so I didn't know what it felt like to be flabbergasted and I didn't even really believe people could be flabbergasted outside of books. That said, I was flabbergasted. Following closely behind Anouk were Oscar and Reynold Hobbs.

"And this is Jasper," she said.

"We've met," Reynold said, with an ephemeral sneer.

"Nice to meet you again," I said, and I threw Oscar the warmest smile in my smile repertoire, but his eyes didn't find my face worth dwelling on, so he missed it.

"What's going on?" I whispered to Anouk.

"They're coming with us," she said, making her eyebrows wiggle.

"Where?"

"Home."

VIII

In the stretch black limousine, both Reynold and his son spent the ride staring out their respective windows. Oscar's three-quarter profile had me transfixed most of the way. What a burden, I thought. Imagine being filthy rich *and* impossibly good-looking. For all that, he exuded a sadness I was unable to account for.

"I've seen your picture in magazines," I said.

"Yeah?"

"And you've always got some gorgeous model hanging off your arm."

"So?"

"So where do I get an arm like that?"

Oscar laughed and looked at me for the first time. His eyes were coffee-colored and motionless.

"What's your name again?"

"Jasper."

He nodded, apparently agreeing that my name was Jasper.

"So how does it feel to be always watched?" I asked.

"You get used to it."

"But don't you feel restricted?"

"Not really."

"You don't miss the freedom?"

"Freedom?"

"Let me put it this way. You couldn't take your penis out and wave it on a public train without it being front-page news. I could."

"Why would I want to wave my penis on a public train?" Oscar asked me. It was a good question. Why would anyone?

Reynold Hobbs coughed, but it was no mere lung-clearing exercise. That cough was meant to put me down. I smiled. You may have all the

money in the world, Mr. Hobbs, I thought, you might own the whole universe and its particles thereof, you might gain interest on the stars and
reap dividends from the moon, but I'm young and you're old and I have
something you don't—a future.

•

"I've heard about this place. It's a labyrinth, isn't it?" Reynold said as we
hiked through the dense bush.

"How did you hear about it?" I asked, and he looked at me as though
I were a shrunken head in an Amazonian exhibit. To him, my question
was the same as asking God how he knew Adam and Eve had taken the
apple.

"Your dad's sure going to be surprised," Anouk said, smiling at me.

I didn't smile back. I was dreading a scene. Normally Dad didn't like
surprise guests, which ordinarily was fine because he never once had any,
but there was no way of knowing how he was going to react. What
Anouk didn't understand was that just because Dad had once written in
a notebook that he wanted to whisper ideas into an enormous golden ear
didn't mean that he hadn't forgotten writing it two minutes later or that
ten minutes later he didn't write in a separate notebook that all he
wanted was to defecate into an enormous golden ear. You couldn't know.

We went inside. Luckily it wasn't a disgusting mess, it was only mildly
vile: books, scattered papers, a couple of days' worth of rotting food,
nothing too off-putting.

"He really is a genius," Anouk said, as if preparing them for the type
of genius who goes to the toilet on the coffee table.

"Dad!" I called out.

"Piss off!" came his throaty answer from the bedroom. Reynold and
Oscar exchanged a silent dialogue with their eyes.

"Maybe you'd better go in and get him," Anouk said.

While Reynold and Oscar made themselves uncomfortable on the
couch, refusing to recline into the cushions, I went to find Dad.

He was lying on his bed, facedown in the starfish position.

I said, "Reynold Hobbs and his son are here to see you."

Dad turned his head toward me and gave me a pretty sneer. "What
do you want?"

"I'm not kidding. Anouk thought you were going into another suicidal depressive phase and was worried about you and so she went through your journals and found the bit about you wanting to whisper big ideas into an enormous golden ear and so she convinced me to go with her and find the biggest, most golden ear in the country and amazingly she pulled it off and now they're waiting for you in the living room."

"Who's waiting?"

"Reynold Hobbs and his son, Oscar. They're waiting to hear your big ideas."

"You're shitting me."

"Nope. Take a look for yourself."

Dad lifted himself off the bed and peered around the corner. If he thought he'd do it without being seen, he was wrong. Reynold turned his head slowly to us and scratched himself listlessly—who knows if he was really itchy or merely playing a part?—and as we approached he shaded his eyes with his hand, as if Dad and I were glowing apparitions too bright for the human eye to bear.

"Hey," Dad said.

"Hey," Reynold said back.

"Anouk's been telling us you've got some great unrealized ideas you thought we'd be interested in," Oscar said.

"We're not wasting our time here, are we?" Reynold asked.

"No, you're not wasting your time," he said. "I swear on my son's life."

"Dad," I said.

"Just give me a minute to get my notes together. Um, Anouk, can you come in here for a sec?"

Dad and Anouk went into Dad's bedroom and closed the door. I wanted to follow them inside, but I didn't want Reynold and Oscar to think I was afraid to be alone with them, even though I was afraid to be alone with them. We all kind of nodded at each other, but nodding gets old after a few seconds. So I said, "I wonder what's keeping them?" and I went into the bedroom, where Anouk sat on Dad's bed while he knelt on the floor, bent over a collection of old black notebooks, frantically turning pages. It was a disturbing sight. I could hear him hiss: he was leaking anxiety. Anouk made a face at me, a face overloaded with dread.

"What are you standing there for?" Dad snapped at me without looking up.

"Are you ready?"

"He hasn't picked an idea yet," Anouk said.

"They're waiting."

"I know!"

"You swore on my life, remember?"

"All right," Anouk said, "let's everybody calm down."

There was a knock on the door. .

"Turn off the light!" Dad whispered to me urgently.

"Dad, they saw us go in."

"Why do I care anyway? This is foolishness."

Dad picked up a handful of notebooks and went out into the living room. Anouk and I followed. Dad sat on the armchair, leafing through one of his notebooks slowly, making clicking noises with his tongue. "So . . . yes . . . the idea . . . I have a couple that I thought you'd be interested in . . ."

He shuffled through to the last page and snapped it shut—seems the idea wasn't there after all, because he pulled out another black notebook, identical to the first. And again, flying through the pages, clicking his tongue, eyeballs sweating. That notebook also failed to produce. Another pocket held a third small black notebook. "I just . . . oh yeah, this is something you'll—no, probably not . . . Hang on . . . just one more second . . . one more second . . . I swear . . . five seconds—five, four, three, two, one, and the winner is . . . um, just one more second." A tiny worm of a smile slid onto Reynold's face. I wanted to stamp it out with the foot of an elephant. At the best of times I hated watching my father squirm in a hell of his own construct, but in the face of derision from outsiders, it was unbearable. Dad was in a frenzy trying to break out of this paralysis of indecision, when Reynold snapped his fingers. Twice. That must be how rich people get things done, I thought. It worked. Dad stopped and immediately read what was written on the page he happened to have open at that exact moment.

"Idea for a cannibal-themed restaurant—every piece of food is shaped like a part of the human anatomy."

The idea hung in the air. It was idiotic. No one responded, because there was no reason to. Dad's eyes dove back to his notebook and continued to search. Reynold didn't snap his fingers again. He didn't have to. Dad started anticipating the fingers and would stop randomly at an idea and read it out loud.

"Drug education—have schoolchildren spend a week living with a junkie in a falling-down squat. Child will watch junkie shoot up, vomit, steal from his own family, break out in sores, and finally overdose. Child will write a report of five hundred words and read it at junkie's funeral, which will be part of the daily school excursion. Every time a junkie dies, the class has to bury him, until association of heroin with death is embedded in the unconscious minds of the children."

He wasn't thinking. He was just spewing out ideas. And none of the good ones.

"Introduce conscription for community service where we let the homeless live in the homes of bankers and take the mentally ill off the streets and let them shit in the bathrooms of those in the advertising industry."

"Next," Reynold said quietly.

"Electronically tag celebrities like cattle, so when they're walking down the street—"

"Next."

"Based on car emissions and usage of water, sprays, and nonrecyclable materials, calculate how much damage each individual is doing to the environment and record it against that person's name and sentence him or her to spend an equivalent in hours or money in doing something to repair the environment."

Reynold's eyes flickered just enough to let you know he was thinking. "How do you make money on that?"

"You can't."

"Next."

"Make every man, woman, and child in this country a millionaire."

Reynold didn't say anything, and he said it with his eyes. His disdain became another entity in the room. "Even if you could do that," he said, "why would you want to?"

It was a fair question. Dad was about to answer when Reynold said, "OK, Martin. We've heard you out. Now I want you to hear us out—is that fair?"

"All right."

"We want to do a television special on Terry Dean. The real story, you know? Stuff we haven't heard. Maybe a miniseries. Over two big nights. The story as you've never heard it before."

The name of his brother made Dad stiffen up so he looked packed in ice. "So who's stopping you?" he said, distressed.

"You are. We have the police and media reports from the time, but everyone else who was there died in the fire. You're the ultimate insider. We can't do it without your contribution. There's so much we don't know."

"Is that why you came?"

"Yes."

So this was how Anouk had convinced these two media giants to come home and listen to my father's inane ideas. What a miscalculation! We all sat for the longest time in the most dreadful, ominous silence, during which I was afraid Dad might try to strangle every neck in the room. He shut his eyes, then opened them again. After several more minutes passed and it became obvious Dad wasn't going to say another word, Oscar said, "Well, we'll be off."

Once they were gone, Dad rose from his chair as if levitating, walked out of the house, and disappeared into the labyrinth. Anouk ran after him. I didn't move for an hour, struck immobile by visions of my father killing himself or doing some fucked-up thing that would get him interned for another round in a mental hospital, and I'm ashamed to say the thought of these appalling things didn't frighten or sadden me as much as they bored me to tears. That's how sick of him I was.

IX

I hadn't seen or heard from the Inferno in almost a week. I played a waiting game with the telephone and lost. It had become, in my mind, a weird surrogate for her, a plastic representation. The telephone was silent because she was silent. I began to hate the telephone, as if she had sent it to me as her delegate because she was too important to come herself.

Shuffling around the labyrinth, I decided to bother Anouk. Shortly after we moved into the house, Dad had given her a spare room to use as a studio. Apart from being both sexy and annoying, Anouk was an artist of sorts, a sculptress. She was really into depicting the subjugation of women, the emasculation of men, and the subsequent ascension of women to a higher plane of consciousness. That is to say, the room was full of vaginas and dissected penises. It was an unsettling potpourri of genitalia; there were thin limping penises dressed in rags, bloody lifeless penises made to look like dead soldiers on a gloomy battlefield, penises with nooses tied around the shaft, charcoal drawings of terrified penises, melancholy penises, penises weeping at the funerals of dead penises . . . but they were nothing next to the victorious vaginas! Vaginas with wings, great ascending vaginas, twinkling vaginas flecked with golden light, vaginas on green stems with yellow petals protruding in place of pubic hair, vaginas with wide grinning mouths; there were dancing clay vaginas, exultant plaster-of-Paris vaginas, blissful candle vaginas with a wick like a tampon string. The most terrifying words you could hear in our house came out of Anouk's mouth when you had a birthday coming up. "I'm making you something," she'd say, and no smile was wide enough to conceal the oceans of dread bubbling underneath.

Anouk was lying on her daybed making SAVE THE FOREST signs when I shuffled in. I didn't bother asking what forest.

"Hey, you free tonight?" she asked.

"Today's not the day to ask me to save anything," I said. "The way I'm feeling right now, wholesale destruction is more in my line."

"It's not for that. I'm doing the lighting for a play."

Of course she was. Anouk was the busiest person I knew. She began every day making long lists of things to do, which by the end of the day she had actually done. She filled every minute of her life with meetings, protests, yoga, sculpting, rebirthing, reiki, dance classes; she joined organizations, she left organizations in a fury; she handed out pamphlets and still managed to squeeze in disastrous relationships. More than anyone I've ever known, she had a life rooted in activity.

"I don't know, Anouk. Is it a professional play?"

"What do you mean?"

What did I mean? I meant that I respect the right of anyone to stand up onstage and speak in a booming voice, but that doesn't make it a tolerable night out. From previous experience I could say without prejudice that Anouk's friends took amateur theater to new, incomprehensible lows.

"Is Dad speaking to you?" I asked.

"Of course."

"I thought after the other night he might have been inclined to murder you."

"Not at all. He's fine."

"He's fine? I thought he was depressed and suicidal."

"So are you coming to the play or not? In fact, I'm not giving you an option. You're coming, that's all there is to it."

•

There's theater, there's amateur theater, and then there's just a group of people who bump into each other in a dark room and make you pay for the privilege of cringing for two hours. This was that kind, and every second hurt.

Anouk was responsible for the operation of a single spotlight, which she swung around the stage as if she were looking for an escaped prisoner going over the wall. Forty minutes in and I had exhausted all my sudden-apocalypse fantasies, so I swiveled around in my seat and looked at the faces of the audience. The faces I saw seemed to be enjoying the play. My bewilderment was indescribable. Then I really thought my eyes were playing tricks on me: sitting in the back row of the hall, perched on the edge of his chair, also seeming to enjoy the play, was Oscar Hobbs.

A loud, unbelievable laugh from one of the actors distracted me. It was the worst pretend laugh I'd ever heard, and I had to see who was responsible. For the next twenty minutes I was held spellbound by this minor character—his inauthentic smile, some plainly hilarious eyebrow acting, and then a whole scene of tearless sobbing—and when the play finished, the lights were turned on, the audience was applauding (perhaps *sincerely*) and I scanned the room in time to see Oscar Hobbs sneak out the back door.

The next day in the morning paper there was, surprisingly, a review of the play. It astonished everyone involved in the production—a play that small and shoddy in a theater that foul and dingy didn't usually attract professional reviewers as much as it attracted homeless people looking for some soup, and having so little faith in the professionalism of their own work, the organizers hadn't bothered to alert the media. The strangest and most suspicious thing wasn't the review itself but the content: it focused solely on the play's lighting: "deeply atmospheric," "moody and arresting," and "bold and shadowy." Everyone who read it agreed it was the silliest they'd ever seen. The actors, the director, and the writer weren't mentioned. Anouk was startled both by having been singled out in the review and by the ugly and childish reaction of her colleagues, who turned on her viciously, accusing her of planting the review, bribing a journalist, and "showing off with the spotlight."

Anouk was confused, though I wasn't. I'd seen Oscar Hobbs at the hall, and it wasn't hard to see his fingerprints all over this thing. What did I make of it? It was no more than amusing. The gods can step down and salivate over the mortals like the rest of us, can't they? Anouk had one of those bodies that demanded, as a man, your rapt attention, and Oscar Hobbs was just a man, after all. As I said, it was amusing, nothing more, and while I enjoy watching the befuddlement of my family, friends, and peers, I can't hold on to secrets for very long. So that night, after Anouk hung up the phone at the end of a long argument with the play's producer, I told her.

"Why didn't you tell me?" she screamed.

"I just did."

She scrunched up her face so her eyes, nose, and mouth were no bigger than a mandarin.

"What the hell does he want?" she said quietly.

I gestured at her body and said, "Take a guess."

"But he can get anyone he wants!"

"Maybe because of something you said to him in the casino. What did you say?"

"Nothing."

"Come on."

"All right," she said. "I told him his soul's got one of those stains on it that smudges when you try to wipe it clean."

•

Two days later I was at work, standing outside the building smoking a cigarette with my boss, Smithy, and I was thinking I'd have to leave the job soon and I'd never forgive myself if I didn't announce my coworkers' faults on the way out. I was wondering whether they'd give me a quitting-in-a-huff party when I saw a Porsche Spyder drive up to a no-stopping zone and stop there. It was the kind of car James Dean died in. It was a nice car. I'd die in there too, if I could afford it.

Smithy said, "Feast your eyes on that."

"I'm feasting."

Oscar stepped out of the car and walked up to us. "Jasper."

"You're Oscar Hobbs!" Smithy said in shock.

"That's right," he said back.

"That must be the problem with being famous," I said. "Everyone tells you your own name."

"Jasper. Can I talk to you a minute?"

"Sure," I answered and, turning to Smithy, excused myself. Smithy nodded at me enthusiastically, still wearing that shell-shocked face, the one that looked as if he'd just found a vagina among his own genitalia.

Oscar and I stepped into a small patch of sunlight. He looked nervous.

"I feel kind of funny coming to see you about this."

"About what?" I asked, sensing the answer.

"Anouk came into my office and really let me have it for that review."

"She did?"

"I also made sure the media reported an environmental demonstration she went on. But she was furious. I don't understand it. She really hates me, doesn't she?"

"It's not personal. She hates the rich."

"How can I get her to like me?"

"If you could demonstrate that you're oppressed in some way, that would help."

He nodded rhythmically, as if to a beat.

"What do you really want with Anouk, anyway? It seems that you're making a lot of effort here. I've seen the women you go for. Anouk's nice, and she has her own style of beauty, but it doesn't really make any sense. You can rake in the über-women anytime you like. What gives?"

"The thing is, Jasper, the world is full of ordinary people. Some are beautiful, some are not. What's rare is extraordinary, interesting, original, and creative people who think their own thoughts. Now, while waiting for this extraordinary woman, if I have to spend my time with an ordinary woman, do you think I'd be with a beautiful ordinary woman or an unattractive ordinary woman?"

There was no need to answer that, so I didn't.

"Women like Anouk are rarer than you think."

After he left, Smithy said, with forced nonchalance, "How do you know Oscar Hobbs?" and I said, "You know, from around," and because

I'm as pitiful as the next man, with the same howling ego, I felt for the rest of that day like someone important.

Still, I was confounded. This man wasn't just running after Anouk like a snorting dragon, he was actually infatuated with her, and she was shooting him down! Power may be an aphrodisiac, but one's own prejudice is a turnoff, and evidently the more potent of the two. I remember her dragging me once to a rally where the speaker said the media barons were in the pocket of the government, and then a month later to another rally where this speaker said the government was in the pockets of the media barons (she agreed with both), and I remember trying to explain to her that it only looks like they are, because by coincidence the government and the newspapers just happen to have the exact same agenda: to scare the shit out of people and then to keep them in constant freezing terror. She didn't care. She decreed her everlasting hatred for both groups, and nothing could persuade her otherwise. I began to think of Oscar's rich and handsome face as an amusing test of the strength and vitality of her prejudices.

•

I arrived home around sunset and walked dreamily through the advancing shadows of the labyrinth. It was one of my favorite times in the bush—the edge of night. As I approached my hut, I saw the Towering Inferno on the veranda waiting for me. We hurried inside and made love and I studied her face vigilantly during it, to make sure she wasn't thinking of anyone other than me. To be honest, I couldn't tell.

Half an hour later a voice was at the door. "Knock knock," the voice said.

I grimaced. It was Dad this time. I climbed out of bed and opened the door. He was in a bathrobe he'd bought months earlier, and the price tag was still hanging off the sleeve.

"Hey, tell me something about that girlfriend of yours," he said.

"Shhh, she's asleep." I stepped onto the veranda and closed the door behind me. "What about her?" I asked.

"Is she on the pill?"

"What business could that possibly be of yours?"

"Is she?"

"As it happens, she's not. She has an allergic reaction to it."

"Great!"

I took a deep breath, determined to bear him with as much patience as I had stored in my depths. His grin drained the pool.

"All right. You win. I'm curious. Why is it great that my girlfriend is not on the pill? And this better be good."

"Because that means you use condoms."

"Dad. *So fucking what?*"

"So—can I borrow some?"

"Condoms? What for?"

"To put on my—"

"I know what they're for! I just—I thought prostitutes brought their own condoms."

"You don't think I can sleep with anyone who isn't a prostitute?"

"No, I don't."

"You don't think I can attract a regular citizen?"

"As I said, no."

"What a son!"

"Dad," I began, but I couldn't think of an end to that sentence.

"Anyway," he said, "have you got any?"

I went into my bedroom and grabbed a couple of condoms from the bedside table and took them back to him.

"Just two?"

"All right, take the whole pack. Have a party. I'm not a pharmacy, you know."

"Thank you."

"Wait—this woman. It is a woman, isn't it?"

"Of course it's a woman."

"Is she in the house now?"

"Yes."

"Who is she? Where did you meet?"

"I can't see what business that could possibly be of yours," he said, and walked off the veranda with a slight lilt in his step.

Strange things were afoot. Anouk was being pursued by a man dubbed by *Guess Who* magazine as Australia's most eligible bachelor, and Dad was sleeping with unprofessional person or persons unknown. New dramas were stirring in the labyrinth.

•

The morning birds, those little feathery alarm clocks, woke me around five. The Towering Inferno wasn't in bed beside me. I could hear her crying on the veranda. I lay in bed, listening to those little deep gulping sobs. It was kind of rhythmic. Suddenly I knew what she was up to. I leapt out of bed and ran outside. I was right! She had her little mustard-sized jar pressed up against her cheek and she was depositing a new batch of tears. It was almost full now.

"This is no good," I said.

Her eyes blinked innocently. That pushed me over the edge. I stepped forward and ripped the jar out of her hand.

"Give it back!"

"You'll never get him to drink it. What are you going to tell him it is—lemonade?"

"Give it back, Jasper!"

I unscrewed the lid, gave her a defiant look, and poured the contents down my throat.

She screamed.

I swallowed.

It was awful-tasting. I tell you, those were some bitter tears.

She looked at me with such intense hatred that I realized I'd done an unforgivable thing. I thought it had the potential to curse me for life, like disturbing a mummy in his tomb. I had drunk tears that were not shed for me. What would happen to me now?

We sat in our respective corners watching the sunrise and the bursting of the day. The bush began to seethe with life. A wind picked up and the trees whispered to themselves. I could hear the Inferno thinking. I could hear her eyelids fluttering. I could hear her heart beating. I could hear the ropes and pulleys lifting the sun into the sky. At nine she rose wordlessly and dressed. She kissed me on the forehead as if I were a son she was duty-bound to forgive, and left without a word.

Not ten minutes later I sensed something, a disturbance. I strained my ears and heard distant voices. I threw on my bathrobe and left the hut and wove my way toward them.

Then I saw them together.

Dad had locked the Inferno in a conversation. Dad, a labyrinth within a labyrinth, was talking at her as if he were engaged in some vigorous activity like a tree-sawing competition. Should I do something? Should I stop him? Should I scare him away? How?

He'd better not be asking her about her allergy to the pill or about her preference for ribbed over flavored condoms, I thought. No, he wouldn't dare. But whatever he was saying, I was certain he was doing me more harm than good. I watched them anxiously for a couple more minutes, then the Inferno walked away while he was still talking. Good for her.

•

That night we were in a pub. It was a busy night, and when I went to get the drinks, I kept getting elbowed. Everyone crowded the bar, trying to get the bartender's attention. Some pushy customers waved their money in the air as if to say, "Look! I have hard currency! Serve me first! The rest of them want to pay with eggs!"

When I returned to the Inferno, she said, "We need to talk."

"I thought we were talking."

She didn't say anything to that. She didn't even confirm or deny that we had just been talking.

"Anyway," I said, "why do you need to preface talking by saying we need to talk? You want to talk? Talk!" I was getting worked up, because I knew more or less what was coming next. She was going to break up with me. Winter had entered my body all of a sudden.

"Go on," I said. "I'm listening."

"You're not going to make this easy for me, are you?"

"Of course I'm not. What am I, a saint? Do you think of me as an especially unselfish person? Do I love my enemies? Do I volunteer in soup kitchens?"

"Shut up, Jasper, and let me think."

"First you want to talk. Now you want to think. Haven't you thought this out? Didn't you at least compose a speech in your head prior to coming out tonight? Don't tell me you're improvising! Don't tell me this is something you're just winging on the spot!"

"Jesus Christ! Just be silent for one minute!"

When I sense someone is about to hurt me emotionally, it's very difficult to resist the temptation to act like a five-year-old. Right then, for example, it was everything I could do to stop myself counting down the sixty seconds out loud.

"I think we need a break," she said.

"A break meaning a lengthy pause, or a break meaning a severing?"

"I think we need to stop seeing each other."

"Has this got something to do with my father?"

"Your father?"

"I saw you talking to him this morning after you left the hut. What did he say?"

"Nothing."

"He didn't say nothing. The man has never said nothing in his life. Besides, you were talking to him for, like, ten minutes. Did he say something against me?"

"No—nothing. Honest."

"Then what's this about? Is it because I drank your tears?"

"Jasper—I'm still in love with Brian."

I didn't say anything. It didn't take a brain surgeon to work that out. Or a rocket scientist. Or an Einstein. Then I thought: I don't think brain surgeons, rocket scientists, or even Einstein are that brilliant when it comes to charting the map of human emotions. And why always brain surgeons, rocket scientists, and Einstein anyway? Why not architects or criminal lawyers? And why not, instead of Einstein, Darwin or Heinrich Böll?

"Aren't you going to say anything?"

"You're in love with your ex-boyfriend. I don't have to be Heinrich Böll to work that out."

"Who?"

I shook my head, stood up, and walked out of the pub. I heard her calling my name, but I didn't turn around.

Outside, I broke into tears. What a hassle! Now I'd have to become rich and successful just so she could regret dumping me. That's another thing to do in this short, busy life. Christ. They're adding up.

I couldn't believe the relationship was over. And the sex! That fortuitous conjunction of our bodies, finished! I supposed it was better this way. I really never wanted anyone to shout at me, "I gave you the best years of my life!" This way, the best years of her life were still ahead of her.

And why? Maybe she *was* pissed off that I had drunk her tears and *was* in love with her ex-boyfriend, but I knew Dad had said something that had pushed her over the edge. What had he said? What the fuck had he said? That's it, I thought. I don't care what he does—he can write a handbook of crime, put in a suggestion box, set a town on fire, smash up a nightclub, be interned in a mental hospital, build a labyrinth, but he absolutely cannot touch one hair on the head of my love life.

He was a stinky concentrated form of pandemonium and I would no longer let him ruin my life. If the Inferno could break up with me, I could break up with *him*. I don't care what anybody says, you absolutely can break up with family.

I went home planning to gather up all the particles of energy I could muster and release them right in his fucking face!

I marched straight into his house. The lights were off. I unlocked the door and sneaked in. I heard a strange sound from his bedroom. He must be crying again. But it didn't sound like mere crying. It sounded like sobbing. Well, so what? I hardened myself against the lure of sympathy. I went and opened the door, and what I saw was so shocking, I didn't have the common decency to close the door. Dad was in bed with Anouk.

"Get out!" he screamed.

I just couldn't get my head around it. "How long has this been going on?" I asked.

"Jasper, get the fuck out of here!" Dad yelled again.

I know I should have, but my feet seemed to be as dumbfounded as my head. "What a joke!"

"Why is this a joke?" Dad asked.

"What's she getting out of it?"

"Jasper, leave us alone!" Anouk shouted.

I stepped back out of the room and slammed the door. This was really insulting. Anouk hadn't wanted to sleep with me and yet she had jumped into bed with my father. And ewww—with *my* condoms! And what was she doing with Dad when Oscar Hobbs had been trying to get into her bed? Was some pitiful soap opera going on? Dad was a man who had spent the majority of his life absent from human relationships, who finally embarked on one with his only confidant, merely to find himself as the dullest point of a love triangle where, if logic prevailed, he would lose her.

Well, this was no longer my problem.

•

The next morning I woke early. I decided the practical thing would be to find a room in a share house with junkies, something cheap and afford-able so I wouldn't drain my meager savings just on shelter. I answered a bunch of ads in the newspaper. There weren't many that didn't specifi-cally ask for, in capital letters, a FEMALE. It seemed to be common knowledge that men hadn't made the right kind of evolutionary leap, the one that allowed them to tidy up after themselves. The apartments and houses that did permit males to exist there weren't so bad, but they all had people living in them. Of course I knew this beforehand, but it wasn't until I was face-to-face with the other humans that I realized I needed to be alone. We were expected to be civil to each other, not just once in a while, but *every day*. And what if I wanted to sit in my under-wear and stare out the kitchen window for six hours? No, the solitude of living in a hut in the center of a labyrinth had ruined me for cohabita-tion.

In the end I decided on a studio apartment and took the first one I saw. One room and a bathroom and a partition between the main area and the little kitchen, which ran alongside a wall. It was nothing to get excited about. There was not one feature of it about which you could say, "But look at this! It has a _____ !" It had nothing. It was just a room. I signed the lease, paid the rent and the security deposit, and took the keys. I went inside and sat in the empty room on the floor and smoked one cigarette after another. I rented a van and drove home to my hut and threw all my possessions worth keeping into it.

Then I went up to the house. Dad was standing in the kitchen wear-ing his dressing gown that *still* had the price tag on. He was whistling atonally while cooking pasta.

"Where's Anouk?" I asked.

"Not sure."

Maybe with Oscar Hobbs, I thought.

The pasta sauce was spluttering, and in another pan he seemed to be overboiling vegetables so as to bleed every last nuance of flavor out of them. He gazed at me with a rare look of affection and said, "I under-stand you were a bit shocked. We should've told you. But anyway, you know now. Hey—maybe the four of us can go out sometime?"

"The four of who?"

"Anouk and me and you and your plaything."

"Dad, I'm leaving."

"I didn't mean tonight."

"No. I'm leaving leaving."

"Leaving leaving? You mean . . . leaving?"

"I've found an apartment in the city. A studio."

"You already found a place?"

"Yeah—put down a security deposit and the first two weeks' rent."

There was a shiver running through him, a shiver I could see.

"And you're moving out when?"

"Now."

"Right now?"

"I've come to say goodbye."

"What about your stuff?"

"I hired a van. I packed everything I need."

Dad stretched his limbs strangely, and in a dull, artificial voice he said, "You're not giving me much say in the matter."

"I suppose not."

"What about your hut?"

"I'm not taking it with me."

"No, I mean . . ."

He didn't finish the sentence. He didn't know what he meant. Dad started breathing heavily through his nostrils. He was trying not to look wretched. I was trying not to feel guilty. I knew that by losing me he was losing the only person who understood him. But I was guilty for other reasons too; I wondered what was going to happen to his mind. And how could I leave him with that face? That sad and lonely and terrified face?

"You need help moving?"

"No, it's OK."

It was as if we had been playing a game all our lives and the game was ending, and we were going to take off our masks and our uniforms and shake hands and say, "Great game."

But we didn't.

Suddenly all my bitterness and hatred for him evaporated. I felt enormously sorry for him. I saw him as a spider who woke up thinking he was a fly and didn't understand he was caught in his own web.

"Well, I'd better get going," I said.

"Do you have a phone number?"

"Not yet. I'll call you when I get the phone on."

"Right. Well, bye."

"See ya."

As I turned and walked out, Dad let out a little rumbling grunt, like the sound of troubled bowels.

FIVE

Author's note: My original version of this chapter went hurtling into the shredder as soon as I discovered among my father's papers the first five chapters of his unfinished autobiography. I'd just finished pouring out my entire story and I was frankly annoyed—mostly because his account covered this period better than my version of the events. Not only was his version more concise, because it did not contain my long digression on the recent glut of calendars featuring sexy priests, but I was irritated that Dad's version of events contradicted much of my own, and even some of the previous chapter (four), which I'd really labored over. Nevertheless, under the influence of my two guiding stars, impatience and laziness, I've not amended any part of Chapter Four, and decided to print Dad's unfinished autobiography here, slightly edited, as Chapter Five. My version of Chapter Five is still around somewhere—I didn't really throw it in the shredder. Hopefully, in years to come it will be of curiosity value—to the highest bidder.

~~My Life by Martin Dean~~
~~A Loner's Story by Martin Dean~~
~~A Loser's Story by Martin Dean~~
~~Born to Be Snide by Martin Dean~~
Untitled Autobiography of Martin Dean by Martin Dean

Chapter One

Why write this autobiography? Because it's the privilege of my class. Now before you start screaming, I'm not talking about working, middle-, or upper-middle class. I'm talking about the real class struggle: the celebrity vs. the ordinary schmo. Like it or not, *I* am a celebrity, and that means that *you* are interested in how many sheets of toilet paper *I* use to wipe my arse, whereas I have no interest in whether *you* wipe your arse at all or just leave it as is. You know how the relationship works. Let's not pretend it's any different.

All celebrities who write their biographies play the same trick on readers: they tell you some terrible degrading truth about themselves, putting you in a position where you think they must be honest chaps, then they turn on the lies. I won't do that. I'll tell you only the truth, even if I come off smelling like lawn fertilizer. And, just so you know, I understand that an autobiography should cover the early years of my life (e.g., Martin Dean was born on such-and-such a date, went to such-and-such a school, accidentally got such-and-such a woman pregnant, and so on), but I won't be doing that either. My life up until one year ago is none of your business. Instead, I'll start from where my life was at the moment when the great change occurred.

•

I was forty-one at the time, unemployed and living off child support even though I was the parent. Admittedly, this is not the spirit that has made our country great, but it is the spirit that has made it so you can go to the beach on a weekday and see it full of people. Once a week I would make myself busy at the dole office showing them a list of jobs I hadn't gone for, and this was taking increasing amounts of energy and imagination. I tell you, the jobs out there are getting harder and harder not to get. Some bosses will hire anyone!

On top of this, I was going through the humiliating process of aging. Everywhere I went I met my memories, and I had that old sinking feeling of betrayal, of having betrayed my destiny. I wasted many months thinking about my death, until it began to feel like the death of a great-uncle I didn't know I had. It was at this time I became addicted to talk-back radio, listening to mostly elderly people who stepped out of their houses one day and just didn't recognize anything, and the more I listened to their interminable griping, the more I realized they were, in their way, doing the same thing I was: protesting the present as if it were a future one still has the option of voting against.

There were no two ways about it: I was in a crisis. But recent shifts in behavioral patterns of different age groups had made it difficult for me to determine what type of crisis I was in. How could it be a midlife crisis when the forties were the new twenties, the fifties were the new thirties, and the sixties were the new forties? Where the fuck was I? I had to read the lifestyle supplement in the Sunday papers to make sure I wasn't actually going through puberty.

If only that was the worst of it!

I suddenly was mortified by how ridiculous I was to live in a labyrinth of my own design. I was scared I would one day be remembered for it, and equally terrified I would not be remembered at all, unlike my fucking brother, who was *still* being talked about, still the focus of my countrymen's affections, still popping up in semischolarly books about the characters that typify Australia, in paintings, novels, comic books, documentaries, telemovies, and the occasional student thesis. In fact, my brother had become an industry. I went to the library and found no fewer than seventeen books that chronicled (incorrectly) the Terry Dean story, as well as countless references to him in books on Australian sport, Australian crime, and those that tackled the tedious, narcissistic topic of pinning down our cultural identity. And the pinnacle of *my* creative life was to build a stupid labyrinth!

I wondered why nobody had stopped me. I wondered why my friend Eddie loaned me the money so willingly, knowing full well that a man who lives in a labyrinth of his own design must necessarily go mad. On top of which, I had not paid him back, and since then he had *continued* to support me. In fact, when I thought about it, he had mercilessly loaned me money ever since I'd met him in Paris, and worse than that, he had brutally, without conscience, never asked for it back. Never! I became convinced that he had an ulterior motive. I worked myself up into a paranoid frenzy about it, and I realized that I hated my closest friend. When I thought about his gestures and expressions in my company, it occurred to me that he hated me too, and I thought friends must hate each other the world over and I shouldn't be bothered by it, but I *was* bothered by this sudden conviction that Eddie actually loathed me. I was bothered by the question of why the hell I'd never noticed it before.

To top this off, I found to my shame that I had all but lost interest in my son as a person. I don't know why, exactly. Maybe the novelty of seeing what my eyes and nose looked like on someone else's face had finally worn off. Or maybe because I felt there was something sleazy, gutless, restless, and horny about my son, something that I recognized in myself. Or maybe because despite a lifetime of my trying to wield my personality as an influence on him, he'd managed to turn out utterly different from me. He somehow became dreamy and positive and took sunsets dead seriously, as though the outcome of the event might not always be that the sun sets but that it might freeze just above the horizon and start going up again. He seemed to be amused by walking in the outdoors, listening to the earth, and fondling plants. Imagine! A son of mine! Isn't that a reason to turn away? Maybe, but to be honest, the reason I lost interest in him is that he'd lost interest in me.

I was increasingly unable to talk to him, or even at him, and more and more regularly the intervals of silence between us lengthened, and then I couldn't utter a single word without disgusting him, or make even a single sound, not even "Oh" or "Hmm." In every look and gesture, I could feel he was accusing me of every possible parenting crime there is short of infanticide. He absolutely refused to talk to me about his love life, sex life, work life, social life, or inner life. In fact, there were now so many subjects he forbade me to discuss, I was waiting for him to outlaw "Good morning." I thought: It's not my conversation he finds distasteful, it's my very existence. If I greeted him smiling, he'd frown. If I frowned, he'd smile. He was fervently working to become my mirror opposite. What ingratitude! After all I'd tried to teach him: that there are four kinds of people in this world, those who are obsessed by love, those who have it, those who laugh at retarded people when they are children, and those who laugh at them right into adulthood and old age. A veritable wisdom bonanza, right? But this ungrateful son of mine had chosen to reject everything, totally. Of course, I knew he couldn't help but be confused by the contradictory directives I'd boomed at him his whole life: Don't follow the herd, I'd preached, but don't be as miserably apart as I've been. Where could he go? Neither of us knew. But look—even if you're a total shit of a parent, you are still burdened by your children, still vulnerable to the pain of their suffering. Believe me, even if you suffer from your chair in front of the television, you still suffer.

This was where I was placed psychologically when the great change occurred.

•

I wasn't feeling well. It wasn't anything I could put my finger on. I didn't feel nauseous and I wasn't in any pain. I didn't have any buildup of phlegm or odd-colored feces. It was completely different from both my childhood illness and the time my mother slipped rat poison into my food. I just felt a little off-kilter, a similar feeling to the one I had when I realized four months late that I'd forgotten my own birthday. But was there really nothing physically wrong with me? Well, there was one thing, though it was more odd than anything else. I detected a faint, strange odor rising out of my skin. Very faint. Hardly an odor at all, really. Sometimes I couldn't smell it. But other times I caught a whiff and yelled out, "There it is again!"

One morning I worked out what it was.

Anyone with an overactive imagination, in particular a perversely negative one, need never be surprised by anything. The imagination absolutely can catch out imminent disasters as they're warming up, especially if you keep your nostrils open. People who can accurately read the future: are they gifted at seeing or gifted at guessing? This is just what my imagination did that morning. It saw all the possible tomorrows, then narrowed them down in a short instant to only one. That one I spoke aloud: "Fuck me! I've got a terminal disease!"

I guessed further—cancer. It had to be cancer; it couldn't be anything other than cancer, because it was always cancer that haunted my waking nightmares, ever since I saw my mother devoured by that king of diseases. Even if you fear death on a daily basis, there are certain deaths that you dismiss—scurvy, giant squid, falling piano—but no one with a brain cell left rattling in his head can ever dismiss cancer.

So! This was it! Death! I always knew that one day my body would kick the shit out of me! My whole life I'd felt like a lone soldier trapped in hostile territory. Everywhere were enemies to my cause—back, legs, kidneys, lungs, heart—and they would eventually conclude that the only way to kill me was a kamikaze mission. All of us were going down.

I rushed out of the house and drove fast out of the labyrinth. Speeding through the green suburbs, I was horrified to see that everything was bathed in gorgeous summer sunlight. Of course it was—nothing brings out sunshine faster than cancer. I took myself straight to the doctor's. I hadn't been for years and I went to the one closest to my house. I needed any doctor, just as long as he wasn't too fat (one must be as suspicious of obese doctors as of bald hairdressers). I didn't need him to be a genius either; I just needed him to confirm what I already knew. DR. P. SWEENY the brass plaque said on the door. I sprinted into his office. It was dark inside, the dark of a room in which everything is brown: the furniture, the carpet, the doctor's mood. Brown. He was there drumming his fingers on his desk, a middle-aged man with a placid expression and a full head of thick brown hair. He was one of those men who never go bald, who go to the grave needing a haircut.

"I'm Dr. Peter Sweeny," he said.

"I know you're a doctor. You don't have to wave it in my face. Don't you know the title is only useful for directing mail, to distinguish you from all the unpretentious Mr. Peter Sweenys of the world?"

The doctor reclined his head a couple of millimeters, as if I had been spitting.

"Sorry," I said, "I guess I'm a little stressed out. So what if you call yourself doctor? You worked hard for the right to plunge your hand inside the human body! Elbow deep in viscera all day, maybe you want to let everyone know you're a doctor so they won't offer you offal or a plate of haggis. What right have I to cast judgment on a man's prefix?"

"You seem pretty wound up, there. What can I do for you?"

"I'm pretty sure I have cancer," I said. "And I just want you to do whatever you have to do to confirm or deny it."

"What kind of cancer do you think you have?"

"What kind? I don't know. What's the worst sort?"

"Well, prostate cancer's the most common for men in your age bracket."

"You're the same age as me!"

"OK—*our* age bracket."

"Well, my cancer won't be the most common, that much I can tell you. What's the worst one? And I mean the absolute worst."

"Do you smoke?"

"Sometimes."

"If I smoked, the cancer I wouldn't want for myself, for fear of kicking myself all the way to the grave, is lung cancer."

"Lung cancer. I knew it! That's the one. That's what I've got."

"You seem pretty certain."

"I am certain."

Even though he was obscured behind his desk, he made a shift as though he'd put his hand on his hip. "All right," he said finally, "I'll order the tests. They aren't pleasant."

"Neither is lung cancer."

"You're right about that."

•

I won't detail the weeks that followed—the intrusive tests, the cruel waiting periods, the stomach-pummeling anxiety. Of course Jasper didn't notice anything, but Anouk sensed something was wrong. She kept hounding me to tell her what it was, but I was tight-lipped about it. I wanted to be 100 percent sure before I told anyone. I didn't want to get their hopes up.

It was a month later when I went back to Dr. Sweeny's office to hear the results. In the waiting period I had been plagued with hope, and nothing I could do could put those pesky optimistic feelings to rest.

"Come in, Mr. Dean. How are you feeling?"

"Let's not waste time. It's cancer, isn't it?"

"It sure is."

In the old days the medical profession didn't tell you that you were dying. It was considered a breach of ethics. Now the reverse is true. Now they can't wait to tell you.

"Lung cancer?"

"I'm afraid so. How did you know?"

Christ! It was true! I was being murdered *by my own body*! I burst out laughing.

Then I stopped laughing—I remembered why I had started.

•

I left the doctor's office in a daze. So! It turned out my lifelong pessimistic stance was entirely justified. Imagine if I had been optimistic all this time! Wouldn't I be feeling ripped off right about now? Yes, I was in for a slow, violent death. And I don't sleep peacefully, so dying peacefully in my sleep was out of the question. The best I could hope for was that maybe I'd die fitfully in my sleep. Oh my God—suddenly all the other possible deaths had slipped into the unlikely. How often does a man dying of cancer suddenly choke to death on a chicken bone? Or get decapitated by jumping up and down on his bed, forgetful of the ceiling fan? Or die from asbestos poisoning or obesity? No, there just wasn't enough time to get really, fatally fat. If anything, my illness was probably going to make me thinner.

Over the following weeks I was an emotional wreck. The slightest thing sent me into tears. I cried at television ads, at the autumn leaves turning brown. One night Jasper came in and caught me sobbing over the death of some idiotic pop star I'd never even heard of. He'd been shot in the head and died instantly, lucky bastard!

What made me cry was the fear that I'd be unable to kill myself when my quality of life dropped below par, when my daily task became choosing between pain and painkillers, between the ravages of the disease and the destruction of the treatment. Even with my lifelong meditation on death, my existence had still seemed something permanent and stable on the planet Earth—something dependable, like igneous rock. Now that cancers were metastasizing to their heart's content, atheism seemed like a pretty cruel thing to do to myself. I begged my brain to reconsider. I thought: Won't I survive somewhere, in some form? Can I believe it? Please? Pretty please can I believe in the everlasting soul? In heaven or angels or paradise with sixteen beautiful virgins waiting for me? Pretty please can I believe that? Look, I don't even need the sixteen beautiful virgins. There could be just one woman, old and ugly, and she doesn't even have to be a virgin, she could be the town bike of the ever-after. In fact, there could be no women at all, and it doesn't have to be paradise, it could be a wasteland—hell, it could even *be* hell, because while suffering the torments of a lake of fire, at least I'd be around to yell "Ouch!" Could I believe in that, please?

All the other afterlife scenarios are just not comforting. Reincarnation without continuance of this consciousness—I just don't see the point in getting excited about it. And the least comforting eternity scenario of all time, one that is growing daily in popularity, one that people never stop telling me about, is that I will die but my energy will live on.

My *energy*, ladies and gentlemen.

Is my energy going to read books and see movies? Is my energy going to sink languidly into a hot bath or laugh until its sides ache? Let's be clear: I die, my *energy* scatters and dissolves into Mother Earth. And I'm supposed to be thrilled by this idea? That's as good to me as if you told me my brain and body die but my body odor lives on to stink up future generations. I mean, really. My energy.

But can't I prolong my existence anywhere? My actual existence, not some positively charged shadow? No, I just can't convince myself that the soul is anything other than the romantic name we have given to consciousness so we can believe it doesn't tear or stain.

So, then, the rest of my life was going to be an accumulation of physical pain, mental anguish, and suffering. Normally I could handle it. But the problem was, until I died I'd be thinking only about my death. I decided that if I couldn't spend one single day without thinking, I'd kill myself. Why not? Why should I struggle against my death? I couldn't possibly win. And even if by some miracle I did beat this round with cancer, what about the next? And the next? I have no talent for futility. What's the point of fighting a losing battle? To give a man dignity? I have no talent for dignity either. Never saw the point in it, and when I hear someone say, "At least I have my dignity," I think, "You just lost it by saying that."

The next day I woke and resolved not to think about anything the whole day. Then I thought: I'm thinking now, aren't I? Then I thought: My death my death my death my death my gruesome painful sobbing death!

Fuck!

I had to do it. I would kill myself.

And I had an idea: maybe I should kill myself publicly. Why not fob off my suicide on one cause or another, pretending to die in protest over, I don't know, the WTO's wasteful agricultural policies, or third world debt, anything. Remember the photograph of that self-immolating monk? Now there's an enduring image! Even if you're killing yourself so your family will be sorry, pick a worthy cause, call the media, find a public spot, and kill yourself. Then even if your life has been a totally meaningless affair, your death doesn't have to be.

The following morning by chance the radio told me that there was a protest on in the city around lunchtime. Unfortunately, it wasn't a protest against the WTO's wasteful agricultural policies or about erasing third world debt, it was about primary school teachers wanting a pay raise and more vacation. I tried to see the bright side. That was as worth dying for as anything, wasn't it? I didn't suppose any of the teachers themselves were passionate enough to self-immolate, but I imagined they'd welcome my contribution to their cause. I found an old canvas bag and threw in a can of petrol, a lighter in the shape of a woman's torso, and some painkillers. I wasn't trying to cheat death; I was hoping to cheat pain.

Sydney is one of the most beautiful modern cities in the world, but I always manage to find myself at the corner of Drab and Bleak Streets, and always in the section of the city where there's nowhere to sit down, so I spent the morning walking and staring into people's faces as I passed by them, thinking, "See you soon!" I was going to die now, but by the look of those triple chins, I knew they wouldn't be far behind.

I arrived at the protest around twelve. It was a poor turnout. Forty or so people were holding up signs demanding respect. I didn't think anybody who had to demand respect ever got it. There were a couple of television cameramen too. They looked young, probably cadets in their first year on the job. Since I didn't require a seasoned journalist who'd ducked sniper bullets in Vietnam to film me, I took a place in the protest next to a couple of angry-looking women I wouldn't want teaching my kid and psyched myself into the state I needed to be in to do myself in. All I had to do was think relentlessly negative thoughts about the inhabitants of the planet Earth. When I felt almost ready, I took out the painkillers but discovered I'd forgotten to bring a bottle of water. I walked to a nearby café and asked for a glass. "You have to eat something," a waitress said, so I ordered a late breakfast: bacon, eggs, sausages, mushrooms, baked beans, toast, and coffee. I ate too much; the food in my belly made me sleepy. I had just ordered a second espresso when I saw someone famous coming out of a restaurant on the other side of the street: an old television journalist. I vaguely remembered that this journalist had been disgraced owing to one scandal or another. What had happened? It was nagging me. Did he wet his pants on TV? Did he lie about the state of the world and say on national television that everything would work out well for everyone? No, that wasn't it.

I paid the bill and walked toward him and was just about to ask him to clarify the details of his public humiliation when a girl came out of the restaurant, flung her arms around his neck, and kissed him passionately. I thought: Sure, I've been kissed, but no one has ever flung her arms around my neck. Women have placed them there gently or lowered them over my head as if they were putting on a jumper, but never flung them. Then the girl pulled away and I recognized her too. Christ, I thought. What do these celebrities do, join forces to double their fame?

Then it hit me. She's not famous! She's my son's girlfriend!

Well, so what? Why should I care? This wasn't very big on the tragedy scale. It was just a teen drama, the type you might see on a nightly soap opera. But by being an eyewitness, I had become a character in the cheap melodrama; I had to play out my part to the end, to the dénouement. How irritating! I just wanted to peacefully self-immolate. And now I had to "get involved."

I dropped the matches and the petrol in disgust and went home, enormously relieved that an excuse for staying alive had dropped in my lap.

•

When I arrived home, Anouk was in her studio, stretched out on the daybed she'd made for herself, propped up on a mountain of pillows. I could always count on Anouk for good conversation. We each had our favorite topics, our default topics. Mine was the gnawing fear of dropping so low in my own estimation that I would no longer acknowledge myself in mirrors, but would pass on by, pretending I hadn't seen me. For Anouk it was always a new horror story from the chronicles of modern relationship hell. She often had me in stitches recounting recent love affairs, and I felt a strange pity for those men, even though they were the ones who left her. She was always creating complications for herself—putting the wrong people together, sleeping with her girlfriends' ex-boyfriends, sleeping with her ex-boyfriend's friends, always just on the line of fair play, teetering on the line, sometimes falling.

"What do you think of this girl Jasper's seeing?" I asked.

"She's beautiful."

"Is that the best we can say about her?"

"I've hardly had two words with her. Jasper keeps her hidden from us."

"That's natural. I embarrass him," I said.

"What's natural about that?"

"I embarrass myself."

"Why are you interested?"

"I saw her today—with another man."

Anouk sat up and looked at me with bright eyes. Sometimes I think the human animal doesn't really need food or water to survive, only gossip.

"Are you sure?"

"Positive."

"Did you tell him?"

"Not yet."

"Don't."

"I think I have to, don't I? I can't sit back and watch my son be made a fool of by someone other than me."

"I'll tell you what to do. Don't talk to him. Talk to her. Tell her you saw her. Tell her she has to tell him or you will."

"I don't know."

"Telling him yourself will be disastrous. If nothing else, he won't believe it. He'll think you're jealous and competing with him."

"Do you think fathers and sons compete for sex?"

"Yes, though not in the Oedipal way. Just in the ordinary way."

Anouk brought her knees up and rested her chin on them and stared at me as if debating whether to tell me I had something stuck between my teeth.

"I've had enough of relationships," she said. "I want to take some time out. I think I've become a serial monogamist. It's embarrassing. What I'd really like is a lover."

"Yes, I think that would suit you."

"A friendly fuck with someone I know."

"Good idea. Do you have anyone in mind?"

"Not sure. Maybe someone like you."

She really said this. And I really didn't get it. Slow, slow, slow. "Someone like me," I mused. "Do you know anyone like me?"

"One person."

"Like me? I wouldn't want to meet him." Jasper? It couldn't be Jasper, could it? "Who do you know like me?"

"You!"

"I'll admit there's a similarity," I said slowly, starting to get the hint. It was coming to me now, as if through a dense cloud. I sat forward in my chair. "You don't mean . . ."

"Yes."

"Really?"

"Yes."

"Really?"

"Yes!"

"No, really?"

That's how it began between Anouk and me.

It became a regular thing. Lying in bed with this young, beautiful woman, I felt a pathetic, adolescent form of pride—this is *me* kissing this neck! These breasts! These are my worn-out hands groping their way along the length of this sublime body! This liaison really saved me. I had begun to perceive my genitals as imaginary beasts in some epic fourteenth-century Scottish poem.

When you sleep with a friend, the trickiest part is getting started. You can't just jump into fucking without kissing, and kissing is very intimate. If you kiss in the wrong way, it sends the wrong message. But we had to kiss, to get the engines warm, so to speak. We never kissed after sex, obviously. What would be the point? You don't warm the engine after you've reached your destination, do you? But then we started doing it anyway. I was confused. I thought a friendly fuck was supposed to be passionate and revitalizing. I was all ready for that. Sex as fun—sinful but harmless, like chocolate ice cream for breakfast. But it wasn't like that at all. It was tender and loving, and afterward we lay in each other's arms, and sometimes we even caressed each other. I didn't know what to make of it. Neither of us knew what to say, and it was to fill an awkward silence that I confided to Anouk my big secret, that I was finally actually dying.

She took it worse than I had imagined. In fact, she almost took it even worse than I did. "*No!*" she screamed, then launched feverishly into a catalogue of alternative therapies: acupuncture, strange-sounding herbs, some terrifying cure called soul-flossing, meditation and the curative potency of positive thinking. But you can't positive-think your death away; you might as well try thinking "Tomorrow the sun will rise in the west. In the west. In the west." It doesn't do any good. Nature has laws which she's maniacal about enforcing.

"Look, Anouk. I don't want to spend the rest of my life fighting death," I said.

She asked me all the details. I gave them to her, as I knew them. She felt so sorry for me, I wept.

Then we made love in a frenzy of desire that was downright violent. We were fucking death.

"Have you told Jasper?" she asked afterward.

"About us?"

"No—about you."

I shook my head feeling shamefully elated, because I was enjoying a fantasy in which he would be sorry for despising me. He would break down and weep, half torn open by remorse. This thought perked me up a bit. Someone else's soul-destroying guilt can be a reason for living.

After this initial discussion, we didn't talk about my upcoming death much, although I could tell it was on her mind by the way she would try to convince me to donate my cancerous organs to researchers. Then one frosty night, while warming our hands on the afterglow of ferocious sex, she asked, "What are you going to do for the rest of your life?"

It was a good question; now that the rest of my life wasn't the few billion years I had assumed it would be, what *was* I going to do? For the first time in my life, I was at a real loss. A total loss. I couldn't even read anymore. What was the point of deepening my understanding of the universe and the shitheads in it when I would no longer be around to snarl at my findings? I already felt my nonexistence with bitterness. There was so much I wanted to do. I thought of all the things I could've been. As I said them to Anouk, each sounded as ludicrous as the next: a mountaineer, a writer of historical romances, an inventor credited with a great discovery, like Alexander Graham Bell, who pioneered phone sex.

"Anything else?"

"There's one thing."

"What?"

"I always thought I would make a really good Rasputin character."

"What do you mean?" she asked.

I dug through my notebooks and showed her an idea I'd had about influencing rich and powerful men with my ideas, whispering spectacular ideas into an enormous golden ear. She latched on to this with a lunatic's energy. She seemed to think that if I achieved just one of my dreams, I would go to the grave feeling satisfied. Does anyone go to the grave satisfied? True satisfaction can't exist as long as there's one itch left to scratch. And I don't care who you are, there's always an itch.

•

Then one empty night Jasper burst into my room with the unlikely news that Oscar and Reynold Hobbs were here to see me. Apparently Anouk had brought home two of the most powerful men on earth. An intense hatred for Anouk surged up in me. What a nasty act of cruelty, giving a dying man his last wish. Don't you realize he doesn't want it? His real wish is not to die.

I went out and saw them. Reynold, imperious and resolute; he even blinked with authority. And his son, the heir apparent, Oscar—sharp and serious, with aesthetically jarring good looks, he was the perfect product of the modern dynasty (in modern dynasties every second generation breeds with supermodels to ensure that the bloodline has high cheekbones). I felt an intense hatred for those two men too, so secure in their destiny. I had finally come around to believing in my death, but I couldn't fathom theirs. They seemed impervious to everything.

Reynold looked at me, sizing me up. I was two sizes too small.

And why were they in my house? To listen to my ideas. How had Anouk pulled that off? It was remarkable. It was the most anyone had ever done for me. I dug out some old notebooks and read a couple of asinine ideas I'd had over the years. It's not important what they were, only that they fell flat. As I read, the two men looked to have faces made of a sturdy wood. There was really nothing human about them.

After hearing me out, Reynold violently lit a cigar and I thought: What is it with wealthy men and cigars? Are they thinking that lung cancer is for the plebs while tongue cancer puts them in a higher echelon? Then Reynold mentioned to me the real reason they were here. Not to listen to my ideas after all, but to get my input on a television miniseries they were hoping to make on, what else, the Terry Dean story.

I didn't know what to say. I couldn't say anything.

Reynold brushed one hand down his thigh and suddenly the son said, "Now we'll be off!"

What teamwork! What superconsciousness!

Then they left.

I went out into the labyrinth, furious at my dead brother, begging the cosmos to allow me to travel back in time just for five minutes, long enough to spit in his eye. I mean, how tireless a ghost was he? He had turned my past into a vast open wound, unhealed and unhealable. Infected and infectious.

It was cold out. I waded through the night as through a river. My disappointment was not so surprising; of course a part of me wanted to succeed. You can't be a failure all your life, can you? Actually, you can. That was the problem right there.

"Marty!"

Anouk. She was running toward me. The sight of her was a great relief. I was no longer angry at her for fanning the flame of my brother's ghost. I had Anouk. I had ferocious passion on my résumé. Our lovemaking was so exciting you'd think we were committing adultery.

"I'm sorry. I thought they might really be interested."

"They just wanted Terry. They always do."

Anouk put her arms around me. I felt desire moving through the rooms of my body, a bright sun casting its light on the shadows of my cancer, and I grew fresh and young and Anouk could feel this was happening because she hugged me tighter and nestled her face in my neck and left it there for what seemed like a long time.

We heard footsteps somewhere in the bush. I pushed her away.

"What is it?"

"I think it's Jasper."

"So?"

"So don't you think we should keep this between us?"

Anouk studied my face for a long time. "Why?"

Somehow I knew he'd take it badly. I was terrified that his hysterics might prejudice Anouk against me, might turn her off the whole idea. She might conclude that sleeping with me wasn't worth the trouble. That's why a couple of days later I went about the bizarre, unenviable chore of interfering in my son's love life. A part of me knew that no matter what I did, no matter how honorable or dishonorable my intentions were, it would inevitably backfire. Well, so what? It's not like I'd be breaking up the world's most rock-solid couple. Isn't their incompatibility evident by the mere fact that she has risen to the moral challenge of acquiring a lover and he hasn't? I'm rationalizing, of course. The truth was, I preferred his storming furiously out of my life to the prospect of Anouk slipping out of my arms.

I couldn't call the girlfriend up, and there was no way of asking Jasper for her phone number without his taking out a restraining order against me, so one morning I woke early and staked out his hut, waiting for her to leave, and when she did I trailed her. The frequency of their relations, if not the seriousness, I was able to ascertain by the adroit way she navigated through the labyrinth. I walked behind her, watching her curvaceous body swing this way and that. As I followed her, I wondered how you go about addressing someone's treachery. I decided you just come out with it.

"Hey, you!" I said.

She turned quickly and gave me the kind of smile that can really castrate a man. "Hello, Mr. Dean."

"Don't give me that. I have something to say to you."

She looked at me with all the sweet, innocent patience in the world. I launched right into it. "I saw you the other day."

"Where?"

"Kissing someone I didn't father."

She let out an uncertain gulp of air and lowered her eyes. "Mr. Dean," she said, but that's all she said.

"So what have you got to say for yourself? Are you going to tell Jasper, or am I?"

"There's no reason to tell Jasper. The thing is, we used to go out together, and I've had a hard time forgetting about him, and I thought . . . well, it doesn't matter what I thought, but he doesn't want me. And I don't want him anymore. And I do love Jasper. I just . . . Please don't tell him. I'll break up with him, but I won't tell him."

"I don't want you to break up with him. I don't care if you're my son's girlfriend or not. But if you are, you can't cheat on him. And if you do, you have to tell him. Look—let me tell you a story. One time I was in love with my brother's girlfriend. Her name was Caroline Potts. Hang on, maybe I'd better start at the beginning. People always want to know what Terry Dean was like as a child. They expect tales of kiddie violence and corruption in the heart of an infant. They imagine a miniature criminal crawling around the playpen perpetrating acts of immorality in between feedings. Ridiculous! Was Hitler goose-stepping all the way to his mother's breast?"

"Mr. Dean, I have to go."

"Oh, well, I'm glad we cleared that up," I said, and as she walked away, I couldn't work out for the life of me what we had cleared up, if anything.

•

Later that night Jasper walked in on Anouk and me in bed. He flipped out. I don't know why it caused him such profound embarrassment—maybe the Oedipal project is most effective in broken families such as ours; the son's desire to kill the father and fuck the mother is less repulsive an idea if it is the mother-substitute the boy desires to sleep with. As if to confirm my revolting theory, Jasper acted very hurt and even furious. I suppose at some point in life we give in to a senseless outburst that serves to rob us of all credibility, and this was Jasper's. There was no logical reason why he should oppose this occasional physical and sweaty union of Anouk's and mine, and he knew it too, but the next thing he came and told me was that he was moving out. We stood in silence for a minute. It was a large minute, not long but wide and cavernous.

I smiled. I felt the weight of my smile. It was exceedingly heavy.

His exit threatened to last a century but was over surprisingly quickly. After he said, "I'll phone you," I listened to the furious song of his footsteps retreating and I wanted to call him back and guilt-trip him into staying in contact with me.

He was gone.

I was alone.

My presence weighed as heavily on me as my concrete smile.

So! He's left me in my dark crevice, in my solitary whirlwind. Children are a complete failure, aren't they? I don't know how people can derive any lasting satisfaction out of them.

I couldn't believe he was gone.

My son!

The sperm that got away!

My failed abortion!

I stepped outside and looked at the stars tattooed on the night sky. It was one of those magnetic nights when you feel everything is either drawn to your body or is repelled by it. All this time I had thought my son was striving to be my mirror opposite, but he wasn't—he had become my polar opposite instead, and that had sent him careering away.

•

A week later I felt lost in a dark and heavy cloud. Anouk hadn't turned up for a couple of days and I sat in her studio, surrounded by plaster genitalia, feeling deeply ashamed because I was bored. What right does a dying man have to be bored? Time was killing me and I retaliated by killing time. Jasper was gone; Anouk had abandoned me. The only person I had left was Eddie, but I really could stand him only for short bursts. It's a shame you can't go out and see people for just ten minutes. That's all the human contact I need to carry me through life for three days—then I need ten minutes more. But you can't invite someone over for ten minutes. They stay and stay and never leave, and I always have to say something jarring like "You go now." For many years I tried the favorite, "I won't keep you any longer," or "I don't want to take up any more of your time," but that never worked. There are far too many people who don't have anything to do and have nowhere to go and who would like nothing better than to squander their whole lives chatting. I've never understood it.

When I heard Anouk's voice calling my name, a gust of pure joy blew through my heart and I shouted, "I'm here! In the studio!" and I felt the pulse of sexual desire fire up. At once I had the imprudent notion that I should take off my clothes. I hardly even remember peeling them off, I was in such a fervor for union, and by the time she came to the doorway I was fully naked, beaming at her. At first I didn't understand the frown on her face; then I thought about how I'd been lurking in ambush among the world's largest collection of genitals, and my own, by comparison, didn't compare. In my defense, the genitals around me were not to scale.

Then she said, "Um, I'm not alone." And who should stick his impeccable head through the doorway but Oscar Hobbs.

In a testament to his unshakable coolness, he launched right into it. "I have some news for you," he said. "I'd like to help you realize one of your ideas."

I felt about to either shatter or freeze into a solid block. "For God's sake, why?" I said briskly, then, "Which one?"

"I thought we'd discuss it. Which one would you most like to see realized?"

Good question. I had no clue. I closed my eyes, took a long breath, and dove into my brain. I swam down deep, and in the space of a minute I must have picked up and discarded over a hundred silly schemes. Then I found the one I wanted—an idea with handles. My eyelids sprang open.

"I'd like to start making everyone in Australia a millionaire," I announced.

"Smart choice," he said, and I understood immediately that we understood each other. "How do you intend to do that?"

"Trust me. I've got it all worked out."

"Trust you?"

"Obviously, since you're a major player in a multinational conglomerate, I can't trust you. So you'll have to trust me. When it's time, I'll tell you the details."

Oscar gave Anouk the briefest of looks before his eyes returned to me.

"OK," he said.

"OK? Wait a minute—are you serious about this?"

"Yes."

In the awkward silence that followed this improbable turn of events, I noticed how the customarily expressionless Oscar was looking at Anouk as if he were struggling against something in his nature. What did it mean? Had Anouk promised him sexual favors? Had she made some strange, unpleasant pact for my benefit? The niggling suspicion compromised my sudden success. That's how it always is—you never get a complete victory; there are always strings attached. Still, I didn't hesitate to accept his offer. That was followed by another unexpected slug in the guts, the crushing look of disillusionment on Anouk's face, as if by accepting Oscar's offer I had proved myself to be less than she imagined. *That* I couldn't understand. This was her idea, wasn't it?

Anyway, I had to accept it. What choice did I have?

I was time-poor.

Chapter Two

We went straight into battle mode. First there was the publicity; we had to whet the public's appetite. Oscar was smart; he didn't mess around. The very next day, before we'd even properly discussed how this ludicrous scheme was going to function, he put my picture on the front page of the daily tabloid with the headline "This Man Wants to Make You Rich." A little clunky, not very elegant, but effective. And that was it for me. The official end to my life as the invisible man.

There was the briefest outline of my idea, without specifics, but most infuriatingly, I was introduced to the Australian public as "Brother of Iconic Outlaw Terry Dean."

I tore the newspaper into ribbons. Then the telephone started ringing and the lowest forms of human life were on the other end—journalists. What had I gotten myself into? Becoming a public figure is like befriending a rottweiler with meat in your pockets. They all wanted details on how I planned to do it. The first to pick up on the story was a TV producer for a current affairs show, wanting to know if I would be interviewed for a segment. "Of course not," I said, and hung up. This was just reflex.

"You have to publicize your scheme," Anouk said.

"Fuck that," I said weakly. I knew she was right. But how could I speak to these journalists when all I could hear in my head, drowning out their questions, was noisy echoes of an old rage? It turned out I was the kind of person who could hold a grudge for a lifetime. I was still fuming over how the media had relentlessly harassed my family during Terry's rampage. What was I going to do? They called and called and called. They asked me about myself, my scheme, my brother. Different voices, same questions. When I walked outside, I heard them calling from somewhere within the labyrinth. Helicopters circled overhead. I went inside and locked the door and climbed into bed and turned off the lights. I felt my whole world was on fire. I'd done this to myself, I knew, but that didn't make it any easier. It made it worse.

The current affairs show ran the story anyway. Oscar Hobbs gave an interview. Apparently he wasn't going to let my misanthropy ruin everything. To my horror, they dug up footage of me from the time of Terry's rampage; because I wasn't watching television then, I'd never seen it. There it was: our town that no longer exists, that I'd burned down with my observatory, and right there on television everyone was alive—my mother, my father, Terry, and even me! Even seventeen-year-old me! It's impossible to believe I was ever that young. And that skinny. And that ugly. On the television I'm all skin and bones and walking away from the camera with the steady steps of someone moving toward a future he doesn't know will hurt him. I instantly formed a love-hate relationship with my former self. I loved me for moving so optimistically toward the future, and hated me for getting there and fucking it up.

The following morning I made my way to the Hobbs building, a hushed, seasonless fortress in the city center, seventy-seven floors of soundproof, smell-proof, and poor-proof offices. As soon as I stepped into the lobby, I knew I had grown old inside my nanosecond of eternity. The people racing past me were so young and healthy, I had a coughing fit just looking at them. This was a new type of working man and woman, wholly different from the breed of worker who waits in a fever of impatience for five o'clock to release him from bondage. These were pathologically stressed-out consumers who worked all the time, in industries called new media, digital media, and information technologies. In this place, old methods and technologies were not even remembered, and if they were, they were talked about fondly, as if discussing the death of embarrassing relatives. One thing was certain: this new culture of workers would have baffled the hell out of Marx.

Contrary to expectations, neither Oscar's nor Reynold's office was on the top floor, but somewhere in the middle of the building. Entering the stark yet stylish reception area, I was all ready to put on my waiting face when the secretary with cone-shaped breasts said, "Go right in, Mr. Dean."

Oscar's office was surprisingly small and simple, with a view of the building opposite. He was on the phone with someone I assumed was his father, who was giving him an earful and doing it so loudly I heard the words "Are you completely stupid?" Oscar raised his eyebrows, waved me in, and motioned for me to sit on a beautiful and uncomfortable-looking flat-backed antique chair. I went to his bookshelf instead. He had an impressive collection of first editions—Goethe, Schopenhauer, Nietzsche (in German), Tolstoy (in Russian), and Leopardi (in Italian)—that called to mind some lines of the last's uplifting poetry:

> What was that acid spot in time
> That went by the name of Life?

Oscar hung up the phone with an expression that was not entirely clear to me. I launched my attack. "Listen, Oscar, I didn't give you permission to start bandying around my brother's name. This has nothing to do with him."

"I'm funding this scheme. I don't need your permission."

"Hey—that's true. You don't."

"Listen, Martin. You should be thankful. Your brother, while he was, in my opinion, a dangerous maniac that Australia has no business celebrating—"

"That's just what he was!" I shouted, thrilled to my bones. For it's a fact that nobody had ever expressed this very obvious opinion.

"Well, blind Freddy can see that. The point is, he is plain adored by this country, and your close association with him gives you the credentials you need to be taken seriously."

"OK, but I—"

"You don't want us to go on and on about it. This is your scheme, this is your turn in the spotlight, and you don't want your long-dead brother overshadowing you from beyond the grave."

"Mate, that's it exactly."

"After this first week, Marty, you'll come into your own, don't worry."

I had to admit, Oscar Hobbs was a real gentleman. In fact, he was charming me more each time I met him. He seemed to understand me right away. I thought: Maybe people need to grasp that nepotism doesn't necessarily mean the ascension of an idiot.

"Anyway, let's get into details. What's your scheme?"

"OK. It's simple. Are you ready?"

"Ready."

"OK. Listen to this. With our population of roughly twenty million people, if everyone in Australia mailed just one dollar a week to a certain address and that money was divided by twenty, *every single week of the year* twenty Australian families would become millionaires."

"That's it?"

"That's it!"

"That's your idea?"

"That's my idea!"

Oscar leaned back in his chair and put on a thinking face. It was the same as his regular face, only a little smaller and a little tighter.

The silence made me uncomfortable. I gave him a few more details to fill it.

"Now what if, after the first week, the people who have just become millionaires from the previous week put in a one-time payment of a thousand dollars as a thank-you. That means after the first week we'll always have a weekly budget of twenty thousand dollars to support the administrative costs of the enterprise."

Oscar started nodding rhythmically. I pushed on: "So by my calculations, at the end of the first year 1,040 families would have become millionaires, by year two 2,080 millionaires, by year three 3,120 millionaires, and so on. Now 3,120 new millionaires in three years is pretty good, but at that rate it would still take roughly 19,230 years for every Australian to become a millionaire, not even factoring in the rate of population growth."

"Or decline."

"Or decline. Obviously, for the number of Australian millionaires to grow exponentially, we need to increase the payment each year by a dollar, so in year two we put in two dollars a week—that's 40 millionaires a week, or 2,080 millionaires for the year; year three we put in three dollars—60 millionaires a week, or 3,120 millionaires for the year; and so on until every Australian is a millionaire."

"That's your idea."

"That's my idea!"

"You know what?" he said. "It's so simple it might actually work."

"Even if it doesn't," I said, "what else are we going to do with this acid spot in time that goes by the name of Life?"

"Martin. Don't say that in an interview, OK?"

I nodded, embarrassed. Maybe he didn't recognize the quote because I didn't say it in Italian.

•

That night Eddie turned up at the house in his usual freshly ironed pants and wrinkle-free shirt with his face that made me wonder if they have Asian mannequins in Asian department stores. I hadn't seen him in a while. Eddie was always disappearing and reappearing. That's what he did. Seeing him, I suddenly remembered my idea that all along he'd hated my guts. I watched him closely. He wasn't giving himself away. Maybe he'd been pretending to like me for so long he'd forgotten that he didn't. Why would he pretend to like me anyway? For what sinister trap? Probably none—to soften up his loneliness, that was all. I suddenly felt sorry for the whole lot of us.

"Where have you been?" I asked.

"Thailand. You'd like Thailand, you know. You should think of going there one day."

"Why the hell would I like Thailand? I'll tell you where I think I'd like: Vienna, Chicago, Bora Bora, and St. Petersburg in the 1890s. Thailand I'm not so sure about. What were you doing there?"

"Did I see your picture on the front page of the paper today?"

"You might have."

"What's going on?"

I told him what was going on. As Eddie listened, his eyes seemed to sink deeper into his skull.

"Look," he said, "I'm not doing anything right now. Things have been a little bad for me lately, as you know. I don't suppose you need any help in there, making people millionaires?"

"Maybe," I said. "Why not?"

It was true Eddie had been down on his luck. He had bungled his life too; the strip clubs he'd been managing (one of which I had partially destroyed with my car in a moment of mental collapse) had been shut down by police because underage girls were stripping. The clubs were also known for drug deals, and one night there was a fatal shooting, the worst kind. Throughout these calamities Eddie had kept remarkably cool, and I suspected it wasn't a façade, either. He had a way of remaining aloof from physical disturbances. It was as though they were happening in a reality he was watching through binoculars.

So when he asked me if he could be a part of the millionaire scheme, of course I said yes. When someone close to you who has never asked you for anything finally does, it's quite touching. Besides, I still owed him all the money he'd loaned me, and this was a way to pay him back.

Considering he had managerial experience, I suggested he take care of the administrative aspect. In truth I was greatly relieved. I only wanted to see the idea realized; I personally wanted nothing to do with administering anything.

"I can't believe we're going to make people millionaires," Eddie said, slapping his hands together. "It's a bit like playing God, isn't it?"

"Is it?"

"I don't know. For a second I thought it was."

If we were playing God in the movie of his life, would it be in character to hand out money? I suppose with an eternity on his hands, even God would run out of ideas eventually.

•

Oscar wasn't keen on the idea of Eddie running the administrative side of the enterprise, but he was inhumanly busy running two television stations, an Internet service, and three newspapers. I couldn't help but be impressed. If you knew how hard these bastards worked, you'd never say anything negative about privilege again, and you wouldn't even want it for yourself. So he okayed Eddie and gave us a large office each in the Hobbs News Building. We were able to pick our own staff, and though we only hired females with great cleavage (a habit from our strip-club days) we weren't just clowning around in there. Eddie got right to it. He really took charge. With Oscar's influence, he obtained the electoral rolls for every state, made a database, and rigged up some system where the names would be jumbled around in the computer much like balls in a lottery bubble. Then, quite at random, the computer would somehow pick the first twenty names. Actually, even though I can't be precise in my explanation of how it worked, it wasn't that complicated. Nothing surprising about that. There's plenty of uncomplicated things I don't understand.

That was it, really. The newspapers publicized the details of the scheme, and by the end of the week the dollar coins came streaming in. Our poor staff was snowed under opening envelopes and counting millions of those round cold dollars. We were also all gearing up for the opening-night party, when the names of the first millionaires would be read out on national television. It was going to be one of those A-list parties where the guests either make a fool out of you or pretend you don't exist. I wasn't looking forward to it. And there was my public role as mastermind behind the unsophisticated scheme; standing next to Oscar Hobbs, I was to read out the list of names, then the new millionaires, rounded up earlier that day by Eddie's crew, would come up onstage and shriek appropriately. That was the plan. Today was Thursday. The party was next Friday. Oscar had organized a deal with all the TV stations. It would be like the moon landing. For one night there was going to be peace between the warring networks. Oscar was incredible—all this he did in between managing everything else.

I was revitalized, but my energy was still easily exhaustible, and I collapsed in bed each night, with Anouk often waiting for me. We quickly wore each other out.

"Are you happy, Martin? Are you happy?" she'd ask.

What an odd question to ask me, of all people. I shook my head. "Happy? No. But my life has become a curious shape that interests me for the first time."

That made her smile with relief.

On the Tuesday before the party, I was sitting motionless behind my desk as if I were some extraneous piece of office furniture when the phone rang. I picked it up.

"Hello?"

"What the hell do you think you're doing?"

"I'm sorry, I don't give interviews."

"Dad—it's me."

"Oh, Jasper. Hi."

"What are you planning?"

"Planning?"

"There's no way you're just making people millionaires for no reason."

"Why do you say that?"

"Because I know you better than you know yourself."

"You think so, do you?"

"It's your opening gambit, isn't it?"

"I don't like talking on the phone. Am I going to see you soon?"

"Yeah—soon," he said.

He hung up and I stared wistfully at the telephone until someone saw me, then I pretended to clean it. The truth is, I missed Jasper: he was the only one who understood that making people millionaires was an entirely calculated bit of shenanigans, simply a means to an end—the end being to get people on my side, then follow that with something that would surprise even Death. Yes, all along this was a conscious strategy for winning their approval, which would be pitted against their unconscious strategy for destroying me. What Jasper guessed was that I had a simple plan:

1. Make everyone in Australia a millionaire, thus winning everyone's support, trust, and perhaps adoration, also having
2. The media barons on my side, while simultaneously
3. Becoming a politician and winning a seat in Parliament at the upcoming federal election and then
4. Commence wholesale reformation of Australian society based on my ideas and thus

5. Impress Jasper, who would apologize, weeping, while I
6. Had sex as often as possible with Anouk and
7. Died painlessly, content that a week after my death construction would begin on
8. Statues erected in public squares to the peculiar specifications of my head and body.

That was it: a plan to put an exclamation mark at the end of my life. Before I died, I would expel all my ideas from my head—every idea, no matter how silly—so that my process of dying would be a process of emptying. When I was feeling optimistic about the success of my plan, the image of my death intertwined with an image of Lenin in his tomb. In pessimistic moments, the image of my death mingled with an image of Mussolini hung from an Esso gas station in Milan.

While waiting for the big night, I hung around the office, slightly annoyed that I had nothing to do. I'd delegated everything. All I could do was work on my look of conscientious deliberation, ask at various junctures "How's it going?" and pretend to care about the answers.

Eddie, on the other hand, was working himself into the ground preparing for the party. I watched him scribbling industriously and I was wondering if he ever felt like I did, like a few misplaced molecules cobbled together to form an implausible person, when I suddenly had a great idea.

"Eddie," I said. "That list of will-be millionaires—are there any in Sydney?"

"Three," he said. "Why?"

"Give me their files, will you?"

•

The first millionaire was in Camperdown. His name was Deng Agee. He was from Indonesia. He was twenty-eight years old and had a wife and a three-month-old baby. The house looked completely deserted. There was no answer when I knocked, but ten minutes later I saw him coming home with heavy shopping bags. Ten meters from the house, the plastic bag in his left hand broke and his groceries went crashing onto the pavement. He looked down at his dented tins of tuna like one heartbroken, as if the tins of tuna just wanted to be friends.

I smiled warmly so he wouldn't recognize me from the newspapers.

"How's life, Deng?" I sang.

"Do I know you?" he said, looking up.

"You doing OK, then? Got everything you need?"

"Fuck off."

He had no idea that in a week's time he'd be a millionaire. It was hilarious.

"Are you happy in this place, Deng? It's kind of a dump, if you don't mind my saying."

"What do you want? I'll call the police."

I walked over, stooped down, and pretended to pick up $10 from the ground. "Did you drop this?"

"That's not mine," he said, and went inside and slammed the door in my face. He's going to make a terrific millionaire, I thought, as if it were necessary for me that *my* millionaires (as I thought of them) be incorruptible.

The second Sydney millionaire was a biology teacher. She had maybe the ugliest face I'd ever seen. I almost cried at the sight of it. I could feel the wind of a thousand doors closing in that ugly face. She didn't see me come into her classroom. I took a desk in the back row and grinned madly.

"Who are you?"

"How long have you been teaching here, Mrs. Gravy?"

"Sixteen years."

"And in that time have you ever forced a child to swallow chalk?"

"No, never!"

"Really. That's not what they're saying down at the Board of Education."

"It's a lie!"

"That's what I'm here to find out."

"You're not from the Board of Education."

Mrs. Gravy walked up and peered at me as if I were an illusion. I looked for a wedding ring on her finger and saw nothing but naked wedges of flesh. I stood and walked to the door. The thought of money's being the only thing in heaven and earth to bring Mrs. Gravy joy was so depressing to me, I almost didn't visit the third Sydney millionaire, but seeing as I had nothing else to do, I leaned my back against the school lockers, a long row of vertical coffins, and opened up the file.

Miss Caroline Potts, the file said.

I don't remember many instances of gasping like they do in the movies, but then fiction has a habit of making the real world seem made up. People gasp. It's no lie. And I gasped on seeing that name, with all its connotations and implications. Connotations: My brother's death. Frustrated desire. Satisfied desire. Loss. Regret. Bad luck. Missed opportunities. Implications: She had divorced or been widowed from her Russian husband. She was not lost in Europe. She had been living in Sydney, maybe for years.

Christ!

These thoughts did not come in any order but arrived simultaneously—I couldn't hear where one ended and another began. They all spoke over each other, like a large family at a dinner table. Of course, reason told me that there could be up to twenty or thirty Caroline Pottses living minutes from each other at any given time, as it's not as unusual a name as Prudence Bloodhungry or Heavenly Shovelbottom. Had Eddie thought it was one of the other Caroline Pottses? I refused to believe it was anyone other than she, because in moments of personal crisis you find out what you believe, and it turned out that I believed in something after all, and it's that I am a ball of string and life is a cat's paw toying with me. How could it be otherwise? Go! a voice screamed. Go!

In the taxi on the way, I read the file over a dozen times. Eddie wasn't very thorough. All it said was: *Caroline Potts 44 Librarian. Mother of Terrence Beletsky, age 16.* Mother! And her son's name: Terrence. Terry. Crap! That took the wind out of my sails. She had named her son after Terry. As if the bastard didn't have enough accolades!

Just incredible!

Caroline lived in one of those buildings that hadn't an intercom system, so you could wander unrestricted right up the shit-colored stairwell, right up to the apartment door. I reached 4A without having thought too much about which would be the greater shock, seeing me or learning that in less than a week's time she was going to be a million dollars richer. I knocked impatiently, and immediately we launched into our old habit of screaming excitedly at each other.

"Who is it?"

"Me!"

"Me who?"

"You wouldn't believe me if I told you!"

"Marty!" she screamed, and that threw me off balance, the fact that after all these years she so swiftly recognized my voice.

She opened the door and I gasped again. Nature had barely laid a finger on her. Then I saw that that wasn't entirely accurate—Nature had given her a bigger bottom and longer boobs, and her face was slightly wider, and her hair wasn't what you would call in good order, but she was still beautiful, she had the same light behind her eyes. Looking at her, I felt as if all the years since Paris had not really happened, that the past eighteen years were like an absurdly long afternoon.

"Oh my God, look at you!" she said.

"I'm old!"

"Not at all. You have the same face!"

"No I don't!"

"Wait. You're right! Your ear's new!"

"I had some skin grafts done!"

"Wonderful!"

"And I'm losing my hair!"

"Well, I have a fat arse!"

"You still look beautiful!"

"You're not just saying that?"

"No!"

"I saw your name on the news!"

"Why didn't you come see me?"

"I wanted to! But after all these years, I wasn't sure you'd want to see me! Besides, I saw a photo of you with a woman's arms around you and she's young and beautiful!"

"That's Anouk!"

"Not your wife?"

"Not even my girlfriend. She's our housekeeper! What about your husband?"

"We divorced! I just assumed you were still in Europe!"

"I thought the same!"

"And hey—we were supposed to meet in Paris a year after that night in the hotel! Remember?"

"I was here! In Australia! Don't tell me you went!"

"I did, actually!"

"Oh my God!"

"I couldn't believe when I saw Terry's name! People are talking about him again! Then I saw it was you! What's this nonsense you're involved in?"

"It's not nonsense!"

"You're going to make every person in Australia a millionaire!"

"You're right! It is nonsense!"

"What made you think of doing such a silly thing?"

"I don't know!" I said. "Wait! You're one of them!"

"Martin!"

"I'm serious! That's why I came!"

"You rigged it!"

"I didn't! I didn't pick the names!"

"Are you sure?"

"Absolutely!"

"What am I going to do with a million dollars?"

"Wait! It says in my file here you have a son! Where is he?"

"He's dead." Those two words that escaped her mouth sounded as if they had come from a different place. She bit her lip and her eyes filled up. I could see her thoughts like subtitles on her face. *Can I talk about this now?* I tried to make things easier for her by guessing, so she wouldn't have to tell me the whole sad story. Let's see—teenagers die in only three ways: suicide, drunk driving, peanut allergy. Which was it?

"Drunk driving," I said, and watched as her face whitened and she gave an almost imperceptible nod. We stood silent for a long moment, not quite ready to put the memory back in its jar. Grief is a strange entity in a reunion.

I felt sick that I had never known her son. I still loved her, and I imagined I would have loved her child too.

She stepped forward and wiped tears from my eyes with her sleeve. I didn't know I'd been crying.

She made a sad sound, like from a tiny flute. The next minute we were hugging, with our hips, and I found sanctuary in her embrace and a cozier sanctuary in her bed. Lying in each other's arms afterward, we set about confiding our secrets and in this way found a method of falsifying history—by ignoring it. We focused only on the present; I confided my plan to run for Parliament and bring about a total transformation of society in the shortest possible time before I was overcome by cancer, and Caroline spoke of her dead son.

Is the mother of a dead child still a mother? There are words for widow and orphan, but not for the parent of a dead kid.

Hours passed. We made love a second time. It was agreed that we were no longer young and fresh, we both had telltale signs of wear and tear, but we were confident that we had been ruined by our personal tragedies in an adorable way—that our sagging faces and bodies wore our heartaches well. We decided we would never be apart again, and since no one knew of our connection, no one would make a fuss and think the drawing was rigged, and we would keep our relationship a secret until after the millionaires' dinner, when we would get married in a small, private ceremony in the middle of my labyrinth. In short, it was a productive afternoon.

•

If you were in Australia and you weren't watching TV the night the names of the millionaires were announced, it was because your eyes had been ripped out by vandals or you were dead. Caroline, Mrs. Gravy, Deng, and the rest of the millionaires became instant celebrities.

The party was held in a cavernous ballroom with chandeliers and seventies floral wallpaper and a stage where I would make my historic speech. The floor-to-ceiling windows looked out on the Harbor Bridge and a big yellow moon hanging over it. It was one of those parties I'd never dreamed of going to, where the partygoers were talking themselves up big, and when they ran out of ways to aggrandize themselves directly, they did it indirectly, by making everyone else small. Reynold Hobbs was there with his young confused bride. People cruelly called her a trophy wife, as if he'd won her in a contest. That just wasn't fair or true. He hadn't won her at all; he'd earned her through hard work and enterprise.

My attention was mostly focused on studying the erratic behavior of my ego in unstable conditions; under the stress of compliments and smiles and repeated blasts of direct eye contact, its propensity was to become engorged. I was so happy I wanted to fold all the people into paper airplanes and fly them into the lidless eye of that big yellow moon.

It was too crowded to pace nervously. I was thinking that my speech would more than likely backfire, and also that I had to tell Anouk about Caroline. Of course I knew it was almost unthinkable that a man like me could reject anyone, let alone a woman like Anouk. How could I tell her I would never taste her again, especially when she gave me the kind of supreme gratification one can get only from freeing slaves or sleeping with a really sexy woman a decade younger than yourself? Luckily, I remembered I was in love with Caroline, so I was able to walk over to Anouk and point her out. Caroline was standing in the corner of the room in a red chiffon dress, pretending not to look at me. Anouk remembered who she was from one of our postcoital confession sessions, and I explained that we were going to get married in a couple of weeks. She said nothing, a loud unpleasant nothing which made my monologue grow louder and incoherent.

"After all," I said, "we don't want to jeopardize our friendship."

Her face became a stone veiled in a smile. She laughed suddenly, a hideously exaggerated laughter that made me take a half step back. Before I had the chance to say anything, to dig myself deeper into a hole, everyone in the room was calling me to make a speech.

This was it. Time to put my plan into action. I stepped up onstage. *After all, you've made them rich.* My head weighed somewhere between a droplet of water and a gallon of air. *Who doesn't love a man who's made you rich? You can't lose.* I stood there, looking dumbly at the eager crowd, stuck in a dizzying immobility.

I searched the crowd for Caroline, who gave me an encouraging nod. That made me feel really low. And then I saw Jasper. I didn't know he was coming and hadn't seen him arrive. Fortunately for me, he had the same expression a dog has when you pretend to throw the ball but still have it in your hand. That gave me the boost I needed.

I cleared my throat, though it did not need it, and began.

"Thank you. I accept your applause and adoration. You're greedy to escape your prisons, and you think that by making you rich, I set you free. I haven't; I have only let you out of your cell, into the corridor. The prison still exists, your prison that you don't know you love so much. All right. Let's talk about me in relation to the tall-poppy syndrome. It's best to address this tricky issue right off the bat. Look, don't cut my head off, you shits. You love me now, but you'll hate me tomorrow. You know how you are—actually, you don't. That's why I'd like to suggest an unusual exercise for the nation, and the exercise is *to love me in perpetuity.* OK? In this spirit, I have an announcement to make. My God, my entire life has led up to this moment. Of course five minutes ago I went to the toilet and my entire life led up to that moment too. But here it is. I am running for Senate. That's right, Australia, I give you my wasted gifts! My squandered potential! I've always led a degraded existence, and now I offer it to you. I would like to be a part of our horrendous Parliament, our collective hoax! I want to put myself among the swine, and why shouldn't I? I am unemployed, after all, and senator is a job as good or bad as any other, isn't it? Just so you know, I'm not tied to any party. I will be running as an independent. And I'll be honest with you. I think politicians are weeping sores. And when I look at our politicians in our country, I can't believe that all of these unendurable people were actually *chosen*. So what can we say about democracy, except that it's not a good enough system to hold people accountable for their lies? Supporters of this inadequate system say, well, punish them at the polls, then! But how can we when most likely the single opponent at the polls is another in a long line of unelectable gormless bandits, and so we wind up voting the liars in again, voting with our teeth clenched? Of course, the most disagreeable thing about being an atheist is that according to my nonbeliefs, I know that all these sons of bitches have no retribution coming to them in the hereafter—that everyone gets away with everything. It's very distressing; what goes around doesn't come around but stays where it went when it first went around.

"Are you all following me? We puzzlingly overestimate our elected representatives. Don't overestimate me! I'll make blunder after stupid blunder! But it is necessary for you to know where I stand on certain contentious issues so you'll know what kind of blunders I'll be making. Well, I am certainly not on the right. I don't care if gays get married or get divorced. Not that I'm not for gay rights specifically, I'm just against the phrase 'family values.' In fact, when someone says the phrase 'family values,' I feel like I've been slapped in the face with a condom from 1953. Well, then, am I on the left? Sure, they're the first to sign petitions and in international affairs will always support the perceived underdog, even if the underdog is a bunch of cannibals—as long as they have less money and fewer resources—and these deeply caring individuals on the left will do anything for the betterment of the disenfranchised except make a personal sacrifice. So you see? I'm neither left nor right. I'm just an ordinary person who goes to sleep feeling guilty every night. Why shouldn't I? Eight hundred million people went to bed hungry today. All right, I'll admit for a while our roles as massively wasteful consumers seemed to be doing us a world of good—we were slimming down, a good half of us had breast implants; frankly, we were looking good—but now we're all fatter and more cancerous than ever, so what's the point of it? The world is getting hotter, the ice caps are melting, because man keeps saying to nature, Hey, our whole idea of a cozy future is to have jobs. That's all we've got planned. What's more, we will pursue this aim at any cost, even, paradoxically, if it means the eventual destruction of our workplace. Man says, Sacrifice industry and economy and jobs? For what? Future generations? I don't even know those guys! I'll tell you something for free—it makes me ashamed that our species, which is so finely ennobled by its sacrifices, winds up sacrificing it all for the wrong things and comes off just looking like a race of people who like to use the hair dryer while taking a bath. I'm only sorry I was born three-quarters through this self-inflicted tragedy and not at the very beginning or at the very end. I'm fucking sick of watching this tragedy in slow motion. The other planets aren't, though—they're on the edge of their suns. The reason we've never had visitors from outer space isn't that they don't exist but that they don't want to know us. We're the village idiots of all the teeming galaxies. On a quiet night you can hear their crackled laughter. And what are they laughing at? Let me put it this way: humanity is the guy who shits in his own pants and then walks around saying, 'So, do you like my new shirt?' What's my point? To let you know I am an environmentalist insofar as I wouldn't like to live in a caldron of boiling piss. Believe me, there's no politics in staying alive. That's why I'm an apolitical person entering the world of politics. But I'm not perfect. Tell me, why have we been infected by that American disease of wanting our politicians to be pure as monks? Society went through the sexual revolution decades ago, but for some reason we judge the people who manage our economy by Victorian standards, and this doesn't seem strange to us. Let me get this out of the way—if I see a chance of having an illicit affair with an intern or a colleague's wife, I will jump at it with both feet. As far as I'm concerned, 'getting away with it' has nothing to do with no one finding out and everything to do with no one falling pregnant. OK? I deny nothing. I admit everything. And let me say this to you too: I will not pretend that I'm not attracted to certain high school girls. Some of them are *seventeen*, for Chrissakes. They're not children! They're sexy, blossoming young women, most of whom lost their virginity at fourteen! There's a difference between inappropriate sex with a minor and pedophilia. It's stupid and dangerous to bundle them up in the same sack.

"What else? OK. I want to put this on the record, right from the outset: if I can give my son advantages—a book of cab charges, for instance, or free vacations—then I will. And why shouldn't I? If you are a mechanic and your son has a car, won't you fix it for him, won't you give him the advantage of having a father who is a mechanic? Or if you're a plumber, are you going to leave your son elbow deep in shit because you want him to do it on his own?

"What's my point? I render all smear campaigns redundant. Why throw dirt at a man caked in mud? For the record, I have been to prostitutes, fathered an illegitimate child—stand up, Jasper, and take a bow. I have lost control of my mind and my bladder. I have broken laws. I have built a labyrinth. I have loved my brother's girlfriend. I believe not in war but in the horrors of war! I believe not in an eye for an eye but in a large cash settlement for an eye! I believe in sexual humiliation education in schools! I believe that counterterrorism experts should be allowed to look up anyone's skirt they like! I believe in standing quietly, thanking our Aboriginal hosts, and every one of us migrating to another country! I believe that inequality is not the product of capitalism but the product of the fact that in a group of two men and one woman, one of the men will be taller and will have straighter teeth than the other, and he'll get the woman. Thus I believe that economics isn't the basis of inequality, straight teeth are!

"When democracy works, the government does what the people want. The problem with that is that people want shitty things! People are scared and greedy and self-centered and only concerned about their financial security! Yes, the truth of the matter is THERE HAS YET TO BE A GREAT DEMOCRATIC NATION BECAUSE THERE HAS YET TO BE A GREAT BUNCH OF PEOPLE!

"Thank you!"

•

So that was my speech, for which I should have been lynched a hundred times over. But I was making them into millionaires and I could do nothing wrong. Even that stupid, incoherent, somewhat obvious and insulting speech of mine won their approval. They lapped it up greedily.

Applauded like crazy. They'd never heard anything like it. Or maybe they had heard only the excited tone of my voice. Either way, I got away with it, and the only thing that night that overshadowed me and my crazy announcement was an impromptu speech by Oscar Hobbs, who wandered spontaneously up to the microphone and announced that he was getting married to the woman of his dreams—Anouk.

Chapter Three

The habits of a man living alone for a lifetime are disgusting and difficult to break. If no one is around to hear it, a falling tree may make no sound, and neither will I make my bed. But Caroline moved into the labyrinth, and now I had to cook! And clean! And share the responsibilities! Honestly, I've never known how people *do* married life. I mean, when I go from the bedroom to the bathroom or the kitchen to the bedroom, the last thing I want to do is stop to have a chat. .

Marriage was just one of many changes, though. How can I describe the most critical period of my life when it comes to me as a series of photographs taken from the window of a speeding train? Did I throw up octopus salad at my wedding or Anouk's? Was it me or Oscar standing still at the altar like one carved out of wood? At whose wedding did Jasper and I get into a heated philosophical argument about thank-you notes? And I don't know whether it was my newfound success or my new life with Caroline, but for some reason I was overcome with very dangerous wishful thinking and, going against everything I believed in, I began a struggle against death—I started fighting the cancer.

I let them suck out my blood; I peed into jars; I was bombarded by X-rays, buried in coffinlike beeping tunnels for CAT scans and MRIs, and underwent a combination of intravenous high-dose chemotherapy and radiotherapy which left me exhausted and breathless, dizzy and lightheaded, with nausea, headaches, diarrhea *and* constipation. I had tingling in my hands and feet. I experienced a continuous noise in my ears which all but drowned out my interior monologues.

The doctors told me to rest, but how could I? I had a new wife and a country to pervert. So I dealt with all this the best I could. To protect my skin from the sun, I wore a hat and sunglasses. I avoided foods with a strong smell. I shaved my head so no one would notice my hair falling out. Blood transfusions gave me the pick-me-up I needed. Unfortunately, chemotherapy treatments sometimes cause infertility. Fortunately, I didn't care. Neither did Caroline, and as we went back to Dr. Sweeny's again and again, together, I remember thinking that she might be the first person who would take a bullet for me, if one came and I didn't want it. Look, I'm not saying our relationship is as passionate as the relationship with the love of your life is supposed to be. It isn't, but I can't hold it against her. I am not actually the love of her life anyway; I am a stand-in, a surrogate for my brother. There was something complete in the way I was compared to him in the eyes of the nation and perhaps now in the bedroom.

So you'll understand why I can't tell you anything definite about those six months when my memories feel like botched memory implants. I don't even remember the election, only that on every street corner were posters of my face peering out with a look of unambiguous rebuke. More than the television and newspaper coverage, nothing was as violent an affront to my former anonymity as those ubiquitous posters.

The unlikely result? I scraped in. That's the wonderful thing about democracy: you can hold public office legitimately while still being despised by 49.9 percent of the suspicious eyes on the street.

Most people overseas think the capital of Australia is Sydney or Melbourne, but what they don't know is that in the 1950s the village idiots opened their own village and called it Canberra. For every sitting of Parliament I traveled with Caroline to this dull city, and it was there I became (I can scarcely believe it myself) dynamic. I was a dynamo. The slugs of Canberra had a repellent force, a force that served to channel my routine chaos and disparity into a vision. I became a visionary. But why wasn't I chased out of there with pitchforks and quicklime? Simple answer: the Australian people were diligently sending in their dollar coins, every week another twenty millionaires were made, and they had me to thank. This financial lure got people all caught up in a shared hysteria, which made them receptive to the ideas that fell thick and fast from my mouth.

I addressed unemployment, interest rates, trade agreements, women's rights, child care, the health system, tax reform, defense budgets, indigenous affairs, immigration, prisons, environmental protection, and education—and, shockingly, almost all my reforms were agreed upon. Criminals would be allowed the option of going into the army instead of being locked up; cash rebates would be offered to those who could demonstrate self-awareness, and the stultified and fearful would be taxed higher; any politician caught breaking just one election promise would be punished in a back alley by a guy named Bruiser; every healthy person would have to look after at least one sick person until he died or got better; we would pick people indiscriminately to become prime minister for a day; all drugs would be legalized for one generation to see what happened. Even my most controversial idea was taken up: rearing any child in a religious belief, freezing the child's mind when it is most vulnerable, would be treated as child abuse. I said all this and people said, "OK, we'll see what we can do." It was unbelievable!

Of course, as a public figure with a national audience for the humiliations that were previously the entertainment of a handful of close enemies, I had my critics. I was called every synonym of the word "insane" and worse. In Australia, the worst insult you can slander a person with, and the easiest way to dismiss every fiber of their being, is to call them a do-gooder. A do-gooder—let's be clear—is a person who does good or wants to do good. Let's be clear about this too, just so there are no misunderstandings: in the eyes of the slanderer, this is definitely an insult, not a compliment, and to be a do-gooder is something shameful, unlike in other places, such as heaven, where it's considered an asset. Thus my critics resorted to this "insult" in order to diminish me. It was only the ugly sneers on their faces that stopped me from thanking them.

Mostly, though, people were on my side. They liked it that I went to the heart of the matter—that my principal reforms were in the areas of loneliness, death, and suffering. At least on some level they seemed to understand my main idea: that we become the first truly death-based society. They accepted that in order to have a proper perspective on life, every single person in the land had to come to terms with the fact that death is an insurmountable problem that we really won't be solving by relentlessly making people—so that the name Smith can perpetuate throughout the eons—nor by hating neighboring countries, nor by chaining ourselves to a God with a long list of dislikes. I half managed to convince people that if instead of singing the national anthem we started each day with a little funeral service for ourselves, if we all resigned ourselves to our inevitable decay and stopped seeking a heroic transcendence of our unfortunate fate, we might not go as far as Hitler, who was so perturbed about dying that he tried to avoid thinking about it by killing six million Jews.

OK, I admit my revolution was a farce, but it was a deadly serious farce. If people laughed or went along with my ideas just to see what would happen, perhaps it was because underneath their chuckling, they saw a grain of truth. Perhaps not. Anyway, I know utopias don't work. Just for society to be a little more fluid and less hypocritical, that was really the sum total of my goal. Now I know it wasn't at all modest; I was reaching for the moon. Still, while churning out millionaires, I continued to soothe the hip-pocket nerve of the electorate and somehow managed to convince people that not to listen to me was a threat to the fabric of society.

Let's make no bones about it. Society was mutating. You could see it · happening, everywhere you looked. Someone even opened up a cannibal-themed restaurant in Surry Hills. I'm telling you, the whole of Australia went crazy. The national obsession became reform. I even think they understood that it wasn't the ideas themselves but the idea of the ideas, the idea that we *might as well* restlessly innovate and wherever possible obliterate our slavish connection with the past. Why? Because the past is always the worst thing happening to the present at any given time.

What delusion and denial came over me at this time of my life! The chemotherapy seemed to be working; the cancer cells were all shrinking nicely. My own death began to recede. I felt so good, I didn't even mind the cruel cartoonists who exaggerated my mouth so it was almost the size of my whole head. They say power corrupts—and how! The me I have always loved, despite my phony self-deprecation, was being mirrored in the eyes around me. It was an egoist's fantasy! My spirit was flying! I was so caught up in my own reformation I didn't realize I was losing the very ingredients that had led me to success—relentless negativity about the human spirit, cynicism and pragmatism about the human mind and how it is constrained. Success had thrown me off balance, and as a result I started having faith in people, and worse—I began to have faith in *the* people. All right. I'll say it. I should've listened to my son, who told me by a look and tone of voice, if not in actual words, "Dad, you're fucking it up!"

And where *was* my dutiful son during all this? Let's analyze him a little: if the first order of business in assuring self-perpetuation is to be greater than the father, the unexpected possibility that I, formerly the embodiment of failure, might suddenly achieve fame and fortune crystallized Jasper's hostility. The higher I rose, the more impossible his mission to supersede me became. In short, my success put him in mortal danger.

I remember very early on, just after the millionaires' party, he called me on the phone.

"What the hell are you doing?" he said when I picked up.

"Hello, son," I said back, knowing how to hit him where it hurts.

"This is going to end badly. You must know that."

"You coming to my wedding?"

"You're joking. Who would marry you?"

"Caroline Potts."

"Your brother's old girlfriend?"

Son of a bitch! Would it kill him to be a little more generous? OK, over the years I had repeatedly molested him with mental violence, but I hadn't done it out of some perverse compulsion, only out of love. He could at least be a little supportive of me in my one single moment of happiness, and not mention my fucking brother. Though it wasn't just Jasper. Every single news article about me, every single one, referred to me as Terry Dean's brother. They just wouldn't let it go. The fucker had been dead for twenty years!

I wanted to make an angry appeal to the Australian people to forget about him, but memory simply isn't that pliable. So I had to grin and bear it, even when I saw Caroline get a dreamy look on her face every time Terry Dean was mentioned.

When Jasper turned up at the wedding, he stared at Caroline as if trying to understand the psychology of a suicide bomber. I didn't see him for a long time after that. He avoided me completely in the chaos and disorder of those days in the limelight. Never once did he congratulate me or even make mention of all my reforms, interviews, debates, speeches, and public coughing fits. He said zilch in regards to my obviously haggard and beaten appearance from all the chemotherapy, and as I began, ever so slightly, to fall out of favor with the people, Jasper ceased phoning me altogether. Maybe he saw that I was suffering from a bad case of hubris and was going to pay the penalty. Maybe he sensed the inevitable fall. Maybe he was ducking for cover. But why couldn't I see it? Why didn't I duck for cover?

When several editorials suggesting that my head was swelling popped up, I should've taken the first space shuttle out of there. And when they made accusations of "extraordinary vanity" just because I carried a mirror in my briefcase (when the eyes of the nation are on you, you can't help but worry there's spinach in your teeth), I should have known that one wrong step would make them lynch me with all their collective souls. I did not, as some people suggested, have a persecution mania. No, I had no such mania for those persecuting me. If anything, I was crazy *not* to see them. Hadn't I said it all my dumb life: that the manner in which people fret about their immortality projects is the very thing that kills them? That the denial of death rushes people into an early grave, and often they take their loved ones with them?

Never once did I think of Caroline or Jasper. If I have made one unpardonable error in my life, it's to deny, *all the time*, that there are people who might genuinely love me.

Chapter Four

One day I turned up at Jasper's work. I had not seen him in many months, not since my wedding, and not since I had subjected myself to medical science. I had not even told him I had cancer, and I thought by telling him in an inappropriate setting like his workplace I could avoid a scene. He was sitting in his office cubicle staring out the window on the opposite side of the room, looking as if he were waiting for humans to evolve to the next level. As I watched him, I had the strange idea I could read his thoughts. They came in a whisper into my head: *Why is it that as soon as we shed fur and learned to stand upright, we gave up evolving, as if smooth skin and a good posture were everything?*

"Jasper," I said.

He spun around and looked at me disapprovingly. "What are you doing here?"

"I've got the big C."

"The what?"

"The big cliché."

"What are you talking about?"

"I've got cancer," I said. "It's found a crawl space in my lungs. I'm fucked." I tried to sound blasé, as if I had had cancer once a month for my entire life and now—what a hassle—I had it again.

Jasper opened his mouth, but no sound came out. We did not move. Fluorescent lights flickered overhead. The wind rustled papers on his desk. Jasper swallowed. I could hear saliva slide down his esophagus. We remained motionless. We were like humans before language, Paleolithic men in an office cubicle.

Finally he spoke. "What are you going to do about it?"

"I don't know," I said.

Jasper understood what most people don't: that the dying still have important decisions to make. I knew he was asking me if I was going to ride it out to the end or beat death to the punch. And then he gave me his view. I was touched.

"Dad, please don't die slowly and painfully. Please commit suicide," he said.

"I'm thinking about it," I snapped, both relieved and irritated he'd said the unsayable.

That night Jasper and Caroline and I sat down to dinner as a family. There was so much we had to say, we couldn't say any of it. Jasper eyed me the whole time. He was looking to catch a glimpse of Death red-handed. I am almost certain now that Jasper and I can read each other's minds, and it is far worse than speaking.

I suggested that he and I go for a drive, even though I had never gone for a drive in my whole life. It was a black night, the stars buried in the clouds. We drove without purpose or destination, and all the while I blabbered an inane monologue about how traffic is nothing but a rioting mob, each member with his own mobile weapon in which he dreams of perpetual motion.

"Hey! Stop the car!" Jasper shouted.

Without thinking, I had driven us to our first apartment, a place where my mental engine had conked out countless times. We knocked on the door, and Jasper told a man in stained boxer shorts that we wanted to look around for the same reason that a person looks through a photo album. The bloke let us in. As we wandered through the rooms, I thought that we had ruined the place by living there, that it had our gloomy residue in every airless corner. I thought we had exuded the essence of our core problems into the air, and our lightly wafting disease of the spirit had probably infected every poor bastard who had lived there since.

Back in the car we drove on, pinballing from one old haunt to an-other—squats, parks, supermarkets, bookstores, barbers, grocers, psychi-atric hospitals, newsagents, chemists, banks, every place that had once housed our confusions. I can't tell you the purpose of this compelling, nonmetaphorical journey down memory lane, but I can tell you that in each place I could see our past selves clear as day; it was as though we were retracing our steps and finding in every vanished footprint our actual feet. There's nothing like a nostalgia trip to make you feel alien from both your past and your present. You also see what's static in you, what you hadn't the courage or strength to change, and all your old fears, the ones you still carry. The disappointment of your failure is palpable. It's terrible to go around bumping into yourself like that.

"This is weird, isn't it?" Jasper said.

"Weird isn't the word."

We looked at each other and laughed. The only upside of the drive was that it turned out our mutual antagonism wasn't as inexhaustible as we thought. In the car we were talking, reminiscing, laughing. It was the only night that I felt in my son I had a friend.

Around three in the morning we were getting tired and losing enthusiasm. We decided to finish up with a beer at the Fleshpot, the strip club I had managed and nearly destroyed with my red sports car some years earlier.

A doorman standing outside said, "Come in! Beautiful dancers, boys! Come in!"

We went in, down the familiar black corridor with the red flashing bulbs, into the club. The room was full of smoke, mostly from cigars, but there was a little curling out of a machine onstage. The strippers were doing their usual sexless thing around poles and in businessmen's faces. You'd never have thought some crazy idiot had once driven a red MG onto the dance floor. I looked around—the bouncer was different. Same bulk, same bozo expression, different face. The girls were different too. They seemed younger than the girls I used to hire. Me! Hiring strippers! With eyes popping out of my head! Me! Unleashed! On a conga line of scantily dressed females barely teetering over the age of consent! Although the truth was, in my two years of auditioning, hiring, firing, and managing girls I had not slept with any of the strippers, except three. In this business, that's nothing.

We took a seat in front of the stage and ordered drinks and sipped them slowly.

"I don't like it here," Jasper said.

"Me neither," I answered. "Why don't you like it?"

"Well," he said, "I don't understand the logic of strip clubs. Brothels make sense. Brothels I understand. You want to fuck, you go there and you fuck, you orgasm, you leave. Sexual satisfaction. Easy. Understandable. But strip clubs—at best, if you don't find them disgusting, you get sexually excited, then because you can't actually fuck these women, you leave sexually frustrated. Where's the thrill in that?"

"Maybe we're not as different as you think," I said, and he smiled. Honestly, with all the noise a father makes about demanding respect and obedience, I don't think there can be a father in the world who doesn't, at the bottom of his heart, want a simple thing: for his son to like him.

"Oh my God," Jasper said. "Look at that bartender."

"What bartender?"

"That one. Isn't he one of the millionaires?"

I took a good look at the thin Asian man behind the bar. Was he or wasn't he? I wasn't sure. I don't want to say anything racist like "They all look alike," but you can't deny the similarities.

"Look at him," Jasper said. "He's working his arse off. Why would a millionaire be doing that?"

"Maybe he spent all the money already."

"On what?"

"How should I know?"

"I know. Maybe he's one of those people who have worked so hard their whole lives they don't know how to do anything else."

We sat there for a while thinking of people who need hard work to give them self-esteem, and we felt lucky we weren't one of them. Then Jasper said, "Wait. There's another fucking one."

"Another fucking what?"

"Another fucking millionaire! And this one's taking out the garbage!"

This one I recognized, as he was in the first batch of winners. It was Deng Agee! I'd been to his house! I'd personally tormented him!

"What are the odds that . . ." My voice trailed off. It wasn't worth saying. We knew what the odds were. Like a horse race with one horse in it.

"Bastard," I said.

"Who?"

"Eddie. He's fucked us."

We drove straight to the Hobbs building and grabbed the files of the millionaires. We read them and reread them, but there was no way of knowing how many friends Eddie had made rich through my scheme. He'd screwed me. He'd really screwed me. There was no way that eventually someone wasn't going to find out about this. That snake! That's friendship for you! It was a truly annihilating betrayal. I wanted to pull down the night with my bare hands.

As we hurried over to Eddie's house, I assumed that Eddie, my so-called friend, had dropped me unceremoniously into the shit on a whim. What I didn't know then, of course, was that it was so much worse than that.

We were halfway up the path to his house, hidden behind a jungle of fern, when we saw him waving from the window. We were expected. Naturally.

"This is a pleasant surprise," Eddie said, opening the door.

"Why did you do it?"

"Do what?"

"We went to the club! We saw all the goddamn millionaires!"

Eddie was silent for a minute before saying, "You took your son to a strip club?"

"We're fucked! And you fucked us!"

Eddie walked into the kitchen and we followed.

"It's not the end of the world, Marty—no one knows."

"I know. And Jasper knows. And it's only a matter of time before someone else knows!"

"I think you're overreacting. Tea?" Eddie put the kettle on.

"Why did you do it? That's what I want to know."

Eddie's explanation was poor. He said, with no hint of shame, "I wanted to do something nice for my friends."

"You wanted to do something nice for your friends?"

"That's right. These guys have had a really rough time of it. You can't imagine what a million dollars means to them and their families."

"Jasper, do you think there's something not right with his explanation?"

"Eddie," Jasper said, "your explanation sucks."

"See? Even Jasper thinks so, and you know we don't agree on anything. Jasper, tell him why his explanation sucks."

"Because if you made all your friends millionaires, why are they all still working at a strip club?"

Eddie seemed unprepared for this excellent question. He lit a cigarette and wore an industrious expression, as if he were trying to suck the smoke into his right lung only.

"You got me there."

He's guilty as hell, I thought, and there's something sinister he's not telling me. He was oozing the worst kind of bullshit—obvious, but not transparent enough to see the reason behind it.

"Answer the question, Eddie. Why the fuck are these millionaires all working in minimum-wage jobs in a sleazy rundown strip club?"

"Maybe they spent all the money already," Eddie said.

"Bullshit!"

"Christ, Martin, I don't know! Maybe they're the kind of people who've worked all their lives and don't know how to do anything else!"

"Eddie. Twenty million people are sending in twenty million dollars every week, and when they find out their money isn't being distributed fairly but is going into the pockets of your friends, whom they will consider *my* friends, what do you think will happen?"

"Maybe they won't find out."

"People will find out! And we'll all go down!"

"That's a bit melodramatic, isn't it?"

"Eddie, where's the money?"

"I don't know."

"You have it!"

"Honestly, I don't."

None of us said anything. Eddie finished making his tea and sipped it with a dreamy look on his face. I was getting madder and madder. He seemed to have forgotten we were there.

"How can we bury this?" Jasper asked.

"We can't!" I said. "We just have to hope no one figures it out."

As I said this, I realized my mother was wrong when she once told me no matter how far down a road you've gone, you can always turn back. I was on a one-way road with no exits and no room to turn around. It was an entirely justifiable feeling, as it happened, because two weeks later everyone figured it out.

Chapter Five

Enter the cannibalistic vigor of the press into my life once again. The story broke all at once, in every paper, on every radio and television station. I was masticated, and good. Leading the charge was none other than Brian Sinclair, the has-been current affairs reporter whom I'd seen with my son's girlfriend.

Caroline and I were eating dinner in an Italian restaurant, at a table by the window. We were digging into an enormous slab of veal in lemon sauce when his slick silver head popped into my line of vision. We locked eyes through the window. As a public figure, I was accustomed to the odd camera pointing at me like a judge's finger, but the slippery eagerness on Brian's face had an effect on me similar to the sudden drop of cabin pressure in an airplane. He signaled furiously at his cameraman. I took Caroline's hand and we bolted out the back door. By the time we got home, the phone was ringing off the hook. That night we saw our backs disappear on the six-thirty news.

As it turns out, the fourth estate has nothing better to do these days than to boast like weekend fishermen. And Brian was there, his arms outstretched, declaring that he had landed the exclusive story of the biggest scandal in Australia's history. He had no trouble linking at least eighteen of the millionaires to the Fleshpot—each a bartender or an accountant or a bouncer or a dishwasher, all running around on camera with their hands over their faces, the physical gesture that's as good as a confession. Yet the story that developed later that night was not what I had expected, mainly because when I confronted Eddie with his crime, he hadn't told me the true nature of his plot. The report was not, as I had anticipated, about Eddie's friends receiving the benefits that belonged in the pockets of ordinary Australians. I knew it was more complicated and dangerous than that when I finally answered the phone and the journalist on the other end asked the out-of-the-blue question "Just what is your relationship with Tim Lung?"

Who?

Here's what I found out. The two nightclubs formerly managed by Eddie and for a short time by myself were owned by a Thai businessman named Tim Lung. So far, out of the 640 millionaires made, 18 had at one time or another been employees of this Tim Lung. Eddie had worked for him for many years and obviously was still working for him. The money Eddie had loaned me to build my labyrinth had in reality come directly from Tim Lung. This man whom I had never heard of had, unbeknownst to me, financed my house. He had given me a job as manager of his club. There was nothing I could say. I was tied to him. Or rather, for some unknown reason, he was tied to me. The evidence was circumstantial yet incriminating. Was that all? No, that wasn't all. It was enough to hang me, but it wasn't all.

Further investigations brought to light that Tim Lung had owned a small fleet of fishing trawlers seized by French authorities for trafficking guns and ammunition from France to North Africa. This meant the work I had done some twenty years earlier, in Paris, loading and unloading crates on the banks of the Seine, was done for this same fucking guy. Tim Lung—he had been responsible for the underworld battle that led to Astrid's death all those years ago! My head was spinning. I kept replaying the revelations over in my head. Tim Lung: I had worked for him in France, he had given me a job in Australia, he had financed my house and had finally called in the favor by ripping off the millionaires scheme. Was that what he'd wanted all along? How could that be possible? And how was anyone to believe the unbelievable fact that I had never heard of him? And how could I never have heard of him? A man whom I had been tied to almost all my adult life? This shadowy Thai businessman turned out to be one of the key figures in my life, and this was the first I was hearing of him. Incredible!

I went online to do a search and found a couple of grainy photos and a link to an old interview on a Thai-language corporate website. He was a tall, thin man in his late fifties. He had a gentle smile. There was nothing about his features to suggest criminality. His eyes weren't even set too close together or too far apart. I turned off the computer, having learned nothing, and not long after the police raided our offices and all the computers were taken. They went on to dig up people I'd known and purposefully forgotten; people I'd worked with in short-lived minimum-wage jobs, inmates at the mental hospital, even prostitutes came out of the woodwork to throw in their two cents. Everyone was on the warpath that led to me.

It was the white-collar crime of the century. I was cooked! I was the personification of everything hated in this country—another fat cat milking decent, hardworking, ordinary Australians of their wages. I was officially a scumbag. A bag of scum! A shitheel. A heel of shit! I was all these things, and more. To my surprise, I was identified racially. A Jew! Even though I had never had any contact with the Jewish community, any more than I'd had with the Amish, the newspapers referred to "Jewish businessman Martin Dean." And for the first time I was accurately called "half brother" of Terry Dean. That's it. That's how I knew I was done for; they were distancing my crimes from those of my iconic brother. They wouldn't stand for me taking Terry's legacy down with me.

A lifetime of my fearing people was finally validated—people proved themselves to be absolutely frightening. The whole country was in a whirlwind of hate, a hatred so intense and all-encompassing, you couldn't imagine any of them were still able to kiss their loved ones at night. This was the instant I felt my destiny—to be an object of loathing—arrive and also the moment I realized there was something to this business of negative energy after all. I felt the waves of detestation profoundly, in my guts. Honestly, you wonder how they ever sneaked the abolishment of the death penalty past a mob like that. I was not unaccustomed to witnessing my countrymen's hatred focused like death rays over the years: I remember the minister whose wife had paid for designer sunglasses with *taxpayers' money*, and that practically was the end of the minister's career. His son's phone bill! Or the MP who was forced to deny claims that she tried to get into the Royal Easter Show for free. The people were upset that she didn't pay her twelve dollars. Twelve lousy dollars! Imagine what they'd do to me!

Of course the appalled faces of my political opponents barely concealed their delight; they adored anything that allowed them to look indignant on behalf of the electorate. It was effortless the way they ground me to dust. They were spared the trouble of having to cook up a scandal to fry me. All they had to do was express shock and act swiftly, to appear to be the one with his foot on my neck. They were all lining up to denounce me, their voices dipped in sewage, pushing each other out of the way to take credit for my downfall.

Oscar was powerless to stop all this, assuming he even wanted to. Reynold had taken over the matter. Anouk tried to reason with her father-in-law and asked him to help me, but Reynold was resolute. "It's too late now," he said. "You can't stop a tidal wave of hatred once it's reached the shore." He was right. There was no point making a foolish protestation of innocence. I knew how it worked. I was already sliced and diced in everyone's mind, so what was I still doing here? You could see it in their eyes—they were astonished that I was still breathing. What a nerve! I considered appealing to the charitable parts of themselves. I even toyed with the idea of telling them I had cancer, but I dropped it. I'd assaulted their pockets, and nothing would soften them to my case.

They could learn that my skin was being peeled away by a blind cook who had mistaken me for a giant potato, and they would cheer. Cheer! It seems that in our society Christianity has made permanent inroads in the eye-for-an-eye department but has made little progress on the practical application of forgiveness.

The biggest irony about this whole thing was that the chemotherapy sessions were over and were successful. So just when I had my life back again, it became unlivable. The Buddhists are right. Guilty men are not sentenced to death, they are sentenced to life.

Sadly, Jasper too was the hapless recipient of a severe hammering. I'm ashamed to say he finally had to pay for the sins of the father. He began receiving messages like "Please tell your father that I am going to kill him!" Poor bastard! He became a death-threat messenger service. And don't think my wife got off any easier. Poor Caroline! Poor babe in the woods! She foolishly agreed to interviews, thinking she could set the record straight. She didn't understand that they had her role clearly defined and would not stand for it to be corrected or amended. By pitting ourselves against the battler, we had lost our talent to be Australians, and thus our right to a fair go was forfeited. They savaged her. My one actual lie was uncovered and it became public knowledge that Caroline and I had grown up together. Thus her being made a millionaire made her look as guilty as I was. She was left weeping on national television. My love! Women spat on her in the street. Saliva! Actual saliva! And sometimes the saliva wasn't even white but the dirty dark-green of long-term smokers. Caroline was not prepared for this; at least I'd had a childhood of persecution to prepare me, many mouthfuls of bitter experience to line my stomach. I started out as a figure of contempt and that's how I ended up—hard to be too upset about it.

And now the saddest part, the tragedy: all my reforms were systematically dismantled, all my innovations, all my warped progress. That was it! The shortest social revolution in history! This little slice of Australian history was going down as a blight. They no longer liked the farce I had orchestrated. It was all coming clear to them now: they'd been hoodwinked. We were right back where we started. Further back, even. They were fast reducing me to a meaningless aberration, rewriting history at supersonic speed. Whole months were wiped out with every thirty-minute current affairs report. Every TV channel had the sad face of a pensioner telling of her sacrifice in sending in her one dollar a week, all the things lost she could have bought: milk, dishwashing liquid, and, with no trace of irony, lottery tickets. Yes, the national lottery was back in business. People had their crummy odds again.

•

In the mirror, I tried to smile; the smile made my sadness look like a permanent disfigurement. It was my own fault! I shouldn't have fought against my meaninglessness any more than I should've fought against those tumors. I should've nursed my tumors until they grew huge and meaty.

I spent the majority of those days stretched out on the floor of my bedroom, my chin resting on the beige carpet until my chin felt beige, and my insides too: beige lungs, beige heart pumping beige blood through my beige veins. I was on the floor when Jasper charged in, intruding on my peaceful beige existence to pass on all the death threats he'd received on my behalf.

"And who the fuck is Tim Lung?" he asked.

Rolling over onto my back, I told him everything I knew, which wasn't much.

"So my mother died on one of his boats in the middle of one of his gang wars."

"You could put it that way."

"So this man murdered my mother."

"She committed suicide."

"Either way, this bastard has ruined our lives. Without him, I might have a mother, and you might not be Australia's newest love-to-hate-him guy."

"Maybe."

"What does Eddie say about him?"

"Eddie's not saying anything."

It was true. The authorities were giving him a hard time too, not only as the administrator of the scheme. Having overstayed his visa, he was already a criminal—they confiscated his passport, called him in for questioning every other day, but had not yet deported him to Thailand, as he was needed for their investigations. Even so, he was the only calm one among us. His calm was natural and impermeable. I suddenly admired him, because even though I suspected that his tranquillity was just a mask, it was the most solid and durable mask I had ever seen.

"This is some mess," Jasper said. "What are you going to do?"

Good point. This was major fraud. Everyone said it: Martin, you will have to prepare yourself for prison. How do you *prepare* yourself for such a thing? By locking yourself in the closet with some stale bread and water? But I'd have to do something. The odds against me were stacking up—stupidly, the state was even reopening the file on *The Handbook of Crime*. It suddenly occurred to them that they had a case after all. I was like a derelict building scheduled for demolition, and everyone was crowding around to watch.

My only hope was to try to pay back some of the money, on the off-chance that would appease the people a little. I would maintain that I had been as duped as they had, that I would do everything in my power to pay back every cent, even if I spent my life doing it. It was a weak ploy, but I gave it a shot. I had to sell my labyrinth. It was heartbreaking to have to part with what I had so meticulously designed and brought to life, not to achieve a dream of happiness but to achieve a dream of deep suspicion and loathing, a dream of hiding, a dream I had realized—it had hidden me loyally for years.

The day of the auction, I was advised by everyone with a mouth not to show up, but I couldn't resist seeing who would be the new owner. Jasper was there too; after all, his hut would be sold in the bargain, the hut that we had both pretended to build with our bare hands. The prospective buyers numbered a thousand. I don't know how many were bona fide bidders and how many turned up just to gawk.

I was overcome with queasy shivers as I arrived. Everyone looked at me and murmured. I yelled out that murmur is the devolution of speech. No one said anything after that. I took my place under my favorite tree, but it didn't soothe my defeat; the enemy was drinking sparkling wine in the middle of the fortress designed to keep him out. People soon got caught in its teeth, though; it was satisfying how many had to be rescued from the maze. That delayed the proceedings. When the auction finally began, the auctioneer made a little speech referring to the house and the labyrinth as "the kingdom of one of Australia's most controversial minds," which gave me an uneasy, anxious feeling as well as a perverse sense of pride. I folded my arms regally, even though I knew they found me laughable and not like some dethroned king. This labyrinth betrayed the extent of my inflated fears, insecurities, and paranoia, so I felt psychologically naked standing there. Did they know they were all gathered in the place that proved my contention that I was the most scared man alive?

In the end, because of its curiosity, insanity, or infamy, my labyrinth and the two properties hidden within went for an astounding $7.5 million, nearly ten times their worth. This predictably convinced both the press and its loyal subjects, the people, that I was a wealthy man, which of course only served to reinforce their hatred of me. The buyers, I learned, ran a chain of overpriced furniture stores, and they intended to open the place as a tourist attraction. Oh well. As indignities go, it's not the worst.

I moved my books and my junk into storage and myself into an apartment Anouk rented for me and Caroline. I didn't even get a chance to offer my $7.5 million to the people like a piece of meat to a dog who'd much rather bite off my leg. The government seized all my assets and froze my bank account. Seized and frozen, and just waiting for the authorities to charge me, I couldn't be more powerless.

So, then—if I was being taken all the way down, I wanted to take someone with me. But who? I didn't bother hating my countrymen for hating me. I saved every droplet in my vast reservoir of fury for my abhorrence for journalists, those phony, self-righteous moral watchdogs in heat. For what they did to my mother, to my father. For loving Terry. For hating me. Yes, I would have my revenge against them. I obsessed about this revenge. That's why I didn't crack. I wasn't ready to fall apart yet. I conceived one last project. A hate project. A revenge project, despite the fact that I've never been good at revenge, even if it is mankind's oldest pastime. I've never been into defending my honor, either. Personally, I don't know how anyone can even say the word "honor" with a straight face. I ask you—what's the difference between "stained honor" and "dented ego"? Does anyone *really* still believe this shit? No, I wanted revenge simply because the media had repeatedly wounded my ego, my id, *and* my superego, the whole shebang. And I was going to get them good.

I borrowed money from Caroline and told her it was for legal expenses. Then I called on a private detective named Andrew Smith. He worked out of his home with his wife and poodle and looked like an accountant, not a private investigator. In fact, he looked like he did

nothing privately. When I sat down in his office and removed the hood
and glasses, he asked what he could do for me. I laid it all out for him.
And consummate professional that he was, he refrained completely from
judging me for my little, mean-spirited, hate-filled plan. He listened quietly, and at the end gave me a thin-lipped smirk where only one side of
his lips raised, and he said, "I'll get right on it."

•

Only two weeks later Andrew Smith came to me with that quasi-smile
of his. He was as thorough in his mission as I'd hoped—he had broken I
don't know how many privacy laws and presented me with a dossier.
While he fed his dog, I went through the files, giggling, gasping, and guf-
fawing. It was an incredible dossier, and if I hadn't had other plans for it,
I could've published it as fiction and made the bestseller list. Now all I
had left was to memorize it.

Then I set off to do the only really nasty thing I have ever done.

The live press conference was held on the steps of the Opera House,
for no good reason. The smell of the harbor and of the media scrum mingled in the cold morning air. Every reporter, current affairs host, shock
jock, and media personality in Sydney had shown up, and we all stood
dwarfed by the bizarre geometry of that iconic theater. This reunion, it
was something. Me and the media, like a divorced husband and wife
meeting for the first time in years at the funeral of their only child.

As soon as I swaggered up to the podium, they posed their loaded
questions, as if defending a high ideal. I cut them off.

"Hermaphrodites of the press. I have prepared a short statement: you
wouldn't know decency if it came up and shat on your face. That's it. I
told you it was short. But I'm not here to explain to you why you are par-
odies of your former selves, I'm here to answer your questions. And
knowing how you all like to shout your questions at the same time with
little or no regard for your comrades who might have small, fragile
voices, I will address each of you individually, and you may ask your
questions that way, one by one."

I gestured to the journalist standing closest to me. "Ah, Mr. Hardy, I'm
glad to see you here and not at your gambling counselor's, where you go
Tuesdays, Thursdays, and Saturdays. What is your question? No? No
question?"

They looked at each other in confusion.

"OK. What about you, Mr. Hackerman? I hope you're not too tired— after all, a man with a wife and two mistresses must have a lot of energy. Your first mistress, twenty-four-year-old journalism student Eileen Bailey, and your second mistress, your wife's sister June, obviously aren't keeping you as busy as one would think.

"What's going on? Where are the questions? What about you, Mr. Loader? I hope you're not going to hit me with a question in the same way you hit your wife—five times, one police intervention. Did your wife drop the charges because she loves you or because she's afraid of you? Anyway, what do you want to know? Nothing?"

I didn't let up. I let loose. I let all the cats out of all the bags. I asked in turn about their marriage counselors, penile implants, hair transplants, cosmetic surgery, about one who had cheated his brother out of his inheritance, about seven who had cocaine addictions and one who'd left his wife just after she was diagnosed with breast cancer. By humiliating them one by one, I turned the assembled crowd into individuals again. They were unprepared, squirming and sweating under the glare of their own spotlight.

"Didn't you tell your psychologist just last week that you've always wanted to rape a woman? I have the recording right here," I said, tapping my briefcase. What were a few defamation and invasion-of-privacy charges when I was going down for fraud? "And you, Clarence Jennings from 2CI. I heard from a certain hairdresser that you only like to sleep with your wife when she's menstruating. Why is that? Come on! Out with it! The public has a right to know!"

They were swinging their cameras and microphones on each other. They wanted to shut them off, but they couldn't miss the scoop when the competition was right there beside them. They didn't know what to do or how to act. It was chaos! You can't erase a live broadcast; their secret lives were dripping through television sets and radio speakers everywhere, and they knew it. They condemned each other out of habit, but then it was their turn in the sick limelight. They stared at me, at each other, disbelieving, ridiculed, like gnawed bones positioned upright. One removed his jacket and tie. Another sobbed. The majority wore terrified smiles. They appeared reluctant to move an inch. Caught with their pants down! Finally! These people had for too long taken on the importance of the subjects they reported on, strutting around as if they were celebrities themselves, yet laboring under the misapprehension that their lives were exclusively their own. Well, not anymore. They were caught in the morality traps they themselves had set. Branded by their own cruel irons.

I gave them a leering wink so they could be certain I had thoroughly enjoyed invading the sanctuary of their lives. Fear was in their throats— they were petrified. It was magnificent to watch the falling of great masses of pride.

"Now go home," I said, and they did. They went off to drown their sorrows in beer and shadows. I stayed alone, with the silence saying everything it always says.

•

That night I celebrated by myself in Caroline's apartment. She was there but wouldn't inhale so much as a champagne bubble in the name of victory.

"Well, that was childish," she said, standing at the fridge eating ice cream from the carton. Of course she was right. Nevertheless, I felt sublime. As it turned out, hateful revenge was the only pure aspiration from my youth that had survived intact, and its satisfaction, however puerile, deserved at least one glass of Moët et Chandon. But the awful inevitability of the situation had dawned on me: they'd be coming for me soon with redoubled strength. I must *right now* choose between the reality of prison and the reality of suicide. I thought I really would have to kill myself this time. I couldn't do prison. I have a horror of all forms of uniform and most forms of sodomy. So suicide it was. According to the conventions of this society, I'd seen my son reach adulthood, so my death would be sad but not tragic. Dying parents are allowed to moan about not seeing their children grow up, but not about not seeing them grow old. Well, fuck—maybe I wanted to see my son graying and shrinking, even if I had to witness it through the foggy frosted glass of a cryogenic deep freeze.

What's that? I hear a car. Shit. I hear footsteps. The haunting percussive beat of footsteps! They stop. Now I hear knocking! Someone's knocking at the door! Suicide? Prison?

•

Well, what do you know: a third option!

I have to finish this off quick. There isn't much time.

I came out of the bedroom to see Caroline curled up on the couch like a long skinny dog. "Don't answer it," she said, not speaking these words out loud but mouthing them noiselessly. I took off my shoes and crept up to the door. The floorboards complained under me. I gritted my teeth, took a few more creaky steps, and peeped through the peephole.

Anouk, Oscar Hobbs, and Eddie were standing there with big convex heads. I opened the door. They all hurried inside.

"OK. I've spoken to a friend in the federal police," Oscar said. "I had a tip-off. They're coming to arrest you tomorrow."

"Morning or afternoon?" I asked.

"Does it matter?"

"Maybe a little. I can get a lot done in five or six hours." That was just bravado. The truth was, I've never been able to get anything done in five or six hours. I need eight.

"And what's *he* doing here?" I asked, pointing at Eddie.

"We've got to get out of here," Eddie said.

"You mean—run?"

Eddie nodded with such energy he lifted up onto his toes.

"Well, if I decide to run, what makes you think I'd run with you? And where could we go anyway? The whole of Australia knows my face now, and it's not something they cherish."

"Thailand," Eddie said. "Tim Lung has offered to hide you."

"That crook! What makes you think—"

"You'll die here in jail, Marty."

That settled things. Not even I would go to jail simply to be able to tell Eddie to fuck off. "But we'll get stopped at the airport. They'll never let me leave the country."

"Here," Eddie said, handing me a brown envelope. I looked inside and pulled out the contents. Australian passports. Four of them. One for me, one for him, one for Caroline, and one for Jasper. Our photos were there but the names were different. Jasper and I were Kasper and Horace Flint, Caroline was Lydia Walsh, and Eddie was Aroon Jaidee.

"How did you get these?" I asked.

"Courtesy of Tim Lung."

Yielding to an impulse, I picked up an ashtray and hurled it against the wall. It didn't change anything substantial.

"But it's still my face on the passport!" I shouted.

"Don't you worry about that," Eddie said. "I have it all worked out."

Caroline put her arms around me and we assaulted each other with whispered questions, each terrified to acknowledge the desires of the other lest they contradict.

"Would you like me to come with you?" Caroline asked.

"What do you want to do?"

"Will I make life hard for you on the run? Will I be in the way?"

"Do you want to stay?" I asked wearily.

"Dammit, Martin, just tell me one way or the other. Do you want me to work on your case from here?" Caroline offered, the idea having arrived at her lips at the same time it struck her brain. I understood that her questions were thinly veiled answers.

"Caroline," Anouk said, "if Martin goes missing, the police are going to give you a pretty hard time."

"So will the public," Oscar added.

Caroline was suffering. The shape of her face seemed to lengthen like a shadow. I watched conflicting thoughts play out in her eyes.

"I'm scared," she said.

"So am I."

"I don't want to leave you."

"I don't want to be left."

"I do love you."

"I was beginning to think . . ."

She put her finger on my lips. Normally I hate it when people shut me up, but I love it when women put their fingers on my lips.

"We'll go together," she said breathlessly.

"OK, we're coming," I said to Eddie "But why did you get a passport for Jasper? He doesn't need to go on the run."

"I think he should," Eddie said.

"He wouldn't."

"The family that sticks together . . ." he said, without finishing. Maybe he thought I'd finish it for him. How could I? I have no idea what happens to the family that sticks together.

•

It was perhaps the saddest moment of my life, saying goodbye to Anouk. It was awful not to be able to say I would see her soon, or even later. There would be no soon. Nor a later. This was it. It was growing dark. The sun was setting with urgency. Everything had sped up. The air was charged. Oscar never forgot that he was taking a risk coming here; he tapped his finger on his leg with increasingly rapid intensity. The sand was racing through the hourglass. Anouk was desolate. We didn't hug so much as we grasped each other. It's only at the moment of goodbye that you understand the function of a person: Anouk had been there to save my life and she had done it, many times over.

"I don't know what to say," she said.

I didn't even know how to say "I don't know what to say." I just hugged her tighter while Oscar cleared his throat a dozen times. Then they left.

Now I am packed and waiting. The plane leaves in about four hours. Caroline is calling me. Though for some reason she is calling me Eddie. Eddie answers. They aren't talking to me.

I think I'll leave this manuscript here in a box in the apartment, and maybe one day it'll be found and someone will have the smarts to publish it posthumously. Maybe it can act as a makeover from beyond the grave. Certainly the media and public will take our escape as concrete evidence of our guilt—they don't have enough insight into human psychology to know that escape is evidence only of fear.

And now, on our way to the airport, we have to stop by Jasper's apartment and say goodbye to him too. How am I going to say goodbye to my son? It was hard enough when he moved out of home, but what words will form the goodbye that says I'm going to live the rest of my days as Horace Flint in Thailand in a nest of seedy criminals? I suppose I'll warm him with the consolation that his father, Martin Dean, will never be eradicated after all, but it will be Horace Flint who will earn himself a grave in some swampy Thai cemetery. That should cheer him up. OK. Now Caroline is really calling me. We have to go. The sentence I am now writing is the last sentence I will write.

SIX

Why, oh why did I go on the run too? Why did I throw in my lot with Dad, after all that had happened between us? Because I'm the dutiful son? You never know. I loved my father, no matter how imperfectly. Is that any reason? I mean, loyalty is one thing, but the man had destroyed my life, after all. That should've reserved me the right to let him tear off into the wilderness without me. He had meddled unforgivably in my relationship. OK, it wasn't his fault I was in love with a girl who was not a girl but a building on fire. And it wasn't his fault either that she chose a man who was not me. I had no case; I *was* me, and embarrassingly so. It wasn't Dad's fault I couldn't strong-arm her affections, that I couldn't think of an offer she couldn't refuse. So she refused me, that's all. Was it my father's fault that this flaming edifice loved her failed ex-boyfriend and sacrificed us on the altar of that love? No, it wasn't. But I blamed him anyway. That's the great thing about blame; she goes where you send her, no questions asked.

That Eddie had rigged the millionaires and dropped Dad in the shit was such a juicy stab in the back that I was dying to tell my girlfriend about it before the news broke, even if, strictly speaking, she wasn't my girlfriend. Maybe it was just a good excuse to see her—the spilling of family secrets. And I needed an excuse. The Inferno had left me, and establishing contact with someone who has left you is a tricky business; it's very, very hard not to come off looking pathetic. I'd already made two attempts at seeing her, and both times I'd come off looking pathetic. The first time I returned a bra that belonged to her that she'd left in my hut, and the second time I returned a bra belonging to her that I'd actually bought that morning in a department store. Neither time was she happy to see me—she looked at me as if I had no business in her line of vision.

The third time I went to her house and left my finger on the buzzer. I remember it was a beautiful day, with shreds of sinewy cloud twisting in fresh wind, the air smelling of a thick, heavy fragrance like the expensive perfume rich women put on their cats.

"What do you want?" she asked impatiently.

"Nothing. I just want to talk."

"I can't talk about us anymore because there is no more us. Well, there is an us, but it's not you and me. It's me and Brian."

"Can't we just be friends?" I asked (already pathetic).

"Friends," she answered slowly, with a puzzled look on her face, as if I'd actually asked her if we could just be fish.

"Come on," I said. "Let's go for a walk."

"I don't think so."

"Just around the block?"

She relented, and on the walk I told her everything that had happened regarding the millionaires, how Eddie had scammed Dad badly by rigging the winners to include most of his friends, and how if anyone found out, he'd be crucified.

I remember at the time I simply wanted to be close to her again, if only for a moment, and spilling our potentially life-destroying secret seemed to be the way to achieve this. It achieved nothing of the kind. In actuality, as a cathartic unburdening of secrets goes, it was intensely unsatisfying. "Your father's crazy anyway," she said, as though that were somehow relevant. When we arrived back at her building, she got serious. I knew this because she took my hand. "I still have feelings for you," she said. I was about to say something. I know this because I opened my mouth, but she cut me off. "But I have stronger feelings for him." So then I was to understand it was a competition for the relative strength of her feelings. Brian was getting all the potent ones; I was getting the leftovers, the tepid, hardly breathing, barely conscious affections. No wonder I couldn't feel them.

Of course I made her swear not to tell anyone the secret I'd told her. And of course she told the man she loved, because without thinking, I had given her a breaking news story to salvage his flagging journalistic career.

So is that why I joined Eddie, Dad, and Caroline on the run? I went along seeking forgiveness? Maybe, though why should I have stayed? I'd just had the worst year of my life. When the Towering Inferno dumped me, I had moved from the spaciousness of Dad's labyrinth into a long thin apartment that was not much more than a glorified corridor with a bathroom and an L-shaped space at the end where you could stick a single bed and anything L-shaped you happened to have lying around. The move from the bush to the city had an unexpected and serious destabilizing effect on me. In my hut, I had been close to the voice of the earth and never had to strive to feel at ease. Now, in the city, I found that I was cut off from all my favorite hallucinations. I'd left myself behind. Banished from the source, I felt entirely at sea.

Then, when Dad became a public figure adored by the nation, I'll admit it—his fame hit me hard. How could twenty million people like that irritating man? I mean, six months before he couldn't get ten friends in a room for a dinner! The world was yet to fall off its hinges, though; one mild afternoon Dad visited me at work, in his suit, stiff as if unable to bend his knees. He stood awkwardly in my cubicle, looking like a house boarded up, and our sad, silent confrontation climaxed with him telling me the awful news. He hardly had to say it. I don't know how, but I already knew. He had been diagnosed with cancer. Couldn't he see I knew as soon as he approached? I practically had to shield my eyes from the glare of death.

These were the strange, turbulent days; Dad married his brother's ex-girlfriend, Anouk married the son of a billionaire, Dad was betrayed by his best friend, I was betrayed by my true love, and he was despised by an entire nation. In the media, the descriptions of him varied: a businessman, a swindler, a Jew. I remember he was often obsessed with his inability to

define himself. Hearing himself compartmentalized in this way only served
to remind him who he wasn't.

Everything was going wrong. I was getting death threats from
strangers. I had to take a leave of absence from work. I was lonely. I wandered the streets endlessly and tried to pretend I saw the Inferno everywhere, but there just weren't enough six-foot redheads in Sydney, and I
wound up mistaking her for some laughable substitutes. Retreating to my
apartment, I became so depressed that when it came time for eating, I
thought: What's in it for me? At night I kept dreaming of a single face,
the same face I used to dream about in childhood, the ugly face contorted in a silent scream, the face that I sometimes see even when I'm
awake. I wanted to run away, but I didn't know where to, and, worse, I
couldn't be bothered doing up my shoes. That's when I started chain-
smoking cigarettes and marijuana, eating cereal out of the box, drinking
vodka out of the bottle, vomiting myself to sleep, crying for no reason,
talking to myself in a stern voice, and pacing the streets, which were
crammed with people who, unlike me, were conspicuously *not* screaming
inside and *not* paralyzed by indecision and *not* hated by every person on
this vile island continent.

I took up my post in bed, under the covers, and stayed there, only
shaken out of a drunken sleep one afternoon to see Anouk's green eyes
peering at me.

"I've been trying to call you for days."

She was dressed in an old undershirt and tracksuit pants. The shock
of marrying money was obviously forcing her to dress down.

"This is very strange, Jasper. I have the exact same feeling as when I
first walked into your dad's apartment after we met. Remember? Look at
this place! It's disgusting. Trust me on this—beer-can ashtrays are a sign
you can't ignore!"

She ran around the apartment, cleaning up energetically, undaunted
by the moldy food and general debris of my day-to-day existence. "You'll
need to repaint these walls to get the smell out," she said. I fell asleep listening to the rising and falling of her voice. The last thing I heard her
say were the words "Just like your father."

I woke a few hours later to find the whole apartment clean and
smelling of incense. Anouk sat with her long legs crossed on the floor,
her shoes kicked off, a sunbeam reflecting off her ankle bracelet. "Too
much has happened. You're overstimulated. Come down here," she said.

"No thanks."

"I taught you how to meditate, didn't I?"

"I don't remember."

"Your dad could never turn off his mind—that's why he was always breaking down. Unless you want to suffer the same mental deterioration, you're going to have to achieve a stillness of the mind through meditation."

"Leave me alone, Anouk."

"Jasper. I'm just trying to help you. The only way you're going to survive all this hatred is if you have inner peace. And to find inner peace, you first have to reach the higher self. And to find the higher self, you have to find the inner light. Then you join the light."

"Join the light. To what?"

"No—you and the light become one."

"What's that going to feel like?"

"Bliss."

"So it's good, then."

"Very."

Anouk went on in this way, about inner peace, about meditation and the power of the mind not to bend spoons but to thwart hatred. She wasn't fooling me. She was only a wannabe guru—hearing rumors of enlightenment was as far as she'd got. Still, we tried to find peace, light, our higher and lower selves, and all those in between. Anouk thought I might be a natural at meditation, since I'd confided in her that I suspected I could read my father's thoughts and often saw faces where there should be none. She seized these revelations zealously, and her frenzied voice became more insistent. Just as in the old days, I was defenseless against her fanatical compassion. I let her buy flowers and wind chimes. I let her buy me books on different approaches to meditation. I even let her drag me to a rebirthing experience. "Don't you want to remember your own birth?" she snapped, as if she were noting forgetfulness as another of my character traits. She took me to a center that had walls the color of an old woman's gums, and we lay in a dimly lit room in a semicircle, chanting and regressing and struggling to recall the moment of birth as if we were trying to remember someone's phone number. I felt like a fool. But I loved being around Anouk again, so I went along with it, and every day afterward, as we sat cross-legged in parks and on beaches, repeating our mantras over and over again like obsessive-compulsives. For those couple of weeks I did nothing but watch my breathing and attempt to empty my mind, but my mind was like a boat with a leak; every time I got rid of a bucket of thoughts, new ones poured in. And when I thought I might have achieved the slightest emptiness, I got scared. My emptiness was not blissful but felt malignant. The sound of my own breathing was faintly sinister. My posture seemed theatrical. Sometimes I'd shut my eyes only to see that strange and terrible face, or else I'd see nothing but I would hear, faint and muffled, my father's voice, as if he were talking to me from inside a box. Clearly meditation couldn't help me. Nothing could help me. I was beyond help, and not even a sudden sun shower could lift me up. In fact, I started wondering what I had seen in nature all that time I lived in the labyrinth. It suddenly seemed to be horrible and ostentatious, and I wondered if it was blasphemous to tell God that rainbows are kitsch.

So that was my state of mind when Dad, Eddie, and Caroline turned up at my apartment building and honked the horn until I went down onto the street. The car just sat there, engine idling. I went over to the window. They were all wearing dark sunglasses, as though they shared a collective hangover.

"They're coming to arrest me tomorrow," Dad said. "We're making a run for it."

"You'll never make it."

"We'll see. Anyway, we just came to say goodbye," Dad said.

Eddie was shaking his head. "You should come with us."

That seemed a good reason to shake *my* head, so I did, and asked, "What are you crazy fugitives going to do in Thailand?"

"Tim Lung has offered to put us up for a while."

"Tim Lung?" I shouted, then whispered softly, "Christ."

That's when an absurd and dangerous idea entered my head with an almost audible pop. Just as I loved the Inferno with clenched fists, I hated Tim Lung with open arms.

I thought: I will kill him. Kill him with an impersonal bullet to the head.

"Are you all right?" Dad asked.

In that instant I knew I was not above the fulfillment of a bloodthirsty fantasy. For months I'd been harboring vile ideas about people (I dreamed of filling their mouths with haggis), and now I knew actual violence was the next logical step. After years of witnessing my father's seasonal dissolutions, I had eons ago resolved to avoid a lifetime of intense contemplation; an abrupt departure into murder seemed the way to go about this. Yes, suddenly I was no longer in the darkness, groping along the endless corridors of days. For the first time in a long time, the path ahead was well lit and clearly defined.

So when Dad said his dried-eyed goodbye for the last time, I said, "I'm coming with you."

II

Take it from me: the thrill and anticipation of voyage is compounded when traveling on a fake passport. And we were taking a private plane— Dad's famous face wasn't going to get out of Australia without a hefty bribe. Hidden under hats and behind sunglasses, we arrived at the airport and went through a security gate straight out to the tarmac. Eddie said the plane belonged to a "friend of a friend," and he handed envelopes of cash to a couple of unscrupulous customs officials, which was to be shared among the corrupt ground crew and baggage handlers. Frankly, everyone we met looked utterly at ease with the transaction.

As we waited for Eddie to finish the dispensation of bribes and the completion of phony paperwork, Caroline rubbed Dad's back while Dad ironed out the wrinkles in his own forehead. Nobody would look at or talk to Eddie. I couldn't help but feel a kind of grief for him. I knew he deserved the alternating fury and cold shoulder he was getting, but his congenital half smile made him look so hapless, so un-Machiavellian, I might have risen to defend his indefensible behavior if only the jury present weren't so predisposed to a beheading. "Once we get in the air, we'll be fine," Dad said, to calm himself down. That surreal phrase stuck in my head: "Once we get in the air." No one else said anything; we were all lost in thought, probably the same thought. The whole time we avoided talking about the future, as it was inconceivable.

We boarded the plane without incident (if you don't count Dad's inhuman sweating as an incident), afraid even to cough so as not to blow our cover. I beat Eddie to the window seat, as this was my first time leaving Australia and I wanted to wave goodbye. The engines started up. We took off with a roar. We climbed the sky. Then we leveled out. We were in the air. We were safe.

"Narrow escape," I said.

Eddie looked surprised, as if he'd forgotten I was there. His gaze drifted past me to the window.

"Goodbye, Australia," he said a little nastily.

So that was it—we had been hounded out of Australia. We were now fugitives. We would probably all grow beards, except Caroline, who would dye her hair; we would learn new languages and camouflage ourselves wherever we went, dark green for jungles, shiny brass for hotel lobbies. We had our work cut out for us.

I looked over at Dad. Caroline had her head resting on his shoulder. Every time he caught me looking at him, he gave me an "Isn't this exciting?" look, as if he were taking me on a father-son bonding holiday. He'd forgotten we were already insidiously bonded, like prisoners in a chain gang. Outside, the sky was a flat color; stark, austere. I watched Sydney disappear from sight with something approximating grief.

Five hours later we were still flying over Australia, over the inconceivably bleak and uninviting landscape of our demented country. You can't believe how it goes on and on. To appreciate the harrowing beauty of the interior you have to be in the middle of it, with a well-stocked escape vehicle. Topographically it's incomprehensible and terrifying. Well, that's the center of our country for you. It's no Garden of Eden.

Then we were flying over water. That's it, I thought. The stage on which our unbelievable lives played out has slipped away, under the clouds. The feeling ran deep inside my body until I felt it settle in and get comfortable. All that was left to think about was the future. I was apprehensive about it; it didn't seem to be the type of future that would last long.

"What does he want with us?" I asked Eddie suddenly.

"Who?"

"Tim Lung."

"I have no idea. He has invited you to be his guests."

"Why?"

"I don't know."

"Well, how long does he want us to stay?"

"I don't know."

"What do you know?"

"He's looking forward to meeting you."

"Why?"

"I don't know."

"Christ, Eddie!"

We were giving ourselves up to the mysterious Tim Lung. Having used Dad to filch millions of dollars from the Australian people, did he now want to thank Dad for playing the sap so amiably? Was it curiosity—did he want to see how stupid a man could be? Or was there some darker purpose none of us had thought of?

The lights in the plane were turned off, and as we flew across the planet in darkness, I thought about the man I'd be killing. From media reports I'd learned that frustrated detectives in Thailand, unable to locate him, made assertions that he was the embodiment of evil, a true monster. Clearly, then, the world would be better off without him. Nevertheless, I was depressed by the realization that murder was the only utilitarian idea I'd ever had.

III

"There's no one here to meet us," Eddie said, scanning the airport crowd.

Dad, Caroline, and I exchanged looks—we hadn't known there was supposed to be.

"Wait here," Eddie said. "I'll make a call."

I watched Eddie's face while he spoke to someone who I assumed was Tim Lung. He was nodding vigorously, bent over in an absurdly servile posture and with an apologetic grin on his face.

Eddie hung up and made another call. Dad, Caroline, and I watched him in silence. Occasionally we gave each other looks that said, "Things are out of our hands but we have to do something, and this knowing look is it." Eddie hung up again and stared at the phone awhile. Then he came over, rubbing his hands together gloomily.

"We have to spend the night in a hotel. We'll go to Mr. Lung's place tomorrow."

"OK. Let's get a taxi," Dad said.

"No—someone is coming to take us."

Twenty minutes later a small Thai woman arrived, so wide-eyed it seemed she had no eyelids. She stepped toward us slowly, trembling. Eddie just stood there like a cow chewing its cud. The woman wrapped her arms around him, and as they hugged, low sobs escaped through her small mouth. I knew Eddie was lost in the moment because he suddenly ceased looking slippery. Their embrace went on and on until it became monotonous. We all felt painfully awkward.

"I have long wanted to meet you," she said, turning to the rest of us.

"You have?" I asked doubtfully.

Then Eddie said, "Ling is my wife."

"No, she's not," Dad said.

"Yes, I am," she answered.

Dad and I were thrown into shock. Eddie was married?

"Eddie, how long have you been married?" I asked.

"Nearly twenty-five years."

"Twenty-five years!"

"But you live in Australia," Dad said.

"Not anymore."

Dad couldn't get his head around it. "Eddie," he said, "twenty-five years. Would that mean you were married when we met in Paris?"

Eddie smiled, as if that were an answer and not another question.

We left the airport bewildered. We were not just in another country but another galaxy, one in which Eddie had been married for *twenty-five years*. Outside, the heat hit us forcefully. We all piled into an old olive-green Mercedes and sped off to the hotel. As it was my first time in a foreign country, my eyes soaked it up—but I'll save you the travelogue description. It's Thailand. You know the sights, you know the smells. You've read the books, you've seen the movies. Hot, sticky, sweaty, it smelled of spicy food, and everywhere there lurked a hint of drugs and prostitution, because like most travelers, we had brought our preconceived notions with us on the journey and did not check them, as we should have, into immigration as hazardous materials best suited for quarantine.

In the car, Eddie and Ling spoke quietly in Thai. We heard our names mentioned several times. Dad couldn't take his eyes off Eddie and his wife. His wife!

"Hey, Eddie. You have any children?" Dad asked.

Eddie shook his head.

"You sure?"

Eddie turned back to Ling and continued speaking softly.

As we checked into the hotel, careful to sign our new names and not the old ones, it struck me that the strangest thing for me was not just to be traveling, suddenly well and truly out of Australia, but to be traveling in a group. I had always imagined leaving Australia would be the ultimate symbol of my independence, and yet here I was, with *everybody*. I know you can never escape yourself, that you carry your past with you, but I really had. Small mercy that I wound up getting my own room, which looked down on an eviscerated dog's carcass.

That night I paced the hotel room. All I could think of was that by now news of our escape would be all over Australia, in every last watering hole, and despite our furtive exit, someone was bound to trace us without too much difficulty. I could easily imagine Australia's reaction on hearing that we had absconded, and at around three in the morning I felt hit by what I was sure was a hot wave of loathing that had traveled from our homeland all the way to our air-conditioned hotel rooms on Khe Sahn Road.

I went out into Bangkok wondering how to buy a gun. I didn't think it would prove too difficult; in my head this was a sordid metropolis, a Sodom and Gomorrah that served really good food. I was in a semidelirious state, only looking at faces, and more specifically at eyes. Most of the eyes I saw were irritatingly innocent; only a few cauterized you just by looking. Those were the ones I wanted. I thought about murder and murderers. My victim was also a criminal; who would cry for him? Well, maybe many people. Maybe he was married too! I thought with a gasp. I don't know why I should've been so surprised; why shouldn't he be married? He wasn't notorious for being ugly and unsociable, only for being amoral. That's attractive in some circles.

It was four in the morning and still oppressively hot and I hadn't yet found a single gun. I walked on, thinking, "Tim Lung—should I kill you straightaway, without even offering you an aperitif?" As I walked, I lit a cigarette. Why not? It's not the number one preventable cause of death in the world for nothing.

I was tired and leaned against a post. I felt a pair of eyes on me. There was something frightening yet strangely invigorating about these eyes. These were the eyes I'd been looking for.

I went over to the young man and we spoke at the same time.

"Do you know where I can buy a gun?"

"Do you want to see a sex show?"

"Yes, please."

He whisked me down the street and took me to Patpong. Large groups of Western men were going into strip clubs and I thought immediately of Freud, who believed that civilization develops in an ever-increasing contrast to the needs of man. Clearly Freud had never been to Patpong. Here the needs of man were scrupulously taken care of, every need, even the needs that made him sick.

I went into the first bar and sat on a stool and ordered a beer. A young woman came and sat on my lap. She couldn't have been older than sixteen. She put her hand between my legs and I asked her, "Do you know where I could buy a gun?" At once I knew I'd made a mistake. She hopped off my lap as if it had bitten her. I saw her talk excitedly to a couple of heavy types behind the bar. I made a run for it, thinking I had slipped into one of those unrealities where you can really hurt yourself, and after a few blocks I stopped running. In effect, these Thai characters were no more criminal than people you'd find at any corner fish-and-chips shop in Sydney, and simply purchasing a gun from them was impossible. In that case, when I met Tim Lung, I'd have to improvise.

When I went down to the hotel breakfast room in the morning, I deduced from the look on Dad's and Caroline's faces that they hadn't slept either. They were wretched, sleepless faces. Faces pinched with worry. Over a large nonexotic breakfast of bacon, eggs, and stale croissants, our banter was light and meaningless, to try to overpower the dark mood. Whatever was in store for us, we wanted to weather it on a full stomach.

Eddie came in without his usual benign expression.

"You ready?"

"Where's your wife?" Dad asked.

"Shut the fuck up, Martin. I've had enough of you. I've really, really had enough."

That silenced us all.

IV

To get to Tim Lung's place we had to catch a long-tail boat down a dirty, foul-smelling canal. As we passed wooden canoes laden with multicolored fruits and vegetables, I shielded my face from threatening splashes of murky water. My first impressions of Thailand were good, but I knew that my immune system wasn't up to the challenge of its bacteria. Once beyond this ragged fleet of watercraft, we were alone in the canal, pressing forward. On either side, sitting lopsided on dusty streets, were houses that looked either semicompleted or semidilapidated. We passed women in large-brimmed straw hats washing their clothes in the brown water, evidently unfazed by the idea of encephalitis nesting in their underwear. Then there were long, deserted, dusty streets and huge trees with sprawling branches. The houses, now grand and flashy mansions, were spaced farther apart. I sensed we were getting close. I tried reading Eddie's face. It was unreadable. Dad gave me a look, the subtext of which was "We've escaped, but into what?"

The boat stopped. We stepped off and walked up a small embankment to a large iron gate. Before Eddie could ring the buzzer, a sharp voice from a tinny intercom said something in Thai and Eddie answered it, looking at me, which gave me the feeling that we were on a road on which to go back was suicide and to go forward was probably suicide. I had goose bumps all over. Caroline took my hand. The gate swung open. We pressed on. Dad said something about the state of his bowels which I didn't quite catch.

Tim Lung's house had "drug cartel" written all over it. It was large, with huge whitewashed walls surrounded by encrusted pillars, gleaming orange and green roof tiles, and an enormous reclining Buddha nestled in a thick bamboo grove. It was reinforced that we were waltzing into a den of thieves when I spotted men hidden in the shade of trees with semiautomatic rifles, eyeing us as if we had come selling a product they knew didn't work. The men wore short-sleeved shirts and long pants. I pointed out the armed men to Dad for his predictable response. "I know," he said. "Long pants, in this weather!"

"This way," Eddie said.

We walked down a set of steep stairs into a rectangular courtyard. Stuck on spikes were severed pigs' heads with sticks of incense sprouting from their foreheads. Nice. On one wall of the courtyard was an extensive mural depicting a city razed by fire. Promising. At the end, large sliding doors were already open. I don't know what I was expecting—snarling Dobermans, tables piled high with cocaine and bags of money, prostitutes sprawled on white leather couches, and a trail of bloodstains leading to the mutilated corpses of dead policemen. What I wasn't expecting was the very last thing in the world I could have been expecting.

Dad saw it first. He said, "What the fuck?"

On both walls, in frames or stuck up with brown tape, were hundreds and hundreds of photographs of Dad and me.

I said it too: "What the fuck?"

V

"Marty! They're photos of you!" Caroline shouted.

"I know!"

"And you too, Jasper!"

"I know!"

"Is this you as a baby? You were so cute!"

Our faces from various epochs peered out at us from all over the room. This perverse exhibition comprised all the photographs Eddie had taken over the past twenty years. There were images of a young Dad in Paris, lean and tall, with all his hair and a strange beard on his chin and neck that couldn't or wouldn't make its way onto his face; Dad, before he started collecting fat cells, smoking thin cigarettes in our first apartment. And there were just as many of me, as a baby and groping my way through childhood and adolescence. But it was the photos of Paris that interested me most: photographs and photographs of Dad with a young, pale, beautiful woman with a demoralizing smile.

"Dad, is that . . . ?"

"Astrid," he confirmed.

"Is this your mother, Jasper? She's beautiful!" Caroline cooed.

"What's this about?" Dad shouted, his voice echoing through the house. Dad was a bona fide paranoiac who had finally discovered, after all these years, that there really *was* a conspiracy against him.

"Come on," Eddie said, leading us deeper into the house.

Dad and I were frozen. Had this something to do with Astrid's suicide? With my mother dying on one of Tim Lung's boats? We were thrust into the role of detectives, forced to investigate our own lives, but our mental journeys into the past were futile. We just didn't get it. We were weakened and exhilarated at the same time. A paranoiac's nightmare! A narcissist's dream! We didn't know how to feel: flattered or raped. Maybe both. We were puzzling at breakneck speed. Obviously Eddie had infused this criminal overlord with an obsession for Dad and me, but what had he said? What *could* he have said? I imagined him in late-night drinking sessions with his boss: "You wouldn't believe these characters. They're insane. They shouldn't be allowed to live!"

"Mr. Lung is waiting for you in there," Eddie said, pointing to double wooden doors at the end of the hallway. He had the colossal nerve to be smirking.

Dad suddenly grabbed him violently by the shirt collar; it looked as if he were planning to pull the shirt over his head—Dad's first official act of physical violence. Caroline pried his fingers loose. "What have you got us into, you bastard?" he shouted, though it wasn't as threatening as he intended. Fury mingled with genuine curiosity just comes out strange.

An armed guard emerged from a doorway to investigate the commotion. Eddie disarmed him with a nod. Disappointed, the guard retreated into the shadows. Apparently Eddie had a nod that was irrefutable. That was news to us. We continued down the hallway toward the double wooden doors in a daze, examining more photos on the way. Until now, I'd never realized how much Dad resembled a dog being pushed unwillingly into a swimming pool. And me—suddenly my identity felt like a less solid thing. I found it almost impossible to connect with the pictorial history of ourselves. We looked like damaged relics of a failed civilization. We didn't look comprehensible at all.

And my mother! My heart nearly burst open looking at her. In all the photos she looked silent and motionless; all the action went on behind the eyes, the kind of eyes that look as if they have come back from the farthest corners of the earth just to tell you not to bother going there. Her smile was like a staircase leading nowhere. Half obscured in the corners of frames, there was her sad beauty, she was resting her head in her hands, her tired eyes clouding over. Perhaps it was coincidence, but in each photo she seemed to be farther and farther away from the camera lens, as if she were shrinking. These images gave me a newfound respect

for Dad—she looked like a distant and imposing woman whom no sensible person would enter into a relationship with. I took one photograph
of her off the wall and broke it out of the frame. It was black-and-white,
taken in a laundromat. My mother was sitting on a washing machine,
legs dangling, looking directly into the camera lens with her strikingly
large eyes. Suddenly I knew this mystery had something to do with her—
here I would receive the first clue as to who she was, where she came
from. One thing was clear to me: the riddle of my mother's existence
would be answered behind that door.

Dad opened it, and I followed close behind.

VI

We entered a large square room with so many pillows on the floor that
part of me just wanted to lie down and be fed grapes. Large indoor ferns
made me feel we were outside again. The walls didn't quite reach the
ceiling and sunlight poured through the space above them, except for
the far wall, which was made of glass and looked out on the overgrown
Buddha in the garden. There, at the wall of glass, was a man, his back to
us, staring out at that Buddha. They were the same build. In the bright
light that came through the window, we could see only the man's giant
silhouette. At least, I think it was a man. It looked more or less like one,
only bigger.

"Mr. Lung," Eddie said, "may I present Martin and Jasper Dean. And
Caroline Potts."

The man turned. He was not Thai, Chinese, or Asian at all. He had
blond scraggly hair and a bushy beard covering pulpy, blemished skin,
and he was wearing shorts and a cut-off flannelette shirt. He looked like
an explorer recently returned from the wilds, enjoying his first taste of
civilization. That's an off-the-point description, though, one ignoring the
elephant in the room, because most of all he was the elephant in the
room, the fattest man I'd ever seen or was ever going to see, an astounding freak of nature. Either he had a hormone disorder or the man
must have eaten fiendishly for decades with the express ambition of becoming the biggest man alive. His body shape was unreal to me—his

hideousness was suffocating. I could no more kill this monstrosity with a bullet than I could dent a mountain by slapping it.

He stared at us without blinking an eye, even while he put out his cigarette and lit a fresh one. Clearly he was planning to stare us into submission. It was working. I felt exceedingly meek, as well as fantastically thin. I looked at Dad to see if he was feeling meek too. He wasn't. He was squinting at the enormous man as if he were one of those magic puzzles that reveal a hidden image.

Dad spoke first, as though talking in his sleep. "Bloody hell," he said, and at once I knew.

Caroline said it before anyone. "Terry," she said.

Terry Dean, my uncle, looked from one of us to the other and broke into the widest smile I had ever seen.

VII

"Surprised? Of course you are," he said, laughing. His echoey, powerful voice sounded like it came from deep within a cave. He limped toward us. "You should see the look on your faces. You really should. Do you want me to get a mirror? No? What's the matter, Marty? You're in shock? Understandable, very understandable. We'll all just wait here until the shock dies down and makes way for anger and resentment. I don't expect any of you to take this lying down. This isn't one of those things you laugh about straightaway, right up front, but later, when it's all sunk in. Don't worry—it'll sink. In a few days you'll be hard-pressed to recall a single day I wasn't alive. But tell me, did you suspect it? Even a little? What am I thinking? Here you are, seeing your long-dead brother after all these years, and not only does he have the effrontery to be living and breathing, he hasn't even offered you a beer! Eddie, get us some beers, will you, mate? And Jasper! I've been wanting to meet you for a long time. Do you know who I am?"

I nodded.

"My nephew! You have your grandmother's nose, did your dad ever tell you that? I'm so happy to see you. Eddie's told me all about you. You must be some kind of rock, living with your dad without shattering into a million little pieces. But you look like you've turned out all right. You look so normal and healthy and adjusted. How is it that you're not crazy! It's crazy that you're not crazy! Though maybe you are. That's what I'm looking forward to finding out. And Caroline! Seeing you comes as a bit of a shock, I'll admit. Of course Eddie told me you'd married . . ."

Terry stared at her for a long moment before snapping himself out of it.

"I know, you're all caught off guard. Drink your beers, you'll feel better. I'll wait until you calm down. There's time. Christ, if there's one thing we all have, it's time. Marty, you're giving me the heebie-jeebies with that look. You too, Caroline. But not you, Jasper, eh? Maybe because you're still young. When you're older, it's a surprise that you can still be surprised. I wonder, what's the bigger surprise, that I'm so wonderfully alive or that I'm so wonderfully fat? You can say it—I don't mind. I like being fat. I'm Henry the Eighth fat. Buddha fat. Let's get it out of the way so we're not bogged down in it. I'm a fat fuck. I'll just take off my shirt so you can see the extent of it. See? OK? I'm a whale. My belly is unrelenting! Invincible!"

It was true. He was so enormous he gave the impression he was indestructible, that he could survive any cataclysm. The zoo of animal tattoos Dad had described to me many years ago had stretched into shapeless swirls of color.

Dad had stiffened. He looked like he wanted to say something but his tongue wasn't cooperating. "Alive . . . fat," was all he could manage.

It dawned on me that Terry was sort of confused himself. He didn't know who to look at. Every now and then he turned and gazed searchingly at me, perhaps his best chance of immediate love and acceptance. He wasn't getting it, because despite the incredible news that a family member so thoroughly mythologized was alive and well, more than anything I felt a bitter disappointment that this had nothing to do with my mother after all.

"Isn't anybody going to give me a hug?"

No one moved.

"So who is Tim Lung?" Dad said finally.

"Tim Lung doesn't exist. Neither did Pradit Banthadthan or Tanakorn Krirkkiat, for that matter."

"What are you talking about?"

"I'm doing it, Marty. I'm finally doing it."

"Doing what?"

"The democratic cooperative of crime."

Dad spasmed as though he'd been jump-started with cables. "You're *what*?!" he screamed. This was the first emotive response he had given.

"Well, mate, the first time I stuffed it up good and proper. Harry was onto something, though. This thing works like a charm."

"I can't believe it! I can't fucking believe it!"

This apparently was a bigger shock to Dad than the news that Terry had been alive all this time.

Caroline said, "What's the democratic—"

"Don't ask," Dad interjected. "Oh my God."

Terry clapped his chubby hands with delight and hopped up and down on his stumpy legs. I was thinking how utterly different he was from the young renegade who had so often appeared in my mind's eye. This fat man was the same sporting hero, the same fugitive, the same vigilante worshipped by the nation?

Suddenly his knees locked up and he looked embarrassed.

"Eddie tells me you've been ill," Terry said.

"Don't change the subject," Dad said, his voice turbulent with emotion. "I scattered your ashes, you know."

"You did? Where?"

"I put them in bottles of cayenne pepper in a small supermarket. The rest I dumped in a puddle on the side of the road."

"Well, I can't say I deserved any better!" Terry laughed loudly and put his hand on Dad's shoulder.

"Don't touch me, you fat ghost!"

"Mate. Don't be like that. Are you pissed off about the millionaires thing? Don't be. I just couldn't resist. As soon as I heard about what you were doing in Australia, Marty, I knew what I had to do. I've been rescuing you from one drama or another your entire life. And helping you has made me who I am. I don't regret it. I love who I am, and just taking those millions in such an obvious scheme was the easiest way for me to rescue you one last time. You see, mate, I wanted you to come here. I thought it was high time we saw each other again, and I was long overdue to meet Jasper."

I could see that Dad's inward rage had almost made its way out. An evil storm was churning in him, and it had everything to do with Caroline. He noticed that she was demonstrating none of the rage; she was

quiet, still literally gaping at Terry in horror and wonder. Terry, meanwhile, aimed his smiling eyes back at me.

"Hey, nephew. Why don't you say something?"

"How did you get out of solitary confinement?"

Terry's face looked empty of thought for a moment, before he said,
"The fire! Of course! And Marty, you told him the whole story. Good for
you! Good question, Jasper, right at the beginning."

"Were you even in solitary?" Dad asked.

We all leaned forward with utter absorption as Terry began.

"I sure was! That was a close one. I almost did get baked—in solitary
there are no windows, of course, but I heard a lot of screaming, guards
shouting orders to each other, and when the smoke came under the door
I knew I was cooked. It was pitch-black in that cement cage, hotter than
hell and full of smoke. I was terrified. I started shouting, 'Let me out! Let
me out!' But no one came. I banged on the door and nearly burned my
arm right off. There wasn't anything I could do, and it took all the psychological effort I could muster to calm myself down enough to settle in
for an unpleasant death. Then I heard footsteps in the corridor. It was
one of the guards, Franklin. I recognized his voice: 'Who's in there?' he
shouted. 'Terry Dean!' I answered. Good old Franklin. He was a good
man who loved cricket and he was a big fan of my rampage. He opened
the door and said, 'Come on!' and in his panic to save me, he let down
his guard. I knocked him unconscious, took his clothes, threw him in the
cell, and locked the door."

"You murdered the man who came to save you."

Terry paused a moment and gave Dad a strange look, like a man deciding whether or not to explain a complex natural phenomenon to a
child, then continued. "After that it was easy. The whole prison was on
fire, and I didn't even have to use the keys I'd stolen—all the doors were
open. Somehow I made my way through the smoke-filled corridors and
out of the prison, I saw the town up in flames and disappeared into the
smoke. That was it."

"So it was Franklin who burned in your cell."

"Yeah, I guess it was his ashes you scooped up."

"What happened next?"

"Oh yeah—I saw you in the fire. I called out to you, but you didn't see
me. Then I saw that you were running into a trap. I shouted, 'Left, turn
left!' and you turned and disappeared."

"I heard you! I thought it was your bloody ghost, you mongrel!"

"Spent a couple of days in Sydney lying very low. Caught a freighter to Indonesia. Worked my way around the globe checking out the other continents to see what they had to offer, and wound up here in Thailand. That's when I started the democratic cooperative of crime."

"What about Eddie?"

"Eddie started working for me at the beginning. I tried to track you down, Marty, but you'd already left Australia. So the best I could do was get Eddie to go and wait near Caroline. I had her address from a letter she'd sent me in jail, and Eddie took a room next to hers and waited for you to show up."

"How could you be so sure I'd go see Caroline?"

"I wasn't sure. But I was right, wasn't I?"

"Why didn't you just get Eddie to tell me you were alive?"

"By then I felt like I'd caused you enough trouble. You were really looking out for me back then, Marty, and you probably thought I didn't notice, but I knew you'd worried yourself sick about me. I figured you'd had enough."

"You told Eddie to make Caroline a millionaire!"

"Of course!" Turning to Caroline, he said, "When I heard about your son, I was so sorry."

"Go on, Terry," Dad said.

"That's it. I had Eddie keep tabs on you. When he told me you were with some nutty lady who you got pregnant and you didn't have any money, I told him to give you some. But you wouldn't take it. I didn't know how to help, so I gave you a job working for me. Unfortunately, it was a bad time—you waltzed right into the middle of a little gang warfare. I didn't know your lunatic girlfriend was going to jump on the boat and blow herself up. It was a nutty way to do yourself in, wasn't it? Sorry, Jasper."

"What else?"

"Anyway. When you took Jasper to Australia, I got Eddie to follow. He came back with some crazy reports. I gave you a job again, running one of my strip clubs, and you smashed the place and wound up in hospital. Then I gave you some dosh so you could build your maze, and that's that. Then you warped the whole of Australia with your strange ideas and here we are. That pretty much brings us up to date."

As Dad absorbed his brother's story, his whole being looked to me like a Hollywood façade, as if I were to take a step around him, I'd see he was only one inch wide.

"When I was in that cell," Terry said, "and thought my death was seconds away, I saw clearly that everything I had tried to do, to tidy up the ethics in sport, was fucking meaningless. I realized that, barring accident, I could have lived for eighty or ninety years, and I had blown it. I was furious with myself! Furious! I tried to reason why I had done it, what I was thinking, and I realized that I'd been trying to leave a trace of myself so that after I was gone, I would still kind of be here. Everything is summed up in that idiotic 'kind of.' And you know what I realized on the very edge of death? That I couldn't give a fuck. I didn't want to build a statue of myself. I had an epiphany. Have you ever had one? They're great! This was mine: I found out that I had killed myself because I wanted to live forever. I had tossed my life away in the name of some daft I don't know what—"

"Project," I said. Dad and I looked at each other.

"Project. Yeah. Anyway, I swore if I got out of there I'd live in the moment, fuck everyone, let my fellow man do whatever he wants, and I swore that I'd follow Harry's advice and stay anonymous for the rest of my days."

Terry suddenly turned to Caroline with clear, serious eyes.

"I wanted to call you, but every time I was about to, I remembered that cell, that death chamber, and I understood that the way I loved you was sort of possessive, and like my sporting rampage, it was a way of barricading myself against, I don't know . . . death. That's why I've chosen to love only prostitutes. There's no chance of getting into that old routine of jealousy and possessiveness. I took myself out of the competition, like Harry said. I'm free, and I've been free since that day. And you know what I do now? When I wake up every day, I say to myself ten times, 'I am a soulless dying animal with an embarrassingly short lifespan.' Then I go out, as the world sinks or swims, and make myself a little more comfortable. In the cooperative our profits aren't outstanding, but we make a fairly decent living, and we can afford to live like kings because Thailand's cheap as chips!"

A long silence followed, in which no one knew where to look.

"Australia loves you," Dad said finally.

"And they hate you," Terry said back.

Despite their divergent paths in life—two diametrically opposed roads less traveled—the brothers had come to the same conclusion, Terry, naturally, through epiphany and the cathartic afterbirth of his near-death trauma, and Dad through reflection and thought and intellectually obsessing about death. Uneducated Terry, the man Dad had once described as being unable to write his name in the snow with his piss, had somehow intuited the traps of the fear of death and with ease sidestepped them, as if they were dog turds on a brightly lit street. Dad, on the other hand, had intellectually recognized the traps but still managed to fall into every one of them. Yes, I could see it in his face straightaway. Dad was crushed! Terry had lived the truth of Dad's life, and Dad never had, even though it was *his* truth.

"So what happens now?" Dad asked.

"You stay with me. All of you."

We looked at each other, knowing that it was a bad idea but that we had no other choice. Nobody moved. We were like a tribe of cave dwellers whose cave had just caved in. As my eyes shifted from my father to his brother, I thought: These sick characters are my family. Then I thought: Career criminals and philosophers have a surprising amount in common—they are both at odds with society, they both live uncompromisingly by their own rules, and they both make really lousy parent figures. A few minutes passed, and even though nobody budged in any direction, I felt like the two brothers were already tearing me apart.

VIII

Life in Thailand was easygoing. They call it the land of smiles. That's not an empty tag: Thais never stop grinning, so much so that at first I thought we'd landed in a vast land of simpletons. Generally, though, the chaos of Bangkok was in harmony with my state of mind. There was only one thing I had to watch out for other than the tap water and those suspicious smiles: Thais have such a deep regard for heads and such a low opinion of feet that everyone kept telling me I should not point my tootsies at people's noggins. They must have thought I was planning to.

A travel guide told me that foreigners can be ordained as Buddhist monks and I thought that sounded like an impressive addition to my résumé, but I found out that monks must abstain from murdering bugs (even if they invade your pajamas), stealing, lying, sex, luxuries, and in-toxicants, including beer and double espressos, and I didn't think that left anything except meditating and the ritual burning of incense. Their philosophy is based on the understanding that all life is suffering, and all life *is*, especially when you abstain from stealing, lying, sex, luxuries, beer, and double espressos. Anyway, I was too full of hate to be a Buddhist monk; in my thoughts I composed letters to the Towering Inferno that had compound words in them like "cunt-bitch" and "whore-nose" and curses such as "I hope you cough your uterus out your mouth." Buddhists generally don't think like that.

I told Terry of my plan to murder Tim Lung and we laughed until our sides ached. It was a great icebreaker. After that, we spent many days and nights together, and I would go to bed with my ears exhausted but buzzing. Like his brother, Terry was prone to unrelenting talking jags, crazy monologues on every conceivable subject. Sometimes they'd be broken by moments of introspection, when he'd hold up one finger as if to put the universe on mute; he'd sway on his fat stumpy legs in open-mouthed silence, his pupils would narrow as though I'd shone a torch on his face, and minutes would pass like this before his finger would come down and he'd continue talking. He did this wherever we went: in restaurants and at vegetable markets, at the poppy fields and in the sex shows. The more time I spent with Terry, the more I saw behind his mis-chievous smile an inner strength and something ageless. Even the breaded-fish crumbs on his beard looked timeless, as if they had always been there.

He had unbelievable habits. He liked to roam the streets to see if someone would try to rip him off. Often he'd let them pick his pockets, then laugh about what was taken. Sometimes he'd stop the pickpockets and tell them what they did wrong. Sometimes he checked into back-packer hostels and partied in a German accent. And he never missed a single sunrise or sunset. One afternoon we watched a dark orange sun bleed into the horizon. "This is one of those sunsets made glorious by the pollution of a congested city. Someone has to say it and it might as well be me—Nature's own work pales in comparison. The same goes for mass destruction. One day we'll all be basking in the glow of a nuclear winter and God, won't it be heaven on the eyes!"

In addition to heroin smuggling and prostitution, the democratic co-operative of crime's main trade was gambling on Thai boxing matches, the national sport. Terry would take me along when he bribed the boxers to take a dive. I remember thinking about his legacy in Australia, how he had been obsessed with fighting corruption in sport, and I was impressed with the way he now shat all over it like this. Often, on the way to the matches, Terry tried to get a tuk-tuk to give the drivers a scare—none would take my mammoth uncle, so we would be forced to walk. He never once got angry; he'd be happy to have the opportunity to stop at a vegetable market and buy a fresh bunch of coriander to wear around his neck ("Better smell than any flower!"). During the boxing match he would ask me all about myself: what I liked, what I didn't, what were my hopes, my fears, my aspirations. Despite prostitutes, gambling, and drugs being his bread-and-butter, Terry was the sort of man who inspired you to be honest. I revealed myself to him as I never had to anyone else. He listened to my confessions seriously, and when I recounted the horror/love story of the Towering Inferno, he said he thought that I had "loved her sincerely, though not really." I couldn't argue with that.

But what thrilled me most about my uncle was that he spoke of the real world—of prisons and bloodbaths and sweatshops and famines and slaughterhouses and civil wars and kings and modern-day pirates. It was a wonderful relief to be out of the philosophical realm for a change, the oppressive, suffocating universe of Dad's thought culs-de-sac and thought outdoor toilets. Terry talked of his experiences in China, Mongolia, Eastern Europe, and India, his forays into remote and dangerous territories, the murderers he'd met in dingy gambling joints, how he picked them to join the democratic cooperative of crime. He talked of his reading and how he started with all of Dad's favorite books, how he'd struggled through them at first, how he'd fallen in love with the printed word, and how he read voraciously in deserts and jungles, on trains and on the backs of camels. He told me of the moment he decided to begin his prodigious eating (it was in the Czech Republic, a cold potato dumpling soup). He saw food as his link to humanity, and while traveling, he was invited to family dinners wherever he went; he ate ritualistically with all races, tasting every culture and custom across the globe. "To be fat is to love life," he said, and I realized that his belly wasn't an impenetrable fortification against the world but a reaching out to embrace it.

Most nights whores entered the house, sometimes two or three together. Their professionalism melted away at the sight of Terry's enormous body, their famous Thai smiles morphing into grimaces on their young, fresh faces. The rest of us couldn't help but feel sorry for these prostitutes as they led Terry to the bedroom like zookeepers conspiring to tranquilize an agitated gorilla. By the time they emerged though, he was vindicated; the girls were happy, exalted. They came out looking strengthened by the experience—rejuvenated, even. And he had his favorite whores too, ones who came back night after night. They often ate with us, and they never stopped smiling and laughing. You couldn't deny that he loved them passionately. He showered them with affection and attention, and I really believed he didn't feel icky that they went off to fuck and suck other men. His love really was uncomplicated. It was love without possessiveness. It was real love. And I couldn't help comparing his love for the prostitutes with my love for the Towering Inferno, which was so bogged down in the issue of ownership, it could easily be argued that what I'd felt for her didn't even resemble love at all.

•

Dad spent the first few months in Thailand remote and surly. On the rare occasions we risked outings and sat in restaurants frequented by Australian tourists, his name would pop up in their conversations, and hearing himself disparaged in the third person nauseated him. He often bought the Australian papers and read them while grinding his teeth, and afterward he wrote long letters to the editors, letters I begged him not to send. As for me, I stayed a mile away from the papers and swore to do so for all time. I've come to the conclusion that reading the newspaper is sort of like drinking your own piss. Some people say it's good for you, but I don't believe it.

Maybe the hate waves from Australia finally took their toll, because Dad started dying again. It was clear that the cancer had reemerged in his lungs and was spreading. Over a period of a few months, his body became the centerpiece in a theater of horror. It looked as if he were being eaten from the inside out. He moved gruesomely from flesh to bone. He became pale and looked as though his essence had been suffused with methane. Eventually he avoided mirrors altogether. He stopped shaving and wandered around Terry's place like a castaway, so thin he was swimming in his clothes. Then, just as suddenly, his trajectory toward death plateaued. He didn't get any better, but he stopped getting worse. It was clear to me that he was waiting for something, waiting to *do* something, and he wasn't going to die until he did it. There's a lot to be said for the power of obstinacy. People often will themselves to stay alive; cripples walk and dead men get erections. Look around. It happens.

At first Terry and Caroline did nothing but plead with him to see doctors and begin another course of chemotherapy, but Dad refused. I knew it was doubtful that I could persuade him to do anything, but I couldn't help thinking of Anouk and her obsessive belief in the powers of meditation. I tried to convince him that the possibility remained that by extreme efforts of concentration he might vanquish the cancer on his own. To humor me, he tried one afternoon. We sat together at the foot of the Buddha. I instructed him that superhuman efforts of the most intense form of mind control were required, but Dad was never able to clear his mind of skeptical thoughts. In the middle of meditation, he opened one eyelid and said, "You know what Mencken said about the human body? He said this: 'All the errors and incompetencies of the Creator reach their climax in man. As a piece of mechanism he is the worst of them all; put beside him, even a salmon or a staphylococcus is a sound and efficient machine. He has the worst kidneys known to comparative zoology, and the worst lungs, and the worst heart. His eye, considering the work it is called upon to do, is less efficient than the eye of the earthworm; an optical instrument maker, who made an instrument so clumsy would be mobbed by his customers.' "

"That sounds true," I said.

"Well, then—what makes you think meditation can override my body's congenital frailty?"

"I don't know. It was just an idea."

"It's a useless idea. Remember how Heraclitus said a man's character is his fate? That's not true. It's his body that is his fate."

Dad pulled himself up, using the Buddha's toes as leverage, and staggered back toward the house. Caroline was standing at the door, watching us.

"How did it go?" I heard her ask.

"It was great. I'm healed. I'll live for another several billion years. I don't know why I never tried it before."

Caroline nodded wearily, then accompanied Dad back inside.

Poor Caroline. On top of her role as primary caregiver, she had her own problems. She surprised herself by succumbing to emotional outbursts and crying fits. She'd been profoundly shaken by the events in Australia. She had always seen herself as somewhat of a thick-skinned, carefree, unself-conscious woman who loved life and never took any aspect of it seriously, least of all public opinion. But the outpouring of hatred focused on her had a serious and permanent destabilizing effect. She had become cautious and introverted; she saw this difference and no longer liked herself. On top of that, the reappearance of Terry, her childhood love, had called her marriage to Dad into question. I wasn't sleeping well, so I was often witness to their midnight soap operas. Caroline would go bleary-eyed into the kitchen to make herself a cup of tea. Dad would sneak down the hallway after her and peer around the doorway. His soupy breathing always gave him away.

"What are you doing?" she'd ask.

"Nothing. Stretching my legs."

"Are you spying on me?"

"I'm not spying. I missed you, that's all. Isn't it romantic?"

"What do you think I'm going to do? Do you think I wait until you're asleep and then . . . what?"

"What do you mean?"

"You know what I mean!"

I tell you, you've never heard so much subtext in your life!

Caroline and Dad shared the bedroom next to mine. Often I'd hear the three a.m. opening of sliding doors. I'd sit up in bed and look out my window at the slim figure of Caroline crossing the lawn to the reclining Buddha. In the moonlight I could see everything. Sometimes she'd rest her head on Buddha's shoulder, and if the night was still and the birds asleep, I could make out the soft sound of her voice drifting into my room. "He's fat and disgusting. And a criminal. He's a fat, disgusting criminal. And he's dead. He's fat and he's dead and he likes whores." Once I heard her say, "And who am I? Look at *my* body. I'm no prize."

The most painful moments came when it was time for bed. We'd be sprawled on cushions on the floor, bloated and drunk from the evening meal. Suddenly conversations would become stillborn dialogues.

Dad: "I'm tired."
Caroline: "Go to bed, then."

Dad would stare at Terry in a faintly sinister way.

Dad: "In a little while."
Caroline: "Well, I'm going to bed."
Terry: "Me too."
Dad: "Me too."

Dad did everything he could not to leave Caroline and Terry alone to-gether. It was awkward, although I suspected he secretly loved the idea of being betrayed by his brother. To be betrayed by his brother was cheap melodrama of Biblical proportions, and it would be a gift to the dying man—a gift that showed life had not forgotten to include him in her grubby comedies. Then one night I saw Caroline sneaking out of Terry's room, her hair messed up, shirt half unbuttoned. She froze at the sight of me. I gave her a weary look—what was I supposed to do, wink? Still, I couldn't bring myself to blame her for her treachery. It was an untenable situation all around. I just wished she could have waited; it wouldn't be long before Dad was out of the way. Cancer thrives on broken hearts; it is a vulture waiting for you to give up on human warmth. Dad often talked about the shame of the unlived life, but it was the shame of his unloved life that was really killing him.

I wasn't sure if Terry was aware of his role in this triangle, and I don't think that in general he knew he had succeeded in doing what Dad had only dreamed about, and that by doing so he had irrevocably cut Dad off from himself. Otherwise, he maybe wouldn't have harassed Dad as much as he did.

Some months after our arrival, Terry got it into his head that it was within his powers to make Dad's final days a constant wonder and joy, and he recruited me to help. He dragged the three of us to bathe naked in the river, then to look at cloud formations, then to bet at a dogfight, then to wallow in flesh and booze at a drunken orgy. Dad seethed about all these interruptions to his dying in peace and threw Terry nothing but odious, hate-filled looks. As for me, I was relieved to be doing something. Maybe it was the sudden freedom of having someone else to worry about Dad, but ever since arriving in Thailand, I'd had an enormous amount of energy. I felt stronger too, as if I could wrestle an animal to the ground. I woke early each morning, spent the day walking from one side of Bangkok to the other, and went to bed late each night. I seemed to need very little sleep. I thrived on the activities Terry meant for Dad to thrive on.

One obscenely hot afternoon, after I had been on my feet for several hours, I lay down in the hammock, stared at that humongous Buddha, and made a sort of mental inventory of my life experiences to see if they in fact wove together seamlessly without my having noticed at the time. I thought if I could decode the order of the past, I could deduce what was coming next.

I couldn't. A shadow fell over me. I looked up at Terry's naked torso. It was always impressive to see him with his shirt off. It made me wonder if he hadn't reversed the usual order of enlightenment and achieved his Buddha-like serenity from the outside in.

"You ready?" Terry said.

"For what?"

"We're going to try kick-starting your father's motor again."

I swung my legs over the hammock and followed Terry into Dad's room. He was lying on the bed stomach down. He didn't acknowledge our presence in any way.

"Look, Marty, don't you find yourself a heavy weight, pinning you down?"

"Look who's talking."

"Don't you want instead to be a leaf blown in the air, or a drop of rain, or a wispy cloud?"

"Maybe I do. Maybe I don't."

"You need to be reborn. You need to die and be reborn."

"I'm too old for rebirth. And who do you think you are, anyway? You're a murderer a hundred times over, you're a drug pusher, a pimp, a gunrunner, yet you take yourself for a visionary and a sage! Why is it your hypocrisy doesn't make you sick?"

"Good question. It's an amiable contradiction, that's all."

God, how these unedifying discussions went on and on.

Terry hauled Dad out of bed and dragged us to a shooting range where you could use pump-action shotguns to hit the targets. Neither Dad nor I had much love for guns, and the force of the action sent Dad keeling over onto his back. Terry bent over him, and Dad looked up, his mouth open, trembling all over.

"Marty, tell me something—where has all this meditating on death got you?"

"Fucked if I know."

"Jasper says you're a philosopher who's thought himself into a corner."

"Does he?"

"Tell me about the corner. What does it look like? How did you get there? And what do you think would get you out?"

"Help me up," Dad said. When he was on his feet again, he said, "In brief, here it is. Because humans deny their own mortality to such an extent they become meaning machines, I can never be sure when something supernatural or religious in nature occurs that I did not manufacture my connection to it out of desperation to believe in my own specialness and my desire for continuance."

"Maybe because you've never had mystical experiences."

"But he has," I said. "Once he saw everything in the universe simultaneously. But he never followed up on it."

"So you understand the nature of the corner now? If men are constantly manufacturing meaning in order to deny death, then how can I know I didn't manufacture that experience myself? I can't know for sure, so I must assume I did."

"But then your whole life you haven't ever really taken your own soul seriously."

"Stop talking about the soul. I don't believe in it, and neither does Jasper."

Terry turned to me. I shrugged. In truth, I simply could not make up my mind about its existence. Dad was right—the immortal soul didn't wash with me. Its shelf life felt overestimated. I believed instead in the mortal soul, one that from the moment of birth is ceaselessly worn away and that will die when I die. Whatever its shortcomings, a mortal soul still seemed perfectly sublime to me, no matter what anyone said.

"Look, Marty. Let it go—the mind that wants to solve the mysteries of the universe. It's over. You lost."

"No, you look, Terry," Dad said wearily. "If I did live wrongly, if I made blunders and still have blunders coming up, I think maintaining the status quo of my deficient personality would be a lot less tragic than changing at the eleventh hour. I don't want to be the dying man who learns how to live five seconds before his death. I'm happy to be ridiculous, but I don't want my life to assume the characteristics of a tragedy, thanks."

I reloaded my shotgun and aimed at the target and, for the first time that day, hit the bull's-eye. I turned back to Dad and Terry, but neither had seen it. They were both unmoving, two brothers standing together but alive in very different worlds.

•

That night I buried myself deep under the covers. The shots Terry was firing at Dad seemed to be missing the target and hitting me instead. It occurred to me that the uncompromising position Dad held in the face of death was likely to be my own someday. Despite my desire to be his mirror opposite, I had to admit there were disturbing similarities between us. I also had a restless inquiring mind that aimed to solve the mysteries of creation, and like him, I didn't know how to find respite from this fruitless, unending investigation. I wasn't so sure Terry wasn't rocking my boat on purpose. He must have known Dad wasn't going to change one atom of his personality, and that's why he was intent on dragging me along for these outings. He was aiming at me and getting me square on. I knew that somewhere within me was a spiritual inclination that Dad lacked, but it was still faint and unresolved. It wouldn't take much to wake up one day and find I'd drifted away from my own center and was now tracing my father's footsteps like a zombie.

There was a knock on the door. I didn't say anything, but the door opened anyway. Terry waddled into the bedroom sideways.

"Damn these narrow doorways. Hey, Jasper, I need to pick your brain. What can we do to make your father's final days wonderful?"

"Fuck, Terry. We can't. Just leave him be."

"I know! Maybe we should go on a trip."

"All of us? Together?"

"Yes! In the country! We could go visit Eddie, see how he's getting on."

"I don't think that's such a hot idea."

"Your father's not doing so good. I think to be in the company of his oldest friend might be just what he needs. And besides, the countryside could freshen him up."

"You can't freshen him up. He's putrefying."

"I'm going to tell everyone."

"Wait—what about the cooperative? Don't you have prostitutes to pimp, opium to grow, guns to trade?"

"The others can take care of things until I get back."

"Look, Terry. Dad doesn't get lost in the beauty of nature. Natural phenomena make him sink into the worst kind of introspection. What he needs is distraction, not a journey into his interior. Besides, you're sleeping with his wife and he knows it."

"I'm not!"

"Come on, Terry. I saw her coming out of your room."

"Look. Caroline's frustrated. Your father doesn't know how to cuddle, that's all. He only uses one arm!"

It was pointless talking to Terry. His mind was made up. We would all of us go to a remote mountain village and stay with Eddie for a couple of weeks. I tore at my hair and overheard him break the news ungently to Dad and Caroline, and though it was a unanimously detested idea, the following morning he herded us all into the Jeep.

IX

During the drive I ruminated on what Terry had told me about Eddie's history. His father had been the only doctor in the remote mountain village where they lived, and as a young man Eddie was expected to follow in his footsteps. It was his parents' dream that Eddie would take over once his father retired, and such was the force of their will, it became Eddie's dream too. Over the years they scraped and sacrificed to send their son to medical school, and he went along, filled with gratitude and enthusiasm.

Unfortunately, things went sour from the first day Eddie opened his medical textbooks. As much as he wanted to pursue "his" dream and please his parents, he found that he was offended by the slop inside the human body. So Eddie spent most of his internship dry-retching. There was really no part of human anatomy he could stomach: the lungs, the heart, the blood, the intestines were not simply repellent symbols of man's animality, but so delicate and prone to disease and disintegration that he scarcely knew how people survived from one minute to the next.

In his second year of medical school he married a beautiful journalism student whom he had won over dishonestly by boasting about his future as a doctor and predicting a prosperous life together. What should have been a happy event was for Eddie a secret torture. He had serious doubts about entering the medical profession but didn't trust that he was inherently lovable enough "as is." Now he had something else to be confused and guilty over: he had begun a marriage based on a lie.

Then he met the man who would change his life. It was two a.m. when Terry Dean stumbled into the emergency room with a penknife stuck in the small of his back at such an awkward angle he couldn't remove it himself. As Eddie pulled out the knife, Terry's open and candid manner, combined with the late-night silence of the graveyard shift, made Eddie confide to his patient his confused feelings—how it felt to be torn between disgust and duty, between obligation and the fear of failure. Basically, Eddie moaned: did he want to be a fucking doctor or didn't he? He admitted that he loathed the idea and it would in all probability drive him to suicide, but how could he get out of it now? How else could he make money? Terry listened sympathetically, and on the spot offered him a high-paying though unusual job: traveling the world and watching over his brother with the aim of helping him out when he needed it. In short, to be Martin Dean's friend and protector.

While it broke his parents' hearts and put an unbelievable strain on his relationship with his young bride, Eddie took the job and set off to Paris to wait near Caroline for Dad to turn up. The most astounding fact of all that was revealed to us was that in all those years, from the moment Eddie met Dad in Paris onward, he couldn't tolerate him. *All those years* he hated my father, and this hatred never once let up. It was beyond belief. The more I thought about Eddie's deception, pretending to like a man for twenty years, the more I thought it verged on virtuosity. Then I decided that people probably pretend to like their family, friends, neighbors, and colleagues for their entire lives, and twenty years is no great trick.

The traffic had been heavy leaving Bangkok, but now we were out of the city, it eased up. We were on an open road flanked by rice fields. Terry drove fast. We passed tiny mopeds with several generations of whole families on them and buses that looked to be veering dangerously out of control. For a while we were stuck behind a slow-moving tractor driven by a farmer who was languidly rolling a cigarette with both hands. Then we began winding up the mountains. As if to finish the story swilling around in my head, Terry gave us an update on what had happened to Eddie since he returned to Thailand.

Eddie's jubilation at having completed a twenty-year mission dissipated as things went almost immediately pear-shaped. After a separation of two hundred and forty months because of Eddie's work, it took just six weeks of togetherness to destroy his marriage. Eddie moved out of his wife's apartment in Bangkok and into a house in the remote village where he grew up. It was a terrible mistake—the ghosts of his parents were everywhere, berating him for breaking their hearts. So what did the fool do? He picked up the thread of his old dream. Dreams can be as dangerous as anything else. If you go through the years, changing with age and experience, and you forget to overhaul your dreams as well, you might find yourself in Eddie's unenviable position: a forty-seven-year-old pursuing the dreams of a twenty-year-old. In Eddie's case it was worse. He'd forgotten that they weren't even his dreams to begin with; he'd got them secondhand. And now he had returned to this outrageously isolated community with the intention of setting up shop, only to find that his father's replacement, now sixty-five years old, had the job well and truly sewn up.

We arrived around sunset at Eddie's place, a dilapidated house set in a small clearing. The hills surrounding it were covered by thick jungle. When Terry turned off the engine, I could hear a river running. We were really in the middle of nowhere. The isolation of the place made me vaguely ill. Having lived in a hut in the northwest corner of a labyrinth, I was no stranger to austerity or solitude, but this was something else. The house made me shudder. Maybe I'd read too much or seen too many films, but when you consider your life in terms of its dramatic attributes, as I did, everything becomes instantly loaded with meaning. A house is not just a house—it is a location where an episode of your life is staged, and I thought this remote house was an absolutely perfect setting for a menacing low point and possibly, if we stayed long enough, a tragic climax.

Terry honked the horn, and Eddie came out waving his arms in a truly berserk manner.

"What's this? What do you want?"

"Didn't you tell him we were coming?" I asked Terry.

"What for? Anyway, he knows now. Eddie! We've come to see how you're getting on. Make up the spare rooms, will you? You have guests."

"I don't work for you anymore, Terry. You can't tell me . . . you can't just come here and expect . . . Look, I'm a doctor now. I don't want any funny business up here."

"My spies tell me you haven't had one patient."

"How did you . . . They're a little suspicious of outsiders. And I haven't lived here for many, many years. It takes time to build a reputation, that's all. Anyway, what's it got to do with you? You can't stay. My position here is precarious enough. The last thing I need is you giving me a bad name."

"My God, Eddie, we're not going to run around the village in our underwear, we just want some peace and quiet, see a little scenery, and anyway, is it so strange for a doctor to take in a dying man and his family for a few weeks?"

"Weeks? You intend to stay for weeks?"

Terry laughed loudly and slapped Eddie on the back.

"Him too?" Eddie asked quietly, looking in Dad's direction. Dad shot a look back that was lifeless and cold. Then Eddie looked at me with a half smile that approximated warmth but was not quite warm. I had recently experienced from the Australian people the concept of hate by association and so recognized the size and smell of it. Terry grabbed his bag and headed into the house. The rest of us followed cautiously. I paused at the door and turned back to Eddie. He hadn't moved. He was standing next to the Jeep, perfectly still. He looked as if he couldn't endure any of us. And who could blame him? Individually we were all quite pleasant people, but together we were unendurable.

I am not aware of what it is about my body that attracts mosquitos of all races and religions, I can only say that I doused my body in insect repellent and lit a thousand citronella candles, but for some reason they just kept coming. I removed the mosquito net from the bed and wrapped it like a shroud around my body. Through the diaphanous netting, I took in my surroundings. To say the furnishings were minimal was an understatement: four white walls, a creaky chair with a broken leg, a wobbly table, and a wafer-thin mattress. A window looked out on the thick vegetation of the jungle. I had insisted on the bedroom farthest away from everybody. There was a back door—good for entering and exiting without having to see anyone, I'd thought.

I felt a mosquito on my arm. They were tunneling through the net. I tore it off in disgust and thought: What am I going to do here? In Bangkok, between the sex shows and the Buddhist temples, there was plenty to keep me occupied. Here, Dad's dying was likely to make all non-Dad-dying thoughts virtually impossible. What was there to do other than watch the man deteriorate?

•

After a silent dinner during which we all eyed each other suspiciously, where the air was thick with secret desires and no one said the unsayable so there was nothing much to be said, Eddie gave me a tour of the place.

There wasn't much to see. Eddie's father had been an amateur painter as well as a doctor and had, unfortunately, found a way to combine his two interests. On the walls hung hauntingly realistic depictions of the bowels, heart, lungs, and kidneys and one of an aborted fetus who, despite his bad luck, appeared to be smiling wickedly. I didn't bother pretending I liked the paintings, and Eddie didn't expect me to. I followed him into his office, a large, immaculate room with wooden shutters. It had the kind of order and tidiness one finds in extremely finicky people and in people who have absolutely nothing to do with their time. As I knew Eddie had been waiting here for weeks on end without a single patient, it was clear which case it was.

"This was my father's office. This is where he saw patients, did his medical research, and avoided my mother. Everything is exactly how he left it. Actually, why did I say that? That's not true. When he died, my mother packed everything into boxes, so I have rearranged everything exactly as I remember him having it."

It was your standard doctor's office: an oversized desk, a comfy padded chair for the doctor, a straight-backed uncomfortable one for the patient, a raised examination table, a bookshelf with thousand-page medical manuals, and, on a side table, perfectly arranged surgical implements from not only this century but the last two as well. Unfortunately, there were more vulgar paintings of body parts on the walls, paintings that seemed to vilify the human as a reputable organism. The atmosphere in the room was heavy, because of either the lingering death of the father or the present-day frustrations of the son.

"When I took up your uncle's offer, my parents broke off all contact with me. Now, here they are."

"Who?"

"My parents." Eddie motioned to two earthenware pots I thought were bookends.

"Their ashes?"

"No, their spirits."

"Less messy."

So the spirits of Eddie's deceased parents were kept on a high shelf. Out of reach of children.

"I wait here every day. Not one single patient has come by. I've introduced myself around, but they're totally uninterested in trying out anyone new. I'm not even sure how much business they throw around anyway. These people don't consult doctors for minor ailments, and hardly even for major ones. But I'm determined to stick it out. After all, I went to medical school, didn't I? So why shouldn't I be a doctor? I mean, what am I supposed to do? Write off those five years of university as a learning experience?"

Apparently Eddie was completely oblivious of the glaring contradiction in his perspective on wasted time. He had chosen to fixate on the five years of medical school rather than the more obvious twenty years of chaperoning Dad and me.

He sat on the edge of his desk and picked something from his teeth with his finger. He stared at me solemnly, as though picking food from his teeth were something he had learned at medical school.

"There're so many things I wanted to say to you over the years, Jasper. Things I could never say because they conflicted with the requirements of my job."

"Such as?"

"Well, as you may have figured out, I hate your father. And that the Australian people bought his bullshit even for one minute degrades them as a nation, and degrades all people everywhere."

"I suppose."

"Anyway, the point is, I hate your father. No, I *loathe* him."

"That's your right."

"But what you might not know is, I don't like you much either."

"No, I didn't know that."

"You see? You don't even ask me why. That's what I don't like about you. You're smug and condescending. In fact, you've been smug and condescending ever since you were five years old."

"And that's my right."

Eddie leered at me menacingly. Now that he was no longer pretending to like us, it felt as if he had become sinister overnight.

"See? Smug and condescending. I've observed you your entire life. I probably know you better than you know yourself. You pride yourself on knowing people and what they're thinking. But you don't know yourself, do you? You know what it is that you especially don't know? That you're an extension of your father. When he dies, you will become him. I have no doubt about that. People can inherit thoughts—they can even inherent whole minds. Do you believe that?"

"Not really." Maybe.

"When I met your father, he was just a little older than you are now. And you know what I see in you? The same exact man. If sometimes you don't like him, it's because you don't like yourself. You think you're so different from him in your core. That's where you don't know yourself. I'm sure every time you hear yourself say something that's an echo of your father, you think it's just habit. It's not. It's him inside you, waiting to come out. And that's your blind spot, Jasper."

I gulped, despite myself. The blind spot. The fucking blind spot. Everyone has one. Even the geniuses. Even Freud and Nietzsche had mile-wide blind spots that wound up corrupting some element of their work. So was this mine? That I was sickeningly similar to my father, that I was turning into him, that I was going to inherit not just his antisocial behavior but his diseased thought processes as well? I was already worried that my depression back in Australia had had echoes of his depression.

Eddie sat on his examination table and kicked his legs in the air.

"It's so refreshing to be speaking my mind. Keeping secrets is exhausting. I would like to tell you the truth, not just about you, but about me and what you and your father and your uncle have done to my life. So you know. It's important that you know. Because when I finish telling you, you'll understand why you must convince everyone to leave this house at once. I don't care how you do it, but you have to make everyone leave. Before it's too late."

"Too late for what?"

"Just listen. When Terry offered me the job of looking after your dad, I took it as a way to escape a future I was uncertain of. 'Help them out when they need help, make sure they keep out of trouble, and take photos of them, as many photographs as you can,' Terry said. That was my mission. Didn't sound too tough. How was I supposed to know it was going to ruin my life? It's my own fault, though, I'll admit. I accepted a devil's bargain. Have you noticed that in books and movies the Devil is always depicted with a sense of humor while God is deadly serious? I think in reality it would be the other way around, don't you?"

"Probably."

"I can't tell you how many times I wanted to quit. But watching your lives was like watching an accident in slow motion. It was compelling. When I was away from Australia, away from your dad and you, I felt I was missing episodes of my favorite TV show. It was maddening. I'd be making love to my wife and thinking, 'What are they up to now? What trouble are they in? I'm missing it, dammit!' And I found I made excuses to return earlier and earlier. And I'd go back to listen to your father's insipid, unending diatribes, but I couldn't drag myself away. I was hooked. I was a junkie, plain and simple. I was hopelessly addicted to you."

Eddie was kicking wildly now and bouncing up and down. I couldn't stop him if I wanted to. I just had to weather this outburst.

"For twenty years I tried to get away, to wean myself off this drug of your family. But I couldn't. When I wasn't with you, I didn't know who I was. I was not a person, I was a nothing. When I went back to Australia and saw you both embroiled in some ridiculous episode, I felt alive. I felt such brightness it practically came out my eyes. My wife wanted a child, but how could I when I already had two children? Yes, I love you both as much as I hate you both, more than you will ever know. I can tell you, after I deposited you two in Terry's lap, I was devastated. Mission accomplished. I knew as soon as I moved home that I could no longer stand to be with my wife. And I was right. She couldn't understand why I was irritable, why I was empty. I couldn't share the emptiness with her and I didn't love her enough for her to fill it with love, so I left her and came up here. You see? I am completely empty, and I've come here in order to try to fill myself. Now do you understand why you must leave? I've come here to find myself again, to find out who I am. I'm building myself from the ground up. Your father is always talking about projects. You were my project. And now I need another one. That's why I need patients. I'm continuing my life where I was interrupted, and obviously I can't do it with you two here. That's why you have to talk your uncle into taking you all out of here."

"Why don't you just throw us out?"

"Well, Mr. Smug, Mr. Condescension, I can't. You might think your uncle's all fun and games, but I've seen the violence he's capable of."

"Terry's pretty stubborn. I don't think I'd have much luck convincing him of anything."

"Please, Jasper. *Please.* Your father's dying. And he is going to do one more crazy thing, and it's going to be a big one. You must know that too. You can feel it coming, can't you? It's like an approaching storm. It's going to be something wild and unexpected and dangerous and stupid. I stay up nights thinking about it. What is he going to do? Do you know? What is it? I must know. But I can't. You see? You *must* leave!"

"I'll try to speak to Terry."

"You don't try, you do. What do you think will happen when your father dies? It's you that will take up his heritage of doing crazy, unbelievable things. And you will turn out to be an even bigger spectacle than your dad. And that's why I promise you, if you don't leave now, I will follow you doggedly for your whole life until you have a son, and then *I* will have a son just so my son can follow your son. Don't you see? This is an addiction that can go on for generations! For centuries! We're at a crucial point here, Jasper. If I don't get off you now, I will be attached to you forever."

That was an unpleasant thought.

"Anyway. That's it. Go speak to your uncle. If you stay, I don't know what I'll do. Slit your throats in your sleep, probably." With that thought he let out a laugh, the kind where you don't see any teeth. "Leave me alone now. I must pray to my parents."

Eddie laid some brightly colored flowers on the floor and knelt in front of them and started muttering. He prayed daily for success, which was bad news—when a doctor in your neighborhood prays for business, you'd better hope his gods aren't listening.

•

I poked my head into Terry's room on the way to bed. Even though I'd knocked and he'd said come in, he hadn't bothered to throw clothes on. He was standing naked in the center of the room.

"Hey, Jasper! What's going on?"

"Never mind. Goodnight."

I closed the door. I wasn't in the mood for chatting to a fat naked man at the moment. Then again, I wasn't in the mood for having my throat slit in my sleep either. I reopened the door. Terry hadn't moved.

"Jesus, can't you knock?"

"Eddie's gone crazy. He's threatening to slit our throats in our sleep."

"That's not especially hospitable, is it?"

"I don't think he wants to kill us, I just think that by being here, Dad and I are likely to push him over the edge."

"So?"

"So shouldn't we get out of here?"

"Probably."

"Good."

"But we're not going to."

"Why not?"

His eyebrows were all bunched up, and his mouth was open as if any second he were going to speak. Any second now.

"Terry. Are you all right?"

"Of course I am. I'm a little agitated, that's all. I'm not used to being agitated. You know, I've been away from my family for so long, it's having a funny effect on me having you two here. I don't feel quite myself. I don't feel quite as . . . free. I've started fretting about you two, if you want to know the truth. And I haven't fretted about anything or anyone in a long time."

"And Caroline? Are you fretting about her too?"

Terry's face turned purple in a split second. Then his eyes went all funny. I felt I was standing outside a house watching someone flick the lights on and off.

"You're a pretty intuitive guy, Jasper. What is your intuition telling you? Mine is telling me that something is going to happen in this house. I'm not sure what. It could be a good thing, though I doubt it. It'll probably be a bad thing. It could even be a *very* bad thing. And maybe we should get out of here, but I'm insanely curious. Aren't you? Curiosity is one of my favorite things. Intense curiosity is like one of those tantric orgasms, a long, maddening, delayed pleasure. That's what it is."

I said goodnight, closed the door, and left him alone in his nakedness, thinking of normal families who have normal problems like alcoholism and gambling and wife-beating and drug addiction. I envied them.

•

I woke early the next morning. My throat was unslit. The sun was hot already at six-thirty. From my window I could see mist oozing out of the jungle. We were at a high altitude, and the mist hid the mountain peaks from sight. I'd had a bad night's sleep, thinking about everything Eddie had said. I knew he was right. Dad *was* planning something, even if he was doing it subconsciously. But didn't I already know what it was? I felt as though I did, but I couldn't quite see it. It was concealed somewhere in my mind, somewhere dark and far away. In fact, suddenly I felt I knew everything that would happen in the future but had for some reason forgotten it, and further, I thought that everybody on the planet also knew the future, only they had forgotten it too, and that fortunetellers and prognosticators weren't people with supernatural insights after all, they were just people with good memories.

I dressed and went out the back door so as not to run into anybody.

At the back of the house, at the edge of the jungle, was a shed. I went inside. There on rickety wooden shelves were paints and paintbrushes. Leaning against the wall were a number of blank canvases. So this was where Eddie's father had painted his disgusting artworks. It appeared to have once been a chicken coop, although there were no chickens now. There were chicken feathers, though, and a couple of ancient broken eggshells. On the floor was a half-finished painting of a pair of kidneys; Eddie's father had obviously got it into his head to use egg yolk to get the right kind of yellow.

I picked up a paintbrush. The bristles, caked in dried paint, were stiff as wood. Outside the chicken coop there was a trough filled with muddy rainwater, as if it had fallen from the sky that way, brown and gluggy. I rinsed the brush thoroughly in the water, flicking the hairs with my fingers. As I did this, I saw Caroline walking from the house down the hill. She was walking quickly, though every few steps she'd stop and stand perfectly still before continuing on her way, as if she were late for an appointment she dreaded keeping. I watched her until she disappeared into the jungle.

I went back into the chicken coop, opened a can of paint, dipped the brush in, and started attacking a canvas. I let my brush float across it, seeing what it wanted to paint. It seemed to favor eyes. Hollow eyes, eyes like juicy plums, eyes like germs seen through a microscope, eyes within eyes, concentric eyes, overlapping eyes. The canvas was sick with them. I had to look away; these thick painted eyes were burrowing into me in a way that was more than simply unsettling: they seemed to be moving something inside me. It took me another minute to work out that they were my father's eyes. No wonder they made me sick.

I put the canvas down and lifted another in its place. The brush started up again. This time it went for a whole face. A smug, self-satisfied face with wide, mocking eyes, a bushy mustache, a twisted brown mouth, and yellow teeth. The face of either a white slave-owner or a prison warden. I stared at the painting and felt a pang of anxiety, but I couldn't work out why. It was as if a thread in my brain had become loose, but I was afraid to pull on it in case my whole being unraveled. Then I realized: the painting—it was *the* face. The face I'd dreamed about in childhood. The imperishable floating face I had seen my whole life. As I painted, I was able to recall details I didn't know I had actually seen before: bags under the eyes, a small gap between the front teeth, wrinkles at the corners of the smiling mouth. I had a premonition that one day this face would come down from the sky to head-butt me. Suddenly the heat in the chicken coop became unbearable. I felt stifled. Being inside a humid chicken coop with that haughty face and a thousand reproductions of my father's eyes was suffocating.

•

That afternoon I was lying in my bed listening to the rain. I felt groundless. Traveling on a fake passport probably meant that I could never return to Australia. That made me nationless. And, worse, the fake name on my passport was one I didn't like, that I was actually sickened by, and unless I organized another fake passport, I might be Kasper until the end of my days.

I stayed in bed all afternoon, unable to force Eddie's words out of my head, his supposition that I was turning into my father. *If sometimes you don't like him, it's because you don't like yourself. You think you're so different from him. That's where you don't know yourself. That's your blind spot, Jasper.* Could that be true? Wouldn't that coincide with Dad's old idea that I was actually him prematurely reincarnated? And now that I was thinking of it, wasn't there perhaps already some frightening evidence of this? Ever since Dad had started dying again, hadn't I gotten physically stronger? Were we on a kind of seesaw—he goes down, I go up?

There was a knock on my door. It was Caroline. She had been caught in the rain and was drenched from head to toe.

"Jasper—you don't want your father to die, do you?"

"Well, I don't have a specific day in mind, but I don't like the idea of him living forever. So yes, if you put it that way, I suppose I do want him to die."

She came over and sat on the edge of my bed. "I've been into the village. The people around here are deeply superstitious, and maybe not for nothing. There are still ways we might be able to cure him."

"You want to make him late for his date with destiny?"

"I want your father to rub this all over his body." She handed me a small jar with a glutinous, milk-colored substance in it.

"What is it?"

"Oil made of fat melted from the chin of a woman who died in childbirth."

I looked at the container. I couldn't tell if it actually contained what she said it did, and I wasn't thinking of the poor woman who died in childbirth, either; I was thinking of the person who melted the fat from her chin.

"Where did you get this, and, more importantly, how much did you pay for it?"

"I got it from an old woman in the village. She said it's great for cancer."

Great for cancer?

"Why don't you do it?"

"Your father isn't listening to me right now. He doesn't want me to help him. I can't even give him a glass of water. You need to get him to rub this oil all over himself."

"How am I supposed to excite him into rubbing a stranger's chin fat on his body?"

"That's what you have to work out."

"Why me?"

"You're his son."

"And you're his wife."

"Things are not so good between us at the moment," she said, without elaborating. Not that she needed to—I was thoroughly familiar with the sharp-edged love triangle threatening to cut us all to shreds.

I procrastinated in the hallway for a while, but finally I went into Dad's room. He was bent over his desk, not reading or writing anything, just bending.

"Dad," I said.

He didn't give any sign he knew I was there. Citronella candles were spread all around the room. He had a mosquito net above the bed, and one over the armchair in the corner too.

"Are the insects bothering you?" I asked.

"Do you think I'm welcoming them like old friends?" he said, without turning around.

"It's just that I have some insect repellent if you want it."

"I already have some."

"This is a new sort. Apparently the locals use it."

Dad turned to me. I stepped forward and put the jar of melted chin fat in his hand.

"You have to smear it over your whole body."

Dad unscrewed the lid and sniffed the contents. "It smells funny."

"Dad—do you think we're similar?"

"In what way—physically?"

"No, I don't know. As people."

"That would be your worst nightmare, wouldn't it?"

"I have one or two worse ones."

We heard a buzzing. We both looked around but couldn't see where it was coming from. Dad took off his shirt and scooped a handful of the melted chin fat from the jar and started smearing it over his chest and belly.

"You want some?"

"No, I'm good."

I started to feel queasy, now thinking of the woman who had died in childbirth. I wondered if her baby had lived, and if one day he might not be annoyed that he hadn't been the one to inherit the fat of his mother's chin.

"Eddie's turned out to be a different sort of bloke than we thought, hasn't he?" Dad said, coating his underarms.

I was tempted to recount Eddie's sick monologue and menacing threats, but I didn't want to add any further stress to his stressed-out body.

"It was still good for you to have a good friend, even if it was all a lie."

"I know."

"Eddie was the first person to tell me anything useful about Astrid."

"Was he?"

"He led me to your Paris journal."

"You read it?"

"Cover to cover."

"Made you sick?"

"Extremely."

"Well, that's what you get for snooping."

As he said this he removed his sandals and rubbed the chin fat between his toes. It made a squishy sound.

"In it you said you thought I might be the premature reincarnation of yourself."

Dad cocked his head to one side, closed his eyes a moment, then opened them again. He looked at me as though he had just performed a magic trick in which I vanish and he was annoyed that it hadn't worked. "What's your point?"

"Do you still believe that?"

"I think it's highly possible, even when you consider that I don't believe in reincarnation."

"That makes no sense."

"Exactly."

I felt an old fury welling up inside me. Who is this irritating man? I walked out and slammed the door. Then I opened it again.

"That's not insect repellent," I said.

"I know. You don't think I recognize melted chin fat when I see it?"

I stood there, my mind a complete blank.

"I was eavesdropping, you little idiot," he admitted.

"So what's wrong with you? Why would you put that crap on your body?"

"I'm dying, Jasper! Don't you get it? What do I care what I put on my body? Chin fat, stomach fat, goat feces. So what? When you're dying, even disgust loses its meaning."

•

Dad was hurrying to his doom, there was no denying that. He looked more ravaged each day. Ravaged mentally too—he couldn't shake the fear that Caroline wanted to go back to Uncle Terry, or that we were all discussing this possibility behind his back. He was paranoid that we were constantly talking about him. This fear soon became a hot topic of conversation between the rest of us. That was how he breathed life into his own delusions and set them free.

Our dinners continued to be as silent as the first; the only noise was

Dad sighing loudly in between spoonfuls of spicy soup. Reading between the sighs, I knew that he was growing increasingly furious because he wasn't getting enough pity from anyone. He didn't want a lot. Just the minimum would do. Terry was no help there—he was still stuck on the idea of giving Dad pleasure and stimulation; and Caroline was even less help— she pretended she'd stopped believing in his death altogether. She applied herself to the unenviable task of trying to reverse the course of his cancer; she was dragging in every sort of witchcraft—psychospiritual healing, visualization, karma repair. All around him was a loathsome form of positivism, anathema to a dying man. And probably because Caroline was obsessed with trying to save Dad's life and Terry his soul, Dad became obsessed with suicide, saying that to die of natural causes was just plain lazy. The more they tried to save him with outlandish methods, the more he insisted on taking the matter of dying into his own hands.

One night I heard Dad screaming. I came out of my bedroom to see Terry chasing him around the living room with a pillow.

"What's going on?"

"He's trying to kill me!"

"I don't want you to die. *You* want you to die. I'm just trying to help you out."

"Stay away from me, you fucker! I said I wanted to commit suicide. I didn't say I wanted to be murdered."

Poor Dad. It's not that he didn't have clear ideas, it's just that he had too many, and they contradicted, effectively canceling each other out. Dad didn't want to be smothered by his brother, but he couldn't bring himself to do his own smothering.

"Let me do this," Terry said. "I was always there for you, and I always will be."

"You weren't there for me when our mother tried to kill me."

"What are you talking about?"

Dad stared at Terry a long time. "Nothing," he said finally.

"You know what? You don't know how to die because you don't know who you are."

"Well, who am I?"

"You tell me."

After some hesitation, Dad described himself as a "seer of limited epiphanies." I thought that was pretty good, but Terry thought he was something else entirely: a Christ figure who couldn't summon the courage to sacrifice himself, a Napoleon who didn't have the stomach for battle, and a Shakespeare who didn't have a gift with words. It was clear we were getting no closer to defining who Dad was.

Dad let out a low moan and stared at the floor. Terry put his wide, thick hand on his brother's shoulder.

"I want you to admit that despite having lived for so long on this earth, you don't know who you are. And if you don't know who you are, how can you be what you are?"

Dad didn't respond in words but let out another moan, like an animal who had just visited his parents in a butcher shop window.

I went to bed wondering, Do I know who I am? Yes, I do: I'm Kasper. No, I mean Jasper. Above all, I am not my father. I am not turning into my father. I am not a premature reincarnation of my father. I'm me, that's all. No one more, no one less.

This thinking nauseated me, and it felt like the nausea was changing the shape of my face. I climbed out of bed and looked in the mirror. I wasn't looking better or worse, simply different. Soon I might not be able to recognize myself at all, I thought. Something strange was happening to my face, something that was not simply the process of aging. I was turning into someone not myself.

There was a loud noise outside. Someone or something was in the chicken coop. I looked out but couldn't see anything from the window, only the reflection of my own slightly unfamiliar face. I turned off the light but even with the moonlight it was too black. The noises continued. I certainly wasn't going to go out there to investigate. Who knew what creatures existed in the jungles of Thailand, and who knew how hungry they were? All I could do was shut my eyes tight and try to go to sleep.

In the morning I sat up and looked out my window. The coop was still standing—I half expected it to be hanging from a giant slobbering mouth. I headed out the back door.

The grass under my feet was cold and wet. The air had a funny taste to it, like an old mint that had lost most of its flavor. I walked cautiously, readying myself to run back to the house if an animal should leap out at me. Inside, the coop was in chaos. The paint cans had been opened and their contents emptied onto the floor and onto my painting of the floating face, which had been torn into little pieces. Who had destroyed my painting? And why? There was nothing to do but go back to bed.

I wasn't in bed five minutes when I heard someone breathing. I closed my eyes and pretended to be asleep. It didn't do any good. The breathing came closer and closer, until I felt it on my neck. I hoped it wasn't Eddie. It was. I turned over to see him leaning down over me. I jumped up.

"What do you want?"

"Jasper, what are you doing today?"

"Sleeping, hopefully."

"I'm going out driving to see if I can drum up some business."

"OK, then—have a good day."

"Yeah. You too."

And still Eddie didn't move. Even though it was exhausting to do so, I felt sorry for him. There's no other way to say it. He looked lovesick. It was a bad look.

"I don't suppose you want to come along. Keep me company?" Eddie asked.

It was a daunting proposition. Spending the day alone with Eddie didn't particularly appeal to me, and visiting sick people even less, but it turned out there was nothing I could imagine as disagreeable as staying in the house with Dad's clanking death.

•

We went traipsing up and down the countryside in the pitiless sun. I thought Australia was hot! The humidity in the mountains was out of control—I could feel beads of sweat forming on my gallbladder. We rode along, not saying much. When Eddie was silent, I felt as if I were the only person alive in the world—although I had that feeling when he was talking too. Wherever we went, people watched us. They couldn't understand a man in his mid-forties wanting to become a doctor—it was a violation of the natural order. Eddie tried to take it in his stride, but it was obviously wearing him down. He had only vicious, unfriendly words to say about the healthy, peaceful inhabitants of this tranquil village. He couldn't stand their contentment. He even resisted the cutesy Thai custom of smiling like a cretin in every conceivable situation, although he had to if he wanted to lure patients. But his smile took up only one side of his divided face. I saw the real one, with the furious down-turned lips and restrained homicidal rage in his blinking eye.

We ate lunch by the side of the road. I could feel no wind, but the branches of the trees moved every so often. After lunch Eddie said, "Did you speak to Terry about taking you all out of here?"

"He wants us to stay. He thinks something bad is going to happen in your house and he wants to see what it is."

"He thinks that, does he? That's bad news for us."

Before Eddie could add any more, we heard the roar of a motorcycle charging at full speed.

"Look who it is," Eddie said.

"Who?"

"That antique doctor. Look how smug he is."

The motorcycle screamed toward us, stirring up dust. It was hard to believe anyone antique could ride a bike so fast. As the doctor came to a shuddering stop, Eddie corrected his posture. It's difficult to look like a winner when you're clearly the loser, but posture plays a part.

The doctor may have been in his sixties, but he had the physique of an Olympic swimmer. I couldn't detect anything smug about him. He and Eddie exchanged a few words. I didn't know what they were saying, but I saw Eddie's eyes widen in a way that darkened his face and made me somehow relieved I couldn't understand the language. When the doctor had sped off, I asked Eddie, "What did he say? Will he retire soon?"

"There's bad news. Fuck! Terrible news! The doctor already has a young apprentice, ready to fill his shoes."

Well, that was the end of that. There was absolutely no use for Eddie in this community, and he knew it.

•

All I wanted to do was sleep, but the moment I returned to my room, I knew it would be impossible, mostly because Caroline was sitting on the edge of my bed.

"I went into the village today," she said.

"Please, no more chin fat."

She handed me a small leather pouch tied with a string. I took it and pulled out a necklace with three strange objects hanging off it.

"A piece of elephant tusk and some kind of tooth," I guessed.

"Tiger's tooth."

"Sure. And what's that third one?"

"A dried-out cat's eye."

"Nice. And I'm to get Dad to wear this, I suppose."

"No, it's for you."

"For me?"

"It's an amulet," she said, and placed it around my neck and leaned back and gazed at me as if I were a sad-eyed puppy in a pet store window.

"What's it for?"

"To protect you."

"From what?"

"How do you feel?"

"Me? OK, I guess. A little tired."

"I wish you could have met my son," she said.

"I wish so too."

Poor Caroline. It seemed she wanted to conduct several conversations but didn't know which to pick.

She stood suddenly. "OK, then," she said, and went out by the back door. I almost took the amulet off but for some reason was overcome with fear of being without it. I thought: The thing that makes a man go crazy isn't loneliness or suffering after all—it's being kept in a state of perpetual dread.

•

The next few days I spent at the mirror, confirming my features with the touch of my hand. Nose? Here! Chin? Here! Mouth? Teeth? Forehead? Here! Here! Here! This inane facial roll call was the only valuable way I could think of to pass the time. Somewhere else in the house Caroline, Dad, and Terry were circling each other like rabid dogs. I stayed well away.

I spent many hours sitting with Eddie in his office. It seemed to me it was *he,* and not I, who had taken on the qualities of an accident in slow motion, and I didn't want to miss the show. Besides, Caroline's gift had put doubts about my health into my mind, and I thought it best if I let Eddie examine me. He gave me a thorough going-over. He tested the dull thumping of my heart, my sluggish reflexes; I even let him take my blood. Not that there was a pathology lab in the area where he could send it. He just filled a vial and gave it to me afterward as a keepsake. He said there was nothing wrong with me.

We were in the office listening to the radio through the stethoscope when something extraordinary and unexpected happened—a patient! A woman came in visibly upset and agitated. Eddie put on a solemn face that for all I know might've been genuine. I sat there on the edge of my seat while the woman gibbered on. "The doctor's very sick," Eddie translated to me. "Maybe dying," he added, and stared at me for a long time, just to show me he wasn't smiling.

The three of us piled into Eddie's car and drove at breakneck speed to the doctor's house. When we arrived, we heard the most awful screeching imaginable.

"It's too late. He's dead," Eddie said.

"How do you know?"

"That wailing."

Eddie was right. There was nothing ambiguous about that wailing.

He turned off the engine, grabbed his doctor's bag, and combed his hair down with his hands.

"But he's dead—what are you going to do?"

"I'm going to pronounce him dead."

"Don't you think that nightmarish howling has pretty much got that covered?"

"Even in a village as remote as this, there are rules. The dead must be officially declared dead," he said. I took a deep breath and followed Eddie and the woman inside.

A dozen or so people were crowded around the dead doctor's bed; either they had come to mourn him or had arrived earlier to watch him die. The doctor that I'd seen a few days earlier tearing around the countryside on his motorbike was now perfectly motionless. The man whose statuesque physique I had envied had caved in. His body looked as if someone had gone in with a powerful vacuum cleaner and just sucked everything out: heart, ribcage, spine, everything. Frankly, he didn't even look like skin and bones, just skin.

I kept an eye on Eddie but he'd made himself look harmless and sincere, which was no small trick considering the vile thoughts going on in his head. The village doctor was gone—now it was between Eddie and the young doctor. I could see Eddie thinking, He shouldn't be too hard to discredit. Eddie straightened himself up, ready to seduce the mourners. It was his first pronouncement as a doctor.

They all spoke to Eddie in quiet tones, and afterward he turned to me and I saw a flicker of derangement, ruthlessness, obstinacy, and deviousness. It's astonishing the complexity that can be perceived in a face at the right time of day. Eddie took me aside and explained that the apprentice had been here when the doctor had died and had already proclaimed him dead.

"He didn't waste any time, the little bastard," Eddie whispered.

"Where's the young doctor now?"

"He went home to bed. Apparently he's sick too."

This time Eddie couldn't contain his glee. He asked directions to the young doctor's house and went off, I was certain, to treat him in as negligent and slipshod a manner as possible.

He drove fast. I caught him practicing his sweetest possible smile in the rearview mirror, which meant he was gearing up to play the tyrant.

The young doctor lived by himself in a hut high up in the mountains. Eddie raced inside. It was a struggle to keep up with him. The young doctor was lying on the bed with his clothes on. By the time I entered, Eddie was leaning over him.

"Is he all right?" I asked.

Eddie walked around the bed as if he were doing a victory dance.

"I don't think he's going to make it."

"What's he got?"

"I'm not sure. It's a virus, but an uncommon one. I don't know how to treat it."

"Well, if the old doctor had it and now the young doctor has it, it must be contagious. I'm getting out of here," I said, covering my mouth as I left.

"It's probably not contagious."

"How do you know? You don't know what it is."

"Could be that something crawled inside them and laid eggs in their intestines."

"That's just disgusting."

"Or else it's something they ate together. I don't think you have to worry."

"I'll decide when and where I worry," I said, heading outside.

The young doctor died two days later. Eddie didn't leave his bedside the whole time. Despite Eddie's insistence that the virus wasn't contagious, I refused to set foot inside the death chamber. I knew the very moment the young doctor died, though, because the same hideous gut-wrenching wails as before echoed through the village. Frankly, I was suspicious of all this showy mourning and finally decided it was just a cultural tic, like those smiles. It's not actually uncontrollable grief, I thought, it's a show of uncontrollable grief. Quite a different thing.

•

That's how Eddie became the doctor of the village. He'd gotten what he wanted, but this didn't soften him up. It was an error of judgment on my part to imagine it would. And it was an error on Eddie's part to imagine that becoming the village doctor by default would warm the villagers to him. We went door-knocking. Some slammed the door in Eddie's face; they thought he'd put a hex on the two doctors, a pox on both their houses. Eddie came out looking like a grave robber. We did the rounds anyway. There were no bites. And it was in no small part because the people didn't seem ever to get sick.

I'd scarcely thought it was possible, but Eddie was becoming even more unpleasant. All this healthiness was getting to him. "Not one patient! All I want is for someone to get ill! Violently ill! What are these people, immortal? They could do with a little motor neuron disease. Show them what life's really about." Eddie meant badly. His heart was in the wrong place.

Thank God for farming accidents! After a few inadvertent amputations and the like, he eventually managed to scrounge up a couple of patients. The people were afraid of hospitals, so Eddie had to do things in the rice fields that I personally wouldn't want done to me in anything other than the most sterile environment. But they didn't seem to mind.

As Eddie began his official career as a doctor, all these years after finishing medical school, I went back to the house to confront the dramas that I was sure would have progressed in my absence to a nice, steamy boiling point.

•

"I'm in love with my husband's brother," Caroline said, as if she were on an American talk show and I didn't know the names of the people involved. She straightened the chair I had unsuccessfully used to barricade the door.

"I know it's hard, Caroline. But can you hold out a little longer?"

"Until your father's dead? I'm so guilty. I'm counting the days. I want him to die."

This explained her feverish efforts to prolong his life: guilt. I had a feeling that when Dad did finally die, she would mourn him more than all of us. In fact, my father's death was likely to ruin this woman. I thought I should speak to him about it, cautiously of course, and entreat him to give her to Terry while he was still alive. The death of her husband could send her over the edge for wishing it. I knew this would be a sore point with him, but for Caroline's sake, for the image of her sad crazy eyes, I had to broach the subject.

Dad was in bed with the lights out. The darkness helped me find the courage to go about my unenviable task. I launched right into it. I pretended that Caroline had said nothing to me and I had just deduced this all on my own. "Look," I said, "I know this must be painful, and I know how you are—the last thing you want to do on the eve of your death is something noble—but the fact of the matter is, Caroline will be destroyed by your death if, as you die, she secretly wishes it. If you really love her, you must make a present of her to your brother. You must bequeath her, while you're still alive."

Dad didn't say a word. As I made this appalling speech, I thought that if someone said this to me, I would probably stick a butter knife through his tongue.

"Leave me alone," he said finally, in the dark.

The next day Terry decided Dad must look at a dead bird he had seen on an early morning walk, and he dragged me along. He thought Dad would look at the still bird and be glad to be moving. It was a childish idea. My father had already seen many dead things, and they'd never made him glad to be alive. They wordlessly invited him to join them in death. This I knew. I wondered why Terry didn't.

"I think you should take Caroline off my hands," Dad said, crouched over the unmoving bird.

"What are you talking about?"

"I don't think she can maintain this farce any longer than I can," Dad said wearily. "We might have gotten away with it had you remained dead, like a good boy, but you had to resurrect yourself, didn't you?"

"I don't know what I have to do with it."

"Don't be obtuse. You take her, OK?"

Terry's body made an unexpected jolt, as if he'd rested his hand upon a high-voltage fence.

"For argument's sake, let's say I agree to this bit of nonsense. What makes you think she'll go along with it?"

"Cut it out, Terry. You've always been a self-serving bastard, so why not just continue the tradition and serve yourself *again*—a helping of the woman you love, who, incomprehensibly, loves you back. You know, I always put my failure with women down to the lack of symmetry in my facial features, and yet here you are, the fattest man alive, and you get her again!"

"So what do you want?"

"Just take care of her, OK?"

"I don't know what you're talking about," Terry said, and his mouth made several odd shapes, though no sound came out. He looked as if he were trying to commit a long and difficult equation to memory.

•

Caroline was sitting under a tree in the rain when Dad and I approached. I knew she was quietly tormenting herself. I thought I could hear her thoughts, fully articulated in my head. She was thinking of evil, whether she possessed evil herself or was possessed by it. She wanted to be good. She didn't think she was good. She thought she was a victim of circumstance and that maybe all people who do evil are also victims of circumstance. She thought not only that Dad had cancer but that he *was* cancer. She wished he would fall in love with someone else and then die peacefully in his sleep. She felt Dad had taken over the story of her life and was rewriting it with messy handwriting so it became illegible. She thought her life had become illegible and incoherent.

This is what I was certain I heard her thinking. I felt so sympathetic, I wished the ground would open up and swallow her.

Dad strode up and laid it on the line. I should have guessed his first foray into noble deeds would blow up in his face. The truth is, his generosity of spirit extended only so far, and while magnanimously sacrificing himself on the altar of their love, he was unable to wipe the hurt look off his face, which killed the point of the whole exercise. It was this hurt look that made her explode.

"No! How can you say that? I love *you! You! I love YOU!*"

Dad pushed on. "Look. Terry was your first love, and I know you've never stopped loving him. It's nobody's fault. When you agreed to marry me, you thought he'd been dead for twenty years. We all did. So why pretend?"

Dad put forth a convincing case and got all worked up as he laid it out. He was so convincing that what seemed inconceivable suddenly became conceivable—and that threw Caroline into confusion.

"I don't know. What do you want me to do? Is it that you don't love me anymore? Yes, maybe it's that." And before Dad could answer, she said, "I'll do whatever you want me to do. I love you, and whatever you want me to do, I'll do."

Dad's resolve was tested here. Why did she keep tormenting him like this? How could he keep it up?

"I want you to admit it," he said.

"Admit what?"

"That you're in love with him."

"Martin, it's—"

"Admit it!"

"OK! *I admit it!* First I started thinking, why does he have to be alive? Why couldn't he have just stayed dead? And the more time I spent with Terry, the more I realized I was still in love with him. Then I started thinking, why do you have to be alive? Why are you dying so slowly? How unjust that someone who loved life, like my son, had to die so suddenly when someone who wants to die, like you, gets to live unendingly. Every time you talk about suicide my hopes jump up. But you never do it. You're all talk! Why do you keep promising suicide if you won't do it? You're driving me crazy with all these promises of killing yourself! Do it or shut up about it, but stop getting my hopes up like that!" Suddenly Caroline stopped and covered her mouth with her hand, doubled over, and vomited. The vomit came through her fingers. When she straightened up, her face was twisted in shame. Every part of her face was magnified by it—her eyes were too round, her mouth too wide, her nostrils the same size as her mouth had been. Before anyone could say anything, she ran off into the jungle.

Dad swayed on his thin legs, and his complexion became what I can only describe as grainy. My life has been an unfair and humiliating series of losing propositions, his face lamented. Love was my noble suicide bid.

Just then Terry came out of the house. "Did I hear shouting?" he asked.

"She's all yours," Dad said.

"What do you mean?"

"Caroline—she's all yours. We're finished."

"Are you serious?"

"Yes. You can be together now. I don't mind."

All the blood drained from Terry's face, and he looked as if he'd just been told the plane he was on was making an emergency landing nose first in a volcano.

"Well . . . but . . . I can't give up my prostitutes. I told you, love doesn't work without possessiveness. No. No way. I can't turn my back on my life now, after so long. No, I can't be with Caroline."

"Don't you love her?"

"Leave me alone! What are you trying to do to me?" he said, and walked off into the jungle, but in the opposite direction to Caroline.

So the triangle had effectively broken up. Nobody was with anybody. The three points were single lines again, parallel, not touching.

Oops. My fault.

I didn't witness the scene later that day between Terry and Caroline, but I saw Caroline afterward, walking as if tranquilized. "Are you OK?" I called out. Every now and then she'd stop and pound her head with her fists. "Caroline!" I called out again. She looked up at me with desperate eyes. Then Terry wandered past my window, looking bulldozed. He informed me that we were going back to Bangkok in the morning. At last, good news. I wondered if Terry's curiosity about the terrible event to take place in Eddie's house had been satisfied by the explosion of the triangle. Either way, I couldn't wait to leave, nor could I spend the rest of the day in that house. I had to get out.

With no other option, I went with Eddie in his car as he went on his rounds. He seemed glad of the company and eagerly delivered a creepy monologue that compared doctors with gods. We visited a few farmers he'd finally discovered had chronic illnesses. After his consultations, to my disgust, he hit on their daughters right in front of the parents, girls who couldn't be older than sixteen. Not knowing enough about the culture, I wasn't sure of the perils of Eddie carrying on in this fashion, but it was hair-raising the way he went about trying to seduce, intimidate, and buy these poor girls. I couldn't find his redeeming features anymore. The man I had grown up with was gone. As we left, he made up words about these girls, "fuckalicious" and "fuck-worthy" being the most common. Every word and gesture of his seemed saturated in frustration and fury. Back on the road, I thought: This man is a grenade waiting to detonate, and I hope I'm not around to see it.

Then he detonated.

I was around to see it.

My forehead was pressed against the car window, and I was wishing that the jungle around us was in fact the interior of a lavish, jungle-themed hotel and any time I liked I could go upstairs to my room and crawl between clean sheets and order room service and take an overdose of sleeping pills. I would have liked nothing better.

"What's this?" Eddie said, breaking my reverie.

It was a girl of about fifteen running down the road waving her arms, signaling us to stop. Here's trouble, I thought.

Eddie pulled over and we both got out of the car. She was motioning for Eddie to follow her. From what I could gather, her father was sick. Very sick. She was in a panic. She wanted Eddie to come right away. Eddie summoned his most professional posture. He translated for me, repeated the symptoms as she described them: fever, vomiting, powerful abdominal cramps, delirium, and lack of feeling in the legs and arms. Eddie grunted and sighed at the same time. Then he shook his head obstinately. The girl started shouting in a pleading voice.

What was he up to?

She turned and grabbed my arm. "Please, *please*."

"Eddie, what's going on?"

"I really don't think I can make it today. Maybe tomorrow, if I have a minute."

"No you understand?" she said in English. "My father. He is dying!"

"Eddie," I said, "what are you doing?"

"Jasper, can you go for a little walk?"

It didn't take a genius to figure out that I was about to be an accomplice in the dirtiest piece of blackmail possible.

"I'm not leaving," I said.

Eddie looked at me with crushing, concentrated hatred. It was a showdown. "Jasper," he said behind clenched teeth, "I'm telling you to get the fuck out of here."

"No way."

Eddie went ballistic, ranting at me with the full extent of his lung capacity. He tried everything to get me to shove off and leave him alone to rape and pillage. I wouldn't budge. This is it, I thought. My first physical confrontation with evil. I was eager to triumph.

I didn't.

He pushed me. I pushed back. He pushed me again. It was getting tedious. I took a swing. Eddie ducked it. Then he took a swing at me. I tried ducking too, but instead of socking me in the jaw, his fist connected with my forehead. I staggered backward a little, and taking advantage of my wobbling, he let fly an unexpected kick that got me in the throat. I fell back and hit my head on the dirt. I heard the car door slam, and by the time I got to my feet, I couldn't do anything but watch the car drive off.

Eddie, that disgusting bastard! That oily, rancid, horny bandit! I felt guilty for my failure to protect that poor girl, but if someone you've known since childhood is so determined to commit a crime he's willing to kick you in the throat, what can you do? Anyway, it was too late now. That fiend had made away with the girl and left me stranded in the middle of nowhere. And where the hell was I, anyway, other than the exact place where all the heat in Thailand gathered for a meeting?

I walked for several hours. Swarms of overexcited mosquitos pursued me assiduously. There was no one in sight, no sign of human life. It was easy to imagine that I was the only one in existence, and it didn't make me feel lonely at all. It's exhilarating to imagine every human dead, to have it in your power to start a new civilization or not. I thought I'd choose not. Who wants the humiliation of being father to the human race? Not me. I could see myself as the ant king, or the figurehead of a crab society—but Eddie had seriously turned me off humans altogether. One person can do that.

I walked on, oozing from the humidity but more or less content in my last-man-on-earth fantasy. I didn't even mind so much that I was utterly lost in the jungle. How many times would this happen in my life? A lot, I predicted. This time it's the jungle, next time it will be the ocean, then a department store parking lot, until finally I will be irretrievably lost in outer space. Mark my words.

But my solitude was short-lived. I heard the chattering of voices coming from the bottom of a hill. I went over the slope and could see a group of maybe twenty people, farmers mostly, in a circle next to a police van.

There was nothing in this scene to suggest it had anything to do with me, but something told me not to go down there. I suppose this is what happens when you feel guilty all the time for no reason.

I stood up on my tiptoes to get a better view. As I did, I saw a shadow creeping up on me. I spun around. A middle-aged woman holding a basket of apples was staring at me. No, she wasn't. She was stealing dark glances at the amulet around my neck.

"Stay down. Don't let them see you," she said in an accent as thick as the jungle around us.

She pushed me to the ground with her long, muscular arms. We lay side by side on the grassy slope.

"I know you."

"Do you?"

"You're the doctor's friend, aren't you?" she asked.

"What's going on?"

"He's in trouble," she said.

So they knew he'd blackmailed the poor girl into sleeping with him. Well, good. I couldn't care less if they threw him in jail so that he could be sodomized for the rest of his life. He deserved it.

"They dug up the bodies," she said.

What bodies was she talking about?

"What bodies are you talking about?"

"The old doctor, and the young one too."

"They dug them up? What made them do a creepy thing like that?"

"They thought it might be a plague of some new virus. A couple of years ago, we had an outbreak of chicken flu. Now there is much vigilance when it comes to multiple deaths of uncertain causes."

Interesting, but what has this got to do with blackmail and rape? I wondered.

"And?"

"They did an autopsy. And I suppose you know what they found."

"A hideous mess of decomposing organs?"

"Poison," she said, looking at me carefully for my reaction.

"Poison?" Poison? "And so they think . . ." I didn't bother finishing the sentence. It was obvious what they thought. And moreover, it was obvious they were right. Eddie had done it, the despicable bastard. To realize his dead parents' dream of his becoming a doctor, he had killed the old doctor and the young apprentice to get them out of the way.

"So the police are going to arrest him?"

"No. You see those people down there?" Did she want me to answer that one? They were right there.

"What about them?"

As she said this, the two policemen got into their van and drove away. The crowd filled in the space where the van had been.

"They just told the police your doctor friend had already moved to Cambodia."

I really wished she'd refrain from describing Eddie as my "doctor friend," although I understood it was good for clarification, as there were three doctors in this story. But was I being unbearably dense? Why had the farmers told the police that Eddie had moved to Cambodia? And why was she excited about it?

"Don't you see? They're going to take the law into their own hands!"

"Meaning?"

"They're going to kill him. And not only him. You too."

"Me?"

"And those other Australians who came here to help him."

"Wait a minute! Those Australians are my family! They didn't do anything. They didn't know anything about it! I didn't know anything about it."

"You'd better not go home," she said.

"But I didn't do anything! It was Eddie! This is the second time Eddie has put a lynch mob onto us. My God—my father was right. People are so single-minded about their immortality projects, it brings them down and everyone around them too!"

She looked at me blankly.

What could I do? I couldn't waste valuable time trying to find the police; I had to get home and warn everyone that an angry mob was coming to tear them apart.

What a dog's breakfast this trip turned out to be!

"Hey, why are you helping me?"

"I want your necklace."

Why not? I had been foolishly superstitious by wearing it at all. I took off the repugnant amulet and gave it to her. She hurried away. I'd worn it only out of desperation, I suppose. If you don't keep your guard up and someone tells you it has magical qualities, you can find comfort in a grain of sand.

•

The group below set off on foot through the jungle. I followed them, thinking of Eddie and my family and of their surprise when the blood-thirsty mob turned up to kill them. I had to make sure the mob and I didn't converge; it was unlikely, not being Thai myself, that I would be assimilated into their number. I would be swallowed whole, as an appe-tizer. So I kept my distance. But I didn't know the way home—I'd have to follow the mob back to Eddie's house. The inherent dilemma was ob-vious. How could I arrive in advance and warn everyone that a murder-ous mob was on the way when I had to follow the mob to get there?

Yet another life-or-death matter. Oh well.

As the group moved, others joined it, forming spontaneously into a mobile crowd, then a pack, a sturdy vessel of revenge. They were a kind of human tsunami, gathering speed and size. There was no dispersing them. It was a petrifying sight. Eerily, they seemed to be gearing up for a silent massacre. This was not a pack with a war cry, this was a tight-lipped group rolling wordlessly forward. As I ran, I thought how I hate any kind of mob—I hate mobs of sports fans, mobs of environmental demonstrators, I even hate mobs of supermodels, that's how much I hate mobs. I tell you, mankind is bearable only when you get him on his own.

Interestingly, it was a democratic crowd. Anyone could join in to mu-tilate Eddie and my family. There were even a few children. That sur-prised me. And some elderly gentlemen too, who despite being timid and frail were not struggling to keep up. It was as if they had been absorbed by the mob and taken on the energy of it, as if their thin, weak bodies were now nimble fingers of a powerful hand. But weren't these people supposed to be Buddhists? Well, what of it? Buddhists can be pushed over the edge like anyone else, can't they? To be fair, Eddie had burst into their inner serenity with poison and murder and blackmail and rape. In-ner serenity isn't impervious to a ferocious assault like that. Incidentally, none of them were smiling like the Buddha. They were smiling like the serpent, like a forty-headed dragon.

Even the sun took on a menacing quality. It was dropping fast. Natu-rally, I thought, this was to be no brightly lit spectacle of raw carnage. It was to take place in the dark.

But what's this? The mob was picking up the pace! I was already pooped, and now I'd have to run at breakneck speed. How annoying! The last marathon I had intended to run was when I beat 200 million spermatozoa for the egg. Now here I was again. In truth, it was kind of exciting. I was so aware of what a relentless thinker I was that action felt surprisingly good. Murderous mob on its way—what are you going to do about it?

The dusk infused the sky with a soft, syrupy red: a head-wound red. As I ran, I wished I had a machete—it was heavy going, tunneling through all that thick vegetation. I was taking furtive passages through shaggy ferns, where the last of the sunlight only made it in random splotches. The jungle with its usual threatening noises had the surround sound of an expensive home entertainment system.

A half hour later I was losing them. Dammit. What was I going to do? What could I do? I ran, I fell, I vomited, I got up again. Why had we come here? Fucking Thais. An Australian mob might kick the shit out of you, but you'd crawl home afterward. This was murder! No, slaughter! My dad! And Caroline! And Terry! All alone up there, isolated and unprepared. I ran on to the point of exhaustion. And the heat. And the mosquitos. And the fear. I'm not going to make it. How can I warn them?

I suppose I could . . .

No.

Unless . . .

I had an idea. But it was foolish, desperate, impossible. I must be out of my mind. Or just my imagination amusing itself. But what an idea! Here it was: Dad and I were connected in deeper ways than just father and son, and I'd long had the suspicion that we were unintentionally reading each other's minds every so often, and so if I concentrated intensely enough, if I only put in a little psychic effort, maybe I could send him a message. Absurd! Brilliant?

The problem was, it was difficult to summon up that kind of concentration while running, and if I stopped and it didn't work, I might lose not only the mob but with them my way home. And everyone would die!

Did I really think we could read each other's minds? Should I risk it? Running through the foliage was getting more difficult; I'd push aside a branch only to have it whip me in the face. The jungle was getting aggressive. The mob was getting away from me. I was wilting in the heat. My family was going to die.

Should I risk it?

Fuck it.

I stopped. The murdering rabble disappeared over a hill. My heart was aching in my chest. I breathed deeply to placate her.

In order to make contact with Dad, I needed to get myself into a deep meditative state. I needed to hurry, of course, but you can't hurry absolute inner quiet. You have to coax it over time. You can't transform the essential qualities of your mind as if you're running to catch a bus.

I got myself in the textbook position. I sat on the ground cross-legged, concentrated on my breathing, and repeated my mantra, "Wow." This brought about a quiet enough mind, but to be honest, I felt a bit blunt in the head. I had some clarity, enough to drift to the edge of consciousness, but no further. I felt a twinge of bliss too—well, so what? I needed to go further than I ever had, and here I was, going through the motions. From everything I had read about insight meditation, I had learned that there was a system to be used—this is how you sit, this is how you breathe, this is how you concentrate on your breathing. But using this system was a routine that seemed the opposite of the true meditative state I needed. Now that I had practiced this meditation thing a number of times, always the same way, with the same breathing, the same concentration, I felt I might as well be working on a factory line screwing tops on Coca-Cola bottles. My mind was peaceful, hypnotized, numb. That was no good.

Trying to calm my excited mind meant that a conflict was going on in my head. That burned up essential energy I needed in order to communicate telepathically with Dad. So then maybe I had to stop concentrating, but how did I achieve a quiet mind without concentrating?

First of all, instead of sitting cross-legged, I stood up and leaned against a tree like James Dean in *Rebel Without a Cause*. Then I listened not to my breathing, as Anouk advised, but to the noises around me. I didn't close my eyes either. I opened them wide.

I was observing the wet, shaggy trees in the late-afternoon sunlight without concentrating. I made my mind astonishingly alert. I didn't just observe my breath, either, but kept an eye on my thoughts. They fell down like a shower of sparks. I watched them for a long time. I pursued them, not where they went but where they came from, back into the past. I could see how they held me together. I could see how they put me together, these thoughts—the true ingredients of the Jasper broth.

I started walking and the silence of my mind went with me, though it was not the absence-of-sound kind of silence. It was a huge, deafening, visual silence. No one had ever told me about this kind of silence. It was really loud. And as I walked through the jungle, I managed without effort to maintain this clarity.

Then my mind became quiet. Really, really quiet. It happened instantaneously. I was suddenly free of inner friction. Free of fear. That freedom somehow helped all my spineless impediments to melt away. I thought: The world is swelling, it is here, it is bursting in my mouth, it is running down my throat, it is filling up my eyes. Strangely, this big thing had entered me, though I was not bigger for it. I was smaller. It felt good to be small. Look, I know how this sounds, but take it from me, this was not a mystical experience. And I'm not kidding myself, either. I'm not a saint. Not for all the breasts in California would I, like Francis of Assisi, purify the lesions of lepers with my tongue, certainly not, but—and this is where I'm heading—I felt something I'd never experienced in my life before: love. I know this sounds crazy, but I think I actually loved my enemies: Eddie, my family, the murdering mob en route to slaughter my family, even the virulence of the recent outburst of hate by the Australian people. Now, let's not get carried away; I didn't *adore* my enemies, and while I loved them, I was not *in love* with them. But still, my instinctive revulsion toward them had evaporated somehow. This excess of feeling frightened me a little—this frenzy of love that tore through the butter of my hate. So then it seemed Anouk was wrong; the real fruit of meditation wasn't inner peace but love. In fact, when you see life in its totality for the first time and you feel genuine love for that totality, inner peace seems like a kind of small, petty goal.

As nice as all this was, I realized I was not communicating with my father. I almost gave up and started wondering where that furious mob had gotten to when suddenly, without even trying, I conjured up Dad's face. Then I saw his hunched body. He was in his room, bending over his desk. I looked closer. He was writing a letter to one of the Sydney newspapers. I could make out only the salutation at the beginning of the letter. "Dear cunts" was crossed out and replaced with "My dear cunts." I was convinced this was not my imagination but a real image of Dad right now, in the present. I thought: Dad! Dad! It's me! A riotous mob is coming to murder Eddie and everyone in the house! Get out! Get everyone out! I tried to send him an image of the rioting mob so he'd know what they looked like when they turned up. I sent him an image of the mob as one common body closing in on the house, armed with Old World farming implements. They had scythes, for God's sake!

Without my permission, the vision faded away. I opened my eyes. It was a clouded-over black night, so dark I could have been underground. All around me the jungle was making formidable groaning sounds. How long had I been here? I had no way of knowing.

I started walking again, pushing branches out of my way, my eyes still full of visions, my nose filled with out-of-place odors (cinnamon and maple syrup), my tongue with out-of-place tastes (toothpaste and Vegemite). I had the sensation of being in the world as never before.

As I walked, I wondered, would they find the house empty? Had Dad heard my warning? Or had I just given up trying to save my family's lives? I walked without knowing where I was going. I let my instinct guide me through the jungle, stomping on luscious plants that gave off a sweet, heady odor. I paused to drink the cold, delicious water of a small waterfall. Then I moved on again, stumbling over hills and through the dense foliage.

I felt no fear. I felt such a part of the jungle that it seemed it would have been rude of the animals to venture out to eat me. Then I moved into a clearing that ran down a long hill where I could see the moon rising. All the eyes of the flowers and the mouths of the trees and the chins of strange rock formations seemed to be telling me I was going in the right direction. That was a relief, because there were no tracks. Somehow the silent mass of vengeful people had left everything undisturbed, as if they had been floating through the jungle like some formless ancient substance.

When I finally found Eddie's place, the lights were blazing inside. The wind was violently knocking at the windows and the doors. The sight of the house made my state of oneness vanish instantaneously. The world was hopelessly fragmented again; the absolute connectedness between me and all living things was gone. Now I felt indifferent to all living things. I couldn't care less about them. The divisions between us were as thick as columns of bone and cartilage. There was me and there was them. Any fool could see it.

Hiding behind a tree, I felt the blood cells racing through my heart. I remembered something Dad had once promised to teach me: how to make yourself unappetizing when the hordes turn up to eat you. I hoped he actually knew this essential skill.

Of course I was too late. The door was wide open, and the mob was already leaving one by one, armed with scythes and hammers and pitchforks. There would be no point facing the mob or its decrystallized form, because presumably it had already done what it came to do. There was nothing to be gained in getting hacked to pieces myself.

Blood covered the hands and the faces of the mob. Their clothes were so stained, they would just have to be thrown away. I waited until the last intruder left and then waited a few moments longer. I watched the house and tried to feel no fear. Even after all Dad had taught me, I was not prepared for such a moment. Nothing had prepared me for walking into a place where my family had been butchered. I struggled to recall any nugget of wisdom from my early childhood that might offer me advice on how to proceed, but I couldn't, so I went forward into the house, emotionally, psychologically, and spiritually defenseless. Of course I had many times imagined them already dead (as soon as I feel an emotional attachment to someone, I imagine his death, so as not to be disappointed later on), but in my mind they were always relatively clean corpses, quite neat in fact, and until now it had not occurred to me to prepare myself by imagining my loved ones' brains splattered against a wall, their bodies lying sprawled in a pool of blood/shit/guts, et cetera.

The first body I saw was Eddie's. He looked as if he'd been run over a thousand times by a champion ice-skater. His face was so cut up I could barely make out it was him, except for his eyes, which had that frozen look of surprise characteristic of Botox and sudden death, staring up at the earthenware pots with his parents' spirits in them, the ones who had purportedly been watching over him. It was easy to see the look of reproach in his eyes. Goodbye and good riddance, Eddie. You took your crumminess to its limit and it collapsed on top of you. Tough luck.

With superhuman effort, my legs took me to the next room. There I saw Uncle Terry on his knees, and from behind he looked like the back of a VW Beetle about to do a reverse park into a tight spot. Sweat poured off the fat folds in his neck. I could hear him crying. He spun around to look at me, then turned back and raised his chubby arm, motioning toward Dad's bedroom.

I went in.

Dad was also on his knees, swaying gently over the mutilated body of Caroline. His eyes were as wide as they could go, as though pried open with matchsticks. The love of his life was on her back, blood seeping from a dozen slashes. Her dead eyes were fixed in an insupportable gaze. I had to look away. There was something disturbing in those eyes. She looked like someone who had said something offensive and wanted to take it back. Later I found out she had died trying to protect Eddie, of all people; she was killed inadvertently, and it was her death that had turned the mob on itself, split it into factions—those who thought that it was OK to kill a middle-aged woman and those who thought it was out of order. That had effectively ended their rampage and sent them home.

We buried Eddie and Caroline in the garden. It had started raining again, and we had no choice but to give them a wet, muddy burial, which was appropriate for Eddie maybe. But watching Caroline's body disappear into the muck made us all sick and ashamed. Dad was having trouble breathing, as if something were blocking his airway—maybe his heart.

•

The three of us drove back to Bangkok in silence, lost in the kind of grief that makes every smile in your life afterward less sincere. On the way Dad sat in absolute stillness, though he made little noises to let us know that every minute left in his life would be an unendurable torture. I knew he was blaming himself for her death, and not only himself but Terry too, for employing Eddie to begin with, and not only Terry but fate, chance, God, art, science, humanity, the Milky Way. Nothing was exonerated.

When we arrived back at Terry's house, we retired to our separate bedrooms to marvel at how quickly the human heart snaps shut and to wonder how we might ever pry it open again. It was only two days later, spurred either by Caroline's murder or by the black dog barking in the manure of his heart, or by mourning crowding out rational thought, or maybe because even after a lifetime of reflecting on death, he still couldn't quite comprehend the inevitability of his own, that Dad suddenly emerged from his grief-induced hypnosis and announced his final project. As Eddie had predicted, it was the looniest yet. And after a lifetime of watching Dad make improbable decision after improbable decision, and being in some way a victim of each one, what surprised me most was that I could still be surprised.

SEVEN

I don't want to die here," Dad said.

"What's the matter?" Terry asked. "Don't you like your room?"

"The room's fine. It's this country."

The three of us were eating chicken laksas and watching the sun set over the polluted metropolis. As usual, Dad was nauseated and managed to make it seem as though his vomiting were a gut reaction not to the food but to the company.

"Well, we don't want you to die either, do we, Jasper?"

"No," I said, and waited a full thirty seconds before adding, "not at the moment."

Dad wiped the corners of his mouth with my sleeve and said, "I want to die at home."

"When you say home, you mean . . ."

"Australia."

Terry and I looked at each other with dread.

"Well, mate," Terry said slowly, "that's just not practical."

"I know. Nevertheless, I'm going home."

Terry took a deep breath and spoke to Dad calmly and deliberately, as though gently chastising his grown-up mentally disturbed son for smothering the family pet by overhugging.

"Marty. Do you know what would happen the minute the plane landed on Aussie soil? You'd be arrested at the airport." Dad didn't say anything. He knew this was true. Terry pushed on: "Do you want to die in jail? Because that's what's going to happen if you fly back home."

"No, I don't want to die in jail."

"That's settled, then," Terry said. "You'll die here."

"I have another idea," Dad said, and at once any glimmer of hope died and I knew that a nice, quiet, peaceful death followed by an intimate funeral and a respectable period of restrained mourning was now out of the question. Whatever was coming was going to be dangerous, messy, and frantic and would drive me to the edge of insanity.

"So, Marty, what are you suggesting?"

"We *sneak* back into Australia."

"What?"

"By boat," he clarified. "Terry, I know you know who the people-smugglers are."

"This is nuts!" I said. "You can't want to risk your life just to die in Australia! You hate Australia!"

"Look, I know this is world-class hypocrisy. But I don't fucking care. I'm homesick! I miss the landscape and the smell of it. I even miss my countrymen and the smell of them!"

"Be careful now," I said. "Your final act will be a direct contradiction of everything you've ever thought, said, and believed."

"I know," he said almost cheerfully, not minding at all. In fact, he seemed enlivened by it. He was up on his feet now, swaying a little, daring us with his eyes to raise objections so he could shoot them down.

"Didn't you tell me nationalism is a disease?" I asked.

"And I stand by it. But it's a disease that, as it turns out, I have contracted, along with everything else. And I don't see the point of trying to cure myself of a minor ailment when I'm about to die of a major one."

I didn't say anything to that. What could I say?

I had to get out the big guns to help me. Luckily, Dad had packed a suitcase full of books, and I found the very quote I needed in his well-thumbed copy of Fromm's *The Sane Society*. I went into his room but he was on the toilet, so I read it to him through the bathroom door: "Hey, Dad. 'The person who has not freed himself from the ties to blood and soil is not yet fully born as a human being; his capacity for love and reason are crippled; he does not experience himself nor his fellow man in their and his own human reality.' "

"It doesn't matter. When I die, my failures and weaknesses die with me. You see? My failures are dying too."

I continued: " 'Nationalism is our form of incest, is our idolatry, is our insanity. "Patriotism" . . . is its cult . . . Just as love for one individual which excludes the love for others is not love, love for one's country which is not part of one's love for humanity is not love, but idolatrous worship.' "

"So?"

"So you don't love humanity, do you?"

"No. Not really."

"Well, there you are!"

Dad flushed the toilet and came out without washing his hands. "You can't change my mind, Jasper. This is what I want. Dying men get dying wishes even if it irritates the living. And this is mine—I want to expire in my country, with my people."

Caroline, I thought. It was obvious that Dad was in the grip of a pain that would arrive forever. He had made himself perpetually vigilant against his own comfort, and this mission to Australia was a directive from a sadness that must be obeyed.

But not only that. By tiptoeing back into Australia as human cargo in a risky smuggling operation, Dad had found one last stupid project, one that was sure to expedite his death.

II

The people-smugglers orchestrated their nasty enterprise out of an ordinary restaurant on a congested street that looked like seventy other congested streets I saw as we drove in. Terry gave Dad and me a warning at the door: "We've got to be careful with these guys. They're absolutely brutal. They'll cut your head off first, ask questions later, mostly about where to send your head." With that in mind, we took a table and ordered jungle curries and beef salad. I had always imagined that fronts for criminal activity were merely façades, but here they actually served food, and it wasn't bad.

We ate without speaking. Dad coughed in between spoonfuls and in between coughs called repeatedly to a waiter for bottled water. Terry was shoveling down prawns and breathing through his nose. The King was glaring at me disapprovingly from a portrait on the far wall. A couple of English backpackers at the next table were discussing the physical and psychological differences between Thai prostitutes and a girl named Rita from East Sussex.

"So, Terry," I asked, "what happens now? We just sit here until closing time?"

"Leave it to me."

We left it to him. All the communication happened wordlessly, according to a preestablished set of rules: Terry gave a conspiratorial nod to a waiter, who in turn gave it to the chef through an open window into the kitchen. The chef then passed the nod on to a man out of our line of vision, who for all we knew passed it on to twenty more men who lined a spiral staircase leading to the mezzanine of hell. After a few anxious minutes, a man with a slightly malformed bald head came out and sat down, biting his lip and staring at us threateningly. Terry produced an envelope brimming with money and pushed it across the table. That softened the smuggler up a little. Grabbing the envelope, he rose from the table. We followed him, our footsteps sounding prolonged echoes as we walked down a hallway that eventually led to a small windowless room where two armed men greeted us with cold stares. One of them molested us, searching for weapons, and when none were found a flabby middle-aged man in an expensive suit entered and gazed at us quietly. His impressive stillness made me feel I was in a story by Conrad, as if I were looking into the heart of darkness. Of course he was just a businessman, with the same love of profit and indifference to human suffering as his Western corporate counterparts. I thought that this man could be a midlevel executive at IBM or a legal adviser to the tobacco industry.

Without warning, one of the bodyguards cracked the butt of a rifle over Terry's head. His massive body crashed to the floor. He was unconscious but alive, his torso heaving with slow, deep breaths. When they aimed the guns at me, I thought how this was exactly the type of room I had always imagined I'd die in: small, airless, and crammed with strangers looking on indifferently.

"You are police," the boss said in English.

"No. Not police," Dad protested. "We are wanted criminals. Like you. Well, not like you. We don't know if you're wanted or not. Perhaps no-body wants you."

"You are police."

"No. Christ, listen. I have cancer. Cancer, you know. The big C. Death." Dad then proceeded to tell them the whole absurd story of his fall from grace and escape from Australia.

I thought it was commonly accepted that stories this ridiculous had to be true, but the smugglers seemed skeptical. As they deliberated our fate, I remembered how Orwell described the future as a boot stamping on a human face forever, and I thought that all around me were boots, people so terrible that the whole human race should be punished for doing nothing to curb their existence. The job of these people-smugglers was to recruit desperate people, strip them of every penny, lie to them before shoving them onto boats that routinely sank. Each year they sent hun-dreds to their terror-stricken deaths. These pure exploiters were the irri-table bowel syndrome of the cosmos, I thought, and looking at these men as if they were examples of all men, I decided I'd be happy to disappear if it meant they also could not exist.

The boss spoke quietly in Thai just as Terry regained consciousness. We helped him up off the floor, which was no easy task. Rubbing his head, he said, "They said it'll cost you twenty-five thousand."

"Fifty thousand," I said.

"Jasper," Dad whispered, "don't you know anything about bargaining?"

"I'm going too," I said.

Dad and Terry exchanged looks. Dad's was dark and silent while his brother's was wide and mystified.

"Plenty of these boats sink long before they get to Australia," Terry said anxiously. "Marty! I absolutely forbid this! You can't let Jasper go with you."

"I can't stop him," Dad said, and I detected in his voice an enthusi-asm to be reckless with my life now that his was over.

"Jasper, you're a fool. Don't do this," Terry protested.

"I have to."

Terry sighed, and muttered that I was more like my father every day. The deal was sealed with a handshake and fifty grand in cold, hard cash, and once the transaction was made, the smugglers seemed to relax and even offered us beers "on the house." Watching these villains, I imagined that I had branched off the evolutionary line at an earlier age and evolved in secret, parallel to man but always apart.

"Tell me one thing, Jasper," Terry said after we left the restaurant. "Why are you going?"

I shrugged. It was complicated. I didn't want the people-smugglers, those fucking ghouls, to double-cross Dad and throw his body into the water half an hour out to sea. But this was not just an altruistic outburst; it was a form of preemptive strike. I didn't want Dad's resentment haunting me from beyond the grave, or little waves of guilt lapping at my future serenity. But above all, it was to be a sentimental journey: if he was to die, either at sea or among "his people" (whoever the fuck they were), I wanted to see it for myself, eyeball to vacant eyeball. My whole life I'd been pushed beyond rational limits by this man, and I was offended by the notion that I could be so implicated in his lifelong drama and not be present for the grand finale. He might have been his own worst enemy, but he was my worst enemy too, and I'd be damned if I was going to wait patiently by the riverbank, as in the Chinese proverb, for his corpse to float by. I wanted to see him die and bury him and pat the earth with my bare hands.

I say this as a loving son.

III

Our last night in Thailand, Terry prepared a feast, but the night was ruined early by Dad's failure to show up. We searched the house thoroughly, especially the bathrooms and toilets, any hole he might have fallen into, but he was nowhere to be found. Finally, on his desk, we found a short note: "Dear Jasper and Terry. Gone to a brothel. Back later."

Terry took it personally that his brother was avoiding him on their last night together, and I couldn't quite convince him that each dying man must perform his own archaic ritual. Some hold hands with loved ones; others prefer unprotected and exploitative third world sex.

Before bed, I packed a few things for the trip. We had taken very little to Thailand, and I put together even less for the return trip—one change of clothes each, two toothbrushes, one tube of toothpaste, and two vials of poison, procured by Terry, who had presented them to me with shaky hands over dinner. "Here you are, nephew," he said, handing me little plastic tubes filled with a cloudy liquid. "In case the voyage drifts on without end or winds up on the bottom of the sea floor and you can look forward only to starvation or drowning, voilà! A third option!" He assured me it was a quick and relatively painless poison, though I pondered the word "relatively" for some time, unconsoled that we'd be howling in agony for a briefer period than offered by the other poisons in the shop. I hid the plastic tubes in a zipped pocket on the side of my bag.

I didn't close my eyes all night. I thought about Caroline and my inability to save her. What a disappointment my brain turned out to be. After everything I had witnessed in my life, I had almost convinced myself that the wheel of personal history spins on thought, and therefore my history was muddy because my thinking had been muddy. I imagined that everything I'd experienced to date was likely to be a materialization of my fears (especially my fear of Dad's fears). In short, I had briefly believed that if man's character is his fate, and if his character is the sum of his actions, and his actions are a result of his thoughts, then man's character, actions, and fate are dependent on what he thinks. Now I wasn't so sure.

An hour before dawn, when it was time to leave to catch the boat, Dad still hadn't returned. I imagined he was either lost in Bangkok, weary at having spent the night bargaining down prostitutes, or else soaking in a bubble bath in a fancy hotel, having changed his mind about the voyage without telling us.

"What do we do?" Terry asked.

"Let's get down to the dock. Maybe he'll turn up there."

It was a half-hour drive to the dock through the stacked-up city and then through ramshackle suburbs that looked like an enormous house of cards that had fallen down. We parked next to a long pier. The sun, emerging over the horizon, glowed through the fog. Above us we could just make out clouds the shape of lopped-off heads.

"There she is," Terry said.

When I saw the fishing trawler, our dilapidated would-be coffin, all the joints in my body stiffened. It was a crappy wooden boat that looked like an ancient relic restored in a hurry just for show. I thought: This is where we're to be stored like the cod livers we are.

It wasn't long before the asylum-seekers, the Runaways, began appearing in fearful, suspicious groups of two and three. There were men, women, and children. I did my own head count as they crowded the dock—eight . . . twelve . . . seventeen . . . twenty-five . . . thirty . . . They kept coming. There seemed no way this little boat could accommodate us all. Mothers hugged their sons and daughters tightly. I felt like crying. You can't overlook the poignancy of a family risking its children's existence to give them a better life.

But here they were! The Runaways! Here they were, demonstrating twin expressions of human desperation and human hope, huddling together furtively, examining the trawler with profound mistrust. They weren't fools. They knew they were riding on a coin toss. They were deeply suspicious that this rusty vessel could possibly be their deliverance. I checked them out, wondering: Will we resort to cannibalism before the journey's done? Will I be eating that man's thigh and drinking that woman's spinal fluid with a bile chaser?

I waited with Terry on the pier. The smugglers appeared as if from nowhere, all wearing khaki. The captain stepped off the boat. He was a slim man with a tired face who stood rubbing the back of his neck over and over as if it were a genie's bottle. He ordered us all on board.

"I'm not going if Dad's not going," I said with enormous relief.

"Wait! There he is."

Dammit, yes, there he was, coming down the dock, staggering toward us.

Someone once said that at fifty, everyone has the face he deserves. Well, I'm sorry, but no one at any age deserves the face my father had as he walked toward us. It was as though the force of gravity had gone haywire and was pulling his face down to the earth and up to the moon at the same time.

"Is that it? Is that the boat? Is that the fucking boat? Is it watertight? It looks pretty loose to me."

"That's her, all right."

"It looks like it couldn't float in space."

"I agree. It's not too late to chuck this whole idea."

"No, no. We'll carry on."

"Right." Fuck.

The sun was rising. It was almost morning. The captain came over and urged us on board again. Terry put a hand on his shoulder and squeezed it like a lemon.

"All right. Remember what I told you: if these two men do not reach Australia in tip-top condition, I will kill you."

"And if he doesn't," Dad said, "my ghost will come back and kick you in the balls."

"That's settled, then," Terry said. "You got it?"

The captain nodded wearily. He seemed used to threats.

Terry and Dad stood facing each other like two men about to wrestle. Dad tried to smile, but his face couldn't support the sudden strain. Terry puffed a little, as if he were climbing stairs, and slapped Dad lightly on the arm.

"Well. This was a hell of a reunion, wasn't it?"

"I'm sorry dying's made me such a shit," Dad said. He looked awkward with this goodbye, and put his hand on his head as if he were worried it would blow away. Then they gave each other a smile. You could see their whole lives in that smile: their childhood, their adventures. The smile said, "Didn't we turn out to be two different and amusing creatures?"

"Just have a nice peaceful death," Terry said, "and try not to take Jasper with you."

"He'll be OK," Dad said, and turning away from his brother, he boarded the boat, which knocked gently against the pier.

Terry grabbed me by the shoulders and smiled. He leaned forward, smelling of coriander and lemongrass, and planted a kiss on my forehead. "You take care of yourself."

"What are you going to do?" I asked.

"I think I'll get out of Thailand. Maybe move to Kurdistan or Uzbekistan, one of those places I can't spell. I'll try setting up a cooperative there. This whole thing with your dad and Caroline has shaken me up a little. I think I need to go on a long, rough journey. See what's up. I have a funny feeling the world's about to go up in smoke. The war has started, Jasper. Take my word for it. The have-nots are getting their act together. And the haves are in for a rough trot."

I agreed it seemed to be developing that way.

"Will you ever come out of the shadows and return to Australia?"

"One day I'll come back and give them all the fright of their lives."

"Come on, let's go home," Dad shouted from the deck.

Terry looked at Dad and held up a finger to say he needed one minute. "Jasper, before you go, I'd like to give you a word or two of advice."

"All right."

"From watching you these past months, I've worked out that there's something you want above all things. You want not to be like your father."

That wasn't something I kept hidden, even from Dad.

"You've probably worked out by now that if you think courageous thoughts, you will cross busy streets without looking, and if you think sadistic, venal thoughts, you will find yourself pulling out the chair every time someone is about to sit down. You are what you think. So if you don't want to turn into your father, you don't want to think yourself into a corner like he did—you need to think yourself into the open, and the only way to do that is to enjoy not knowing whether you're right or wrong, play the game of life without trying to work out the rules. Stop judging the living, enjoy futility, don't be disillusioned with murder, remember that fasting men survive while starving men die, laugh as your illusions collapse, and above all, always bless every single minute of this silly season in hell."

I didn't know what to say to that. I thanked him, hugged him one last time, and boarded the boat.

As we set off, through a heavy curtain of black engine smoke, I waved goodbye to Terry until he disappeared from sight. I looked at Dad to see if he was sad to never see his brother again, and I noticed that he was turned in the opposite direction, gazing out at the horizon and smiling an inappropriately optimistic smile.

IV

The terrible ocean! Weeks and weeks of it!

It seemed impossible for the captain to get the boat under control. Large waves threatened us on all sides. The trawler was tossed appallingly. It felt like she wasn't just rocking back and forth but wheeling and spiraling and looping, doing mad circles in space.

Below deck, the portholes were welded shut and painted over with black tar. The floors were lined with soiled cardboard, and the passengers slept on mattresses as thin as sheets. I remembered how when I first arrived in Thailand everyone told me not to point my feet at anyone's head. Now, in this cramped space, people were crowded together so closely that you ended up putting your feet not just at the heads of strangers but right into their faces too, day in, day out. Dad and I were jammed into a tight corner, sandwiched between bulky sacks of rice and a chain-smoking family from southern China.

In that hot and sweaty cage, the only oxygen we inhaled had been exhaled by other passengers. To be below deck was to be submerged in a nightmare. The crush of limbs and skeletal torsos was oppressive, especially in the suffocating darkness, where voices—peculiar, chilling, guttural sounds—made up conversations from which we were estranged. If you had to go outside for air, you didn't so much move among them as were pushed remorselessly from one end of the hull to the other.

Sometimes, Dad and I slept up on the hard, ridged deck, using as pillows coils of wet, heavy rope caked in mud from one sea floor or another. It wasn't much better up there; the days were stinking hot, it rained steadily, and who'd have imagined mosquitos could make it this far out to sea? They gnawed us incessantly. We could hardly hear ourselves swear at God against the loud, throbbing engine, which was belching out clouds of black smoke relentlessly.

At night we lay staring up at the sky, where the stars swam in shapes somehow made menacing by sobs, screams, and howls of delirium, mostly from Dad.

There's nothing pleasant about the final stages of cancer. He was confused, delirious, convulsing; he had severe throbbing headaches, giddiness, slurred speech, dizzy spells, nausea, vomiting, trembling, sweating, unbearable muscle pain, extreme weakness, and sleeps as heavy as comas. He made me feed him from a pill bottle with an unreadable label. They were opiates, he said. So Dad's various immortality projects had given way to the more important mortality project: to die with the least pain.

No one liked having the sick man on board. They knew the journey required strength and stamina, and besides, no matter what religion you followed, a dying man was a bad omen in every one. Perhaps because of this, the Runaways were reluctant to share their provisions with us. And it wasn't just Dad's health that bothered them—we emanated the smell of the alien. They knew we were Australians who had paid enormous sums of money to enter our own country illegally. They couldn't wrap their minds around it.

One night on deck I was awoken by a voice shouting, "Why you here?" I opened my eyes to see the ship's captain standing above us, smoking a cigarette. His face was a pulp novel I didn't have the energy to read. "I don't think he make it," the captain's voice persisted as his foot nudged Dad in the stomach. "Maybe we throw him off."

"Maybe I throw you off," I said.

One of the Runaways stood up behind me and shouted something to the captain in a language I didn't recognize. The captain backed off. I turned around. The Runaway was around the same age as me, with large, beautiful eyes that were much too big for his drawn face. He had long curly hair and long curly eyelashes. Everything about him was long and curly.

"They say you're Australian," he said.

"That's right."

"I would like to take an Australian name. Can you think of one for me?"

"OK. Sure. How about . . . Ned."

"Ned?"

"Ned."

"All right. I am now Ned. Will you please call me by my new name and see if I turn around?"

"OK."

Ned faced away from me and I called out "Shane!" as a test. He didn't fall for it. After that I tried calling him Bob, Henry, Frederick, and Hotpants21, but he didn't even flinch. Then I called out "Ned!" and he spun around, grinning madly.

"Thank you," he said politely. "May I ask you a question?"

"Shoot."

"Why are you here? We would all like to know."

I looked behind me. Others had emerged from the cabin below to wash their filthy lungs in the night air. Dad was sweating and feverish, and Ned held out a wet rag for my inspection.

"May I?" he asked me.

"Go ahead."

Ned pressed the wet rag against Dad's forehead. Dad let out a long sigh. Our fellow passengers yelled out questions to Ned, and he yelled back before waving them over. They shuffled closer, crowded around us, and wet our ears with a spattering of broken English. These strange ancillary characters, called in at the last minute to make a guest appearance in the epilogue of a man's life, wanted to understand.

"What's your name?" Ned asked Dad.

"I'm Martin. This is Jasper."

"So, Martin, why do you go into Australia like this?" Ned asked.

"They don't want me there," Dad said weakly.

"What did you do?"

"I made some bad mistakes."

"You kill someone?"

"No."

"You rape someone?"

"No. It was nothing like that. It was a . . . financial indiscretion." He winced. If only Dad had raped and killed. Those crimes would at least have been worth his life, and possibly mine.

Ned translated the phrase "financial indiscretion" to the others, and as if on cue a thick curtain of cloud parted, allowing the moon to illuminate their blank confusion. Watching them watching us, I wondered if they had the slightest clue what to expect in Australia. I supposed they knew they'd be living an underground existence, exploited in brothels, factories, building sites, restaurant kitchens, and by the fashion industry, who would get them sewing their fingers to the bone. But I doubted they were aware of the adolescent competition among political leaders to see who had the toughest immigration policies, the kind you wouldn't want to meet down a dark alley. Or that public opinion was already set against them, because even if you're running for your life you still have to wait in line, or that Australia, like everywhere, excelled in making arbitrary distinctions between people seem important.

If they knew this, there was no time to dwell on it. Surviving the journey was the only priority, and that was no easy trick. Things were getting steadily worse. Supplies were dwindling. Wind and rain battered the boat. Enormous swollen waves threatened to capsize us at every moment. There were times we could not let go of the rail or we would have been thrown overboard. We felt no closer to Australia than when we started, and it became hard to believe that our country even existed anymore, or any other country, for that matter. The ocean was growing bigger. It covered the whole earth. The sky got bigger too—it was raised even higher, stretched to breaking point. Our boat was the smallest thing in creation, and we were infinitesimal. Hunger and thirst shrank us further. The heat was a full-body fat suit we all wore together. Many were trembling with fever. We spotted land once or twice, and I screamed in the captain's eardrum, "Let's pull in there, for Chrissakes!"

"That's not Australia."

"Who cares? It's land! Dry land! We won't drown there!"

We pushed on, cutting a foamy trail through an ocean bubbling with hostile intentions.

It's surprising just how placid the dying human animal can be in such a circus. I never would've believed it. I thought we'd be tearing each other's flesh off, drinking the blood of our brothers, but it wasn't like that at all. Everyone was too tired. Sure, there was crying and a fair amount of bitter frustration, but it was sad and quiet bitter frustration. We were tiny, shrunken creatures, too frail for any kind of serious protest.

Most of the time Dad lay motionless on deck, looking like a scary stuffed toy you give to a child on Halloween.

I stroked his forehead gently, but he summoned up just enough energy to shrug me off.

"I'm dying," he said bitterly.

"Another couple of days and I'll be dying too," I said, to cheer him up.

"I'm sorry about that. I told you not to come," he said, knowing full well he hadn't.

Dad was trying to act remorseful for having selfishly aligned my fate to his. But I knew better. I knew something he would never admit—that he had never fully shaken off his old, sick delusion that I was the premature reincarnation of his still living self—and now he thought that if I died, he might live on.

"Jasper, I'm dying," he said again.

"Jesus Christ, Dad! Look around! Everyone here is dying! We're all going to die!"

That burned him up. He was furious that his death was not being regarded as a tragic isolated spectacle. To die among the dying, as a number, was really a thorn in his side. Mostly, though, it was the constant praying to God that was getting under his skin. "I wish these idiots would shut up," he said.

"These are good people, Dad. We should be proud to drown among them."

Nonsense. I was talking pure nonsense. But Dad was determined to leave the earth in a belligerent state, and there was nothing I could do to dissuade him. Even with his life packed and its passport stamped, he rejected the religious world for the umpteenth time.

We were the only ones not praying, and the Runaways' positivism really put Dad and me to shame. They still had the feeling that lovely things were stirring in the air. They were giddy in their ecstatic flight, blissful because their gods were not the inner kind, who can't really help you out in a tangible, nonephemeral crisis like a sinking boat; their gods were old-fashioned, the kind who direct the whole of nature to the desires of the individual. What a lucky break! Their gods actually listened to people, and sometimes intervened. Their gods dealt out personal favors! It's Who you know! That's why their private experience had none of the cold terror of ours: we envisaged no big thumb and forefinger descending from the heavens to pluck us out of harm's way.

I tended to Dad in a sort of trance. In the dark he laid out countless ideas about life and how to live it. They were slightly more confused and puerile than his usual diatribes, though, and I realized that when you're falling, the only thing you have to hold on to is yourself. When he talked, I pretended to listen. If he wanted to sleep, I slept too. When Dad moaned, I gave him painkillers. There wasn't anything else to do. He was suffering, his far-off eyes farther off than ever before. I knew he was thinking of Caroline. "Martin Dean—what a fool he was!" he said. It gave him some comfort to talk about himself in the third-person past tense.

Ned sometimes gave me a break. He took my place and gave Dad water and took over pretending to listen to his ceaseless droning. On those occasions I crawled over the half-conscious bodies of my companions to get to the deck for a breath of air. Above me the sky opened up like a cracked skull. The stars were glistening like beads of sweat. I was awake, but my senses were dreaming. My own sweat tasted of mango, then chocolate, then avocado. This was a disaster! Dad was dying too slowly and in too much pain. Why didn't he just kill himself? Why do staunch atheists put up with so much futile agony? What was he waiting for?

Suddenly I remembered. The poison!

I ran down and climbed over the human mattress and whispered feverishly in his ear. "Do you want the poison?"

Dad sat up and looked at me with glowing eyes. Death can be

controlled, the eyes sang. Our vital powers were somewhat recharged, contemplating the poison.

"Tomorrow morning at dawn," he said. "We'll do it together."

"Dad—I'm not taking the poison."

"No, of course not. I didn't mean that you would take it. I just meant that I'd take it and you'd watch."

Poor Dad. He always hated loneliness, and now he was faced with the deepest, most concentrated form of loneliness in existence.

But at dawn it was raining, and he didn't want to commit suicide in the rain.

When the rain cleared, it was too hot to end it all.

At night he wanted to let out his final breath in the warm glare of the sun.

In short, he was never ready. He vacillated interminably. He always found a new excuse not to do it: too rainy, too cloudy, too sunny, too choppy, too early, too late.

Two or three days of agony passed in that way.

•

It finally happened just after sunset around two or three weeks at sea. A wave of foam crashed below deck. We were half drowned. The shrieking didn't help anything. When the ocean settled, Dad sat up in the dark. He suddenly had trouble breathing. I gave him some more water.

"Jasper, I think this is it."

"How do you know?"

"I just know. I was always suspicious of the way in movies people knew when their time was coming, but it's true. Death knocks. He actually knocks."

"Can I do anything?"

"Take me up top, wait until I'm dead, and push me off the boat."

"I thought you didn't want a watery grave."

"I don't. But these bastards have been eyeing me like I'm just one big lamb chop."

"Cancer hasn't exactly made you appetizing."

"Don't argue with me. Once I'm dead, I don't want to spend another minute on this boat."

"Understood."

The Runaways didn't take their eyes off us. They spoke to each other in quiet, conspiratorial tones as Ned helped me get Dad out of there.

Up on deck his breathing grew easier. The Pacific air seemed to do him some good. The vast movement of the ocean pacified him. Well, at least I'd like to think so. These were his final moments, and I'd like to think that at the end he ceased to find his cosmic insignificance insulting, that finally he felt something whimsical in meaning nothing, that it was even somewhat amusing to be an accident in the appalling wasteland of space-time. This was my hope—that, staring out at the ocean's majestical performance in surging blue and facing the mad sea wind, he might have cottoned on to the idea that the universal stage show was a bigger drama than he could ever have dreamed to land a key role in. But no, he didn't put his existence into perspective at all—he was humorless about it right to the end. He went to his death a martyr to his own secret cause, unwilling to denounce himself.

I record his last minutes in the sad spirit of a biographer too close to his subject.

The night was silent, save for the creaking of the boat and the gentle lapping of the water. The moon hung brightly above the horizon. We were heading straight for it. The captain was steering us into the moon. I imagined a hatch door opening. I imagined us drifting inside. I imagined the door slamming shut behind us and the sound of crazy laughter. I imagined these things to distract me from the reality of my father's death.

"Look, Martin, look at the moon," Ned said. "Look at how it has been painted on the sky. God is truly an artist."

That gave Dad a burst of energy. "I hope not, for all our sakes," he said. "Honestly, Ned, have you ever actually met an artist? These are not nice people. They're selfish, narcissistic, and vicious types who spend their good days in a suicidal depression. Tell him, Jasper."

I sighed, knowing this speech by heart. "Artists are the kind of people who cheat on their mistresses, abandon their legitimate children, and make those who are underprivileged enough to know them suffer terribly for their efforts to show them kindness," I said.

Dad raised his head to add, "And you proudly label God an artist *and* expect him to take care of you? Good luck!"

"You lack faith."

"Have you ever wondered why your God requires faith? Is it that heaven has a limited seating capacity and the necessity of faith is God's way of keeping the numbers down?"

Ned looked at him with pity, shook his head, and said nothing.

"Dad, give it a rest."

I gave him another couple of painkillers. After swallowing, he gasped and fell unconscious. Ten minutes later he began ranting deliriously.

"Hundreds . . . millions . . . Christians salivating . . . heaven a fancy hotel where . . . won't be bumping into Muslims and Jews at the ice machine . . . Muslims and the Jews . . . no better . . . no budging . . . modern man . . . good teeth . . . short attention span . . . supposed to be . . . turmoil of alienation . . . no religious worldview . . . neurosis . . . insanity . . . not true . . . always religion among creatures . . . who . . . die."

"Save your energy," Ned said. He could have said "Shut up" and I wouldn't have held it against him.

Dad's head fell back into my lap. He couldn't have had more than a couple of minutes left and he still couldn't believe it.

"This is really incredible," he said, and took a deep breath. I could tell by his face that the painkillers were kicking in.

"I know."

"But really! Death! My death!"

He slipped into sleep for a few minutes, then his eyes sprang open with a blank expression behind them, as bland as a bureaucrat's. I think he was trying to convince himself that the day he died was not the worst day of his life but just an average so-so day. He couldn't keep it up, though, and groaned once more through clenched teeth.

"Jasper."

"I'm here."

"Chekhov believed that man will become better when you show him what he is like. I don't think that's turned out to be true. It's just made him sadder and lonelier."

"Look, Dad—don't feel pressured to be profound with your dying words. Just take it easy."

"I've said a lot of drivel in my life, haven't I?"

"It wasn't all drivel."

Dad took a few wheezing breaths while his eyes rolled around in his head as if they were searching for something in the corner of his skull.

"Jasper," he croaked, "I have to admit something."

"What?"

"I heard you," he said.

"You heard what?"

"In the jungle. When they came. I heard your voice warning me."

"You heard me?" I shouted. I couldn't believe it. "You heard that? Why didn't you do anything? You could have saved Caroline's life!"

"I didn't believe it was real."

We didn't say anything for a long while. We both gazed silently into the moving waters of the sea.

Then the pain started up again. He howled in agony. I felt afraid. Then fear grew into panic. I thought: Don't die. Don't leave me. Don't leave us. You're breaking up a partnership. Can't you see it? Please, Dad. I'm absolutely dependent on you, even as your opposite, especially as your opposite—because if you're dead, what does that make me? Is the opposite of nothing everything? Or is it nothing?

And I don't want to be mad at a ghost, either. That'll never end.

"Dad, I forgive you."

"What for?"

"For everything."

"What everything? What did I ever do to you?"

Who is this irritating man? "It doesn't matter."

"OK."

"Dad, I love you."

"I love you too."

There. We said it. Good.

Or not so good—strangely unsatisfying. We'd just said "I love you." Father and son, at the deathbed of the former, saying we love each other. Why didn't that feel good? This is why: because I knew something that nobody knew or would ever know—what a strange and wonderful man he was. And that's what I really wanted to say.

"Dad."

"I should have killed myself," he said between clenched teeth; then he repeated it, as if it were his private mantra. He would never forgive himself for not committing suicide. In my mind, that was appropriate. I think all people on their deathbeds should not forgive themselves for not committing suicide, even one day earlier. To let yourself be murdered by Nature's hand is the only real apathy there is.

His actual death was quick—sudden, even. His body trembled a little, then spasmed in fear, he gasped, his teeth snapped shut as if trying to bite death, the lights of his eyes flickered and went out.

That was it.

Dad was dead.

Dad was dead!

Unbelievable!

And I never said I liked him. Why hadn't I said it? I love you—blah. How hard is it to say "I love you"? It's a fucking song lyric. Dad knew I loved him. He never knew I liked him. Even respected him.

Saliva was left unswallowed on his lips. His eyes, devoid of soul or consciousness, still managed to look dissatisfied. His face, deformed by death, damned the rest of humanity with a twist of his mouth. It was impossible to believe that the long, inglorious tumult in his head was over.

A couple of the Runaways came forward to help me throw him off the side.

"Don't touch him!" I screamed.

I was determined to perform the burial at sea by myself, without assistance. It was a worthless idea, but I was stubborn about it. I knelt down beside his body, cupped my arms underneath him. He went all sinewy in my hands. His long, loose limbs dangled over my shoulders. The waves swelled up, as if licking their lips. All the passive, sunken faces of the Runaways looked respectfully on. The wordless ceremony roused them from their own languid dying.

I put my shoulder into it, flung his body over the edge and buried him in the roar of waves. He floated momentarily on the surface, bobbing up and down a little like a carrot thrown whole into a boiling stew. Then he went under, as if taken by invisible hands, and went off hurrying to greet himself in strange corners of the sea.

That was it.

Goodbye, Dad. I hope you knew how I felt.

Ned put his hand on my shoulder. "He's with God now."

"That's a terrible thing to say."

"Your father never understood what it's like to be part of something bigger than himself."

That shit me. People always say, "It's good to be a part of a something bigger than yourself," but *you already are*. You're part of a huge thing. *The whole of humanity*. That's enormous. But you couldn't see it, so you pick, what? An organization? A culture? A religion? That's not bigger than you. It's much, much smaller!

•

The moon and the sun had just begun to share the sky when the boat approached the shoreline. I made eye contact with Ned and waved my arms around majestically, motioning to the bushland that surrounded the cove. Ned stared blankly at me, not understanding that I was suddenly overcome with the irrational feeling that I was his host and, almost bursting with pride, wanted to show him around.

The captain stepped out of the darkness and urged everyone to return below deck. Before I disappeared, I paused at the top of the steps. There were silhouettes on the shoreline. They stood frozen in clusters along the beach, dark figures wedged like poles in the wet sand. Ned joined me at the railing and clutched my arm.

"They might be fishermen," I said.

We watched silently. The human statues grew in size. There were too many of them to be fishermen. They had spotlights too, and were shining them right in our faces. The boat had made it to land, but we were sunk.

V

The federal police and coast guard were all over the beach. They took no time in rounding us up. The coast guards strutted and shouted to one another like trout fishermen who had unexpectedly landed a sperm whale. The spectacle of them sickened me, and I knew my fellow travelers were in for a nightmare of bureaucracy they might never awaken from. To be poor and foreign and illegal and at the mercy of the generosity of an affluent Western people is to be on very shaky ground.

Now that Dad was absolutely gone, no longer there to make my life a living hell, I automatically took on that role myself. Just as I had always feared and Eddie had predicted, with Dad dead, it was up to me now to be indecent with my future. That's why it seemed perfectly natural on that beach at dawn not to do what I didn't do.

I had plenty of opportunities to speak up, to explain that I was an Australian and had every right to walk free. I should have separated myself from the Runaways. I mean, there's no law prohibiting an Australian from returning to Australia on a leaky boat. Theoretically, I should be able to return from Asia propelled by a giant slingshot if it works, but for some reason I chose to say nothing. I simply kept my mouth shut and allowed myself to be rounded up with the others.

But how was it that they mistook me for a Runaway? My father's genetic hand-me-down black hair and olive skin worked marvelously with the inability of my own countrymen to shake the idea that we are overwhelmingly Anglo-Saxon. Everyone assumed I was from Afghanistan, Lebanon, or Iraq, and no one thought to question whether I was. So away we went.

•

And that's how I came to the strange prison surrounded by a seemingly endless stretch of desert on all sides. They call it a detention center, but try telling a prisoner he's only a detainee and see if he feels consoled by the distinction.

They had difficulty classifying me, as I refused to speak to them. They were dying to deport me from day one, but they didn't know where to. Various interpreters hounded me in many different languages. Who was I, and why wouldn't I tell them? They guessed country after country, save one—no one ever guessed that my point of origin and point of destination were the same.

For weeks, when I wasn't in English classes pretending to struggle through the alphabet, I wrote my story, on pages stolen from class. At first I wrote crouched on the floor behind the cell door, but I soon realized that between the hunger strikes and the suicide attempts and the recurring riots, I was hardly noticed. They thought I was just depressed; you were allowed, if not encouraged, to mope in your cell. As far as they were concerned, I was just a sad, unwanted enigma left unsolved.

When Ned received one of the coveted temporary protection visas, he kept hounding me to admit my citizenship. The day he left, he begged me to leave with him. And why didn't I? What was I doing in this awful place? Maybe I was just fascinated—you never knew when someone might slash himself, or swallow detergent or pebbles. And there were three hearty riots in my time; a burst of furious energy compelled the Runaways to try impossible things like pulling down the fence, before they were torn away by the strong hands of the guards. After the last riot settled down, the administration built stronger walls and a higher-voltage electric fence. I thought about what Terry said, that the have-nots are getting their act together. I wished they'd hurry.

Every now and then I tried to convince myself I was in this prison as the ultimate protest against government policy, but I knew I was only rationalizing. The truth was, Dad's lack of existence terrified me. This was an aloneness that required time to adjust to. I was hiding in here, avoiding facing up to the next step. I knew staying was perverse, shameless, and cowardly. Still, I couldn't leave.

As usual, God comes up in many conversations. To the guards, the Runaways let out endless proclamations: "God is great!," "God will punish you," and "Wait until God hears about this." Sickened by the treatment of the Runaways here and in their homelands, contemplating with horror the sad state of compassion in the world, one night I spoke to this God of theirs. I said, "Hey! Why is it that you don't ever say, 'If one more man suffers at the hands of another, it's all over. I will finish it.' Why don't you ever say, 'If one more man cries in pain because another man is standing on his neck, I'm pulling the plug.' How I wish you would say that, and mean it. A three-strikes-and-you're-out policy is really what the human race needs to pull its act together. It's time to get tough, O Lord. No more half measures. No more ambiguous floods and unclear mud slides. Zero tolerance. Three strikes. We're out."

I said all this to God, but there was so much silence afterward, a cold silence that seemed to get caught in my throat, and I heard myself suddenly whisper, "It's time." Enough was enough. It was during English class, in a small, bright room with a U-shaped arrangement of long desks. The teacher, Wayne, was standing in front of the blackboard instructing the class on the use of clauses. The students were silent, though not respectfully so; it was the bewildered silence of a group of people who had no clear idea what they were being taught.

I stood up. Wayne looked at me as though readying himself to take off his belt and start whipping me with it. I said, "Why are you bothering to teach us about clauses? We won't need them."

His face turned pale, and he tilted his head back as though I had just grown a meter taller. "You speak English," he said dumbly.

"Don't take it as a testament to your teaching abilities," I said.

"You've got an Australian accent," he said.

"Yeah, mate, I do. Now tell those mongrels to come in here. I've got something to say to them."

Wayne's eyes widened; then he did an exaggerated dash from the classroom like a cartoon tiger. People act like children when you surprise them, and bastards are no exception.

Ten minutes later they came running in, two guards in tight trousers. They had looks of surprise too, but theirs were already beginning to fade.

"I hear you've been running off at the mouth," one said.

"Let's hear it," the other commanded.

"My name is Jasper Dean. My father was Martin Dean. My uncle was Terry Dean."

Their looks of surprise got all freshened up. They hauled me away, down the long gray corridors into a stark room with only one chair in it. Was that for me, or would I be forced to stand while an inquisitor drilled me with his feet up?

I won't detail all seven days of the interrogation. All I will tell you is that I was like an actor trapped by contract in a bad play with a long run. I said my lines over and over and over. I told them the whole story, though leaving out all mention of Uncle Terry being alive. It wouldn't have done me any good to resurrect him. The government leaned heavily on me to tell them Dad's whereabouts. They had leverage too: I had committed two crimes, traveling on a false passport and consorting with known criminals, although the second was not actually a crime but just a bad habit, so they let it go. I was hounded by groups of detectives, and agents from ASIO, our unimpressive spy agency, which Australians know very little about because it is never the subject of movies or television shows. For days I had to put up with all the clichéd tricks in their repertoire: the staccato questioning, the good cop/bad cop routine and its variations (bad cop/worse cop, worse cop/Satan in a clip-on tie), performances so terrible I wanted to boo. We don't torture people in our country, which is a good thing unless you're an interrogator pressured to get results. I could tell one of them would have given anything to be able to tear out my fingernails. I caught another gazing forlornly at my groin while dreaming of electrodes. Well, too bad for them. Anyway, they didn't need to torture me. I played along. I spoke myself hoarse. They listened themselves deaf. Pretty soon we were all running on empty. Every now and then they let me pace the room and shout out things like "How many more times do I have to say it?" It was embarrassing. I felt silly. I sounded silly. It was so corny. Movies have made real life corny.

They searched my cell and found what I'd written, two hundred pages about our lives; I had only gotten as far as my early childhood, when I learned the Terry Dean story. They studied the pages intensely, read them carefully for clues, but they were looking for Dad's crimes, not his flaws, and in the end they thought it was nothing but fiction, an exaggerated story of my father and uncle composed as a clever defense; they concluded that I had depicted him as a lunatic so no one could find him guilty of anything by reason of insanity. They ultimately couldn't believe in him as a character, saying that it was impossible for a person to be a megalomaniac *and* an underachiever. I can only assume they didn't understand human psychology.

In the end they gave the pages back to me; then they interviewed all my fellow travelers to see if my story of Dad's death held up. The Runaways confirmed it. They all told the same story. Martin Dean was on the boat, he was very sick, and he died. I threw his body into the sea. I could tell this news was a tremendous disappointment to the authorities—they hadn't caught me out lying. Dad would have been the ultimate prize for them. The Australian people would have loved to see my father served up to them on a plate. Dad's death left a conspicuous hole in their lives, an important vacancy that needed filling. Who the hell were they going to hate now?

Eventually they decided to let me go. It wasn't that they had no real interest in charging me but that they wanted to shut me up. I'd seen firsthand how the Runaways were treated inside the detention center, and the government didn't want me talking about the systematic abuse of men, women, and children, so they bought my silence by dropping the charges against me. I went along with it. I don't feel bad about my complicity, either. I couldn't conceive that the facts would make a difference to the voting public. I can't imagine why the government thought they would. I guess they had more faith in people than I had.

In exchange for my silence, they gave me a dirty little one-bedroom apartment in a dirty government housing block in a dirty little suburb. The federal police flew me from the desert into Sydney and dropped me off here, and, along with the keys to my grubby, minuscule flat, handed over a box of papers raided from my old apartment when we'd skipped the country: my real passport, my driver's license, and a couple of tele-phone bills they hinted I should pay. When they left me alone, I sat in the living room and stared out the barred windows into the apartment opposite. It seemed I had not done all right out of the government. I had blackmailed them for this shitty place and a welfare allowance of $350 a fortnight. It seemed to me I could've done a lot better.

I caught sight of myself in the bathroom mirror. My cheeks were sunken; my eye sockets went deep into my head. I'd gotten so thin I looked like a javelin. I needed to fatten myself up again. Apart from that, what was my plan? What was I going to do now?

I tried calling Anouk, the only person left on the planet I had any connection with, but this proved far more difficult than I'd anticipated. It's not easy getting in touch with the richest woman in the country, even if she once cleaned your toilet. Her home number was unsurprisingly un-listed, and it was only after calling the Hobbs Media Group and speak-ing to several secretaries, that it finally occurred to me to ask for Oscar instead. I received a few noes before one young woman said, "Is this a prank call?"

"No, it's not a prank call. Why shouldn't I speak to him?"

"You really don't know?"

"Know what?"

"Where've you been living the last six months, in a cave?"

"No, a prison in the middle of the desert."

That got me a long silence. "He's dead," she said finally. "They both are."

"Who?" I asked, my heart freezing block-solid.

"Oscar and Reynold Hobbs. Their private jet crashed."

"And Mrs. Hobbs?" I asked, shaking. Please don't let her be dead. Please don't let her be dead. In that moment I realized that of all the peo-ple I had ever known in my whole life, Anouk deserved to die the least.

"I'm afraid so."

I felt everything pour out of me. Love. Hope. Spirit. There was noth-ing left.

"Are you still there?" the woman asked.

I nodded. No words to speak. No thought to think. No air to breathe.

"Are you OK?"

This time I shook my head. How could I ever be OK now?

"Hang on," she said. "Which Mrs. Hobbs do you mean?"

I gulped.

"Reynold's wife, Courtney, was on the plane, not the other one."

"So Anouk?" I gasped.

"No, she wasn't with them."

I sucked all that love, hope, and spirit back into my lungs with one deep breath. Thank you!

"When was this?"

"About five months ago."

"I have to speak to her. Tell her Jasper Dean is trying to call her."

"Jasper Dean? Son of Martin Dean?"

"Yes."

"Didn't you skip the country? When did you get back? Is your father with you?"

"JUST LET ME SPEAK TO ANOUK!"

"I'm sorry, Jasper. She's uncontactable."

"How's that?"

"She's traveling at the moment."

"Where is she?"

"We think she's in India."

"You think?"

"To be honest, nobody knows where she is."

"What do you mean?"

"After the plane crash, she just vanished. There're a lot of people who want to talk to her, as you can imagine."

"Well, if she calls in, can you tell her I'm home and I need to speak to her?"

I left my telephone number and hung up. Why was Anouk in India? I supposed she was mourning out of the spotlight. Understandable. The spotlight is the last place anyone wants to mourn. Anouk would be well aware that as a widow, if you're not a mascara-running hysteric, the public will just assume you're a murderer.

I felt desolate, unreal. Dad was dead, Eddie was dead, now even the indestructible Oscar and Reynold were dead, and none of it made me feel especially alive. In truth, I didn't feel much of anything. It was as if I had been anesthetized head to toe, so I didn't feel the contrast between life and death anymore. Later, in the shower, I wasn't even certain I knew the difference between hot and cold.

A day into my new life and I already hated it. There was no way I could become anything other than permanently disgusting in this disgusting apartment. I resolved to get out of there. And go where? Well, overseas. I remembered my original plan—to drift aimlessly through time and space. For that, I needed money. Problem was, I didn't have any money and didn't know how to go about making it fast. All I had to sell was the same as everybody else who hasn't an asset to his name: I could sell my time or I could sell my story. Having no marketable skills, I knew my time wouldn't fetch me one dollar over minimum wage, but with not one but two infamous men in my immediate family, my story might get me a higher price than most. Of course I could've gone the easy route, agreeing to a television interview, but I'd never squeeze the whole story into the twenty minutes of a television half hour. No, I had to keep writing it down to be sure the story got told right, without leaving anything out. My only chance was to finish the book I'd started, find a publisher, and set sail with a hefty advance. That was my plan. I took out the pages my interrogators had read and dismissed as fiction. Where was I up to? I hadn't gotten very far at all—I had a lot of writing to do.

I went out to the shops to buy a couple of reams of A4 paper. I like white pages—they shame me into filling them. Outside, the sun was a hand of light slapping me in the face. Looking at all the people, I thought: What a strenuous life. Now that I had nobody I was close to, I'd have to make do with some of these strangers, turn a couple of them into either friends or lovers. What a lot of work life is when you're always starting from scratch.

The streets of my city felt like a foreign country. The toxic effects of being in a detention center were still with me, because I found out that while I needed individuals, I was terrified of crowds, with an intense physical anxiety that left me hugging streetlamps. What was I afraid of? They didn't mean me any harm. I suppose I was afraid of their indifference. Believe me, you don't want to fall over in front of man. He won't pick you up.

I passed a newsstand and my heart sank—everything had gone public. Dad was officially declared dead. I decided not to read any of the tabloid eulogies. "Bastard Dies!" "Woo-Hoo! He's Dead!" and "The End of a Scumbag!" didn't seem worthy of my $1.20. Anyway, I'd heard it all before. As I walked away, it occurred to me that there was a certain unreal quality to those headlines, like a prolonged déjà vu. I don't know how to explain it. It felt as if I was either at the end of something I'd thought endless or at the beginning of something I could have sworn had started long ago.

The next few days I sat by the barred window and wrote day and night, and as I did, I remembered Dad's ugly, pontificating head and laughed hysterically until the neighbors banged on the walls. The phone rang nonstop—journalists. I ignored it and I wrote ceaselessly for three weeks, each page a fresh unloading of nightmares that it was a great relief to be rid of.

•

One night I was lying on the couch, feeling displaced, like an eyelid trapped inside an eye, when I heard the neighbors arguing through the walls. A woman shouted, "What did you do that for?" and a man shouted back, "I saw it on TV! Can't you take a joke?" I was using up what felt like my last remaining brain cell trying to work out what he'd done when there was a knock at the door. I answered it.

Standing there with enviable posture was a young, prematurely balding man in a double-breasted pin-striped suit. He said his name was Gavin Love, and I accepted that at face value: I couldn't think of any reason someone would call himself Gavin Love if that wasn't his name. He said he was a lawyer too, which lent his Gavin Love story all the more weight. He said he had some papers for me to sign.

"What kind of papers?"

"Your father's things are being held in a storage room. They're all yours. You just have to sign for them."

"And if I don't want them?"

"What do you mean?"

"If I don't want them, I guess there's no point signing."

"Well . . ." His face was blank. "I just need your signature," he said hesitatingly.

"I understand that. I'm not sure I want to give it to you."

Right away his confidence evaporated. I could tell he was going to get into trouble for this.

"Mr. Dean, don't you want your inheritance?"

"Did he have any money? That's what I really need."

"No, I'm afraid not. His bank account is empty. And everything of value would have been sold. What remains of his possessions is probably, well . . ."

"Worthless."

"But worth a look, though," he said, trying to sound positive.

"Maybe," I said doubtfully. Anyway, I didn't know why I was torturing this poor dope. I went ahead and signed my name. It was only later I realized I'd signed "Kasper." He didn't seem to notice.

"So where is this storage room?"

"Here's the address," he said, handing me a piece of paper. "If you'd like to go now, I could give you a lift."

•

We drove to a lonely-looking government building stuck out near furniture warehouses and packaged food wholesalers. A guard in a little painted white cubbyhole had carte blanche on the raising and lowering of a wooden beam at the entrance to the parking lot. Gavin Love rolled the window down.

"This is Jasper Dean. He's here to claim his father's estate."

"I'm not here to claim anything," I said. "Only to give it the once-over."

"ID," the guard said.

I pulled out my driver's license and handed it over. The guard examined it and tried to equate the face on the license with the face attached to my head. They weren't a clear match, but he gave me the benefit of the doubt.

We drove to the front of the building.

"You'll probably be awhile," Gavin Love said.

"Don't worry, I won't ask you to wait."

I got out of the car, and Gavin Love wished me luck, which he seemed to think was pretty decent of him. A small, pudgy man in a gray uniform opened the door. His pants were pulled up higher than what I deem standard practice.

"Can I help you?"

"My name's Jasper Dean. My father's possessions are stuffed in one of your airless rooms. I've come for a poke around."

"His name?"

"Martin Dean."

The man's eyes widened a little, then contracted. He went into the office and came out with a large blue ledger.

"Dean, Dean . . . here it is, Room—"

"One-oh-one?" I asked, thinking of Orwell.

"Ninety-three," he said. "This way."

I followed him to an elevator. He got in with me. We didn't have much to say to each other, so we both watched the lift numbers illuminate in turn and I saw that he mouthed each number silently. On the fourth floor we got out and walked down a long, brightly lit corridor. About halfway down he said, "Here we are," and stopped at a door.

"There're no numbers on these doors. How do you know this is ninety-three?"

"It's my job to know," he said.

That was no kind of job. He took out a set of keys and unlocked the door and pushed it ajar.

"You can close the door behind you if you want."

"That's OK," I said. It didn't look like the kind of place you want to be closed into.

The room was dark and cluttered and I couldn't see the end of it—I imagined it stretched endlessly to the brink of existence. I couldn't think how they'd managed to get everything in here: books, lamps, maps, photographs, furniture, empty picture frames, a portable X-ray machine, life jackets, telescopes, old cameras, bookshelves, pipes, and potato sacks filled with clothes. The space was entirely occupied by Dad's possessions, everything jumbled up together and in complete disarray—papers on the floor, cupboard drawers emptied and turned over. Obviously the authorities had searched for clues of Dad's whereabouts and where he had left the money. Every dusty cubic meter was occupied by Dad's worthless junk. I felt a kind of diluted heartache navigating through the maze of bric-a-brac. None of the anxiety that he had infused each item with had ebbed away. I could smell his intense frustration everywhere. I was taken over by the delusion that I was walking around in my father's head.

It really was a no-man's-land. I felt I had stumbled upon undiscovered continents—for example, a large blue sketchbook had me captivated for hours. Inside there were designs and sketches for unbelievable contraptions: a homemade guillotine, a large plastic collapsible bubble worn on the head so you could smoke in airplane toilets, a question-mark-shaped coffin. I also found a box filled with thirty or forty teen romance novels as well as his unfinished autobiography, and underneath a manuscript in his handwriting entitled "Love at Lunchtime," a nauseating story of unrequited love written for thirteen-year-old girls. I felt completely lost. I felt I was meeting a few more of his well-hidden selves for the first time. Even before the idea of writing a book about him had occurred to me, even before I had set down one line, I had seen myself as his unwilling chronicler. The only thing I was an expert on was my father. Now it seemed there was a life to him I hadn't known. In this way he mocked me from beyond the grave.

The guard appeared in the doorway and asked, "How are you getting on in here?" I didn't know quite how to answer the particular phrasing of that question, though I said I was getting on fine.

"I'll leave you to it, then," he said, and left me to it.

What was I supposed to do with all this rubbish? The journals were worth keeping, certainly. Without them, I might never prove to anyone that my life with him had been as manic as I remembered it. And not only for outsiders—for myself too. I took them and his autobiography, placed them by the door, and continued scavenging.

Underneath a moth-eaten duffel coat I found a large wooden crate, rotted away at the corners. It looked damaged by water and time. A padlock was hanging off it, and a crowbar lay on the floor. The authorities, looking for missing millions, had cracked open this crate and rummaged through it. I looked closer. On the side was some yellowing paperwork written in French, with Dad's name and, underneath, an address in Australia.

I opened it up.

On the top was a painting. In the dim light, I couldn't make it out at first, but when I did, I was so shocked I may even have said something like "What the—?"

It was the painting I'd painted in the chicken coop in Thailand. The painting of the disembodied face that had haunted me my whole life. The painting that had been destroyed.

My head was spinning. I looked again. It was definitely my painting. How could this be?

I lifted it up to see what was underneath. There were more paintings of the same face. That was strange. I had painted only one. Then I understood.

They weren't my paintings. They were my mother's!

I took a deep breath and thought it out. I remembered Dad's green notebook, his Paris journal. Dad had bought Astrid paints, brushes, and canvases and she had become obsessed with painting. The words of his journal were etched in my mind. I recalled that he had written: *Each painting a rendition of hell—she had many hells & she painted them all. But hell was just a face—and it was just the face she painted. One face. One terrible face. Painted many times.*

A moment of terror stretched into a solid minute of terror and kept going. I looked again at the face; it was like a big bruise, purple and splotchy. Then I studied all the paintings carefully. It was undeniable. The lashes on the lower eyelid, curled like fingers; the nose hairs like nerve fibers; its eyes in a trancelike state; the oppressive closeness of its flattened nose; its uncomfortable gaze. It looked as if the face threatened to break out of the painting and actually come into the room. I also had the uncomfortable feeling that I could smell it—its odor poured off the canvas in waves.

My mother and I had painted the same face, that same ghoulish face! What did it mean? Had I seen these paintings in my youth? No. The journal said she had given up painting after my birth, and since Dad and I left Paris just after her death, I definitely hadn't seen them. So Astrid had seen a face and painted that face. And I had seen the same face and also painted it. I examined the paintings again. With sharp edges and horizontal lines broken up to make its geometrically off-putting head, done in a vile green and thick, wavy lines of black and red and brown, it wasn't a passive face she'd painted, it was face as function—the function being to scare you.

I turned away from the paintings and tried to work it out. It was totally reasonable to assume that (a) my mother was haunted by the face in the same manner I was or (b) my mother hadn't seen it floating in the clouds but had actually known the person it belonged to.

Pacing the warehouse, I forced my way through the junk and came across an old broken cabinet. In the bottom drawer I found half a packet of Marlboros and a lighter in the shape of a woman's torso. I lit a cigarette but was too preoccupied to inhale. I stood there in that place totally immobilized by thought until the cigarette burned my fingers.

My eyes sprang open. I hadn't realized they'd been closed. An idea had been inserted into my brain. But what an idea! What an idea! Why didn't I think of it straightaway? I circled the room shouting, "Oh my God, oh my God," like a contestant on a game show. I examined the paintings again. This had never happened to me—a lightning-bolt moment! It was incredible! "Why assume I'm turning into my father," I shouted, "when there's an equal chance I'm turning into my mother?" I stomped my feet to shake up the whole building. The thought was absolutely liberating. What had I been worried about all this time? And even if I was turning into my father, it wouldn't ever have been the *whole* of me but only a section or a subsection—maybe a quarter of me would turn into him, another quarter into my mother, one eighth into Terry, or into the face, or into all the other me's I hadn't met yet. The existence of these paintings suggested a scope to my being I had not previously imagined. I think you can appreciate my indescribable joy. The period when my father threatened to dominate my personality—the Occupation—was a mirage. It had never been just me and him. I was a goddamn paradise of personalities! I sat down on a couch and closed my eyes and pictured myself. I couldn't see anything clearly. Wonderful! That's how it should be! I am a blurry image constantly trying to come into focus, and just when, for an instant, I have myself in perfect clarity, I appear as a figure in my own background, fuzzy as hair on a peach.

I suddenly knew what it meant. My mission was clear: fly to Europe and find my mother's family. The face was the starting point. This was the first clue. Find the face, I thought, and I'll find my mother's family.

In a daze, I grabbed as many of the canvases as I could handle and called a taxi and took them home. I stared at them all night. I felt a mixture of feelings so conflicting in nature I was threatened with being torn apart by them: a deep grief for the loss of my mother, a snug feeling of comfort that we were close in mind, spirit, and psychosis, an abhorrence of and revulsion for the face, a pride that I'd uncovered a secret, and a furious frustration that I didn't understand the secret I'd uncovered.

Around midnight, the phone rang. I didn't want to answer it. The journalists wouldn't leave me alone. The phone stopped ringing and I heaved a sigh of relief. My sigh was short-lived. A minute later the phone started up again. This was going to go on all night. I picked it up.

"Mr. Dean?" a male voice said.

I supposed I'd better get used to that. "Listen," I said, "I'm not giving interviews, quotes, comments, or sound bites, so why don't you go hound a gang-raping footballer."

"I'm not a journalist."

"Who are you, then?"

"I was wondering if we could meet."

"And I was wondering who you are."

"I can't say. Your phone is probably bugged."

"Why would my phone be bugged?" I asked, looking suspiciously at the phone. I couldn't tell whether it was bugged or not.

"Could you be outside Central Railway Station at nine o'clock tomorrow morning?"

"If the phone's bugged, won't whoever is listening be there too?"

"You don't need to worry about that."

"I'm not. I thought you might be."

"So will you be there?"

"All right, then. I'll be there."

He hung up. I stared at the phone awhile, hoping it might start speaking on its own, explaining to me all the things I didn't understand. It didn't.

•

At nine o'clock the next morning I was at Central Station, waiting for God knows who. I sat on a bench and observed the people who hurried into the station to catch the trains and the people who hurried out of the station to get away from the trains. They seemed to be the same people.

A car honked its horn. I turned to see a black Mercedes with tinted windows. The driver was leaning out of his window, beckoning me with his finger. I didn't recognize him. When I didn't move, he stopped with his finger and started beckoning me with his whole hand. I went over. Even standing right up against the car, I couldn't see who was in the backseat.

"Mr. Dean, would you get in the back, please?"

"Why should I?"

"Jasper! Get in!" a voice called out from the back. I smiled instantly, which felt strange because I hadn't smiled for a long time. I opened the back door and dived in, and as the car moved off, Anouk and I hugged for ten minutes without speaking and without letting go.

When we pulled away, we stared at each other with our mouths half open. There was simply too much to say to know how to go about saying it. Anouk didn't look like a rich widow. She was wearing a silk sari of deep red and had shaved her head again. Her enormous green eyes peered crazily out of her skull like symbols of an ancient catastrophe. Her face looked both old and young, foreign and familiar.

"You must think I've become paranoid with all this mystery stuff," she said. "But it's awful, Jasper. Everyone wants me to put on a brave face, but I don't have one of those. I only have a distraught face. After Oscar and now your father it's the only one I've got left."

I sat trying to think of a way to start speaking. I squeezed her hand instead.

"I own it all, Jasper. I don't know how this happened. I'm the richest woman in Australia."

"The richest woman in the world," the driver said.

"Stop listening!"

"Sorry, Anouk."

"I won't let anyone call me Mrs. Hobbs. Well, that's another story. But isn't it funny that I'm so rich?" It was more than funny. It was more than ironic too. I hadn't forgotten how we'd met—she'd been running a key along Dad's sports car because she outright hated the rich. "But you're so thin!" she exclaimed. "What's happened to you? I've only heard bits and pieces."

I asked the driver to stop and he pulled the car over in a dead-end alley. Anouk and I climbed out, and standing in the alleyway next to a sleeping drunk clutching a broken television set, I told her everything about Eddie and Terry and the democratic cooperative and Thailand and poison and the murdering mob and Caroline and the people-smugglers. By the time I got to the boat trip she was biting her lower lip, and at my description of Dad's death she sucked it into her mouth. For the rest of the story she kept her eyes closed and left a sad, bittersweet smile on her face. I didn't mention my mother's paintings, because I needed to keep something just for myself.

"As for me," she said, "I'm in hiding. Everyone wants me to make a decision as to what to do. Am I going to take on running this megabusiness or aren't I?"

"Do you want to?"

"Some of it might be kind of cool. It might be fun to run a movie studio. I produced a short film once, do you remember?"

I remembered. It was a dreadful, pretentious mesh of abstract images and obvious symbolism about a rich man who convinces a poor woman to sell him her breast, and once he's bought it, he sits with the breast in his favorite armchair, stroking it, kissing it, trying to make the nipple erect, but when the nipple doesn't rise, in frustration and despair he throws the breast on the barbecue and eats it with tomato sauce.

"What do you think, Jasper? You think I could run a movie studio?"

"Absolutely."

"I'm giving a lot away to friends—the music companies, the book-stores, the restaurants, the hotel chains, the cruisers—and my dad always wanted an island, but I'm going to wait for his birthday."

"Aren't you keeping anything?"

"Of course. I'm not a bloody fool. I'm keeping the newspapers, the magazines, the radio stations, the cable and free-to-air TV stations, and the movie studio for myself. Can you believe it, Jasper? The most powerful propaganda machines in the history of civilization, and they've fallen into our hands!"

"What do you mean, our?"

"That's what I want to talk to you about. What are you going to do now?"

"I want to go to Europe and search for my mother's family. But I need money. Anouk, can I have some money? I won't pay you back."

Anouk suddenly peered up and down the alley, and I thought that it doesn't matter whether you're a celebrity or a wanted criminal, excess attention makes you paranoid. She leaned forward and solemnly uttered, "Of course, Jasper. I'll give you whatever you want."

"Really?"

"On one condition."

"Uh-oh."

"You have to help me out."

"No."

"You'll have lots of power."

"Power? Yuck."

"Please."

"Look. I really just want to leave the country and live the rest of my days floating in an anonymous fog. I don't want to help you with—what is it you want help with?"

"With the media."

"What media?"

"All of it."

"I'm going to Europe. I don't want to be stuck in some office."

"This is the twenty-first century, so if you want—"

"I know what century it is. Why do people always tell me what century it is?"

"—so if you want to keep moving, you can. You'll have a laptop, an assistant, a mobile. You can do it all on the road. Please, Jasper. I don't trust anyone else. You've never seen so many people who want so much so openly. They all have their hands out, all my old friends included. And no one will give me an honest opinion. You're the only one I can count on. And besides, I think your father was preparing you your whole life for something like this. Maybe for this exact thing. Maybe he knew all along. This feels like fate, don't you think? You and me, we're completely the wrong people to be in this position—that's what's so great about it."

"Anouk, this is crazy. I don't know anything about newspapers or television!"

"And I don't know anything about being a media mogul, but here I am! How is it possible that I'm in this position? And why? I didn't claw my way to get here. I fell into it. I feel I'm supposed to do something."

"Like what?"

She made a very hard and serious face, the kind that makes your own face hard and serious just from looking at it.

"Jasper, I believe that life is based on love. And that orderly love is the fundamental law of the universe."

"Which universe is that and where is it? I'd love to pop by and say hello."

Anouk sat on the edge of an empty beer keg. She was radiating pure joy and enthusiasm. Yes, she might have been pretending to hate this strange turn of events which had transformed her into a rich and powerful woman, but I wasn't buying it.

"I believe that a person's thoughts often manifest into actual events—that we think things into existence. Right? Well, think about this: one of the illnesses that has become an epidemic in the Western world is an addiction to news. Newspapers, Internet news, twenty-four-hour news channels. And what is news? News is history in the making. So the addiction to news is the addiction to the outcome of history. Are you with me so far?"

"I get it. Go on."

"In the past couple of decades, news has been produced as entertainment. So people's addiction to news is the addiction to its function as entertainment. If you combine the power of thought with this addiction to entertaining news, then the part of the hundreds of millions of people, the viewing public, that wishes peace on earth is overshadowed by the part of them that wants the next chapter in the story. Every person who turns on the news and finds there're no developments is disappointed. They're checking the news two or three times a day—they want drama, and drama means not only death but death by the thousands, so in the secret parts of himself, every news-addicted person is hoping for greater calamity, more bodies, more spectacular wars, more hideous enemy attacks, and these wishes are going out every day into the world. Don't you see? Right now, more than at any other time in history, the universal wish is a black one."

The homeless man in the gutter had woken up and was moving his half-open eyes furtively from Anouk to me, a bored smile on his face, as if to say in response to Anouk's theory that he'd heard it all before. Maybe he had.

"So what do you intend to do?"

"We have to wean people off their addiction, or else there'll be hell to pay."

"We."

"Yes, Jasper."

I looked at the drunk in the alley to make sure I wasn't imagining all this. Did I want to help Anouk in her plan? Sure, I could take control of the newspapers and put in fun headlines like "This Newspaper Makes Independent Thinking Impossible" and pursue Anouk's aim of combating this addiction to "news" by making news dry and boring—limiting broadcasts and reporting banal and positive events (grandmothers planting new gardens, football stars eating dinner with their families) and not allowing mass murderers their turn on the celebrity wonder wheel.

However, the last thing I wanted was to take on a public role doing anything. The general public was still apt to turn apoplectic with rage at the mention of my father, and thus people would hate me for whatever I did. All I wanted was to melt into vast crowds of non-English-speaking people and taste the many flavors of women filling tight-fitting T-shirts in all the cities of the globe. And Anouk wanted the news division to be under my control?

"Anouk, I'll tell you what. You start without me. I'll give you a call in six months, see how you're getting along, and then maybe I'll come and help you out. But it's a big maybe."

She made a weird sound in her throat and started breathing hard. Her eyes somehow got rounder. I almost weakened. It's hard enough to go through life disappointing yourself every second day, but disappointing others takes it out of you too. That's why you should never answer the phone or the door. So you don't have to say no to whoever's on the other side.

"OK, Jasper. But I want you to do one thing before you leave."

"What's that?"

"Write an obituary for your dad that I can print in the paper."

"What for? People don't care."

"I care. And so do you. And I know you—you probably haven't let yourself grieve in any way for your father. I know he was a pain in the arse, but he did love you and he made you what you are and you owe it to him and to yourself to write something about him. Doesn't matter if what you write is flattering or insulting. As long as it's true and it comes from the heart and not from the brain."

"OK."

We climbed back into the car, and the homeless man watched us with smiling eyes that said in no uncertain terms that he had just overheard a conversation between two people who took themselves too seriously.

•

The car pulled up outside my building and we sat in the backseat facing each other, with barely a blink between us, barely the slightest movement.

"Sure I can't convince you to stay in Australia for a few months?"

It was obvious that what she needed more than anything was to have a friendly face around, and I felt bad because I was taking mine to Europe.

"Sorry, Anouk. This is something I have to do."

She nodded, then wrote me a check for $25,000. I was eternally grateful, but not so grateful I didn't wish it were more.

We kissed goodbye, and I almost fell to pieces watching the black

Mercedes disappear from sight, but I pulled myself together, out of habit. I walked to the bank and put the check in my account. I would have to wait three days before I could access the money to buy myself a one-way ticket to somewhere else. Three days seemed too long.

When I got home, I lay on the couch and stared at the ceiling and tried not to think about the fact that there were cat hairs on the couch that weren't there yesterday. Not having a cat, I had no explanation for it. Just another of life's inscrutable and pointless mysteries.

I tried to go to sleep, and when I couldn't go there, I tried to get sleep to come to me. That didn't work either. I got up and drank two beers and lay down on the couch again. My mind took over and dug up a few fragile images that seemed ready to crack if I thought about them hard enough. I decided to think about the future instead. In three days I would be on a plane to Europe, just as my father had once been, at roughly the same age, when almost everyone he knew was dead. Well, you have to follow in people's footsteps sometimes. You can't expect every cough, scratch, and sneeze to be your own.

Around midnight I started working on the obituary for my father that Anouk could print in the paper. After staring at a blank page for two days, I began.

<u>Martin Dean, 1956–2001</u>

Who was my father?

The offal of the universe.

The fatty rind.

An ulcer on the mouth of time.

He was sorry he never had a great historical name like Pope Innocent VIII or Lorenzo the Magnificent.

He was the man who first told me that no one would buy life insurance if it was called death insurance.

He thought the best definition of thoroughness is having your ashes buried.

He thought that people who don't read books don't know that any number of dead geniuses are waiting for their call.

He thought that there seems to be no passion for life, only for lifestyle.

About God—he thought that if you live in a house, it's of only nominal interest to know the name of the architect who designed it.

About evolution—he thought it was unfair that man is at the top of the food chain when he still believes the newspaper headlines.

About pain and suffering—he thought that you can bear it all. It's only the fear of pain and suffering that is unbearable.

I took a break and read over what I'd written. All true. Not bad. This was coming along nicely. But I should be more personal. After all, he wasn't just a brain in a jar spitting out ideas, he was also a human being with emotions that made him sick.

He never achieved unlonely aloneness. His aloneness was terrible for him.

He could not hear a mother calling for her child in the park without calling out too, sick with the ominous feeling that something awful had happened to little Hugo (or whoever).

He was always proud of things that shamed others.

He had a fairly complex Christ complex.

His worldview seemed to be something like "This place sucks. Let's refurbish."

He was impossibly energetic but lacked the kind of hobbies that actually required energy, which is why he often read books while walking and watched TV while pacing back and forth between rooms.

He could empathize with anyone, and if he found out someone in the world was suffering, Dad had to go home and lie down.

OK. What else?

I looked over what I had written and decided it was time to get to the heart of the man.

The concept of Dad's death ruined his whole life. The very thought of it struck him down like some toxic jungle fever.

My God. This topic made my whole body feel heavy. Just as Terry had realized that the terror of death had almost killed him, Dad had often repeated his conviction that it was the base cause of all human beliefs. I saw now that I had developed a nasty mutation of this disease, namely, the terror of the terror of death. Yes, unlike Dad and unlike Terry, I don't fear death so much as I fear the fear of it. The fear that makes people believe, and kill each other, and kill themselves; I am afraid of this fear that could make me unconsciously manufacture a comforting or confusing lie that I might base my life on.

Wasn't I going off to chase the face from my nightmares?

Wasn't I going on a journey to learn more about the face? And about my mother? And about myself?

Or was I?

Dad always maintained that people don't go on journeys at all but spend a lifetime searching for and gathering evidence to rationalize the beliefs they've held in their hearts since day one. They have new revelations, certainly, but these rarely shatter their core belief structure—they just build on it. He believed that if the base remains intact, it doesn't matter what you build on it, it is not a journey at all. It is just layering. He didn't believe that anyone ever started from scratch. "People aren't looking for answers," he often said. "They're looking for facts to prove their case."

This made me think of *his* journey. What was it all about? He may have traveled the globe, but he didn't seem to go very far. He may have dipped himself in different pools of experience, but his spirit stayed the same flavor. All his plans, plots, and schemes centered on man in relation to society, or larger—to civilization, or smaller—to community. He aspired to change the world around him, but he saw his being as solid and unchangeable. He wasn't interested in testing the limits within himself. How far can someone expand? Can his essence be found and enlarged? Can the heart get an erection? Can your soul pour out your mouth? Can a thought drive a car? It hardly seems to have occurred to him.

Finally I knew how to revolt against my father's ways! The nature of my anarchy was clear. Like Terry, I would live as though on the edge of death, as the world sank or swam. Civilization? Society? Who cares. I would turn my back on progress, and unlike my father, I would concentrate my attention not on the outside but on the inside.

To get to the bottom of myself. To get to the bottom of thought. To get beyond time. Like everyone, I'm saturated in time, I'm soaking in it, I'm drowning in it. To annihilate this profound, all-encompassing, psychological trick would really be an ace up my sleeve.

I had communicated my thoughts successfully to Dad from the jungle in Thailand, though he chose not to believe it. That means the manipulation of thought exists. That's why you have to be careful what you think. That's why most doctors quietly admit that depression, stress, and grief affect our immune systems, as does loneliness. In fact, loneliness is linked to higher death rates through heart disease, cancer, and suicide, and even to *accidental* death, meaning that feeling lonely may lead to fatal clumsiness. See your doctor if loneliness persists.

We ignorantly indulge in negative thoughts, unaware that thinking over and over again "I suck" is probably as carcinogenic as sucking down a carton of unfiltered Camels. So then, should I rig up a device where I can give myself little electric shocks every time I have a negative thought? Would that work? What about self-hypnosis? Even in my fantasies, beliefs, ideas, and hallucinations, can I stop my mind from running in old grooves? Can I emancipate myself? Renew myself? Replace myself like old skin cells? Is that too ambitious? Does self-awareness have an off switch? I have no idea. Novalis said that atheism is when you don't believe in yourself. OK, in this respect I am probably an agnostic, but either way, is this my project? To test the limit of the power of thought and see what the material world really looks like? What then? Can I be of the world and in the world even when I have crashed through time and space? Or do I have to live on a mountaintop? I really don't want to. I want to stay at the bottom and bribe seven-year-olds to buy me half-price tickets for the movies. How do I deal with such incompatible desires? And I know that to achieve enlightenment I'm supposed to witness the dissolution of my wants, but I like my wants, so what's a guy to do?

•

I packed my bags and manuscript and put in a photograph of Astrid, my mother. She was remarkably beautiful. I have that on my side. Society hangs its tongue out at the sight of a pretty face; all I have to do is walk up the tongue into the mouth that will tell me everything I need to know.

This woman touched lives, and not just my father's. Some would be dead. Some would be too old. But somewhere were childhood friends, boyfriends, lovers. Somebody would remember her. Somewhere.

Neither Dad nor I had much love for religion, because we preferred the mystery to the miracle, but Dad didn't really love the mystery either—it was like a pebble in his shoe. Well, I won't ignore mysteries like he did. But I won't try to solve them, either. I just want to see what happens when you peer into their core. I'm going to follow in my own stupid, uncertain footsteps. I'm going to wander the earth awhile and find my mother's family and the man who belongs to the face in the sky and see where these mysterious affinities take me—closer to understanding my mother or to some unimaginable evil.

I looked out the window. It was dawn. I made myself a coffee and reread the obituary one last time. I needed a conclusion. But how do you conclude a life like his? What did he mean? What idea could finish this off? I decided I should address all those thoughtless, ignorant people who had called Dad a bastard without even knowing he actually was one.

Martin Dean was my father.

The act of writing this sentence knocked the wind out of me. All of a sudden I felt something I'd never felt before—privileged. I suddenly felt better off than a billion other sons, privileged that I had had the good fortune to be raised by an odd, uncompromising, walking stew of ideas. So what if he was a philosopher who thought himself into a corner? He was also a natural-born empathizer who would have rather been buried alive than have his imperfections ever seriously hurt anyone. He was my father. He was a fool. He was my kind of fool.

There's no way to sum him up. How could I? If I was only a part of him, how could I possibly ever know who *he* was a part of?

I wrote on:

> My father has been called a lot of terrible names by the people of this country. OK, he wasn't a Gandhi or a Buddha, but honestly, he wasn't a Hitler or a Stalin either. He was somewhere in the middle. But what I want to know is, what does your view of my father say about you?

When someone comes into the world who reaches the worst depths that humans can sink to, we will always call him a monster, or evil, or the embodiment of evil, but there is never any serious hint or suggestion that there is something *actually* supernatural or otherworldly about this individual. He may be an evil man, but he is just a man. But when an extraordinary person operating on the other side of the spectrum, the good, rises to the surface, like Jesus or Buddha, immediately we elevate him to God, a deity, something divine, supernatural, otherworldly. This is a reflection of how we see ourselves. We have no trouble believing that the worst creature who has done the most harm is a man, but we absolutely cannot believe that the best creature, who tries to inspire imagination, creativity, and empathy, can be one of us. We just don't think that highly of ourselves, but we happily think that low.

That should do it. A nice confusing off-the-point conclusion. Well done, me. I popped this in the mail to Anouk at the Hobbs News Division, went to the bank to check that the money was in my account, then caught a taxi to the airport. This time I was leaving the country under my own name.

"I'd like to buy a ticket to Europe," I said to the unsmiling woman at the counter.

"Where in Europe?"

"Good question. I haven't thought about it."

"Really," she said, then leaned back in her chair and looked past me, over my shoulder. I think she was looking for a television camera.

"What's the next flight that gets me in the Europe vicinity?"

She stared at me another couple of seconds before typing at lightning speed on the computer keyboard. "There's a flight leaving for the Czech Republic in an hour and a half."

The Czech Republic? For some reason I had thought she was going to say Paris, and then I'd say, "I believe Paris is lovely this time of year."

"You want the ticket or not?"

"Sure. I believe the Czech Republic is lovely this time of year."

After I bought my ticket and checked in my bags, I ate a $10 vegetable samosa that tasted worse than a seven-course meal of postage stamps. Then I went to the phone box and looked in the white pages to see if Strangeways Publications still existed and if Stanley was still running it, the man who had published Harry West's *The Handbook of Crime* all those years ago.

It was there in black and white. I called the number.

"Hello?"

"Hi. Is that Stanley?"

"Yeah."

"You still publishing books?"

"Men's magazines."

"I've written a book I think you might be interested in."

"Men's magazines, I said. You deaf? I don't publish books."

"It's a biography."

"I don't care. Of who?"

"Martin Dean."

I heard a sharp intake of breath on the other end. It was so sharp, it almost sucked me right into the receiver.

"Who are you?"

"His son."

Silence. Then I could hear the sound of someone moving a number of papers around a desk, and the sound of someone stapling something that didn't sound like paper.

"Jasper, isn't it?" Stanley said.

"That's right."

"You want to come into my office?"

"I'm just going to put it in the post, if that's all right with you. I'm about to head overseas and I don't know how long I'll be or if I'll ever be back. You go ahead and do whatever you want with it."

"All right. You got my address?"

"I've got it."

"I'll look forward to reading it. Hey, I'm sorry about your dad."

I hung up the phone without responding. To be honest, I didn't know if he was sorry Dad died or if he was just sorry that he was my dad.

Right now I'm sitting at the airport bar, drinking an expensive Japanese beer for no good reason. Sitting at the next table is a woman with a cat in a little cat carrier. She's talking to the cat, calling him John. People who name their pets ordinary human names depress the hell out of me. I listen to her carry on and it gets worse. The cat's name isn't just John. It's John Fitzpatrick. That's too much.

Now that I've told our story in all its fist-eating, gut-wrenching, seat-edging, nail-biting, lip-pulling, chain-smoking, teeth-clenching detail, I wonder: was it worth it? It's not like I want to start a revolution or finish one that's dragging on. I wasn't a writer before I began, but writing a book makes a writer out of you. Anyway, I don't know if I want to be a writer. Herman Hesse once said, "True creative power isolates one and demands something that has to be subtracted from the enjoyment of life." That doesn't sound like much fun to me.

An announcement just told me my flight is boarding. I'll write a few last words before I pop this in the postbox to Stanley. What could be an appropriate thought to finish on?

Maybe I should conclude with some semiprofound observation about my life.

Or about how sometimes dropped anchors hit slow-moving fish.

Or about how often the swallowing of saliva is really the suppression of a violent longing.

Or about how people mourn the recent dead but never mourn the long-term dead.

Or about how idiot savants surprise their doctors, losers blame their fathers, and failures blame their children.

Or about how if you listen closely, you discover that people aren't really ever *for* something but instead are just opposed to its opposite.

Or about how when you're a child, to stop you from following the crowd you're assaulted with the line "If everyone jumped off a bridge, would you?" but when you're an adult and to be different is suddenly a crime, people seem to be saying, "Hey. Everyone else is jumping off a bridge. Why aren't you?"

Or about how when women who've had extensive plastic surgery die, God greets them with puzzlement, saying, "I've never seen that woman before in my life."

Or should I finish on a positive note and say that even if you find yourself with no loved ones left to bury, it's good to be optimistic and carry a shovel with you, just in case?

No, none of that seems right. I've run out of time anyway. My plane's boarding in ten minutes. This paragraph will have to be the end of it. Sorry, whoever you are. Hey—that's a question: who might actually read this if Stanley actually publishes it? Anyone? Surely there's got to be one measly person out of six billion who has a couple of days to spare. One bored soul out of the shocking number of humans cluttering up this lit-tle blue-green ball of ours. You know, I read somewhere that by the year 2050 there will be another couple of billion. What a conceited outburst of humanity! I tell you, you don't have to be a misanthrope to be chilled at the idea of that many people bumping into each other on the street, but it helps.